A SHARE OF EARTH AND GLORY

AUGUSTA WELLES—The plantation brat who grew to passionate womanhood. She was the silk-skinned beauty who posed for Parisian artists while she longed for her beloved Carolina land . . .

TOM RAVENEAU—The Southern gentleman with a fashionable taste for gambling. Far from her sun-drenched home, he introduced Augusta to a London of brittle gaiety and smiling enemies . . .

SIR ADAM TREVAYNE—The English aristocrat, trapped in a marriage he despised, drawn to the frank young American heiress . . .

LORD HARRY—The wickedest man in Europe, he was called—and Augusta knew both his cruel bondage and the glorious freedom he could offer . . .

GANNON MURDOCK—The childhood friend, the overseer's son who hated Augusta even as he desired her. The reckless man who would claim her and everything she possessed as his own rightful prize . . .

A Share of Earth and Glory

KATHERINE GILES

A JOVE BOOK

A SHARE OF EARTH AND GLORY

A Jove Book / published by arrangement with
the author

PRINTING HISTORY
Jove edition / March 1982
First printing

ISBN: 0-515-04756-2

Jove books are published by Jove Publications, Inc.,
200 Madison Avenue, New York, N.Y. 10016.

To
Helen R. Holt
Margaret S. Holt
Beverly Lewis
who helped more than they know

Courage! And shuffle the cards.

—Lola Montez, her motto

A Share of Earth and Glory

PROLOGUE

The Barony, 1835

Heaven from all creatures hides the book of Fate.
—Alexander Pope,
An Essay on Man

As I sit here, pen in hand, so much comes flooding back out of memory, more vividly than I would ever have thought possible. I have only to close my eyes, and I see the Barony as I first saw it in childhood—a great white house with many-columned piazzas, and broad flights of stairs, and four chimneys that seemed to touch the cloud-flecked South Carolina skies. A shake of my head, and a dozen years pass, and I see my cousin Melinda in the moonlight, emerging like a ghost from the dark woods near the Barony. Then suddenly memory sweeps me across the sea to London, and once again I hear the waltz at Almack's and the riffle of the deck in a gambling hell—a thousand pounds to be won or lost on the turn of a card. And in another moment I have crossed the Channel, and I hear the crash of pistols through the foggy dawn in the Bois de Boulogne.

Where, then, do I begin my story? I could begin with a certain evening in my grandfather's youth when he won the Tear of Venus, that beautiful diamond with its halo of ruby and emerald chips and its chain of gold. Or with my birth in London in 1821, of an American father, Mr. August Welles, and a gray-eyed, hollow-cheeked English beauty, the former Miss Lydia Greshame. Or even with my first sight of the Barony, five years later.

But something keeps telling me to start with Gannon Murdock. Gannon, whom I loved and feared as only the very young can love and fear. Gannon, whose wrath pursued me across the seas and over the years. Gannon, who swore his oath of vengeance against me—against all the Welles family— on that summer day so long ago.

He was our overseer's son—dark, aloof, brooding, given to fits of rage that contrasted sharply with moments of joy, magnanimity, and great, unrestrained laughter. I long ago became accustomed to thinking of Gannon in terms of his anger, his resentment, the threat of violence I so often felt in his presence. But that was only one side of him, and now memory returns me to that spring afternoon, soon after my fourteenth birthday, when quite possibly he saved my life.

Everything about that afternoon is clearly impressed on my mind. It happened that my parents and various companions were either occupied or nowhere about the house, and I was at loose ends, so finally I went up to my room and put on sandals and an old shift and headed out for a stream where I frequently bathed. The day was hot, even for South Carolina, and as I crossed the green cotton fields, sweat flooded over my body. By the time I reached the shady grove where the stream ran clear and fresh over the pebbled bottom, my shift was clinging uncomfortably, and without thinking about it, I began pulling it off. Then I stopped and glanced about. I saw no one. The hands had left the fields for the day, and there was no reason why I should not bathe nude, as I had so often done throughout my childhood. Yet a new-found modesty stopped me, and I smoothed the shift back down, thinking, *not yet, not till I'm in the water*.

For a moment I stood on the bank of the stream, looking down at my fourteen-year-old body with a certain wonder. The changes of recent years had come slowly enough for me to accustom myself to them, and yet sometimes I felt caught by surprise on the verge of womanhood. I could not quite believe that those long, newly shaped legs, the narrow waist, the ripening breasts were really mine. Was it possible that I, the chubby, awkward child, was even becoming beautiful, just a little? I rose on the balls of my feet and arched my back, tensing my muscles and feeling the strength of my growing body. It was possible. At fourteen, all things were still possible.

Laughing quietly at myself for reasons I did not wholly understand, I kicked off my sandals and sat down on the grassy bank of the stream to dangle a toe, a foot, a calf into the water. To my sun-heated skin, it felt surprisingly cool, and I gasped as I put in the other leg and eased myself thigh-deep into the stream. Shivering, I embraced myself and felt my nipples rise. Now I was glad that I had found no one to come here with me. Only when I was alone could I permit myself this feeling of sensuous unity with the water and warm air and sunlight that bathed me, with the very woods and fields of the place that I loved above all others on earth—the Barony.

I belong here, I thought, as I began pulling off my shift. *I belong here, and I'll always come back. No matter where I go, no matter what happens, I'll come back.*

Half-naked, I paused. The sunlight on the water dazzled me, and I tilted my head back and closed my eyes, trying to see the future. But of course there was only one imaginable future. The heavens would turn, and the seasons of my life would come and go as regularly as the ticking of a clock. In another two or three years, perhaps at a ball or a party, someone wonderful would come into my life. He would marry me, but nothing would really change, and life would go on as it always had, growing sweeter with every passing year. I would come to this same stream to bathe, and in time I would bring my children here, just as my mother had brought me, and I would sit on the bank, watching them laugh and splash. . . .

My dream was shattered by a cry: "Gussie! Look out! *Cottonmouth!"*

It took me an instant to comprehend what was happening. Opening my eyes and whipping my shift down, I turned and saw Gannon Murdock on the stream bank. Bare-chested, his face strained with alarm, he was racing toward me. Then I looked upstream and thought I saw a long dark shadow coming toward me through the water.

I understood. Death was coming toward me. Death, that ended all dreams. Death in the form of two venom-ladend fangs in cotton-white jaws.

A scream tore through my throat like a claw. I felt my legs thrashing through the water, saw myself reaching toward Gannon, who seemed ever so far away, while in my mind's eye I saw the snake's brown length with the black bands, saw the pits on each side of the spadelike head, saw the fangs in the widening mouth. As in a dream, it seemed to take me forever to reach the bank, though Gannon was now leaning down from it, extending his right arm, and still I could not stop screaming. His hand caught my right forearm, and I felt the massive force of his tug as I was drawn up from the water and through the air. My feet hit the ground. As I slammed against Gannon, he stumbled back from the stream and fell to earth, and I found myself sitting within his arms, my knees to my breasts, my feet kicking in a frenzy against the backs of my thighs.

"Gussie, it's all right! It's all right now, you're safe!"

For a moment the breath went out of me, and it seemed that I would never catch it. Then it came back, and with it came tears, and I melted, weeping, against Gannon's bare chest.

"It's all right, Gussie, it's all right. Ain't nothing gonna hurt you. I'm here, and I ain't gonna let nothing hurt you. It's all right."

Death was gone, for a time at least, but still I sobbed, could not stop sobbing, welcomed the arms that enclosed me and the hand that gently stroked my shoulder.

Gradually my weeping slowed.

And then, maddeningly, Gannon began to laugh. "My God, princess, how you do carry on! We got you out all right, didn't we? What the hell you carrying on for?"

Fear turned to anger, and I began thumping on his chest with my fist, but Gannon only laughed harder. Tears returned, and I heard myself wail, "Goldang you, Gannon Murdock!"

The grove rang with Gannon's laughter. And the worst of it was that I began to laugh with him.

Hadn't that always been the way of it? Mean Gannon, fierce Gannon, wicked Gannon—but so often there when I needed him. We were never really close—how could we be, when he was three years older than I, and, moreover, a creature of snakes and toads and pet cur dogs, whereas *I* was only a *girl!* But he was part of the Barony. He was *our* Gannon.

From the day of my arrival at the Barony, he had been the scourge of us younger children, both our protector and our enemy. I still hear his scornful voice after he had frightened his sister Janthina and me by tossing a "spider" at us: "Dumb girls, don't even know a nice old daddy longlegs when you see one!"

But, oh, how we tormented him in turn! Hiding his borrowed copy of *Frankenstein*—"Just when I got to the good part!" Stealing his clothes when he went bathing in one of the Barony's streams, then alerting the people in the slave quarters, so that as Gannon came running home after dark, cursing and snarling and holding a fringe of leaves fore and aft, a hundred or more men, women, and children hooted and hollered him on his way.

And then, waiting for Gannon's revenge. "Look out, he's coming, he's coming! Gannon's coming!" With shrieks of delicious terror we fled in all directions, around the barn and the stables and the paddock, legs pumping until they ached.

"Gannon Murdock," his mother would call out, "what are you doing, chasing after them children? You're supposed to be looking after them. Don't you know you always look after the little ones, no matter what?"

And, now that I think of it, he did remain amazingly patient with us. *He* might occasionally bully us, but let no other try, and I do not think he would have let harm come to us in a thousand years. Perhaps it was no wonder that as we reached the ages of twelve and thirteen, Janthina came to adore him. "My big brother is really *something!*" she would say. "It ain't no wonder that every gal 'tween here and the Sea Islands is flaggin' her tail at'im. *He* is *something!*"

In my most secret heart, almost hidden even from myself, I had to agree. One day when he came riding by, I found myself staring up at him, so high in the saddle, so darkly handsome, so beautiful that my breath caught in my throat. When he saw the look on my face, he knew my thoughts better than I did myself, and he burst out laughing. I tried to save my dignity in the only way I could think of—I yelled, "Pooey on you, Gannon Murdock! You're nothing but a—" and I let fly a swarm of naughty words and phrases, half of which I did not even understand. This so delighted Gannon that he howled with mirth, kicked free of his stirrups, and swung from the saddle. I, thinking he was throwing himself at me, turned and ran. When I looked back, he was lying in the grass, helpless with laughter.

Oh, yes, he was my enemy from the beginning, my very dearest enemy. But for an hour or so on that spring afternoon we declared a truce. And to this day I still wonder if, on that afternoon, he did not save my life.

Later, when he had calmed me and cast me out of his arms, I asked him if there had really been a snake. By then, I was sitting cross-legged by the stream, while Gannon, still bare-chested, and dappled by the sunlight through the leaves, lay on his back beside me, his eyes closed and his hands behind his head.

"Was there really?" I asked. "Was there really a cotton-mouth?"

"I said there was. Why shouldn't you believe me?"

"Lots of reasons. It wouldn't be the first time you scared me with a snake or a dead rat or some such like."

"Gussie, like I told you, I'd just had a dip myself. I went off a little ways to dry off, and when I was pulling on my britches, I saw you and remembered the snake I'd spotted upstream." Gannon grinned.

"What's funny?"

"You. Coming out of the water. The look on your face."

The remark gave me an excuse to touch him, and I gave him a little slap. At seventeen, his face still had some of the delicacy of boyhood, but the strength of the man showed in the high, broad forehead, the full cheekbones, the strong jaw. His eyebrows were thick, almost bristling, yet well-formed, and his eyes deep-set. His mouth was wide, full-lipped, and almost sensuous. Except for a ring of light tan just above his low-slung britches, he was burned a rich brown almost as dark as some of our Negro hands; and across his chest, and thick between the two sun-darkened nipples, lay a rough diamond of coarse black hair. To me he was a picture of grace and power: broad shoulders, a deep chest well-padded with firm muscle, a belly hard-looking and flat. When I saw how his tummy moved when he laughed, I felt a strange warm tug deep in my own, and my entire body seemed to blush at the thought that, if he had arrived a moment later, I might have been without my shift.

"Gannon," I said, looking down at him, "you're pretty."

"I'm what?"

"You're beautiful."

"Jesus Christ, Gussie!"

I laughed at his embarrassment, though I was hardly less embarrassed myself.

"Men ain't beautiful," Gannon said flatly, "ever!"

"Some are. My mamma says that's one reason she married my daddy."

Gannon made a sound of disgust, but he was trying not to smile, and I sensed that he was pleased in spite of himself.

"Who do you aim to marry, Gannon?"

"Don't be silly. Who the hell would have me?"

"My mamma says Lou Belle Fickett, over on the Butler place, has got her cap set for you."

I had said something wrong. Gannon's face slowly soured. His lips pursed a time or two before he spoke.

"You mean, Gannon Murdock is only an overseer's son, so he's stuck with marrying some white-trash gal?"

"Why, Gannon Murdock!" I was a little shocked. "Lou Belle Fickett isn't white trash. She's a very nice girl, even if she is only . . ." Too late I realized my mistake.

Gannon sat up beside me and turned around to stare morosely into the stream.

"Even if she is only an overseer's daughter," he said. "Like I'm only an overseer's son."

"But I didn't mean it like that," I protested. "Everybody knows you come from a good family."

"A good family, hell. I know what folks think of us." A hundred remembered insults were in Gannon's voice. " 'The Murdocks—maybe they was good people once, but look at them now. And that Gannon Murdock—too big for his britches. Don't know how to keep in his place.' "

"But people don't think that!"

"Oh, yes, they do. They don't only think it, they say it. To my face, when they got the guts. They say it enough that sometimes I think—maybe it's true."

"No—"

"But I'll tell you something, Gussie." Gannon turned to face me, his eyes obsidian, all softness gone. "It's only true if a man lets it be true. And I ain't gonna let it be true. You think I'm gonna spend my life being some rich man's overseer, like my daddy?"

I had no answer. Perhaps I had assumed exactly that: that Gannon would follow in his father's footsteps.

"Well, I ain't. I don't give a damn what people say or what they think, I got it in me to rise."

"Why, of course you do, Gannon," I said, as if I had known it all along.

"You know what I been doing, Gussie? Hiring out my free time. And soon as I get my stake—"

"What? What are you going to do?"

"Head west. Head out for Alabama or Mississippi, 'cause that's where the future is. Buy me some of that government land cheap and plant cotton. And then maybe some day . . ."

"Some day you'll come back here."

"That's right. Come back here and let 'em all see what an overseer's boy has made of hisself. Maybe I'll even buy the Barony."

The idea shocked me. "But you couldn't do that!"

"Why not? You ain't got no brothers to take over from your daddy, and four or five years from now, you'll be leaving—"

"No, I won't!" The possibility that I might leave the Barony forever, that there might not even be a Barony for me to return to, had never occurred to me.

" 'Course you will. You'll marry some rich old boy that'll take over his daddy's plantation, and you'll go to live there and never again set foot on this place. Someday the Barony has to pass on to somebody else. Why not to me?"

No. Never. The Barony had been in the Welles family for over a hundred years. The Welles family had fought Indians and pirates and the Carolina Proprietors themselves, that they might hold the Barony. They had held it through revolution and war, and it was inconceivable that they should ever lose it. My name would change with marriage, of course, but the Barony would still be mine and my children's. Here I would live and here be buried.

I drew up my knees and rested my forehead on them, closing my eyes as if to shut out Gannon's vision of the future.

"I'm never going to leave here, Gannon."

"You leave every summer and every winter. You're not here more'n half the year, as it is."

"That's not what I mean. I mean, this is my home. And I'll always be able to come back here."

"Maybe." I felt Gannon's hand on my shoulder, felt it give me a friendly squeeze. "Maybe so, Gussie, but things do change. And when you meet the right fella, you'll change your mind."

"Never!"

Somewhere, distantly, thunder rumbled, threatening the bright day. I heard Gannon climbing to his feet, and when I looked up, he was pulling on his shirt.

"Gannon, why are you so nice today? Most of the time you're so goldang mean."

Gannon grinned. "I'm mean 'cause that's my nature—half bear and half 'gator and born to be hanged. But you ain't a bad kid, princess." Gannon pulled on his boots. "You still gonna have yourself a dip?"

"I don't know."

"Well, if you do, take more care. You never know what's

upstream floating toward you . . . or downstream in the shadows . . . just lying in wait.''

Gannon started off through the woods and soon vanished among the trees.

For a time I merely sat on the bank of the stream, looking into the water as if it were a crystal that could show me the future. But now I saw nothing. Thunder rumbled again, closer, and a breeze swept through the woods like a wave of apprehension. Bad weather was moving in.

''Nothing's going to change,'' I murmured aloud to myself. ''Not ever.''

For Gannon had done something more cruel than he could have known. He had thrown all my certainties, all my sweetest hopes, into doubt. And I could not help remembering his words: *''You never know what's upstream floating toward you . . . or downstream in the shadows . . . just lying in wait. . . .''*

BOOK ONE

The Death of Innocence

~~~~~~

To our bodies turn we then, that so
   Weak men on love revealed may look;
Love's mysteries in souls do grow,
   But yet the body is his book.
                  —John Donne, *The Ecstasy*

          To be wise and love
Exceeds man's might.
            —Shakespeare, *Troilus and Cressida*

1 ⌁⌁⌁⌁⌁

Ah, but I do get ahead of my story.

As I have said, I was five years old before I even saw the Barony. In 1817 my father had gone to London as secretary to Mr. Richard Rush, the American minister to Great Britain. But much as he enjoyed England, he missed South Carolina—or perhaps I should say the Barony—and when, in 1825, Mr. Rush returned to the United States to become Secretary of the Treasury, my father was eager to follow him. Early the next spring we bade adieu to my maternal grandmother and boarded the ship.

My principal impression of the voyage is of its discomfort. It seemed to take forever, for there was little for a child to do and our small stateroom was damp and chilly. New York City was little better—a bath was almost as difficult to obtain in a hotel as it had been on shipboard. After a few days in New York, I was dragged, weeping, aboard a packet to Washington City, where we fared just as poorly, and then aboard another to Charleston. There we rested two days in the Welles family's city residence—actually in the nearby suburb of Wraggboro—and I have a sharp memory of spending long hours soaking in luxuriously hot and soapy baths.

On the third morning, we set out by carriage for the Barony. To me, it was a magical trip, because never before in my life had I seen anything like the gray veils of Spanish moss that festooned the oak trees along the road, never anything like the vast cotton and rice fields. My father happily lectured us on "claying" and "sprout flows" and "the open trunk system," but I heard scarcely a word. The morning was warm and sweet, and I was busy watching chickadees and redbirds and the rabbits that scampered ahead of us. I knew then that my father was right. Nowhere, absolutely nowhere in the world, was there another place like South Carolina.

We reached the plantation in the early afternoon. As our

carriage approached, the black people greeted us first, children running alongside the carriage and older people waving to us from the fields. Then we turned onto a road of crushed white shells that led straight north, through a long, broad park, directly to the house. The road circled in front of the house, and by the time we arrived there, the family was standing out in front waiting for us.

A tidal wave of love seemed to sweep us out of the carriage. It swept us up the long stairs to the piazza and through the open double doors of the entrance hall. My grandfather, a heavyset, silver-haired man who made me think of Father Christmas, tossed me into the air and caught me, until my "new" grandmother, protesting, seized me and whirled me about. My father embraced my Aunt Nickie, a pretty lady with a soft French accent, and did the same to big, stern Uncle Thaddeus, his older brother. Everyone embraced my mother, not least those colored folks who came rushing into the hall—and there were far more colored than white. My mother was at first startled—what English servants had ever behaved like this?—and then delighted.

And I was delighted to see that there were children. There was my cousin Melinda, a year and a half older than I, the prettiest little girl I had ever seen. There was a strange little fat boy, Horace Blakely, who was Melinda's cousin, though not mine. And there were several black children—two of them, Pearl and Rufus, immediately made me their personal charge and tried to drag me off to play.

After we had freshened up from the journey, we were served dinner. The grownups ate in the dining room, and we children—Melinda, Rufus, Pearl, Horace, and I—ate in the cellar kitchen, and it was surely the most riotous meal I had ever experienced. Afterwards, we were herded back upstairs for a nap, all five of us stretched out across the same bed. After repeated warnings from Pearl's mother, Polly, who was the chief housemaid, we finally sank into calm and quiet. And before long, I found that only I was still awake.

I felt deserted, betrayed. How could my companions possibly sleep on this glorious day! I poked at Melinda a time or two and shook Rufus and Pearl and Horace, but they merely made small sounds of protest and turned away from me. Frustrated and unable to lie still, I sat up and started to get off of the bed.

At that very instant, the door opened a crack, startling me.

As I held my breath, it opened a little farther, and a face peered in.

It was a boy—a *big* boy, I saw as he slipped into the room, all of eight years old. He had a ragged mop of black hair, and shiny dark eyes, and his cheeks were burned to a dusky rose. His shirt was tattered, his oft-mended pants were held up by a string, and his feet were bare. My first thought was that he must be a gypsy.

Before I could speak, he held a finger to his lips, then beckoned to me. I slipped off the bed and, when he beckoned to me again, followed him barefoot out of the bedroom.

Silently we made our way to the stairs and down them. I was careful to follow his lead, stepping on certain edges and corners, as if to avoid those places that squeaked. From somewhere below, we heard adult voices and laughter, and again the gypsy boy signaled me to be silent.

We reached the downstairs. The door to the piazza was already open, and in an instant the boy was through it, and I followed after him. Then we were running down more stairs and away, away, away over grass, and away from the house. When we reached a garden hedge, he slowed down, and after a single glance at me, continued to lead the way, while I obediently followed.

Ahead of us, waiting, stood a little girl of about my age. Like most of the children I had seen at the Barony, she wore only a shirt that barely reached her legs. She had scabby knees and was as dark as the gypsy boy, and I knew intuitively that she was his sister. As we approached her, she smiled shyly.

The boy looked at her with the infinite scorn I would come to know so well. "Who says I don't dare?" he sneered, and walked off.

The little girl's dark eyes were the merriest I had ever seen. "Ah know yew," she said in an accent I barely understood. "You're Augusta. Will yew play with me? Mah name is Janthina."

But I was hardly listening. I was gazing after the boy who had stolen me right out of the crowded house and away from all the others. The brave gypsy boy.

That is how I left my infancy and entered my childhood—led out of my family's sheltering house by Gannon Murdock.

And now there is so much I would like to tell. I would like

to tell about the crisp December days when we brought in the cotton, every man, woman, and child at work in the fields from dawn to dusk . . . about the smell of hot syrup in the kitchen, where we children stood about, hoping to lick the pan after Matty, the cook, had put up the latest batch of preserves . . . about the excitement of trips to Charleston—the late-night parties, the shopping expeditions through crowded city streets, the noisy, thrilling horse races at the Washington Race Course.

Those were the wonderful years, the growing years, the years of innocence. But of course innocence begins its slow death long before childhood ends.

It was Gannon who, the spring I was eight, brought us the news about Uncle Thaddeus, the news that threatened to tear our family apart.

At that time, my uncle's prospects could hardly have been brighter. While my father was in England, Uncle Thad had married Monique de Garinet—my Aunt Nickie—the older daughter of one Alphonse de Garinet, who had immigrated to America in hope of enlarging his fortune. Aunt Nickie was a striking woman with a full, svelte figure and a lovely face, its heart shape emphasized by the dark lock that fell over her forehead. She had brought a respectable amount of money to the marriage, and Uncle Thad, though no one knew it at the time, had used it to make some extremely profitable investments. Later, Monique's younger sister, Laure, had married Josiah Blakely, a planter with a small but prosperous place, and had borne him a son, Horace. When Josiah and Laure were carried off by a fever, Aunt Nickie and Uncle Thad naturally took Horace in. Meanwhile, as my grandfather had grown older, Uncle Thad had virtually taken over the running of our family cotton-and-rice factoring business in Charleston, and to some extent the plantation as well. Though willing to share with my father, he naturally expected to be my grandfather's principal beneficiary. His future was assured.

Then, on a spring day in 1829, we learned the nature of Uncle Thad's investments.

The day was otherwise perfectly ordinary. That morning Melinda and Horace and I had our lessons: the three R's from my mother, and geography and French from Aunt Nickie, who insisted that one was never too young to learn "the only truly civilized language in the world." Pearl and Rufus and

Gannon's sisters, Janthina and Sarah, studied with us—but not Gannon, who usually preferred to read his books by himself. After lessons and dinner, Aunt Polly herded the seven of us to the creek where we all bathed together.

And there Gannon appeared. He was so obviously excited that we all stopped shouting and splashing to look up at him. Even Aunt Polly, sitting on the bank with her needlework, looked at him with curiosity.

"I guess you all ain't heard yet," he said.

"Heard what, boy?" Aunt Polly asked.

" 'Bout Mr. Thad. My daddy was just over to the Butler place talking to Mr. Fickett—"

"What about my daddy?" Melinda, waist-deep in the water beside me, asked.

"He's in trouble, bad trouble, with the law, and he's gonna go to jail."

"Boy," Aunt Polly said, "what you telling us! What you mean, Mr. Thad go to jail?"

"He got caught," Gannon said gleefully. "He got caught bringing in illegal slaves from Cuba."

Aunt Polly's eyes were large with consternation. That a gentleman should in any way connect himself with the slave trade was unthinkable. "Gannon, boy, you go spreading talk like that, you the one be in trouble!"

"But it's true. He's gonna go to jail—"

"It isn't true," Melinda wailed, "it isn't!"

"They say he's been slave-trading for years." Gannon looked at Melinda and Horace and me with great satisfaction, as if a point had been proved once and for all. "And my daddy says that there ain't nothing lower than a slave trader, smuggling poor damn niggers into the country from down in the islands. So now they gonna lock him up for good."

Melinda's face screwed up, and tears came to her eyes. "It's not true! It's not true!"

"Boy," Aunt Polly said fiercely, "you better get away from here and stop spreading your lying tales!"

"But it *is* true!"

"It's not! It's not!

Melinda scrambled up onto the bank, and for a moment she seemed about to attack Gannon. Warily, he backed away.

"Well, you don't have to be a crybaby about it."

"Now, what you expect," Aunt Polly asked, "you coming here and saying her daddy gonna go to jail!"

"It's not true!" Melinda wept. "My daddy isn't going to jail! He isn't!"

Aunt Polly tried to embrace and comfort Melinda, but my cousin would have none of it. She pulled loose and, still weeping, ran for the house. Aunt Polly turned on Gannon.

"Gannon Murdock, you are ornery and a bully and got a evil tongue!"

Gannon looked genuinely aggrieved. "How was I to know she'd be such a crybaby? I just thought you all would want to hear about what's going on!"

It so happened that my grandfather and Uncle Thad were in Charleston at the time, and if my parents had any idea of what was happening, they showed no sign of it. I was afraid to mention the subject, but the household seemed strangely tense and quiet.

Uncle Thad arrived back at the Barony that afternoon, and my grandfather the next evening. He was hardly through the front door when he summoned Uncle Thad into the library. At first, voices were kept low, but before long they rang out with no thought of who might hear.

"I am telling you for the last time, Thad," my grandfather said angrily, "I am leaving you the factoring business and nothing more!"

"But I have a right—"

"You have forfeited your right! You went into the slave trade—very well, you can support yourself as a common tradesman. But you'll get not one acre of the Barony, not one black servant, not one field hand!"

"You long ago promised me the Wraggboro house. You promised me—"

"August will get the Wraggboro house, the Barony, the Tear of Venus, and everything else I have."

When Uncle Thad spoke again, his voice almost broke. "I stayed here and worked for you, worked like a goddamn dog, while *he* spent all those years in England—"

"Serving his country, sir, while *you* stayed here and trafficked in human flesh. Do you really think I would trust you with our black people after what you've done?"

"But the Barony is *mine!*" my uncle roared hoarsely. "And I am going to have it! One way or another!"

"No, Thad. And don't you dare say a word that sounds like a threat, or you'll get nothing at all. Oh, I'll try to save you from prison, if I can—but I'll be damned if I'll support your foul dealings."

My grandfather was as good as his word. Somehow he did keep my uncle out of prison, and when he died a year later, not long after my grandmother's death, he left Uncle Thad only the factoring business. Everything else went to my father. And though Uncle Thad was too shrewd to break with my father, nothing was ever quite the same between them again.

Soon after we had found out about Uncle Thad's involvement in the slave trade, we left the Barony for the summer, and it was late fall before I saw Gannon again. He was almost twelve by then, and very strong for his age and handy with tools. I found him repairing the paddock gate. "Ha!" I said in an attempted jeer. "Ha! You said they were going to put my Uncle Thad in jail. That just goes to show how much you know, Gannon Murdock. *Nobody* can put *my* Uncle Thad in jail!" Expecting anger, scorn, or even roughhousing from Gannon, I was prepared to run. But he only turned dark, disillusioned eyes on me.

"Yeah," he said after a minute. "They say he made thousands out of the trade, and didn't nobody even take a dollar of it back from him. But if me or my daddy ever once done such a thing and got caught, they'd lock us up and throw away the key. They'd say, what else can you expect of trash like that? Teach 'em a goddamn lesson."

It was true. Even at eight I knew it was true.

Gannon went back to work. I watched him for a moment. Then, feeling oddly ashamed, I turned and left.

My father loved Gannon. I know that now.

I know now that my father wanted a son and that at some point he realized he would never have one. Nor, it seemed, would he have the consolation of a nephew of his blood and name, for Uncle Thad and Aunt Nickie also failed to produce a male heir.

Probably I benefited from this situation, though I did not know it at the time. I remember the happy hours my father spent teaching me to ride, and shoot, and sail our sloop, the *Maid of Athens*—I was a tomboy if ever there was one. But the ages of twelve and thirteen and fourteen came, with all the dismays and delights of those years, and, no, I was not his son but very definitely his daughter. And increasingly my father spoke of his hopes for Gannon Murdock.

But how can I explain his fondness for a boy who showed more disaffection for us with every passing year? As Gannon's bitterness grew—as his resentment took on darker hues and he turned to drinking and gambling and brawling—why did my father still love him? I can only think that behind the scapegrace behavior my father saw something valuable—intelligence, courage, aspirations—and, hating waste, he longed to see Gannon make the most of those qualities.

But he was doomed to disappointment.

I think he began to realize that his hopes were for naught on a Saturday evening in late autumn of 1835, the same year that Gannon had warned me about the cottonmouth.

For some forgotten reason, my parents and I were up quite late that night. We were in the library when we heard horses and a pistol shot announcing the arrival of guests. Of course, we were startled, even frightened. My father said, "Stay here!" as he hurried out into the entrance hall, but nevertheless my mother and I followed him. When he threw open the doors, we saw a carriage and half a dozen young men on horseback down below in the moonlight.

I recognized some of the men: Hamilton Butler, Beau Legree, Dexter Raveneau. Beau Legree got down from the carriage, and Dexter helped him pull another man out of it. My mother cried out when she saw that it was Gannon. They had evidently brought him to our house because the rest of his family was in Charleston for a few days—and also perhaps as a personal challenge to my father, who had so often defended him.

Gannon's wrists and ankles were tied, and he dropped to his knees. Beau and Dexter grabbed his upper arms and dragged him up the steps, across the piazza, and into the hall. Beau flung him down at our feet.

"You've been told before!" Beau all but shouted in my father's face. "Keep this here trash in line or get him the hell out of the district. You can tell his pap, if he can't keep his boy home, the next time I see him I'll kill him!"

To me, Gannon looked half-dead already. He wore no coat, and the back of his shirt was dark with blood. His face was one massive bruise, the lips blood-encrusted and the eyes swollen almost closed. And yet, with a whimper that had a note of defiance in it, he tried to raise himself up on his elbows.

"I said I'll kill him, goddamn it," Beau repeated as we

paid no attention to him. "He comes near me or my sister again, I'll kill the son of a bitch!"

My father's voice was quiet but steely: "You will correct your language, sir."

Beau's normally red face grew redder. "I got provocation—"

"You are in my house and standing before my wife and daughter. Do not give *me* provocation. Now, tell me what happened."

"What's it look like? I whipped hell out of him, and he got off easy. If I'da had my way, I'da used the hog knife on him and made him sing soprano—"

"Get out of my house."

My father was not a particularly big man. He was tall, but not as tall as Beau, and very slim, with delicately chiseled features. He had thick chestnut hair, richly highlighted, like my own, and his deep-brown eyes, as he looked at Beau, seemed to burn with autumn fires. He had the habit of command, and when he gave an order, his voice was like a whiplash.

Beau stared at my father a few seconds before trying to go on.

"You tell him to stay out of my way—" Beau began.

"*Out!*"

The bluster went out of Beau. His jaw moved silently. He turned and strode out of the hall, but he paused at the door like a child who has to have the last word: "I'll kill him!" And then he was gone.

Dexter remained with us. He was grinning. "Don't blame old Beau too much for his bad manners, Mr. Welles, sir. He's got pretty good reason to be upset." I had never liked Dexter Raveneau. He was a mean-eyed youth, about nineteen, with a thin brutal face and high cheekbones that seemed to give him a perpetual squint, and he seemed to be enjoying this nasty little scene.

"What good reason?" I asked. "What happened?"

Dexter glanced at my mother and me, his grin twitching, but his answer was directed at my father. "I'll tell you later, Mr. Welles, sir, if it's all the same to you."

"But I want to know!" I objected.

"Augusta," my father said in his quiet whiplash voice, "that is enough."

My mother and I soon had Gannon untied. She decided he should be moved as little as possible and that for now we would keep him in the house. While she went to prepare a room and send for the doctor, my father and Dexter lifted Gannon to his feet and, though he said a few words of protest, carried him into the library and laid him face-down on a sofa. When the two men had returned to the hall, I asked, "Why did they do it, Gannon?" but he only shook his head and sobbed with pain. Then I heard Dexter speaking in a low voice, and I hurried to the side of the door to eavesdrop.

". . . caught him and Julie Anne Legree together tonight when we all was over at Beau's to play some cards," Dexter was saying. "I reckon Beau had an idea that something was going on, 'cause when he realized his sister wasn't in the house, he got in a real uproar and took us out with him to look for her. Only he didn't let us do no shouting around—he wanted us to catch 'em before they knew it. Well, we caught 'em all right, there in the garden. Gannon had little old Julie Anne leaned back against the trunk of a big old willow tree. Her skirt was up, and he had her panting like a bitch in heat, just begging for it. 'Oh, Gannon, take me! Oh, darling, I love you so much, I want you so, darling—' "

"I get the idea," my father said dryly.

Dexter laughed. "And I got to admit he's got something to make a bitch beg all right. We'd caught 'em two minutes later, he'da rogered her good. . . ."

It was the kind of talk I had rarely heard, but I knew what it meant, and I stood there frozen. After a moment, I realized that Dexter was still speaking.

". . . and I reckon Beau would'a deprived him of some parts right then and there if I hadn't stopped him. We convinced him just to whip Gannon, and I got to say he sure did whale hell out of him. We figured we'd better get him home 'fore Beau killed him off."

"Well, I do thank you, Dexter."

I heard Dexter leaving, but I continued to stand right where I was, stunned. A world I had only dimly perceived before—a world of animal passions, of lust and hatred and pain—had suddenly become real for me. And it frightened me, frightened me badly.

I did not move until I heard a sound behind me. Turning, I found that Gannon was on his feet, and all thought of what I had just heard fled. Gannon's head was down, and his battered face was twisted with pain. Leaning on a table to support himself, he was moving toward the front door.

"Gannon, you mustn't!"

His voice was little more than a whisper. "Let me be."

"You mustn't get up! You're going to stay here, Gannon, right here in the house where we can look after you. We'll take care of you—please, *I'll* take care of you, Gannon!"

"Oh, Gussie—" Suddenly he lurched against me. His head fell against my shoulder, and I felt his blood and tears on my neck. An arm went around my shoulders, clinging to me, and, "Oh, Gussie, Gussie, Gussie!" he sobbed, as one hurt child might to another.

What happened between us in that moment? I was not really close to Gannon Murdock—Gannon himself had seen to that. Yet in his pain he was reaching out to me for something—for understanding, help, solace—and I felt my heart swelling and aching in answer to him. I did not care what he had done to Julie Anne Legree, I did not care how bad he was—he was *our* Gannon, he was *my* Gannon, and in that instant not even the angels could have torn him from my arms.

But Gannon himself was no angel. As if in sudden anger, he thrust me away.

"I'm going home."

"No, Gannon!" I blocked his way. "My mamma is getting a room ready for you. She said you shouldn't move. Let us help you, Gannon—"

The look in his dark eyes cut me off, a look of absolute malevolence. I knew he hated himself for his moment of weakness, yet I was totally unprepared for what came next.

"I don't want *nothing* from you," he said venomously. "I don't take *nothing* from no goddamn Welles. Nothing that I don't earn—or that I can't steal!"

Shocked, I backed away from him. Then I realized, as he did, that we were not alone. Looking around, I saw my father in the doorway, white-faced, staring at Gannon.

My father could forgive Gannon for that, of course. He could understand the bitterness in the boy's soul, and he tried to explain it to me.

"He blames us," he said sadly. "He blames me, he blames your grandfather, I suppose he blames every Welles."

My father had finished checking to see that the *Maid of Athens* was secure, and we were on the landing, looking out at the river on a gray December day.

"But why?" I asked. "What has he got to blame us for?"

"I've told you, Augusta. The Murdocks once had one of the biggest plantations in this part of the country—a large part of the Barony was theirs. But over the years they had bad luck and used bad judgment. Crops failed, business ventures crumbled, debts piled up—debts largely owed to the Welles family, since we acted as the Murdocks' cotton factor. By Gannon's grandfather's time, there was little left.

"It's been a sad comedown for them, Augusta. And I suppose Gannon looks about and sees what he thinks should have been his. He might have been wealthy, been raised a gentleman like his forebears. Instead, he finds himself scorned as trash. And so much of what the Murdocks once had fell into Welles hands that he probably feels we took advantage of their bad luck, perhaps even cheated them."

"But we didn't!" I said indignantly.

My father shrugged. "Who knows? From what I've been told, some of the earlier Welleses were pretty unscrupulous in building the Barony, if no more so than their rivals. If I were in Gannon's position, I might feel the same way."

I tried to understand. "Then why doesn't his daddy feel that way? Mr. Murdock doesn't blame us, does he?"

"Doesn't he?"

It was one of those moments of revelation when a child's world is changed forever. *"Doesn't he?"* my father had asked, and suddenly, for the first time, I saw that, yes, Mr. Murdock did blame us. Perhaps he himself did not know how much he blamed us. He and my father were friends. In private they called each other by their first names, Laird and August, and they often shared a drink at the end of the day. Mr. Murdock, with his ramrod backbone and his iron bar of a mustache, had always seemed a stern but kindly figure to me. He helped make my world safe.

But now I was certain, without being told, that it was his sense of injustice, his hidden resentment, that Gannon had inherited and expressed so openly.

If that were true, I thought in bewilderment, was it possible that Mrs. Murdock blamed us, too? And Gannon's younger sisters, Janthina and Sarah, and his baby brother, little Ross— would they one day also come to blame us?

My father smiled, as if reading my mind. "Don't let it bother you too much, Augusta. Sometimes blame and friendship, even hatred and love, can be very oddly mixed. After all these years, the Murdocks are a little like family to us. Whatever our differences, they'll always be our friends, I'm sure, and we'll always be theirs.''

But it was not to be.

The final disappointment came the next spring, when I caught Gannon in the wine cellar.

Such a small thing caused the incident—a petty rudeness, a thoughtless word, once too often. The Butlers had come to Sunday dinner, and Gannon was on hand to care for the horses. When he had greeted young Zelda and tried to help her down from the carriage, she had interrupted him with ''Don't touch me, boy,'' and a disdainful curl of her pretty little lip. I, looking at Gannon's stricken face, had felt a knife in my heart, but Zelda had not even noticed.

That evening, when I was sent down to the wine cellar to fetch a bottle of madeira, Gannon was there.

The cellar, which was on a lower level than most of the other basement rooms, was a cool, musty place with a number of tall bottle-racks. A small, high window lit the room but dimly, and I was through the doorway and down the stairs before I even saw Gannon. Half-crouched behind one of the racks, he had an open wine bottle in one hand, and for an instant he seemed about to hurl it at me.

I did not cry out. I stood perfectly still until I found my voice. ''What are you doing here?''

''You better get out of here, Gussie.'' Gannon took a long drink from the bottle.

''What are you *doing* here!''

''Go on, get me run off the place. See if I give a damn.'' He smashed the bottle down on the stone floor, and broken glass flew through the room.

I realized then what I should have known instantly. ''You're stealing, that's what you're doing! You're stealing from our wine cellar!''

Gannon stepped toward me. ''You shut your ugly little mouth.''

''You're stealing from us, and I'm going to tell my daddy!''

''Bitch!''

As I backed away from him, he sprang at me, grabbing me by the shoulders. His dark eyes were terrifying. I cried out and struggled to get away, but he only drew me closer and told me again to shut my mouth. His wine-scented breath, warm on my face, nauseated me. I beat on his chest with my fists, but he stopped me by wrapping his arms around me and drawing me tightly up against him, while I continued to twist and turn, trying to get away.

Suddenly the look in Gannon's eyes turned into something else, something that I recognized as even more dangerous than his anger. His breath caught, and I felt him hardening against me. One arm moved down my back, then swiftly up my side to stroke my breast, and alarms, like the jangling of fire bells, went off throughout my body.

"Gannon, let me go!"

He did not seem to hear me. One arm locked me to him, and the hand continued to touch me as I had never been touched before.

"Damn you, Gannon Murdock, damn you, damn you!"

"By God, princess, you done turned into a woman, and I'm gonna treat you like one. Think I ain't good enough for you? Like that damn Zelda? I shoulda done this at the stream, when you and the cottonmouth went swimming." His mouth crushed cruelly down on mine.

"Damn—damn—damn you!"

The wine cellar was only a few steps from the servants' hall, the kitchen, and my father's office, and it was inevitable that my cries would be heard. Suddenly my father appeared in the doorway. Coming down the few steps in a single stride, he spun Gannon away from me and struck a blow that slammed the boy sprawling back against a wine rack. Bottles fell from the rack, and Gannon sank to one knee. He did not try to defend himself. My father yanked him to his feet and put all his weight behind a blow to the stomach that sent him, retching horribly, to the floor.

For a few seconds my father stood motionless over him. Then, seizing a bottle from the rack, he raised it for a blow that would surely kill, and I found myself screaming, "No, no, no!" and clinging to his arm.

Slowly the wildness went out of his eyes. I felt him relax. And I knew it was over.

As if I were the guilty party, I was sent to my room and ordered to stay there. My mother questioned me, but I was too shaken to say much.

More than an hour passed before my father came to my room. He looked as haggard as if he had passed a week without sleep.

"Augusta," he said, "there is one question which I must ask you, and I apologize for it. Have you ever in any way encouraged Gannon?"

"No!" My voice shook. "I hardly ever talk to him. Or even see him, any more."

"Sometimes, though, without meaning to, a girl will give a man certain ideas—"

"No, Daddy, I just caught him stealing from our wine cellar, and he grabbed me, and—" I blushed at the thought of what Gannon had said and done.

My father nodded as if satisfied. He turned to look out a window, and as the waning daylight hit his face, I was shocked. He looked so much older than his forty-one years. It made me want to comfort him, but I did not know how.

"I suppose you know that Gannon was drunk, Augusta?"

"Yes, sir."

"Otherwise, it might never have happened . . . though I don't know . . . I just don't know any more. I had high hopes for Gannon at one time. I think you know that."

"Yes, Daddy."

"He comes from good stock. I thought he had it in him to improve himself. And I did want to help."

For the first time, I began to understand the depth of my father's disappointment in Gannon.

"Well, we can't have everything in this world." He shrugged as he turned from the window, and his shoulders seemed heavy. "Augusta, I thought about sending Gannon away. I even talked to Mr. Murdock about it. But I hate to do that. After all, this place is home to the Murdocks, just as it is to us."

"I understand, Daddy."

"But I have made it clear to both Gannon and his father that an incident such as this must never happen again. From now on, Gannon is not even to speak to you. In fact, he is not even to approach this house without permission. If he does, he must go away from here. And I mean for good."

I thought he was trying to reassure me, but I hardly knew how to respond. "Yes, Daddy," I said.

"And henceforth, I want you to stay strictly away from that young man. Stay as far from him as possible, never look at him, never speak to him, and what happened . . . well, I'm sure it won't happen again."

"Yes, Daddy."

With that, he left. Supper was waiting downstairs, but I was not hungry. I wanted only to be alone for a while longer to absorb what had happened to me.

My years of innocence, I dimly realized, were drawing to an end. Gannon Murdock, the boy I had teased with childish jokes, and tried to comfort in his pain, and secretly adored, no longer existed. This older Gannon, with his poisoned soul, was a danger to me, a threat, and somehow I sensed that the worst was yet to come. But he had reminded me of something I had not thought of for a long time. I remembered that beautiful spring afternoon when he had pulled me out of a stream and warned me of the cottonmouth. And afterwards we had sat and talked and laughed in the sunlight, he bare-chested and so darkly handsome, and I in my thin cotton shift. And for a little while Gannon Murdock and I had been such good friends.

2 ~~~~~

Fortunately I had a distraction from troubling thoughts of Gannon Murdock.

Every spring, around the time of my birthday, we gave a party at the Barony. Indeed, my birthday parties were something of an institution in those days. Friends and neighbors would come from miles around, some from as far as Columbia and Savannah. We might have to feed a hundred and fifty or more people, and many of them would stay one or even two nights. All of this required considerable preparation, and I had thought for little else.

The great day was the next Saturday, and on Friday afternoon, the first guest arrived—Tom Raveneau.

Tom was everything his younger brother, Dexter Raveneau, was not—a natural aristocrat. With his deep blue eyes, his sandy hair that turned different shades of gold, his long narrow nose and square chin, he was undeniably handsome— so handsome that everybody *knew* he would marry my cousin

Melinda, for two people so beautiful could only be meant for each other. And whereas Dexter was quite content to stay home and run the Raveneau plantation, Tom preferred to get an education and see something of the world.

And he was gallant—gallant with the ladies, gallant in his chivalry. At twenty-one, he had already fought and wòn three duels and succeeded, as he put it, in killing no one. For who would want to kill a friend, he asked, and he had never fought with anyone but friends. He was, in short, the very image of his own father, my father's best friend; and when the elder Tom died, the younger quite naturally inherited a portion of my father's heart.

For my part, I looked on him as an older brother with all the irritations thereof, and I was surprised by my flush of pleasure at seeing him. But he quickly managed to turn that pleasure into something else.

"Well, tyke," he said as he stepped down from his carriage, "how old are you this year? Fourteen?"

Tyke—would he never stop calling me by that silly pet name? "Fifteen," I said, "and I am no tyke."

"Fifteen!" He shook his head in mock amazement. "I could have sworn you were just turning fourteen. Or maybe only thirteen. Are you sure you've counted right, tyke?"

I hated him when he teased me, and therefore did not deign to reply. I stuck my nose up in the air and walked grandly away—which only drew his laughter.

"Tomorrow I'll bring you the fox's ears for a birthday present, tyke."

Oh, no, he would not! I'd show Mr. Tom Raveneau who was a tyke!

The next morning I was up at dawn. A good many of the guests had arrived by then, and though it was hardly the season for one, the day was to start with a fox hunt. My mother was dismayed at the thought of my joining in the chase, but my father suppressed his own unease and let me saddle up my beloved horse, Wanderer. And no ladylike sidesaddle for me! How could I truly join in the chase on a sidesaddle? No, sir, I put on a full-skirted riding outfit and mounted as my father had taught me.

As soon as it was light enough, we gathered at the paddock, the hounds milling about our horses' legs, and my father made a short speech offering the hospitality of the house. He had hardly finished when we heard a horn signaling that the boys were about to release the fox they had captured, and we moved out. Before long the hounds picked up the scent, and it was tallyho and away!

Never will I forget that hunt, the best of my life. At a touch of my reins on his flank, Wanderer leapt to full gallop, and soon I was flailing away at him and shouting my joy. For what's better than riding full-tilt, breakneck, hell-for-leather through the fields, jumping streams, vaulting walls, spraying mud, to the braying of the huntsman's horn and the roaring and ringing and baying and bugling of those Carolina black-and-tans!

What matter that the fox got away? A marvelous ride!

The hunt lasted much of the morning, and we were lucky there were no ruined horses. At last we returned to the house, and as I dismounted, sweaty and muddy and sore, yet ever so happy, Tom came riding up beside me.

"Great hunt, tyke. Too bad you had to miss it."

I looked at him with astonishment. "What are you talking about? I was in the lead the whole time!"

"Funny. *I* didn't see you."

The Welles gorge rose. "And I don't see you bringing me back any fox's ears either, Mr. Tom Raveneau!"

I considered this a most stinging rejoinder, but, maddeningly, Tom merely laughed at me again and turned away.

Well, I would show him yet! I would *show* him!

The Lord knows I did try. I was ready to run races, shinny up trees, pick fights to "show" Tom Raveneau. I even joined in with the boys chasing the greased pig, though I never laid a hand on it. "Augusta," my mother said, "what in the world has gotten into you! You are fifteen years old now. Can't you start behaving like a lady?"

"Oh, let her be, Lydia," my father said. "It's a party, and there won't be many more where she can have this kind of fun."

In the afternoon there was a gander-pulling, which I was resolved to win. Galloping by the pole where the gander dangled from its bound legs, I did at least manage to grab its greased neck, but somehow it slipped away from me, and the laughter and applause for my effort simply made me more angry for my failure.

"Tyke," I heard Tom's cool voice at my side, "you don't really think you're going to win that gander, do you?"

"I don't see you even trying, Tom Raveneau, so don't you tell me you can do any better!"

It was, of course, the wrong thing to say. Smiling, Tom took the reins of my horse. He mounted, and a moment later he took the gander's head off quite effortlessly—thus winning the fluttering, bloody bird.

Infuriating!

But early that evening, before supper and the ball that would end the day, I thought I saw my chance at last.

As part of the day's entertainment, a cockfight had been arranged. Gannon Murdock had bragged that he had a three-time winner that could beat anything Beau Legree cared to pit against it. Because of the scandalous whispers concerning Gannon and Beau and his sister Julie Anne, this fight was regarded as a grudge match, and it attracted a lot of attention. Melinda and I were determined to see it, and when we went out to the torchlit barn where the pit had been set up, there were three or four dozen white men and a number of blacks waiting for the fight to begin.

As we entered the barn, I saw my father and Uncle Thad on the far side of the pit. Beau and Gannon were on opposite sides, facing each other, and Tom was standing near Gannon. We tried to be inconspicuous, but my father's gaze soon fell on us.

"We want to see the cockfight," I said quickly. "It's *my* birthday party, and I want to see it! Just this once!"

I was sure Uncle Thad, frowning at Melinda, was going to object, but my father merely looked amused. "All right, Augusta, maybe you should see one. Just this once."

Melinda and I were allowed to come to the walls of the pit. Gannon never looked at me. He was cheerfully showing off a large cock called Gray Murder. In spite of the trimmed wing, hackle, and rump feathers, it struck me as ugly, bedraggled, and mean-looking. In contrast, Beau's cock, a White Pile called Whirlwind, was one of the handsomest fighting birds I had ever seen.

I found myself moving closer to big, red-faced Beau, allying himself with him. "Come on, Murdock," he said, "seventy-five dollars only gets you a hundred against a four-time winner. You can do better than that."

"Mr. Legree, *sir,"* Gannon said in his scornful way, "I came here with seventy-five dollars in my pocket, sir, and that is what I am willing to bet."

Beau shrugged. "What about you, Tom? Who are you backing?"

Tom shook his head. "I don't know. I like your bird, Beau, but I've seen them both fight, and . . . I've just got a feeling Gannon's bird is going to win."

That was what I wanted to hear! That Gannon's mongrel-looking bird should win against *any* Legree bird was unthinkable. Yes, I would show Tom Raveneau!

Without another thought, I snapped, "I'll bet you it doesn't!"

Tom looked at me in surprise, as did quite a few other people, including my father. Oh, I was in fine form that evening.

"I'll bet you it doesn't," I repeated. "I'll bet you Beau's cock will win."

Tom smiled at me. *"What* will you bet me, Augusta?"

The question took me by surprise. "Why, I—nothing! I—I'll just bet you, is all."

Tom shrugged and turned away. "Well, then, if you 'just bet me, is all,' it doesn't really matter whether you bet me or not, does it, tyke?"

There was some laughter, and I felt my face redden. Oh, no, he wasn't going to do that to me!

"I'll bet you my horse, Wanderer, against whatever you think he's worth."

At my side, Melinda gasped. The words had been spoken before I could stop them, and I regretted them instantly. I wanted to "show" Tom Raveneau, to beat him, to put him in his place; but Wanderer was my dearest possession in all the world, and to risk losing him . . .

"I don't think you want to do that, Augusta," Tom said, no longer smiling.

I could not back down at that point. "I do! I'll bet Wanderer against—against whatever you think it should be."

Tom looked at my father, as if asking what he should do. Now my father was tight-lipped, and Uncle Thad had the faintly amused smile.

My father said, "The horse is Augusta's. She may do with it as she pleases."

Tom looked at me for a long moment. "You're sure, Augusta?"

I was not at all sure, and Melinda was whispering, "Don't! Don't!" in my ear. But I forced myself to say, "Of course I am. Why do you think I said it?"

"All right. Wanderer, against whatever your father says he's worth. You're on."

I had one bad moment at the very start of the fight. Beau and Gannon entered the ring and advanced slowly toward each other, holding their birds out before them. Before the birds were within three feet of each other, Gannon's Gray Murder began to peck and spur at Whirlwind, and by the time they were a foot apart, it was in such a frenzy that Gannon seemed hardly able to hold it. Whirlwind, however, until it was almost breast to breast with its opponent, did not seem game at all. Then suddenly it started pecking and spurring with the same frenzy, and Beau and Gannon backed away from each other. They hunkered down, held the straining cocks on their marks, and waited.

Mr. Butler, the judge of the match, swept his hand down, yelled *"Hey-y-y-y!"* and the birds were released.

In a flurry of feathers, each bird went for the other, rising from the floor. They met, and the white flurry and the gray all but merged. They rose higher still, their heads striking at each other and their steel spurs slashing the air. Then down they came, falling apart.

Almost instantly they were at it again, wings beating, beaks striking, spurs slashing. But this time Beau's cock got higher than Gannon's. A spur whipped through the air like a razor. Blood poured from Gray Murder's head and neck, and for a moment I thought the fight was over.

I was wrong. The birds went at each other again and again, while the rest of us cheered them on. Only Gannon was silent, wearing a slight, grim smile. His bird was certainly game, but it did seem to be tiring.

The moment came when it refused to fight. Whirlwind went for it twice, and twice Gray Murder darted away. There were boo's from the crowd. After Gray Murder had retreated a third time, its hackles rose ever so slightly, just enough to show some white feathers, and the booing grew louder.

"That's not a bad bird, Murdock," Beau said. "He won for you three times—it'd be a shame to kill him now. You want to concede?"

"Not yet, Mr. Legree, sir." Gannon still wore his grim smile.

He and Beau climbed back into the pit. They picked up their birds and, just as before, advanced toward each other until the birds were almost touching. This time, Whirlwind went into a frenzy first, and Gray Murder showed only a small part of its former strength and determination. It seemed clear to me that I was going to win my bet with Tom.

The birds were separated and put on their marks. Mr. Butler gave the order to release them.

The end came so quickly and shockingly that I could hardly believe it. The birds met in midair, a blur of gray and white feathers, but this time, in a final, supreme effort to gain ascendancy, the gray rose well above the white. As blood sprayed from Whirlwind, Melinda and I squealed and jumped back from the pit wall. The birds fell to the floor, Gray Murder still stabbing with his spurs. There were yells around the pit, urging the birds at each other, but suddenly both of them were still.

Gray Murder fluttered slightly. He was alive. But Whirlwind was obviously dead. He lay as if broken, one of Gray Murder's spurs thrust through his left eye and caught in his skull.

I've lost Wanderer. The thought hit me sickeningly. Whatever I had been trying to prove to Tom, whatever I had been trying to "show" him, I had failed utterly. And in the process, I had lost my dearest possession. *I've lost Wanderer*. . . .

Gannon whooped his victory. Beau knelt over the birds and managed a grin. "I'll be damned," he said softly. "I said you had a good bird, but if that don't beat all."

Gannon whooped again. "You think that damn batch of white feathers could beat Gray Murder? You call that damn thing a gamecock, boy? Christ, you just plain murdered your own bird, putting him in the same pit with Gray Murder."

I've lost Wanderer. The sickness in my stomach grew. My throat hurt.

"All right, Murdock, here's your money."

"Christ, and you call yourself a breeder and trainer. Why, you couldn't train a bird to beat chicken feed!"

Beau's face darkened. "Boys, you ever notice how it's always the mongrel dog that bays the loudest?"

Gannon swung his fist with such force that, when he missed, he staggered sideways and nearly fell over the side of the pit. Before he could attack again, several men grabbed him. For a moment it looked as if he might throw them all off.

"You heard what that son of a bitch said about me!"

"Yes," one of the men said, "and we heard what you said, too."

For a moment, it seemed that Gannon would explode, and the hands that held him tightened. Then the breath went out of him, and he relaxed.

"All right. I guess I was baying pretty hard. Been drinking some. My apologies, goddamn it."

It hardly sounded like an apology at all, coming from Gannon, but I suppose it was the best he could do.

Bets were paid off, and the men drifted out of the barn and back toward the house for supper and the ball. Melinda still at my side, I stayed right where I was, feeling sick from my loss. Wanderer . . . no longer mine. Tom was talking quietly to my father, and the two of them came over to me.

"Well, tyke?" Tom said.

"You won." I turned away for fear Tom would see the pain in my eyes.

"Augusta . . . I'm not going to take Wanderer."

"You won," I said again.

"Call it my birthday present to you. Your father says it's all right if I give you Wanderer for your birthday."

No. I was not going to accept any gallant gestures from Mr. Tom Raveneau. Not in a thousand years.

"You *won!*" I insisted. "You won fair and square, and I don't want that dumb old horse any more! You can just take him away any time!" Oh, I was in wonderful form that evening.

Tom shrugged. "I hope you'll change your mind, tyke. Miss Melinda, honey, may I see you back to the house?"

Giving me a regretful look, Melinda took Tom's arm, and they departed.

My father shook his head sadly. "Sometimes you're as bad as Gannon. Stubborn, proud, unable to win or lose or even accept a gift graciously. I think your mother is right. It's time you grew up and learned to behave properly, young lady."

I walked back to the house with him, feeling as miserable as I ever had in my life, hating myself and detesting Tom Raveneau.

But the worst of that long, troublesome day was still ahead of me.

Gannon Murdock came to the ball.

Since the Murdocks were *our* people, the whole family

was, of course, invited to my birthday ball. But considering
what had happened in the wine cellar so recently, Gannon
might have had the tact to stay away.

I was watching Tom and Melinda dance, as was almost
everyone else in the ballroom, when my father, standing near
me, swore softly. I followed his gaze, and there in the
doorway stood Gannon. "Remember what I told you, Augusta," my father said. "Stay away from him. If he wants to
dance with you, make an excuse."

He gave Gannon only a perfunctory greeting, and my
mother gave him the coolest of smiles. But Gannon seemed
not to notice. He grinned and nodded and acted as if he were
receiving the warmest welcome in the world.

Why on earth had he come here!

I soon found out why. Leaving my parents, he came farther
into the ballroom. His eyes swept across it as if he were
looking for someone, but he did not appear even to notice
Tom and Melinda, and his eyes hardly flickered as they swept
past me. Then they halted. Gannon began to smile again.

He was looking directly at Julie Anne Legree.

She was sitting between her mother and father, and Beau
was standing by them. Gannon caught her eye. He tilted his
head back and gave her a long sideways look and an amused,
half-suppressed smile. It was a meaningful look, and I thought
Beau was going to throw himself at Gannon.

Julie Anne's eyes widened as if she were terrified. She was
the most demure young woman I knew, and it seemed impossible that Gannon had once almost seduced her. She quickly
lowered her eyes, and even in the dim light of the ballroom I
saw her cheeks flush rosy-red.

Gannon was utterly shameless. He strode over to her. He
held out his hand to Julie Anne, and her parents smiled. They
had probably heard nothing of the scandal—they had been in
Charleston at the time, and who was to tell them? Surely not
Beau or his friends. Julie Anne stood up and slid into Gannon's
arms for a waltz.

But how could she, I asked myself, astonished. Gannon
had all but destroyed her reputation, and now that the scandal
was dying down and she had a chance to regain her good
name, he was reviving it again. Bringing back all the nasty
whispers and titters, just to get even with Beau Legree for a
well-deserved insult. How could she let him do this to her?

When they danced by me (and where had Gannon learned to waltz like that!) I saw her face, and I understood.

Julie Anne Legree *did not give a damn* about any scandal! All she knew was that she loved that terrible Gannon Murdock with all her heart. Loved him no matter how shabbily he treated her love. Would go on loving him, hopelessly. I fought back tears. Her love and my pain seemed to be the same thing, and I wanted to comfort her.

"Miss Augusta, honey, a pretty girl like you shouldn't be standing here like this at her birthday ball. Would you do me the honor . . ."

It was Hamilton Butler, but I hardly heard him. Gannon and Julie Anne had gone by, and once again I was looking at Tom and Melinda. *Men,* I thought, *they're all the same! All of them! Arrogant, and—and selfish—and cruel!* Tom was looking deeply into Melinda's eyes, and she was smiling up at him. He whispered something to her, and she laughed. They were alone in their own world, and that was the way I saw them: everything else in the ballroom faded away before my very eyes, and they were alone together, dipping and turning and gliding to the strains of a waltz.

"Miss Augusta, honey . . ."

And then at last I understood what had been troubling me all day. I understood my pain.

I was in love with Tom Raveneau.

It was a hopeless love, a futile love, because he belonged to Melinda and could never be mine. But in spite of that, in spite of everything, I loved him desperately, frantically, with all my heart and every bone in my body.

"Miss Augusta . . ."

My heart dissolved in tears, and I fled from the ballroom.

The next morning my mother had a surprise for me.

"How would you like to have your cousin Melinda stay on with us?"

"You mean, for a visit?" I was delighted.

"I mean for the rest of the spring, or even longer."

"I'd love it!"

I imagine it was largely because of my behavior the day before that Melinda was asked to stay. She was almost a year and a half older than I and a great deal more ladylike. No doubt my parents thought she would be a good influence.

But whatever their reasons, I could not have been more

pleased. Melinda was my best friend in all the world, and I adored her. She was gay, she was funny, she was beautiful. Her dark hair was silken, her complexion had the soft smoothness of a flower petal, and who could resist those large, lustrous brown eyes, so innocent and merry? But most of all, I loved her smile. She was rarely without it, and the play of it on her face was enough to lighten any heart. I, in contrast, had "the Welles mouth," an inverted U that I hated. "There go snooty ole Miss Gussie," Pearl once yelled when she was angry with me. "Snooty ole Miss Gussie with her nose turn up and her mouth turn down."

Everybody laughed at me, and in consequence, I spent hours in front of a mirror trying to imitate Melinda's smile. I kept at it, in fact, until one day Aunt Chloe, the housekeeper, caught me at it. "Chile," she said, "what in the world is you doing to yourself?"

Too embarrassed to tell the truth, I said, "Nothing. I think I've got a pimple coming out. I was looking for it."

"Well, don't you know you make faces like that, sometime you gonna get *stuck* that way? Don't you know your face get stuck and freeze, and you ain't never gonna get it back right again? Now, don't you let me catch you making no more of them faces!"

She never did, and I never captured Melinda's smile, though I knew my brown eyes were a bit like hers.

No matter. I had Melinda herself, and she helped make the year that followed one of the best of my life. We had a month together at the Barony, playing with Janthina and Pearl and Rufus and our other friends, while the jessamine and dogwood and magnolia bloomed. Then, early in May, we moved to the house in Wraggboro, where there were parties and summer balls, and we spent hours sailing the *Maid of Athens*. LIfe could hardly have been more pleasant.

I did suffer, of course. I continued to love Tom Raveneau, and he continued to be Melinda's beau. But I accepted that, and in consequence my pain mellowed and sweetened. It even occurred to me that in a year or so the young men would begin to take me seriously. One of these lads would love me as Tom loved Melinda. I would reciprocate with the deepest affection, and he would never guess the tragic love that would always remain in my secret heart.

Ah, fifteen! Of all the lovely things Melinda and I did that year, I think the talks were the best, those dreams of a bright and endless future that was on the verge of opening up for both of us. We talked as we roamed the beaches and sailed the *Maid of Athens,* but the best talks of all came in the evening when we were alone in our room.

"When do you think you'll marry Tom?" I asked one evening.

Melinda rolled over on the bed. We were both in our thin summer nightgowns, and I was sitting in a rocker with my feet up on the bed. "When do you think, Mel?"

"Oh, pshaw," she said, "what makes you think I'm going to marry Mr. Tom Raveneau?"

"You're in love with him, aren't you?"

"Rrmpf," she said into a pillow.

"Well, aren't you?"

"I guess so. He certainly is the handsomest thing on two legs, and I like being with him better than anyone else. So I guess I love him."

"A lot?"

"Quite a lot. Yes, I think so. Quite a lot."

"I'll bet you're married to him by next spring. I'm surprised he hasn't asked for your hand already."

"Maybe he isn't in love with me."

"Oh, he is so! Anybody can see that. He doesn't call you silly names like 'tyke,' and he comes calling on you all the time."

Melinda hugged her pillow. "You mean he comes calling on *us.* He's like part of the family, almost. You know that."

"Just the same, when he asks for your hand, will you give it to him?"

Melinda's smile was dreamy, a smile of sweet anticipation. "Yes," she said. "Yes, I guess I will."

And I would be left with my tragic secret.

"Will you have lots of children?" Children that could have been mine. Oh, Tom, Tom, Tom. . . .

"Children? I don't know. If the good Lord smiles on us."

"Well, He's almost bound to smile sooner or later if you try hard enough."

"What do you mean, try hard enough? If we *want* them enough—"

"If you want them enough to keep on trying."

"That's silly. Tom and I will have children because we want them. We won't have to *try* to want them."

"But you will have to try to *make* them, won't you? After

all, you don't think babies come from a cabbage patch, do you?''

"Of course not. They come from their mamma's tummy.''

"Well, somebody has to put them there, doesn't he? *Some-*body has to put the cake in the oven. You know that, don't you?''

Melinda's frown deepened, and she sat up. "Of course. God does it.''

"Melinda!''

"I mean, if you want a baby hard enough and the good Lord smiles on you—''

"Melinda, don't you know anything? People get babies by making love!''

She looked confused. "Well, that too, I suppose. But if you make love but don't really want a baby, I don't think the good Lord is going to smile—''

"Oh, don't you ever think that!'' Close as we were, we had never discussed such matters before, and I was just beginning to sense the extent of my cousin's ignorance.

"Mel, do you know what making love is?''

"Certainly I do. It's hugging and kissing and saying sweet things.''

I shook my head. "It's a lot more than that, Melinda.''

I do not think I was especially precocious about sex, but by that time I did have what might be called a working knowledge. After all, I had been raised on a plantation, and my mother and Aunt Polly had given me a certain amount of instruction. My mother did not believe in the nonsense about a husband instructing his bride on the wedding night.

That night I instructed Melinda. I gave her a fairly detailed and accurate account of the ways and means of sex, while she sat on the bed and stared at me in consternation.

"But I don't think you *have* to do that to have a baby!'' she wailed.

"You surely do! How do you think *you* got here?''

Melinda shook her head. "Mamma just said that she and Daddy *wanted* me so much. She said the good Lord—''

"The good Lord smiled on them, I know. But God helps those who help themselves.''

"But it seems so . . . so . . . so *vulgar*, Gussie! I don't think I could *do* that with a man!''

"But it's not bad at all! My mamma says—''

"I don't care!'' Melinda hid her face in a pillow. "I don't

want to talk about it any more! I just don't want to talk about it!''

We sat quietly for a time. I was sorry I had upset my cousin so badly. The truth was that, whatever I told her, I was not at all certain that *I* could ''do that with a man,'' and in informing Melinda, I was trying desperately to reassure myself.

I sat on the bed and put an arm around Melinda's shoulders. ''I didn't mean to get you all worried, Mel.''

''I just don't think I could do it, Gussie. I just don't think I could.''

''Others do. And if we're going to get married and have children, we'll have to, or else we'll be old maids all the rest of our lives.''

That prospect was appalling, and we spent a few moments in contemplation of a ruined future.

''Maybe I could try it just once,'' Melinda said.

If she could, maybe I could.

''You said it only hurts the first time, didn't you? But not after that?''

''Yes.''

''And after that, it's . . . nice?''

''Yes.''

''Well, then . . . maybe twice.''

That wonderful year. Tom Raveneau and I soon made our peace. When I mentioned that Wanderer was still in our stable, he again offered me the horse as a gift, and I managed to accept with some grace.

August and September were the most dangerous months on the low-country plantations, and we were kept away from the Barony. October brought relief from the heat, and November the first frost, and it was time to return. Melinda went with us, and we continued those talks about the mysteries of love which were still so alien to us. Everyone worked hard at bringing in the cotton, and the air was pungent with smoke from the smokehouse and from the fields where the rice stubble was burning. And before we knew it, Christmas was on us, the happiest of all times at the Barony.

A month passed like a wink of the eye, and it was the ''gay season.'' Back to Wraggboro again! Back for Race Week and the Jockey Club Ball and the three Saint Cecilia Balls! Ah, that was the way to meet young men! But one day at the races

I caught Tom looking at me and smiling. My heart leapt, and I knew I still loved him.

Why did everything have to go so wrong? Why did our little world have to fall apart? I feel now as if, like those first sinners, we were about to be expelled from paradise.

By my sixteenth birthday, I sensed a change. Something seemed to be amiss between Melinda and me. We still got along well, but increasingly she was quiet and withdrawn, and in the weeks that followed my annual party, she was often nervous and tearful. When I tried to find out what was troubling her, she would retire to our room and sleep.

Then, sometime in June, after we had returned to Wraggboro, I became aware of something called "the Panic." I did not altogether understand it, but it seemed that President Jackson had ordered that only gold and silver or the notes of specie-paying banks be accepted in payment for public lands. As a result, investors were rushing to turn in bank notes for hard cash in order to make their land-office payments. This "bank run" was causing more banks to fail every day, and investors— in land, in banks, in a great many things—were being broken along with them.

My father was not badly hurt by the Panic, but apparently Uncle Thad was. Indeed, as my father explained to me in a Wraggboro drawing room one afternoon, he had so overextended himself in land-speculation, among other things, that he was in danger of losing everything he had.

"Like everyone else, he needs cash to keep up his payments, or he'll lose his investment. I simply can't afford to give him all he needs, and I'm not going to mortgage this house or any part of the Barony." My father hesitated. "Augusta, I was brought up to believe that a man should shelter his family against financial considerations, and ordinarily I wouldn't discuss this matter with you. But in a way, you are directly involved. You see, I'm considering turning the diamond over to him to use as collateral . . ."

The diamond. He was referring to the Tear of Venus.

". . . but because you are to inherit it, I thought I should ask how you feel about the matter. I can't pretend there isn't a certain risk, but I'm sure we'll eventually get it back."

No. Something told me that if my father turned the Tear of Venus over to my uncle we would never see it again. Suddenly I had a tremendous sense of loss—as if the diamond

were a symbol of all the good things that might slip away
from us.

Even so, I agreed immediately: "Well, of course, Daddy."

Everything was changing. All that spring my mother had
become increasingly ill; with what, I had no idea. And in
spite of that, my father was determined that we should return
to England! But why, I asked, why now, of all times? It was
the cholera epidemic which had lately been sweeping the
country, he said: he wanted to get my mother and me away
from it for the next year or two, until it died down. But that
meant I would miss the next gay seasons, my first seasons as
an "almost grown-up" young woman. To me, it all seemed
so unfair!

But there was no altering my father's decision. We would
leave in late July or August, he said, just as soon as he had
put his affairs in order. At my insistence, he did agree,
despite the season, to a final week or two and one last party at
the Barony.

That's when the tragedy happened.

On the Friday night before the party, I was awakened by a
nightmare. As so often happens, the dream faded almost
immediately, but I still recall that it had something to do with
a stream where I was wading and the approach of a long, dark
cottonmouth along the pebbled stream bed. I dimly realized
that I was dreaming of something that had happened long
before, but that did not diminish my fear in the slightest. I
cried out. Cried out again. The cottonmouth was coming ever
closer, and somehow I had to get away.

With another cry and a final desperate effort, I tore myself
out of the dream before the snake reached me.

I lay still, whimpering, panting, heart thundering.

It was only a dream, I told myself, only a dream. I was
lying in my own bed in the dark of night, with my cousin
Melinda only a few inches away, and I could feel the rumpled
pillow under my cheek. A dream could never hurt me.

I gave a last sob and a long, relieved sigh. The fear was
fading a little, but I still wanted reassurance. I whispered my
cousin's name: "Melinda."

There was no answer. I knew I should not awaken Melinda, and there was really no need, so after a moment I merely
reached out to touch her.

My hand touched only the still-warm pillow.

It took me another moment to realize that I was alone.
Then, opening my eyes, I sat up and gazed at the empty side
of the bed. Hardly believing my cousin could really be gone,
I peered into every shadow. I whispered again, louder,
"Melinda!"

Silence.

For a few seconds I sat perfectly still, afraid to move, but
telling myself that everything was all right. After all, Melinda
might have gone down to the kitchen for something to eat.
Or, unable to sleep, she might have gone to fetch a book and
a lamp. This fear I felt was only the residue of a nightmare.
And yet, and yet . . .

"Melinda!"

I slipped out of bed. I went to the door and looked out into
the dark hallway. Seeing no one, I crossed to the stair hall. The
creaking of a stair told me that Melinda was only a little way
ahead of me, and, relieved, I hastened to catch up.

As I reached the stair hall, I heard the click of a closing
door. I stepped out onto the landing and stood dead still.
Melinda was nowhere in sight, and the click had sounded like
the outside door. But why in the world would my cousin be
leaving the house in the middle of the night?

I hurried down the stairs. Slowly, as quietly as possible, I
opened the door.

Melinda's white-robed figure was clearly visible in the
bright moonlight. She had just reached the foot of the steps
from the piazza, and she was hurrying away from the house,
her robe fluttering about her.

I watched with dismay, not daring to follow or to cry out.
If my parents had known about this, if my uncle or aunt were
to find out . . .

Somehow I knew that my nightmare was not yet over. It
was only beginning.

Sleep was impossible. I had to know that Melinda was safe,
and why she had done such an unbelievable thing. Uncounted
times I crept downstairs and looked out the door hoping to
see her reappear. I watched, too, from the upstairs verandah
outside my room. But there were only the wheeling stars above
and the darkness below and the pulsing, thrumming sounds of
the warm summer night.

By the time dawn was about to break, my worry had
become an agony. I put on a robe and slippers, intending to

go out and find my cousin, but first I took one last look from the upstairs piazza. To my relief, there she was at last, emerging from the nearby woods and running back toward the house. If only she could cross the last few hundred feet without being seen! I hurried downstairs to meet her.

She waved to me as I came out of the house. There was a mischievous look in her eyes, part guilt and part amusement, and I sensed suppressed laughter. We fell into each other's arms and hurried back into the house. Neither of us said a word until I had closed our bedroom door.

"Melinda Welles, where have you been!"

Laughing, she tossed off her robe and flounced onto the bed. I was almost in tears as I joined her.

"Melinda, I have been up all night worrying about you! How dare you go out at night like this! And not even dressed! *Why*, Melinda, *why* would you do such a thing!"

"Oh, Gussie, if you only knew."

"Well, you tell me!"

Sitting up, she put an arm around me and tried to draw me to her, but I was in no mood to be hugged. "Oh, Gussie, darling, you won't tell on me, will you? Will you, Gussie?"

"Of course not. But you could have been hurt or killed. You know my Daddy says we shouldn't go out alone at night."

"Darling, I was perfectly safe. And I wasn't alone."

I was almost afraid to ask my next question. "What do you mean, you weren't alone?"

"I was with Gannon Murdock."

I felt as if I had been hit in the stomach, and my nightmare fear returned.

"You were with Gannon . . . all night?"

"Yes."

"Where?"

"In the barn. The one between us and Gannon's house. We were up in the loft."

"Oh, Melinda . . ."

The fear grew, sickening me.

"It's all right, Gussie."

"But you and Gannon—"

"I love him, Gussie."

"But you can't. You can't possibly. He's bad. He's wicked and cruel."

"No, darling Gussie. He's good and gentle and kind. He's the sweetest, loveliest man in all the world, and I love him."

How in the world could she say such things about Gannon Murdock? Gannon Murdock, who could be trusted with no woman?

"But what about Tom?" I asked. "You're going to marry him."

Melinda laughed. "No, Gussie. I like Tom, and I hope we'll always be friends, but I know now that that's all we are and all we ever will be."

"But everybody thinks—"

"Everybody can think what they please. I am going to marry Gannon."

Melinda and Gannon. The very thought of such a match made me want to cry. "Melinda, you know your daddy won't let you, not in a thousand years."

I felt Melinda stiffen. "He must." Her voice shook, and there was fear in it. "He must, Gussie."

"But he won't—"

"He's just got to! When he gets here today, I'm going to tell him that Gannon wants to ask for my hand. I'm going to marry Gannon, Gussie, and he's just got to let me do it!"

The tears came at last. "Melinda, Gannon is no good—"

"Now, now, darling Gussie . . ."

"He's only trying to hurt you . . . to hurt us all!"

Melinda held and rocked me. "No, darling, you're wrong about Gannon. I know he's proud, and sometimes he's spiteful, and sometimes he's even mean. But we've got each other now, and he's putting all that behind him. We're going to have a good life together, Gussie. Don't reckon it'll be easy, because you're right—we can't expect much from my daddy, and we'll be poor at first. But we've got such plans, Gussie. We'll be all right, just you wait and see."

I let her rock me until I could control my tears.

"How did it happen, Mel?"

"Oh, we just saw each other here and there when you weren't around. He couldn't come near the house, of course, and I knew I shouldn't be talking to him, but he made me laugh and feel happy and excited, and I guess I did the same for him. And finally he dared me to meet him at night . . . said he'd be waiting every night till I came . . . and finally I—"

"Oh, Mel. And last night . . ." I had a growing suspicion. "Last night wasn't the first time, was it?"

"No, Gussie, it wasn't."

Now I understood Melinda's long afternoon naps. "But why didn't you tell me—your very best friend?"

"Oh, you know why, Gussie. I knew you'd try to make me stop. Besides, it seemed kind of private. Just between Gannon and me."

". . . Mel?"

"Yes, Gussie?"

We both knew the direction my questions would go next. "You didn't even get dressed."

She leaned back on the pillows, drawing me down with her. She was quiet for a moment, considering how best to answer me.

"You didn't even get dressed, Mel."

"Well, dear, there doesn't seem to be much point in putting clothes on . . . if you're just going to take them off again."

"Oh, Mel . . ." Sickened, I hid my face against her shoulder. "But how could you? How could you bring yourself to . . .?"

Melinda stroked my head comfortingly. "I don't know, exactly. He held me in his arms that first night and kissed me, and . . . I wasn't nearly as scared as I'd thought I'd be. And after a while—"

I buried my face deeper, trying to shut out the visions that came unbidden. "Mel, Mel . . ."

Her voice was soft and dreamy. "You were right, Gussie. It did hurt some, that first time, but after that—oh, Gussie, there is nothing more wonderful in all the world. We've been making love most of the night, and yet even now, when I think about it, I start wanting to be with Gannon again. I want to feel his lips on mine, his hands touching me. I want to be a gift for him. I want to be flung out and naked and aching under him, and feel him taking my gift and giving himself to me. I want—I want—"

"Oh, don't, don't, don't."

"Let me tell you something, Gussie. When you find a love of your own, don't you be afraid of it. Don't turn it down, don't run away from it. I don't care if the world is coming to an end, or the sun is burning out, or the moon is falling from the sky. Pay it no mind. When you find love, Gussie, just take it, and let the rest of the world go hang. Take it, Gussie, take it . . . take it. . . .''

Her voice drifted off. After a moment, I realized she was asleep.

My tangled emotions kept me awake for a long time, but as I lay in Melinda's arms, one thing became clear to me. Much as I hated the idea of her marrying Gannon, I would do anything I could to help her. Her happiness was far more important than my opinion of Gannon Murdock.

But how could I help her? No matter what she said, it was inconceivable that Uncle Thad, that big, brutal, thundering man, would allow his older daughter to marry a mere overseer's son. When he learned of her love for Gannon Murdock, his anger was bound to be terrible.

Only one bright thought occurred to me. It appeared that, whatever else happened, Melinda was not going to marry Tom Raveneau.

Perhaps I would have a chance with him after all.

3 ～～～～～

They arrived in the late afternoon: Uncle Thad, with his Welles mouth turned grimly down at the corners; Aunt Nickie, whose dark compassionate eyes always seemed to see more than she was willing to tell; and the latest addition to the family, little Lucy, a smiling year-old toddler.

And Cousin Horace. Poor, fat, towheaded Horace, with his slow mind and his terrible stutter.

My father greeted them cordially. My mother had remained abed today, he explained, to save her strength for the party that evening. Some of our boys took the bags into the house, and Melinda's family went upstairs to settle into their customary rooms.

''When are you going to talk to your father?'' I asked.

Melinda's face was drawn with apprehension. ''Right now,'' she said.

"Maybe you should wait until tomorrow after the party."

"No. I've got to know what he'll say. I *can't* wait. Oh, Gussie, he simply *must* let me marry Gannon!"

She followed her family up the stairs.

Among the young, at least, love is selfish. I wish I could say that I remained in worried suspense all the time Melinda was with her family, but the truth is that after the first few minutes I gave her very little thought. From the time I had awakened that morning, I had thought of little else but Tom Raveneau. How would he react on learning about Melinda and Gannon? Was there any chance at all that he would forget Melinda and come to love me? He was supposed to come out to the Barony for the party, and the day seemed to stretch out endlessly as I waited to see him.

Finally I decided I would stand on the piazza and watch the approaching carriages no longer. I had had little enough sleep the night before, or rather that morning, and I would go upstairs and rest. Besides, from my bedroom window I could more easily see Tom coming.

I had just reached my room when I heard Melinda cry out. Her anguished wail told me what had happened. The door across the hall flew open, and Melinda came running toward me. Uncle Thad stood behind her. As she rushed past me into our room, his big strong-jawed face twisted with rage. He stared at me for a moment, then marched toward the stairs. I followed Melinda into our room and closed the door.

She lay on the bed sobbing. "He said no, Gussie! He said never, never would he let me marry Gannon! And I know he never will!"

When Melinda had calmed somewhat, I tried to comfort her.

"Maybe it's not as bad as it seems. Maybe when he thinks about it and gets used to the idea—"

"No. He thinks Gannon is the lowest thing on earth, no better than any old sandhiller, and he said he'd rather see a child of his dead before letting her marry such a man."

"Is your mamma against Gannon?"

"I don't know. But I don't think she could ever hate him the way my daddy does."

"Then maybe she'll take your side. Maybe she'll persuade your daddy to let you marry Gannon."

Melinda shook her head. "No, he won't ever let me." She

burst into fresh tears. "And he's *got* to, Gussie, he's just *got* to!"

Pearl tapped at the door and stepped into the room.

"'Scuse me, Gussie, but your daddy say for you to come down to the library right now."

I nodded. "I've got to go, Mel. Now, don't you worry, we'll find a way."

"He won't even let me speak to Gannon, Gussie, to tell him what he said. He said I was never to go near Gannon or speak to him or even look at him again."

"Is that what's troubling you?" Pearl asked, going to Melinda. "Why, you poor thing!"

"Gussie, how can I tell him—"

"Pearl can tell him. Nobody's said Pearl can't go near Gannon or talk to him. Isn't that right, Pearl?"

"That's surely right," Pearl agreed. "But, Gussie chile, your daddy and your Uncle Thad is in that library waiting for you, and ain't neither of them in a mood to be *kept* waiting."

"All right, I'll go down right now. You see if you can do anything for Melinda."

For my father and Uncle Thad to send for me at this moment could only mean that they wanted to discuss Melinda, and I had no wish to tell all I knew. Hence, as I went down the stairs, I already felt guiltier than I had reason to feel, and my knees shook.

When I entered the library, my father was sitting in a deep leather chair, while Uncle Thad paced with hard, heavy steps. ". . . and meet secretly, unchaperoned," he was saying. "Let's not deceive ourselves, August. This is a matter of family honor, yours as well as mine."

"Thaddeus," my father said, "you needn't lecture me on honor." He turned to me. "Augusta, I suppose you have some idea of what has happened?"

"Yes, Daddy."

"It's quite important that we find out how far this little affair has gone, and perhaps you can help us."

"I'll try, Daddy."

"You and Melinda have been close for a long time, and I'm sure you often confide in each other. Has Melinda ever said anything to you about having . . . carnal relations with Gannon Murdock?"

"No, Daddy," I lied, and my guilt became real.

"Has she ever said anything to you that might suggest that she has had such relations?"

"No, Daddy."

My father looked at me for a long moment without speaking or smiling. At such times I could almost believe he was reading my secret thoughts.

"Augusta, how long have you known about this . . . relationship between your cousin and Gannon?"

It was a relief to tell the truth. "Just since this morning."

My father looked surprised. "So short a time! Do you have any idea of how long it's been going on?"

"Not long. Since sometime this spring, I think."

"Since spring," Uncle Thad said, "and she only told you about it this morning? And you two thick as thieves?"

My father threw him a hard look. "Thad, we agreed that I would ask the questions. Augusta, how did she come to tell you, after all this time?"

"She told me because I'd find out anyway. She said she was going to ask Uncle Thad if she could marry Gannon."

"But—your uncle is right about this—since you two are so close, why didn't she tell you before?"

"I don't know. I guess because she was in love and was afraid that if anybody found out—"

Uncle Thad snorted at the word *love*.

"In any case," my father said, "she knew perfectly well that both of you girls were to keep your distance from Gannon. Isn't that true?"

"Yes, sir."

"Then why do you suppose she broke that rule?"

"I don't think she meant to. I think it was just an—an accident!" Anything to defend Melinda.

My father sighed and turned again to my uncle. "Thad, I don't think there's any point in continuing with this. We've learned all we're going to learn."

"Oh, no, we haven't." Uncle Thad seemed to swell with wrath. "August, I'm not going to cause a disturbance while you have guests here. But as soon as I get that girl home, I'm going to have her examined by someone I can trust to tell me the truth. And if I find that she's been ruined, I'm coming back here, August, and I'll kill that boy. I mean it. I'll kill him."

"All right, you'll kill him. And by doing so you'll certify

your daughter's ruination to the community, and pay the price."

Frustrated, Uncle Thad shook his head. "For God's sake, am I simply to stand by and do nothing?"

"I didn't say that. The minute I leave this room, I'm going to find Gannon. I'm going to tell him the same thing I told him in respect to Augusta. He is never again to approach Melinda or to speak to her. If he does, I shall take appropriate steps."

"Or I will, by God. If I get home and find he's ruined my girl, I don't care what you say, he's going to hear from me again. I'm going with you to speak to that boy, August."

After a moment's hesitation, my father nodded. "You might as well. If you're going to live here next winter, he had better know who he'll have to deal with." He smiled at me. "Thank you, Augusta. You've been very helpful."

The two men left the room.

"I'm going to have her examined," Uncle Thad had said, *"and if I find that she's been ruined . . . if I get home and find he's ruined my girl . . ."*

He would soon know. And whether or not he killed Gannon, he would most certainly punish Melinda. That punishment was too terrible to contemplate, and I wanted to save her from it, but how? I could think of no way in the world.

I stood there in the library, feeling as if I were being torn apart, until I could bear my anguish no longer. Choking on my tears, I ran from the house, ran for a place where no one would see me weep.

I ran, as it happened, straight to Tom Raveneau.

I think I have suggested that I was not the most disciplined young lady in South Carolina, but only my disturbed state of mind accounts for my behavior that afternoon. We had a house full of guests and, for the moment, only Aunt Nickie and me to look after them, yet I fled without a thought. I rushed out onto the piazza and down the steps just as Tom was bringing his carriage up to the house. He gave me a startled look. Before he could stop, I sprang into the carriage, grabbed the reins from his hands, and we were off.

I headed back down the road away from the house, then east on the Charleston road, but I really had no idea of where I was heading. Tears were streaming down my face, and when I saw another carriage coming toward us, I turned off on a side road. I did not slow down until Tom said, "Augusta, Rascal has had enough." Then I pulled off the road into a grove of trees where we could not be seen.

Tom took the reins from my hands and put an arm around my shoulders. "Why the tears, tyke?"

How could I tell him? Did I have the right? I was not prone to self-sacrifice, and I wanted Tom for myself, but if he asked for Melinda's hand, would that save her? Would he want to marry her if he knew what she had done? The questions overwhelmed me, and all I could do was blurt out the most important.

"Tom, do you really love Melinda?"

He stared at me for a few seconds, then burst out laughing. "What a thing to ask!"

"Please! I want to know!"

He shook his head as if dumbfounded. "Why, honey, everybody loves Melinda."

"But do you *love* her? Really love her?"

"Why do you want to know?"

"Because she needs help from someone who loves her very much."

"Well, I suppose I love her *that* much," Tom said with a certain discomfort. "I'd be glad to help her if I could. But I'd help any friend. You surely know that."

My tears had stopped. I stared at him incredulously. "I'm not talking about a friend. I'm talking about *Melinda!* The girl everybody says you'll most likely marry!"

He frowned. "Everybody says too damn much. Why should I marry Melinda? Just because people say we look good together? It so happens that I'm not in love with Melinda, and I have no intention of marrying her."

There are moments when the world seems to stand still, and then spins on, never again to be quite the same. This was one of them. Tom did not love Melinda. Any more than Melinda loved Tom. As I stared into those fathomless blue eyes, all was a vast stillness.

Never before in my life had I done what I did next. In fact, except for a few childish kissing games, never before in my life had I kissed a man other than my father. But now, without a thought of what I was about to do, I put my hands on Tom's shoulders, rose slightly from the seat of the carriage, and pressed my mouth fully and firmly on his.

I could not have been more surprised by what happened

then. The instant our lips touched, a shock went through me, and every part of me, body and soul, leapt to new and vibrant life. An arm encircled my shoulders, laying me back in the corner of the carriage seat, and as Tom's mouth answered mine, I seemed to be carried away on a warm tide. My head whirled, my sight blurred, and with a cry more of fear than of pleasure, I tore myself free.

For a few moments we were silent and I kept my face averted. When Tom spoke, his voice was husky.

"Why did you do that?"

"I love you." The words were as spontaneous as the kiss.

Tom laughed softly. "God knows, tyke, nobody can accuse you of being coy."

I wanted to cry. "Now you'll think I'm shameless."

"No, tyke, not shameless. You're just very young—"

"I am *not*," I protested, "and if you ever call me tyke again, I'll—I'll murder you!"

I felt his handkerchief on my wet cheek. "You're right," he said. "You're not a tyke any more. And I promise never to call you by that name again."

Then, gently, he drew me back into his arms, and I knew he was going to kiss me. I felt his warm breath on my face, felt his lips moving lightly over my eyes, over my cheek, to my mouth. I was frightened of what was about to happen, and yet I longed for it, I welcomed the tide that flowed through me as his lips moved against mine, I wanted only to melt away in Tom's arms forevermore.

But the kiss came to an end, and I opened my eyes to look into his, their deep blue now misted over.

"No," he said, "you're no tyke, no child, any longer."

"Do you . . . care for me at all?"

His answer was to touch his mouth to mine again—hesitantly, lightly, almost unwillingly—and a tremor went through me. Then, as if he were unable to stop himself, his mouth bore down and turned on mine, and as he gathered me more closely into his arms, the tremor became an earthquake, and I thought I might die of this measureless pleasure.

"I love you," Tom said, when at last we moved apart. "I love you with all my heart. Does that answer your question?"

I nodded. No words were possible.

"I think I've loved you since a moment last winter at the races when I looked at you and realized you'd become a woman.

I've fought it, because, woman or not, you're still so damn young—"

"Not so young, Tom."

"—and I know your father won't give his blessing until you're older. But one day I'm going to marry you, Augusta, if you'll have me."

"I'll have you, Tom. I love you so very much."

Our mouths met again for another of those soul-searing kisses that I thought I could hardly survive.

It was true enough that my father would not allow me to marry so young. He had said repeatedly that he did not believe in early marriage and that I would have to be at least eighteen before he would give his consent. But somehow I would endure the wait, now that I knew Tom was mine. From now on, I would hardly let him out of my sight. He would call on me daily in Wraggboro, I would dance with him at every ball, he would be my partner, my beau, for the gay season—

Suddenly I remembered. I would not be here for the gay season.

Tom saw the stricken look on my face. "Darling, what is it?"

"Tom, they're taking me away. To England."

For a moment he merely looked at me, his expression a reflection of mine. Then he said, "But surely they won't make you go. You can stay with your aunt and uncle while your parents are gone. Even if your father won't let us marry yet, when you tell him about us . . ."

Yes, there was that hope—a slim one, but I clung to it. For how could I ever give up this sweetness, I thought, as once again Tom's lips came to mine.

That lovely afternoon: the sunlight through the pines and the breeze so soft, and I so innocent in my young passion, feeling so daring and yet so fearful. "Now," Tom said a little later, as I lay aching in his arms, "what was that you said about Melinda needing help?"

I was ashamed that once again I had forgotten all about Melinda. "She wants to get married, but Uncle Thad said no."

"Oh? Who's the man?"

"Gannon Murdock."

Tom looked surprised. He laughed and shook his head as if he could hardly believe what I'd said. "No wonder her daddy turned her down. Gannon Murdock! My God!"

"But she loves him, Tom."

He nibbled at my eyelids, sending little shivers through me. "She'll get over it."

"Like you'll get over me?"

"Don't ever say that, Augusta."

Unwillingly, I drew myself out of his arms. "And now you'd better take me back to the house, Mr. Tom Raveneau, or my daddy will *make* you marry me."

"It would be worth it."

When Tom picked up the reins and started back, my earlier misery was all but forgotten. I was in love, and was loved in return, and I was giddy with happiness. A new optimism filled me, and it was impossible to believe that I would not find a way to make Melinda as happy as I was.

And now, once again, I hear a waltz. It lifts me and swings me and whirls me about the floor of the Barony ballroom, and I arch back against Tom's right hand. The lamps of the ballroom streak by, faces are swiftly passing blurs, and the only face I really see is Tom's, as I look up into his deep blue eyes.

I suppose that at that very moment Gannon was somewhere out in the darkness, watching the bright windows of the Barony and listening to the distant music.

But I was aware only of Tom and the waltz and the gaiety of the night. Oh, yes, sometimes I saw Melinda's white, stricken face, which she tried so hard to control, but in my own happiness I persisted in my hope that all would be well.

The evening was going beautifully. Though it was the wrong time of the year for a plantation party, because so many families had left the countryside for the summer, all afternoon guests had kept arriving. We must have had fifty or more people in the house that evening, quite enough for a ball, and after supper the little orchestra had struck up the first tune, and my father and mother had led the first dance.

"Don't forget," Tom whispered, smiling down at me as I whirled in his arms, "don't ever forget that I love you, Augusta Welles."

"And I love you, I love you," I boldly whispered back.

And somewhere out there in the darkness Gannon was coming closer, ever closer. . . .

The evening wore on to the sound of waltzes and polkas and country dances. Tom's presence, as he danced with other young women, was sweet torture. Why must he smile at them like that! why laugh at their silly little jokes! But I dared not dance with him too often, for my father was watching, and I sensed that I had best not test his indulgence too far.

A last dance, and I pretended to be oblivious of Tom. Soon many of our guests would be departing for home, and others would be retiring for the night. But first Julie Anne Legree had a suggestion. She and Zelda Butler drew me aside. "Gussie, Zelda has never even seen the Tear of Venus. Is it here in the house? Do you suppose . . .?"

A marvelous idea! The Tear was so seldom worn that it had never occurred to me, but tonight I would wear it for Tom! I hurried to my father and whispered in his ear. He smiled and nodded, and a moment later held his hands over his head for attention.

"It has been suggested to me," he said, "that some of the ladies here have never seen a certain article of jewelry and that they might take pleasure in viewing it."

The ladies were indeed interested, and, chattering happily, we followed my father into the library. The library had always seemed a dark room to me—a room of dark leather bindings, leather-topped tables, deep comfortable chairs—but tonight we were having a party, and it was brightly lit. We all watched as my father unlocked a cabinet and took out a flat box.

I suppose that by that time Gannon was standing right outside the house.

We gathered about my father in a semicircle, some peering between the shoulders of others, all of us falling silent. My father held the box out before him. Then slowly he lifted the lid so that the box opened toward us.

Dazzling light flashed and flared from the box as the lid went up, and the room was filled with oohs! and ahs! The Tear of Venus lay on a bed of black velvet. In shape it was a pear, and it did indeed suggest a single great teardrop from the eye of a goddess. Hanging from a gold chain, it was set off by a nimbus of gold and silver filigree embedded with chips of emerald and ruby. But none of that sparkling halo touched the Tear itself. The Tear existed as a thing apart on the black velvet, filling our eyes with a dance of blue, scarlet, green, every color of the rainbow, and the purest white fire.

My father put the open box on a table for a few minutes, so that everyone had a chance to look at it. Then he lifted the necklace by its chain, and the ladies drew back as if he had flashed a magic charm before their eyes. He turned to my mother, offering the necklace to her, but she smiled and shook her head. He glanced about the room and asked, "Who will be first?"

The ladies made sounds of delight as they understood what he meant. Mrs. Legree was closest, so my father stepped behind her and fastened the chain at the back of her neck. A full-length mirror had been brought to the library, and she stepped up to it to admire herself. All the other ladies exclaimed their approval.

One after another they wore it, each for a minute or two, until it was Melinda's turn. If she was misty-eyed as my father fastened the chain around her neck, if her chin trembled a little, no doubt the others thought she was carried away by the beauty of the necklace. She played her part well. She looked at herself in the mirror, smiled, preened a little, then danced away, swinging her skirt and humming a waltz, while the others laughed and applauded her performance.

I never got to wear the diamond for Tom. As Melinda returned to my father so he could remove the necklace, I glanced out the open window. Not twenty feet away, angry-eyed and defiant, stood Gannon Murdock.

For a moment we stared at each other. Then, as Gannon came a few steps closer, I knew I had to get him away from the house before my father or Uncle Thad saw him. If I failed, any last chance for Melinda and him would vanish.

I moved away from the window. As casually as possible, I edged my way around the room to the door. Fortunately, the entrance hall was at that moment deserted. I hurried out onto the piazza and down the steps.

"Little Gussie," he sneered as I ran to him.

"Gannon, you've got to get away from here!"

"Little Gussie. *Miss* Augusta Welles. You come out here to talk to the white trash, Gussie? You come out to bless the goddamn buckra with your presence?"

Torches had been lit for the departing carriages, and Gannon's face, damp with sweat, glistened in their light. He had been drinking—I could smell the whiskey on his breath—but he looked sober, as if his anger had burned the liquor away.

"Gannon," I said desperately, "if my father sees you out here—"

"You know what they did, Gussie? Because of me and

Melinda? They came over there, they came right into the house. And right in our own house they told me to stay away from her. Like I was some kind of mongrel, gonna spoil her for them. Told me—''

His voice was rising.

"Be quiet, Gannon, please, be quiet!''

"Told me what he'd do to me, your uncle did, if I even once looked at her. Laid his goddamn hands on *me,* the old bastard, and threw me against the wall! Like I was nothing but a handful of shit he was dirtying up our house with!''

I do not think I had ever before in my life witnessed such an overwhelming anger—not even when my father had caught Gannon holding me in the wine cellar. Gannon seemed to loom over me like some dark elemental force of nature that could never be stopped, could never be held back.

"Oh, Gannon—''

"And I took it. For her sake, I just stood there and took it. Knowing that all I had to do was just open my mouth once, and it would rip that old bastard's heart out.''

I understood now. Knowing he could disgrace Melinda in her father's eyes, Gannon had kept silent. He had endured the humiliation of that visit. But afterwards, he had sat brooding, feeling the shame, sick with it, now and then taking a drink that did not help at all, while the shame ate like poison, deeper and deeper. Until finally he had been unable to stand it any longer, and he had come here. Why? God only knew. To stand outside and hate us. To put his everlasting curse on us. To see Melinda, if only at a distance.

"Go home, Gannon. Please go home.''

He ignored me. His eyes were on the windows of the library. "I saw what you all were doing in there. Parading around in that necklace, wasn't that it? Showing them all the Tear of Venus, the famous *Welles* diamond. The Welles diamond, hell. You know where that diamond came from, Gussie?''

I was close to tears. "Gannon, for Melinda's safe—''

"It belonged to my granddaddy, did you know that?''

Yes, I had heard that story at some time in my childhood, but I had hardly thought of it until this night.

"It was the *Murdock* diamond, Gussie, until your granddaddy won it away in a game of cards. And there were plenty that said your granddaddy wasn't above a bit of cheating in those days—twice he had to fight a duel because of it. Did you know that, Gussie? Did you know that in his younger days your granddaddy had a name as a goddamn cheat?''

"That's not so! You get away from here, Gannon Murdock!''

"A goddamn cheat who took our diamond, who really *stole* that damn diamond—''

Tears came. "No!'' I threw myself at him, pounding his chest, pushing at him, trying to force him to leave. "Go away, Gannon, you go away from here—''

"Thieves! Cheats! Liars! Dirty goddamn thieves!''

Gannon had completely lost control of himself. Refusing to yield to me, he shouted at the top of his voice toward the open windows of the house. I have no idea of what I said then—I begged him to leave, I pleaded with him, I implored. Tears were streaming down my face. He stood like a rock as I shoved at him, he still shouting, his hands gripping my shoulders. As I twisted in his grip, I heard cloth tearing, more from my own efforts than from his. There were shouts, cries, footsteps behind me. Gannon had stopped yelling and was staring over my shoulders. I slipped from his hands and dropped to one knee, clutching at my dress to hold it closed over my bare breasts.

Suddenly the night was utterly silent. Slowly I raised my head and looked about. Tom and Gannon, both of them half-crouched, faced each other over my shoulders. Behind Tom stood my father, looking stunned, and Melinda, her face a mask of tragedy. Behind them stood all the others—my mother, Aunt Nickie, Uncle Thad, Horace, a number of the guests.

Tom made a move toward Gannon, and Gannon said, "You touch me just once! You just touch me!'' He held out his arms as if inviting Tom to touch him, and Tom froze.

I do not know how Gannon's father happened to be there. Neither he nor Mrs. Murdock were at our party that evening. Perhaps he had followed Gannon. In any case, he did step into the light of the torches. He said, "Gannon, you get home. Right now.''

Neither Gannon nor Tom moved. They continued to stare at each other.

My father came forward. He took my arm and pulled me to my feet. "Augusta, go back into the house. And stay there.''

"It's not Gannon's fault,'' I said quickly. "He didn't mean anything!''

"I said, go back into the house.''

I moved away, but did not leave. The guests, realizing that this was none of their affair, returned quietly through the open door.

"Laird," my father said, "you know what I told you."

"But it's not his fault," Mr. Murdock said. "You heard what the girl said, August—"

"You know what I told you," my father repeated. "I said that if Gannon ever again touched Augusta—if he ever so much as approached this house without permission—"

"Daddy, please! It was my fault, really it was!"

"I told you he'd have to go. You know I meant that, Laird. And you know I'm a man of my word."

Mr. Murdock was breathing very hard, as if he had run a long distance. "Mr. Welles, sir," he said after a moment, "this is my son's home, the same as it's Mrs. Murdock's and my other children's and mine."

My father shook his head. "Not any longer. He's no longer welcome here."

"Then I'm not either," Mr. Murdock said heavily. "I'm not either."

Gannon turned to his father in alarm. "Pa—!"

"You shut up. Mr. Welles, sir, you told my boy to stay away from your women, and as far as I know, he did. Your own girl says that what happened wasn't his fault, and she should know. So I'm standing behind my boy. We're a family, Mr. Welles, and if you run him off, you run us all off."

My father nodded, as if he understood. "It's your decision, Laird. But I am not running you off."

Mr. Murdock's laugh was bitter. He said, "The hell you ain't, Mr. Welles—sir," and my father looked as if he had been spat upon. He started to say something further, but Mr. Murdock was already walking away.

What can I say of the look that passed between Melinda and Gannon then, of the naked pain in their eyes, of the longing and the despair? They seemed to be reaching for each other while being drawn ever farther apart, and I could feel the anguish in Melinda's heart. Was there no hope for them now or forevermore?

Melinda moaned softly, fought back her tears. Gannon turned away and followed his father into the darkness.

4 ~~~~~

Clutching at my torn dress and turning my tear-stained face away from eyes that tried not to stare, I ran back into the house and up to my room. As I washed my face, guilt overwhelmed me, and I could only think, *What have I done! What have I done!*

Hurriedly, I changed into another dress. I had just finished when Melinda came into the room. She closed the door and slumped against the wall.

"Melinda!"

As I tried to embrace her, she pulled away from me and threw herself face-down on the bed, an arm around her head to cut out the light, as if trying to make the whole cruel world disappear.

"Mel, I'm sorry!"

She did not answer or look up. When I touched her back, I felt the silent, convulsive sobs that shook her body.

"I didn't mean it to happen, Mel! You've got to believe me. I only wanted him to go away before he got caught."

She shook her head, but I had no idea of what she might mean, or if the motion were only a sign of pain. I wanted desperately to comfort her, but had no idea of how to do it. And what comfort would she want from me now?

"Mel—"

She raised her head from her arm. "They want you downstairs," she said in a tearful whisper. "People are leaving."

"But Mel—"

Her face was hidden again, her voice muffled. "Go away, Gussie."

No, she wanted nothing from me now. Perhaps least of all from me.

When I arrived downstairs, I found that my parents were bidding our guests goodnight. I also realized that I had become the object of scandal. I was, after all, a young lady of sixteen years who had gone out into the night to rendezvous (so it seemed) with our overseer's son (of all people!) and who had managed (in a quarrel? a mischance? a moment of passion?) to get the front of her dress ripped open. I was sure that for many of our guests the incident made the party a total success.

Naturally, we all tried to act as if nothing untoward had happened. But my father's face was pinched and pale, and his eyes were too wide, and my mother's manner was too briskly pleasant. We were all glad to see the last guests depart for their homes or their beds.

I wanted only to return to my room and to Melinda, but first my parents escorted me into the library.

"Now," my father said, "tell us exactly what happened."

I could hardly tell them everything without causing more trouble. I merely said that I knew my father and Uncle Thad would be angry if they saw Gannon so close to the house and that I had gone out to send him away.

":Your dress, darling," my mother said. "You haven't told us how Gannon came to tear it."

"Actually . . ." I groped for some way to mitigate the incident. "Actually, *I* tore it. He was shaking me—I can hardly blame him—and I twisted to get away from him, and somehow *I* tore it."

My mother seemed to accept that. I could not tell if my father did. He looked unwaveringly at me for a moment, one of those moments when he seemed to read my mind.

"Augusta, I told you not to go near Gannon and not to talk to him. If you hadn't gone out there, he might very well have wandered off before long. He had caused no trouble before you disobeyed my orders."

"But I didn't mean . . . I didn't mean . . ."

I found myself enfolded in my mother's arms and weeping on her shoulder. It did not matter that I had not meant to cause trouble but to prevent it. I had disobeyed orders, and this was the result. Gannon and his family were leaving the Barony, and any ghost of a chance that he and Melinda might yet have married had surely vanished.

I felt my father patting my head. "You meant well," he said gently, "and that forgives a lot of things."

But how did one forgive oneself?

"Listen to me, Augusta," my father went on, "Gannon must leave here. But it's not the worst thing in the world for a young man to go off on his own—often it's the making of him. And perhaps, just perhaps, tomorrow I can persuade Mr. Murdock to stay.''

I went from my mother's arms to my father's. "Oh, try, Daddy, try!" If only he could persuade Mr. Murdock! That would undo at least part of the trouble I had caused.

"I'll do my best."

At last I was released from the library, and I hurried upstairs, hoping to make some kind of peace with Melinda. But I had forgotten that I would be unable to talk with her alone that night. We had long before asked Julie Anne Legree to stay the night and share our bed, and Julie Anne wanted to discuss the evening's excitement. When at last I had silenced her, and the lamps were out, I felt the bed shaking on Melinda's side. I turned and fitted myself to her back. This time she did not draw away from me, but I sensed it was not the right time to talk. Yet I wanted to comfort her in some way, and I contented myself with holding her tightly until her silent weeping eased into sleep.

When I awakened in the morning, my very first thought—my only thought—was of Tom Raveneau.

Had it really happened? Was it true that he loved not Melinda but me? Had we really held each other and kissed and declared our love?

I had to see Tom. I had to see him and talk to him as soon as possible and assure myself that nothing had changed since yesterday afternoon, that he really did love me as I loved him.

Stretching luxuriously, I found that one side of the bed was empty. Julie Anne was still asleep, the look of a sweet child on her face, but Melinda was already up and gone. That brought back to me her terrible predicament and all that had happened during the previous evening, and I felt guilty for not thinking of that first. But surely things were not as bad as they seemed—I could not be this happy and not believe there was a way to make Melinda happy too. I had to see and talk to her, as well as to Tom, as soon as possible.

When I arrived downstairs, the household was in a whirl, for our remaining guests had to be fed breakfast and seen off on their journeys home. Some of them had brought their own servants, and the house seemed to rattle with manservants and maids, more of them than of us. Ben, Chloe, and Polly— butler, housekeeper, and chief housemaid—managed to be in all places at once, and I was told repeatedly to keep out of the way. When I went down to the kitchen, Matty, the cook, was shouting orders to her daughter Tilda, who also told me to keep out of the way, and when I went outside the house, Polly's husband, David, who was bringing the guests' carriages to the door, shouted, "Out of the way, Miss Gussie, out of the way!" Everything everywhere was in happy commotion.

I finally found Tom with my father and a couple of other men strolling around the house. The instant I caught his eye, I knew it was all true—that he did love me. There was, I thought, a special sparkle in his eye and a flush on his cheek, and he seemed to be concealing a secret smile.

Of course there was no hope of drawing him away from the other men to talk to him alone—such a thing wasn't done—so I went in search of Melinda. But it looked as if I would find no opportunity to speak to her alone either. At the breakfast table she sat between her grim-faced daddy and her pale-faced mamma, and afterwards they continued to flank her, as if keeping her under surveillance. She appeared calm that morning, but hollow and washed out—rather, I thought, like someone who had accepted the fact that she was going to the guillotine. Finally I found a chance to whisper to her, "The gazebo in the flower garden," and she nodded.

It was only long after breakfast, when most of the guests had departed, that Melinda escaped from her parents and came out to meet me. I had been waiting in the gazebo for what seemed like hours.

She pulled off her sunbonnet and dropped down on a bench. "Daddy's been watching me like a hawk," she said, "but I guess he got tired of it. I told him I wanted to find you, and he let me go."

I, I am ashamed to say, went immediately to what concerned me most. "Melinda! I've been dying to tell you something, but I haven't had a chance!"

"Tell me what, Gussie?" She smiled wanly.

I sat down on the bench beside her. "About Tom and me! When he got here yesterday, I jumped into his carriage and drove off with him, and—and he's in love with me, Mel!"

She stared at me. "What do you mean, you drove off with him?"

"Just that! Just the two of us! And the next thing I knew, we were sitting there in the woods, the two of us all alone, and he kissed me, and—and he told me he loved me! Just like that!''

"Why, Gussie!"

"And I'm in love with him too, Mel. I have been for a long time, but I never said anything, because I thought he belonged to you."

"Why, Gussie Welles!" Melinda laughed softly and put her arms around me. "And you say he kissed you?"

"More times than I can count."

"And you love him!"

"So much!"

Melinda continued to laugh and to rock me in her arms. "Oh, Gussie, I am so happy for you."

"The only trouble is, Daddy has always told me I have to wait till I'm eighteen to get married, and I don't think I'll *ever* get that old!''

"Oh, you will. And sixteen is a little young to marry, I guess."

"But you're planning to get married, and you're not much older than me.''

"A year and a half. It seems like a long time."

It did indeed seem like a long time, and Melinda seemed to have grown even older in the last day or two—so much older since yesterday afternoon.

"Mel, about Gannon . . .''

Her arms fell away from me, and her smile faded. She looked sick.

"I'm sorry about last night," I said.

She closed her eyes and shook her head. "It wasn't your fault. I know you were only trying to help. But it probably would have happened anyway. That's why Gannon came to the house. He was hurt and angry and likely drunk, and he came to the house to make trouble. Don't blame yourself, dear."

That was my cousin Melinda—always generous, always forgiving. In her place, I would have been ready to commit murder.

"But don't give up hope," I said.

"There is no hope."

"Yes, there is! Your daddy can't make you marry anyone else but Gannon if you don't want to."

"But he can keep me from marrying Gannon—especially now that Gannon and his whole family are going away."

I insisted on optimism. "Melinda, listen to me. I talked to my daddy last night. He said that today he would try to persuade Mr. Murdock to stay. And if the Murdocks stay, you can bet that Gannon will be coming back to visit. And you'll be here! Melinda, we're going to get you married to Gannon yet!"

Her eyes closed, Melinda slowly shook her head. She looked sick again.

"But why not!"

"Gussie, there's something that maybe you don't know. When my daddy gets me home tomorrow, he's going to have some of the women give me . . ." She choked on the words. "He's going to have them give me an . . . examination."

"Oh!" I had completely forgotten.

"Oh, Gussie!" Suddenly Melinda leaned forward, her head between her knees, breathing hard, as if she were in danger of fainting. "Gussie, I don't think I can bear that examination! I can't, I can't bear it! And when he finds out! . . . Oh, God, Gussie, I can't bear for him to find out! I can't bear for him to know, I can't bear what he'll think, what it'll do to him! Oh, Gussie, *I can't bear it, I can't bear it!*"

Her voice was filled with sheer terror, and when she raised her head, so were her eyes. Her face was frighteningly red, and she was breathing harder than ever. "Melinda, don't!" I cried, seizing her shoulders. "Melinda, stop! Please! It's going to be all right!"

"No, it's not. Oh, Gussie, I'd rather die than go through that examination. I'd rather die than have him find out. I love my daddy, Gussie, I love him! And I'd rather die right now—"

"Stop it! Stop it!"

I shook her with all my strength, until she broke out in a long agonized wail, then held her tightly.

What had Uncle Thad done to her, I thought with horror, that she should literally prefer death to disgrace in his eyes? For the first time in my life I began to comprehend the emotional blackmail by which so many men—fathers, husbands, lovers—rule their women, and parents their children. Melinda truly loved her father—and he had used that love to reduce her to this craven, terrified thing.

I had to help her. Somehow.

Gradually I calmed her, but when she ceased to weep, she

seemed like an ill old woman, even sicker than my mother. At seventeen.

She said she wanted to go to our room and lie down, and I led her back to the house. Fortunately, we met no one before I had her in the room. Then I went looking for my mother. She, too, was lying down, saving her strength, for the previous evening had drained her.

"Mamma," I said, standing by her big canopied bed, "do you know about the—the examination that Uncle Thad wants done on Melinda?"

She frowned. "Yes, I do."

"You must tell Aunt Nickie not to let him do it. The whole idea has got Mel upset."

"I'm afraid that Melinda's being upset is not going to stop your Uncle Thad."

"Mamma! Listen to me! You must not let him do it. Aunt Nickie must not let him do it. We've all got to stop him. We've got to keep Mel here and not let her go home!"

My mother looked directly into my eyes and saw the truth. "Oh, my God," she said softly. "Oh, that poor child."

"Will you speak to Aunt Nickie?"

"Yes. Of course. I don't know if we can stop him, but if there's any way at all, we'll do it. We must. We must."

Melinda pleaded sickness and did not appear at Sunday dinner. Her father sighed heavily but raised no objections. While my father was saying grace, I looked at my mother at the far end of the table. When our eyes met, I saw the determination in hers, and when I looked across the table at Aunt Nickie, sitting on my father's right, I thought I saw the same thing in the set of her jaw. I felt a sudden rise of hope, for both of those ladies, ordinarily so gentle, could be tigerish where their children were concerned.

Hence I was feeling much happier when, half an hour after dinner, Tom whispered a few words that caused a wild fluttering of my heart. But, yes, I would do it! By that time most of the household was groggy from full stomachs and the afternoon heat, and it was a simple matter to wander away from the house unnoticed, disappear into the woods, and reach my destination unseen. One last look around, and I darted into the barn. And there, in the dim light and the pungent animal smells, I awaited Tom.

He appeared ten minutes later.

For a long moment we merely stood there and looked at each other. He was hatless and in shirt sleeves. A shaft of sunlight turned his sandy hair to gold, and his eyes, hot on me, were blue fire.

I remember the beat of my heart. I remember closing my eyes. Then his arms were around me, my body was arching against his, and I was swept away, my mind reeling and the sweet hot fires running through me from breasts to thighs. His mouth was against mine, and my lips parted—oh, I was learning!—and lightning flashed through me. I saw the fine texture of Tom's cheek as we kissed, and the very barn smells in the hot damp air were like a perfume that made me want to dissolve into his body. I became aware of my thighs as his thighs trembled against them, of my breasts as they moved against his chest. He murmured my name as his hand slid down the small of my back, and it was almost more than my senses could bear—I thought I was going to faint.

Before that could happen, I took my mouth from his, sighed, and drew away from him.

"Tom," I said, when I could speak, "maybe one good thing has come out of this—this trouble with Gannon and his family."

"What's that, sweet?"

"My father will have to hire a new overseer, and that will take time. That means we can be together a little longer before they take me away."

"We'll never be apart, if I can help it. The first chance I get, I'll speak to your father about us. Maybe you won't have to go to England."

He drew me tightly to him again.

"Oh, Tom . . ."

We dared not remain alone together for too long, and within the hour I insisted that we return to the house. No one was in sight as I peered out of the barn door, and we quickly scooted out.

"Well, what are you two doing here?"

My father's voice. I nearly jumped out of my shoes. He had just come around the corner of the barn.

"Just looking around," I said, and added quickly to change the subject, "Daddy, may Tom stay on with us while we're here at the Barony?"

It was an ill-considered diversion, for my father's eyes

definitely took on a measuring look. But then he smiled and said, "Tom knows he's always welcome here."

"Why, thank you, sir," Tom said.

We started walking back toward the house, Tom and my father on each side of me. I took my father's arm, as if *that* might allay any suspicions.

"What are *you* doing out here, Daddy?"

"I've just been talking to Mr. Murdock."

That brought it all back—Melinda's problem and all that had happened the previous night. The fact that my father now fell silent and blank-faced was not promising.

"Did you persuade him to stay, Daddy?"

"Augusta, I asked him to hear me out and give me no answer until he had taken time to think things over. And then I simply made the best case I could for him to stay."

"Did he seem receptive, sir?" Tom asked.

"Not really." My father sounded disheartened. "He did hear me out, but he never said a word. And afterwards he just went back into his house and closed the door. Augusta, it's possible that Mr. Murdock will come around yet, but I can't hold out much hope."

But I had to have hope. I had to cling to any shred of hope I could find. It was hope for Melinda.

When we got back to the house, I left Tom and my father talking together and went to look for my mother. I found her sitting alone in the south parlor, and I sensed at once that all was not well. Since she had become sick, her face had become thinner, and her finely sculpted features—her high cheekbones, the graceful line of jaw and chin—had grown more prominent. Now she sat, eyes closed, head resting on her fingertips, and her face looked more spare, more pale than ever, a portrait carved in ivory.

"Mamma," I said, "are you sleeping?"

She opened her eyes and raised her head from her fingertips. "No, Augusta, I'm not sleeping. Just resting."

"Have you . . . has Aunt Nickie spoken to Uncle Thad yet?"

"We both spoke to him. Just now. At considerable length." My mother sounded weary. "We pointed out that no woman should be forced to submit to such a barbaric indignity. We appealed to his pride in his family and in himself: what would he think of himself for doing such a thing?"

Her tone told me what I wanted to know. I felt sick. "But he's going to do it anyway."

My mother nodded. "So he says. Or insists, rather."

I gave a little cry and shook my fists. I wanted to throw something, to break something.

"But don't you worry, Augusta." The strength returned to my mother's voice and the determination to her eyes. "We are not done with Thaddeus Welles yet. We shall speak to him again and again, and if need be yet again. I shall have your father speak to him, too. We are not going to let this thing happen."

A few minutes later, I passed Pearl on the stairs.

"Have you seen Melinda, Pearl? How is she?"

Pearl shrugged. She did not look at me. "She be all right, don't you worry. She resting in your room." There was something evasive in her manner, and I watched her as she continued down the stairs and out of the house.

When I got to our room, I found Melinda lying on our bed. She seemed calm enough, but she was hollow-eyed and unmoving.

"Mel," I said, "how are you now?"

Ever so slightly she shook her head.

"Are you all right?"

She nodded.

"Mel, *every*thing is going to be all right. Daddy talked to Mr. Murdock about staying on, and your mother and mine are both going to talk to your father—"

"They already have," Melinda said softly. "I heard them."

And heard what my father had said, his insistence on going through with the examination.

"But they're going to talk to him some more, Mel, and Mamma says my daddy will talk to him, too. Everything's going to be all right, Mel, I'm sure it is."

Melinda's eyes closed. "No."

I wanted to cry. "But you can't just give up hope!"

She did not answer. The abject terror of the morning was gone, but this apparent acceptance of defeat seemed almost as bad.

"Mel, I am not going to give up hope, and neither are you!"

She lay as still as a corpse. One might have thought that she had not heard a word I said.

"Is there anything I can do for you, Mel? Anything at all?"

"No," she said. "Pearl is taking care of everything."

I awakened sometime during the night with no sense of having slept at all. It was as if I had lain in my bed for an hour or more, thinking constantly that Uncle Thad had to be stopped, that he *must* be stopped—and suddenly my eyes were open, and I was staring at the dark wall.

I sat bolt upright, my heart pounding. Somehow I knew that Melinda was no longer with me even before I looked at the other side of the bed.

I knew instantly where she had gone, of course, and as I hurried out of bed, I thought, *Oh, Lord, not tonight!* *"Pearl is taking care of everything,"* Melinda had said, and now I understood: Pearl had been carrying messages between her and Gannon, helping them arrange a secret meeting. I understood, too, Melinda's wish to be with Gannon, but how could she be so foolish as to endanger any last chance of curbing her father's intentions?

Surely, once again, she could not be too far ahead of me. In robe and slippers, I stole out into the hall. I whispered her name sharply two or three times, but there was no answer, no sound at all.

As I hurried down the stairs, the house remained utterly silent. Out on the piazza, I found the night moonlit, as it had been forty-eight hours earlier, but this time Melinda was nowhere in sight. Racing toward the barn, I thought of my father's warnings about going out at night, but nothing was more important than finding my cousin and bringing her back to the house.

The door of the barn was ajar, and to my surprise, a thin ray of light filtered out from it. When I looked in, Melinda was there, as I had expected, and so was Gannon. They were both dressed for travel, and by the light of the lamp, Gannon was hitching bundles to the backs of two mules.

"Gussie!" Melinda cried out as I entered the barn, and Gannon looked around, startled. "Gussie, what are you doing here?"

"I woke up and found you gone," I said. "Melinda Welles, have you gone out of your mind?"

"Oh, don't be angry with me, Gussie," Melinda said, and as she came to me and wrapped her arms around me, she was smiling, and happiness had returned to her eyes. Over her shoulder I saw Gannon watching me tensely.

"But what—what are you doing!"

Melinda backed away and held my shoulders. "The only thing we can do. We're running away together. My daddy will never let us get married if we stay here. And if he gives me that examination tomorrow and finds out that I'm not—that we—"

"He ain't gonna find out nothing except that you're gone," Gannon said. "Unless little Gussie here has got a big mouth."

Melinda gave me a little shake. "Oh, Gussie won't say anything. Will you, Gussie?"

"No, but—but what will happen to you, Mel?"

"We're going west," she said excitedly. "By the time everybody wakes up, we'll be miles away. Gannon says we'll travel at night for a few days and stay off the main roads in the daytime. He has lots of friends, and he knows places where we can stay until we're far away from here."

"But after that—"

"Gannon has some money, and he owns these two mules that are worth something, and if we have to, we'll stop and work from time to time to make our money last. And—and Gannon is awfully good at playing cards—"

"Oh, that's no way to make a living!"

"Please listen to me, Gussie! Everything is going to be all right. I know it won't be easy, in fact, it'll be awfully hard at times, but—"

"There's a future in the West, Gussie," Gannon said quietly. "I told you that once, remember? Land's cheap in Alabama and Mississippi, and some say it's the richest soil in the world. There is one great big *pie* out there, Gussie, and Melinda and me, we're gonna carve us out the biggest piece of that pie you ever did see. It's there for the taking." He smiled and held out a work-calloused hand. "That is, it's there for the taking if you got the right kind of hands for it. Maybe this ain't a gentleman's hand, but the frontier ain't no place for a gentleman. I've got the right kind of hands for the job."

As he withdrew his hand, his smile faded. "And don't you worry none about Melinda, Gussie. I'll take care of her. You can count on it."

I had never thought to hear such a speech from Gannon.

Gone from his voice was all the old bitterness, the resentment, the spite. Gone, too, was the gypsy boy's scorn with which he had treated me for as long as I could remember. But that had been mere childishness, after all, and we were grown up now. All three of us. And I realized that Gannon was asking me not merely to keep silent about this elopement, but to give it my blessing. Somehow that brought tears to my eyes.

I had never dreamed that I would say it: "I think Melinda is right. I think you're a good man, Gannon Murdock."

He gave me a quick grin. "You're a spunky kid, Gus," he said. "Just don't step on any cottonmouths."

For a moment we just stood there, looking at each other, wondering when we would all meet again. Then Melinda embraced me one last time.

"We'd better be going, Gussie."

"Write!"

"Oh, I will, just as soon as we're settled."

"I'll be waiting every day!"

"Now, dear, don't cry. One day you and Tom will come to see us, and—"

Something terrible happened to her voice. It became a long wail of despair. And as she looked over my shoulder, I saw in her eyes the death of every dream.

"You're not going anywhere," Uncle Thad said, coming through the door. "Not anywhere at all."

5 ◌◌◌◌◌◌

How had Uncle Thad come to be there? Had he heard my sharp whisper of Melinda's name in the hall? Had he been lying awake, suspecting, fearing, that Melinda might try to run away with Gannon?

I have no idea. And I have no idea whether he spoke his next words in irony or in malice. As he came toward us, a big tousled figure in robe and slippers, he uttered a short, bitter laugh. "You did very well, holding them until I got here, Augusta. Oh, yes, Augusta, you've been a great help."

Whatever Uncle Thad's meaning, Gannon heard betrayal in those words. As his eyes moved from Uncle Thad to me, I saw the dismay in them turning to a kind of pained bewilderment at the idea that I, even I, could have done this thing to Melinda and him. Only a moment before, we had made our peace, he had thought we were friends, and now once again I was one of *them*, the Welles family, the enemy. I said, "Gannon, I didn't!" but there was no belief in his eyes.

"And you, girl," Uncle Thad said, looking at Melinda. "What the hell do you think you're doing?"

Under his gaze Melinda writhed like a creature on fire. "Daddy—"

"Doing to me and to your mamma and to yourself as well. Seventeen years we've brought you up right, and you've come to this. Trying to throw yourself away, to destroy all my plans for you, a good marriage, wealth, a future—"

"Mr. Welles," Gannon said, "I'll give Melinda all that! I don't mean to do no wrong by her! I want to marry her!"

"Daddy, if you'll only listen—"

"No. Go back to the house. I'll deal with you later."

Melinda pressed herself against Gannon's chest as if to protect him. "Daddy, I love Gannon!"

"Love?" As Uncle Thad stepped toward Melinda, he wore a faint smile that made the glitter in his eyes all the more frightening. "Don't you ever say that to me. Don't you ever speak to me about love, don't you ever say that word to me again."

"Mr. Welles," Gannon said desperately, "I swear to you, I'll make Melinda happy, if you'll just give me a chance!"

"Happy?" Uncle Thad laughed contemptuously. "What does a pup like you know about happiness? A jug of whiskey, a willing wench, and somebody's head to pound on—that's happiness to you. Sandhiller happiness!"

Gannon's eyes sparked. "I'm no sandhill trash, and you know it. I'm a Murdock—"

"Sandhiller happiness," Uncle Thad repeated. "White-trash happiness for an overseer's whelp. But not with my daughter. Now, get your hands off her."

Melinda and Gannon made no move to part, and I do not know what Uncle Thad might have done if my father and Tom had not arrived at that moment. My father looked at once alarmed and confused with sleep. Tom moved protectively to my side, but said nothing.

"What is it?" my father asked. "Thad, what's going on? We saw the light out here—"

"What does it look like? This is what happens when I put my daughter into your keeping."

My father looked at Melinda and Gannon and the mules and began to understand. "Oh, no . . ."

"Yes. And I'm going to do something about it. Once and for all."

My father shook his head. "Thad, I know you're upset, and I don't blame you. You have every right. But I think we'd best let this lie until morning. Let tempers cool."

"No. We finish it tonight. I'm not going to sleep until it's finished."

"Mr. Welles, sir," Tom said respectfully, "Mr. August is right—"

"I said tonight. You'd best rouse up some of the women, August. Chloe and Matty, and maybe someone else who isn't too thick with them. I don't want any collusion, I don't want any lies. I want the truth."

"Daddy!" I said in alarm. "Don't let them!" Melinda's cry, as she hid her face against Gannon's shoulder, tore my soul apart.

Sleep was gone from my father's eyes. He looked shocked. "But how can you even think of such a thing!" he said. "My God, what kind of people are we? Your own daughter!"

Uncle Thad shook his head sharply. "Do you think I want to do it? But I've got to know! And I'm going to know *now!*"

Melinda cried out one last time—a cry of pain, of defeat, of utter desolation. Then, tearing herself from Gannon's arms, she ran out of the barn and was lost in the outer darkness.

"Well," Uncle Thad said softly, and he sounded like a lost soul, "I reckon that just about tells me everything."

"It tells you nothing," my father protested, "nothing at all."

Uncle Thad ignored him. He turned again to Gannon. "You had her, didn't you, boy? You ruined my daughter."

But Gannon was staring at me. "You," he said, "you were supposed to be her friend. Her best friend."

"Gannon," I said desperately, "I didn't tell!"

He didn't seem to hear me. "She trusted you! Her best friend! She trusted—"

The next thing I knew, I was in his hands.

I do not think he knew what he intended to do to me then. I do know that he was acting only out of a grief that he could not contain. To this day, I have never believed that Gannon Murdock actually meant to harm me.

But harm me he might have, without ever knowing what he was doing. I was helpless in his hands, unable to escape as he lifted me from the floor and shook me with all his strength. "Her friend!" he repeated, as if the words were a curse. "Her very best friend!"

Tom swore and tried to wrest me away from him. But Gannon released me only when my father brought a slashing blow down across his arms and threw him back against a mule.

"I think you're right, Thad," he said in sudden anger. "I've had enough of this scoundrel. Yes, I think we had best finish this tonight!"

Gannon Murdock had taken many a beating in his nineteen years, but surely none worse than the one he received that night. Ordered back to the house, I paused in the dark of the woods to look toward the lighted door of the barn. I heard Uncle Thad's voice, his words muffled but his anger clear. I heard Tom's temperate, reasoning tones. I heard my father's sharp, clear order: "Tie him!" Gannon was silent.

The first crack of the whip—I had no doubt what that sound was—brought my hands to my ears, but there was still no sound from Gannon. Somehow I knew it was Uncle Thad who wielded the whip—Uncle Thad, who would be merciless. I heard the crack again and again despite my hands, and no hands in the world could have stopped the cry that suddenly rent the air. The cry was repeated with every whip crack, then became unending. I could stand it no longer. I turned and ran.

Lights were appearing in the house. Aunt Nickie spoke to me as I entered the hall, but I fled past her and up the stairs to my room, where I threw myself across my bed.

It seemed like hours before I heard my father talking to my mother and Aunt Nickie outside the room, and I knew that Gannon's ordeal was over. A moment later, my father came into the room, my mother with him, and sat down on the bed beside me.

"It had to be done," he said. "Even if Gannon hadn't touched you, it had to be done."

Gannon's cries still rang in my ears. "Will he be all right?"

My father's silence alarmed me.

"Daddy—!"

"Augusta, you're too old not to be told the truth. Physically, Gannon will be all right, I'm sure, except for a few scars. But the whip can do things to a man's spirit."

I sat up on the bed and tried to see my father's eyes in the dark, but he kept his head averted.

I wept then. Laid my head on my father's shoulder and wept. For, whatever Gannon thought of me now, I remembered the youth who had once wept on *my* shoulder . . . but who, in the end, had thrust me away to stand on his own feet, his pride unbroken. That was the Gannon whom Melinda loved. And my father was telling me he had been humbled at last.

The silence was broken by a disturbance in the hall. A light appeared, silhouetting Uncle Thad's big frame in my doorway. Aunt Nickie was calling his name and appeared to be trying to draw him back, but he ignored her. "Melinda?" he called. "Melinda, you get yourself out here!"

"She's not here, Thad," my father said.

"I want her, right now. I've got Matty out here, and Chloe has gone after one of the other women—"

"Oh, no!" My mother and Aunt Nickie spoke together. "No, Thad," Aunt Nickie said, "you are not going to do this! Not to my daughter!"

"They're right, Thad," my father said, rising to his feet. "You shouldn't do such a thing, and certainly not tonight."

"Yes, tonight. And if what I suspect is true . . . August, I am going to cure that boy for all time."

"No, Thad, you are not!" I don't think I had ever heard my father raise his voice to my uncle before, and rarely to any other man. But now it was his turn to thunder. "No, Thad, you are not going to cure anybody of anything on this plantation! And you are not going to conduct your—your examination of that girl here. You've had your vengeance, Thad! Now, for God's sake, man, go to bed and let the rest of us get some sleep!"

At that instant, light from a candle struck my uncle's eyes, and all the resentment he felt for my father was naked in them. When he spoke, his voice was surprisingly soft.

"August," he said, "you are not going to tell me how to

run my family, not at the Barony or anywhere else. Now, I want my daughter!''

My father had done what he could, and he knew it. Out in the hall, Aunt Nickie was sobbing. My mother clasped her hands before her bowed head, her eyes closed. My father turned to me.

''Augusta . . .?''

''I don't know,'' I said. ''I haven't seen her since she left the barn.''

''She isn't here, Thad,'' my father said. ''You can see that.''

Uncle Thad turned toward the hall.

''Nickie, where is she? You have any idea?''

''No. She's not in our room.''

''Well, damn it, she's got to be hiding somewhere in the house. Where *is* she?''

A chill of apprehension swept over me. I was instantly certain that Uncle Thad was wrong, that Melinda was nowhere in the house. If she had been, surely she would have been right here, in our bedroom.

Suddenly—I knew not why—Uncle Thad was no longer the greatest threat in the world. ''We've got to find her!'' I said, springing up from the bed. ''Oh, Lord—Mamma, Daddy, we've got to find her!''

Melinda was nowhere in the house.

With a growing sense of panic, we went through every room—first, the upstairs bedrooms, then down through all the first-floor rooms, repeatedly calling her name. Then, lamps in hand, we searched the house yet again, from the attic rooms to the cellars, but nowhere was she to be found.

When at last we gathered in the entrance hall, even Uncle Thad's eyes held fright. Yet he said with great certainty, ''I know where she is. There's one more place, and she's got to be there.''

We all knew where he meant. Surely at this time Melinda would want only to be with Gannon.

My father accompanied Uncle Thad to the overseer's house, and I followed them—nothing in the world could have kept me back. As we approached the house, we saw that lights were still burning.

In one bound, Uncle Thad was up on the piazza and loudly

banging the brass knocker. Mr. Murdock, his eyes stony, answered the door at once.

"Murdock," Uncle Thad said, "I'm looking for my daughter."

"You dare come here?" Mr. Murdock asked. "After what you did tonight, you dare come here?"

"I said, I'm looking for my daughter. I've come to get her."

"Well, you won't find her here."

Mr. Murdock started to close the door, but Uncle Thad kicked it open again. As he shoved his way into the passage, Mr. Murdock grabbed at him, but my father said, "Laird, please!" and held him back.

We could hear Uncle Thad's boots thump as he went from room to room and up the stairs. He seemed to be trying to drive his heels through the floors, and no doubt he ignored any furniture he overturned. Mr. Murdock stood perfectly still except for his clenching jaw, as if knowing that if he let himself slip, if he heard any outcry from his wife or children, he very well might kill.

Fortunately it took but a few minutes to search the little house. When Uncle Thad came back down the stairs and out the front door, he never looked at Mr. Murdock, but he must have felt the hatred that glowed in our overseer's eyes.

The door closed, shutting off the light from the passage, and the two men came down off the piazza.

"Oh, Christ," Uncle Thad said, his voice breaking.

"It'll be all right, Thad," my father said. "She's somewhere nearby. We'll find her."

Next we searched the house servants' quarters, since they were close to the big house, and the servants were recruited to help us. Torches were lit, and we went through all the other nearby outbuildings. Nothing was overlooked, and torches explored every shadow as the search grew wider. Tom and I even returned to the barn, and I climbed up to peer into the darkness of the loft.

There was no answer to my hushed call of Melinda's name.

The search spread farther still, out to the quarters of the field hands and their families, and there I led the way, for I, of course, knew best which of the young people Melinda might have turned to. But I saw only bewilderment in their faces, as they shook their heads and told me no, no, they had no idea of where Melinda might be. Soon almost every man and woman on the plantation was looking for her.

It was David who found her—David, the chief coachman, Aunt Polly's husband.

It was perhaps an hour before dawn, and I was completely exhausted. Tom and I had returned to every single place where Melinda and I had ever played, yet I still could not comprehend the reality of her disappearance. She *had* to be somewhere nearby. Wearily, clinging to Tom's arm, I followed him along the river path, heading upstream toward the plantation landing.

Ahead of us, in the darkness, I heard an anguished cry.

The cry was repeated. David's voice was at first unrecognizable. "Oh, my Lord, no," he was saying. "Not dis poor chile! Oh, no . . ."

Tom started running, dragging me along the trail through the darkness.

"Oh, my Lord, my Lord . . ."

I suppose I knew then, if I had not before. The grief that began to well up was almost more than I could bear.

"Oh, my Lord, Mr. Tom . . ."

I could see but dimly at first. David was knee deep in the river. Two other men stood on the bank. David was trying to take something, a sodden whiteness, from the water.

Oh, not Melinda! I screamed inwardly. *Please, God, please, not Melinda!*

Tom jumped into the water and, with David, leaned over that whiteness. Carefully he took it from David's hands, carefully turned it over in his arms, and gently lifted it.

As he carried her up onto the bank, I saw her face, pale as the moon. Melinda.

She looked so small, so shrunken, that she might easily have slipped away from Tom's arms. Her eyes were slightly open, and for a moment I had a wild thought that she must still be alive. But then David, with a sob, touched those eyes and ever so gently closed them.

A moment later I realized that he was holding me, supporting me and trying to soothe me, as we followed Tom, Melinda in his arms, back to the house.

Dear God, must I remember everything that followed? My aunt's cries of protest and pain and grief when she saw her daughter lying dead in Tom's arms? The agony in my uncle's eyes, an agony I would never wish even on that terrible man? Cousin Horace Blakely's tear-drenched chubby face? My parents' anguish?

Why? I asked myself. Why had she done it? For, remembering Melinda's state of mind the previous morning, I was certain that she had taken her own life. But why could she have not kept at least some glimmering of hope? Why had she yielded to despair?

An hour or so after dawn found me lying on the bottom steps of the piazza with my head in Pearl's lap. On my face, Pearl's tears mingled with my own.

"Why, Pearl?" I asked. "Why?"

Pearl did not answer at first, just stroked my hair. A new day had begun, but we saw none of the people in the fields or at their chores, heard no sounds from the outbuildings. The Barony was in mourning.

"Why, Pearl? Why did she have to throw away even the tiniest chance?"

"Reckon she figured there wasn't no tiniest chance. And, knowing Mr. Thad, reckon she was right."

"But if she had just waited . . ."

"Don't reckon she figured she could wait no longer, Gussie, chile."

I lifted my head so that I could look at Pearl's face.

"What do you mean?"

Pearl closed her eyes, and her lips pursed and trembled. I thought she was going to cry again.

"What do you *mean?*"

Pearl wiped her eyes with her hand. "Well . . . I reckon she was . . . 'bout three month along."

It seemed to take forever for Pearl's meaning to come clear to me.

"No," I said in a voice that could not have been fainter.

Pearl nodded.

"Why didn't she tell me?"

"Don't reckon she wanted to tell nobody."

"She told you."

Pearl shook her head. "She don't tell me nothing, but I got a good eye for it. I can 'most always tell. And I see how she been acting, so I look at her real good, and I say, 'Miss Melinda, you got something you want to tell me? Maybe I can help.' And she turn all pale and act like she don't know what I'm talking 'bout. So I say, 'Honey, I see your eye when you look at Mr. Gannon. He the one, ain't he?' And she bust out crying, and then I know I'm right.''

Everything made sense. Of course Melinda had killed herself. What else would she have done? Never in the world could she have admitted to her father that she had committed the sin of love, that she was bearing the child of that love.

Better to die.

"Does Gannon know?" I asked.

Pearl shook her head. "She don't want to worry him or scare him or make him feel like he marrying her 'cause he got to. She say telling him ain't gonna make her no less with a baby.''

I thought about it and came to a decision, the only one possible.

"You mustn't tell anybody, Pearl. Not anybody at all. Not Gannon or even your mamma or mine. It can only add to everybody's unhappiness, and I think it would kill Aunt Nickie if she found out. It's got to be our secret.''

"Don't you worry none, Gussie, I ain't going to tell nobody else. I only tell you, 'cause I got to tell somebody, and you her friend.''

"Our secret. Forever.''

"I am the resurrection and the life, saith the Lord. He that believeth in me, though he were dead, yet shall he live. And whosoever liveth and believeth in me shall never die.''

The next thing I remember is those words being spoken over Melinda's coffin in the nearby village church, where the funeral was held two days later. The church was crowded, for every neighbor who could attend had come. Even the Murdocks were there—except for Gannon, of course, and little Ross, who was too young—for at this hour the quarrel between our families was irrelevant. But principally I remember our own family, the white and the black, united in sorrow.

Even with the minister's eulogy, the service was mercifully short. When it was over, the six pallbearers carried the coffin from the church and placed it in the wagon that would carry it to our family graveyard. The minister and our family and the other mourners followed in carriages, and when we reached the Barony, our people from the quarters joined the cortege. The day was so hot, the sky so blank and blazing, that it was actually a relief to reach the shaded graveyard, and as I climbed down from the carriage, I was pleased to see that

Melinda's grave was under the wide-spreading branches of a magnificent oak.

"Man that is born of a woman hath but a short time to live and is full of misery," the minister intoned as the pallbearers brought the coffin to the grave. "He cometh up and is cut down like a flower. He fleeth as it were a shadow, and never continueth in one stay. In the midst of life we are in death. . . ."

Holding the coffin with ropes, the pallbearers slowly lowered it into the grave.

"Unto Almighty God we commend the soul of our sister departed, and we commit her body to the ground. Earth to earth, ashes to ashes, dust to dust . . ."

I heard Aunt Nickie's sobs and could barely hold back my own. Pearl and Rufus, standing near me, appeared to be in terrible pain. Who had brought Melinda to this, I asked myself. Who had brought her to this early grave? I, Gannon, Melinda herself—we all bore a measure of blame. And surely, most of all, Uncle Thad, for the fear he had inspired in the daughter who had loved him. But who was I to stand in judgment? My uncle, too, was suffering.

"Come, ye blessed of my Father, inherit the kingdom prepared for you from the foundation of the world. Grant this, O Father, for the sake of thy Son—"

"Get him away from here!"

Until Uncle Thad's outburst, no one had noticed Gannon. He had made his way through the circle of black people from the quarters and had stood outside our own circle, a solitary mourner, excluded. By what supreme act of will he had dragged his whip-crippled body from his bed and all the way to the graveyard, I could not imagine. But now, in shirt sleeves, his face glistening with sweat, he stood with his feet braced apart, swaying as if he might fall at any instant.

"Get him away from here, August," Uncle Thad repeated angrily. "Murdock, you get your boy away. How dare he desecrate my daughter's burial by coming here?"

There was a shocked murmur among the mourners, and as Mr. Murdock hurried around the grave toward my uncle, his face was ashen under its weathering. "Mr. Welles, my boy meant no desecration. He came here to pay his respects, is all."

"Get him away from here. If I ever lay eyes on him again, I'll kill him."

Anger flared in Mr. Murdock's eyes, but quickly died.

Grief, like love, excused many things. He hurried toward Gannon.

And Gannon began to laugh.

We could not believe it at first. We all thought it must be some sound of grief, of pain, the uncontrolled weeping of a mourning lover. But, no, Gannon Murdock was laughing, throwing back his head and laughing like a madman. "Son," Mr. Murdock said, hurrying to him and holding him, "Son, you come along with me, now!"

Suddenly Gannon's laughter stopped, and with surprising strength, he threw his father off. His dark-browed face belonged to an angry gargoyle.

"Yes, you'll kill me!" he cried. "You've taken everything else from us—why not our lives!"

"Son," Mr. Murdock said, trying to silence Gannon and lead him away, "Son, come away!"

Again, Gannon thrust his father away. "Thieves, liars, hypocrites, all of you! Year after year, you've taken! From my father, my grandfather, his father! Taken our land, taken our people, and now our home!"

"Murdock," my uncle said, "I told you! Get him away from here!"

"You've taken everything else, you took Melinda away from me—"

"She was never yours!" my uncle shouted, as my father tried to restrain him.

"She was mine, and you took her from me. She'd be alive if it wasn't for you."

"I said I'd kill you—"

"Yes, you better. 'Cause I'm here to tell you something, Mr. Welles. This is a promise, so hear it well."

For an instant, Gannon hesitated, as if he realized the enormity of the commitment he was about to make. Then he spoke: "Everything you ever stole from us—you hear me, now, I say every damn thing—*I'm gonna take it back!*"

There was something about those words, and the way that Gannon said them, that stilled the crowd of mourners, that seemed to bring even my uncle up short.

Gannon looked about the crowd. "You all heard me, you all be my witnesses. Everything the Welleses ever took from the Murdocks—the land, the people, our home—it's gonna be ours again. That and the Barony and everything else, 'cause I'm taking it *all* from them, the same as they took it all from

us. That's my promise. And if I can't have Melinda . . . ''
Those terrible eyes moved to mine. "I'm not good enough for
a Welles? That's too bad. Because maybe I'll just have me
one before I'm through. Yes, that's a promise too, Gussie.
We'll finish what we started in the wine cellar that day. I
promise you—''

Gannon might truly have died then, at my father's hands if
not at Uncle Thad's. But as my father rushed toward him,
Mr. Murdock raised his arm and, with a single blow, knocked
his son to the ground.

Only then did we hear from Gannon Murdock the true
sounds of grief.

6 ~~~~~~

Now I must pause to reflect. Having written the foregoing
pages with such candor, I blush at the thought of what I have
yet to tell, and I ask myself, why in the world am I doing it?

After all, it should by now be evident to any Gentle
Reader who might happen across these pages (which God
forbid!) that they are meant for no eyes but my own. As the
world turns these days, there seem to be ever fewer men
capable of understanding, let alone forgiving, such a story as
mine. Indeed, it would hardly be too much to say that only
another woman could understand. Then why write it?

Perhaps the answer is simply this. We live in a world of
mendacity. I learned early that most men live lies—some
forced upon them, others seized upon, unwillingly or eagerly—
and I have lived more than my share. But the worst lies, the
most degrading of all, are the ones we tell ourselves. And by
putting my story down on paper, perhaps I shall be able to see
it more clearly and honestly, perhaps I shall be able to move
beyond nostalgia and self-justification and nightmare, and
thus come better to know the truth about myself. Perhaps I
shall become a more honest woman.

Gentle Reader, I can but try.

* * *

What to say of the hours that followed?

We returned to the house. As was customary, our friends and neighbors had brought food, and my father served wine and whiskey. But our guests did not stay long, and I thought I knew why. When an older person dies after a full and useful life, there is much to be celebrated as well as mourned. The end comes to us all, and a good life has been successfully completed. But there was no sense of completion or acceptance when we buried Melinda. A young woman whose earthly life was just beginning had died violently, senselessly, tragically, and in its secret darkness, each heart wanted to cry out, *God, why did You let it happen?*

By late afternoon, the house seemed empty. No servants were anywhere to be seen. Aunt Nickie had collapsed after the return from the graveyard and had been put to bed, and my mother was with her. The dining room and the entrance hall, as I went through them, were silent. No sound of Melinda's laughter now, or ever again.

Instead, a quiet sobbing. It seemed to come from the library, and when I entered, I found Cousin Horace curled up at the end of a sofa. I had never been particularly close to him, and hardly knew how to comfort him, but I wanted to try.

"What am I going to d-do without her?" he asked. "She was just like my s-sister," he said, "just like a r-real s-sister to me."

"You've got Lucy," I said, sitting down with him and stroking his soft blond hair.

"Aw, she's just a b-b-baby. Mel and me, we t-t-took care of each other."

"I know you did."

"She always st-stood up for me. Like when Beau Legree made fun of how I st-st-stut . . . how I talk, she said she'd scratch his eyes out if he didn't st-stop."

"She would have, too."

"She even st-stood up for me 'gainst Uncle Thad sometimes." He began to weep again. "Oh, I wish I'd died 'stead of Mel!"

"No, you don't, Horace. It was a terrible thing to happen to anybody. Don't ever wish yourself dead."

"But I do! G-G-Gussie, Uncle Thad hates me—"

"Why, Horace Blakely, that's not so! Uncle Thad loves

you, just the same as he loves us all." How I wanted that to be true!

"He does not!" Horace turned a wet, round face toward me. "He-he-he thinks I'm st-stupid! Gussie, is it my fault I'm st-stupid?"

What a terrible thing for a boy to believe of himself, I thought, even if it were just a little true. It made me feel guilty for every childish slight I had ever given Horace. Somehow I had to make it up to him.

"Horace," I said, "you are not stupid."

Eyes down, he shook his head. "Oh, I know I am."

"No, Horace, you are not."

"I been hearing all my life how st-stupid I am."

"Horace, *I* said you are *not*."

His head continued to shake. "All the fellows think I'm st-stupid, and the girls l-laugh behind my back when I go by, and Uncle Thad is *al*ways telling me how st-stupid I am. So I guess I ought to know."

"*Horace!*" For some reason I did not understand, I was becoming a little angry, and tears were coming to my eyes. "Horace Blakely, I told you—"

"'Cept for Aunt Nickie, old Mel was the only one who ever told me I *wasn't* st-stupid. But just the same—"

"Horace Blakely!" I did shake him then. Took his shoulders and shook him hard. "Now you listen to me, and you listen good! If I ever again hear you call yourself stupid, I'll—I'll never speak to you again! If Melinda told you you're not stupid, then you're not! Did Melinda ever lie to you?"

Horace looked at me with bewildered eyes. "No," he said, "no, Melinda never l-lied to me."

"Then you remember that. And from now on, whenever someone calls you stupid, I want you to say to yourself, *No, I am not stupid. I know I am not stupid, because Melinda told me so! And Gussie says so too!* For the rest of your life, Horace! Do you understand me?"

Horace stared at me, and I was afraid my words had been lost on him. Then he said, "I . . . I understand."

"And you promise? You promise you'll always tell yourself that?"

"I p-promise."

"Then say it. Say, 'I am not stupid.' "

"I am not . . . I am not . . . st . . . stupid. . . ."

His face came apart like a paper mask dissolving in tears, and as Horace collapsed weeping into my arms, I could hold back my own tears no longer.

Even the brightest of the days that followed seemed dark. I had only to look across the quiet, empty room Melinda and I had shared to have the dull ache in my soul turn to pain. I had only to touch a dress we had made together, or remember her bathing with me in the stream, or think of her in a beau's arms swaying to a waltz. Impossible to believe that she was gone, and yet she was only a dream that would never be fulfilled now, a beautiful promise that would never be kept.

But meanwhile life went on. My father wanted us to move back into town before the departure for England. "The sickly season will soon be on us," he reminded my mother, "and since you're not well . . ."

"Nickie prefers to remain at the Barony for the time being, and so do I. Here we can look after each other, with a minimum of callers and social obligations. We simply don't feel up to coping with the city."

My father reluctantly agreed. "But I want you back in Wraggboro by the end of the month."

"In a couple of weeks. We'll be fine, dear."

And so we stayed on, long after the womenfolk on most plantations had left. Tom stayed on too, doing his best to make things easier for us. Mr. Murdock had agreed to stay out the month, until Gannon could travel more easily, and Tom worked with him.

Then one day about a week after Melinda's death, something happened that filled me with guilt.

My comfort, if not my consolation, during that period was Tom, though he was quite busy and I saw less of him than I would have wished. But after dinner, when the hands were out of the fields and the shops were closed, I would finally manage to be alone with him.

We would wander away from the house, sometimes down to the landing for an hour or so, where we would watch the river rolling lazily by. Sometimes, hand in hand, we walked through the gardens. Or we sat on the bank and dangled our feet in the stream where Melinda and I had bathed. We rarely mentioned my cousin, because to do so was painful, but she was never far from our minds.

Nor was the thought far from our minds that we might soon

have to part. "I'll speak to your father about us," Tom said more than once.

"Not yet."

"But why not?"

"It's too soon after . . . after . . ." Too soon after Melinda's death. Somehow it seemed wrong. It was not that I loved Tom any less, but my emotions had been given over almost entirely to Melinda: I still mourned her, and would for a long time to come. I needed Tom to lean on, I loved being at his side, but the few kisses we exchanged could not have been more chaste. Though neither of us said a word about it, I was sure he understood.

Thus the incident, when it happened, was totally unexpected. We had wandered out to the garden after dinner with no particular thought of where we were going. Finding ourselves in the flower garden, we entered the shade of the vine-covered gazebo. We sat on a bench side by side, our arms entwined, both of us sleepy from the heat. A scent of oleander was in the air, and the only sounds were the distant shouts and laughter of children playing. For the first time since Melinda's funeral, it occurred to me that perhaps, after all, happiness was still possible.

Tom withdrew his arm from mine and put it around my shoulders, drawing me closer to him. I felt his lips against my forehead. I smiled and lifted my mouth to be kissed. His lips touched mine. . . .

And it happened again, that thing that had occurred so unexpectedly in Tom's carriage and yet again the next day in the barn. Suddenly I found myself being carried mindlessly away on a tropical tide, a mounting crest of desire.

With a cry, I turned away from Tom and hid my face in my arms on the bench.

"Augusta, what is it?" Tom asked, baffled.

How could I tell him my shame?

His hands were on my shoulders, but I resisted them. "What is it?" he asked again.

"How can I feel like this when she's . . . when Melinda is—"

"Augusta, there's nothing wrong with the way you feel."

"But she's only been . . ." I could not say *dead*. "She's only been gone a week. And I loved her. How can I be so selfish, so wicked?"

"You're not selfish or wicked. You're human. And you love me too, don't you?"

"Yes, but . . ."

He lifted me from the bench and tried to pull me back into his arms—and I wanted to be in them. I wanted to throw myself against him and forget everything else in the world. But how could I do such a thing, how could I even think of such a thing, when it was so wrong?

"Augusta, let me hold you—"

"Oh, no-o-o!"

I slipped from his hands and ran from the gazebo.

But my own passions were not so easily escaped. They followed me to my room, where I threw myself face-down on my bed, feeling like a wretched sinner whose demon refuses to be exorcised—and who secretly wishes to keep him.

Melinda, forgive me!

There was no peace in that room, no hiding from myself or from my demon. All I could think of was Tom—Tom, so close to me, holding me, caressing me, kissing me. I wanted to cry his name aloud, I wanted to call him to me, I wanted . . .

Melinda, forgive me!

"Why, there's nothing to forgive, Gussie, dear."

Even today I would almost swear I heard her voice, sweet, mildly amused, comforting. I have little belief in returns from the Other World, and now I am sure that the voice came from my own fevered imagination. But at that moment it was utterly real to me. *"Why, there's nothing to forgive."*

Oh, but there was. Now, however, I felt that Melinda would have understood.

The next afternoon, when Tom found me in the gazebo, neither of us had to say a word. He looked into my eyes, and he saw, and he knew. His hair, gold in the sunlight, turned a darker gold as he entered the vine-covered enclosure, and his eyes once again were blue flame. The perfume of flowers mingling with a faint male musk sent my mind spinning, and I found myself sliding into his arms.

Grief and joy, love and sorrow, make one of the headiest wines known to mankind, and in the next few days I drank of that wine as never before. Drunkenly, wantonly, I sought my lover's arms at every opportunity. That first afternoon, a sudden thunderstorm broke over the Barony, but the lightning was nothing compared to the flashes of our passion, or the thunder to the pounding of our hearts. When the storm had passed and we dared linger in the gazebo no longer, I wondered how anyone could miss seeing my love-dazzled eyes and kiss-bruised lips.

That evening after supper, we met in the darkness down by the river landing, and the next morning we spent an hour together in a patch of woods far from the big house. And in whispers between kisses and caresses, we plotted further meetings.

No need to record all—only that at each meeting we grew bolder. Inevitably, one afternoon my loose summery frock slipped from my shoulder. That evening, while Tom's lips burned across mine, it slipped from my breast. But despite a superficial boldness, no Melinda was I, to tumble naked into my lover's bower and consummate my love at the very first chance. No, mine were days of delightful suffering and nights of sweet frustration.

Meanwhile, the greatest danger to our secret meetings was Horace. For I discovered to my consternation that, ever since that afternoon in the library when I had tried to comfort him, poor Horace had become quite smitten with me. Electing me to take Melinda's place in his heart—if that were possible— he constantly sought me out, and how dared I let Tom stroke my thigh and kiss my breast, when at any instant Horace might appear? Thus Horace became the unwitting guardian of my virtue.

Yet Tom and I did meet, at least once or twice a day, and only the ever-perceptive Pearl guessed our secret. Tom repeatedly asked for permission to speak to my father, and I decided to allow him to do so as soon as we returned to Wraggboro.

That day approached. My father announced that he had found a first-class overseer, who would soon arrive, and we would be at the Barony only two or three more days.

Then, too soon, it was Tuesday, the first of August. I awakened very early that morning, long before dawn. Hearing an odd rumbling sound outside, I hurried to the window. At first I did not know what to make of the carriage and the big mule-drawn covered wagon, but then I realized that the Murdocks were leaving. They had sold many of their possessions in the past two weeks, and now everything they owned was in the carriage or the wagon or walking alongside.

Gannon Murdock must be in that wagon, I realized. I had

not known at the funeral that I was seeing him for the last time, and now he was riding out of my life forever.

Or so I thought.

Tom and I had no opportunity to meet secretly that day. He had volunteered to do Mr. Murdock's work until the new overseer arrived, and I was kept busy with preparations for the return to Wraggboro and the trip to England which, of course, everyone assumed I would be making too. In her weakened condition, there was little my mother could do, so a great deal fell to me, and suddenly there were a hundred things that needed doing—clothes to be selected, clothes to be given away, clothes to be packed, and unpacked, and packed again. Pearl helped me, and we could hardly look at each other without bursting into tears.

That evening after supper, Tom and I did manage to find a few minutes alone on the front piazza. We were about to dare a kiss, when Horace joined us. I could barely hide my exasperation, but I had vowed never to do the slightest thing that might make the boy feel unwanted. So I smiled and greeted him—and went to bed that night unkissed.

And awakened to the sound of the fire bell.

For a moment I merely lay in the dark, trying to comprehend the meaning of that bell. Then a muffled cry and the thump of feet out in the hall brought me to my senses. Leaping from my bed, I pulled a robe over my nightgown and stepped into slippers. As I entered the hall I smelled smoke. Aunt Nickie was at her door.

"What is it?" I asked. "Is it the house?"

"We think it's the overseer's house," she said. "Go find out how bad it is, Augusta. I'll stay here with your mother, and if she has to be moved . . ."

I heard no more. By then I was in the hall, running down the stairs.

The first alarm had come from the house-servants' quarters. By the time I was outside, a second alarm was ringing in the field quarters, and a flickering light glowed from the direction of the overseer's house. I saw my father, Uncle Thad, and Tom running toward that light, and, awkward in my floppy slippers, I followed them.

When I got there, they were standing in front of the burning house. My father and my uncle had their nightshirts tucked into their pants, and Tom had torn his shirt down the front in his haste to pull it on. Bucket brigades were forming, and a rosy glow showed from the upper interior of the building.

"How do you figure it started?" my father asked.

"Probably sparks from the kitchen house," Uncle Thad said. "That's how it usually happens."

"But, my God, the Murdocks have been gone for hours. And Laird would never leave a fire burning in the kitchen."

"Then maybe somebody set the place on fire deliberately," Uncle Thad said angrily. "Who knows how it started?"

"Gentlemen," Tom said, "I think we'd better get to swinging those buckets."

From that moment on, we all worked as we never had before in our lives. Soon every able-bodied man and woman on the plantation was there, carrying buckets of water up from the river to the mounting inferno. Before long it became clear that there was no chance of saving the house—our task was to save the other buildings. Hence we not only tried to diminish the fire but also watered down every nearby roof.

Messengers were sent to neighboring plantations, and wagons began to arrive with more hands and more buckets, a hundred more black people to bring water up from the river, their masters working at their sides. I tried to do my share, swinging buckets in one of the brigade lines until I was too tired to keep up with the others. Then I carried my own buckets of water up from the river, my slippers flopping until I lost first one, then the other. Shirts were discarded. Strong brown shoulders glistened in the firelight. My hands grew raw, my back ached, and my lungs begged for air, but pride kept me going.

Finally I could go on no longer. I had filled my bucket from the river and taken but a few staggering steps when I fell to the ground and found it impossible to get up. As I lay panting and sobbing, someone touched my shoulder, and I looked up to see my father kneeling beside me. Tom, in his ripped shirt, stood nearby.

"You'd better go on back to the house, Augusta," my father said. I tried to protest that the fire was not out yet, but he was gently insistent. "You've been working hard for over three hours, and I'm proud of you, but now I want you to get some rest." He looked up at Tom. "Tom, see that she gets safely back to the house."

Tom said "Yes, sir," and my father departed.

I sat where I was for a few minutes until my breath grew

less ragged, then washed my raw hands and my face in the river. Tom and I turned our backs on the overseer's house, now crumbled into a great bonfire with a dark chimney thrusting up through it, and started back along the dark path to the Barony big house.

When we were out of sight of the others, I leaned against Tom's side, and he wrapped a strong arm around my waist. A strange melancholy, not unpleasant, filled me. Never before had I felt as I did that night, so aware of life's fragility, so freed from the petty conventions that bound our lives. Melinda was gone, and my life, I somehow realized, was but a brief moment before I followed her. But for that moment I would live with all the intensity of the great blazing fire we had been fighting.

We stopped by the barn and looked back. The inferno still reached high into the night sky, but we were hidden from its light. In the darkness Tom drew me into his arms and lifted my face for a kiss. As his mouth moved against mine, I felt a long rippling of muscles from his bare chest to his hardening thighs, a tension that flowed into me and brought me back to quivering life. Tomorrow I would be weary and every bone would ache, but for now I had the comfort of my love's tall, lean body, and its strength was restoring my own.

For long moments we stood together like that, hardly moving, the tension, the want, the need growing. With one hand Tom drew me more tightly to him, while with the other he sought my breast through my flimsy cotton gown. "I'm not going to let them take you away from me, Augusta," he whispered. "I'm going to keep you here and marry you, and nothing in the world will keep us apart."

His hand moved from my breast to the neck of my gown, and his finger was like a flaming taper burning my flesh as it pulled away the lacing. Then my gown was open, and I was hiding my bare aching breasts against the light golden fleece of his chest. His hand covered a burgeoning nipple, and as he put his mouth aslant mine to give me a long, thought-shattering kiss, I found myself twisting and moving against him, trying to be a part of him, trying to embed myself in his very soul.

"Sweet Jesus, Augusta," he said, "if only you knew what I feel for you."

Perhaps I did know. I knew that even this closeness was not enough, that I loved this man, that I could not bear the thought of being separated from him, not for a year, not for a day. But some thread of sanity told me that we could not continue clinging to each other half-naked in the darkness without being discovered, and I tried to draw away from him and cover myself.

"The barn," he said. "Let's go into the barn."

"They'll miss us," I said fearfully.

"No, they won't." His lips returned to mine. "We won't stay long. Augusta, if you love me . . ."

I could not resist that plea, or those lips. I let him lead me into the barn and close the door behind us. Finding my way through the pitch-blackness to the ladder, I climbed up with Tom close behind me. I felt my way across the loft and flung open the big loft doors. The moon was long gone, but the sky was flooded with starlight.

The loft was stifling hot, and I dropped my robe to the floor. My gown had come open again, and I started to pull it closed.

"Don't do that," Tom said, coming to me. "Don't ever hide yourself from me, Augusta. You're too beautiful, every part of you. These eyes . . . this mouth . . . this throat . . ."

His kiss, moving over my face, barely touched me, but I felt it in every part of my body, and the want which had abated returned quickly, stronger than ever. My gown, as he brushed it from my shoulders, slipped to my waist, and once again I was in his arms. Suddenly he bent and lifted me, cradling me in his arms, and the stars whirled in the heavens. *He'll hurt me*, I thought, hardly knowing what I meant, yet whatever he intended to do, I did not want him to stop.

As he settled me down on the same mound of blanket-covered staw that Melinda and Gannon had used to make love, I slipped my arms out of my gown and let it settle about my hips. For a moment Tom sat beside me, looking down at me, and I wondered if I could possibly be as beautiful to him as he was to me.

"Augusta . . ." A whisper, a sigh, and I was in his arms again. But none of our intimacies had prepared me for what followed—the lips that wandered freely over face and throat, breasts and belly, stinging me like sparks from the fire, the magic touches that made my body leap and quake, the nibbling teeth and searing tongue that filled me with a longing that was almost more than I could bear.

Then for a moment he left me. His back to me, he pulled off his shirt, kicked away his boots, slipped off the rest of his clothes. My heart pounded with unexpected panic. Turning toward me again, he knelt at my side, sitting back on his haunches, hands on spread thighs. And beautiful though he was, I dared look only at his starlit face and his broad shoulders and chest.

"Augusta," he said softly.

Everything for days had led to this moment. I knew what he wanted to do, what I wanted to do, here, in the loft where Melinda and Gannon had made love . . . on the very same bed of blankets and straw . . . where they would never make love again.

In a rush, all my guilt returned. How could I be doing this when not even a blade of grass grew yet on Melinda's grave? It was wrong, wrong! How could I commit such a sacrilege against my dearest friend? As Tom tried to take me back into his arms, I thrust him away.

"What is it?" he asked. "You're trembling."

Refusing to look at him, I shook my head. Even in guilt, my body still throbbed with longing.

"Am I frightening you, darling?"

"No!"

"Then . . ."

Suddenly Melinda's words came back to me, those words that were cut so deeply in my memory, and I seemed to be hearing her speaking them all over again: *"Let me tell you something, Gussie. When you find a love of your own . . . I don't care if the world is coming to an end . . . When you find love, Gussie, just take it, and let the rest of the world go hang. Take it, Gussie, take it. . . ."*

My guilt vanished. The only thing that mattered was *now*, our love, and the joys that were yet to come.

Ah, if only it could have been that easy, a young girl's dream of being taken by her beloved at last. But the reality is always different, and gentle though Tom was, I found myself shivering with apprehension, shaking like a frightened animal. Even as our mouths pressed together and Tom's hand moved from one swollen breast to the other, I wanted to cry out, *"Stop! Oh, I can't! Stop, please stop!"* But then his touch was moving down over my trembling belly and lower to discover secrets, and I found myself, legs high, frenzied, kicking my gown away.

As naked as Adam and Eve, we lay together, as natural as

the beasts of the forest, alone in our lair of love, while Tom continued to stroke my frightened body, continued to caress it as it had never before been caressed. "It's all right, darling," he whispered, "it's all right. I won't harm you, Augusta, I won't ever harm you."

Gradually my trembling diminished, and something like rational thought returned. So this was what Melinda had experienced, this absolute nakedness of body and soul, this vulnerability, this feeling of total surrender. This intimacy that granted every secret of one's body to the beloved, that held nothing back, that filled every corner of one's being with delight. No, with more than delight. With an expectation of ecstasy, a demand for some ultimate fulfillment, that was almost an anguish. With a mewling cry, I tried to pull Tom closer, and found him rising up over me.

My trembling returned. Eyes tightly closed, I found myself crying out, "Not yet! Not yet!" and fighting him as he forced my thighs apart and moved between them. When I pounded on his shoulders, he seized my wrists and held me still. "Tell me to stop, Augusta," he said, "and I'll stop. Tell me to stop."

I said nothing.

As he brought himself to me, I gasped and tried to draw away. But I was his captive, and as he pressed on, gently, gently, desire surged, and I rose to meet him—and in one painful instant the last barrier was broken.

For a moment, passion vanished and the night stood still. I was alone in my darkness, alone with my hurt. Then came the knowledge that I was not as I had been, that I never would be again. The child who had roamed the paths of Barony plantation was gone forever.

Slowly I opened my eyes, slowly became aware of Tom again, of our entanglement on the bed of straw, of his hard male presence deep within me. Murmuring my name and whispering endearments, he kissed my eyes and stroked my breasts. And it began all over again, that mounting need, the need to be one with the other, to touch the soul with the flesh.

Tom felt my response to his presence and, laughing softly, answered, probing deep and hard. No holding back then. The battle was joined, no quarter given, and I felt I was wrestling with a naked angel, an angel who struck with irresistible strength while I met every blow, an angel whose heart thundered against mine, an angel who filled my body with heavenly fire. With kisses and caresses and all the strength of his driving, pounding body, he raised me to ecstasy and beyond, lifted me, soaring, to heights I had never dreamed of. I could not bear this, I thought, I could not bear this. Yet bear it I did, until in one final shared moment the full moon seemed to rise again, and, as I cried out, it exploded, filling the heavens with its glorious light.

Afterwards, I wept a little, though I did not know why.

"Augusta, do you regret—"

"No. Never, dearest. Don't you see I'm smiling?"

With passion spent, a degree of modesty returned, and I clung to Tom and pulled a blanket over us, as if to hide from his gaze. I was content to lie in his arms and feel his body touching mine while his hand gently stroked my cheek, my shoulder, my breast, and his lips moved over my face. We would rest a little while, I thought, then dress and return to the house before our absence was discovered. But how little I knew of passion.

All too swiftly the hours passed, as I learned its lessons—the lesson of fright and fervor, the lesson of easy joy, and a final lesson, almost cruel as we strove to raise the moon, almost painful in that last explosive moment. But the night had to end, no matter how we tried to prolong it, and as we sensed dawn approaching, we slowly, reluctantly pulled on our clothes. There would be other nights, and once more all was right with the world. Tragedy had been left behind, and my love and I had each other, and it was impossible to believe that my father would keep us apart.

Tom closed the loft doors, and in darkness we made our way down the ladder. Outside, there was still a glow from the overseer's house, and the stench of smoke hung in the air, but there was also a freshness, a cleansing breeze. All my fatigue was returning, but I was comfortable with it. Arm in arm, we walked slowly toward the house.

We were halfway up the steps before I realized there was a light in the library. My heart skipped a beat. Even if I had not been missed, Tom surely would have been, and here we were, entering the house together at dawn. What excuse could we possibly make?

"Don't worry, Augusta," Tom said, reading my thoughts, "I'll speak to your father about us. Right now."

But we were not even noticed as we entered the library.

"Yes, it's gone!" my uncle was saying, his voice harsh. "Any damn fool can see that! It's gone!"

My father looked about blindly. His jaw hung loose, and his eyes were wide and glazed with shock.

Uncle Thad laughed angrily. "Well, don't you understand? While we were out fighting the fire, somebody came here and—"

"They must have deliberately set the fire, as a distraction," my father said, recovering his wits. "Then when we were all out of the house—"

"What does it matter? You've lost the diamond. And I need it, August. Maybe it's nothing but a trinket to you, something to show off at parties, but if it had come to me as it should have—"

"Maybe we'll get it back."

Uncle Thad laughed again, contemptuously. "Do you really believe that?"

"And I still have money. I'll find a way to help you."

Then I saw: the cracked wood of the once-locked cabinet where the door had been pried open. And on the table the open box, the Tear of Venus no longer resting on the black velvet.

This time it was Gannon Murdock's voice I heard: *"Everything you ever stole from us—you hear me, now, I say every damn thing—I'm gonna take it back!"*

Gannon Murdock's revenge had begun.

BOOK TWO

The Worldly and the Wicked

It was a dream of perfect bliss,
Too beautiful to last.

—T. H. Bayly, *It Was a Dream*

There is a method in man's wickedness—
It grows up by degrees.

—Beaumont and Fletcher, *A King and No King*

1 ˄˄˄˄˄˄

"Soit sage," Aunt Nickie used to admonish us children, *"soit sage!"* But what sixteen-year-old girl in love was ever wise, or good, or even entirely in her right mind? Gannon Murdock might be seeking revenge, or, as Melinda had said, the world might be coming to an end; but the only thing I really cared about was Tom Raveneau and my determination never to be parted from him.

However, everything seemed to conspire against me. Tom had no opportunity to speak to my father on the morning of the fire, nor was there any immediate need, since no one had seen us enter the house together. Apparently Tom had not been missed during those early hours, and my father's entire concern when we entered the library was to locate the constable and the Murdocks and, if possible, to retrieve the Tear of Venus.

I went to the kitchen, where Matty was already preparing breakfast, and then to bed. When I awakened, my father and Uncle Thad had left in pursuit of the Murdocks, and my mother informed me that the next morning we would be leaving for the city.

Thus Tom and I would not be seeing each other for several days, for he was staying on at the Barony until the new overseer arrived. When we met in the flower garden gazebo that afternoon, we were both conscious that each kiss might be the last until we met again. "But it won't be for long," Tom said, as I melted in his arms. "And we can be married before your parents sail for England. In less than a month."

On Saturday evening my father and Uncle Thad arrived wearily at the house in Wraggboro. They had located the constable and then gone looking for the Murdocks. The Murdocks had not been difficult to locate, having traveled only twenty-odd miles.

"They were staying with some relatives," my father said, when we had all gathered in a parlor. "Naturally, these relatives claimed the Murdocks had all been there the whole time. But Laird and Gannon didn't pretend to be surprised when we confronted them. Not surprised or gratified or anything else. They said as little as possible and had faces like closed doors."

"But we know it was them," Uncle Thad said.

"How do we know?" I asked. "How can you be sure?"

"Your uncle and I went back to the Barony," my father said. "We talked to our people and found several who had seen Laird and Gannon skulking around the fire and the big house that night. They probably didn't go very far after they left the Barony. Sent the rest of the family on, then doubled back."

"Then why don't you have them arrested?"

"We could hardly do that, when they have witnesses to the fact that they were miles away."

"But if we know they were at the Barony—"

"Legally, we don't know. Because *our* witnesses are slaves. No slave can bear witness against a white man in a court of law, as I'm sure you know well."

I did know, but it was one of those matters to which I had seldom given the slightest thought.

With sadness, I recognized that the Tear of Venus would never be mine, and I remembered my earlier foreboding that if it were lost, all else might follow it. But I had other things to think about. And on Monday evening, his work at the Barony done, Tom came to the house in Wraggboro.

The Wraggboro house was huge, a three-story brick building surrounded by gardens, with brick outbuildings at the back. Its piazza-flanked entrance hall led to a large, high-ceilinged, chandeliered central hall with a beautiful staircase spiraling unsupported, as if floating on air, to the upper floors. Its many rooms easily accommodated the entire Welles family, and yet Tom and I could find virtually no place to be alone.

At supper I could hardly eat. Afterwards, when we saw my father entering his office, we knew our chance had come.

"I'll go with you," I said.

"No, Augusta."

"But, Tom, I want to *tell* him—!"

"This is for me to do, darling. For me alone."

I was left waiting outside the door of my father's office for what seemed like hours, though common sense told me it was only a few minutes. Then the door opened, and my father motioned me to enter.

The instant I saw Tom's face, I knew the interview had not gone well. He was trying to smile, but without much success. My father settled into his chair at his desk and asked me to sit down.

"Augusta," he said, "I needn't tell you that I'm not altogether surprised. And in some respects, I could not be more pleased."

Hope sprang anew. "Then, Daddy—"

My father silenced me with an upheld hand. "But you know, Augusta, that I have always been against early marriage, and you're only sixteen."

"Going on seventeen!"

"Sixteen and a few months," he said gently.

Tears came to my eyes and a catch to my voice. "But Daddy, you said we'd be gone at least a year and maybe two whole years or even longer—"

"A lot can happen in a year," my father said in the same gentle tone. "And besides, there are other considerations."

"What other considerations?"

My father glanced at Tom. "I don't think we need go into those."

Tom shrugged. "That's all right, sir. I think Augusta is entitled to know." He turned to me. "I have some debts, Augusta. They're only gambling debts, just paper debts actually, but even so—"

"I have noticed," my father said, "that gambling debts are generally considered paper debts only up to a certain point. Then our friends begin to get restless."

Tom cleared his throat. "Well, of course that's true. But a great deal of my debt is to my brother. He's covered twenty-odd thousand for me, almost half—"

"*Twenty thousand!*" The words leapt from my lips before I could stop them. I was used to the idea of gentlemen gambling, but twenty thousand dollars, and that only half!

Tom was speaking: "Your father feels that my debts should be cleared up before we marry."

My father nodded. "I do indeed. Tom has promised me that he will clear up his debts and hereafter keep his gambling within reason. And after that . . ."

"After that, we can be married?"

"After that," my father said with a touch of impatience, "we may reconsider the matter and weigh all factors."

"But—but why? Why can't I just stay here with Aunt Nickie and Uncle Thad, and when Tom has paid his debts—"

My father sighed. "Tom, would you please leave the room for a few minutes?"

Tom said, "Yes, of course, sir," and stepped out of the office, closing the door behind him.

I expected a storm, but none came. Instead, my father said, "Augusta, I'm sorry. I'm afraid I haven't made matters clear to you. I meant everyhting I said about your age and Tom's debts and the present cholera threat. But even if these facts were otherwise, I would still insist on your coming to England with your mother and me."

"But why, Daddy? I don't understand! Why is it so important that I go to England with you?"

"I don't feel that I can tell you that. Not yet. I can only say that in time you will know, and I can only hope that you will agree then that I have done the wise thing."

Unable to speak, I shook my head in frustration. No words could have expressed the depths of my disappointment, but my father must have seen it in my eyes.

"I must ask you, Augusta," he went on, "not to resist me any further in this. I've suggested to Tom that when his debts are paid he might visit us in England. And if at sixteen your love can't survive separation . . ."

I agreed. I would say nothing more about not going to England. But what in the world, I wondered, could my father be holding back from me?

It was dark when Tom and I went out into the gardens, where we could cling together unseen.

"I'm sorry, Augusta," he whispered to me, "I did my best."

"He said you might visit us."

"I will. As soon as possible. But your father is right. I've got to start winning again and clear up my debts."

"Oh, please, Tom! Don't gamble any more! If you go on losing, we'll never be married!"

Tom's laugh was faint. "Darling, including my debt to Dexter, I owe over forty thousand. How am I going to pay that off if I don't gamble? But don't you worry," he added with careless confidence, "I'll take care of it."

"When do you think you'll be coming?"

"Well, I can't promise anything, sweetheart, but maybe in the early spring."

"Oh, Tom . . ." Seven months or more without seeing Tom. What all could happen in seven months?

"Believe me, darling, before you know it, I'll be coming to see you. No, not to see you—to marry you." His lips sought mine.

And so after eleven years we returned to England. In those days, of course, we did not yet have transatlantic steam packets. The *Great Western*, with its tall funnel and its sidewheels, had been launched on the very day that Melinda had been laid to rest, but it had not yet reached America, and it would be another three years before the Cunards launched the *Britannia*. Hence, even after we had reached New York, we still had five long, tedious weeks ahead of us on one of the dozen American sailing packets then plying the Atlantic.

In October we did at last reach London, where my father's solicitors had taken a beautiful three-story red-brick house for us in Harley Street. My maternal grandmother had long since passed away, but we were soon called on by some chilly cousins who seemed even more distant than they were; they had never approved of my mother's marrying a mere rustic American.

But what need had we for them? In the weeks and months that followed, I learned that others had quite a different view of my father. One of our first callers was the elderly Lord Brougham, who had defended Queen Caroline at her trial for adultery in 1820. "With the exception of Mr. Richard Rush himself," he told me, "your father did more than any other man to mend relations between America and England after the war." Another caller, only a little older than my father, was handsome, witty William Alvanley, known as the perfect Regency buck. "I suppose you've heard about poor George Brummell, haven't you, August? Gone quite mad, I'm afraid. He's in a charity asylum in Caen. . . ." And there was Comte d'Orsay, surely the most elegant man alive, who traded reminiscences of Byron with my father—Comte d'Orsay, who considered a fifty-thousand pound gambling debt a trifle, while my Tom had to worry over a mere forty thousand dollars!

In October, however, much of this still lay ahead of me.

We had hardly settled into the London house when my father told us he had located a country house in Hampshire, to which we would soon repair. He was a sporting man, and there one could ride to the hounds almost every day of the week and still be within a few hours of London.

Even I, who had largely been kept ignorant of financial matters, began to wonder how we could afford this extravagance, when my father had been so worried about how he could help Uncle Thad. But at last I began to understand. My mother, it seemed, "had money." It was not money my father felt he could lend to my Uncle Thad, however, and it was suggested to me that one day this income would be mine. Meanwhile, it permitted my parents to live as they pleased.

Life at Ashtonfield Park, as our country home was called, could hardly have been happier. We had scarcely arrived there when my mother almost miraculously began regaining her strength, and my father returned from each morning of riding or shooting with a ruddy glow of health on his cheeks. We were quickly accepted into the local society, and I met several young ladies who, like me, had been raised in the shadow of the stables and therefore were allowed an occasional ride to the hounds. Not a week passed without one or two dinner parties, and in good weather there were long drives through the woods and fields.

There were young men, too, of course, but though I might acknowledge the charms of an Englishman, my heart belonged exclusively to Tom, and for a long time I kept my promise to write to him daily. When news was in short supply, I fell back on one of my few talents, a good eye for line and color, illuminating my pages with watercolor portraits of our neighbors, architectural renderings of our house, and views of the countryside. Tom's letters were less frequent and sometimes arrived two or three at a time after a lapse of a month, but that only made them more precious.

Christmas came and went, and it was a new year, and I confess: those first months in England were among the happiest of my life. Even Tom's absence added something to their sweetness, for my father was right, I *was* still very young at sixteen, still not quite ready for marriage, and simply to long for Tom was heaven enough in itself. How many nights did I lie awake reliving that one night in the loft, wondering if it could possibly have been as glorious as I remembered it?

But my happiness was not to last. It rested on the assumption that I would be seeing Tom again before long, and by January I realized that he had not said a thing about his spring visit in his ever-less-frequent letters. I wrote to him about his plans, and weeks later received his reply.

My dearest Augusta,

I want to assure you at once that, in the main, all goes well—in fact, in some ways better than one might have expected—and I look forward with a joy I cannot express to our reunion.

However, I am forced to question the wisdom of a trip to England at this time. Though the price of rice has, surprisingly, risen somewhat, that of cotton has fallen drastically. . . .

Stunned, I read on. In order that we might wed as soon as possible, Tom said, it seemed wise at this time to hang on to every cent possible and reinvest it in the most profitable way. Dexter had opened up a number of new acres to cultivation in the last few years, and they planned to open up still more. With any luck, Tom said, he would be able to afford a visit at the end of the summer, probably in August.

In August! But that meant I would not have seen him for a whole year!

"Now, dear," my mother said briskly, "in some ways it's just as well that Tom has been delayed. You are going to be a very busy young woman from now on, you know."

"Why? Why would I be too busy for Tom?"

"Why, this is *your* spring, dear! This summer is *your* season, my sweet! You must be presented to the queen!"

A few days later, I was bustled back to London, and the weeks that followed were as hectic as any I had ever known. From my portfolio I selected a hundred sketches of morning gowns, evening gowns, riding costumes, underskirts, bodices, redingotes, anything I might need in the months to come. I pored over magazines, looking for ideas. Melinda and I had designed most of our clothes, but never before had I taken the task so seriously. Seamstresses, milliners, glovemakers, shoemakers had to be engaged. Materials had to be selected. Fittings had to be arranged. In short, in a very little time the impossible had to be accomplished.

But somehow it was done, and one fine morning our carriage joined the procession along Piccadilly to St. James

Palace, where I was presented to the nineteen-year-old queen.
Her large blue eyes were merry, even on this formal occasion, and two little white teeth, protrusive, bit into her lower
lip as she held back laughter. *Why, she's only a girl,* I
thought with delight as I curtsied to her. *She's only a girl
. . . a little older than I . . . just starting out.*

Suddenly I was in a different world. I was no longer the
child of the family, who peeped down the stairs from the
landing at all those fine ladies and gentlemen who were on
their way in to dinner—I was one of those ladies! Grown up!
Though my father was still firmly against my marrying before
I was eighteen, in bringing me out he had in effect announced:
"Gentlemen, here she is!" And the gentlemen came calling!

And there was so much more. There was the theater, the
opera, the ballet. There were picnics *al fresco* and excursions
on the steamboats of the Thames. And there was Almack's,
perhaps the most exclusive social organization in the world.
My mother, I learned, was a favorite of some of the patronesses
of Almack's—Lady Willoughby D'Eresby, Lady Londonderry,
the formidable Lady Jersey—and that brought invitations
to those famous assembly rooms, where we danced amid gilt
columns and mirrors, under gaslit chandeliers, to an orchestra
thumping and fiddling on a balcony.

But how, one might ask, could I truly enjoy this when Tom
was three thousand miles away? I can only confess—I loved
it!

Yet, all through that spring and summer, a growing worry
nagged at my mind. As Tom's letters became less frequent, I
wondered: Was it possible that the glorious night which I
remembered so vividly had faded in Tom's memory? Was it
possible that that night had never meant as much to him as it
had to me?

What if it had not been the first such night for Tom?

Worse, what if it had not been the last? What if there had
been other nights since, with other girls?

Had I, like so many before me, been a fool?

In late July my father came to me with a grim look on his
face. "Augusta, has Tom said anything more to you about
visiting England this autumn?"

I had to admit that Tom had not even mentioned the matter
in a long time.

"I don't know if I'm right in doing this, but I think you
should be prepared."

My father showed me a letter my mother had received from Aunt Nickie. With plummeting hopes, I read:

> . . .I dislike spreading rumors, but you have asked me to tell all. It is said that Tom has been gambling heavily again and that his losses have been catastrophic. . . .

The next letter from Aunt Nickie came off the packet only a few days later.

> . . .again, I detest this kind of gossip, Lydia, but I do think you should be fully informed. I have heard that the Butlers will announce the engagement of their daughter Zelda to Mr. Tom Raveneau any day now. And from what I have seen of the deportment of those two together, I would say it is highly likely. Well, if one loses heavily enough at the card table, I suppose that is one way of restoring the family fortune. . . .

That evening I took pen in hand and informed Tom that he might consider himself free. Though I wept, my hand was steady, and I did not allow my tears to touch the page.

In the next month I received two short letters from Tom, but I scarcely glanced at them. Then it was the middle of September, and I knew my final letter had reached him and that I would never hear from him again.

My parents were tactful and kind. I, however, felt sick—sick with the shame of a foolish girl who has let herself be used and abandoned. Never again, I vowed. Never again would I let such a thing happen.

In October we returned to Ashtonfield Park, for it was cub-hunting time, time to train the new hounds. I was grateful that nothing was said about a return to South Carolina, for I hoped never again to set eyes on Tom Raveneau—or if I must, that it would be as a wife and mother who had forgotten that he had ever existed. Meanwhile, I tried to lose myself in rural pleasures, in long rides with the whiff of gunpowder on the autumn air, and evenings of dancing and charades and whist. And yet, though I smiled most of the time in those days, inwardly I wept a great deal.

On a November evening, when the Hunter's Moon was rising, I wept for the last time.

We had gone to bed rather early, for my father was riding in the morning. Though the night was chilly, my casement windows were flung open, and moonlight flooded my room. As I lay in my bed, I remembered the November moon back at the Barony, and suddenly I was stricken with homesickness. If only I could return not only to the Barony but to a far more innocent time, a time when proud Gannon, wicked Gannon was not yet our enemy, a time when we children were still untouched by tragedy, a time when all the bright promises were still unbroken, still to be kept. But no tears or prayers could ever take me back to that happier day.

I must have slept, if only for a little while. Suddenly I was wide awake, my heart pounding, and the light in the room had subtly shifted, as if the moon had risen farther. But what had awakened me? I listened.

There was no sound, not even a creak of the house. But I sensed that someone—something—was near, though I saw nothing in the shadows of the room.

"Who is it?" I asked in a fearful whisper. "Who's there?"

As if in answer, a dark figure suddenly appeared crouching in my open window, silhouetted by the moonlight. I gasped and started to scream.

The next few seconds seemed to last forever. The scream never left my throat. As light and swift as a cat, the dark figure sailed through the air toward me. I never heard it hit the floor. A hand went to my mouth, and an arm encircled my shoulders. "Not a sound, my love," said a dear familiar voice. "Not a word, not a sound, not a thing—but this!" As the hand left my face, a hard mouth crushed my lips.

"Oh, Tom!" I said when I could breath again. "Oh, my Lord, Tom—it's you!"

2 ◦◦◦◦◦◦

"Yes, it's me," he said, laughter in his voice, "but if you were expecting someone else—"

"How did you get here? How did you find my room?"

"I've been watching the windows, my love, and biding my time, and now . . ."

Again his mouth came down on mine, his arm tightening around my shoulders, and a hand swept down my side to hip and thigh, holding me so firmly I could not escape. I kicked and squirmed, I pounded at him, I tried to claw him, and all I got for my efforts were blankets kicked aside, a torn neckline, and the hem of my gown thrown high on my legs. And still he kissed me, while I tried to pull my mouth away and cursed him and, as a sudden hot thrill raced through my body, began kissing him back.

"Oh—*damn* you, Tom Raveneau!"

"I have been damned, my sweet. Life has been hell without you."

"Oh, yes, and I'm sure that Zelda Butler did her best to ease your discomfort!"

The rogue had the nerve to laugh.

"Well, isn't it true you've been having a mighty active social life, Mr. Raveneau?"

"From what you've written," he said, nuzzling my throat, "you've had a merry time yourself."

"That is entirely different, and you know it!" Oh, I thought, as I continued struggling, why had he caught me in an old flannel gown instead of something silken and pretty! "Aunt Nickie said you were practically engaged to Zelda!"

"I'm surprised at Miss Nickie for spreading such gossip," he said, holding me down. "Augusta, you know how people get wrong ideas. Like with me and Melinda. Even you thought we'd get married. Now, isn't that so?"

"Just the same . . ." Oh, Lordy, I thought as his kiss

moved about my throat and his hand swept over me, sending lovely tremors all through my body, oh, Lord-a-mighty, if he doesn't stop doing that. . . . "Just the same, you wrote so little—and took so long to come."

"I came as soon as I could. I was about to leave when I got your farewell letter."

"Liar!"

Abruptly he released me, and I fell back half-naked in the moonlight. When I reached to pull my gown back over my legs and breast, he took my hands. "No," he said. "I've told you, Augusta, don't ever hide yourself from me. I made you mine long ago, and you have nothing to hide."

His eyes, ordinarily so brightly blue, were dark and limpid as he looked down at me on the bed, and when he spoke again his voice was husky. "You'd forgive me for taking so long to come to you if you knew how much I've missed you. God, Augusta, how I've longed for you. . . ."

How could I ever have doubted his love, I thought. How could I ever have doubted that, when the time was right, he would come to me?

Again he took me into his arms, and this time I did not resist. In spite of the chill of the room I felt as if a summer-warm Carolina stream were flowing through me. As he kissed me, his hand slid under my torn gown to hold my breast, fingers moving over the peaked nipple, and that was right, that was good, because we were becoming as one again, the long breach healed.

Eagerly, too eagerly at first, we kissed, hungry kisses, burning kisses. His hands moved over me, rediscovering each part of my body, and only when they became too bold did I stop him.

"We're going to be married," he whispered in my ear. "As soon as possible."

"But your debts . . ."

He put a finger to my lips. "Darling, I haven't any debts. Not a debt in the world."

"But Aunt Nickie said you were gambling and losing heavily—"

Releasing me and sitting up, he flung off his coat. "You lose one time, you win another. My luck turned, just as I always knew it would."

As he pulled off his stock and unbuttoned his waistcoat, I realized what he had in mind.

"Tom, you mustn't!"

He silenced me with another kiss. "Darling, tomorrow afternoon I shall arrive here supposedly for the first time. I shall ask your father for your hand in marriage. And until we're married, we may never have another chance to be alone together like this. All I ask of you is an hour or two tonight. Just an hour or two."

I remembered how our "hour or two" in the loft had lasted almost until dawn and how easily we might have been caught.

"Tom," I said weakly, "what we did that night . . . I've sworn that . . . that I never will again . . . until we're married."

"Augusta, I love you, and I'll never do anything you don't want me to do. You know that. I just want to hold you . . . touch you . . . have you in my arms for a little while."

"Well . . ." Surely, as long as we were careful, there was no harm. "Only a little while."

A moment later Tom was sitting beside me, naked in the moonlight and as beautiful as I remembered him. He smiled as I reached up to touch his face, to trace the line of his throat and shoulder, to run my fingertips through the light golden fleecing of his chest and over a nipple as taut as my own. He lifted my hand to his lips, then rolled into my arms, crushing my breasts with his chest.

I had thought I remembered the quaking, the hot lava flow, the volcanic forces that were released within me by Tom's lovemaking, but memory only hinted at what he did to me now. For a time, as fearful as if we had never been together before, I resisted the most intimate of his touches. But a moment came when, quivering, trembling, aching with desire, I could no longer deny him—or myself—and I lay open to every kiss, every caress.

"Augusta," he whispered. His exploring touch, going farther, ever farther, had found me ready, and I knew what he wanted.

"Oh, no!"

"Only for a moment or two."

"I don't dare."

"I'm not asking for everything. Only to meet for a moment— like a kiss. Is that so much to ask? A kiss?"

I could resist no longer. I wanted that moment, that kiss, as much as he. As we lay on our sides facing each other, I raised a thigh up over his hip and let him bring himself to me. He gave me, as he had promised, little more than a warm, moist, probing kiss, as our mouths, too, met, but my mind reeled and the world rocked until, with a sob and a moan, we slipped apart.

But I could not stop with that, I thought. I would die if I stopped with that. Just once more, for a moment or two . . .

This time he rolled me onto my back, and as he settled between my raised thighs, he entered, strong and hard, all the way into me, his fully impaled captive.

"Augusta, darling," he whispered, holding me tightly and stroking me from breast to thigh, "darling Augusta, to be with you like this again . . . to be with you, to be part of you, to love you as I do . . ."

All resistance left me. Like a single heartbeat, we began to make love, and as our pleasure soared, I didn't care, I didn't care, I did not want this ever to end. Not until once again we reached that state where moons explode and stars shower from the heavens, and I would know nothing but our shared bliss.

Oh, to be young and in love for the first time and to lie naked in the moonlight with one's darling. Little by little, my shyness was vanishing, and that night I allowed myself to look at him fully and directly for the first time. And he was beautiful in every part—not only his face, but the strong column of his neck, his broad shoulders and chest, his soft, silken manhood in its nest of blond fleece, his long, shapely thighs and calves. Even his feet and hands were gracefully formed, as if made to give me pleasure. Only a little while, we had said, but the first hour led to another, and that one to yet another, and even then we could not bear to part. Each time we thought we had exhausted passion, we had only to lie resting in each other's arms for a time to find the will, the need, the savage hunger returning, and again we made love, gently and sweetly one moment, fiercely and greedily the next.

"You must leave," I implored him when I heard a stirring in the house, "you must!" For my father would be abroad at any time, and it would be impossible for Tom to leave unseen. He finally did pull his clothes back on, but even after he had swung out onto the ivied wall of the house, he lingered at the window another minute.

"Today," he said. "This very afternoon I'll come and ask your father for your hand."

"Go!"

He leaned in to kiss me one more time, and I could not resist. " 'Sleep dwell upon thine eyes,' " he whispered, " 'peace in thy breast! Would I were sleep and peace, so sweet to rest!' "

And then he was gone.

Ah, but I had a surprise for Tom.

By chance, we were all in the east parlor the next afternoon, when the butler announced that Mr. Tom Raveneau was at the door, and my parents, who rarely lost their composure, could hardly have looked more astonished. My mother gasped and said, "How dare he!" and my father was literally shaken. Flushed, he looked at me, as if gauging my reaction. I shrugged and smiled and said, "Well, my goodness! Let's ask him in. He's come a long way."

I must say that Tom carried off his arrival well. After the infrequency of his letters and the length of his silence, he could hardly have expected an enthusiastic welcome, but he did not appear to notice the frigidity of my mother's smile or the bleakness in my father's eyes. He kissed my mother's cheek and shook my father's hand and then turned to me, and I surprised my parents by the warmth of my greeting—as if he were still a dear old friend or a well-liked older brother.

"I do apologize for not letting you know I was coming," Tom said, "but I wanted to surprise Augusta."

"He simply must stay for dinner, Mamma!" I said. "No, better yet—now that he's here, Tom must stay on at Ashtonfield Park with us! Oh, please, do ask him to stay!"

Tom pretended to demur, but my enthusiasm prevailed; for the time being, at least, he would stay, and we must send a servant to fetch his luggage from the nearby inn immediately. My father seemed amused by my attitude, but my mother's eyes showed disappointment. They asked me if I were so lacking in pride.

The afternoon proceeded pleasantly. Tea was served, and we demanded of Tom all the news of home and told him of our latest adventures in England. Later, my father went to write some letters, and my mother also found an excuse to leave Tom and me alone together, but I surprised her by insisting that, no, she must not leave us but must help me show Tom the grounds of Ashtonfield Park—there would be just enough time before dinner. I was determined not to be left alone with Tom—yet.

After dinner, my mother and I left the men with their cigars and their port. When they left the table, they did not join us. I heard the door of my father's study closing after them. I felt the weight of my mother's disapproval, but she said nothing. Her jaw hardened, and her eyes had their I-shall-wait-and-see look.

After half an hour we heard the door of the study open, and Tom, with an excited, pleased look on his face, came into the parlor where my mother and I sat. My father, following him, also looked pleased. "My dears," he said, as he put his hand on Tom's shoulder, "I've been having a little chat with Tom, and I'm sure you know what it was about."

"Why, no," I said innocently. "Why, no, Daddy, what?"

My father smiled and patted Tom's shoulder. His faith in the young man, the son of his great good friend, had been vindicated. "Tom tells me his fortunes have improved a great deal since we last saw him. And, as you'll no doubt have guessed, he's come here today to ask me for your hand in—"

"What!" I leapt from my chair so abruptly that both Tom and my father reeled back a step.

"I said, Augusta, that Tom has come here today—"

"To ask for my *hand?*"

"Why, yes—"

"After hardly writing for months, after having taken up with Zelda Butler and—and—"

"Augusta!" Tom yelped. He looked as if I had shot him between the eyes.

"—and goodness only knows how many others, he has the nerve—"

My father's jaw sagged. My mother could not have looked more delighted.

"He has the *nerve* to come here and ask you for my hand? He has the nerve, when we haven't even seen each other in fifteen months, when we haven't even been alone together since he walked into this house this afternoon? He is so arrogant that he thinks all he has to do is ask you for my hand, and I am going to leap into his arms? Well, I'll tell you something—"

"Augusta," Tom said, "please!"

"I'll tell you something, Mr. Tom Raveneau. If you want

me now, after the way you've behaved, you are going to have to come courting me! You are going to have to try to win me, and someday *maybe*, just *maybe*, Tom Raveneau, I shall consider marrying you!''

Snooty ole Miss Gussie had never had her nose higher or her mouth more turned down than at that moment, as she marched proudly out of the room.

Of course, I did marry Tom.

But, oh, if only life were more like a play, with all the actors making their entrances and exits conveniently on cue! Or should I say, if only life were *not* so much like a play, with its intermission between the betrothal at the end of Act One and the marriage at the beginning of Act Two! But, alas, life is full of intermissions, and its entrances and exits are usually ill timed, and its denouements are often inappropriate.

Yet never would I willingly have missed the fun of the months that followed. Tom was soon forced to give up the idea that he could visit my bedroom at night. That was much too dangerous a game, even if I had wanted to play it, and I told him he would find my door locked and my window barred. Though I wanted him as much as he wanted me, I had told him he must court me, and court me he did.

In January, when the holiday season was past, he asked my permission to speak to my father again, and this time I gave it. We became officially betrothed.

My mother and I returned to London to prepare for the nuptials. A wedding dress had to be ordered, my trousseau had to be filled out, lists of invitations had to be drawn and redrawn. At my father's urging, Tom had agreed that we would stay in England at least a year after the wedding, and so a suitable house had to be found. After considerable searching, we located one in Mayfair, not far from the Harley Street house, and Mrs. Belknap, our housekeeper, saw that it was staffed by her own well-trained nieces and nephews.

Almost unbelievably, the day finally came. The marriage ceremony was performed at a church near my parents' house, by my father's old friend, the Bishop of Bath and Wells. Tom and I were man and wife at last, and off on our wedding trip.

When did I first realize the truth about my mother? I think it dawned on me slowly during the following year. Certainly I had no inkling at the time of our wedding trip, or I could never have been so happy then and in the months that followed.

We made the seven-hour trip to Brighton by private coach, arriving quite late in the evening. The bridal suite, filled with flowers, awaited us, and a cold supper of chicken and lobster and champagne was wheeled in on a cart. As soon as we were alone, we separately and modestly slipped from clothes to robes, performed our ablutions, and, ravenously hungry, attacked our supper. Never had food tasted so good. When we had finished, we sat back, half-naked, yawning with satisfaction. But the night was far from over, and, his robe slipping away, Tom reached for me.

I suppose we were a fairly typical bridal couple, for we saw little of Brighton that year, and Brighton saw little of us. Yet we returned to London without any particular regret, for we had our new home to look forward to.

There followed the gayest summer season I had ever known. Soon after our return to London, we joined my parents on a trip to Epsom for Derby Day. Fortunately, my parents had friends there, for the inns were filled and virtually every spare bed in every home had been rented, and people even erected tents among the hedgerows. And then, to everybody's horror, snow fell before and all during the race, the only time in the history of the Derby that such a thing had happened.

There were races all over the country during the summer. At the end of that week, there was the Oaks at Epsom, and there was the Thousand Guineas at Newmarket and the St. Leger at Doncaster, and Tom and my father had to see—and wager on—all the best known. But more to my mother's taste and mine were the dinner parties of the season. If we were not attending one, we were planning or giving one, and ours—my mother's and mine—were as successful and gay as any in London.

Perhaps I should have guessed about my mother when, near the end of the season, she fell ill and I had to take her place as hostess at one of her parties. But even then, she did seem to recover.

In autumn we returned to Ashtonfield Park. My parents' house was large enough for Tom and me to have an apartment of our own, and my father seemed eager to keep me nearby. All in all, we had a good winter, full of fine, fast hunts in the mornings, jolly visits in the afternoons and evenings, and quiet, cozy lovemaking at night. If only, I thought, oh, if only, now that my mother was well, she could recover more of her strength.

But she did not. The four of us had planned a trip to Brighton in the spring, but my mother was too weak to go. She urged Tom and me to go alone, and "have a second bridal trip, children," but instead we decided to delay our trip till late summer, at the end of the season. To be near her, I willingly yielded to my father's request that we move into the Harley Street house. I think that by then I knew the truth, for I said nothing about a return to America.

But something else was nagging at my mind.

Was it possible, I asked myself, that Tom was growing tired of me?

Six months earlier, such an idea would have been unthinkable. Now it was inescapable. I told myself that I was being a silly little fool, that Pearl's mother, Aunt Polly, had warned me that most couples make love more often in their first year of marriage than in all the rest of their lives. Furthermore, I certainly did not expect thunder-and-lightning ardor every time we made love—nor did I want it! But surely, when we made love, his mind should stay a little more with me . . . he should seemed a little less distracted.

I could not help wondering if he were worried about something. Had there been bad news from home? He laughed and said that, on the contrary, his fortunes were prospering. He gambled a great deal—had he perhaps been losing heavily? He assured me he had not. Was it me? Was I displeasing him in some way? He kissed me tenderly and asked me what in the world I was talking about.

Never mind, I thought. Everything would be all right. My mother was getting better, and we were all still having wonderfully good times. And, remembering our first wedding trip, I could not doubt that the second one would put everything to rights.

But then my mother went into decline again.

When I saw the frightened look in my father's eyes and heard the doctors whispering the old familiar phrases—". . . chronic wasting disease . . . increasing anemia . . ."—I could no longer hide the truth from myself. My father had brought my mother home to England to die. That was why he had insisted on my making the trip with them—so that my mother might have me near at the last. He had thought the truth too cruel for a young girl to live with for long, and perhaps he had been right. But then we had all been blessed: for a time my mother had had a remission. Now, once again, she was sinking.

She summoned me to her bedside. Never before had her face been so wasted, but the beauty of those fine bones remained, and her voice was surprisingly firm.

"I'm sorry I shan't be going to Brighton with you this year, darling."

I wanted to weep. "Mamma, we are certainly not going without you!"

"Don't be silly, dear. This is just a passing indisposition, and I shall soon be better. Next year we shall all make the trip together. No, you go—"

"No, Mamma, I won't!"

"You'll do as I ask." She gave me a penetrating look. "Augusta, what is wrong between you and Tom?"

"Why, nothing, Mamma!"

"Perhaps it's just as well that your father and I won't be going with you. I know you've been looking forward to a second bridal trip, and I think you need one."

"No, Mamma!"

"Yes. I want you to make this trip, Augusta. I want it very much. Please. If you want to make me happy, please go to Brighton with Tom."

I could not refuse her. Tom and I went to Brighton alone. And there, God help us, we met Adam and Jewel Trevayne.

Sir Adam Trevayne, Baronet, was surely the handsomest man I had ever met, not excepting Tom. In his late twenties, he was a little taller than Tom but no broader, a lean whip of a man. His dark brown hair came to a peak on his high forehead and flowed back over his head in thick gentle waves. His eyebrows flared and curved like a beautiful bird's wings. His nose was long and straight, his chin was square and slightly notched, and every plane and proportion of his face had a look of hard perfection. His long-fingered hands were enough to make any woman shiver, and so was his voice—a soft, cello-smooth baritone.

He had only one flaw—his eyes.

It was not merely that they were so light a gray as to appear washed out. It was the total indifference in them. They were the eyes of a dead man.

We had hardly arrived at the Norfolk Hotel when he and

Tom fell into conversation, and Tom told me soon afterwards that "a real gambling man can sniff out another before he's even in sight." Perhaps I should have known then that our "second wedding trip" would be less than a total success.

From our very first evening in Brighton, Tom gambled at every opportunity, and goodness knows there were plenty of them. Though there were laws against gambling, there was never any problem in finding a game—anything from écarté and hazard to all-fives and put. But what Tom loved most of all was the private game, right there in the hotel.

I had looked forward to long walks, arm-in-arm, along the Steyne; to intimate suppers in our rooms; and above all, to making love as we had on our bridal trip—leisurely, fiery, repeated lovemaking with no fear of interruption, a true meeting of the souls through the naked bodies. But when Tom did make love to me, it was almost perfunctorily, as if even at that moment his mind were elsewhere.

In the gaming room. With Adam Trevayne.

A few nights after our arrival at Brighton, I awakened to find Tom putting on his clothes in the dark. When I asked him what was the matter, he said he could not sleep. "Well, you come back here," I purred, "and we'll do something to make you sleep."

"But darling," he whispered, bending down to kiss me, "a man can't be doing that *all* the time."

Once he could have. But now Adam was downstairs waiting. And then there was Jewel. Lady Jewel Trevayne.

Any woman would have found Adam fiercely attractive, especially if she were an unfulfilled wife. Even I could not deny the sudden warmth that went through me when I looked at him—until he turned those dead, indifferent eyes on me. And Jewel had much the same effect on men.

There was nothing dead or indifferent about her eyes, however. Deep violet in color, they seemed to sparkle with energy and mischief. Shorter than I, she had a fuller figure, a svelte, sensuous figure that took a man's breath away—and she used it for that purpose. She was the most outrageous flirt and tease I had every seen, with a way of giving a man a suggestive up-from-under look, while running her tongue over her lips, that could only be described as completely naughty, an open invitation to bed.

I first met Jewel at a card game in the hotel, soon after our arrival at Brighton. I had no intention of spending all my time alone while Tom gambled, so I went with him. To my relief, there were a number of women present in the card room, but my relief was short-lived when Jewel appeared. At least she showed no favoritism in her flirting, and Tom did have the grace to look embarrassed as she leaned over his shoulder at the card table, her breast brushing his cheek, while Adam looked on with complete indifference.

Why Jewel should have taken to me, I had no idea at the time, but she did. Certainly I offered her no encouragement, for at first I quite disliked her. And yet it was convenient to have someone with whom to explore the pleasures of Brighton—shops and band concerts and dipping in the sea—rather than languishing in my room or sitting around bored while the men gambled. And I had to admit that, as I became accustomed to her, I enjoyed much of her risqué chatter and gossip. It often seemed to me that she was trying to find out if she could shock me, but I was determined not to be shocked.

That was a mistake. I found out what Jewel had in mind a few days before we were to return to London.

At the close of an afternoon of wandering the sunny streets from shop to shop, we wound up by paying our admittance to the famous pier and looking at the sundial and the brace of cannon and the new weighing machine. I paid little attention to Jewel's chatter as we sat down on a bench to rest, but suddenly I realized she was talking about Tom. She went on at some length about what a marvelously handsome man he was, and finally asked bluntly how he was in bed. I smiled, because I had become used to outrageous remarks and questions from Jewel. I told her, truthfully enough, that, though I did not think it any of her concern, Tom had given me some absolutely wonderful times.

"I can believe it," she said. "Is he the best you've ever had?"

"Jewel, dear," I said primly, "he is my one and only husband."

"And your only lover, you mean? You've never had anyone else?"

I felt a flush coming to my face. "Of course not."

"Then how can you be so sure he's all that wonderful? I mean, you have no basis for comparison, have you?"

"I don't feel the need—"

"Now, I can assure you that Adam is an extraordinary lover. And," she gave me a sly look, "I can also assure you that he has the wherewithal to be one. Nothing grotesque, mind you, just—well—quite large, once aroused. Tell me, is Tom very large?''

"Jewel!'' I laughed, but she had at last managed to shock me.

She did not seem to notice. ''Of course, size isn't everything,'' she chattered on. ''I do enjoy a big man, but skill is much more important, and Adam is the most skillful lover you'll ever meet.''

"Well, I don't intend to meet him as a lover.''

"Oh, no?'' A bright, naughty look came to Jewel's eyes. ''Tell me the truth. Haven't you even once wondered what it would be like to make love with Adam?''

"No!'' I said. ''No, I have not!''

She looked at me for a long moment, an impish smile coming to her face. ''Well, you're thinking about it now.''

The worst of it was, now she was right. After what I had been through with Tom lately, the thought, once Jewel had put it into my mind, was not easily banished.

"Jewel, I don't think we should talk like this any more.''

"Can you deny that you're attracted to Adam?''

"He is a very attractive man, but there are many such men, thank goodness, or the world would be a dreary place. I can find a man attractive without wanting to go to bed with him.''

"On your word of honor, Augusta—tell me you are quite certain you would *not* enjoy going to bed with my husband.''

My face warmed. ''Oh, Jewel . . .''

Jewel laughed. ''There, you see?''

"But I didn't mean . . .''

"Darling, I'll tell you something.'' She leaned close to me, eyes aglitter and the mischievous smile still on her face, and whispered into my ear. ''Adam and I have talked a great deal about you and Tom. And my husband would *adore* going to bed with you!''

I should have simply stood up and walked away. The conversation had gotten completely out of hand. But I was more shaken than I would ever have expected.

"Please, Jewel—''

"And if you want to know the truth,'' Jewel went on, ''*I* would adore going to bed with your Tom!''

I should not have been shocked. I knew perfectly well that Tom and I had wandered into a rather racy crowd. But I had certainly never expected to receive a suggestion such as Jewel appeared to be making.

"Well," she said, standing up from the bench, "time to get back to the hotel. You haven't forgotten that you and Tom are having dinner with Adam and me in our rooms this evening?"

"Jewel, I don't think . . ." I looked for a way to beg off. "I've been out in the sun too much this afternoon, and I'm getting a headache . . ."

"Oh, my dear." Jewel took my hand as I stood up and gave me a close, confiding look. "You think about what I've said and come to dinner anyway. And after dinner, if you still have a headache . . ." Her voice lowered confidentially. "You have Tom take you back to your rooms. Let him rejoin us. Then a little later perhaps Adam will visit you to see how you're feeling . . . and, if you wish, do anything he can to make you feel better."

Jewel smiled and patted my hand. She could not have made her meaning plainer.

I think I was still in a kind of shock when Tom and I were dressing for dinner. I hardly knew how to say what was on my mind, and finally I just blurted it out. "Tom, I do not like them. I do not like them at all."

Tom smiled. "Now, who's this you don't like?"

"Sir Adam Trevayne and Lady Jewel. I do not like them. Do we have to have dinner with them?"

"Well, of course we do. We're expected."

"She wants to go to bed with you, you know. And she wants me to go to bed with her husband."

"Wha-a-at?"

He looked at me, grinning as if I had said the most incredible thing in the world, and I told him as nearly as I could remember exactly what Jewel had said. When I had finished, he burst out laughing.

"Darling, don't you know Jewel by now? She was teasing you. Of course, if you *did* plead a headache after dinner, she would think you were accepting her suggestion, and the joke would be on you when Adam never turned up."

"I thought of that possibility. But I think he would turn up. Tom, what incredibly nice people we have for friends."

"Oh, now, darling . . ."

Suddenly I had an inspiration. Rising from my chair, I

threw myself into Tom's arms. "Tom," I said, "let's go home!"

"We are going home, Augusta, in just a few days."

"No! I mean home to America! Home to the Barony! Everything was so wonderful at the Barony, and if we can just go back there. . . . Tom, we're Americans, we don't belong here with these people! Please, darling, let's go home."

"We will, Augusta, we will, just as soon as we can. But we have to wait until your mother is better."

"Oh."

How cruelly selfish I felt at that moment. For the past weeks I had been so absorbed by my own problems that my mother's had faded in my mind, and in that moment I had forgotten them altogether.

But something good was happening. I was in Tom's arms, and he was giving me more real tenderness than he had in months.

"You're right, Augusta," he said, as his mouth roved my face, "America is the place for us. And we will go back just as soon as possible. And, darling . . ." His arms tightened around me, and his voice thickened with emotion. "Darling, I know this trip hasn't been what you wanted it to be. And I know that's been my fault. I wanted to renew our marriage too—my God, I didn't come here to play cards, I came to get away from gambling, and to be with you. But when I met Adam . . . it's been as if some demon were compelling me. Night and day, I haven't been able to get gambling out of my mind. But from now on, it's going to be different, Augusta. I swear it. It's going to be different."

Perhaps Jewel's invitation, and Adam's alleged interest in me, had disturbed Tom more than he cared to admit. Because from that moment on, things *were* different.

Tom made love to me that night as he had not in months, and he continued to do so during the few days that remained of our second bridal trip. We saw almost nothing of the Trevaynes, or of Brighton, but remained in our rooms like newlyweds, enjoying our greatest intimacy in more than a year. How right my mother had been to send us off alone together, I thought, and how pleased she would be with the result.

"It's going to stay this way, Augusta," Tom pledged on

the morning we started for home. "I'm never again going to let us be drawn apart."

My happiness continued until that afternoon, when our private coach entered Harley Street. Then, ahead of us, on the pavement before my parents house, I saw that fresh straw had been spread to muffle the sound of iron-rimmed carriage wheels. That meant that my mother was still seriously ill, and my joy faded.

As the coach drew up before the house, I had the feeling that a dream of happiness was turning into a nightmare. I dared not understand what it meant when I looked at the door and saw Mrs. Belknap arranging the black crepe.

I screamed something, I have no idea what. I threw open the coach door and leapt down without waiting for Tom. I raced up the steps to the door. "My mamma!" I cried. "No, not my mamma, not my mamma!"

Mrs. Belknap turned a grief-swollen face to me. "No, not your mamma, poor lamb," she said, "not your mamma yet. 'Tis your poor dear father that's passed away."

3 ~~~~~~

In less than a month I lost both of my parents.

Cholera had claimed my father—the same dreadful cholera that had been so prevalent in America the year we had left. Five years before that, it had killed thousands in England, almost eight thousand in London alone, but it had died down, and my father had thought we would be safe from it, now it had killed him.

Mercifully, it had done its work quickly. My father had reached the point of complete collapse within hours, and his heart had been unable to take the strain. He was dead soon after the message of his illness had been sent to us in Brighton.

That message had never reached us. There was not yet a magnetic telegraph to Brighton, the semaphore telegraph was out of order, and the railway, with its fast mail delivery, would not be in operation until the next year. The message had gone by coach, and somehow it must have gone astray or been delivered late—after our departure.

With my father's death, my mother seemed to lose her will to live. Each day I saw her growing thinner and smaller and weaker, as if she were literally fading away.

And then she was gone.

It was as if both of my parents had been taken from me at a single blow, a blow far more devastating, even, than the death of Melinda.

I remember very little of the next six months. I have a vague memory of being given laudanum and being put to bed after the second funeral. Mrs. Belknap and Tom, I was assured, would take care of everything that needed doing. I remember hours of weeping—tears of grief, tears of rage— and the feeling that I was once again a small child, deserted and lost and far from home. I had only Tom, and much as I loved him, he could not give me what had been taken away.

It was as if time stood still in those months, while I remained confined to the dark room of my grief. The house itself, with its drapes drawn, was dark, and I seldom left it, spending more time in bed each day, while the strength drained from my body.

Tom was a model of patience. No one could have been kinder or more understanding, and not once did I hear a cross word or a sigh from him. I could not expect him to share altogether in my mourning, of course, and as the autumn wore on and he attended to his own affairs, we saw less and less of each other.

We did not go to the country that autumn. I had no wish to go anywhere beyond the dark rooms of the Harley Street house—unless it was back home to America, and to do that, we had to wait until I regained my strength. Christmas and the New Year passed almost unnoticed, and increasingly Tom and I lived almost as strangers. And then an event occurred that drew me back into the world.

Tom, as usual, was out. He was frequently out until all hours, with the result that we sometimes went for several days seeing little of each other, and I thought nothing about it. But that night I was feeling lonely and restless—the signs of returning life—and I found myself waiting for him. Unable to concentrate on a book, I wandered about the house, returning time and again to the front hall. It was quite late, and I must have looked out the door at least a dozen times, but the gas street lamp, glowing dimly in the fog, revealed nothing. I was about to close the door for the last time and go to bed, when I heard the clatter of hooves on stone and the rumble of a clarence. I felt silly to be seen waiting, so in case it should be Tom, I closed the door most of the way and peered out into the street.

Sure enough, the clarence—or growler, as we call them because of their noise—came to a halt, the fog swirling about it. The door opened, and Tom got out. As he turned to say something to whomever was still in the carriage, I heard the peal of a woman's laughter. I froze.

I would have recognized Jewel Trevayne's laugh anywhere.

But the man who leaned out of the carriage to speak to Tom was not Adam Trevayne. For a moment his face was shadowed. Then he looked up toward the door. And despite the fog and the dimness of the gas lamp, never in my life could I have mistaken that face.

The face of Gannon Murdock.

"Everything you ever stole from us . . . I'm gonna take it back!"

I had hardly thought of those words since we had come to England, yet now they rang in my ears as clearly as if I were hearing them for the first time. Oh, no, I thought, Gannon had already had his revenge. He had taken the Tear of Venus—wasn't that enough? Then why was he here?

He drew back into darkness, and the carriage pulled away. Tom came up the steps, raising an eyebrow in surprise as I opened the door for him. "Up so late, my love?"

I closed the door and stood there for a moment, hardly knowing what to say. I had the oddest sensation of emerging back into the world, of truly looking at Tom for the first time in months, of events occurring to which I must react, and swiftly.

Tom looked puzzled. "What is it, dear?"

"What were you doing with Gannon Murdock?"

"Gannon . . ." He looked at me as if he must have heard wrong.

"Gannon Murdock! What is he doing here?"

"As far as I know, he's doing nothing here. Who in the world told you I was with Gannon Murdock?"

"Why, you were with him just now, with him and Jewel Trevayne, in the growler. I saw him—"

"Augusta, you saw Adam Trevayne. I happened onto Adam and Jewel in Leicester Square and spent part of the evening with them. But you certainly did not see Gannon Murdock." He laughed. "Good Lord, I haven't even thought of Gannon in years."

"Tom, I *saw* him," I insisted. "He leaned out of the carriage and spoke to you. He looked up at the house, he looked straight at the front door—"

"Augusta, you could have seen very little by lamplight in the fog. Some trick of the light fooled you. Has something put Gannon into your mind lately?"

"No, but I could have sworn . . ."

Tom put an arm around my shoulders and patted me. "Gannon Murdock is past history, Augusta. I haven't forgotten his threats, but you have nothing to fear from him. Believe me, even if he were to show his face in London, I wouldn't let him hurt you in any way. Not ever."

Perhaps that was why Tom had denied that Gannon had been with him: to save me worry. Or perhaps he had told the simple truth: that the dim light and the fog had tricked me. I had, after all, seen Gannon for only a few seconds. But those few seconds had been so vivid. . . .

The words still echoed in my mind: *"Everything you ever stole from us . . . I'm gonna take it back!"*

When did I first become suspicious of Tom and Jewel?

Perhaps it was a day or two later, when Tom admitted he had been seeing Jewel and Adam without telling me. "Only a few times, actually, and I know you don't care much for them, especially after Jewel's prank at Brighton, so I didn't say anything. But really, you should get to know her better, Augusta. She's a very high-spirited, intelligent woman."

The jealous pang I felt may have helped bring me back to life, because I began to long for Tom as I had not in months. I had been such a fool. I had nearly lost my husband once, to the gaming tables, and I had won him back. But then, in my grief, I had let him slip away again, and I suspected that to win him back a second time might be far more difficult.

I did not care. I vowed to do it, no matter how difficult the task or how long it might take.

I started by taking stock of myself, and when I looked into

a mirror, what I saw came as a shock. My hair looked dead and stringy. My complexion was not merely pale but sickly sallow. My hollow cheeks looked like my mother's before her death. There was little to remind Tom of the girl he had fallen in love with.

I determined to do something about myself—fast.

For a time, Mrs. Belknap and the other servants were certain that grief had driven me mad. Knowing I needed exercise, I would do almost anything to get it. Thus there was no more lying abed until afternoon, no more Ophelia-like wandering about the house in nightgown and robe; I was more apt to be found racing up and down the stairs like a child and coming to a sudden guilty halt when a maid popped into view.

The very efforts I was making seemed to raise my spirits. Within ten days I could see a difference in myself, and within a month, so could Tom. One evening I found him looking at me as he had not since the final days of our trip to Brighton. I took his hand and led him up the stairs. An hour later, after the final sigh and while we still lay entangled upon the bed, he raised his head from my breast to look at me with a certain wonder. "Well, my dear," he said, "welcome back to the world!"

So much for you, Lady Jewel, I thought.

But of course it was not that easy.

In the months after I emerged from deep mourning, we saw a great deal of Sir Adam and Lady Jewel Trevayne. Since Tom had joined their circle, a circle known for its hedonism at a time when England was growing more "respectable" by the hour, I could look forward to no more invitations to the Wednesday-evening balls at Almack's, and Tom would see less of his club. This was quite acceptable to him, since he much preferred the gambling hells of Jermyn Street and Leicester Square—the more disreputable, it seemed to me, the better. Tom's character had facets I had not previously suspected.

When I reminded him of his promise that we would return to America as soon as possible, he demurred. "After all," he said, "we haven't seen much of England together these last months. It's hard to say when we'll get back over here. We ought to stay at least until next fall."

But not to see England. To be with Jewel.

There were incidents, classic incidents, that untold thousands of betrayed women would recognize.

When the betrayed one sees her husband and the other woman meet, their greetings are much too casual—indifferent, almost to the point of rudeness—yet neither appears to notice or to be offended.

Later, there are significant glances between the pair. Lovers always think they are unobserved and that their glances are meaningless to anyone else in the room. They are always wrong.

Then, one day on entering a room, the wife sees the couple standing much too close together. Startled, they jump apart. The woman has an excited, guilty look in her eyes. The man is unconvincingly nonchalant.

Two or three incidents, a half-dozen, a dozen, and for a long time the wife continues to call herself a silly, jealous fool, and to insist that the only one guilty of anything is herself. But some incidents are almost impossible to deny.

Such an incident occurred at Brighton in July.

At Tom's insistence, we made the trip with the Trevaynes that summer, and stayed at the same hotel. We made an odd foursome. Jewel exhibited such sisterly fondness for me, one would have thought I was her dearest friend. Adam, on the other hand, was the very picture of studied indifference, if not contempt. Surprisingly, I found myself even more resentful of him than of Jewel. Perhaps it was simply that I found him as attractive as ever—and attraction, when impermissible, can generate the most implacable hostility. As for Tom, he seemed to notice none of this. He was enjoying the stay at Brighton thoroughly, and if he hardly displayed the ardor of a newlywed, he did take care not to desert me as he had done the year before. For that reason alone I had hope that my fears were foolish.

But then one night, toward the end of our stay, they seemed to be confirmed.

I could not sleep that night. After dinner, the men had gone to play cards, and I had retired early. But thoughts of Tom and Jewel disturbed my peace, and finally, against my better judgment, I dressed again and went downstairs to the card room.

Tom was not there.

The half-dozen men sitting around the table were playing chemin de fer. I knew all of them but one, a pale, ginger-haired man on the far side of the table, sitting next to Adam. About twice my age, he had a long, narrow, high-templed face, hooded eyes under thick V-slanted brows, and a long bony jaw with a narrow, square chin. I suppose he was handsome after his fashion, as predatory animals often are. He announced his wagers with that casual arrogance of the wellborn Briton that inspires instant hatred in every good Scot, Welshman, and Irishman, and from the way he swayed over the table, he appeared to be drunk.

No one seemed to notice me until the hand was played out. Then, all but the ginger-haired man started to rise, until I motioned them to sit down.

Adam gave me a worried look. "I believe Tom went out for a breath of fresh air, Mrs. Raveneau," he said.

"*Who* went out for a breath of fresh air?" the ginger-haired man said, and, yes, he was drunk.

"Mrs. Raveneau's husband."

"Oh. Oh, yes, young Ravenel. Our blond Adonis. Left long ago."

"Just a little while ago, Harry, and the name is Rave*neau*."

Harry shrugged. "Ravenel, Raveneau—"

"Mrs. Raveneau, I don't think you've met the Earl of Huxton. My lord, I'd like to present Mrs. Tom Raveneau. Mrs. Raveneau is the daughter of Mr. August Welles, the well-known Charleston aristocrat who—"

Harry—the Earl of Huxton—burst out laughing. "Charleston aristocrat? My dear boy, there is no such thing as a Charleston aristocrat! 'S ridiculous as speaking of a—a *Liverpool* aristocrat! There is simply no such thing."

"*Harry!*"

Adam Trevayne was the last person in the world from whom I would have expected a defense, but his hot flash of anger appeared to sober the ginger-haired man.

"Oh, I say, old boy, have I sinned? Least offensive man in the world, you know, when I'm not in my cups. I say, Miz Ravenel, I must 'polgize—"

I heard no more. I had turned and left the card room. I went back up the stairs to the next floor.

And there I found them.

They were standing in the dimly lit corridor, Jewel in the door to her suite, Tom just outside. His back was to me, but his blond hair caught the lamplight. He was fully clothed; Jewel was not—she seemed to be wearing a robe, though she was half-hidden from me. She moved as if her hand were on Tom's chest. He lifted his hand to her throat and moved it down, I could have sworn, inside her robe. His head lowered toward her as if he were kissing her. She laughed softly. Then she saw me.

For an instant, she seemed to freeze. Then she smiled at me, though her barely moving lips were whispering something to Tom. Slowly he looked around. He, too, smiled at me, then looked back at Jewel. I heard him murmur goodnight, and Jewel whispered goodnight, first to him, then to me.

Tom, still smiling, came to me.

"What are you doing still up?" he asked, putting an arm around my shoulders.

"Looking for you."

"Well, you've found me. Let's go to bed."

Neither of us said another word until we were in our bedroom. Then I spoke the words aloud for the first time:

"Tom, are you having an affair with Jewel?"

He gave me that look of innocent surprise I had come to know so well. "What in hell ever put that idea into your head?"

"Are you?"

Pulling off his coat, he stepped closer to me and looked directly into my eyes: "No."

"Are you in love with her?"

"Good God, no. Augusta, I was coming up to bed when I saw Jewel looking out into the corridor for Adam. I assured her he'd be up soon. That's all."

I wanted to believe him, oh, how I wanted to believe him. I had loved him so, and I still did, and I did not want my fairy-tale romance to end, not ever. I did not want to lose my Prince Charming.

"Darling," I said, "make love to me."

Why? Was I challenging him? Did I think that if he were incapable it would prove that he had recently been with Jewel? Or was I merely asking for reassurance, for the physical symbol of his love? Even now, I do not really know. I do know that an odd glitter came to Tom's eyes, and he had an odd little smile on his face, as if I *had* issued a challenge, and he was about to take it up.

Without haste or hesitation or another word said, he began to undress me. As my clothes fell away from my body, his lips burned their way down my neck and over my shoulders, his hands slid over my breasts and down my back, and my mind began to blur. I was losing myself in this age-old ritual, the act of love, and I wanted it to happen, I longed for it to happen, I reached out for my lover, helping it to happen. There was no Jewel, no Adam, there was only my lover and my love, about to become one and the same.

Before his clothes were shed, it was already evident that he was not incapable, and by the time he was naked, I was completely ready for him. I let him lay me back onto the bed. He lifted one of my legs to the bed and left the other dangling to the floor. Thrusting a knee under my raised leg, he moved closer to me. And gave himself to me.

No. Did *not* give himself to me. For he gave me only his body. I wanted to believe he was giving himself to me, I tried to believe it, because I was giving all of myself, both body and soul. But I think now that he was only trying to prove that he could satisfy me. And so he worked on me—yes, *worked* on me—half standing up, not embracing me, but looming over me, his hands doing their work, bending down from time to time for his lips to do theirs, methodically *working* to bring me to the frenzy that I myself wanted to achieve—but not alone! For both of us, both of us!

I gasped, sobbed, cried out. "Oh, God, I love you so much!"

"Yes, you do . . ."

"I do, I do!"

"Because I can do this for you."

"No! Oh, no! For, oh, so much more!"

"Didn't think I could be this good, did you?"

"Oh, Tom, please . . .!"

"Want me to stop?"

"Oh, no! No, never!"

He laughed.

It was as if I were not his beloved but his victim. And when at last I lost myself completely, and he followed me into that oblivion that had once been so glorious, his final cry was not of love and pleasure—but of triumph.

Later, I continued to lie awake in the darkness long after Tom was asleep, and never before in my life had I felt so lonely.

*　　　*　　　*

I had not seen the last consequence of my trip down to the card room. The next afternoon, when Tom and I had returned to our rooms to refresh ourselves, there was a knock at the door, and a maid delivered a large basket of flowers. When Tom unfolded the accompanying note, his face brightened.

"They're from Henry Wycherley."

"Who?"

"The Earl of Huxton. Lord Harry, they call him." He frowned. "He apologizes for his ungentlemanly behavior toward you last night. What's that about?"

"Nothing. A drunken joke. When Adam—"

But Tom was not really interested. His face brightened again. "He's inviting us to a dinner party in London next week."

"How thrilling." I would have been content never to see the ginger-haired man again.

"Augusta, you don't understand. It's quite a thing to be accepted into Lord Harry's circle. He's sometimes called the Wickedest Man in Europe."

"Oh, what a distinguished title!"

"He's also very rich. They say he has something like thirty thousand acres around Huxton Hall alone. He's in railways, mills, real estate, half a dozen things. He owns a good part of London, and he has houses in Paris, Rome, Venice, I don't know where all."

"Well, all I know is, your Lord Harry is a boorish, drunken lout, and I am really not interested in him."

"I am, though. We're going to accept this invitation, Augusta."

"Must we?" I sighed, but I knew Tom would insist.

Thus it was that a week later we presented ourselves at Lord Harry's house in Belgravia. As we were led into a crowded drawing room, I was happy to see a few people I knew—Lady Blessington, Comte d'Orsay, Lord Petersham— and Lord Harry greeted us cordially. "Ah, Adonis! Welcome to our revels. And is this Venus . . . or Proserpina?"

Venus and Proserpina—who had quarreled over Adonis. The reference to Jewel and me was so obvious, the insult so unexpected, that I was stunned and said nothing as Lord Harry brought my fingers to his lips. But was it possible that he knew nothing about Tom and Jewel? His smile was innocent as he said, lowering his voice, "But one so lovely could only be Venus. Dear lady, I have been *long*ing to express my regret for my rude behavior at Brighton. I *do* hope you'll find it in your heart to forgive me. I could not *bear* that one so lovely should be anything but a friend.''

I found myself murmuring something appropriate and staring at Lord Harry. He was a tall man, shallow-chested but broad. He had a world-weary voice and a limp-wristed manner, but to consider him effeminate would have been a dangerous mistake. He had the look of a sportsman, and I suspected that physically he was very strong. Despite his alleged ''wickedness,'' there was not the slightest sign of dissipation in those sparkling brown eyes or that long, unlined face.

At dinner I became convinced that he did know about Tom and Jewel. One guest had failed to arrive, leaving thirteen at table, which I took to be a bad omen. And with that many people it could have been no accident that Jewel was seated next to Tom and Adam next to me.

Yes, Adam and Jewel were there, as I should have expected, and I saw Lord Harry observing us, his eyes alight with amusement as Tom beamed meaningful looks at Jewel. When he turned toward me to see my reaction, I flushed and looked down at my plate.

''To hell with them all,'' Adam muttered. ''Don't give them the satisfaction.''

''What?'' I said, startled. ''What did you say?''

He had his usual look of indifference mingled with contempt.

''Nothing, Mrs. Raveneau,'' he said. ''Nothing worth repeating.''

The dinner should have been delightful. At least two dozen candles made the silver and chinaware sparkle, and waiters and footmen kept the dishes flying. There were half a dozen entrees, including fresh oysters and cutlets of veal and lamb, as well as *flancs*, *relevés*, and *entremets*. This was followed by roasts and game birds and delicious sweets, and finally the table was cleared for dessert, ices, coffee, and liqueurs. All the while, I chattered and laughed as gaily as the others, but secretly I watched Tom and Jewel and fought back tears.

At length, the meal ended. Lady Blessington, who was acting as Lord Harry's hostess, rose at her end of the table, and we ladies rose with her, following her from the dining room and leaving the gentlemen to their final drink. We gossiped among ourselves for a while, until the gentlemen joined us. As Tom entered the room, I saw his eyes seek out

Jewel, saw her gaze meet his, saw the heat lightning that flashed between them.

I did not think I could take much more. More guests were arriving, some of them from other dinner parties, and other guests were leaving for after-dinner visits to other houses. We had invitations which gave us an excuse to leave, and I found Tom and told him I wanted to do so.

"No," he said flatly.

"But Tom—"

"I've been looking forward to dinner at Lord Harry's for a long time. So far, I barely know him, but before the evening is over—"

"But darling, I'm not feeling well!"

He gave me an impatient look. "Augusta, this is important to me. Please don't ask again. We're staying."

Before I could say anything more, he walked away.

I had to be alone. Another minute, and I would no longer be able to conceal my distress. Half-blinded by tears, I groped my way along a wall and through a doorway into a drawing room that seemed to be empty. There for a moment I almost gave way to my grief.

"Well, well, Mrs. Raveneau," said an American voice. "It's been a long time, hasn't it, princess?"

Oh, no, I thought, *oh, dear God, no! It cannot be, not he!*

But when I turned, it was he, once again.

Gannon Murdock.

He looked much the same, yet so different. This was no hard-handed overseer's son in a tattered shirt and muddy brogans. In his slate-colored suit with the high-collared coat and the tight trousers over black Wellington boots, in his white-silk roll-collared waistcoat and his high stock of wine-red satin, he was as fashionably turned out and impeccably tailored as Brummell or d'Orsay had ever been.

Yet this was truly Gannon Murdock, God help me, *my* Gannon Murdock.

How long my gaze remained locked with his, I do not know. Then slowly a smile came to his compressed lips, and that broke the spell. I rushed past him through the doorway.

The adjoining room had become crowded, but Tom was only a few feet away, and I went to him. "Please," I said, "Tom, I beg you—"

"Why, it's the Barbarian at last!" Lord Harry said somewhere behind me. He had a fondness for nicknames, it seemed.

"I'm sorry I missed dinner, Harry," Gannon said.

"But at least you're here. I daresay Mrs. Raveneau has little opportunity to talk with Americans, and I thought—"

"Tom, I'm ill," I said. "I ask you again, please take me home!"

People were looking at us, and Tom tried to hide his anger. "Augusta," he said in a lowered voice, "I told you I do not *wish* to go home—"

"But of course you don't," Lord Harry said, "and there's no need for you to leave. Mrs. Raveneau, if you're indisposed, I'm sure one of the ladies will be glad to see you home—"

"No. No one. If you'll get me a carriage—"

"But of course." A footman seemed to materialize from nowhere. "Sims, get Mrs. Raveneau a carriage. Mrs. Raveneau, we'll see your husband safely home later, if that is agreeable."

"Yes . . . yes . . ."

But it was not that easy to escape from Gannon Murdock.

Not a minute later I was in a hansom cab headed north toward Harley Street, but we had not even reached Hyde Park Corner when suddenly the door opened, and Gannon leapt in. With a startled cry, I tried to escape out the opposite side, but his arm encircled my shoulders and held me prisoner.

"Don't worry," he said, as the cab continued on, "nobody saw me."

I was frightened, more frightened than in all reason I should have been, and he must have felt my trembling. I tried to pull myself from his arms, but he continued to hold me tightly. When lamplight briefly lit his face, I saw his hard, challenging grin.

"Why are you running so hard, Mrs. Raveneau?"

Somehow I managed to answer in kind. "Why are you pursuing me, Mr. Murdock?"

"Curiosity. I saw my own little Gussie Welles back there, and it damn well pleased me to speak to her."

"Well, you've spoken to me. Having satisfied your curiosity, you may feel free to leave this cab at once and allow me to go home alone."

Gannon's dark eyes glittered. "No curiosity of your own, princess?"

"None whatever. The last time I saw you, you swore

revenge on my family. You proved you meant it by turning to arson and larceny. That is all I need to know about you, Gannon Murdock, now and forever more.''

Those dark eyes stared at me. "By God, that's the only way you see it, isn't it?''

"It's the only way I need to see it, Mr. Murdock.''

"Never mind the rights and wrongs of it. Never mind that a young woman lies in her grave—''

"Gannon, that is not fair!''

"Not fair?'' Gannon's voice grew harsh with anger. "You tell me I'm not being fair, when Melinda lies dead, thanks to you—''

"No!''

"Yes, thanks to you. You laid her in her grave—''

"I did not!'' The injustice of the charge brought fresh tears to my eyes, and again I struggled to escape from the cab, but Gannon held me securely.

"You did your part. You led them to the barn that night and held us till they could get there." He quoted my uncle's words: "'You did very well, Augusta. Oh, yes, Augusta, you've been a big help.' ''

It was too much, all too much. Tom, Jewel, the past months, this evening, and now Gannon. Ceasing to struggle, I turned my face away and tried to hide my tears.

"Gannon," I said in a thin voice, "Gannon, whatever you think of me, please try to believe me. I loved Melinda too. I don't know why my uncle said what he did that night, but I did not betray you.''

"Didn't you, Gussie?'' His voice was flat and unbelieving.

"I swear to you, *I did not betray you*!''

Gannon's hand tightened on my shoulder. I felt the power of his body tensed against my side like a bomb on the verge of exploding. Then his hand loosened, his arm slipped away, and he slumped in his corner of the seat. For long minutes the only sounds were the horse's hoofs and the creaking of the hansom.

"I've believed differently for too long," he said at last. "Much too long. And even if it were true, it wouldn't change a thing. It wouldn't stop me from doing what I've got to do.''

"Revenge," I said.

"Call it revenge, call it justice. I promised to take back what should have been mine, and I still intend to do it.''

I could no longer hide my tears. "Then do it and be

damned! I'm not begging you for anything, Gannon Murdock. But I think you know that I never wronged you—not purposely. And if you think my father did, your revenge comes too late. He's dead now too.''

Gannon was silent for so long that I thought our argument was finished. I was about to ask him to leave the cab when he spoke.

''But Thad Welles isn't dead.''

Of course. I should have realized. However much Gannon blamed the rest of us, he blamed my uncle most of all.

My laugh was sardonic. ''Poor fool. Do you really think you can hurt my uncle?''

''I know I can. Think back, Gussie. Thad Welles figures your father cheated him out of the Barony, and he'd give his very soul, if he had one, to get it back.''

Suddenly I was alert and on guard again, my tears ceasing. I knew that Uncle Thad had considered himself cheated, but that he might actually try to recover the Barony had never occurred to me.

''But the Barony isn't for sale.''

''Isn't it? He's made your husband more than one offer—''

''No!'' Tom controlled my affairs, of course, as any husband would, but he had never mentioned such a thing to me.

''Yes, he has. But Tom hasn't sold to him yet, and if I have anything to say about it, he never will. I've guaranteed him I'll top any offer Thad makes. I figure that, short of killing him, my taking over the Barony is about the worst thing I could ever do to Thad Welles.''

''But Tom won't sell to either of you. The Barony is mine. He would never sell without my consent.''

Gannon laughed. ''He'll sell.''

He won't, I thought, *he mustn't! I won't let him!*

Never had I felt my longing for the Barony more keenly than I did that night. If only I could get back there, I thought, if only I could be with Pearl and Rufus and all the others once again, everything would be all right. No matter what terrible things had happened to others at the Barony, it was home to me, and once there, nothing too bad could happen to me, ever again.

Dreaming of the Barony, I almost forgot Gannon's presence. Then, as we approached Harley Street, I felt him slip his arm back around my shoulder. He brought his face close to mine, as if examining me in the lamplight. Brushing a finger across my still-damp cheek, he said, "Do you want to know the real reason I followed you?"

I turned my head aside. "Please don't touch me like that."

He ignored my request. "To tell the truth, Gussie, until tonight I couldn't have given less of a damn if I never saw you again. But then I saw you going into that room. Only I didn't see you at all. I saw Melinda. For a moment I thought I was going mad, and I almost cried out her name." He turned my face toward him, and his fingertips moved down my cheek to my throat. "Do you know you look even more like Melinda than I remembered? Same hair, same nose, something about the eyes."

I shook my head. "She was beautiful."

"You've caught up with her, princess."

Then his mouth was on mine, and I knew I should fight him, but there was no fight left in me. His mouth was firm, gentle, demanding, giving. But I knew he was not really kissing me at all. He was kissing Melinda. And the kiss went on and on.

I told myself I had felt absolutely nothing during that kiss. Not true. As Gannon's mouth turned on mine, a wave of sweet feeling swept through me, and somehow I was back at the Barony again. I saw Gannon sitting high in the saddle against the blue sky. I felt him weeping and bleeding on my shoulder. I felt myself being drawn from a deadly stream into his bare sun-warmed arms. And for the briefest instant, my lips answered his.

When he whispered, "Good night, princess," and slipped out of the hansom, I was weeping again.

4 ~~~~~~

Tom slept late the next day, and I had no opportunity to speak to him until afternoon, when he was about to leave the house. "Really, Augusta," he said, as I detained him in the front hall, "I told Adam Trevayne I'd meet him at his club, and I'm already late."

"This won't take a moment," I said, "and Sir Adam can wait. You'll be interested to know that Gannon Murdock rode home with me in the hansom cab last night."

His eyes hardening, Tom turned away from the door and stared at me. "At your invitation?" he asked.

"Don't be silly. I do not invite my enemies to ride with me. He forced his way into the cab, and there was no way I could get rid of him."

"By God," Tom said softly, "Gannon forgets himself."

"It's of no importance," I said. "I do not wish to discuss the manners of an ill-bred overseer's son."

"Did he behave improperly in any other way?"

Remembering the kiss, innocent though I wanted to believe it, I flushed. But I said, "Of course not. And it hardly behooves you to speak of behaving improperly after—after the way you've been carrying on."

"Now, what in the world do you mean by that?"

"You know perfectly well. You and Jewel Trevayne. You couldn't have flaunted your feelings for each other more openly than you did last night."

"Good God," Tom said with a show of disgust, "I've told you before, to me Jewel is simply—"

"I know. A high-spirited, intelligent woman."

"Exactly. And you could learn a few things from her, my dear."

"Oh, I have, I have. But I don't wish to talk about Jewel Trevayne. I want to talk about Gannon Murdock—and my Uncle Thad."

Tom sighed and smiled as one does when forced to make time for a child. "Very well, but quickly. I really must be on my way."

"Gannon tells me my uncle has offered to buy the Barony."

Tom nodded. "I believe I did mention that to Gannon."

"Why did you never tell me?"

"Because the matter never came up. Darling, why don't you do as other wives do? Leave business matters to your husband and not bother your sweet little head with them." He turned toward the door. "Now, if you'll permit me—"

"Wait, please. Gannon said he had guaranteed to better any offer my uncle might make. Is that true?"

"Yes, it is. But since I know how much the Barony means to you, and I haven't the slightest intention of selling it, the entire matter is academic. Any other questions?"

"Yes. Where in the world, in four short years, did Gannon Murdock get enough money even to think of buying the Barony? Did the Tear of Venus make him that rich?"

Tom laughed at my ignorance. "Hardly. He won the money."

"You mean—gambling?"

"Of course. It's a lot faster way of making money then raising cotton or cane—though Gannon is doing all right at that too. He sends his winnings to his father in Mississippi, where the old boy invests in land and slaves. Gannon is pretty close-mouthed, but I get the impression that they've built something big, maybe as big as the Barony."

"Built it on a gambler's winnings," I said contemptuously.

Tom shrugged. "Augusta," he said, with studied patience, "am I free to go now?"

"One last question. That night last winter when you denied that Gannon was with you in the clarence—why did you lie to me?"

He looked at me for a moment as if considering whether to maintain the lie. Then he shrugged again. "You were having a difficult time, and I knew how you felt about Gannon. I didn't want you to be worried."

"By the knowledge that you were consorting with my self-proclaimed enemy?"

"Augusta, that business was a long time ago. Gannon has forgotten all about it."

"He hadn't forgotten about it last night."

Tom smiled. "Talked about old times, did you?"

"He made it perfectly clear that, one way or another, he intends to have the Barony. One way or another, he's going to persuade you to sell."

Tom's voice rose with impatience. "But I have told you, Augusta, that I have no intention of selling, and if you do not mind, my dear, I would prefer not to discuss the subject any longer. Now, Augusta, I *must* be on my way!"

He left me staring at the closed door.

George Sand, knowing something of my history, once asked me why I put up with the events of the following months. The answer was not that divorce was extremely difficult in England and impossible in South Carolina. The answer was simply that I wanted to save my marriage. I no longer expected perfect bliss, and I had known all along that Tom and I might experience less-than-perfect interludes. But I thought that, if only I remained patient and understanding, all would come right in the end.

Therefore I resolved to be an amiable mate, Tom's friend and companion in his sport. I would not remind him that we had talked of returning to the Barony in the autumn. I would laugh and smile and keep my tears to myself, and perhaps in the spring . . .

In the months that followed, we saw a great deal of Gannon Murdock. Adam and Tom and their friends traveled in a kind of pack about London, drinking and gambling, and, as often as not, it was Gannon and Adam who delivered Tom home at dawn. Sometimes Tom and Adam allowed Jewel and me to accompany them to certain gambling hells where, if women were admitted at all, we were taken to be prostitutes—to Jewel's delight—and Gannon would be there. And of course there were the dinner parties and the house parties in the country. Time after time, Gannon appeared, a popular guest.

Gambling was the chief preoccupation of our circle—gambling, discreet love affairs, and indiscreet gossip. Most nights, when the party was over, the men would retire to the card room and the ladies either to bed or to a quiet drawing room where they could whisper and titter over who had taken up with whom.

Sometimes I would slip away from the women to look into the card room. Tom had his good nights and his bad nights, but Gannon was almost always ahead. His methods amused Tom but angered me. The men often took turns naming the game, and Gannon almost invariably called for poker, which was virtually unknown in England. Furthermore, he would from time to time call for variations—just to make the game more interesting, he said—which no one had ever heard of and which no one but he really understood. More than once, deep in the night when coats and stocks had been abandoned, and Gannon sat in shirt sleeves with an old broad-brimmed planter's hat slanted against the light, I heard that Carolina purr, "The name of the game, gentlemen, is poker . . . five-card draw . . . deuces wild. . . ." And he would then proceed to rob everybody blind.

It was after such an incident that I had one of my rare conversations with Gannon. It occurred at the Trevayne's country home. I am told that some of the poker variations which are now becoming popular were actually invented by

Gannon, and that night he introduced one involving some cards being dealt face up and others face down. It seized the men's fancy to the extent that they played it all night, while Gannon raked a small fortune across the table.

I watched with disgust for some time. Then, as dawn approached, I went out onto a terrace for fresh air. I had been there only a few minutes when I heard Gannon's voice—"Good morning, Mrs. Raveneau"—and looked around to see the glow of a cigar coal in the dark.

"Sorry if I interrupted your meditations," he said. "I just stepped outside for a smoke. I hope you don't object?"

I stared at him for a moment, ignoring his question and trying to make out his face in the darkness. I said, "You know you're no better than a thief."

He laughed softly. "Why, Miss Augusta."

"Those men gamble for sport. You're here only to take their money."

Since that night in the hansom, Gannon had always been polite but distant with me, and I could hear the courteous smile in his soft voice. "Different people play for different reasons, ma'am. Sir Adam, it's true, plays for sport. Lord Harry plays as a means of manipulating people. Your husband plays for blood—and money. Personally, I have no interest in blood."

"My husband is not a professional gambler."

"That's true, though he is about as good as any professional I've ever met. Except for one thing. He seems to think he can voodoo the cards. Sometimes, sitting across the table from him, I get the feeling I'm not playing Tom at all, but some demon inside him who's trying to make magic. But there is no magic over the cards, Miss Augusta. And in the long run, the cool-headed gambler whose only magic is the odds is going to beat that demon every time."

"You admit that you're a professional gambler, that you play only for the money, not for the sport?"

"I would never contradict a lady," Gannon said, that maddening smile still in his voice, "but, Miss Augusta, there's something you don't understand. Everybody plays to win. Everybody wants to beat me and take *my* money. They know by now they haven't got much chance, but that just makes me more of a challenge. I never put a gun to a man's head for his money in my life."

Because I could not immediately refute his logic, I only

became more angry. The important fact was that he was still my enemy—and Tom's.

"Well, I'd like to put a gun to your head, Mr. Murdock," I said. "If I were a man, I'd challenge you to a duel and shoot you like a dog."

Gannon stared at his cigar coal for a moment, and when he spoke, a note of sadness had entered his voice. "No, you wouldn't, Gussie."

"I'd shoot you so fast—"

"A couple of times when I was a kid," he went on, ignoring me, "I issued challenges. I was turned down, of course, because I wasn't a gentleman. But I've had to fight twice since. Once a no-good drunken sandhiller drew on me over a card table, and I wounded him. The other time, a very nice man, who got the idea I had cheated him, challenged me. I gut-shot him, and a few days later he died in screaming agony." Gannon shook his head as if to clear it of the memory. "I'll still defend myself and my own, Gussie. I'll kill for them if I have to. But after killing that man, I swore to God I'd never fight another duel." He managed a forlorn laugh. "So don't talk to me about shooting people down like dogs, Miss Augusta. Duels are only for fools, drunks, and gentlemen."

How had he mastered the knack of making me feel ashamed?

Tom's voice broke the silence: "Augusta?"

In the first light of dawn, he was coming out onto the terrace. His face went blank, and his eyes flashed between Gannon and me when he saw that we were together. His automatic jealousy irritated me: it was based on nothing more than a broken convention and the knowledge that, since he himself had cheated, it was possible for him to be cheated on.

"Mrs. Raveneau," Gannon said, "has been passing judgment on me, Tom. It seems that she believes with Lord Chesterfield that 'Whoever plays deep must necessarily lose his money or his character.' Since I haven't lost my money, she's drawn the obvious conclusion."

I made no attempt to hide my scorn. "Not only has our overseer's son learned to speak like a gentleman," I said, "he has become well-read."

Life came back to Tom's face. "Well, I guess he has a lot of time for reading on all those ocean voyages, don't you, Gan?"

"I do indeed." Gannon turned to me. "You see, Mrs.

Raveneau, I learned something useful. People get very bored on ocean voyages, and to wile away the time, they like to gamble. And a two-week voyage on a steam packet gives me just enough time to examine the prospects, read a few good books, and shear the sheep clean.''

Tom laughed. ''Gannon's invented a new profession, Augusta—the professional transatlantic gambler.'' He actually sounded admiring.

''When can we hope to see you return to that profession, Mr. Murdock?'' I asked.

''Not before spring. I don't favor winter voyages, and since the *President* went down last March, steam packet travel has fallen off. The passenger lists don't look as rich and promising as they used to.''

I was not surprised. Despite the time saved in travel, many people were fearful of the steamships. Several notables, including Tyrone Power, the famous Irish actor, had disappeared with the *President*, making it the most sensational news event of the year.

''For your sake, Mr. Murdock,'' I said, ''we shall look forward to the time when the passenger lists are more promising.''

''I do thank you, Mrs. Raveneau. With all respect for present company, I can assure you that your kindly interest in my departure is no more acute than my own. And now, if you all will excuse me . . .''

Gannon went back into the house.

''Good lord, Augusta,'' Tom said, ''I know you don't care for Gannon, but you don't have to be outright rude to him.''

In addition to his other failings, I was beginning to suspect that my husband simply was not very bright. ''Tom, darling,'' I said, ''please try to get it through your head that Gannon Murdock is not our friend. He may have found a good tailor and read a book or two, but he is the same Gannon Murdock who swore vengeance on the Welles family in our graveyard.''

''You forget, honey, I am not a Welles.''

''But I am, and you're married to me, and you've got what he wants. A plantation, a house in Wraggboro—''

''And you, honey?'' Tom said mockingly. ''Didn't he say he just might have you too? Is that what you two were up to out here alone in the dark?''

''Tom, be serious!''

"Why, I am being serious, honeychild. Maybe more serious than you know." He put an arm around my shoulders. "Now, don't you worry your pretty little head any more. I've known Gannon Murdock all his life, and there's not a thing he can do to you or to me. I know how to handle him. Trust me, darling. Trust your husband."

He did not understand. He simply did not understand.

That was the year that Uncle Thad took Aunt Nickie and little Lucy to France. They visited us twice—for a few days in late August, while on their way, and again in October, on their return.

Uncle Thad was in his late forties and as massive and implacable looking as ever. He smiled, but his eyes were cold, and I had the feeling that he still considered me implicated in Melinda's death. He was in no way overtly unpleasant to me and actually seemed to enjoy visiting with Tom, but he left most of the socializing to Aunt Nickie and little Lucy.

Aunt Nickie, by then in her early forties, was still slim-waisted, and the few wrinkles she had gained only added character and beauty to her heart-shaped face. She was as delighted as a child at the thought of seeing her native France again after twenty-four years, and during both visits, she spoke French with me constantly.

Lucy, at five, showed every sign of becoming as beautiful a young lady as Melinda had been. But where was Cousin Horace, and how was he? Oh, Horace was fine, Aunt Nickie informed me with a trace of sadness, but he had elected to stay home. He had lost a little weight and looked better, but he could not defeat his stutter, and he and Thad were more at odds every year. It was hard for me to imagine a nineteen-year-old Cousin Horace.

I delighted in both visits; it was such a pleasure to play with little Lucy and to show Aunt Nickie about London. But I soon realized that, as far as my uncle was concerned, the trip to France was simply a pretext to approach Tom personally about buying the Barony and, for that matter, the Wraggboro house. "It's not enough that he lives in the house as if it were his own," Tom told me after a meeting with my uncle, "he wants to *have* it. He wants it to be *his*. But most of all, he wants the Barony." Uncle Thad had no more forgotten his obsession with the Barony than Gannon Murdock had forgotten his.

The night before he was to return with his family to America, Uncle Thad closeted himself with Tom in the study one last time.

"You do know, don't you," Aunt Nickie said, as we sat together in the drawing room, "that at this very moment your uncle is doing his best to buy the Barony from Tom."

I knew that.

"I have told him time and again, 'Thad, you are wealthy. If you can afford to buy the Barony, you can buy any other plantation. Forget the Barony. It belongs to Augusta. We don't need the Barony.' But no. It must be the Barony, only the Barony."

"But that's understandable," I said. "I feel exactly the same way. I *love* the Barony!"

"No, you do not understand. Your uncle's love for the Barony has very little to do with it."

"Then why?"

"In a way, I am to blame."

"But how? How in the world?"

"You really cannot know what your uncle was like in the old days, when I first arrived in America."

Then she told me a tale I had heard before, but twice-told tales often gain new significance as we grow older.

When my aunt, with her father and sister, had first arrived in America in 1817, my uncle was quite a different person from the man I had always known. Far from grim, he usually had a smile spread across his broad face, and his practical jokes were notorious. He had little interest in either planting or factoring, preferring to spend his days hunting and fishing and his evenings in conviviality with his friends. My grandfather fondly referred to him as an "amiable lout."

Mlle. Monique de Garinet was to change all that.

Having said little to her other than "*Enchanté, mademoiselle,*" with an execrable accent, my Uncle Thad proceeded to fall in love with the lady. He saw her frequently, for the de Garinets had come to the Welleses with a letter of introduction and were under their sponsorship. But how could he ever expect her to take him seriously as a suitor? He had never been a great gallant with the ladies, and in Mlle. Monique's presence, he found himself tongue-tied. How could he ever express the love he felt for her?

He found a way.

The occasion was a Friday-night card party in a private

home, where the nine or ten guests included Thad and one of Mlle. Monique's rejected suitors, a certain Mr. Chauncey Parker. By the age of thirty, the slim, dapper Mr. Parker had achieved quite a reputation as a duelist; he had fought and won seven times and five times had killed his opponent. His skill at cards, however, left something to be desired, and his luck that evening was as bad as Thad's was good. A wish to get back a little of his own may have led to his unfortunate remarks, or perhaps he was merely drunk and morose and looking for someone to kill. He was said to be that kind of man.

In any case, Mr. Parker, his eye on Thad Welles, made some slighting remarks about "the Frenchies" who had recently come to Charleston, and the room immediately became quiet. The de Garinets were known to be friends of the Welles family, and such an affront was more than sufficient cause for a challenge. But Thad, smiling, appeared to be paying no attention.

Mr. Parker went on to make various observations on the depraved manners and morals of "Frenchies," while the rest of the party wondered how much it would take to provoke Thad. They soon found out.

"Now, you take for example that there Mamzelle Moe-nique de . . ."

That was enough.

Whatever Mr. Parker said next has been forgotten. What is remembered is that Thaddeus Welles, still smiling but with eyes bright with anger, stood up and walked to where Mr. Parker was sitting. And, not with a glove or a handkerchief but with the back of his hand, he dealt Mr. Parker a blow that hurled him halfway across the room.

They met at dawn the next morning at the Washington Race Course. And there Thad Welles, in the first duel of his life, shot Mr. Parker dead.

"I was appalled that such a thing should happen," Aunt Nickie said, "but when I asked Thad why he should have killed a man for my sake, he at last found his tongue. If I would marry him, he would give me a kingdom and make me its queen, and our sons would be princes and our daughters princesses." She smiled at that distant memory. "Oh, your uncle was very romantic in those days. Very romantic and very handsome. You have no idea."

Thinking of Uncle Thad's dream of a kingdom for his lady,

I felt guilty. "Aunt Nickie, am I selfish to want to keep the Barony, when Tom and his brother already have a plantation?"

"No," Aunt Nickie said, "you are not selfish. Augusta, I would love to see your uncle get anything he wants, but not at your expense."

"But Uncle Thad seems to want it so much—"

"Even so, the truth of the matter is that your uncle is a city man, a tradesman. However much he might deny it, he loves the sharp bargain, the profitable deal. And he's good at it! Your grandfather was right—trade is where he belongs."

"Then why does he want the Barony so badly?"

"Because he has always felt he was cheated out of something that was rightfully his, something he had promised me, and he is not a forgiving man. And the Barony is *Welles* land! He's always felt it was the best thing in the world he could give me—and his children."

Our conversation was interrupted by the sound of a door opening, and a moment later Tom and Uncle Thad entered the room. Both men had an air of suppressed excitement that alarmed me.

"Augusta, Miss Nickie," Tom said, "I'm sorry we deserted you for so long, but we have some news that may interest you."

Oh, no, I thought, *what has he done*!

As if in answer, Tom looked at me and said, "The Wraggboro house. Thad has made an excellent offer for it, and I have accepted. After all, we really don't need it, Augusta—I have my own house in Charleston, and your place is with me."

"Why, of course, darling," I managed to say.

"And this way," Aunt Nickie said consolingly, "the house is still in the family. It's still the *Welles* house."

"Of course, Aunt Nickie. I wouldn't want it any other way. I'm so glad."

But I was not glad. My feeling of shock was greater than I would have expected.

Once again, as when my father decided to turn the Tear of Venus over to my uncle, I had a tremendous sense of loss. Melinda had died. My parents had died. The diamond had been stolen. The Wraggboro house had been sold. I was thousands of miles from home with a husband who had turned from me to another.

One by one, all the good things of life were slipping away from me.

5 ~~~~~

But I was still determined not to lose Tom. I would be patient, I told myself. This same thing had happened to other women, and they had survived to retrieve their happiness, and so would I.

In November, Lord Harry invited us to Huxton Hall for a foxhunt weekend. Tom was reluctant to take me, but I insisted on going, because I had not ridden hard and fast for a long time. Unfortunately, the weekend began going bad at the very start.

We were still outside, looking at Lord Harry's house, if it could be called that—it was a huge old edifice of dark stone that had grown up a little at a time over several centuries and yet had gained a certain Gothic grace—when Adam started to speak to Tom. Then, seeing me, he broke off as if unpleasantly surprised.

" 'Tis only I, Sir Adam," I said lightly, "come to join in your revels, as Lord Harry would put it."

With apparent effort, Adam broke off his stare. "I'm sorry. I simply didn't expect to see you, of all people."

"But why not? I understand other women will be here. Isn't that Lady Jewel I see coming toward us?"

"Are you staying for the entire weekend? In the house or the shooting box?"

"For the entire weekend, of course, and in the house."

Adam's face was sullen and somehow disappointed. "How nice for you," he said. He threw Tom an angry look and walked away without another word.

"What in the world is the matter with him?" I asked.

Tom seemed embarrassed. "Oh, nothing. That's just Adam. One of his moods."

My unease continued at dinner that evening, though it was hard to say why. Hunts hosted by Lord Harry were considered special, and most of the gentry of the surrounding countryside were there, good solid respectable people. But mingled with them were some of the most rakish and raffish of our London circle, and it made for an odd mixture. I looked about for Gannon Murdock and was relieved not to see him.

Most of the party soon headed for bed in order to be up early for the hunt, and when I arose the next morning, I felt better. After a hot cutlet breakfast, we went out to the stables, where I watched the assemblage with growing excitement: the horses and grooms and milling hounds, the men in their caps and cravats and mahogany boots, and all the whippers-in and earth stoppers and terrier men necessary for a good hunt. I was glad to see that I was not the only woman riding, though of course we were few.

But once again Adam Trevayne introduced a sour note.

"What the devil?" He glared at me from his saddle.

"Is something wrong, Sir Adam?"

"Women on a hunt—of course something's wrong! Tom, are you actually going to let her ride?"

"Try and stop her," Tom said. "And if you let her ride astride like a man, she'll keep up with you all day long."

"Well, she's not a man, and she's not riding astride. She could easily get hurt."

"Sir Adam," I said, "I do not think that is any concern of yours."

"With all respect, madam, it is my concern. I came here to hunt, and if you'll pardon my saying so, nothing can spoil a hunt like a female. They're so damned eager to prove they're as good as any man that they ride jealous. They do it on a saddle never meant for jumping fences and timber, and they proceed to break their silly necks."

"Sir Adam, if you will kindly mind your own silly neck, I shall take care of mine!"

Tom laughed, and Adam moved away from us. Of course he was perfectly right, but nevertheless I vowed silently that I would *show* Adam Trevayne a thing or two, I would! I would *show* him! Oh, yes, fifteen-year-old Gussie Welles, seething with indignation, was back in the saddle that morning.

Before long, the cry of the hounds and the double-note sound of the huntsman's copper horn signaled that the fox had been found, and we were off, following the hounds and the huntsman's cheers.

It should have been wonderful. The trouble was my horse. Lord Harry had lent me a lovely little mare, but she had no speed, no heart, no fire. She was truly a *lady's* mount and not meant for a real hunt at all.

What happened was my own fault. I *was* riding jealous, and angry as well, and I deserved to "break my silly neck." I was overworking the poor creature, trying to keep up with the others, and I was careless at a piece of broken fence. I failed to make the jump, and the next thing I knew I was hurling through the air, curling up to roll and protect myself from flailing hooves, and knowing that, when I hit, any little stick might pierce my body and take my life.

I hit. Rolled. Felt the mare's leg brush me. Thumped against a tree trunk. Wondered if I were all right.

I lay there for a minute. Then looked up, dazed, to see the mare calmly eating grass.

I would have smiled and thought, *Well, Gussie, gal, that's your third bad fall, and you've lived through it again,* but, no, Adam Trevayne robbed me of that sweet moment.

Having seen me fall, he came galloping back. White-faced, he threw himself down from his horse, fell to his knees, and started to gather me up in his arms. "Oh, my God—Augusta—Mrs. Raveneau, are you all right?"

"Perfectly," I said, thrusting him away in my humiliation, "except that that *pony* Lord Harry gave me couldn't outrun a one-legged tortoise, so I thought I might as well sit here a while and rest."

The instant Adam realized I was unhurt, he was furious. "What in hell did you think you were doing! If you can't even clear a bit of fence, why did you try!"

"I thought it was all broken down!" I said, tears in my eyes. "I didn't see—"

"You didn't see! You simply *had* to try to break your neck and scare the wits out of me!"

"I have *told* you, Sir Adam, my neck is not your concern!"

"Well, that animal you were riding is my concern! The way you women abuse a good horse—"

"I did nothing of the sort! Now, if you'll kindly leave me alone—"

"Gladly, madam, gladly!"

Adam went off to rejoin the others, but I had lost my taste for the hunt. With the help of a passing groom, I remounted my little mare and rode slowly back to the stables.

From then on it was as if the party were continuing without me. Somehow I managed to jest and laugh, but at times I could hardly see through my blurred eyes. My humiliation before Adam Trevayne had been the last straw, and I could no longer pretend to myself that I had been anything but miserable for months.

After supper that evening, there was the usual hunt ball, given to propitiate those ladies who did not ride, and I dutifully put in my appearance. But I did my best to avoid dancing, for my sore body was as nothing compared to the tension and knotting I felt within. Whenever a gentleman looked toward me, I avoided his eyes and moved away.

Adam Trevayne, however, was not so easily put off. Two or three times I evaded his approach, but toward the end of the evening he managed to corner me.

"The waltz, Mrs. Raveneau?"

I sought an excuse, but Adam was a difficult man to refuse. Against my will, I found myself being guided into the circle of his arm and onto the ballroom floor.

"I'm sorry," he murmured, his lips hardly moving, and, still somewhat indignant, I looked up into his pale gray eyes.

With a sense of shock, I realized that his eyes had changed. There was pain in them. They were alive. Alive under those beautiful bird-wing eyebrows in that incredibly handsome face.

"I'm sorry," he said again, "for my behavior this morning. I had no right."

"You had every right," I said, "because I was riding jealous, and riding badly, and abusing that horse."

"I wasn't as concerned for the horse as I may have sounded. Frankly, Mrs. Raveneau, I was terrified that you might have been hurt. And if that had happened . . ."

I hardly took in his meaning. I could only gaze into those eyes, no longer distant and contemptuous, that had so strangely returned to life.

"Tell me," Adam said, "why did you come to this affair?"

"Why . . ." The question surprised me. "We were asked!"

"That's not what I mean. I'm here because Jewel insisted that we come, and why should we not? But you've never entirely joined in our, ah . . . our revels, and it's been obvious to me that your heart has never really been in them. And I, of all people, could hardly blame you."

"Are you telling me that *you* have no heart for Lord Harry's . . . revels?" I asked incredulously.

"Need one have heart to indulge in them?" Something of

the old contempt appeared in Adam's eyes and voice, together
with a profound sadness. "They pass the days . . . and the
nights."

Suddenly I understood Adam's eyes—the deadly ennui
they had always held. He no more cared to be a part of Lord
Harry's shabby, decadent circle than I did. But *"Jewel insisted,"*
he had said, and it was true: I knew her ways all too well.

In those few moments, while we waltzed, my feelings
toward Adam Trevayne underwent a change that I would
never in this world have expected. A shiver went through me,
and I felt as if something frozen within me were melting as I
moved into warm, sunlit waters.

"I'm sorry," Adam said, drawing me closer into his arms.
"It is really none of my affair why you are here."

"Do you think badly of me for being here, Adam?"

"Dear Augusta, never in this world could I think badly of
you."

How long did we dance after that, one waltz after another,
in complete disregard of convention? I could look into his
eyes without flinching now, and I thought, *Not so close,
Adam, oh, don't hold me so close, you've always been unbear-
ably beautiful, you've always awakened forbidden warmths
and tremors, and now, with those suffering eyes . . .*

But then I found I hardly cared. On the outside, my flesh
might be bruised and aching, but deep within, the tensions
were easing and the knots were dissolving—dissolving in the
new, deep warmth that was flooding through my entire being.
We floated on the waltz, dipped and crested, whirled and
whirled again, and floated on, and I felt more alive than I had
in months. *But, oh,* I thought, as the warmth grew, and we
whirled to the throbbing, pounding seductions of the music,
*oh, I should not be feeling this way in any man's arms but
Tom's.* I must not feel this way, because it was wrong, and
anyone who looked at me would see what I felt, anyone who
looked would know, but I hardly cared, I hardly cared at all.

"Augusta," Adam whispered, "I have a suggestion."

"Do tell me."

"A most improper suggestion."

"Oh, then you must not tell me after all!"

"I propose that in the dead of night you and I flee this dull
circle of conventional sinners for a happier clime."

"This very night? Where shall we go?" I tried to match his
lightness, but my voice was perilously uneven.

"I propose that we flee to an emerald-green Greek isle that I know, where we shall drink retsina and ouzo, and I shall watch you bathe naked in the wine-dark sea—"

"Sir Adam!"

"—and emerge like Aphrodite from the waves to make love on the sparkling white sand." The pain that glistened in Sir Adam's eyes belied his smile and the lightness of his voice. "It's only a dream, dear Augusta. But sometimes our dreams make it possible to go on living. Don't deny me my dreams."

Oh, the visions Adam conjured up. I knew I should banish them, but I had been lonely for so long, and to find myself now in the arms of another sufferer and one so attractive . . . I could see him standing tall and naked like a Greek god on the sun-drenched sands as I went toward him, emerging from the sea, salt water dripping from my bare breasts, belly, thighs. "No, Adam," I whispered, "I'll not deny you your dreams." But, oh, I thought, how wicked of me to share them!

We could not dance together forever. At last I made Adam conduct me from the floor. As he bowed over my hand, he looked up and spoke so softly that only I could hear. "We shall meet . . . later."

Oh, no, I thought, we must not! But before I could say the words, he had turned and left.

The ball was over. At another time we might have danced until dawn, but it had been a long day, and Lord Harry had other plans for the night. As Tom and I passed him, he said, "Cards?" and Tom nodded. *Please, no*, I thought, *not tonight. I need you. I need you with me.*

Quickly, most of the guests departed. Some left for their homes, while others went to Lord Harry's shooting box, a converted inn a half-mile away. Considering the size of Lord Harry's house—there must have been at least two dozen bedrooms—it seemed to me that curiously few of the guests were staying there for the night.

If Tom had observed me dancing with Adam, he said nothing about it. He took me to our room, and as I sank down on the bed, all the new life Adam had awakened still throbbed within me. "Now, you make yourself comfortable," Tom said, "and I'll be back in a little while."

"Please," I said weakly.

"Please? Please what, dear?"

I held his hand to my cheek. "Please don't leave me."

"I won't be gone long, dear," Tom said, giving me a pat on the head. "I promised Lord Harry I'd play some cards, just a few hands, and then I'll be right back."

He tried to pull away, but I clung to his hand. "Please stay with me a little while before you go," I said. "Come to bed for just a little while."

"Augusta, dear, there isn't time for that. But there will be time when I get back, I promise you. Now, be a good girl." He pulled his hand free from mine.

He's going to Jewel, I thought, as he left the room. That was why he had not wanted to come to bed with me. Oh, yes, he would play cards, but there would also be Jewel.

I got ready for bed, though I was certain that in my state I could never sleep. Yet my head had hardly touched my pillow when I fell into sleep as if to escape into its darkness.

When I awakened, I had no idea of how long I had slept. The lamp still burned, and outside it was still dark. I was alone in the bed. I thought of the men at cards . . . of Jewel. . . .

I decided to look for Tom. I would find the card room, and if, as at Brighton, Tom were not there. . . . I put on a robe and slippers.

The moment I stepped out into the hall, closing the bedroom door silently behind me, I had an odd sense of throbbing life, of quiet wakefulness, throughout the house. A lamp burned on a sconce, dimly lighting the hall, and another light flickered behind a door that had been left ajar a few yards down the hall.

Suddenly the door of the next room opened. A woman darted out, followed by the sound of male laughter, and hurried along the hall, her back to me. She was wearing only the flimsiest gown and no robe or slippers, and she quickly slipped in through the door that had been left ajar.

For a moment I could only stand where I was, stunned by such outlandish behavior. Then, reminding myself of my mission, I moved on.

As I passed the slightly open door from which the woman had appeared, I heard voices in conversation, at least two men and a woman. Passing the door she had entered, I heard other voices, male and female.

Dear Lord, I thought, is nobody in this house asleep? And what are they doing?

As if in answer, somewhere, distantly and mockingly, a woman laughed.

Then I understood.

I understood why the party included some of the most scandalous members of our London circle.

I understood why so many of the guests had been sent home or to the hunting box, though some of the bedrooms of the house remained empty.

I understood why Adam had been surprised to see me accompanying Tom and to learn that I was staying in the house.

I think I have made clear that I was anything but a prude. I was quite aware that even in the best circles some husbands and wives did have *affaires de coeur*. My parents had observed such affairs with amusement, if not always approval, and I was aware that my mother had always made sure that certain ladies who came visiting while their husbands were off shooting grouse had rooms conveniently close to certain gentlemen whose wives might be off counting grouse feathers. No, I was certainly not a prude. But such matters were to be conducted, if at all, with a certain style and discretion, and I was hardly prepared for the kind of house party where the guests played musical beds in the middle of the night.

I felt angry and humiliated. Even if he no longer loved me, how dared he—my husband—subject me to this? When I found him, I would demand that we leave as soon as possible and never return.

I went down the stairs. Here and there a lamp burned in a shadowed room. Carpets and tapestries muffled all sound. Huge old portraits on the walls and empty suits of armor stared at me, but I saw no one. I intended to find the card room if I had to comb the house from top to bottom, but its corridors were so complex and strange to me that I was not at all sure I could find my way back to my bedroom.

Somewhere I heard a piano. Beethoven. The first movement of the "Moonlight Sonata."

The sound, wistful, airy, romantic, was oddly reassuring—what terrible thing could possibly happen to the melodies of the "Moonlight Sonata"?—and I followed it.

I found the music room. A single lamp gave the only light.

Adam, in a robe, sat at the piano, a glass of brandy at hand. He glanced up at me, but continued playing.

I leaned against the piano, absorbing those lovely, mesmeric arpeggios and feeling the anger and humiliation drain out of me. Adam's robe was open in a V to his waist, and he wore nothing under it, but in this house, that hardly surprised me. I watched those long-fingered, lightly hirsute hands caressing the keys, and looked at the chest, smooth as alabaster, and shivered. Closing my eyes, I remember my vision of a Greek god on a sun-drenched beach.

He reached the soft final chords of the movement, chords like a whispered, repeated summons. When I opened my eyes, he was reaching for his brandy. "Please don't stop," I said.

He sipped the brandy and shook his head. "I play better when I haven't been drinking. I'm afraid I've drunk a great deal tonight."

"I never would have guessed."

He stood up from the piano, and for a long moment we merely looked at each other. Then he slowly came around the piano toward me. I held my breath and stared at his bare chest. He did not stop until he was almost touching me, looming over me like fate.

He said, "You do know I'm in love with you, don't you?"

His closeness made me feel faint. I said, "You mustn't tell me such things, Adam."

"But it's true. I've loved you almost from the day we met, but I've never dared to say anything. Then this evening as we danced, I sensed that you were . . . not totally indifferent."

I closed my eyes for a moment. I dared not speak.

"Do you know what I've been doing tonight, Augusta?"

I shook my head.

"I've been thinking about us. About you."

"Please, Adam . . ."

"About Aphrodite rising out of the sea and walking over our island. Aphrodite escorted by doves, with green grass and wild flowers springing up behind her in her footsteps. Aphrodite bringing the gift of love."

"Please . . ." As he stepped closer still and leaned over me, I put my hands against his chest to hold him back, but he seized my elbows, and his body touched lightly against mine. I wondered if he had any idea how vulnerable I was.

"When I saw Tom come down the stairs and I knew you were alone, I tapped on your door."

"Adam, you shouldn't—"

"You didn't answer. So I went away and drank."

"Adam, I'm looking for Tom—"

"You're trembling, Augusta. Why are you trembling?"

I felt as if I were dreaming. His body pressed me back against the piano so that I could not escape, and his mouth slowly came down on mine. The room whirled, and my soul was filled with the music I had heard. As Adam raised his head, I looked up into pale gray eyes that implored. My lips were swelling, my breasts were growing heavy, my legs felt too weak to support me. All the deep warmth Adam had brought to me earlier came flowing back through me, and, my body atremble, I was melting, melting. . . .

"Oh, Adam," I whispered, "no . . . no . . ."

I tried to resist as he gathered me into his arms and brought his mouth down on mine again. I felt the surge of his passion as he pressed against me, and I knew I must escape at once, but my own body longed to betray me. Even as I protested and tried to thrust him away, I found myself moving against him, twisting and turning as his fingers touched my back and his kisses burned my throat.

"I've wanted you for so long," he murmured, "for so very, very long."

"Oh, please, Adam, no," I moaned, "I don't want this to happen. Please, Adam."

"But you do, you know you do."

As he held me to him and kissed me, one hand swept open my robe and slipped my gown from my shoulder. The hand slid down over my bare flesh, and there was no denying the passion-swollen nipple his fingers passed over or the ache deep within as he lifted, probed, stroked.

"I want you, darling," he said, his breath warm in my ear. "I want you as you want me, and now . . ."

My hair whipped about my face as I shook my head and cried denials, though every touch, every kiss, inflamed me more. I found myself with my fingers in his hair, returning his kisses even as I tried to turn my face away. Then, suddenly lifting me high in his arms, he covered my breast with his mouth, and the swift stab of my desire almost robbed me of reason. In a dreamlike state, I seemed to float with him as he carried me, turning, turning, across the room in a dizzying whirl, and though I cried, "No more, no more!" I clung to him as fiercely as he to me.

"Oh," I moaned as he lowered me again, "I'm so ashamed."

"There is nothing for you to be ashamed of."

"But I'm so weak!" Even as he laid me back on a couch and began to lift the hem of my gown, I could hardly believe this was happening.

"Love is not weakness. Love is strength. And I love you, Augusta. I love you, and I'm going to make you love me."

"But it's wrong, it's wrong!"

"Less so for us than for others."

"Please . . ."

Kneeling between my thighs, he bent down to kiss my breast again. He moved up over me, his mouth covered mine, and our tongues met. His knees moved my legs apart, and as we kissed, his hand swept up between my thighs like loving fire, ever more intimately, touching me as no man but Tom had ever done before. If he had taken me then, while I hardly knew what he was doing, could I have resisted? I had never dreamed that any man other than Tom could arouse such desire in me.

"Augusta," he sighed. "Oh, darling Augusta . . ."

He lifted himself from me and threw his robe open.

Even at that moment, prepared as I was, his appearance was like a physical blow. His was the only naked male body aside from Tom's that I had seen since reaching womanhood, and the abrupt sight of it recalled me to reality. Despite my deep longing, despite my unfulfilled hunger, I truly did *not* want to be unfaithful to Tom, I did *not* want to give up my dream of regaining happiness with him, and almost in spite of myself, I resisted Adam more fiercely than ever.

I tore my eyes away from him and resisted, crying, "No, no, no, no!" as he stroked my bare thighs and kissed my naked breast. Resisted, twisting beneath him, as he slid over me, hard and demanding, trying to take me. Resisted by covering myself from those urgent thrusts.

He whispered soft, soothing words, but I only struggled more furiously, wailing my despair. I begged, I pleaded. Tears burst from my eyes, and I felt my face twisting into ugliness as I wept. *"No, no, no . . ."*

And then hands no longer brutal were helping me sit up

and covering my nakedness, and Adam was saying, "Oh, my
God . . . oh, God, Augusta, I am so sorry . . . oh, God,
Augusta, forgive me . . . forgive me. . . ."

"Augusta, forgive me. If I hadn't drunk so much . . . I
swear to you I'll never again do such a thing, never again try
to touch you."

Passion still ached within me, but my tormentor was once
again my comforter, and I sat curled up in the curve of his
arm, weeping my heart out.

"I'm sorry," I said brokenly, when I began to regain
control of myself. "It was more my fault than yours."

"No, Augusta—"

"I realized this evening that you were unhappy too. And I
began to like you, Adam, more than I should. And I let you
see . . . how I felt. And I shouldn't have. . . . Oh, Adam, I
am so unhappy!"

"Tell me, Augusta. Tell me."

It all came spilling out then, on a flood of fresh tears. I
knew I had no right to speak of my husband in such a way,
and certainly not to Adam Trevayne, but I could not help
myself. I hated Tom's obsession with gambling, I said. I
hated his neglect. I hated his affairs with . . . I hesitated.
"With Jewel," Adam said quietly, and I choked on my tears.
"Tell me," he said, his cheek to my head as if I were a child,
"tell me what happiness means to you, Augusta."

I tried to tell him. Still half-weeping, but sometimes smil-
ing through my tears, I told him about my childhood at the
Barony, with its vast fields and towering big house and the
broad, placid river winding down to the sea. I told him about
Pearl and Rufus and Aunt Polly, about Wanderer and the
Maid of Athens. I told him about young Gannon Murdock and
Janthina and our fun and deviltry . . . and about the Tom I
had known in those days, so tall and blond and shining.

"Make him take you home, Augusta," Adam said, when I
fell silent. "Make him take you back to your Barony."

"Oh, if only I could!"

"England is no place for either of you. You've fallen in
with the wrong people. We're no good for you, Augusta, no
good at all."

"You're good for me, Adam. I feel so much better just
from having talked to you. But now you tell me. What does
happiness mean to you?"

He hesitated, stroking my hair, then said, "The thought that one day you'll find the happiness you're looking for."

"Oh, no! It must be something for yourself."

"Unless you'll consent to run away with me to our emerald-green Greek isle, my dear, I fear happiness is lost to me."

"No, that can't be true! Adam, do you still love Jewel?"

"I don't know. I thought there might be something left—until I met you."

I ignored the last. "If you don't love her, why do you stay with her?"

Adam went on stroking my hair. "Augusta, please don't blame Jewel too much."

"But if she makes you unhappy, and you have no hope—"

"The situation is my own fault. I have no excuse."

"I can hardly believe that."

"But it's true. I knew what Jewel was before I married her, knew but refused to admit the truth to myself. You see, Augusta, I come from a very conservative family, very respectable, pillars of church and state. But Jewel's family is quite different. Her father was one of the greatest dandies and rakehells in London, and her mother is said to have been more than a match for him. And Jewel has always been very much their daughter—pretty, gay, irresponsible, game for any lark that anyone dares. She was sixteen when I fell in love with her. I was twenty years old, and sober, shy, and scholarly."

He really did not know what she saw in him, he said, but she seemed as much in love with him as he was with her. His father, however, disapproved vehemently and threatened to disinherit him, leaving his fortune to Adam's younger brothers. But in the end he gave his consent, and less than a year after meeting her, Adam married Jewel.

"I was happy, I can't tell you how happy. Jewel bore three children in the first four years—oh, yes, we have children, two sons and a daughter whom I love dearly. But then, a few months after the birth of our third child, I caught her making love with one of my friends. Caught them in the act, in my own bed."

"Oh, Adam . . ." For a few seconds the terrible deadness returned to his eyes.

"By that time, my father was dead. Because I had married Jewel, he had put control of our family fortunes into the hands of my uncle, a childless widower. When I approached him about a divorce, he would not agree. To my astonishment, his sympathy was entirely with Jewel. I had been warned about her, I had known her background, I had known the kind of person she was. Why should she suffer just because she was behaving like the innocently amoral slut—my uncle's words—she had been brought up to be? I had made my own bed, and now I could damned well lie in it. And if I insisted on pursuing the matter, he would cut me off without a penny, and that meant my children as well.

"I had my children's right to consider. I gave up all thought of divorce. As for Jewel . . ."

Jewel took the attitude that Adam was behaving like a petty, narrow-minded prig. Why did he say she no longer loved him? Of course she still loved him. She had only done what thousands of other civilized women had done. Once she had given Adam a healthy son and heir, she had decided it was time to enjoy the world. And if Adam had a brain left in his jealous head, he would do the same.

"And that's really all there is to the story, Augusta. I loved Jewel more than I can possibly tell you. But something was lost, something precious, something that can never be recovered."

"Adam, I am so sorry."

I was still cozy-warm, curled up in the circle of his arm with my head on his shoulder. My passion had diminished to embers deep within, an almost comfortable glow. I could see the rise and fall of Adam's chest in the V of his robe, and the robe had fallen away from one long leg, as softly hirsute as his hands and forearms. When I looked up at his face, the pale gray eyes under the flared brows had lost some of their pain, as if telling his story had given him a measure of peace.

"Don't pity me, Augusta," he said. "My uncle was right—I made my own bed. And once I knew the truth about Jewel, I learned to take my pleasure where I find it, just as she does, and it's not all that bad. Make no mistake about it, my dear, I am no martyr, suffering for love. But just the same, sometimes I wish . . ."

"I know, Adam," I whispered, "I know."

With a sigh, he lay his head back on the couch, closing his eyes, and extended his legs. I was a warm ball, my knees on his lap.

"Tell me, Augusta, if there had never been a Tom in your

life or a Jewel in mine, and if tonight had happened just as it did . . . do you think . . .?''

There was no need for him to complete his question. My heart pounded harder as I thought of Adam as I had seen him only an hour or two earlier—rising up over me, his robe open, ready to make love. But now my fear was gone, and in memory I could see him as he truly had been, as perfect in form as in face—a Hermes by Praxiteles, perhaps, but a Hermes aroused. I could see the fine symmetry of the marble-smooth torso; the flat belly, every muscle under the taut skin defined by the light from the lamp; the hard columns of thigh and manhood, aquiver with desire. He had truly been my vision of a Greek god, fit for a goddess.

With dismay I realized that fires never properly quenched were flickering again. But now I was on guard against them.

"I don't think . . . I should tell you."

"Then you think we would have. We'd have made love, and afterward I'd have stolen you away to my emerald-green Greek isle." His lips brushed the top of my head. "There really is such an island, Augusta. I've never taken Jewel there, and now I never shall. I shall never take any woman there if I can't take you, and I shall never again be able to think of my island without thinking of you—Aphrodite rising from the sea."

In one swift movement, Adam removed his arm from my shoulders and sat hunched forward, hiding his face in his hands. "Christ, Augusta, how much we have missed and now will never have—"

"Don't say that!" I seized his shoulders and leaned against his back, trying to comfort him. My breasts throbbed between us. "Please don't say that, Adam!"

I felt him shaking, but I could not tell if he were weeping or not. After a moment, he straightened, and his voice was low but steady. "I'm sorry. Of course that's not true for you. One day you and Tom will go home to America and raise a family, and you'll have all the happiness anyone could ever want."

Oh, how I wanted to believe that!

"But we'll always be friends, won't we, Adam?"

"Always. And if ever you need me . . .''

He turned to me, taking me back into his arms, and for a moment we held each other tightly. The warmth within me glowed still higher, and I wondered why I could no longer have with Tom the sweetness I now shared with Adam.

Adam's hand moved to my cheek. Very gently, he tilted my head back, and once again I was looking into his eyes.

"Augusta, I know I promised you I would never again touch you, but I wonder—"

I heard myself saying, "Kiss me goodnight, Adam. Just one kiss that I can remember always."

Even as his face lowered to mine, I realized I had made a mistake, that I was in far greater danger than I had known. Adam's kiss seemed to go through every part of me, flowing, heating, turning me to liquid. I felt his hand hovering over my breast, wanting to touch me. If it had, I think he could then have touched any place he wished, any place at all, for one by one my defenses were falling. Adam had suffered far longer than I, and if he needed me as Tom did not, if that beautiful godlike body, so full of desire, needed mine . . .

But he was true to his promise. The hand that hovered over my breast did not touch it. As Adam slowly lifted his face from mine, his hand returned to my cheek. I did not move, could not move.

"I, too, shall always remember," he said

"Goodnight, Adam," I murmured.

"I'll take you to your room."

It was nearly dawn as we went up the stairs and along the hallways, and the servants were rising. There might have been a few men in the card room still, but all the bedroom doors were closed, and there was no sound from behind them.

We arrived at my room. Adam leaned down and whispered to me, "My darling, this has been one of the most precious nights of my life, the most precious in many years." His kiss was light and gentle on my forehead. "Goodnight, dear Augusta," he murmured, and he moved away from me as if forcing himself to leave by strength of will.

I backed toward the door and, reaching behind me, opened it. I heard a sound. When I looked around, I saw Tom.

I was safe.

The lamp was still burning, and Tom was in his shirt sleeves. He stared at me, at Adam, at me again, his face turning blank and wooden. I nodded at Adam. He nodded back and continued to move away as I closed the door.

A crooked smile came to Tom's face. "Well, well, well," he said. "So that's how it is. First Gannon, and now Adam, and how many others?"

I hit him.

Stepping forward with my left foot, I brought my open right hand up and around, and I hit him with every ounce of my strength. The blow was like a thunderclap. Tom's back arched, and he fell back, tripping over a corner of the bed and falling loudly to the floor.

"How *dare* you!" I said, as he looked up at me in astonishment. *"How dare you!"*

He held up an arm as if afraid I might attack him again. "Augusta, I didn't mean—"

"How dare you, after all you've put me through! After all you've made me suffer!"

"Augusta, I'm sorry—"

"After the way you've been carrying on with Jewel in front of me and everyone else! How dare you!"

Tom scrambled to his feet and backed away from me. "Listen to me, Augusta, I have something to tell you—"

"How dare you, after bringing me to this house of—of assignation—"

"Listen to me, goddamn it!"

For the first time, I realized there was more than shock or accusation in Tom's eyes. That moment had passed. Now there was something else.

Fear.

"All right, I'm listening. What is it?"

His face twitched. He paced the room, glancing at me, glancing into dark corners, his face working as if he could not find the right words. His fear spread to me.

"Tom, what is it?"

His voice was barely audible. "We've got to leave."

"Good. I'd like nothing better than to leave this house at once."

"Not this house. We're leaving—leaving England!"

An unexpected wave of hope swept over me. "Leaving England? We're going home to America?"

"No, goddamn it, not to America!"

"Then where?"

His eyes darted about wildly, and I had the strange feeling that he had given no thought to where we would go. Then his eyes focused to me, and he laughed. "Italy!" he said, as if the answer had been revealed to him "Yes, of course, that's where we'll go!"

I listened, unbelieving. "Where?"

"To Italy, Augusta! We're going to Italy!"

6 ⌁⌁⌁⌁⌁

I have seen Italy, but not with Tom Raveneau.

I soon realized why he was so eager to depart from England and to leave a false trail. For over a year his gambling and spending had grown even wilder, and his creditors were hard after him. Some of his gambler-friends were very dangerous men, and he could only hope to get away from England for a time and recoup at the tables. In this endeavor Lord Harry was his accomplice.

Action recharged Tom with confidence and energy. He actually seemed happy, as we hurried back to London and packed for the journey. Arrangements were made for the shipment or storage of the rest of our belongings, and the bewildered house staff was paid off; at least we had money for that. I later learned that Tom had told some people that we were returning to America, others that we were going to Italy, still others Bavaria—anything to spread confusion as to our true destination.

Like sneak thieves, we left the house in the middle of the night, and when we were aboard the packet to Calais, I learned that we were even traveling under assumed names.

"From now on, my dear, you are no longer Augusta Raveneau. You are Liane Duhamel, and I am your husband, Julien."

"But why?" I asked, though I had begun to suspect. "Why in the world—"

"A lark. From now on, we are French."

"But we could never in the world pass for French!"

"Your Aunt Nickie says your accent is perfect. As for me,

I am of an emigré family that moved to England during the Revolution. Don't worry, Augusta—I mean Liane—I have it all worked out.''

It was evening a few days later when we arrived at our place of refuge, Lord Harry's *hôtel* in Paris. We descended from our carriage in the rue Saint-Honoré to find ourselves facing huge iron gates in a tall stone wall. While a footman pulled down our trunks, Tom banged the iron knocker and yanked a pull-rope. He announced our names—M. and Mme. Duhamel—to a servant who had come running, and, as Lord Harry had instructed him, asked for Mme. de Laurence. A moment later we were within the gates.

The house took my breath away. It loomed above us like a great medieval castle. A light appeared at a window here and there, and though the wings sprawled wide, the paved court-yard went around it on both sides with plenty of room for carriages and coaches.

One side of a tall double door was open, spilling dim light into the courtyard. We went up granite steps and through the door to find ourselves in a hall so big it could have held our little house in Mayfair. Its ceiling was roof-high, perhaps fifty feet above us. Two marble staircases ascended to the second-floor landing, which was overhung by the third-floor balcony. Doors on each side of the hall led to the wings, and a door between the staircases led to the back of the house.

From this last door came a young woman. Though she could not have been many years older than I, the disillusionment in her blue eyes made her seem so. Her hair, pale blond, was braided and pinned up at the back with a simplicity that only enhanced her beauty. Her eyebrows were darker than her braided hair and her lashes darker still. Her rather strong jaw contrasted with a full, lovely mouth.

She looked at us with indifference and hardly seemed to hear as Tom, smiling, spoke to her and handed her Lord Harry's letter. She broke the seal and read, her face expressionless, while Tom said a few more gracious words in poor French.

"You are not French, monsieur?" she said, refolding the letter.

"Of French lineage, though raised in England." Tom said. "Madame is French."

Mme. de Laurence and I smiled automatically at each

other. She indicated the luggage the porter had carried in. "This is all you have brought with you?"

"Some other things will follow," Tom said.

"You have brought no servants?"

"Ah—no—"

"No matter. I shall assign someone to you. We shall be most happy to make you as comfortable as possible." She turned to me. "And now perhaps you would like to refresh yourselves?"

"Oh, yes," I said. "After such a trip—"

"Of course. Your rooms are ready for you. We have been expecting you for some weeks now."

Both Tom and I must have looked startled. "Mme. de Laurence," Tom said, "I wonder if there's isn't some confusion. We ourselves only knew a few days ago that we were coming here. Are you perhaps expecting other guests?"

"No, monsieur. Lord Harry tells me in this letter that you are the guests I was told to expect. Perhaps he had intended to invite you to Paris before this."

"Yes, of course," Tom said, "that must be it." But with foreboding I remembered Gannon Murdock's words: *"Lord Harry plays as a means of manipulating people."* Had Harry been directing our lives more than we knew?

Mme. de Laurence issued orders to the porter and led the way toward a marble staircase. At that moment a man in evening dress appeared at the top of it, hurrying down toward us. He slowed as he came, and halted a step or two above us.

He looked at me, only at me. He looked into my eyes, looked me up and down, then looked into my eyes again. And smiled. At my side I felt Tom make a startled motion, then restrain himself.

There are men who cause apprehension on sight. This was such a man. He was approximately my height, which was why he had remained on the steps. A walking stick in one hand and an opera hat in the other, he stood as if to block our way. His well-tailored black suit of English cut and his *surtout* did not hide the fact that he was broadly and powerfully built. His face was round, his eyes narrow. His complexion was swarthy, and his black hair and thin, pointed mustache seemed painted on his head.

"Good evening, my friends," he said, his French strangely accented. "Mme. de Laurence, we are to have more guests?"

Mme. de Laurence had been standing as one does when

faced by a potentially dangerous animal—quite still and with eyes averted. Now, with as few words as possible, she introduced us to this man, M. Louis Paoli, and added with subtle emphasis, "They are Lord Harry's guests, M. Paoli. His very special guests."

"Ah!" M. Paoli said, as if delighted. "Then we may expect to have my dear friend Harry's company again very soon, may we not?"

"Perhaps. He has not informed me."

"I look forward to it." Paoli made a motion of casting dice. "He owes me five thousand from his last visit."

"Monsieur enjoys a game of chance?" Tom asked quickly.

Paoli looked at Tom as if he were an upstart. "Only with those who have something worth winning, monsieur."

Tom flushed but maintained his smile. "Fortunately, even when I have had little to lose, I have never found that that kept me for long from winning."

Paoli's lip curled. He looked at me as boldly as he had before. "When I have decided you have something worth winning, monsieur, then perhaps I shall give you the opportunity to lose it." He stepped down the stairs and walked toward the door without giving us another look. "Meanwhile, I am off to the Comédie Française, my friends, and I leave you in the good hands of the comtesse."

Tom looked questioningly at Mme. de Laurence. "Comtesse?"

Mme. de Laurence shrugged, her eyes more disillusioned than ever. "By the grace of my late husband," she said. "It is unimportant."

We followed her up the marble stairs and soon found ourselves in a pleasant three-room suite—a spacious sitting room and a bedroom, separated by a dressing room. Lamps had been lit within, and the porter and an assistant scurried in with our luggage. A maid appeared with pitchers of hot water, another began our unpacking for us, and Mme. de Laurence told us that a supper would be sent up whenever we were ready. When she turned to leave, I followed her out into the hallway.

"Mme. de Laurence, I don't mean to pry into anything that's not my concern, but I don't understand. Is M. Paoli also a guest here?" I felt it might be wise to know more about the man.

"I'm sorry," Mme. de Laurence said. "I assumed that

Harry—Lord Harry—had told you. As you can see, this is quite a large house and requires a large staff. Lord Harry maintains it by having 'paying guests' in the apartments he doesn't use. M. Paoli is here with two or three servants most of the time. Sometimes his business associates, or Lord Harry's, stay with us.''

"In other words," said Tom, who had appeared in the doorway, "we are guests in a very fancy *pension*."

"If you wish, monsieur."

Tom laughed and went back into the apartment.

"And you, madame," I said, "you are . . . *la femme de charge?*"

Mme. de Laurence smiled briefly. "The housekeeper? No, I am Lord Harry's hostess."

"And M. Paoli. I could not identify his accent. And what does he do?"

The smile faded. "M. Paoli doesn't encourage inquiry into his affairs. He's Corsican and calls himself . . . a businessman. But tell me, where did you learn to speak French?"

The question caught me off guard, and my look confirmed her suspicions. "Oh, Lordy," I said in English, "I told Tom it wouldn't work. Is my French that bad?"

"No, my dear," she said in accented English, "and that is the difficulty. No Parisienne would ever speak such meticulously accurate French. You are English?"

"American."

She leaned toward me confidentially and patted my arm. "Don't worry," she said, returning to French. "Say as little as possible to anyone in this house for the next few weeks. We shall take you out into the streets of Paris, and in a month you will be more French than I."

"Oh, I do thank you, madame."

She looked at me searchingly. "You are in trouble, perhaps?"

"Why, I . . ." Mme. de Laurence seemed to be growing more sympathetic, but I was far from ready to confide in her.

"Never mind, Mme. Duhamel. I shall help you if I can. But may I give you some advice—in confidence?"

"Why, of course."

"This is no place to bring an end to your troubles. Your husband may think that Lord Harry is doing him a great kindness in letting him hide here—if that is the case. But when Harry gives something, he always asks for payment in return—and like the devil, he always collects. You know, don't you, that some people call him the Wickedest Man in Europe?"

"Yes."

"They have reason . . . as I know all too well."

"Madame . . ."

She would not let me question her. Insisting that she must leave immediately to see to our supper, she hurried away from the door and down the stairs.

The gambling continued.

It started again the day Lord Harry arrived in Paris, less than a week after us. Until then, Tom was like a man half-dead, sleeping the days away, showing no interest in Paris, simply waiting. But the moment Harry appeared, the light was rekindled in Tom's eyes, and he was filled with energy, a man resurrected.

Meanwhile I, to my delight, had found a friend, my first real friend since Melinda's death. I had begun to like Céleste—Mme. de Laurence—that very first evening, when she warned me against Lord Harry and volunteered to help me. We soon learned that we could talk comfortably together—though we avoided the subject of our pasts—and make each other laugh. And somehow each of us sensed in the other an ally.

Though she was reluctant to talk about Lord Harry, it was Céleste who told me why he was called the Wickedest Man in Europe.

"Because he *is* wicked."

"But *how* is he wicked?" I tried to think of something truly nasty. "Is he a flagellant? Does he patronize child-prostitutes?"

"He may have tried both. He says he finds such things uninteresting."

I was increasingly skeptical. We were lounging about Céleste's sitting room on that sunny December afternoon, and wickedness seemed abstract and unreal. "Then how is he wicked?"

"He is said to have worshiped the devil."

"Ah, black magic! Voodoo! I had no idea Lord Harry was a religious man."

"You laugh, but . . . All right, I'll tell you something. You know that here in Paris, Harry is somewhat circumspect. But north of the city he has a château—his 'hunting lodge,' he calls it—and there he sometimes holds Adam-and-Eve nights.''

''What in the world is that?'' I asked, though from my experience at Huxton Hall, I could hazard a guess.

''Call it a charming bit of history relived. Over a hundred years ago, Philippe d'Orleans, the Regent of France, and his friend Madame de Tencin, held orgies at Philippe's château. Madame de Tencin called them Adam-and-Eve nights. The guests dined naked until Madame had the lights put out, and from then on it was, as you say in English, catch-as-catch-can.

''Harry read of this and was inspired. But of course he is not so crude. I am told that the guests are carefully selected and dine in their robes. Then they are blindfolded and led about the château until they have no idea whom they may encounter in the dark. *Then* the lights are put out and the robes are abandoned for an hour or so. After that, the lamps are lit again for an hour of refreshment, and this is repeated perhaps three times before dawn breaks. And one may never know whose kiss that was in the dark, whose breast, whose thigh. . . . Is that wicked enough for you?''

''Wicked enough?'' I pretended to consider the matter. ''Well, it's *naughty* enough, I suppose, if one has a taste for naughtiness. But it certainly doesn't sound like much fun. Just think of all those anonymous sweating bodies groping around in the dark. Think of the barked shins, the blacked eyes, the stubbed toes, think of the curses and the howls of pain—'' Céleste burst out laughing, and I continued, ''No, my dear, I'm afraid you have yet to convince me that our Harry is anything worse than a naughty little boy.''

Céleste's smile faded. ''It would be a pity if you really believed such a thing. I have tried to warn you about Harry, but if you don't believe me—''

''If you want to convince me, tell me something truly wicked.''

For a moment she sat staring at her clasped hands. Then she said: ''Very well, I shall do that. I shall tell you a very small story. About a year ago a young couple came to Paris from Bordeaux. He was to join his uncle's law firm here. He was very enthusiastic, and she was very proud of him, and they were most happy. Unfortunately, they were one of those couples who are so conscious of being from the provinces that they simply must prove they are not provincial. They are educated, superior, *au courant* in every way. 'How can you possibly call Delacroix the greatest living French painter! Why, he can't hold a candle to Ingres! Really, my dear fellow, when one tries to take a Sand or a Balzac seriously— what has become of our standards!' In short, they were priggish, pompous, and pretentious . . . and very, very young . . . and so happy to be together and just starting out in Paris.

"Can you guess what happened to them?"

I did not want to ask. Céleste's eyes had become the eyes I had seen on the evening of our arrival, and once again she looked much older than her years.

"Someone gave them a letter of introduction to Harry— perhaps out of malice, because anyone who really knows Harry knows he would detest such a couple from the minute he laid eyes on them.

"But he never let his real feelings show. Oh, no. He gave them dinner, he took them to the opera, he introduced them to those very luminaries they had thought they despised. It becomes quite a different thing, you know, when George Sand is laughing at your little joke or Balzac is sniffing around your bosom. And of course Harry made sure that the young man met beautiful women who pretended to consider him much too fine a prize for a mere country girl, and she met handsome men who taught her that she was far too good for a mere bumpkin from Bordeaux.

"How much more need I tell you? He was seduced a time or two, and she nearly so a half-dozen times, and when Harry considered the time ripe, he gave a party for them at his château. It was no trick at all to get them both drunk, put him into a bed with several girls at once, and then lead her to the little Judas-window in the wall. And no trick at all after that to put her weeping into bed with one man after another, as she tried to take her revenge, and let him look in at the moment she was carrying on with four or five.

"Afterwards he cut his wrists but was saved at the last moment. She has not yet been saved. She is still half-mad and being cared for in a convent.

"Tell me, do you still think that our Harry is nothing but a naughty little boy?"

The afternoon was passing and the room had darkened. I said, "I think that is the wickedest thing . . . no, the evilest thing . . . I have ever heard of."

"Then remember my warning, Liane. Whatever trouble you or your husband may be in, hiding with Harry is like hiding with the devil. His price is your soul. If you are wise, you will take your Julien and run . . . run. . . ."

But of course I could do nothing of the kind. There was no way in the world that I could persuade Tom to desert that green-baize-covered table.

Meanwhile Céleste and I grew closer. She had promised to take me out into the streets of Paris to improve my French, and together we explored the city as few people ever do. There was no accurate map of the entire city, but there were thirty bus lines, with delightful names like the Doves and the Gazelles and the Reunited Women, and more than three hundred buses. Fashionable Parisians seldom used them, but what did we care? They had cushioned seats, and there was no standing, and for a thirty-centime fare we could travel almost anywhere we wished.

In Paris, I began to learn for the first time about poverty. I had been aware of rich and poor in Charleston, but it had been inconceivable to me that anyone might actually starve there; and in London I had been mostly sheltered by my father and my husband from knowledge of the wretched hovels, the narrow back alleys, the crumbling tenements where so much of the population lived. But in Paris, traveling about with Céleste, I saw for myself.

The wealthy residential districts were at the western end of the city and south of the Seine in the Faubourg Saint-Germain. The entire central and eastern part of Paris was inhabited by working people and the poor, and while slums could be found almost anywhere in Paris, they were especially concentrated in the center of the city in the area around the rue Saint-Denis. There one found narrow winding streets, often without sidewalks and always wet from open sewers. Tenements had been built story on story until one had hardly a glimpse of the sunlight. Everywhere beggars plucked at our arms, and workers fought for jobs. "Please, madame," I heard a woman imploring at a shop entrance, "I am an excellent seamstress—" "No work." "Just one blouse, madame—" "No work." My child is starving—" "No work!" Céleste crammed a few francs into the woman's hand, and she ran weeping along the crooked street. "And tomorrow," Céleste said sadly, "one more prostitute."

Oh, yes, I learned much more than the venacular of Paris and the argot of its streets.

Christmas and the New Year passed with little celebration at the house on the rue Saint-Honoré, and in January, Céleste announced that I was ready for my graduation test. She would take me to visit a friend who knew nothing about me. "If he doesn't suspect you're not a native of Paris," she said, "you will have passed."

Thus it was that on a frosty afternoon we found ourselves at 17 rue des Marais-Saint-Germain. At Céleste's knock, the door opened to reveal a hard-faced middle-aged woman who pursed her lips and crossed her arms over her bosom.

"Good day, Jenny," Céleste said cheerfully. "Will you tell monsieur—"

"Monsieur is busy," Jenny said.

"But will you tell him—"

"Monsieur is at work."

"Jenny, will you please—"

"Monsieur must not be disturbed."

"*Please*, Jenny."

A quietly amused male voice sounded from within: "Who is it, Jenny?"

"It is Madame de Laurence," Jenny said, looking over her shoulder, and she added meaningfully: "Again!"

"Well, show her in."

Jenny stepped aside and disappeared as we entered the house. The man who came to greet us wore an expensively tailored gray suit with a black cravat and a blue waistcoat. In his early forties, he was not much taller than I and gave the impression of being frail and delicate, but that was an illusion caused by the fineness of his features. A thick shock of dark brown hair rich with red highlights surmounted a broad, noble forehead, and he wore a full but neatly trimmed mustache. His eyes were large and dark, his complexion was oddly Oriental, and his straight, sharp nose suggested aristocratic hauteur. Both eyes and mouth were narrowed by the habit of concentration and gave the impression of extraordinary will power and controlled passion.

"Eugène!" Céleste said, going to him, and they clasped hands and exchanged kisses on the cheek. "If you are really too busy to see us—"

"Of course not. Jenny guards me like a dragon."

"As she should! But we were nearby, and I could not

resist." Céleste looked around and smiled at me in such a way that I knew she had a surprise in store. "Eugène, I would like to present to you my new and very dear friend, Madame Duhamel." The gentleman smiled and stepped forward to take my hand.

"Madame . . ."

"And Liane, I would like to present to *you* my very dear friend—Monsieur Eugène Delacroix!"

I was stunned. Céleste and I had visited the Louvre to view some of M. Delacroix's most famous paintings—*Dante and Virgil in Hell, The Massacre at Chios, The Death of Sardanapalus, Liberty Leading the People*—but not once had she even hinted that she knew this great man. As yet, I had no idea of how they had met, but I sensed between them the warm afterglow of old intimacies.

His studio was not at all the paint-bespattered chaos one usually expects of an artist. It was as clean and orderly as the man himself. Every cabinet, brush, and easel was in its place, and the only decorations were some sketches and studies pinned to the walls. A furnace roared, making the room tropically hot, and it struck me that M. Delacroix was a kind of exotic flower. Then, watching the grace with which he moved, I corrected the thought: he was a Bengal tiger wreathed in orchids.

The afternoon passed quickly. Jenny served coffee and cakes, but M. Delacroix, noticing my diffidence, insisted I sample his brandy, and soon my tongue was loosened. But Céleste almost tied it again with her flattery:

"Hasn't she the loveliest complexion, Eugène? Could even you do justice to a complexion like that?"

M. Delacroix looked closely at my cheek. "I should love to try. Of course, flesh reveals its true color only in the open air and above all in sunlight, and I look forward to seeing madame again on a brilliant spring day."

"He'll pay you five francs a session for modeling, Liane, and that's a very good rate. Just think of all the fares we can pay on the Doves or the Gazelles with five francs!"

But the best of the day was yet to come.

"I wonder if I can persuade you ladies to stay for supper."

"Oh, we wouldn't want to put you to the trouble, Eugène."

"But you wouldn't. It will be very informal. I'm having a

few friends in, nobody you don't know, Céleste. George, Frédéric, a few others . . .''

George Sand. Frédéric Chopin. I was dreaming. I had died and gone to heaven.

That evening was one of the most delightful of my life, the happiest time I had had since the early months of my marriage. It was a mélange of laughter and chatter and argument and music and still more laughter.

The first people to arrive were a young sculptor called Alfred and a model, Madeleine, who were there partly to assist Jenny. Then came Mme. Elizabeth Boulanger, the painter, who was said to have been M. Delacroix's mistress for a short time. After that came Pauline Garcia Viardot, the singer, and her husband, Louis Viardot, the art critic. And at last, Mme. George Sand and M. Frédéric Chopin.

We ate. We laughed. We talked. Céleste, who really did know everybody, drew me into one conversation after another, though that was really unnecessary with George there. Oh, yes, she was almost immediately *George* to me. I was glad I had been reading her latest novel, *Horace*, in the *Revue indépendante*, but it would have made no difference if I had not. When George turned from her arguments with M. Delacroix to talk to me, I found myself babbling away like a child, voicing every opinion, every feeling, as if it might really matter to that sympathetic woman. Her large dark eyes seemed to glisten with *my* emotions, her full lips pursed with *my* pain, her long-nosed oval face tilted back with *my* laughter. Despite all one reads of her smoking cigars and wearing male attire, she was the most *motherly* woman I had ever met.

M. Delacroix called for attention. M. Chopin was at the Pleyel piano which had been installed for just such occasions as this. Pauline Garcia Viardot, a young woman of about my age, stood beside him, and when she smiled, her plain Spanish face was transformed to something irresistibly charming. For almost an hour she sang Mexican songs to M. Chopin's accompaniment, filling the house on the rue des Marais-Saint-Germain with the most glorious voice in Europe—the voice that the divas Rosine Stoltz of the Paris Opéra and Giulia Grisi of the Théâtre des Italiens, fearing for their own careers, had vowed should go unheard from Paris stages.

The evening wore on. As other guests arrived, each was introduced to me by George or Céleste or M. Delacroix.

Some of the names were unfamiliar to me—Arsène Houssaye, a writer; Pierre Leroux, an editor—but how could I not know the name of Honoré de Balzac, as infamous in Charleston as it was famous in Paris? That chubby little man with the sparkling eyes and the wide, tickly mustache kissed his way up my arm from my fingers to my elbow, all but vowing eternal love, and such was his enthusiasm for everything he did, I think he half-believed himself.

When the time came to leave, I was almost weeping with happiness. While Alfred, the sculptor, looked for a hackney for Céleste and me, we gave George our firm promise that we would dine with her and Frédéric in a few days' time at her apartment in the rue Pigalle. Then we were off, humming Pauline's sad Mexican songs until tears ran down our cheeks and we had to cheer ourselves up with airs from Rossini.

"But how in the world did you come to know Monsieur Delacroix and George and—and all these people?" I asked, as the hackney clattered toward the rue Saint-Honoré.

"Oh, Harry knows everybody. When he introduces you to one or two, you soon meet others."

I sensed a sudden reticence on Céleste's part, but I was in no mood to examine it. I could hardly wait to tell Tom about the evening. He was an educated and civilized man, after all, far more versed in literature and the arts than I, and when I told him about the people I had met—!

The minute we arrived back at the house, I went looking for him. Céleste followed me through the grand dining room and the gallery toward the back of the house. As we approached the card room, we heard raised voices, and I thought, *Oh, no! Lord, don't let anything happen to spoil this evening!*

A dozen men were in the card room when we entered. Several of them, including M. Louis Paoli, were on their feet. M. Paoli's face was twisted, and his hands were shaking. Tom, a pile of chips and franc-notes before him, was grinning, which seemed to increase M. Paoli's rage.

"You laugh at me, monsieur?"

"Not at all, Louis—though I must admit that where I come from, we contend that there is nothing more amusing than a bad loser."

"Monsieur may find himself less amused on the field of honor."

Tom's blue eyes glittered, and though he never ceased to smile, his voice took on a new edge. "I have been on the field of honor, monsieur, several times. And I have never failed to walk away—from a fallen opponent. But monsieur need not worry. A Carolina gentleman never fights—except with another gentleman.''

For a long silent moment it appeared that there would be not a duel on the field of honor, but murder in the card room. M. Paoli nearly always had a big, strong male companion with him, and now that companion's hand darted toward his sleeve, until M. Paoli's abrupt motion stilled him. Tom's hands gripped the table, ready to throw it over. Lord Harry, perfectly relaxed, appeared to be on the verge of laughter. Nobody made another move.

M. Paoli relaxed. He even smiled, though there was no humor in his voice when he spoke. ''Very well. You have proved your point. As you warned me several weeks ago, nothing keeps you for long from winning. But as I warned you, monsieur, when I decided you had something worth winning, perhaps I would give you the opportunity to lose it. Well, you have something, monsieur.'' As M. Paoli turned to leave the room, he looked directly at me, his eyes hard and cold. ''And I swear to you that I shall most certainly take it from you.''

Behind me Céleste uttered a little cry. Tom grinned and raked his fingers through his winnings. M. Paoli and his companion strode out of the room. ''Gentlemen,'' Lord Harry said, ''I believe the game is *vingt-et-un*.''

When I looked around, Céleste, too, had left the room. I hurried after her, saw her going up the marble stairs in the main hall, and followed her up to her apartment. When I entered, I found her huddled, white-faced, on her bed.

''Céleste, what is it?''

She composed herself and spoke with studied calm. ''Liane, I told you the evening you arrived, and I tell you again. This is no place for you. You should take your husband and leave. Vanish. Disappear.''

''But why? You warned me against Lord Harry, not against Monsieur Paoli. Why should we fear Monsieur Paoli?''

''Because your husband has insulted him as no other man ever has—and lived. And in return for that, he wants you.''

''Well, he certainly shan't have me.''

''Listen to me. The evening you arrived here, you asked about Monsieur Paoli. Now I shall tell you about him.'' Though the room was warm, Céleste shivered. "He trades in lives, Liane. In human lives."

"In human . . ." I was not sure I understood. "Do you mean slaves?"

"Women. Preferably beautiful white women, but women of any color. And pretty little boys. For the brothels of Hamburg and Marseilles, and the slave markets of Africa and South America."

The horror of what Céleste was saying began to dawn on me. "A slaver? A slaver of women?"

"His men find a pretty shopgirl, a seamstress, a house-maid, someone without protection. She disappears. If she interests Monsieur Paoli, he amuses himself with her for a time. And after that . . . Marseilles . . . or Algiers . . ."

"But how do you know—"

"I know from living in this house. If it were not for Harry, I myself would long ago have been in Monsieur Paoli's hands. But for some reason Paoli respects Harry, perhaps even fears him, and I am under Harry's protection. That's one reason I dare not leave him. If I ever did, Monsieur Paoli would surely find me, and then—"

"But, Céleste, aren't you really saying that I dare not leave this house either? That I should stay here and hope for Lord Harry's protection?"

Céleste had no answer. Her arms enfolded me, and she buried her face in my lap.

But I could not believe what she had said. I was no shopgirl, no housemaid, no woman without protection. I was an American. I was Augusta Welles Raveneau, no matter what name I might use. Such things as Céleste had mentioned simply did not happen to people like me. I had Tom, I had a great plantation to go home to, and I was safe, forever safe.

Then why did I still see M. Paoli's eyes glaring into mine? M. Paoli's eyes, so hard and cold?

7 〜〜〜〜

I found it difficult to believe that I was really in any danger from M. Paoli, and when I told Tom what Céleste had said, he scoffed. "It was only a little gambler's tiff. Tonight maybe Paoli will win a little, and then he'll be happy as a lark." And sure enough, whenever I saw Tom and M. Paoli together in the days that followed, they were gaming, joking, and laughing like old comrades.

I failed to interest Tom in my new friends. When I spoke of M. Delacroix, he merely shrugged, and when I mentioned George Sand and Balzac, he yawned and said somthing about preferring Washington Irving or James Fenimore Cooper.

Meanwhile, however, I was happy. I am certain this information would come as a surprise to any Gentle Reader who happened onto these pages, but it is true. A human being, in any given set of circumstances, has only a limited capacity for unhappiness, and I had reached mine. Tom's gambling no longer greatly concerned me. Nor did the fact that he never truly made love to me and only rarely importuned me—a time or two of taking his pleasure to celebrate a win or console himself for a loss. He showed no sign of remembering Jewel, or any real interest in any other woman. He never spoke of returning to America, but I did not even need that reassurance. I had found my own escape from all that had troubled me—my new friends.

I had no illusions about my place among them. George was interested in me because she sensed an unhappy marriage, evidence that wedlock was a barbarous institution. Frédéric liked me because I was ravished by his music. Eugène put up with me because I was decorative and adored him, and artists adore being adored by the decorative. Both Céleste and I were clever enough to appear to be admiring pupils who asked no awkward questions and lived only to serve these geniuses, and in doing so we learned a great deal.

And there was Adam.

How many nights did I lie awake wondering if I had made a fool of myself with him? Had he been sincere, or had he merely been trying to seduce me, failing only by a slight miscalculation?

At the end of January, I learned the answer. Tom and I had easily avoided those of Lord Harry's London friends who had visited Paris and who might have recognized us, but Adam had made a shrewd guess as to where we had disappeared and had come looking for us. When we met in the grand salon, he spoke to us cordially but showed no special interest in me. He had come to Paris alone, he said, for a short vacation. He sat at table with us for the next few days, went to the theater in the evening, and played cards with the men at night. There was plenty of opportunity for him to approach me if he wished, but he was so unfailingly proper that I might have thought the incident at Huxton Hall had been nothing but a drunken aberration. But it was not, as I learned when he found me in the gallery on the morning he was to leave.

"I've hardly had a chance to talk to you," he said.

"It seems to me that you've avoided a number of opportunities," I replied a trifle coolly.

His eyes were pained. "Don't say that, Augusta. You know what I mean. I dare not let myself be alone with you for any length of time. Even now, in this room . . ."

Oh, God, I thought, *he does love me. I think he truly does love me!*

"Someday, Augusta, there will be a chance for us. I cling to that thought. Someday a chance."

I had not realized he was coming closer to me. Suddenly he seemed to envelope me. His arms pulled me to him, his mouth pressed on mine, and I lost myself in the moment. But the moment did not last. He thrust me away, and only just in time. From the doorway Lord Harry called, "Your carriage is ready, Adam."

"Right away, Harry," Adam said with false cheer, then lowered his voice. "I'll come back when I can. Meanwhile, if you need me for anything—anything at all—send word. I'll come. I won't fail you."

That night I dreamed of Adam Trevayne.

The days passed. Paris went wild during carnival and Mardi gras, then settled down for Lent. Lord Harry was absent more often than not, attending to his affairs in London, but now the gaming continued without him. Tom and M. Paoli were becoming close friends. Adam returned for a few days in early March, and we spent more time together, but we did not exchange so much as a kiss. He renewed his promise to help me if ever I needed him, and returned to London. And I went on being happy with Céleste and my other new friends.

I had not the slightest idea that the end had come at last.

I was awakened at dawn that morning by the beating of my heart. I lay still for a time, faintly alarmed, listening to that steady *a-thump! a-thump! a-thump!*, wondering what I might have dreamt. I had awakened in the same way quite often in the preceding weeks.

From somewhere in the room I heard a sound—a muted whimper, perhaps, or a sob.

I whispered, "Tom?"

There was no answer. When I reached out, he was not beside me. I sat up and looked around.

"Tom?"

He still did not answer. Sitting hunched over in a chair near a window, he was little more than a shadow in the gray light of early morning.

"Darling, what is it?"

He shook his head without raising it, and my feeling of alarm grew stronger.

"Has something happened? Tom—"

"They're breaking me."

"You've lost before, if that's what you mean. You'd better come to bed. You'll win when you play tonight."

He shook his head again. "You don't understand. This time I've lost everything." He stood up and began to pace, his arms over his chest as if he were cold, and his voice held the same fear that I had heard that morning at Huxton Hall. "If they'd just extend my credit, I could win it all back. I always have before. But they won't, goddamn them all, they say it's time to settle accounts, it's time to pay up or—"

"Tom, what are you talking about!"

He whirled on me, his fear turning to anger. "I lost tonight, don't you understand? I lost, goddamnit, and those bastards are breaking me! They've taken every damn cent I can lay my hands on and one hell of a lot more! They've backed me into a corner, and not even Harry will advance me a goddamn sou! Don't you understand what that means, goddamn it? They're breaking me!''

"You don't mean they've—''

"Yes! That's exactly what I mean! I mean we've got nothing left, no money, nothing at all! At least nothing I can get my hands on in time—a few acres of land and some slaves back in Carolina—''

"Tom, you're not going to sell the Barony!''

"The Barony!'' His laugh was pitying. ''What Barony are you talking about? The Barony was gone long ago!''

I sat dazed, still unable to take in what he was saying. He continued to pace and shake his fists and rail at his gambling friends, but I could only think, *What does he mean? The Barony gone? How? What has happened?*

"The Barony . . .''

I must have said it aloud. "Yes, gone, goddamn it, how many times do I have to say it? If it hadn't been gone, maybe we wouldn't have had to get the hell out of England.''

"But . . . how? Was it Gannon—''

"Hell, yes, it was Gannon, that smooth-talking, cardsharping bastard. Who the hell else did you think it would be? What the hell do you think he's been after for the past five years? Hell, yes, it was Gannon! . . .''

Tom ranted on, but I hardly heard him. With my eyes closed, I was seeing a whip-crippled nineteen-year-old boy in a graveyard, seeing his half-mad face and hearing his vow: *"Everything you ever stole from us . . . I'm gonna take back! . . . The land, the people, our home—it's gonna be ours again. . . .''*

He had done it.

Gannon Murdock had gotten his revenge. He had the Barony—my Barony—with all my people, with Pearl, Rufus, Aunt Polly, and all the others. He had the great white mansion I had loved almost from infancy . . . my horse, Wanderer . . . my boat, the *Maid of Athens* . . . and my dreams. . . .

Yes, most of all, my dreams . . . dreams of going back to the Barony with Tom . . . of raising a family at the Barony . . . of my children roving the fields with Pearl's children and playing in the same streams I had.

All my dreams gone, lost across a green-baize-covered table.

I lay quietly back on the bed and wept.

When my tears stopped, the light at the window had grown

brighter. Tom had sat down again, and I could hear him shivering, though the morning was not that cool. "Have we *nothing* left?" I asked.

"Nothing here in France. Nothing to pay off my debt."

"I have a little jewelry—"

"If you wore much jewelry, you'd know the best pieces are already gone. Anyway, they wouldn't be worth nearly enough."

So he had lost my jewelry too. "How much do you owe?"

Tom muttered something too softly for me to hear.

"*How* much?"

". . . Maybe . . . four, five thousand . . ."

Five thousand at least, then. "Francs? Or dollars?"

"Pounds."

Oh, no! Oh, my God, no! "But how in the world are you going to pay it?"

"I don't know. I could never borrow that much."

"But *your* plantation—your share—you can borrow against that!"

"Augusta, I can't even prove that I own part of a Carolina plantation. Oh, I could, of course, given enough time, but—"

"Then how in the world do they expect you to pay?"

Tom raised his shaking voice. "Augusta, I don't know! I only know that Paoli says I'd damn well better pay in the next day or two, or—"

"Or what?"

He was silent.

"Or what, Tom?"

Tom's voice was faint again. "Or he'll have me killed."

No. That was unbelievable. It was absurd. "Tom, nobody kills a person who owes them so much money!"

"Some people do. Why do you think we left England? But I've paid that off. We don't have to worry about that."

" 'Don't have to worry'!" I didn't know whether to laugh or to weep again. "You have just told me that Monsieur Paoli will kill you if you don't pay him something like—like a hundred thousand francs, and you say we don't have to worry? Tom, what are we going to do?"

He buried his face in his hands and remained silent.

"But there must be something we can do!"

Hours seemed to pass before he spoke, his hands muffling his words: "There is only one thing we can possibly do."

"What's that? Run away?"

"No. You don't run away from Paoli. But Harry said . . ."

Harry. I felt a clutching sensation at my heart. "Harry said what?"

"Harry knows I have a plantation. He has some idea of its worth. He'll give me a loan against my share so that I can pay Paoli."

"Then there is no problem! You're saved! Tom, sell him your share if you have to! I don't want any plantation, if it means your life!"

"But he'll only do it on one condition."

"Well, what is that? We'll fulfill it somehow. Tom, darling, we'll find a way—"

"That you spend a night with him."

Once again I was sure I was not hearing correctly, or not understanding. Surely Tom could not really mean . . .

"One night," he said. "Just one night."

He did.

"Tom," I said, "are you asking me . . . ?"

He hid his face. "Of course I'm not asking you to do such a thing. I'd never in a thousand years ask you to do such a thing." He hunched farther forward. He seemed to be crumbling in on himself. Then suddenly he straightened and burst out, "But goddamn it, *we are talking about my life!*"

He meant what I thought he meant. And he wanted me to do it—spend a night in another man's bed.

I wondered if this was what Lord Harry had been planning all along. Again I remembered Gannon's words: *"Lord Harry plays as a means of manipulating people."* And Céleste had said, *"Hiding with Harry is like hiding with the devil. His price is your soul."*

I continued to sit on the bed, and Tom paced the room. The morning grew brighter. A maid brought my usual breakfast, but I could not touch it. Tom told me again and again that it was unthinkable that I should spend a night with Lord Harry, that he would never allow it, that he would kill Lord Harry and Paoli both before he would let such a thing happen. But then in a moment of fright he burst out, "For God's sake, Augusta, it's not as if you were some kind of frightened virgin! You're an experienced married woman! There's nothing you don't know or haven't done!"

Again and again I silently vowed that I would refuse.

But of course I would not. It did not matter how Tom had gotten us into this situation. It did not matter what he said or did out of fear. He was my husband, and his life was in jeopardy, and that was far more important than my petty sensibilities and vanities.

"All right," I said at last. "If there is no other way, I'll do it."

I had some conditions of my own to impose.

I wanted as few people as possible to know about my night with Lord Harry—not the other guests, not the servants, no one. I wanted the night to take place somewhere else. Lord Harry's "hunting lodge," his château outside Paris, would do. If such precautions were hypocritical, then so be it. I was not prepared to flaunt my sins.

I sent Tom away. I did not want him to see me leave the house or return to it. I did not want to see him again until my ordeal was over. In fact, I was not sure that I wanted to see him again, at all, ever.

I spent the entire day in our apartment, sleeping much of the time in order to escape the thought of what was to come. Céleste sensed that something was wrong. She was the one person in the world in whom I could confide, and I told her of the bargain Tom and Lord Harry had struck.

"Oh, Liane, I should have warned you!"

"You did warn me. You warned me that Lord Harry was a devil. Though it does seem that he's more interested in my body than my soul."

"But I should have foreseen . . . I should have known . . ." Céleste sank down and wrapped her arms around my waist, and I found myself in the odd position of comforting her, rather than the other way around.

In the late afternoon a carriage came for me. I took the few things I might need in a small bag. As I entered the courtyard, I gave thanks that Tom was nowhere in sight. Céleste, her eyes haunted, was the only person to see me off.

The carriage headed north, up past the hill of Montmartre and into the country, and all the way to Lord Harry's château I felt as if I were on the way to my execution. The château itself, when we arrived, proved to be a lovely place—very old, ivy-covered, rambling, with walled gardens and a fountain. But I hardly saw it in the dusk of evening. The pit of my stomach felt like cold lard, and I was certain I was going to be sick.

A servant led me into the château and up dark stairs. He

opened the door of a lighted room and placed my valise within, and as I stepped inside, I heard the door close behind me.

"Welcome, my dear," Lord Harry said.

I was in a large, high-ceilinged bedchamber. A fire crackled in a fireplace that stretched out along one wall. The far end of the room had a curtain partially drawn across it, and behind the curtain I could see the corner of a bed on a dais. In the center of the room a table had been set with snow-white linens, shining silver, and sparkling crystal, and several bottles of champagne were nestled in a large silver ice bucket. Beautifully arranged on the table was a variety of cold foods on ice—lobster, oysters, the usual seafoods men seemed to think appropriate for occasions such as this.

"I trust you have not yet had supper?"

"I'm . . . I'm not hungry."

Lord Harry smiled. "Perhaps you will be later. If you'll sit with me now . . ." With his ginger hair, his narrow high-templed face, and his thick V-slanted brows, he had never looked more like the devil he was. He stood tall and animal-handsome in a richly brocaded robe, his cheekbones highlighted and his eyes aglitter in the candlelight from the table. "Please, Augusta, do sit with me."

We sat down. Lord Harry opened a bottle of champagne, and I sipped at a glass, hoping it would settle my stomach. As he ate and drank, he talked as casually as if the evening were the most ordinary in the world. ". . . do hope you've been enjoying Paris . . . sorry I haven't been here more often to look after you . . . Céleste tells me she's introduced you to a few interesting people . . . and have you heard the latest about Balzac and Madame Hanska? . . ."

Suddenly my stomach rebelled. I leapt up, knocking over my chair, and looked wildly about the room. A basin stood on a side table. I ran to lean over it, retching violently, though my stomach was empty of anything but wine. Tears ran down my cheeks, and I could not stop until I felt Lord Harry's hand supporting my forehead and heard him soothing me: "It's all right . . . it's all right . . . you'll be fine . . . it's all right."

Gradually, I calmed down. My stomach relaxed. Harry fetched cold water and another bowl so I could rinse my face, then led me back to the table. A few tears still flowed, and I whispered, "I'm sorry, I'm sorry," while he reassured me.

"Some German bitters," he said, holding out a small glass of brown liquid. "There's just a touch of opium to settle your stomach."

I drank gratefully and felt better. When I blinked away the tears that still crowded my eyes, I saw Harry sitting with his chin on his palm, hiding a wry smile behind his fingers. "I'm sorry," I said again. "I'm not at all experienced at . . . at this kind of thing. It seems you've made a bad bargain."

"Have I, Gussie?"

I resented his using that old pet name. "I wish you wouldn't call me that."

"I'm sorry, Augusta. I'm afraid you have a very poor opinion of me."

That needed no answer.

"Actually, Augusta, you could do far worse than me, you know. Monsieur Paoli would never be satisfied with your husband's life in return for the money owed him. No, he would insist upon material reparation as well. I'm not at all certain I could protect you from him, and when he was through with you. . . . It might be argued, my dear, that I am saving you from a fate far, far worse than death, and all I ask in return is my *droit du seigneur*."

"Lord Harry," I said, "we have come here for one purpose only. Shall we get on with it?"

Harry laughed. "Spoken like a true professional. But first I would like to know something. Just why do you hold me in such low regard?"

I faced him. "You have to ask that? Considering the way you use people, the way you manipulate them, the way you degrade them?"

Harry's eyes widened. "Oh, dear me! No wonder I'm called the Wickedest Man in Europe! And exactly how do I degrade them, my dear?"

"I have heard a story about a young lawyer and his wife from Bordeaux. They came to Paris about a year ago."

Harry stared at me for a moment. "Possibly what you heard was true."

"I'm sorry to hear that."

"But do you really think that genuine innocence could be so easily led astray? No, Augusta. That young lawyer and his chit of a wife simply found their own level. All I did was give them the opportunity. And when they got there, they didn't like what they saw."

"No, Harry," I said wearily, "they didn't find their own level. You pulled them down to yours."

Harry's smile grew pinched. "And why in the world would I want to do that?"

"I don't know. Maybe because you want to believe the rest of the world is no better than you are. Or maybe just because you're bored and you like to step on ants and pull the wings off flies."

"Wrong on both counts, my child. Would you believe me if I told you I admire virtue and honor and integrity above all other things—and hate hypocrisy?"

"Harry, my dear, do you want me to be sick again?"

Harry laughed and sat back in his chair. He cocked his head to one side and looked at me appraisingly. "You really don't want to go to bed with me, do you?"

I stared at the table top. "A bargain was made. I agreed to it. I . . . I don't think you'll find me . . . very good, but . . . I'll do my best. I'll try to . . . deliver value."

"It really is quite interesting," Lord Harry mused. "Most women don't find me unattractive. You would be surprised at the number of quite nice ladies—and I am not being ironic, they *are* nice—who, just once, would enjoy being in your place."

"I'm sorry, Harry. I'm not one of them."

Harry leaned forward against the table. "I know you're not. And furthermore, my dear child, I have no intention of making love to you against your will. Laugh if you must, but I respect you far too much to insist on your keeping our bargain. However . . ." Harry's fists clenched, and an angry sparkle came into his eyes. "However, I am still going to teach that contemptible pup you call a husband a lesson or two. I am going to ask you to remain here with me overnight. You may sleep alone, if you wish, or we can play chess or gaze at the moon or whatever you please. And afterwards you may tell your husband that nothing occurred between us, and possibly he'll even believe you. But he'll always know, in spite of all his pretentions of being . . ." Harry's voice became a mockery of Tom's. "Of being 'a fine Carolina gentleman and Charleston aristocrat,' that in truth he is the kind of man who would sell his own wife in order to pay a gambling debt and save his skin!" Harry's jaw clenched, and his hand clutched spasmodically at a napkin. With an angry laugh, he threw it down on the table. "Oh, you needn't worry. I'll keep my end of the agreement, whatever you do, because I've given your husband my word. And whatever you may think of me, I do have a code of honor. But he'll always know.''

How long did we sit in silence, Harry sneering his contempt, and I mute with shame?

A bargain had been struck. I had agreed to it. And I had my honor too. There was only one thing I could do.

I got up from the table. I walked to the end of the room and went behind the curtain that concealed the bed.

In the shadows, I began taking off my clothes.

Slowly, piece by piece, I took them off, with numb, fumbling fingers. Shoes and stockings. Dress and corset. Underskirt. Drawers.

I was trembling with near-panic. I could not do this, I could not. Never before in my life had I felt so vulnerable in my nakedness. I was unable to drop my last piece of clothing, but held it in front of me below my belly.

I heard Lord Harry move his chair back from the table. A moment later he appeared at the edge of the curtain. With one hand he held the curtain back so that the candlelight struck me. He stood there unmoving, silhouetted by the light.

I let my last piece of clothing fall to the floor.

8 ~~~~~~

A carriage and driver were waiting before the door of the château when I went out into the gray dawn of the next morning. Wearily, I climbed into the carriage, and we set off. I did not look back. I felt a thousand years older than when I had arrived.

By the time we reached Paris, the bustle of the day had begun, but at the house on the rue Saint-Honoré no one was in sight except Céleste. As the carriage went through the open gate, she hurried down the front steps to meet me.

She said nothing. She helped me down from the carriage,

took my bag, and led me into the house. Still no one appeared, for which I was thankful, and I was even more thankful when we reached the apartment and Tom was not there.

Céleste knew what I needed, and a big tub of steaming hot water awaited me. We hardly said a word as she helped me undress. My hand on her shoulder, I stepped into the tub and lowered myself carefully into the water. When she knelt and began washing me with a sponge, something seemed to break inside me. Crying her name, I reached out to cling to her and hide my face against her shoulder.

I do not wish to exaggerate the unhappiness of the night I spent with Lord Harry. In all fairness, I must admit that he had proved to be a gentle and considerate lover, and skilled beyond anything I could have imagined. But even so, I had been put into the bed of a man not of my choosing, and I had sacrificed an innocence as precious as the one I had given Tom. Never mind that Tom had sent me to that bed—my greatest infidelity was to myself, and I was left with a feeling of shame that Céleste would never be able to wash from my soul.

She helped me get out of the tub and dry myself. I put on a soft flannel gown, and she helped me into my bed, covered me up, and kissed my forehead as if I were a child. And I slept.

I awakened in the early evening to find Tom sitting on the side of the bed. The drapes had been drawn back, and the light from the window put a halo around his ever-handsome blond head. He was misty-eyed and smiling, and as I sat up, he tried to embrace me. But a sudden feeling of revulsion came over me, and, pretending I was still half-asleep, I thrust him away.

"Darling," he said, "you are all right, aren't you?"

"Of course," I said, rubbing my eyes. "Why wouldn't I be all right?"

"You've saved me, you know. No man ever owed his wife more than I do."

"Oh, please, Tom . . ." Must he remind me?

"It's true. And I'll never be able to thank you enough. Or repay you adequately."

"You can repay me."

"How? Only tell me how."

As if he didn't know, I thought bitterly, but I kept my

feelings from my voice. "Take me home, Tom. Take me home to America."

When he put a hand on mine, I had to struggle not to snatch mine away. "I will, dear. And very soon now."

"How soon?"

"Well, you know I have to repay Harry."

Of course, I thought. The use of my body for a night covered only the interest on the debt, not the debt itself. After all, who ever heard of a five-thousand-pound-a-night whore?

"But as soon as that's done, darling—"

"You mean you're not going to stop gambling?"

Tom made a gesture of hopelessness. "Augusta, I really have no choice."

"You could sell your share of the plantation and pay Harry back. But if you go on losing—"

He laughed, "I'm not going to lose, darling. I'd have been all right as it was, if only they'd given me a bit more credit."

Would the man never learn? "But you can't know that for certain!"

"Oh, but I can. You see, Harry not only covered my debt to Paoli—before he left for his hunting lodge yesterday, he gave me a stake. Just a small one, but . . ." Aglow with success, Tom reached into his coat pocket, pulled out a handful of franc notes, and tossed them onto the bed. "How do you like that? That's almost ten thousand, and I started out last night with only a couple of hundred. Now do you think my luck hasn't turned?"

I stared at the notes. Tom laughed again. "You really can't believe it, can you?"

I said slowly, "While I was away last night . . . lying in another man's bed . . . you were gambling?"

Tom's grin vanished. "Augusta, you've got to understand—"

"You were gambling? With money borrowed from the man you had sold me to?"

"Augusta, I didn't *sell* you!" He sounded shocked. "What do you mean, I *sold* you?"

"Is there another word for it?"

He ignored the question. "And what did you expect me to do? I was *worried* about you, can't you understand that? I was worried *sick*, and I couldn't just sit here waiting for you to come back! I had to *do* something, I had to do something or go mad! Augusta, *I* went through *hell* last night! Is that so hard to understand?"

"I understand," I said dully. "I understand."

"Augusta, darling . . ."

Again, he tried to take me into his arms, and I thrust him away. The last thing in the world I wanted at that moment was to have him touch me.

"Augusta," he said, "I love you. You're a brave and wonderful girl. I only want to show you how much I love you." He moved closer to me. "Augusta, right now. I want to show you . . ."

Did he think he could wipe out what had happened by making love to me? Did he think that would make me his again and no longer the toy of the last man who had had me? Was he trying to give comfort and reassurance to me—or to himself?

"I'm sorry, Tom," I said. "I'm still very, very tired. Later perhaps."

"Of course," he said, and he seemed torn between disappointment and relief. He quickly gathered up the franc notes and stuffed them into his coat pocket. "But very soon. I understand, darling." He gave me a kiss on the forehead—quickly, as if he sensed that I might flinch away from him. "And, darling . . ."

"Yes?"

"Remember—I love you."

But did he really? Or did he, with a perversity we all share, merely want what he could no longer have?

Certainly he was the most solicitous of husbands for the next week or two. But I, like a sick animal, wanted only to be left alone to nurse my wounds and to heal, and I found myself turning cold and shrinking away whenever he came close to me.

We were most apt to encounter each other in the early morning hours when he came upstairs from the card room or in the evening before or after dinner. One evening he found me sitting on the bed. I did not know he was in the room until I felt him sitting down behind me. Before I could move, his arms came around me, gently but with the strength of chains. I sat within that embrace as if I were frozen.

"Now, that's not so bad, is it?" he asked.

"Tom, I'm sorry."

"Of course it's not so bad." His lips on my neck felt like a spider. I shuddered.

"Darling," he said, "it's been almost two weeks since that night . . . and months since you and I . . ."

"I'm sorry, Tom, I can't help it! But I'll get over it, really I will! I just need time!"

"Yes, of course. Time." His voice turned indifferent, and his arms slipped away from me.

"Please be patient with me, darling!"

"I am the very model of patience," he said, getting up and going to the door.

"Tom, I love you!" *Did I?*

Smiling coldly, he looked back at me. He shrugged and left the room.

After that, his attitude toward me changed. Outwardly he was still the thoughtful husband, patient and understanding, but he began to make a show of it. Once he addressed me as "tyke," and when I said, "I thought you promised not to call me that," he replied with a patronizing smile, "And *I* thought *you* had grown up." Sometimes he would start to touch me, and then, as if catching himself in the act, jump back, holding up his hands and laughing "Oops! mustn't touch!" as if it were all quite a joke.

Harry, on seeing him do this, withered him with a look. Since my night with him, Harry had treated me with unfailing courtesy and never, with so much as a word, reminded me of what had happened. In fact, to my surprise, he had even become protective.

One evening, for example, the two men nearly came to blows over me. There were two full tables in the card room that evening, and I had stopped by to watch for a while. Standing behind Tom's chair, I saw that he was not doing very well, which usually made him irritable. His glass was empty, and at the end of a hand, he said, "Augus—ah, Liane, get me another drink."

I looked at the glass, wondering what he had been drinking. Before I could ask, he said, "I told you, goddamn it, get me a drink!"

"Oh, Julien," Harry called pleasantly.

Harry was at the other table and on the far side of the room, yet he had heard. Instantly he had risen to his feet, smiling, the genial host. He motioned to Tom that he wanted to talk to him and headed for the door. Tom, always obsequious to Harry, was instantly on *his* feet and hurrying after him.

I followed at a slower pace. When I entered the next room,

the two men were squared off, and Harry was white with
anger. (Would I never understand the man?) "Don't you ever
again let me hear you speak to your wife in that manner in
this house!"

Tom looked stunned. "Harry, for God's sake, I only—"

"I mean it. Never again."

Tom's face reddened, and he began to tense. There was
only so much he would take, even from Harry.

"Maybe you've forgotten something. She's still my wife!"

"And maybe you've forgotten something. This is still my
house!"

Harry turned and walked back toward the card room without giving me a glance. Tom, hard-eyed, started to follow.
Putting out a hand to stop him, I said, "Tom, I'm sorry . . ."

There are certain words which, though we hear them often
enough behind our backs, ladies are not supposed to know.
Men like to pretend they are nothing but good earthy, masculine words, but in truth they usually convey such dislike and
contempt that I find them difficult to write and have avoided
doing so even in the privacy of these pages. And Tom used
one now.

I said, "I'm sorry, I didn't mean to make trouble."

Tom never looked at me. He merely said, in a low ugly
voice I had never heard before, "Shut your fucking mouth."

Shut your fucking mouth. It was as if he had balled up his
fist and hit me squarely in the face.

I hated to talk about Tom, because it seemed disloyal, but I
had to talk to someone, and by this time I had few secrets
from Céleste. "I don't understand," I said to her the next
day, when we were alone in her apartment. "It's as if,
instead of trying to draw me back to him, he's trying to drive
me away!"

"Maybe he is."

"But why would he want to do that?"

"Because every time he looks at you, he remembers the
terrible things he's done. A bad conscience makes a bad
enemy—whether it's your own or somebody else's."

Céleste could see the situation more objectively than I.
Was she right?

She certainly did seem to be. One morning I was awakened
from a bad dream by the oddest sensation between my legs.
For a few seconds I lay perfectly still, my heart pounding

with fright. Then I realized that a hand was stroking me. With a little scream, I thrust it away and covered myself with my gown.

"What the hell," Tom said. "You wouldn't always have done that. I can remember when you would have wakened up purring like a pussy cat."

"I'm sorry, darling," I said. "I was having a bad dream, and you startled me."

Naked beside me in the dawn light, he was swollen with desire. Seizing my hand, he drew it to him.

"Please, Tom . . ."

He would not let go. "Honeychild, it's been months."

"I know, but . . ."

"A husband has his rights. I mean, I don't care how many other men you've spread for—"

I cried out.

"—you're still my wife. Oh, Christ, now don't start crying."

He released my hand and rolled away from me. I looked at him. Once he had appeared so beautiful to me, a man impossible not to desire. Now, though he had changed very little, he appeared crude and threatening, as if my view of him were affected by the way he treated me.

"If only you could be . . . a little slower with me," I said. "If only you could be a little gentler and take a little more time—"

"For God's sake, Augusta, that's part of your problem. We've been married for three years now, and you can't get it through your head that married life is not one long bridal trip. You've been around a while, honeychild, but you still expect people to treat you as if you were a sensitive virgin."

Was there some truth in that? Did I expect to be treated forever like a bride, and was I being overly sensitive? I tried to understand how Tom might feel.

"I'm . . . I'm sorry, Tom," I said after a moment. "Maybe you're right. If you'll give me a moment to get ready . . ."

"Forget it. I wouldn't want to put you out."

"But you won't put me out. I *want* to, Tom, really—"

"Yes, and it'll be like making love to a corpse. The fact is, you've got no real passion, Augusta."

We lay quietly for a time, Tom on his back, still uncovered, staring morosely at the ceiling. This sad, painful time would pass, I thought. It was important to believe that. I could not have gone on living if I had not believed that.

And suddenly I realized something that I should have known all along. Tom was suffering too. He was torturing himself fully as much as he was torturing me, as a punishment for having sent me to Harry. Why had I not realized that before?

As I sat up in the bed and looked at Tom, a wave of tenderness such as I had not felt in weeks swept over me. Why had I thought him crude and threatening? To me, he was very beautiful and very human, my blond Adonis, and somehow I must let him know that I loved him in spite of everything— no, *because* of everything, for our suffering would make us grow wiser and worthier.

I lay back down, my head on his chest, and my tenderness grew. He did not move, but when I kissed his nipple and passed my hand down over him, I felt his thrill of pleasure, and I began fondling him as earlier he had fondled me. With a little moan, he came back to readiness.

He could have had me then. He could have had me, and all would have been well.

"Tell me something," he said, "what was it like?"

I did not understand. "What? What do you mean?"

"You and Harry. What was it like?"

I lifted my head from his chest and looked at him. He lay perfectly still, his eyes closed.

"What was it like, doing it with Harry? You know what I mean. Did you *like* doing it with him? What did it *feel* like—"

I screamed. My nails drew blood as they ripped down his chest. I began pounding his chest, pounding his shoulders, slapping his face. He grabbed my wrists and threw me onto my back. His face was twisted with anger.

"Don't you ever do that to me again! Don't you ever hit me again, you bitch, or I'll kill you! Do you understand me? I'll kill you!"

He flung me aside and left the bed. I lay where I was, weeping.

Again I must admit, with some astonishment, that I remember a considerable amount of happiness during this period of my life. I think I must have been like a sparrow during a hard winter, finding happiness and a chance of survival in every crumb that came my way.

I am afraid I have done Tom an injustice and inadvertently painted him blacker than he was. As I have said, he, too, was suffering, and I should have given him credit in these pages for those moments that kept me hoping our lives would take a turn for the better. An unexpected kindness from him now and then was enough to bring tears to my eyes.

Then there was my birthday. It went quite unnoticed on the rue Saint-Honoré, but not on the rue Pigalle, where George herself baked me a cake, and there were presents, and we all sang songs. And even Eugène, though he was ill with laryngitis all that spring, found an hour to drop by and kiss the birthday girl.

Ah, but it was Céleste who, a few days later, gave me the best present of all.

I had gone back to filling my hours by doing charcoal sketches and watercolors—city scenes, landscapes, and dress designs. My dress designs particularly interested Céleste, who selected two or three for herself. I discovered to my chagrin that she was a far better seamstress than I—*I*, who had thought myself the best! But she had little talent for creating a design, so together we made a good team, and we enjoyed many hours of sewing together.

After the birthday party, Céleste insisted that I take a selection of my dress designs and other work to Eugène. She had arranged for him to look at it: That was her present.

I was embarrassed by the very thought of taking my amateur dabblings to the great man, and the minute we entered his studio, I saw I was right. Eugène was a kindly person, despite his air of hauteur, but he had already been quite indulgent with Céleste and me, and he did not like having his time wasted. In such a situation, he could be scathing.

"Please," I said, "I really don't think you want to look at these, Eugène. I know you're not feeling well."

"Nonsense," Céleste said. "Eugène has told me he is longing to see your work. Tell her something nice, Eugène. She's melancholy and needs cheering up."

"As a teacher and a critic," Eugène said in a voice hoarse from his illness, "I never tell anything less than the truth, and Liane had better be prepared for it. Besides, she is not melancholy. Melancholy is too profound an emotion for any woman to experience. She may be *sad*, yes, but she is *not* melancholy."

Oh, God, I thought, how charming he was today! "Eugène,"

I said, "I'm *sure* you're much too busy for this. Can't we just—"

"Yes," he said, snatching my portofolio from my hands, "can't we just get *on* with it!"

He sat on a tall stool at a drafting table, opened the portfolio, and began looking through its contents. Celéste and I found chairs and sat quiet as church mice. Eugène looked through my work with an air of indifference, pausing now and then to cock his head this way and that, then shrugging and pursing his lips as he moved on to the next picture. I longed to look over his shoulder and comment, but I was afraid even to move.

I saw that he had looked at all my clothes designs and was looking at my landscapes. He did not appear impressed. "You've got to learn how to put violet into your shadows. These watercolors give no indication that you've ever really *looked* at a shadow."

So much for my landscapes.

"Elegant," I thought—I was sure—I heard him murmur, as he looked again at one of my dress designs. "Yes, really, not bad at all."

He went on looking, while my heart sang.

"Not *good*, actually," he said, as he reviewed some more of the designs. "In fact, quite *bad*, when you get right down to it, but promising, promising." But I had heard him the first time: *"Elegant!"*

"Come here, Liane. I want to show you something."

Without asking my permission, he began marking up my work. And in the next two hours I learned more about drawing than I had in all my life.

So it was that, thanks to Céleste, I became Eugène Delacroix's pupil—his only pupil that spring. The art of practical dress and costume design, he said, was virtually lost. Women's clothes were becoming more wretched by the hour, and only a few English gentlemen still remembered how to dress. He would be committing a mortal sin, he said, if he did not encourage and teach the only truly talented designer of women's clothes he had ever met. My mission in life, he informed me, was to *save the Parisiènne!* I'm sure his hyperbole was simply part of his kindness—he knew I had troubles with my husband—but the fact remains that from that day on I had the run of his studio even when he was not there—and the benefit of his genius when he was. It was a privilege I did not abuse until. . . . Ah, but everything in its time.

In May, Adam paid another of his short, infrequent visits to Paris. As before, we had almost no opportunity to talk in Harry's house, but I arranged that he, Céleste, and I should meet for supper at George Sand's the evening before he was to leave. After supper, George, Frédéric, and Céleste gave us some time alone in the sitting room.

"Something has happened between you and Tom in the last two months," he said, as we sat knee to knee. "I can feel it. He hasn't been treating you well."

I had no intention of telling him what had happened. I said, "Oh, the usual ups and downs. Nothing to worry about."

He shook his head. "I see the way he behaves toward you. But one day, Augusta, I'll be able to take you away from him."

"I'm afraid that day is a long way off."

"Augusta, do you ever think of that night . . . at Huxton Hall?"

Oh, why had he to mention that? I had not thought of that or of anything like it since the night with Harry. My only moment of vulnerability had been those few minutes with Tom before he said the words that seemed to rob me of my womanhood. But now I remembered that one brief glimpse of Adam: the lamplight glistening on his bare chest as he rose up over me . . . the spread thighs, the readied manhood . . . my Greek god, my Hermes, wanting me, needing me. . . .

Adam looked concerned by my silence and perhaps by the mist in my eyes. "Augusta, I'm sorry. I never should have mentioned it."

"It's all right. Yes, I remember, Adam. And you needn't apologize for what happened, ever. Because I was grateful to learn . . . that I could still be loved."

"You still are loved, my darling. And someday . . ."

Oh, the care I took in letting him kiss me farewell—the care not to feel too much.

After he left, George, Céleste, and I found ourselves alone together. "Dear God, what a handsome man!" George said. "You're lovers, of course?"

"Not at all," I said primly. "Just very good friends."

"But my child, what a waste! Céleste, isn't it a waste?"

"Mm," Céleste said, eyes slitted, a catlike smile on her face. "And I promised myself that if Liane didn't sleep with him this time while he was here, *next* time he came to Paris, I'd invite him to park his shoes under *my* bed!"

"You will not!" I snapped with sudden jealousy, and both women doubled over with laughter.

Yes, I was happy. Within my world of pain, I built my secret little paradise.

My fool's paradise.

My last illusions were shattered in June.

George and Frédéric had gone to her country château at Nohant in May, and in June, Eugène went to join them for a few weeks; but Jenny, his housekeeper, had come to accept me, and I used the studio daily. It gave me a chance to get away from the house and work without interruption. By then I had made other friends in artistic and literary circles, and I particularly enjoyed having suppers with Alfred and Madeleine, the young sculptor and the model I had met that first evening at Eugène's. When my work was done, on that June day, I met them in the garret room in the Latin Quarter where they lived together, and we spent an enjoyable evening at a nearby artists' café.

As a result, I arrived back at the house rather late, so I went directly to our apartment. Tom was not there, nor had I expected him to be. He would be in the card room. Lamps had been lit for me, and there was a large pitcher of water by the basin so I could wash, and I proceeded to get ready for bed. My clothes off, I looked at myself in a mirror. Madeleine had said, only half-joking, that if my figure were as good as she suspected, she could get work for me modeling anytime I wished, and Alfred had said that if it were as good as *he* suspected, he would like to portray it in stone. Now, as I pulled a gown over my shoulders, I decided that my figure *was* good, perhaps as good as Madeleine's.

Someone appeared behind me in the mirror. With a startled cry, I whipped my gown down over my body and spun around.

Tom, sullen-eyed, stood in the doorway. "You can't even stand having me look at you any more, can you?"

"I didn't know it was you. You surprised me."

"Yes, of course. Men wander into your bedroom all the time, don't they? Or you into theirs."

Oh, please, I thought, *don't let him start that kind of talk.*

"Tom, what do you want? You're usually in the card room at this time of night."

He shrugged. "I just thought you'd like to know something. I'm free."

"Free?"

"That's right, free. I don't owe Harry a cent. In fact, I'm now way ahead of the game. I've got a damn good stake."

It took a moment for the meaning of his words to come home to me, and then I felt a joy I had not known in months.

"A stake? You mean we can leave now? We can go home to Charleston, to our friends, to your plantation?"

Tom leaned back against the doorjamb and crossed his arms and his ankles. His smile was brief. "I haven't got a plantation."

My joy faltered. "What do you mean?"

"I sold out to Dexter. I didn't get a lot, since I'd already sold most of my half to him, and he's a tight bastard, but together with what I've won . . ." He shrugged.

"But that's all right," I said. "As long as we can get back to America! Oh, Tom, I'm so happy!"

I went to him, wanting to cling to him, but he moved away as if to avoid me.

"And what would we do in America, Augusta?"

"Why . . ." It came to me: Gannon's dream, Melinda's dream. "Why, we can go west, Tom! Go out to the frontier, where nobody knows us! Oh, darling, I know I've been a terrible wife to you for weeks now, but it's this place. It's . . ." I tried to explain. "Tom, if only we can go out to the frontier where nobody knows us, we can forget everything bad that's happened and be like *new people!* We can be *clean* again! And I'll be a good wife, you'll see. Oh, darling, we'll buy a little land and plant cotton and—and all we need to start out is a few acres and some seed and a couple of mules— Tom, I'll pull the plow myself if I have to! Darling, we're young yet! We can do it—"

"Augusta." Tom held out his hand in a gesture I remembered all too well from a night at the Barony five years earlier. "Augusta, does that look like the hand of some damn yeoman farmer? That's the hand of a gentleman, Augusta. It was never meant to touch dirt, and if I have anything to say about it, it's never going to."

"But Tom . . ." What was he saying? Was he saying that there was no dream left for me, that it was gone, all gone?

"Do you really want to go back to America, Augusta? Back to Charleston?"

"Yes . . ."

"Good. I'm glad I can be of help to you." He lifted my right hand. Taking something from his pocket, he slapped it into my palm. It was a thick roll of bills. "That's more than enough to get you back to Charleston. I'm sure your Uncle Thad will be glad to take you in."

I looked at him in confusion. "But you're coming with me."

"What for? You don't want me."

What was he saying? That he was sending me home to live in my uncle's house as a grass widow? To be without him, without a family of my own? To be alone, perhaps for the rest of my life?

"You don't want me," Tom went on, "and I don't want you . . ."

No!

". . . don't want you, don't need you, and am damn sick and tired . . ."

No!

". . . and if going back home is what you really want . . ."

No!

I found myself weeping and pleading with him while I tried to thrust the money back into his pocket. I did not want to go back to America without him! He was my husband, and I needed him! "Please, Tom! Please! Don't make me go away!"

I do not know what all I said, but somehow I got the money back into his pocket. He looked at my swollen face with a kind of angry triumph.

"You'll start behaving like a wife again?"

"Yes!"

"And stop this goddamn wounded-fawn act?"

"Yes!"

"And try to grow up a little?"

"Yes!"

"Fine." He started unbuckling his belt. "Take off that damn gown and get on that bed. Right now."

Instantly that terrible coldness came back to me. "You mean you want . . . ?"

"You're my wife, remember?"

"But can't we wait—"

"Wait, hell. I used to be able to drive you crazy, honeychild.

I want to find out right now if I still can or if Harry has ruined
you for good.''

"But . . . I'm so upset, darling. You can see that. If only
you can give me a little time—"

"Oh, for Christ's sake!" He whirled away from me.

"Tom, wait!"

He strode through the apartment toward the door of the
sitting room, while I followed him, begging him to stay. As
he opened the door, Céleste shied back as if she had been
about to knock. Stepping toward her, Tom gave her a hard grin.

"Well, well. Another of Harry's little whores. I don't
suppose *you* would mind spreading those slim white thighs
for me, would you, sweetheart?"

Céleste's eyes widened with shock.

"Well, how about it, sweetheart? What's your price for a
night—"

"*Cochon!*"

Céleste hit him every bit as hard as I had seven months
earlier at Huxton Hall. But this time he did not fall to the
floor. He reeled back and seemed to bounce off the wall.
Then with a cry of anger, he grabbed Céleste by the hair,
lifting her and pulling her head back, and he raised a rocklike
fist that would surely smash that lovely face forever.

"I say, old boy, I wouldn't do that."

At the sound of Harry's voice, Tom froze. When I looked
out into the hall, Harry was drawing a derringer from his
pocket.

"Let go of her, old boy."

Tom slowly relaxed. His raised hand came down and the
other slipped from Céleste's hair. He forced a grin. "Sorry,
Harry, but the women have been giving me a hard time.
Sometimes they need a scare thrown into them. A bit of
discipline, you know, so I—"

Harry smiled pleasantly. "Tom, old boy, I feel duty-bound
to warn you. If you ever so much as lay a hand on either of
these young ladies again—if you so much as touch *either* of
them—I shall most certainly blow your foolish head off. Do
you understand?"

Tom turned slowly to me. He looked as if all the worst
thoughts he had ever had about me had been confirmed.
Never in my life had I seen such hatred in a man's eyes.

There was a clicking sound as Harry drew back the cock on
the little pistol. "I asked, do you understand?"

Tom's eyes never wavered from mine. "I understand, Harry."

"Oh, good." The pistol clicked again as Harry lowered the cock. He tossed it into the air, caught it, and put it back into his pocket. "Now, do come down to the card room. The game is *vingt-et-un*."

Harry walked toward the stairs. Tom followed after him.

I was awakened by the sound of Tom packing his belongings. I lay perfectly still, unwilling to believe what I was hearing—the heavy tread from room to room, the curt, half-whispered orders, the thump of luggage dropped to the floor. He could not be leaving me, he could not!

When the servants had left and the apartment door had closed, Tom came into the bedroom, a lamp in his hand. His face was hard in its light.

"It's dawn," he said. "The game is over."

I, poor fool, whispered, "Come to bed, Tom."

He barely smiled. "I've had it out with Harry. You two seem to have grown mighty close since that night."

"That's not true! Tom, what's he been telling you? You know I only went to him because you sent me!"

"Yes, I seem to recall I had a powerful lot of trouble persuading you. Anyway, I told him it was you or me, and since he won't turn you out, I'm leaving. His isn't the only game in Paris."

"But you can't leave me here!"

"Can't I? I offered you passage back to Charleston. You still don't want it?"

"Not without you."

"So be it."

As he stepped closer to the bed, something in his eyes made me cower back behind the sheet. He put the lamp on a table, then put his foot up on a chair seat and leaned down toward me.

"I'm going to leave you now," he said, that faint smile still on his face, "but first there's something I want to tell you."

"Please, Tom, don't leave me—"

"I'm going to tell you, and then I'm going to give you a little something to remember me by. Do you still say you love me?"

I mumbled something, I know not what, through my tears.

"Well, I don't love you."

"Oh, Tom, you don't mean—"

"I do mean it. I don't love you now, and what's more . . ." He seemed to brace himself. "What's more, I never did."

Tears blurred my sight. "But you *did* love me," I whispered. "You told me that day in your carriage that you loved me with all your heart."

"Yeah, after you came on to me like a bitch in heat. But I didn't love you then, and I don't now."

"You're lying! You made love to me—"

"*I* made love to *you?* Is that what you call it when you drive a man crazy by throwing yourself at him every chance you get? When you lead him up into a barn loft and drop your clothes and proceed to fuck hell out of him, so that he feels that he's *got* to marry you?"

Were those wails of anguish mine? Was it possible for a human being to feel this much pain? Every word he spoke was like a fiery whiplash cutting through me. And what was he doing to all my lovely memories!

"What are you crying about, bitch?"

"Tom, you did love me! You came all the way to England to ask for my hand!"

"Because I damn well thought I should do the right thing. And by God, I've been paying for it ever since."

"Oh, no, no, no, no . . ."

"Paying for it, I said. And, honeychild, I'm going to tell you something more."

"No more," I wept, "no more!"

"Yes, more. What I've been paying sure as hell wasn't worth what I got. Oh, you know how to throw yourself at a man so he can't get away, but when it comes to giving a man some real pleasure—"

"No, please . . ."

"—you haven't got the slightest idea of how to start. Jewel Trevayne and any of a dozen others I've known *all* put you to shame, honey. And God, if you knew how they laugh at you behind your back!"

Even then, I think I was begging him to love me, begging him not to leave me, begging him to do anything that would stop this terrible pain.

"Don't worry," he said. "Like I told you—I'm not going to leave without giving you something to remember me by."

The chair under his foot fell over as he came at me. I recoiled from him as he ripped the sheet from my hands and off the bed. Then he was over me, ripping my gown open, and I realized what he meant to do.

"So you can't stand my touch any more? Scream, and I'll hurt you, honey, I'll hurt you bad. And if you fight me, I may kill you yet."

He did hurt me. But at least it did not last long. A few seconds, and he uttered a choked cry and spent himself.

Afterwards, while I lay with my face pressed into my tear-drenched pillow, I realized that he, too, was sobbing like a heartbroken child. "Here," he said, tucking a few franc notes under my cheek. "It's more than you're worth, but any whore ought to get something."

I heard footsteps. And then silence.

I lay there thinking, *No, no, no, he can't be leaving me, he can't, no, he will be back, he can't leave me, he loves me and won't leave me . . .*

But he was gone.

I threw myself out of the bed. Without even stopping for a robe to cover my torn gown, I ran from the apartment and along the hall. I came to the head of the marble stairs in the great central hall. Looking down into the shadows, I saw Paoli on one side of the hall and Tom, talking to Lord Harry, on the other. Tom started for the open front door.

I cried out his name as I ran down the marble stairs, cried it out again and again, but he did not look back. Paoli and Harry came toward me as I ran for the front door, and somewhere behind me Céleste called, "Liane!" When I reached the front door, a carriage was going out through the gate.

Running down into the dawn-gray courtyard, I cried out again: "Tom!"

The carriage was gone.

I looked around from tear-blinded eyes. Paoli and Harry had come out the front door. Céleste hurried to me and hugged me tightly. Harry made a gesture, and when I looked again, the gateman was doing his work.

The great iron gate thundered shut.

BOOK THREE

La Vie Passionée de Liane Duhamel

There are defeats more triumphant than victories.
—Montaigne, "Of Cannibals," *Essays*,
tr. Charles Cotton and W. C. Hazlitt

Woman is woman's natural ally.
—Euripides, *Alope*, tr. M. H. Morgan

1 ~~~~~~

As Céleste led me back up the steps toward the door of the house, my anguish had a dreamlike quality. I told myself that this was not happening, this *could* not be happening, not to me, not to Augusta Welles Raveneau of Charleston and the Barony. And yet it *was* happening. Once again, I found myself in a waking nightmare.

Céleste took me back upstairs and put me to bed. She offered me laudanum from a large bottle which I kept for occasional sleepless nights, but I did not want it. Like an amputee who looks at the stump of an arm with disbelief, I was having quite enough difficulty grasping the significance of this hour; I knew intuitively that dulling my pain, and the pain yet to come, would not help me.

Somehow I slept. When I awakened, Céleste was sitting in a nearby chair reading a book. Thinking I heard Tom moving about in the next room, I raised my head, but it was Harry who came through the doorway.

"Tom," I said groggily. "Has Tom come back?"

"Good Lord," Harry said, feigning wide-eyed surprise, "would you want him to come back?"

I let my head sink down onto my pillow. "You would never understand, Harry. He's my husband, whatever he's done. And I have never stopped dreaming—"

"Well, if you really want him back," Harry said, "don't worry about him. I know his kind. The chances are he'll turn up like a bad penny in a day or two, and oh, yes, he'll be full of contrition and promises of good works to come. But he won't have changed, not really."

In my heart I knew Harry was right. Tom would never change. But he was all I had in this world to cling to—my one chance for the home and family and kind of happiness I had always dreamed of.

For a week or more I hardly left the apartment. I felt

imprisoned by my growing sense of guilt. I had been "bad," and now I was paying for it.

It was not that I accepted Tom's version of our history: I did not, and I refused to believe I had seduced him. But was I wrong? *Had* I led Tom on more than I realized? Everything I had ever heard about women being the guardians of virtue came back to me, and my guilt grew.

When I tried to explain to Céleste how I felt, she became angry. "Liane, you know that's complete nonsense! You didn't destroy your marriage, your husband did! He threw away your fortune and sold your body, and from then on he couldn't face either you or himself. You have nothing in the world to feel guilty for."

"Then why *do* I feel this way?"

We were in my sitting room that afternoon, and Céleste arose from her chair to confront me. "Because you've been taught to, don't you know that?"

"Well, of course—I've been taught to know right from wrong—"

"No, no, no, it's not that at all. This is a man's world, my dear, and if they can get *you* to take the blame for anything, anything at all, why should they blame themselves? How convenient for them to believe that their passions are ungovernable but ours are not! But it's a lot of stupid nonsense, and you know it." She threw herself back down in her chair and turned away from me as if avoiding my eyes. "And furthermore, it's an insult to those who are truly guilty—those who've earned the *right* to feel guilty!"

I stared at her. "The *right*, Céleste?"

"The right, my dear." Her laugh was uncharacteristically harsh. "Oh, Liane, you don't even know what guilt is!"

Without thinking, I said, "My God, Céleste, what have you done?"

She did not answer. Her eyes had the disillusioned look I had noticed when we first met.

"I'm sorry. I shouldn't have asked."

She shrugged. "It doesn't matter. I've never told anyone the whole story. Maybe I owe it to you."

"You don't owe me anything."

"Oh, I think I do. Because what Harry did to you and your husband wasn't so different from what he did to me and mine. Or to that couple from Bordeaux, for that matter. The only real difference is that in my case things turned out so much worse. And I was to blame.''

"Céleste, whatever happened to you, I'm sure you're blaming yourself more than you should.''

"No, I'm not.'' Céleste closed her eyes for a moment, as if considering how to begin. "You know, of course, that my husband is dead.''

"You told me the evening we arrived here.''

"What would you say if I told you I killed him?''

I had a sick, sinking feeling. "Céleste, no.''

"Judge for yourself.''

Again, she closed her eyes for a moment before speaking.

"It began as a jest, or so I thought, and it seemed harmless enough at the time—a mere piece of flattery, a bit of gallantry.

"Liane, I was so innocent, so naive in those days. I was an eighteen-year-old village girl, raised by a very strict and elderly aunt and uncle, and hardly able to believe that someone like Valentin could love me. He was so handsome, and rich by my standards, and he even had a title—he was a *comte*. His father was dead, and his mother lived on a magnificent country estate that would one day be Valentin's, along with a great deal of money. But I, I brought absolutely nothing to the marriage but my love, and perhaps I can't blame his mother for thinking I was a fortune hunter.''

"I'm sure your love was worth more than any fortune.''

"Perhaps,'' Céleste said bitterly, "but it wasn't worth a man's life.''

"The first year of our marriage, we were the happiest young couple in Paris. Then, somehow, through friends, we met Harry. The Wickedest Man in Europe, they called him, but, oh, what a delightful fellow he was!

"Soon after we met him, he gave a ball, and it was the grandest affair I could have imagined. A great buffet of champagne and caviar, a magnificent orchestra, the ballroom awhirl with dancers in beautiful gowns. Statesmen, artists, social leaders from all over Europe were here. The king's minister, Comte Louis Molé, came, and Louis Philippe himself stopped by for an hour.

"Valentin and I were the very least of the guests, but it was as if we were the guests of honor, and how I danced that night! One gallant after another swept me around the floor, showering me with compliments, and in the early morning hours, when I was in Harry's arms . . . he told me I was the most beautiful woman at the ball. He said that every man in the room wanted me, and he most of all. He said he was absolutely determined to seduce me.

"How I laughed! I had been hearing much the same words the whole evening long. I said, 'Sorry, milord, but I'm afraid you'll be wasting your time. I love my Valentin too much. I could never be unfaithful to him.'

" 'If you're so certain,' he said, 'perhaps you would like to make a little wager. I shall seduce you within six months.'

" 'So long a time!' I said. 'I'm sure I shall die, just waiting for this thrill!'

" 'My dear,' he said, 'I promise you: Within six months I shall not only seduce you, but you will be looking forward to each visit to my bed as eagerly as if it were your first.'

"I said, 'And what are the stakes?' 'Why the stakes are the pleasure itself, madame,' he said. 'If you win, you lose—if you lose, you win.'

"You see, a jest. Nothing more. Of course, I was aware of Harry's reputation—it was a well-known joke that a good many women had gone to his bed, some quite eagerly, to pay off their husbands' and lovers' gambling debts . . ."

Inwardly, I cringed. I was hardly unique, it seemed. No, I was just another conquest, another in a long list of prizes Harry had brought to bed.

". . . But I didn't have to worry about Valentin's gambling debts. Because, you see, *I* was the one who haunted the card room during the evenings we spent here. Not my husband, Liane, but *I!* I was the one who destroyed us.

"We had plenty of money to gamble, or so it seemed to me, and what was a dozen francs lost now and then, especially since sooner or later I would win it back? The *game* was the thing! If you don't gamble, I doubt that you can understand. You sit there blank-faced, apparently composed, and all the time your heart is pounding, your brain is throbbing, and you are *willing* the fall of the cards! And when they fall in your favor, *you* have done it, *you* have controlled fate! And when you lose. . . . Ah, but there is always the next time! You *must* have a next time in order to prove that you can still do it! It's a lust that for some people can equal any lust of the flesh."

Oh, I knew. I remembered the look in Tom's eyes.

"We came to this house almost nightly, and while Valentin

talked to the other guests, I played, just as your Tom did. And I won and I lost. No more than twelve, fifteen, twenty francs at a time. I kept telling myself that I was never far behind and sometimes a little ahead. I was having fun, and what was the harm?

"Then one night I lost a thousand francs. I had to tell Valentin about my losses. He was angry, of course. And when we calculated what I had lost *before* that night, my God, *that* came to over a thousand francs!

"My dear, we were not poor by any means, but two thousand francs was a lot of money to us. How in the world could I ever hope to win it back?

"Never mind, my husband said. He had been one of the best cardplayers in his region. Maybe he could retrieve some of the money.

"He did better—he won back all two thousand francs in a single evening. And perhaps that was the worst thing that could have happened to us.

"We were at last gambling together, Valentin and I. The next evening I broke even, and Valentin won another three hundred. The evening after that, we lost a total of eight hundred, but that was all right, we said—we were still fifteen hundred ahead. *Ahead?* We were five hundred behind again! But never mind that, we would soon win it back. Valentin had shown that he could win at Harry's tables, hadn't he?

"And after that he *did* win! Won and lost, won and lost, playing at every opportunity, and mostly right here in this house.

"Finally a night came when Valentin lost a couple of thousand and laughed about it, and I saw Harry smiling at me across the table. Something about that smile brought me to my senses. I realized that Valentin had become even more addicted than I. And I will give myself this much credit: after that, I did try, I tried desperately, to make him stop. But I failed. And the fact remains that *I* am the one who got him started.

"I'll tell you something that most people don't realize, Liane. Money has very little reality to people who gamble heavily. When you're pushing money back and forth across the table—a hundred francs, a thousand, ten thousand, in and out of your hands time after time—how can it possibly mean anything? How can it be real? It becomes real again only when you've lost everything and know you'll never get it back.''

"Or, worse," I said, "you've even gone into debt, and payment is demanded." Oh, I knew.

Céleste nodded. "Yes, Harry trapped us in exactly the same way he trapped you and Tom. But oh, my dear, the ending was so different.

"Valentin came to me and told me he had lost everything and owed a great deal. He had asked his mother for help, but she would do nothing for him. She didn't realize the seriousness of the situation, he said, that simply *as a matter of honor* he might have to forfeit his life if he couldn't pay his debts. Romantic foolishness, his mother had said, and she had refused to listen.

"But there was a way out. Of course you know what it was."

Oh, God, no! I thought. *Not Céleste too!*

"Valentin asked nothing of me. The decision was mine. I knew that everything that had happened was my fault, and I loved my husband very much. So I agreed. I, too, went to the château. But afterwards. . . .

"Valentin had thought his luck at cards would turn, he told me later. But now he was even deeper in debt than before, and God only knew what would happen to him—and to me too, since Monsieur Paoli had set eyes on me. It would be best, perhaps, if we both died.

"You see, Paoli and Harry didn't have to threaten Valentin with death, as they did Tom. They held a different sword over him—his honor. He was a *comte*, a *chevalier*, a man of honor, and that meant more to him than anything else in the world.

"At first I couldn't even get Valentin to admit that Harry had made his offer again. But when he did, I told him that I would spend another night at the château on one condition. He must give me his word as a man of honor that never again would he gamble. Not a franc, not a centime.

"He gave me his word. And I spent a second night with Harry." Céleste closed her eyes and covered her face.

I said, "Céleste, you needn't go on."

She said, "They tell me confession is good for the soul. I want to tell you.

"I'm sure Valentin fought to stay away from the tables, and the struggle must have been hell for him. But maybe a true addict can't be saved from his vice. Somehow I had escaped, but the lure of the tables was too much for Valentin. He went back. And lost.

"Again, he came to me and begged my forgiveness. Said he could not go on living if I withheld it. And I gave it to him, because I loved him so much. But then he . . . he . . .'' The words came out painfully: *"He himself* . . . suggested . . . that if only I would . . . go to bed with Harry one more time . . .

"I refused. He called himself a man of honor, I said, yet he couldn't keep his word to his own wife. I told him, 'Valentin, I love you, and I would lie and steal and, yes, even whore to feed you and keep you alive. But I will not be made a whore to fill the pockets of your gambling friends!'

"But I was lying, Liane. That was not the real reason I refused to go to Harry a third time. Not the real reason at all. The *real* reason was . . .''

Céleste's hands clutched at each other, and her eyes were older than I had ever seen them.

"I don't know exactly how to explain this, Liane," she said. "But you see, I had never thought of myself as a very passionate person, and . . . Valentin's lovemaking . . . *our* lovemaking . . . had always been rather naive and . . . unimaginative. And I really think I preferred it that way. I mean, I know I would have been shocked if Valentin had done some of the things that Harry did, and he would have been shocked, even frightened, if I . . .

"I don't mean that Harry was cruel in any way. On the contrary, no man could have been a more thoughtful and patient and—and generous lover! But I had never before experienced such ways of making love. He would bring me to one crest of desire after another.''

Céleste's laugh was sadly ironic. "Oh, I did learn so much that first night. And when Valentin told me about his losses the second time . . . Liane, I still told myself that going to bed with Harry was the last thing I wanted to do. But I didn't merely give consent. *I offered to do it!''*

Céleste leaned forward in her chair, her face in her hands. "And now do you understand the *real* reason I refused to go to Harry a third time? I refused because deep within me a part of me *wanted* to go. And I was afraid that if I did go, I would go still again . . . and again . . . and again. I was afraid that from then on I would be his whenever he wanted me. I would be his captive, unable to resist.

"You see, Harry was winning the bet he had made months before, the bet I had never taken seriously! Somehow he had looked into me and found my weakness, he had looked into me and found a deep well of need, a hunger I had never known existed—something I had been taught to fear and hide away from myself, something another woman might have turned into a gift of love for her beloved. And Harry was using it to corrupt me. Or, as he would say, he was letting me see my true self, letting me find my own corruption.

"But I loved my husband. I loved him with all my heart, and I wanted to save my marriage. So when he asked me to go to Harry a third time, I refused. I gave in to fear and shame and panic. I looked at Valentin's white, stricken face and screamed at him that he was no man of honor, that he was just another filthy whoremongering degenerate who was trying to drag his wife down to his own level. Then I picked up my needles and my thimble and went out to find work.

"When I returned to our apartment that evening, I found him. He had hanged himself."

"I don't see how you can live here," I said a little later, breaking the silence. "After what Harry did to you, I don't see how."

"Why, my dear!" Céleste lifted a delicately curved eyebrow. "Don't you know that Harry is the kindest of all men?"

"Kind? He's a demon."

The irony left Céleste's voice. "Perhaps. But think of what he did for me. My husband's death almost destroyed me, and I had no one to turn to, nowhere to go. By that time my aunt and uncle were dead. My husband's mother would willingly have seen me in my grave—or in Monsieur Paoli's hands. There was only Harry. And I had already decided to join Valentin—I had even fastened up the noose—when Harry came to our apartment and stopped me.

"Yes, I'd be dead if it weren't for him. He took me in and fed and clothed me and saw to it that I was cared for like an invalid. At that time I was like you—I thought I could never bear to be touched by a man again, and Harry never so much as hinted at wanting me in his bed. When I began to recover, he put me to work as his hostess. He pays me well, and you know how light my duties are.''

"Are you suggesting that he has a conscience?''

"No, I don't pretend to understand him. I can only tell you that from the day of Valentin's death, he's been as kind as he was cruel before. It was he who introduced me to Eugène, and I think he knew—even planned—what would happen.''

Céleste smiled at the recollection. "Eugène taught me that I was not so uninterested in men as I had thought. And I learned that Harry was by no means the only man in the world who knew how to make love.'' She laughed.''Not that there was anything more than friendship and affection between Eugène and me. I'm not very likely to fall in love again.''

"Why do you say that? You're young—''

"Not in my heart. And I've put all that behind me.'' Céleste spoke lightly, but I saw the mist in her eyes. "Oh, I do have feelings, of course, and when the urge is on me and I find someone I really like, maybe I'm a naughty girl for a night or two, but . . . I have no right to love. Not after what I did to Valentin.''

"After what *you* did to *him!* But you did nothing to him!''

"I told you, I killed him. I started him gambling. I started the disintegration of his character. Even then, if I had been more patient and understanding, he might not have hanged himself.''

"That's right, *he hanged himself!* Céleste, *you* didn't kill him! Don't you understand, your lovely husband took the nastiest revenge on you he possibly could. He left you penniless and helpless in a world full of Harrys and Paolis. Worse, he left you with a soul filled with guilt—guilt that was *his,* not yours! I'm sorry, Céleste, but in the end your beloved Valentin was just like my Tom. He was exactly what you told him he was—just another filthy degenerate who was trying to drag his wife down to his own level!''

Céleste's face had turned chalk-white, and for an instant I thought her heart was failing. Then slowly she crumpled forward, putting her face into her hands, and began to sob— long, hard, racking sobs.

Oh, how Harry had manipulated us all, I thought, as I went to her and took her into my arms.

Gradually, as I rocked her, Céleste calmed. "He wasn't always like that,'' she said. "Believe me, Liane, my Valentin wasn't always like that.''

"Of course he wasn't. Any more than Tom. Tom was just a nice young man with a few human flaws, like the rest of us. But those flaws were like loose thread-ends in a piece of fabric. And when Harry found them—"

"He sat back, laughing to himself," Céleste interrupted.

"Yes, and began pulling at the thread-ends. Pulling at them until everything came unraveled. And I hardly knew Tom any more."

"Then surely Harry is right: why would you want him to come back?"

I had no answer. I only knew that, unlike Céleste, I could not go on forever being the recipient of Lord Harry's favors. One way or another, I had to escape from the house on the rue Saint-Honoré.

2 ～～～～

To my surprise, my relations with Harry, whom I should have loathed, were perfectly amiable—which was just as well, as long as I was dependent on his generosity. He continued to act as if the night at the château had never happened. He told me that the apartment I had shared with Tom was mine for as long as I cared to keep it. When Céleste pointed out that I would need at least a little money beyond what Tom had left me, he said, very well, I could consider myself in his employ as Céleste's assistant. But as far as I was concerned, all this simply meant that I was receiving free room and board and an allowance, and was thus becoming indebted to Harry. My determination to leave his house never diminished, but how was I to do it?

I took stock of my resources, such as they were. I was an attractive young woman—no need for false modesty. Céleste half-jestingly suggested a career on the stage, but I could neither sing nor act, and as far as dancing was concerned, the great Marie-Sophie Taglioni had nothing to fear from me. Could I be a seamstress, then? I was an expert, if hardly

Céleste's equal, but Paris was filled with seamstresses looking for work. I remembered the woman Céleste and I had
seen near the rue Saint-Denis: *"My child is starving—"* *"No
work!"* *"And tomorrow,"* Celeste had said, *"one more
prostitute."*

I even turned to Harry for advice. "What am I going to do,
Harry?"

"Yes, Gussie, what *are* you going to do?"

I recall him leaning back in his chair behind the huge mahogany desk in his office, his fingers laced behind his head,
smiling at me like a big, friendly, ginger-haired Satan. "If
you care to return to England, you can always go to work in
the mills. Of course, you'll have to work thirteen hours a day,
six days a week, for a mere five or six shillings—about a
quarter of what a man would get on the same job—so you'd
probably do much better in the coal mines."

"Harry, please—"

"But, actually, I think a young woman like yourself might
be more comfortable as a nanny, say, or even a governess.
And who knows, you might meet some bright young fellow
belowstairs and the two of you would end your days as
housekeeper and butler. Bless me if I wouldn't be tempted to
hire you for one of my establishments, if I should find an
opening."

"Harry, be serious."

"My dear, I am being perfectly serious. You are now
living at the very edge of the great maelstrom of poverty into
which millions vanish, few ever to return. But fortunately
there is hope. I have discerned, for instance, that Adam
Trevayne is quite interested in you. I'm sure he would be
happy to tuck you away in a comfortable little villa in St.
John's Wood and keep you nicely for the rest of your days.
Does such a prospect appeal to you, my dear?"

To be a rich man's mistress, "tucked away" in a little villa
for the rest of my life? Oh, dear God, no!

One possibility remained: my dress designs. Eugène really
did think I had talent, though he found fault with all my work
and insisted that I was not yet ready to sell it. But I had to do
something about my situation, so I decided to approach one
of the better-known dressmakers of Paris, a certain Mme.
Colombier. I selected five designs, all of which Eugène had
(grudgingly) pronounced very good, and with Céleste accompanying me, I confronted the dressmaker in her office.

"Every schoolgirl with a box of crayons imagines she's a designer," she grumbled. Mme. Colombier—in English, Mrs. Dovecote—looked like a giant dove herself, with her magnificent overblown bosom and her beadlike eyes. "But you say you've studied with Monsieur Delacroix—not that *he* knows anything about dress design—so let's see what you've got. Is this all you've brought?"

"I didn't want to burden madame—or bore her—"

"Never mind." Mme. Colombier started to glance hurriedly through the designs, then paused and started over again, more slowly. A hungry look came to her eyes. "Not bad. You have talent. You're only beginning, but I believe in encouraging talent. I might offer you fifteen or twenty francs for the lot."

"*Twenty fr—!*" I was shocked by the niggardliness of the offer.

"I can be generous. I might even make it twenty-five, five francs each, if you'll promise to keep working hard and bring me more."

"Madame, I don't think . . ."

I tried to take the designs from her hands, but she hung onto them, staring at them, and the look in her eyes turned from hungry to gluttonous.

"Yes, my dear, I'll take them all!"

"I think not, madame. Another time, perhaps I'll have something more worthy of madame's attention."

"Thirty francs. Forty, if you like!"

"No! No!"

Somehow I managed to gather up my portfolio and get out of the office, and Céleste came hurrying after me. "I think," she sighed, "you may now expect some very familiar-looking dresses to appear in Paris, and you will not get a sou for your work." I did not reply. I was too close to tears, and I lacked the nerve to try another dressmaker.

When July came, Tom still had not reappeared, and I was still asking, "What am I going to do, Harry?" On his advice, I had written to my father's solicitors in London and Charleston to find out if there were any assets Tom had overlooked, but I had little hope.

One day in his office I had another thought. "Harry, is there any reason for me to go on being Liane Duhamel?"

"Perhaps not, but . . ." Harry considered the matter. "Who knows your real name and background?"

"As far as I know, only Céleste." I had, of course, confided in her some time ago. "Monsieur Paoli must suspect something, though—he heard me calling Tom by his real name on the morning he left. But to everyone else in Paris, I'm French."

"Then why not keep it that way for the time being? It will save tedious explanations to a lot of people, and you can always go back to being Augusta when it suits your convenience. I think you would be wise to keep as many possibilities open as you can."

As he spoke, I heard a sound at the door and turned around to see hard-eyed M. Paoli standing there, smiling at me. With his black painted-on hair and mustache, he looked like an evil doll. I wondered how much he had heard.

"I am sorry to interrupt," he said in his Corsican-flavored French, "but I have information which may interest madame."

"And what would that be, Louis?" Harry asked.

Paoli looked at me. "Naturally, I would like to do all I can to be of assistance to madame, and to that end I have put my people to work. And they assure me that there is in Paris no one who answers to the name and description of Monsieur Julien Duhamel."

"We do thank you, Louis. If that's your information, I am sure it's accurate."

"However," Paoli continued, still looking at me, "not long ago a gentleman of his description, answering to the name Mr. Tom Raveneau, was seen in the gaming houses near St. James Palace, in London. He has since departed for America. As you know, Harry, I have associates everywhere from Constantinople to Rio de Janeiro. And I do not think Monsieur Duhamel—or Raveneau—will be able to elude us for long."

Whatever Tom had done to me, I certainly did not wish M. Paoli on him. "Please," I said, "don't follow him for my sake."

Paoli bowed. "For such a lovely lady, how can one not—"

"Monsieur Paoli, please, I want Tom—Julien—left alone!"

"As you wish." Paoli continued to smile, but his eyes were no less hard and cold than they had ever been. "To serve," he said, "is its own reward." And he left the room.

*   *   *

When Eugène returned from Nohant in July, his throat was much improved, and he could resume working with me more comfortably. He was furious when I confessed that I had tried to sell some of my designs.

"Of course that old cow tried to steal them from you! She'll steal every little thing she can remember of your designs, you can depend on it! And you deserve it! I have told you that *I* will decide when you are ready to show your work! *I* will tell you whom to show it to! *I* will see that you get the best possible price! Now, get back to work, and hereafter follow my orders!"

I did as I was told. It seemed my best chance for leaving Harry's house as soon as possible.

Once again, in the months that followed, I found that the human heart snatches at happiness like a starving animal at any scrap of food. At the house in the rue Saint-Honoré my duties were undemanding—helping plan menus, presiding at table now and then, mediating between the guests and the staff—but I threw myself into them with a will so that I could give no thought to my precarious position. During my hours in Eugène's studio I worked harder than I ever had in my life. And on those evenings I had to myself . . .

Ah, those evenings, those nights! I was in love with Alfred and Madeleine that summer, as much as they were in love with each other, and many an evening I went to their garret room in the Latin Quarter to worship and adore. He was a tousled stonecutter's apprentice who wanted to carve something more beautiful than the *Pietà*, and she was the taffy-haired nymph who would inspire him. He was built like a bull—"In every way!" Madeleine confirmed enthusiastically—with muscles enlarged and hardened by his work, while she was as delicate-looking and supple as a wildflower. Loving them both, I wanted them to stay always just as they were—"Forever wilt thou love, and she be fair!"—though in my heart I knew that could not be. Alfred cared only for Madeleine, but she had a roving eye, and I really did not think she could help herself.

Some of my most delightful times were spent with those young artists and writers, as yet unknown, to whom Alfred and Madeleine introduced Céleste and me. We often took bread and cheese and wine up to their room, and there we celebrated the eighteenth birthday of Dumas the Younger and listened to twenty-year-old Henri Murger read his poems.

Some nights the party grew so large and riotous that we wound up racing through the dark streets, singing and dancing and drinking wine, while we dodged the police and ducked the chamber pots hurled at us from the upper stories. If Tom could have seen me, he never would have believed it!

But it appeared increasingly unlikely that Tom would see me, or I him. July passed, and August, and still he did not return or send word. I soon heard from London, and later from Charleston, that he had overlooked nothing of my estate: I was penniless. At the end of August, I forced myself to write to Uncle Thad, asking for help. At the same time, I wrote a much more guarded letter to my English cousins, suggesting that they might help me with some recent difficulties. That letter was quickly answered: They were most sorry to hear of my difficulties and trusted I would soon find them alleviated, and they hoped I would call on them when next I was in London. Well, they never had liked my mother for marrying an American, and now they had their revenge. So be it. My cousins and I wrote each other off for good, and I waited for a reply from Uncle Thad.

More and more, during that summer and autumn, I had the feeling of being stalked by M. Paoli. It was hard to say why, for actually I saw little of him. But when we did meet, he would look at me with that same insolent intensity he had displayed on the evening of our arrival, and like Céleste on that evening, I found myself standing quite still, with eyes averted, as if I were being viewed by a predatory animal.

When I spoke of this to Céleste, she said, "You haven't forgotten the night he quarreled with Tom in the card room, have you? I know Paoli—he swore then that he was going to have you, and you can be sure that *he* hasn't forgotten. To a man like Paoli, such a vow is a holy obligation."

The feeling of being stalked intensified greatly in October when several times I encountered M. Paoli on the streets of Paris. Such a thing had never happened before, and I could not believe the meetings were mere happenstance. After the first meeting, I pretended not to see him, but hurried along the street until I dared look back and found he had dropped out of sight.

Adam returned to Paris in November, but not to stay at Harry's. "I've borrowed a friend's apartment near the place d'Orléans," he explained, when I noted he had no luggage. "But where is your husband?"

While we sat in a small drawing room, I hesitantly gave him the barest facts. As I spoke, Adam's lean, hard body grew so tense I thought he would burst out of his coat. "Why didn't you write to me?" he asked indignantly. "Why didn't you tell me you needed help?"

I laid a hand on his arm. "But I don't need help, Adam. Harry lets me live here and pays me for helping Céleste. I have plenty of time for my own work, and Eugène charges me nothing for instruction. And I don't want you worrying about me."

"Until you are mine, my love, and entirely mine, I shall never cease to worry about you."

He would be in Paris only a week, and then he had to return to England to attend to his estates. A great many people were dependent on him, and I had learned that Adam was not one to shirk the responsibilities that went with great privilege. He would be gone at least six months.

But we had our week, and we made the most of it. There were carriage rides in the afternoons, theater in the evenings, visits with friends. George and Frédéric had taken two apartments on the place d'Orléans not far from Adam's borrowed apartment, and we had dinner with them. There was an evening *chez* Eugène. And all through the week, not once did we encounter M. Paoli on the streets.

Then why did I sometimes have the feeling of being watched?

Adam had borrowed his friend's apartment, he said, in the hope that we could spend a few hours alone together without fear of interruption. But until our last evening together, I refused to visit it unchaperoned. Those late-night rides with him, trembling in his arms as he held me and kissed me in the darkness of a cab while taking me back to the rue Saint-Honoré, were temptation enough. It had been so very long since I had been kissed like that, with such tenderness and yearning, and if Adam had known how weak I was . . .

Had he ever gone further than a few goodnight kisses, I never would have gone alone with him to his apartment. But his pleas finally swept away my resistance, and I agreed to have supper with him there on his last night in Paris. The supper, catered by the Pavillon Henri IV and enjoyed by candlelight, was lovely. At first, due to the circumstances, there was an unfamiliar tension between us, but it was quickly eased by a little wine, some laughter, and a kiss or two so chaste that I could not believe there was any danger.

But there was danger, of course. Foolish girl, who thinks she can be alone with a man to whom she is deeply attracted, eat and drink with him, laugh and sigh with him, and be perfectly safe. When we had finished the last sweet and savored the rich, steaming coffee, and taken a deep breath of the cognac's heady bouquet, what was more natural than that we should rise from the table and go to a window to look at the stars? And slide into each other's arms for a kiss, a moving, tasting, feeling kiss that extended from our lips down the length of our bodies? It was a kiss such as I had not experienced since being in Adam's arms at Huxton Hall a year before, and as if from a great distance, I heard Adam implore God, while his mouth moved against mine, and a hand moved down over the small of my back, sending floods of warmth through me.

"Stay with me tonight," he whispered.

"Oh, no," I moaned.

"I'll make love to you as I've never before made love to any woman. You are the temple wherein I'll worship, and tonight I'll bring such love to that temple that never again will you be able to refuse me. We'll live and love forever, you and I—"

"Oh, no, Adam, don't . . ."

"Augusta, darling . . ."

What recalled me to sanity? I do not know. I did know that if I let Adam continue, he would soon pick me up and carry me into the bedroom. And I wanted that. I wanted to forget Tom and Harry and M. Paoli, I wanted to lose myself in Adam's arms and forget every bad thing that had ever happened to me, I wanted to give myself up to his love and live only for that.

And yet I kissed him gently one more time and stepped out of his arms. How I found the will to do it, or what angel whispered in my ear, I have no idea; but swaying like an inebriate, I turned and walked away, catching myself on the back of a chair before I could fall.

"I'm sorry, Adam," I said, when I could speak. "I shouldn't have let that happen. It was unfair to you."

"Listen to me." He took my shoulders and turned me so that I had to face him. "Augusta, I love you. I know I promised I wouldn't take advantage of any feelings you might have toward me, but Tom is gone now, he's been gone five months—''

"He may come back yet."

"You can go on saying that forever. But meanwhile, you have a life to live, and you love me—''

"Adam, please try to understand. I *want* to love you, I want that with all my heart. But I have *no right* to love you. Neither of us has the right—''

"Augusta, we do!"

"No. Not yet and perhaps never. Adam, I do have such love *for* you that I don't know how I left your arms just now. But we're both married. You have a wife who does, I think, love you in her fashion—''

"But who gives me complete freedom."

"And I have a wandering husband who may return at any time. And I think he may still have a kind of love for me, too—he wept when he left me."

"Nevertheless, he did leave you."

"Yes, he did, and I may never see him again. But until I know . . . oh, Adam, I never should have come here tonight. Please take me home."

Once Adam's eyes had held the indifference of the dead. Now I rarely saw them holding anything but pain. I was glad when he closed them.

"Stay, Augusta."

"No—''

"Stay a little longer. I promise I won't try to make love to you beyond a kiss, an embrace. But I'll remember every kiss, every embrace, until I see you again."

"Adam, I shouldn't. To love when one cannot love, should not love, must not love—that can lead to such suffering!"

"I don't care. Far better to suffer hell in your arms than to seek heaven in the arms of another."

I stayed.

I planned to stay only an hour or two. I stayed most of the night.

If I had the slightest doubt as to the sincerity of Adam's love, it was forever banished. For as we lay back together on a couch, talking softly and kissing from time to time, my defenses crumbled, just as they had at Huxton Hall. Why did I cling to that last degree of fidelity, I wondered, when I was already unfaithful each time we kissed? What did I owe Tom, who had deserted me in such a cruel fashion and would probably never return? Would making love to a man I cared for so deeply be any worse than spending a night with Harry? A hundred justifications occurred to me, and if Adam had been intent on seduction, he might well have succeeded. But he knew I was not one of those doll-women who protest only in order to be conquered, and, truly loving me, he did not take what was not given freely.

It was still dark when the hansom cab Adam had kept waiting for us all night rolled into the courtyard of Harry's *hôtel*. Inside the great hall, a single lamp burned, hardly piercing the gloom. I turned to Adam for a last moment in his arms. "Six months," he said. "I'll do everything in my power to be back within six months. And then . . ." One final lingering kiss, and he left my arms to return to the breaking dawn. I closed the door.

"Madame," M. Paoli said.

I spun to face him. He stood in the doorway across the hall to my right, almost hidden by the shadows. Behind him was one of his big muscular male companions, wearing an overcoat, muffler, and gloves. The man gave me a knowing smirk, then went up a marble staircase. Paoli walked slowly toward me, his footsteps on the stone floor echoing through the hall. His collar was loose, he wore a smoking jacket, and he had dark circles under his eyes.

"I am sorry if I startled you, madame. Paris can be dangerous at night. I am happy to see you safely back within these walls."

Now I knew why I had had the feeling of being watched all during the past week. No doubt M. Paoli's man had had to hurry to arrive back at the house before us. The thought angered me so, I did not trust myself to speak. Giving Paoli a defiant look, I started for the stairs.

"I have news for you, madame, concerning your husband."

Only those words could have pierced my anger and swung me around to face Paoli again. A wisp of a smile played over his face and vanished.

"I fear, madame, that I must express my condolences."

Surely, I thought, Paoli was playing some kind of joke. "You don't mean—"

"It happened some weeks ago in New Orleans. A tall blond man calling himself Mr. Tom Raveneau was found dead—"

"Oh, no!"

"Yes, madame, stabbed to death in a back alley."

"But there may have been a mistake!"

"No, madame. There can be no doubt that the victim was a man who sometimes called himself Julien Duhamel."

Something in Paoli's manner, something satisfied, even triumphant, behind the apparent sympathy, told me the truth.

"You had him killed, didn't you?"

Paoli's eyebrows arched. "I, madame? What an odd thing to say!"

I was shaking as if I had a fever. "You had him killed! You murdered him in cold blood, as surely as if you had stabbed him yourself!"

"Surely madame's grief is excessive?"

"You're not even denying it, are you? You murdered my husband!"

"Come, madame, it is unseemly to pretend there was any love lost between the two of you. You know you're better off without him. You're free of him now, you need wait for him no longer—"

"You're a monster!"

Paoli's eyes widened and his jaw set. His shoulders bunched as if he were having trouble restraining himself. "That may be," he said, "but I am a monster who demands respect. I always pay my debts—and I always collect them. And if you believe I freed you of your husband—you owe me something for that, madame."

We stared at each other. I was trembling so hard I could barely speak. "What do you want of me?"

Paoli stepped toward me. He put a finger under my chin and raised it slightly. He spoke slowly, each word distinct: "You know what I want."

Tears came to my eyes. I had all I could do not to scream the words: "I am not a whore, monsieur. Even if I did owe you anything, I would never pay like that."

"You paid Lord Harry. Now perhaps the effete English baronet pays you. One day you will pay me."

"Never!"

"I have been known to wait ten years for a single night with a woman. I shall wait."

"When I tell Harry—"

Paoli burst out laughing. "My dear, you have nobody now

to protect you but Harry and me.'' His words carried a mocking note. ''And if my dear friend Harry is called the Wickedest Man in Europe, *I*, madame, am called the Most Dangerous.'' He laughed again, and the tone of his voice was pure threat. ''Now, to go bed, woman, and dream of paying your debt.''

It took all my strength to walk up the marble staircase. Twice I looked back, and Paoli was still standing down below, watching me. He watched me all the way to the top of the stairs, and I still felt his gaze on me when I was out of his sight.

3 ﹋﹋﹋

A few days later I received a letter from Uncle Thad confirming Tom's death:

> I would have informed you before, but a Raveneau cousin arrived from New Orleans with the news only a short time ago.
>
> I am sure you realize that your situation has caused a considerable amount of scandal in Charleston. All that is really known here is that Tom Raveneau arrived home last August, having left his wife in Paris, and almost immediately thereafter departed for New Orleans. I did not see him or hear about his return until after he had left, or he would have had to answer to me. Dexter Raveneau, whatever he knows of the situation, at least has the sense to keep his mouth shut. . . .

So Tom was truly dead. I was a widow and, in a way, fortunate to be free. But I had never wished anyone a fate such as Tom's, and remembering our early happiness, I could not rejoice.

I returned to the letter:

Now, I am quite willing to send you funds to come home. But your return is bound to keep tongues wagging for a time, and we must have a firm understanding that, since I am the head of the family, you will submit yourself to my judgment in all things. For instance, it would be in the best interests of all concerned if, after a decent period of mourning, you married again. Of course, under the circumstances, that might be a little difficult in a respectable city like Charleston. But young Horace is in many ways a fine lad in spite of certain shortcomings. You are not blood relatives, and I am sure you could settle him down and turn him into an adequate provider. . . .

I stopped, hardly able to believe what I was reading. I, marry Cousin Horace? Poor, slow-minded, stuttering Horace, so sweet but so pathetic? How could Uncle Thad even think of such a thing? And yet, as I read on, he made clear that my agreeing to such a marriage was a condition of his helping me.

I turned to a letter from Aunt Nickie, which had arrived at the same time:

. . . so good to hear from you again and to know that you are safe and have work that is not too taxing. The Earl of Huxton sounds like a kind man. Of course, we both know it is difficult to say everything one might wish to say in a letter. . . .

She meant that she sensed my reservations and also that Uncle Thad would be curious about anything said in letters exchanged between us.

. . . sorry to say that there has been increasing conflict between Horace and your Uncle Thad—many scenes and angry quarrels, until Horace finally moved out of the house. He actually lives in a warehouse loft and makes a living of sorts by sweeping out stables, offices, shops, whatever he can find. I cannot imagine what will ever become of the boy. Thad says he is increasingly convinced that Horace is not only slow but also just a trifle "tetched." I resist the idea, but perhaps it is so.

And this was the young man my uncle wanted me to marry. Did he perhaps think that by marrying me off to Horace he could subjugate us both? Or was he actually trying to discourage me from coming home? Aunt Nickie was obviously, if not openly, warning me.

One thing was clear to me: even if I avoided marrying Horace, to move from the house in Paris to the house in Wraggboro would simply be to move from one hell to another. It would mean putting myself under my uncle's domination, perhaps for the rest of my life, and I could not do that. Somehow I had to find my own escape from the house on the rue Saint-Honoré.

Céleste said I was mad to think of leaving the house. "Once you leave here, anything can happen to you. You could disappear, and who could prove that Paoli had you kidnapped?"

"Who could prove it if he had me snatched off the street right now? If Monsieur Paoli wanted to do such a thing, he could have done it already."

"Well, at least wait until Harry's back in Paris. I think that Corsican beast may show a little more restraint with him here."

I agreed. In any case, I had to find a way of making a living before I moved out.

"You and Madeleine have both said I could find work as a model."

True, Céleste said, but that was a poor livelihood. Perhaps, but at least it might provide a start for me until I could sell my designs at a decent price. Would Céleste please tell me what to do? How to get started? Yes, she sighed, if I insisted, she would help me.

It was easiest to start, she said, by working with friends, and therefore she went with me to Eugène and asked if he could use me. He protested that I should continue to devote as much time as possible to my studies and not waste it earning a few francs. But I was so determined to find work that he finally yielded and said to return one afternoon the next week.

I did, and Céleste accompanied me to bolster my confidence. As soon as we were in the studio, she stepped behind a screen and, as casually as if she were going to take a solitary dip in a Carolina stream, began pulling off her clothes. I, however, undressed with only slightly less self-consciousness than I had felt that night at Harry's château, though I did manage to walk out from behind the screen with some semblance of dignity. I even managed to retain some appearance of indifference while Eugène walked around me, inspecting me as if I were a side of beef. But when he merely nodded and said, "You'll do," I felt myself shriveling. Perhaps in my vanity, I had hoped for another *"Elegant!"* But Eugène, ever a blunt critic, was not paying me to bask in his admiration.

There followed the most strenuous afternoon I had experienced in ages. Eugène was looking for something—some form, some design, some new pose. He had us sit on a low rug-covered platform and move from one position to another. "Each in a different pose," he said impatiently, "and when I tell you to move, move to a different position at once. If I don't like it, I'll tell you to move again. Now, *move!*" A sketchbook across his forearm, he sent his charcoal flying over the paper. "Move, Céleste—*not* you, Liane. . . . All right, both of you, *move!* Move again, Liane. . . . Liane, extend your left leg more. Straighter, straighter! . . . Hold it, hold it! *Sacristi!* Can't you *hold* it?" I "held it" until every muscle, every nerve, every bone was in agony.

After the first two hours, Céleste dressed and Eugène paid her, but she stayed another hour rather than simply leaving me naked and on my own. During the fourth hour, after she had finally left, I was trembling with fatigue, so tired that I would hardly have cared if Eugène had sketched me sitting on his chamber pot.

Yet when I went back behind the screen to dress, I was happy. I was about to be paid the first money I had ever earned—*really* earned; for the money that Harry paid me for doing so little hardly seemed to count. Five francs, earned in four long, grueling hours of work!

When I came out from behind the screen, I found Eugène frowning at the sketches he had not thrown away. He stopped to count out some money from a purse and hand it to me.

Three francs.

He saw my eyes widen and my smile fade. "What's the matter?"

I felt oddly numb. "Nothing. I just . . . I thought Céleste said something about five francs a session."

"Céleste was overly optimistic. I do pay five francs now and then, but the usual rate for women is three or four francs. And you're hardly experienced, you know."

That was true enough, but. . . .

I had had it all worked out. I would do at least ten sessions a week, and at five francs a session, that would give me over two hundred francs a month. I would get the smallest, cheapest room I could find in the Latin Quarter and eat inexpensively and work very hard at my designs every evening. And maybe by spring, or by next fall at the latest, Eugène would say, "Liane, you're ready!"

But at three francs a session, how could I do it? How could I possibly do it? I turned away from Eugène so that he would not see me blinking back my tears.

"I am not cheating you, Liane," Eugène said quietly, as if he understood my disappointment.

"I know, Eugène. And I do thank you. Will you need me tomorrow?"

"Next week, perhaps."

Céleste was angry when I told her. "Hardly more than half what you expected! Why, he's often given me five for a full session!"

"But you're experienced."

Céleste shook her head sadly. "Liane, don't you think you should give up this idea?"

"No! If other girls can make a living at modeling, so can I. Céleste, I am not going to be beaten!"

Oh, such brave words!

The next morning Céleste took me looking for work. "Put on something clean but old and drab," she said. "You want to look as if you'll appreciate getting the work."

I was lucky. I found work in the teaching studio of M. Paul Delaroche that very morning. "You're not exactly a pocket Venus, are you?" the master's assistant said. He was a young man, a full head shorter than I, who somehow managed to make me feel cowlike. "Had any experience, Margot?"

"Yes," Céleste said quickly, "and she's nobody's Margot, little man. She modeled for M. Delacroix just yesterday afternoon."

"Can you be here regularly, Margot? Monsieur Delaroche wants somebody he can count on for two sessions a day for the next several weeks."

"Oh, yes!" I said, hardly believing my luck at finding regular work so soon.

"Good. Be back here before one o'clock."

Céleste and I were back, and I was undressed, well before one o'clock. The dozen students who drifted into the studio paid little attention to me at first, and as the assistant posed me sitting on a dais, I realized I was going to be more at ease before a whole class than before a single painter. Céleste stayed a short time, greeted a few friends, and left.

To maintain a single pose for four hours, even if the pose is simple and one is given several rest intervals, is even more tiring than striking a series of poses, and the afternoon seemed endless. My mouth became parched and my muscles cramped, but somehow I managed to remain perfectly still throughout the session. When it was over, the assistant said, "We'll see you in the morning," and paid me my three francs.

But the next morning I found I no longer had the job.

"I'm sorry," the assistant said, smiling falsely up at me through the barely open doorway, "but we won't be needing you after all. We've made other arrangements."

My heart sank. "Did I do anything wrong? Nobody said anything."

He sighed and rolled his eyes heavenward. "You tall ones never are very bright, are you? I said, we won't be needing you, Margot, dear, and I really don't think explanations are necessary."

The door closed in my face with unmistakable finality.

As I returned home, I felt more than disheartened. I felt devalued, as if I had become worth a little bit less as a human being. I had been dismissed, rudely and without explanation, and the experience had left me so benumbed that I could not even get angry about it. Was this how people treated each other out in that workaday world of which I knew so little?

Céleste, when I told her what had happened, shrugged off the matter. "Probably an old favorite of Monsieur Delaroche came looking for work, and after all, you're still new."

"Then why didn't his assistant just tell me that?"

"Because the little pig wanted to feel important, and treating you badly was one way to do it. But what's the difference? You'll find another job."

I did, but it was not easy. I learned what it was like to go from studio to studio all day long, day after day, being repeatedly refused. I learned that it was not enough to have a pretty face or a good figure, however useful those assets: artists preferred experienced models, and whenever possible, old friends got the work first.

I was probably fortunate to get work again as soon as I did: a full day with a master who needed a model for a class, a half-day with a painter who used me for the kind of quick-studies Eugène had done. I spent another afternoon with Eugène. He referred me to another painter, and Madeleine got me yet another job. But as Christmas approached, I still was not getting nearly enough work to support myself. "You'll get more jobs and jobs that last longer as you build up your own clientele," Madeleine told me. "And if you want to build it up quickly, Liane," she winked at me, "be 'nice' to them!"

No doubt she was right. I soon found, to my dismay, that though an artist might be all business during his workday, the minute he set his palette aside and began cleaning his brushes, he usually ceased to look on me as a nude model and saw me instead as a naked woman alone with him in his studio. More than one made clear that we might arrive at a mutually advantageous arrangement. But I simply was not made for giving or taking such trivialized pleasures, and that avenue to success was closed to me.

There was little demand for models between Christmas and the New Year, and after the New Year I still failed to find steady work. And to make matters worse, I had virtually abandoned my own studies. After walking from studio to studio all day long, after spending long hours shivering in an ill-heated studio, I could do nothing when I arrived home but sink into the sleep of exhaustion. And after a month and a half of this, I found that I had earned less than sixty francs. I was in despair. Never would I escape from that house and the watchful eye of M. Louis Paoli.

Then Harry returned to Paris.

He came back on a cold, dreary day in January. I had returned to the house that day after a long afternoon in a drafty studio at the Ecole des Beaux-Arts, and I was looking forward to nothing more than a tub of warm water and a little supper before going to bed, when a maid informed me that monsieur awaited me in his office. Reluctantly, I went back downstairs.

As we traded greetings, Harry looked at me with concern. "You're ill," he said, settling me into a chair.

"No, Harry, only tired."

"I can understand why. What's this nonsense Céleste has told me about your looking for work? Don't I pay you enough?"

"More than I earn."

"But you want to get away from this house—and from me."

Too weary for the self-serving lie, I shrugged. "And from Monsieur Paoli."

"Yes, I understand about Louis. And I know, of course, about Tom's death. I shall not offer my condolences." Harry sat down behind his mahogany desk. With his elbows on the gleaming top, his fingertips making a steeple, he looked at me pensively. "Are you utterly determined to ruin your health in this mad quest for independence?"

"I would simply prefer to live somewhere out of Monsieur Paoli's sight, somewhere—forgive me—with fewer unpleasant memories."

Harry's fingertips touched silently half a dozen times. "Perhaps I can help you."

"You've helped me quite enough."

He ignored my irony. "Yes, perhaps I can help you, but on one condition. No more of this modeling, young lady. You rest and get your strength back, and I'll try to find you something more worthy of your talents."

Unexpected gratitude warmed me like the bath I had been looking forward to. "Thank you, Harry."

"Your thanks are premature."

The next ten days or so were a wonderful grace period: no trudging through the wet city streets, no shivering before classes of students, no fending off unwanted advances at the end of the day. Despite my wish to escape the house, I hardly set foot outside. I tried to repay Céleste a little for her many kindnesses by relieving her of as much work as possible—everything from acting the hostess at table to supervising the refreshments in the card room at night.

At the end of that period Harry again summoned me to his office. "You still wish to find work and move out of this house?" I did indeed. "Then I may have something for you. Do you think you might be able to teach some manners, not to mention letters and figures, to three very young brats?"

The position Harry had found for me was better than anything I could have hoped for. He had arranged for me to be a part-time governess in the family of a British diplomatic employee. I would do all my tutoring in the mornings, and evenings I would help entertain the children and tuck them in bed. I would have every afternoon off from one to six, and I would have two evenings a week as well, which would give me time for my studies. I would live with the family and receive my board, of course, and on top of all this I would receive a stipend of two hundred francs a month.

I could hardly believe it. Where did this munificence flow from?

"You know Mr. James Scarborough, don't you, Augusta?"

Yes, I did, and I felt a slight qualm at the mention of his name. Since Harry's return to Paris, Mr. Scarborough had come to the house three or four evenings, and I had the feeling that he was escaping an unhappy home life. In his early thirties, he was a slim, coltish man of medium height, who gave the impression of wiry strength. His smooth pink cheeks made him look younger than he was, and his soft brown eyes under heavy, arched brows gave him a rather shy, eager-to-please look which undoubtedly endeared him to many a lady, if not to his wife. He had seemed quite taken with me, in his diffident way, and I had found him very likable, but I had sensed a situation which might best be avoided. However, I was not going to miss an opportunity such as this, and when he arrived that afternoon to take me to meet his wife and children, I was eagerly awaiting him.

My nerves were drawn tight all the way to the Scarborough house in the rue de Rivoli, but the minute I saw the children I felt better. They came bounding down the stairs into the front hall, two smiling girls and a small boy who immediately assured me that he already knew his alphabet and "lots of words." We were already becoming friends when a stout English nanny appeared, reminded them of their manners, and shooed them back up the stairs again.

Mrs. Scarborough was a different matter. As I walked into the drawing room and she rose to meet me, I sensed antagonism—directed, if not at me, then at the world. She was one of those pretty women who seem to strive not to be pretty: her brow was pinched by a constant frown, her full lips were compressed thin, and her brown hair was pulled tightly back and braided and bunned as if she were trying to give her round face a severity it otherwise lacked.

She acknowledged our introduction with little more than a nod, then took my letter of recommendation from her husband and read it. When she had finished, she looked at me again, still frowning. Her eyes were a catalogue of resentments.

"I understand you want a great deal of time off."

"I'm a student, madame—"

"I know, an art student." She gave the term a vaguely disreputable sound. "I'm told you speak English very well."

"I was born in England. I've spent almost half my life there."

"That, at least, is promising." She glanced at the letter. "Your last employment was also your first, and you held it less than a year?"

"Yes, madame." Harry had obtained the letter from a friend who was in his debt.

"Your employer gives you high praise. Why should you wish to leave such a position?"

"As the letter says, the family is going to America. I prefer to stay here."

"I don't blame you. A barbarous country. First my husband wants to hire a Frenchwoman for a governess, and next he'll want an American."

"I want a French governess," Mr. Scarborough said patiently, "so that the children will have the best opportunity to learn the language."

"I know, I know." Mrs. Scarborough sounded as if she did not believe a word of it, and my heart sank. She glanced at the letter again. "This says you're a widow, Madame Duhamel. What happened to your husband, if one may ask?"

"He died of a fever. He left me very little to live on, and so . . ."

"Perhaps you don't know how lucky you—" She caught herself and broke off, closing her eyes for a moment, as if trying to regain control of her emotions. "Forgive me, Madame Duhamel. That was unkind, and I've been very rude. I suppose there's no harm in giving you a try. When can you start?"

"Why, madame, any time! Tomorrow! Today!"

"Perhaps you would like to see your room. . . ."

Goodbye, Harry! I thought, my heart soaring again like a bird breaking cover. *Goodbye, M. Paoli, goodbye!*

4 ～～～～～

Lies! My new position, my salvation, was founded entirely upon lies! But have I not written that I have lived more than my share? I am sure that any fire-and-brimstone moralist would say that I earned the worst that happened to me. But *I* can only say that I was happy that evening and ready to love the Scarborough family with all my heart, because thanks to them, and to Harry, I was at last leaving the house on the rue Saint-Honoré.

Céleste was delighted for me, yet sorry that I was leaving. "But when will I see you again?"

"Any afternoon at Eugène's. And Sunday you must come to see my new room."

"Oh, but I'll still miss you so!"

Harry came up to my apartment and watched with sardonic amusement as I packed. "But why are you taking everything?" he asked. "Why not wait and see if you like your new position?"

"No, Harry, I shall love my new position. And everything I have must go with me."

"Nevertheless, your apartment here will be waiting for you, if you should want it."

I stayed long enough to have supper and to bid farewell to some of the guests and the staff. Then I was off to the Scarborough house. Looking back across the courtyard as Harry helped me up into the carriage, I saw M. Paoli standing before the door, his gaze fast on me. Harry glanced at Paoli, then smiled at me. "Don't worry. He won't harm you. I promise."

I shivered. I could not leave the courtyard quickly enough.

The rest of the evening had a festive air about it. Though Mrs. Scarborough still wore pursed lips and a frown, she did give me a kind of smile, and I found myself hoping we would become friends. And Mr. Scarborough looked as pleased and grateful as if he had feared I might not return. The children were still up despite their nanny's protests—"Well, it's a special evening," Mrs. Scarborough said—and they insisted on "helping" me unpack and put away my belongings.

Afterwards, as Nanny and I tucked them into bed, the children and I became further acquainted. There was Ellen, nine years old and very shy; Clarissa, eight, and the most outgoing; and David, six, and full of wonder at the world. "Will you stay with us forever?" he asked from under the covers.

"Not forever, silly," Clarissa said from her bed, "just till we learn French and get married."

"I'm never going to get married," Ellen said sadly. "Married people fight." For an instant I felt a chill in my heart, but when I went to my room, it vanished.

I loved my room. As one who was less a servant than a paid guest, I was neither belowstairs nor under the eaves, but on the top floor near the nursery. And while my room was quite plain and modestly furnished, it was spacious and had a comfortable bed and a small fireplace. There were adequate cabinets and a table on which I could work during the evenings, and I had the feeling that even if it were years before I enjoyed success at my chosen employment, I could be happy here. A book in hand, I settled down in my chair, not to read but simply to feel at home.

A sound disturbed me and I realized I had dozed off.

There was another sound and another—a thump, a crash, from somewhere below me.

Alarmed, I rose from my chair and stepped out into the dark hall. Somewhere a door slammed and I heard muffled voices.

"Milly, will you get back in here?"

"I will not!"

"Millicent, goddamn it . . ."

I could not tell where the voices were coming from—a room, a hallway—except that they were down below. The walls and floors of the old house were thick, and yet, perhaps by some freak of echo, the voices did reach me.

"That's right, curse me!"

". . . am not cursing you . . ."

". . . don't know why I gave in to you . . . let you bring that woman here . . . a common jade in this house."

"She's no such thing! Where the hell did you get such an idea—"

"You can see it! And *you* wouldn't have anything to do with her if she weren't!"

"Milly, you're drunk!"

" 'Course I'm drunk!" Broken sobs floated up through the air. ". . . don't know why I married you . . . curse the day we met."

". . . no great prize yourself, you know."

". . . hate you! Hate you!"

"Good God, you'd drive any man away . . ."

I knew I should not listen, but for a minute I felt paralyzed. Then, as I was about to go back into my room, the nursery door swung open. A small pink-gowned figure emerged from the darkness, darted across the hallway, and threw her arms around my waist while burying her face against me. It was Clarissa, the younger of the two girls. I held her tightly and stroked her head. "It's all right," I whispered, "it's all right."

"They always fight. All the time."

"It's all right, darling. Let me take you back to bed."

I led her back into the dark nursery, put her into her bed, and kissed her goodnight. When I crossed the hallway to my own room, there were no more voices from down below.

Oh, dear Lord, no, I thought, as I closed my door. *Let there be peace in this house. Let me find a haven here.*

An all-too-familiar feeling of desperation swept over me. I had failed to sell my designs for a decent price. I had failed to make a living as an artist's model. And now apparently Mrs. Scarborough wanted to be rid of me. But if she turned me out, where would I go, what would I do next?

Please, Lord!

The next morning, the incident I had overheard seemed unbelievable. I went down the stairs fearing the worst, but the household was sunny and cheerful, and the children's laughter sounded from behind the kitchen door. Mr. Scarborough had already left for work, and I had breakfast in the dining room with Mrs. Scarborough. She was as smiling and friendly as anyone could wish, questioning me about my studies and expressing awe that I, a woman, should associate with so distinguished an artist as Eugène Delacroix.

After my third cup of tea, the children took me to their

schoolroom, where I examined their collection of books and tried to discover how advanced they were in their studies. They soon confirmed my impression that they were a bright and eager lot, and I was certain that I would have no difficulty in instructing them. In fact, the morning flew by so quickly and joyfully that we were all sorry to see it end.

That afternoon, when I went to Eugène's studio for the first time in weeks and told him of my new situation, he grumbled that I should be working at my studies full-time rather than zookeeping little demons, but he was pleased to see me nonetheless. And I, when I at last got to work, had a happy surprise. I had feared that my skills might have deteriorated, but I discovered instead a new firmness and sureness in my lines. Well, Eugène conceded, taking a little time off sometimes allowed one's lessons to sink in.

I took care to arrive back at the house well before six o'clock. Dinner with Mr. and Mrs. Scarborough was pleasant enough, though Mrs. Scarborough's smiles of the morning had disappeared and her frown had returned. After dinner I taught the children a few French words and played with them until their bedtime. The rest of my evening I spent in my room, sketching and reading, uninterrupted by any shouts or cries from the floors below.

Such, more or less, was the pattern of my days during the weeks that followed. If only I had known precisely how Mrs. Scarborough regarded me, my situation could hardly have been better. But I never knew if she was going to approach me with friendliness or suspicion; and twice more within a few days I heard her drunken cries and imprecations against me in the middle of the night.

It was after the last of these three incidents that Mr. Scarborough came to take me home one evening from Eugène's studio. I hardly noticed the cab in the dark street as I stepped out the door at 17 rue des Marais-Saint-Germain, until he leaned out and called my name: "Madame Duhamel!" I hurried to him, welcoming the ride.

"Madame," he said, when we were underway, "I felt I must speak to you alone. I want to apologize for Mrs. Scarborough and reassure you."

"Why, monsieur, I have no idea of what—"

"You needn't pretend, Madame Duhamel," he said, "or Liane, if I may call you that. You must have heard Mrs.

Scarborough last night. When I went upstairs, I saw the light under your door.''

"Monsieur, I try not to listen to things that are not my affair.''

His soft brown eyes were unhappy. "You are very generous, madame—Liane—and I do hope you'll try to understand. Mrs. Scarborough is not really a bad woman. In some ways she's an excellent mother. But she is subject to these irrational jealousies which drive her to drink.''

"I'm sorry, monsieur.''

"But I want you to know that you have nothing to fear. Whatever Mrs. Scarborough may say when she's had a glass too many, your job is secure. When she's sober, she herself is delighted with your work.''

"I'm so pleased . . .''

As if in pain, Mr. Scarborough closed his eyes and covered his face with a hand. We rode in silence for some time before he spoke.

"You have no idea what a lonely man I am, Liane.''

"I'm so sorry, monsieur.''

"Mrs. Scarborough and I . . . we haven't lived . . . as man and wife . . . for quite a long time.''

I was embarrassed by these revelations and hardly knew what to say. "I'm sure your children . . . and your friends . . .''

"Help me? Of course they do.'' He gave me a sad smile and fleetingly touched my hand. "Can I count you among my friends, Liane?''

"Why—why, certainment, monsieur.''

"Among my very best friends?''

I tried to sound gay. "Ah, but I do not yet know you well enough, Monsieur Scarborough!''

He smiled, and when his hand touched mine again, it lingered a little longer. "Well, we must remedy that. When we're alone, you might call me James, you know.''

It was my turn to hide my face. "Oh, no, monsieur!''

"It will be our secret. Do call me James.''

"Oh, monsieur, I think not. It would not be proper.''

He patted my hand. "Try, Liane. You won't find it difficult.''

We chattered harmless banalities the rest of the way to the house, but I could not still the faint sense of alarm that had arisen in my breast.

Nor was it stilled the next evening, when again I left

Eugène's studio to find Mr. Scarborough waiting for me in a cab. There was no way to avoid his invitation to join him.

"I was passing this way," he said, as the cab started off, "so I thought we might as well ride together."

"But is it wise, monsieur? Madame . . ."

Mrs. Scarborough had not remarked our simultaneous appearance at the house the evening before, and I had no wish to arouse her suspicions.

"You're right," Mr. Scarborough said, giving my hand a firm squeeze. "I had best leave you before we arrive at the house. But I enjoyed our conversation last night so much that I couldn't resist the opportunity for still another."

I disliked this hint of conspiracy, but it was hard not to like Mr. Scarborough. His soft brown eyes glistened with pleasure and his pink cheeks flushed as we talked, and he seemed ever so much younger than he was. I found it impossible not to unbend to his entreaties that, when we were alone together, I call him by his Christian name, and I almost thought of him as another of my young charges.

Nevertheless, I was dismayed and a little annoyed the next evening, when I looked out the window of Eugène's studio and saw a cab come to a halt. It was Thursday, my evening off, and Céleste and I had planned to join Alfred and Madeleine for supper. With a slight feeling of guilt, I departed by a back way and left Mr. Scarborough waiting in his cab in the street.

Undiscouraged, he appeared yet again the next evening. I put on a cheerful face as I stepped up into the cab, but I decided it was time to bring the practice to a halt.

"Mr. Scarborough—James," I said as we approached the house, "I do have one favor I would like to ask of you."

"Then please do, my dear Liane."

"You've been very kind and brought me home three times this week, but I really do think this should be the last time. I am not at all certain that Mrs. Scarborough would approve."

"Why can't we have our little secret? It's harmless enough."

"In our eyes, yes, but perhaps not in hers. And I would be very foolish and wicked to do anything that might cause her pain."

Mr. Scarborough sighed. "I suppose you're right, but you don't know how much these little tête-à-têtes mean to me, Liane. You see me as a cheerful fellow, but you and the children are among the few people on earth with whom I'm happy.''

I patted his hand. "I'm sorry, James."

"I don't suppose Monsieur Delacroix would allow me to visit with you in his studio, would he? Or perhaps we could meet at Lord Harry's?"

"I'm afraid not."

"But, Liane, we have so much to offer each other." His eyes desolate, he moved closer to me. "You a young widow, I a man in my prime who has not had a true wife in longer than I care to tell you. My dear, do you know how difficult that can be for a man?"

"I . . . I think I may have some idea."

"Then you'll forgive me if I . . ."

The next thing I knew, his arms were encircling me and his mouth was pressing down on mine. At first I was so startled that I could not move. My every suspicion, every worry had proved valid. Regaining my senses, I fought to thrust him away.

"Please!"

"Forgive me, Liane," he said, breathing hard but still not releasing me. "Forgive me, but I had to. Don't you know you've been my salvation in that house? Don't you know it's you and you alone who have saved my sanity?" He drew me back to him again.

"Oh, Mr. Scarborough . . . James . . . please don't do this—"

"I don't ask much. A little love, a little tenderness. Is that so much to ask?"

His mouth pressed down again until I tore mine away. "James, don't! I'll have to leave. I don't want to, but I'll have to."

"Where would you go?"

"I don't know. I have friends. I can go to them anytime. Tonight!"

Perhaps he sensed my determination, for his arms slowly loosened, allowing me to slip away from him. "No. No, Liane, I don't want you to leave, and I'll do nothing to drive you away. But I want you to think about something. Will you promise me to think about it?"

"Yes, yes," I said desperately, wanting only to be far away from him, "what is it?"

"You're a woman with very little in this world aside from

your beauty. I am a man with a great deal to give and very few people to give it to. I want to give to you, Liane. I can give you a home of your own. Every comfort. And my love. Will you think about that?"

"Yes . . . yes . . ."

"Then, one more kiss, my darling."

I gave him the kiss while he held me close in the darkness of the cab, his hand moving over me far more boldly than I would have expected or wished. And if, at my present remove, having kissed him seems unwise, I know I did it because I wanted to end the episode as quickly as possible and because I still saw Mr. Scarborough as a very lonely, much-put-upon man whom I liked a great deal in spite of my apprehensions.

"That shall not be our last kiss," he said as he released me. "That shall not be the last, I swear it."

But it had to be!

As we got out of the cab, I saw Mrs. Scarborough looking down at us from a widow. How long had the cab stood there before the door of the house, I wondered. And how long had Mrs. Scarborough stood at the window, watching?

The very thing I had wanted to avoid had happened. As always, the storm broke after the children were in bed and I had retired to my room.

". . . you and that woman alone in that cab!"

"Good heavens, Milly, I only brought her home—"

"And sat there with her right outside our door, sat there brazenly for how long?"

"For a minute or two, perhaps—"

"Mr. Scarborough, I was watching you! I was at the window watching you and that—that Jezebel!"

I no longer shrank from listening to these ravings. I was the one being defamed, after all, and my position was at stake. But if I was to keep it, I had to find a way to allay Mrs. Scarborough's jealousy, and I decided to approach her on a woman-to-woman basis.

I found an opportunity the next morning, when she was finishing her correspondence. She looked up at me from her escritoire, her eyes bitter and unforgiving, as if I had confirmed her every suspicion.

"Well, what is it?"

I hardly knew how to begin. "Madam—Mrs. Scarborough—I thought I should explain . . ."

"Well, get on with it."

"Mrs. Scarborough, you were very kind to give me work as governess to your children. I thought I should explain that I meant no disrespect in accepting a ride home from Mr. Scarborough."

"I do not wish to discuss the matter."

"I really would not know how to refuse such an offer from an employer—"

"I *said,* I do not wish to discuss the matter!"

"I only want—"

"Enough!" Mrs. Scarborough's hand slammed down on the desk as she rose to face me. "Madame Duhamel, you have been employed here, as you have mentioned, as our children's governess. You will confine your attention to them, or you will leave. Do you understand?"

"Yes, madam, but . . . I only wanted . . ."

It was useless. I turned to leave before I lost all dignity.

"Wait!"

Reluctantly, I halted. To my surprise, when I looked at Mrs. Scarborough again, something in her eyes had changed. The bitterness, the lack of forgiveness, seemed to be fading. It was as if she were struggling to communicate something to me in spite of herself.

"Madame Duhamel, I believe you may have overheard words not meant for your ears. If I have been unfair to you in any way—"

"Yes, Mrs. Scarborough?"

"Then it is important that you realize . . . ." She bit her lower lip and her face contorted as she sought the words she wanted. "My husband . . . may not be . . . altogether . . . what he seems."

Astonishing words! With a shake of her head, she fled from the room, and I was left staring after her.

Oddly enough, the incident gave me hope. In some way, Mrs. Scarborough seemed to realize that, whatever furies pursued her, they were not of my making. There had even been a note of fellow-feeling in her voice at the last.

However, I was not soon to hear it again. In the next two days her frown deepened, her lips compressed tighter than ever, and her voice grew taut with acrimony. On Monday afternoon she seemed ready to come to blows with me.

"And where do you think you're going?"

"Why, I . . .'' I was at the front door, about to leave for my usual afternoon at the studio.

"Madame Duhamel, I have calls to make this afternoon, and Nanny is in bed, sick with the grippe. Just who do you think is going to look after the children?"

"I'm sorry, Mrs. Scarborough, I didn't realize there was a problem. Of course I'll—"

"You're being paid two hundred francs a month and yet you're never here afternoons."

"Madam, I am not *supposed* to be here afternoons," I said defensively, hating the quaver in my voice. "And I have never been asked—"

"You shouldn't have to be asked. For two hundred francs you should be here every afternoon. If you want to keep your job, you're going to be here today."

"Madam, of course."

There were other servants who could have looked after the children, but I did not care to argue with Mrs. Scarborough. And so it was that she did precisely what she wished least to do—left me alone in the house with her husband.

By alone I mean, of course, that the servants never intruded unless rung for, the children were having their nap, and Nanny was in bed sick: there was little chance of our being interrupted. I was in the dining room having one last cup of tepid after-lunch tea when Mr. Scarborough appeared. He startled me so, I leapt to my feet. He looked as surprised as I. The house was utterly silent. Then, smiling, he was coming toward me, and before I could say a word, he had gathered me up in his arms, and I felt his lips on mine.

He would have made love to me then and there if I had let him. But after that first kiss, I fought him—struggled to free myself from his arms, while he whispered, "Oh, my darling, my everlasting darling!" in my ear and worked to subdue me.

"Please," I cried, "let me go!"

"Not after the way you warmed to that kiss!"

"Mr. Scarborough, please, it's just that I do like you!"

"Of course you do! You've proved it! And you don't think I'm ever going to let you go, do you?"

"You don't understand!"

"Ah, but I do, my love. I felt those lips answer mine just now. There is only one more bridge to cross, my sweet, and you're as eager to cross it as I."

"No, Mr. Scarborough!"

When I struck out at his chest, he finally let me slip away from him. He looked honestly puzzled.

"Liane . . . darling, I'm sorry. I . . . I thought . . ."

"Please! Please don't say anything more!"

"You came into this house like a saving angel—"

"Mr. Scarborough, there is something I must tell you!"

He looked at me for a moment as if anticipating what I was going to say. "Is there someone else?"

"Yes!" I had feared a moment such as this and had already considered this defense.

"Who?"

"A man I've known for several years—you don't know him. He's in England at present, but he'll be here soon."

"Why haven't you mentioned him before?"

"Because I need this job, Mr. Scarborough, and I was afraid you wouldn't keep me on if you thought I might be leaving."

"But can't this—this gentleman friend of yours provide for you—"

"I have my pride, Mr. Scarborough, and I'll be kept by no man but my husband."

"I see. And when do you plan to marry?"

"He expects to come into some money," I said vaguely, "and then . . ."

He looked so bewildered and lost as he turned away from me that I actually felt sorry for him.

"And I had such hopes, Liane."

"I'm sorry, James."

"Perhaps you don't know . . . I had a seat in Parliament not long ago. People in both parties spoke of me for the cabinet. There was no limit to how far I could go. But the pressures of homelife—"

"I am sorry."

"Then I met you. You were the light in my darkness. I knew I could still accomplish great things. I knew that with you to give me comfort and strength . . ." His eyes, oddly unsteady, turned on me again. "I don't think you've yet learned what real love is. If you were to give me a single hour alone with you—"

"Mr. Scarborough, please try to understand. You are a dear, kind man, and I shall be forever grateful to you for allowing me into your house. But there can be nothing between us but friendship. Though I do value that friendship more than I can say!''

He shook his head, and all the force seemed to go out of him, as if he recognized defeat. ''When a woman values a man's friendship, he can have little hope for love.''

''But true friendship is love, in a way.''

''Yes, but I had dreamed of so much more.'' He shrugged. His eyes were moist. His smile was rueful and not unkind. ''Please do not worry, my dear—I shall say nothing about your fiancé to Mrs. Scarborough.''

He turned away from me and left the room before I could thank him.

The days that followed did seem to suggest that my difficulties with Mr. Scarborough were over. Thereafter, he scarcely gave me a glance. He never again appeared in a cab outside Eugène's studio and never said a word to me that was not polite but properly distant.

My relations with Mrs. Scarborough also improved immediately, and to my surprise, we soon became good friends. I was at a loss to understand why this should be, until I noticed one simple little fact. Not once since I had come to the house had Mr. Scarborough gone out in the evening—until our final scene on that Monday afternoon. Then suddenly he was going out again, off to Harry's or the Jockey Club or somewhere else. And that signified to Mrs. Scarborough that he had lost interest in me and perhaps was after other game.

Céleste, whom I saw at least twice a week, confirmed this. ''He asked me if it were true that you planned to be married, and I said it certainly was. I told him, not only that, but the gentleman in question was one of the handsomest men in Europe, and it was said by the ladies who knew, that once he had made love to you, you were forever spoiled for any other man.''

''Céleste! You didn't lead him to think I had *slept* with Adam!''

''I let him think what he pleased. And sometimes I wish I hadn't, because from that moment he's been after me like a puppy dog in heat. Tedious, my dear, tedious.''

Suddenly the world was good to me again. My mornings and evenings with the children were a delight. Eugène was actually becoming enthusiastic about my designs, and Céleste and I spent afternoons in fabric shops exploring the possibilities of bombazine and Indian muslin and corded silk and tulle and cassimire and dozens of other materials. One afternoon Mrs. Scarborough joined us, and no three women could have had a happier few hours together. When we stopped on our way home to introduce her to Eugène, she was properly awe-struck and aglow with pleasure, and from then on she was Milly to me, whenever we were alone.

But nothing lasts forever, it seems, and I had been in the house little over a month when Milly got bad news. Her father was ill, and she was wanted in London as soon as possible. As she began her preparations for the trip, her quarrel with Mr. Scarborough resumed.

"You are planning to take Nanny and the children and Madame Duhamel with you, aren't you?" I heard Mr. Scarborough ask, as I crossed the hallway after tucking the children in.

"Oh, yes, you'd love that, wouldn't you? Nobody but the servants to know that you're bringing your doxies right into our own house."

"For the love of God, Milly, if you believe that, why don't you just leave them all here! Maybe together, the children and Nanny and Madame Duhamel can keep Poppa and the household pure!"

"I intend to do just that. Not that it will help."

Two days later, Milly set out for London. The day of her departure proceeded much like any other. The children were restless because of their mother's absence, and I volunteered to stay home that afternoon, but Nanny assured me I would not be needed. And so I went to the studio as usual and, after several well-spent hours, hurried back through the wintry gaslit streets toward the rue de Rivoli.

I arrived home so chilled that, when Mr. Scarborough offered me a large drink of brandy before dinner, I gratefully accepted. He suggested that we eat together, since he thought that few things were as dull as an excellent meal eaten in solitude. He poured wine, a Bordeaux which I thought had a rather odd taste, but the food was good and the meal enjoyable. Toward the end of it, however, I felt a great lassitude coming over me, and I had to apologize when I found myself nodding. And when Mr. Scarborough offered me another brandy with my coffee, I thought I should refuse, but somehow lacked the will or the energy. I smiled, raised my glass to whatever toast he had proposed, and drank.

I seem to remember that little David wandered into the dining room about that time, something he rarely did. "Oh, look,'' he said in a faint and distant voice. "Oh, look, Poppa. Madame Liane is falling asleep.

I shall not—cannot—dwell for long on what happened next. There was a moment of blinding clarity on the stairs when I found myself supported by Mr. Scarborough's arm, then darkness encompassed me again. The darkness parted once more as I stared down at my half-clothed body and fell forward onto my bed. I felt hands tugging at my underclothes, and then . . .

There was a long time-without-time, a vast black emptiness. When at last a sense of time returned, there were dreams. Frightening dreams, sensual dreams, painful dreams, dreams swirling and blindingly bright and fading into darkness before I could grasp them. What was happening to me, what was I doing? Who was this in my arms—what man, what phantom, what strange beast? Why was I so terribly frightened?

My head pounded sickeningly. Light pressed against my eyelids like hot metal. Small bleating sounds came from my throat.

Slowly I raised my head and opened my eyes. Stretched out before me like an unfamiliar war-scarred landscape lay my naked body, bathed in red light from a shaded lamp. Bruised and aching, soiled and used, my belly and thighs were covered with red nail scratches, my shoulders and breasts with the blue marks of tooth and fang, as if I had been savaged by a wild animal. The voice in my throat belonged not to me but to some wounded prey.

Mr. Scarborough laughed.

I wanted to cover myself, but barely had the strength to move. My head pounded harder from the mere effort of looking at Mr. Scarborough. Standing by the bed in the red light and grinning down at me, he seemed less a human being than a creature from hell. He was even thinner and more wiry than I had thought, every muscle distinct under his paper-thin skin. His narrow ears looked almost pointed. The dark hair was sparse yet long and shaggy on his chest, forearms, loins, and thighs, and his male weapon arched out, long and thin and needlelike. If I could have looked down at the floor, I was sure I would see cloven hooves.

He was saying something to me, I had no idea what. He picked up a goblet of wine and drank, spilling some of the dark liquid over his chest, then seemed to do a little dance in the hellish light. Or perhaps he merely staggered, in his sodden glee.

He set the goblet down and leaned over me, his grin widening. ". . . loved it, didn't you?" he said. "Christ, how you squirmed. After you, Céleste next . . . everybody knows, Harry's Harlots! Harry's Whores! Too goddamn good for Jamie Scarborough, are you? But you loved it just now, didn't you? And I'm not through with you yet, bitch." And he threw himself on me again.

The next moments—the next hour?—were a lifetime. Never had I dreamed that a human being could feel so helpless, so degraded, so monstrously *used*. I was no longer human; I was mere animal flesh, alive and bleeding, the defenseless object of his lust. Again and again his claws furrowed my buttocks and thighs and his teeth raked over my breasts, and only when I thought I was about to die did he shudder and slow and drop his inert weight upon me. Then, after a moment, he sighed, rolled off me and onto his back, and began softly to snore.

Those strange little bleating noises were still coming from my throat. I was only dimly aware of them. I thought perhaps I was weeping.

Somehow I managed to crawl from the bed and stumble to the bowl and pitcher. I poured water and and began to scrub, scrub, scrub, scrub, but I felt that never again in my life would I be clean. This was far worse than my night with Harry. This was a different world, a different universe of sin. Why, that had been mere childish naughtiness, compared to this. Now I was truly dirty, so befouled that all the tears in the world would never wash away the stain.

And then I saw the scissors.

They were my largest pair of sewing scissors, lying on the table in the red light—a great heavy pair meant to cut through the strongest fabrics.

I picked them up. The blades made a sweet swishing-clicking sound as I opened and closed them.

I went to the bed. James Scarborough still lay flat on his back, arms flung out and legs apart, his manhood rapidly shrinking. Opening the scissors, I grasped the flaccid flesh, all of it, and drew it up with my free hand. I closed the blades on him. Tightened the blades. The sounds from my throat were louder than ever, drowning out his snoring.

I could not do it.

With a scream, I reversed the scissors in my hand and raised them like a dagger, high over his chest. My shadow danced against the ceiling and wall. I tried to bring the scissors down.

I still could not do it.

I tried to jam the scissors into his throat—pressed in the points until the skin broke and blood ran. And still I could not. With another scream, I flung the scissors across the room.

I remember little after that. Somehow I got dressed and found myself out on the street. The gas lamps still burned, hardly piercing the darkness. Where could I go at this hour? To Céleste? Yes, I had to find Céleste. And Harry had said my apartment would be waiting for me. A place to curl up and hide and weep for all I had lost.

How I ever got there, I do not know. The night was murderously cold, the wind whipping through the streets, whistling around corners, and freezing the tears on my cheeks. I must have lost my way, for the journey seemed endless. Again and again I slipped on the ice and fell sprawling. Once, when I was on my hands and knees, a man kicked me over, groped about my body in search of a purse or reticule, then staggered off into the darkness. Somehow I got back onto my knees again. My hands were bleeding. The big carts that collected the contents of the Paris cesspools each night rumbled by, stinking and dripping their contents, on their way to the canal boats at La Villette. I struggled on hands and knees across their wake, crawling back to the house in the rue Saint-Honoré.

After hours, or so it seemed, I finally arrived at my destination. I fell one last time and dragged myself to the big iron gates. Grasping the bars, I pulled myself to my feet and began to cry out. I rattled the gates, cried for help, found the pull-cord and hung on it. A shadowy figure, shaking a fist and shouting angrily, appeared from the gatehouse and ordered me away. I kept on rattling the gate and sobbing until he came close enough to stare at my face through the bars.

"Madame!"

He opened the gate, helped me across the courtyard and up the steps, and unlocked the front door for me. Did I need more help? I shook my head, and the door closed behind me.

How strange it was there in the vast front hall! Two or three lamps burned. Male laughter drifted from the direction of the card room. Nothing had changed. I felt like a visiting ghost.

A voice inside me cried out: *Céleste, help me!*

Taking one of the lamps, I crawled up the staircase as I had crawled through the streets of Paris. No one appeared. At last I reached my apartment.

Céleste, help me!

With no fire in the fireplace, the apartment was cold, and it seemed terribly barren without my few familiar things. But it was mine, my place, a place for me to go to and hide, hide from the outside world forever.

Céleste, please!

I stumbled into the bedroom, set down my lamp, and leaned against a table, my head hanging down. When I raised it, I found myself staring into a mirror. My face was almost black. My clothes were torn, my hands were still bleeding, and I was covered with frozen mud and filth. That terrible bleating sound began coming from my throat again.

I dropped my ruined clothes to the floor. There was water in the pitcher, as if I had been expected, though it was frozen over the top. I washed again, slowly, carefully, my tears dropping into the bowl. I had no nightgown, but when the filth was gone, I wrapped a blanket around myself.

Céleste, help me!

Then I saw the bottle.

I would have sworn I had taken it with me to the Scarborough house. I thought I had left absolutely nothing behind when I had quit these rooms. But there it was, standing not far from the pitcher and basin, as if it had been awaiting my return all this time.

My bottle of laudanum.

With trembling hands I picked it up. I fumbled out the cork and brought the bottle to my mouth.

I did not wish to die. But I could not bear to live.

I swallowed. And swallowed. And swallowed. . . .

The bottle slipped from my fingers. It seemed to take forever to hit the floor.

The single blanket around me, I rolled onto the bed. I was no longer cold. I had what I wanted now.

Sleep . . . endless sleep . . . oblivion. . . .

5 ～～～～

No!

Perhaps that one syllable reverberated somewhere deep in my soul all along. Some part of me did not want to die. But, oh, the pain of living! Why could I not leave all that behind?

No!

Yes. I was content to sink ever deeper into eternal darkness, to forget, to cease to dream, to cease to be. Goodbye, goodbye. . . .

Damn you!

At first I thought the voice was my own: it seemed a voice from my fading dreams. But then it came again, stronger: *"Damn you! Damn you! Damn you!"*

Bright white light flashed through my mind. Flashed and flashed again. *Let me alone!* I thought angrily. *Let me sleep, sleep, sleep.* . . .

When the light flashed still again, my cheek warmed to a blow: someone was slapping me. My eyes opened wide for a moment, to gaze on Céleste's angry, tear-stained face. "Damn you, you little fool! Damn you, damn you, damn you!" Her hand slashed across my face again and again, sharp and stinging.

My eyes closed. Darkness swept over me.

"No, damn you, don't you sleep!"

"Let me be."

"No, no, no—"

"Wanna sleep . . ."

"Wake *up,* damn you!" *Slap! Slap! Slap!* "Wake up, damn—"

"GO 'WA-A-AY, CELESTE!"

"That's right, get mad! Get angry, damn you! Get mad!"

Without having any idea of how it had come about, I found myself bent over, hanging from my hips in someone's strong grip, while I gagged and retched. Fingers stabbed deep into

266

my throat, and hot liquid rushed out. Someone lifted me, poured some other liquid back down my throat, then bent me forward to vomit again. The sick pounding in my head was even worse than it had been earlier.

"That's enough," said an unfamiliar voice. "You must keep her moving now. Do not let her sleep. Talk to her. Slap her if she dozes off. But above all, keep her moving."

"Is she out of danger now, Doctor?" That was Harry.

"No. She has a long way to go yet. And her heart could give out. Simply fade away."

Darkness, darkness, blessed darkness . . .

"Wake up, damn you!"

Held up by the arms, my head lolling on my shoulders, I was walked, and walked, and walked. But always I seemed to be in the same place, the floor moving under my feet, passing beneath me, moving, shifting, and turning around, and passing beneath me again.

"If I hadn't come up here," Céleste wept, "if I had stayed downstairs a little longer. . . . But somehow I had a feeling. . . . Liane, dearest, what *happened* to you?"

For some reason, only one answer seemed possible: "I think . . . I stepped . . . on a cottonmouth."

But of course that meant nothing to them, and I myself hardly knew why I had said it.

Dawn broke, and still they kept me walking, walking, walking. The doctor left and returned and left again. Harry left and returned. Maids came and went. The terrible pounding in my head became a steady ache. My mind slowly cleared and my drugged torpor became a natural fatigue. Would they never let me lie down? Never, ever again? And besides . . .

Suddenly the pit of my stomach was cavernous. "Oh, Lord, Céleste," I heard myself groan, "I am so *hungry!*"

Céleste began to laugh hysterically. "Oh, thank God, thank God!"

"Give her some clear broth," the doctor said. "Yes, some nice, warm clear broth, and in a few hours she'll be as good as new."

He was wrong.

But what did rape mean to him, a male? How was he to know that I had been subjected to the worst kind of slavery a woman can endure—the forced, uncaring, *contemptuous* use of her body, the breach of her most precious physical intimacy, an intrusion that went far deeper than her most vulnerable flesh? How could he understand that to rape a woman's body is to desecrate her soul?

Finally, they let me sleep—a long, deep, dreamless sleep. At one point, drifting to the surface, I awakened to see Céleste bending over me. "It's all right," she whispered when I tried to speak. "Don't say anything. You've told us what happened. Just rest." Later I awakened again to see her sitting nearby reading a book, and still later to see her dozing in a chair. She never left me.

Hours passed, days, nights. I had no idea of how many. Time had little meaning for me. My personal possessions had been retrieved from the Scarborough house, but I rarely dressed, seldom spoke, never left my bedroom. I cried a great deal for no apparent reason, but I cried hardest the night my monthly flow began. Cried not with joy but with sheer, simple relief. I was not carrying James Scarborough's child. *That* punishment, at least, I had been spared.

Céleste, worrying terribly, tried to help me—"Liane, darling, you must take hold of yourself!"—but there was little she could do. I found myself walking about the apartment, stooped and shivering, my head down and my arms clasped around my bosom. How could I explain to her that I felt myself withering and aging into an old woman? After all that had happened, how could I not feel old, old, old?

Days came and went, and even the brightest of them seemed dark. At some point, I hardly knew when, Harry went back to England. George came to see me several times, but I was barely able to speak to her. My despondency grew so deep that I had no thought of ever recovering from it.

Then one night a strange thing happened. It began as a dream I had had in different forms a number of times before. I found myself in an old shift, standing thigh-deep in a stream that wandered through a pleasant grove of trees on the Barony. The day was warm and bright, and some kind of celebration was going on, for an orchestra was playing and the stream banks and grove were teeming with people, everyone I had ever known.

But something was wrong. Somewhere nearby but unseen was an evil presence, a presence that grew more powerful and deadly with every passing moment. What its nature was and whether it was upstream or down, I had no idea, but I felt its approach like a dark shadow. My heart began slamming with a nightmare beat, and I cried out for someone to help me.

But no one seemed to hear my cries. On one bank, Mrs. Butler and Mrs. Legree pretended not to see me, though they gave me surreptitious glances as they talked together. "And when a man leaves his wife," Mrs. Butler was saying, "I always ask, 'Why, what was wrong with *her* that she couldn't hold her man?' That's what I always ask. 'What was wrong with *her?*'" "Oh, my dear, I couldn't agree more," Mrs. Legree said. "And furthermore, whenever I hear of some nice man making improper advances to a woman—even if he becomes violent and perhaps even *forces* her—why, I say, 'What did she do to *provoke* him to such behavior? What did *she* do to lead him on?'" "Exactly!"

"Please," I cried out to them, "help me!"

They gave me a last frosty glance and turned away.

Tom now stood on the bank, shaking his head. "You're not worth it," he said. As he covered his face with his hand, tears ran down between his fingers. "You're not worth it, you slut. First Adam, then Harry, then Jamie Scarborough, and God only knows how many others—you're not worth it."

I knew it was true, I was not worth it. But still I held out my hand and begged "Please! Please!" while he turned his back on me and walked off.

"That's the way of it, Gussie, dear girl," Harry said, strolling along the bank not far away. "People do find their own level, you know."

"Harry, help me!"

"Why, I have helped you, dear girl, I really have. I helped you into the stream, didn't I? I can hardly be blamed if you don't like what you've found there." Chuckling to himself, he strolled away.

"I'm sorry, Augusta," my father said, taking Harry's place. "I'm sorry I had to go away and leave you."

"Daddy, you should have *told* me," I cried, reaching for him. "I didn't know it would be like this. You should have *told* me!"

He shook his head sadly. "You're a proud, stubborn girl, Augusta. Sometimes you're as bad as Gannon. We pretty much get what we deserve in this world, you know."

"And you had your chance," Uncle Thad thundered. When I whirled toward his voice, he was standing on the other bank with fifteen-year-old Horace beside him. "You had your chance and you refused it. If you had done what any decent, respectable woman would have done, you would have come home and married Horace!''

''But I couldn't—''

A familiar mocking laugh sounded behind me, and when I looked around again, Gannon Murdock stood in my father's place. He was in shirt sleeves, a broad-brimmed hat shadowed his face, and a cigar dangled from his fingers.

''I told you I'd take it all, Gussie,'' he said, with a twisted smile more rueful than triumphant. ''I told you how it would be. The Barony is mine now. All mine.''

''Gannon, please!''

''I also swore that one day I'd have you. But hell—'' He shrugged and turned from me. ''Who would want you now?''

The music faded and the crowd vanished. As Gannon walked away, he passed a man who had been hanged—a young man dangling from a noose tied to a tree limb. Somehow I knew he was Céleste's husband. The bulging eyes in the purple face rolled toward me, the long black tongue lolled from the mouth, and he grinned at me and winked.

And I knew what he meant.

He meant that the joke was on me.

Everything that had happened to me—my husband's desertion, my ''infidelity'' with Harry, my abuse at James Scarborough's hands—*I* was expected to take the blame for it! I was bad, I was fallen, I was ruined, ruined, ruined! Because *they* all said so!

''But it's not fair!'' I screamed. *''It's not fair!''*

No one answered. I was alone with the approaching evil, and now I could almost see my punishment: Paoli's fanged cottonmouth jaws opening wide. And I cried out again, less in fear than in anger, *''It's not fair!''*

Yes, anger. Suddenly I was so *damned* angry! *Filled* with anger! Saving, scalding, healing anger, anger that brought tears, anger that burned and cleansed!

How dared they look down on me so! How dared they judge me with such self-righteousness! How dared they pursue me with their contempt even into my dreams!

I knew then that I had been dreaming, but my anger remained with me and grew even as I awakened. ''It's not fair!'' I cried aloud, and Céleste, who slept beside me during those grim weeks, at once embraced and tried to soothe me: ''Liane! It's all right! You've been dreaming!''

"It's not fair, it's not, it's not!"

How dared they, after all they had done to me! To Melinda! To Céleste!

To Melinda, my childhood friend, my adored cousin, driven to suicide by a father whose love was not bread but a stone.

To Céleste, very nearly driven to suicide by an "honorable" husband who sold her to another man, hanged himself, and left her with nothing but a legacy of guilt.

And to me, Augusta Welles. Abused. Deserted. Raped. Driven to such despair, so diminished in my own eyes that I, too, had attempted suicide.

"It's not fair," I cried out in the dark, as Céleste and I clung together, "it's not fair, and I *won't* let them do this to me! Never, never, never again! I swear to Almighty God, *never again!"*

Men like James Scarborough might find it convenient when their prey simply lay down and died, but I was damned if I was going to be so accommodating! I intended to survive. And suffer not one instant of guilt for doing so. No more accepting the victim's role, no more suffering without striking back. I was going to make my way in the world, and God help the man who tried to stop me. I swore by all the powers of heaven and earth that from that hour forth, I would be the ruler of my own destiny, the mistress of my own fortune.

And then I lay in the dark, wrapped in Céleste's arms, and wept.

My tears must have continued for all of an hour, until I realized that they were no longer the tears of anguish or defiance or self-pity, but of relief. Oh, dear Lord, how good it was to get all that out! I was finished with it, done! I was a different Augusta, a stronger Augusta, no matter what happened to me next! I suddenly felt reborn! Resurrected! Alive!

For a long time afterwards, Céleste and I lay huddled together. We talked quietly and laughed at stupid little jokes, and I enjoyed that wonderful clear-lunged feeling that sometimes follows a good cry. Finally I said, "Céleste, do you know what I've been thinking?" though in truth I had hardly been thinking at all.

"What's that?" she asked.

"I've been thinking it would be stupid for us to sell my designs to someone like Madame Colombier."

The idea had come to me out of the blue. I felt Céleste stiffen at my side and hold her breath.

"Obviously," she said after a moment, as if she knew exactly what I had in mind.

"But we'll need money. I have only a few hundred francs—"

"I've saved a few thousand. Not enough, but I'm sure we can borrow from Harry."

"But I can't ask you to invest all your savings, not if we go halves. That wouldn't be fair to you."

"Nonsense. The designs are yours, and they're the most important thing. But I'm a far better patternmaker and seamstress than you, and I just happen to have a little money."

"Well, if you're sure . . ."

We talked about it. Oh, how we talked that night, laying our plans! In the darkness of that room, a whole new life seemed to be opening up for us both, and I felt a happy excitement such as I had not experienced in ages.

"We have an awful lot of work ahead of us, Céleste."

"Oh, yes."

"I have *got* to stop this moping around! My mother never would have stood for it!"

Céleste laughed softly and yawned.

"Tomorrow I must go to the studio. I'll tell Eugène our plans. He may not like them, but I don't think he'll refuse to help us, do you? . . . Céleste?"

But Céleste was asleep.

I lay awake for some time, contemplating the future. In that first flush of enthusiasm, success seemed inevitable, and I thought of the rewards it might lead to. Security, recognition, satisfaction. And one day maybe . . .

The Barony.

Oh, Lordy, I thought with rising excitement, would it be possible for me to make the Barony mine again? Such an ambition seemed almost too grand to be imagined.

And yet . . . why not? If Gannon could do such a thing, why couldn't I? Why shouldn't I, with Céleste's help, restore my lost fortune, why shouldn't I once again have money and the power that went with it? And when that day came . . .

Yes, I would do it! I would return to America. I would go back to the place of my innocence, the one place on earth I loved above all others, and somehow I would find a way to make it mine again. *So watch out for me, Gannon Murdock* I thought. *Because I'll be back! It may take me half a lifetime* or even longer, but I'll be back and I'll take the Barony from you, one way or another, as surely as you took it from me!

I drifted into sleep, dreaming of a great white house with four chimneys that stood tall against a Carolina sky.

When I awakened, Céleste was gone. Later she said she had known it was all right to leave me, because I was sleeping with a smile on my face.

6 ~~~~~~

Céleste went with me to Eugène's studio that afternoon. "Our intention is quite simple," she told him. "It is to be the very best, the most exclusive, the most successful dressmakers in Paris."

Eugène, lounging back on a sofa like an Oriental potentate, smiled. Though he knew something of my ordeal, he said nothing about it. He radiated warmth and kindness, as if delighted by my return from an arduous journey.

"The *most expensive* dressmakers in Paris," he said.

"Exactly."

Eugène looked at me. "But you must not expect overnight success. It will take you at least a year or two to become established. And meanwhile Liane must continue her studies."

"Oh, I have no intention of stopping them," I said, "ever!"

"Then I'll do what I can to help you. You must be seen in the right places, you must meet the right people. It will be very, very boring for a man of my temperament, and I hope you'll understand what an extraordinary sacrifice I'll be making on your behalf. But somehow I shall force myself to do it in the name of our friendship."

He spoke jestingly, but I knew he more than half meant what he said, and I vowed never to forget his kindness.

Céleste had carefully kept M. Paoli away from my apartment while I was recovering. That evening, when I spoke with him for the first time since my departure for the Scarborough household, I allowed him to see no pain, no humiliation, no weakness in my eyes.

"I'm so sorry," he said with his usual faint, false smile, "so very, very sorry."

Increasingly, M. Paoli made me think of a great sinister doll. His black-button eyes were mindless. Human in form, he was less truly human than he was the wooden puppet of some malevolent force.

"Sorry for what, Monsieur Paoli?" I asked coolly. I stood blocking my doorway.

"Why, for . . . for your . . ."

"For my indisposition, Monsieur Paoli? That's very thoughtful of you, but it's really nothing. I'm quite well now."

"I'm glad. Madame Duhamel, I want you to know . . ."

"Yes, Monsieur Paoli?"

"Perhaps our friend Lord Harry has told you that Monsieur Scarborough departed for London the morning after . . . after your ordeal. But he will find his flight to be futile."

My heart lurched. "I don't understand."

"There is no need to dissemble, dear lady. I know everything that has happened. And I promise you, you shall not go unavenged."

The November night when I had returned to the house and found M. Paoli waiting for me had come to seem like a dream. But now the memory returned in full force. I remembered Paoli's flat, merciless voice as he spoke: *"Mr. Tom Raveneau was found dead . . . stabbed to death in a back alley."* And his parting words, as I turned to go up the steps: *"Now, go to bed, woman, and dream of paying your debt."*

"Monsieur Paoli," I said, struggling to keep my voice level, "I think I have made clear to you that I do not care to have you for my avenging angel."

"Your avenging angel? But no, madame. A debt is owed and I simply pick up the note."

"My notes are not transferable, monsieur, and I'll have no dealings with . . . with . . ."

M. Paoli's hard eyes challenged me. "With what, madame?"

I wanted to say, *"With a common criminal and murderer,"* but I confess I dared not. I found myself merely closing the door, oh, so slowly. And as I leaned on it, my heart racing, I could hear Paoli laughing on the other side.

* * *

I was relieved when, a few days later, Harry returned to Paris. Odd, how that ginger-haired devil who had contributed so much to the misery of my life had come to represent safety to me, but he did. The moment he came through the front doorway, I felt I could snap my fingers at Paoli.

The feeling did not last very long.

As soon as Harry had a few minutes to spare, we met in his office. While he sat behind his great mahogany desk, his hands prayerfully together and the lamplight making the long planes and hollows of his face more satanic than ever, I told him of the plans Céleste and I had made. I half expected sneers and discouragement, but he actually seemed pleased.

"Eugène is right," he said. "It will take you a year or two to become established. We must map out a campaign."

"Then you approve?"

He opened his long-fingered hands. "My dear, I shall regret the loss of the two most charming hostesses in Europe. But I shall watch your ascent to fame and fortune with the most eager curiosity, and I shall do my utmost to help you."

"Sometimes, Harry, I think that, wicked or not, somewhere concealed within your heart you have a hankering to be kind."

"Nonsense. You once accused me of acting out of boredom. You were right. My every act is part of my eternal war against boredom. And now, Augusta, I have some interesting news for you from London."

A grim tightening about his eyes and mouth put me on my guard. "Yes, Harry?"

"It seems that your friend Mr. James Scarborough . . . ."

In that moment of shock there was no elation, no triumph, no sense of justice done. Only a deeply sick feeling and a vision of M. Paoli's dark, soulless eyes.

"Murdered, did you say, Harry?"

"Yes. Tortured and mutilated. His detached parts stuffed into his mouth and his lips sewed shut. It is a peculiarly Mediterranean method of. . . . Augusta?"

I fell forward in my chair, suddenly faint.

"Augusta, are you all right?"

"Yes," I said, when I could speak again. I straightened and sat very quietly for a few moments, breathing deeply and trying to regain my composure.

"I'm not sorry he's dead, Harry. I wanted to kill him myself."

"Of course."

"But to die in such a way . . ."

Guilt sickened me. *I* had wanted to kill James Scarborough in that same barbaric fashion. I had even brought the scissors to his flesh. It was as if Paoli had guessed my thoughts and had had the deed done for me.

"Monsieur Paoli had him killed," I said.

"I should not be at all surprised."

"He seems to think he's my avenging angel. And he's made clear that he expects payment from me."

"Louis always expects payment. And he usually gets it."

I remembered what Céleste had told me more than a year earlier. "Is it true that he's a slaver of women?"

"It is true. I have seen them in the holds of his ships."

Oh, God, I thought, *the infinite villainy of man.* "Harry, something must be done about him."

"Yes, I've been thinking the same thing for quite some time, as a matter of fact."

"But what?"

"Kill him, I suppose."

I was not sure I had heard correctly. *"Kill* him, Harry?"

Harry shrugged. He spoke as casually as if he were making the most ordinary, everyday decision. "I shall miss him, of course. For some reason, Louis has always looked up to me, and that is very flattering. It has allowed me to hold him in check and observe him, and he has made a most interesting pet. But what else can one do when a bad dog starts slipping his leash? Yes, I am afraid the dog must die."

"You don't propose to—to have him . . ."

Harry looked at me and laughed. "To have poor old Louis done in like Jamie? Of course not, Augusta. Sooner or later I shall find a pretext for putting him out of his misery in a perfectly honorable fashion, one that will please him."

For some reason, Gannon Murdock's words echoed in my mind: *"Duels are only for fools, drunks, and gentlemen."*

"Harry, I don't want you to do this for me."

Harry smiled. "You prefer Louis's bed—and a slave ship afterward?"

I had no answer.

"Don't worry, Augusta. I shan't do the deed for your sake only. And the way Louis lives, fate itself may intervene and solve the problem."

*　　*　　*

But I had little time to worry about such things. Céleste and I were too busy launching our new career, and there followed the busiest spring of our lives.

Céleste wanted to rent an atelier and send out notices to all the "best people," but, no, Harry had other plans for us. Any woman with a sewing basket could call herself a dressmaker, he said, but to *show* the public that she was the *première couturière* was altogether a different thing. I had to become quite obviously the best-dressed woman in Paris. Céleste, too, would wear my dresses in public as much as possible, but since I was the designer—the "font of all this beauty," Harry said mockingly—attention must be focused on me. In short, Harry intended by dint of his own efforts—and mine—to make me a public figure.

And I must say we succeeded. Suddenly there was not an evening when I was not at the theater, a dinner party, a fashionable restaurant. Whenever I was not with Harry, he arranged for me to be with some other well-known man-about-town. And Eugène, too, sacrificed considerable time to be with me and did his best to set tongues wagging about this oh-so-gorgeously dressed young beauty with whom everybody wanted to be seen.

But who *was* I, people were soon asking, *what* was I? Why, I was a designer of dresses, said those who knew, and Eugène was quick to affirm that I had no equal in Paris. I did everything in my power to prove that this was true. Every dress I wore I had designed myself, and I can honestly say that each and every one was spectacular. Red silk embroidered with white floral motifs, worn over one of the new crinolines. White silk covered with a green tunic embroidered with gold metalic threads. A riding costume of dark wine broadcloth, with a severe shoulder-wide collar, worn with a matching broad-brimmed, white-plumed hat. Bertha collars of the finest lace, double skirts opening in a triangle in front, all the latest fashions, but each with my own distinctive touch.

There was only one thing wrong with all this activity. It produced no results whatever. In the first six or eight weeks, I received a hundred invitations and a thousand compliments, but barely a hint that anyone might actually buy one of our creations. When Céleste imposed on her friendship with the famous courtesan, Marie Duplessis, by suggesting that the latter would look magnificent in one of our gowns, all she got was a blank stare followed by protestations that, much as Marie admired our work, she had all the dresses she needed.

Surely, I said, it was now time to send out announcements, as Céleste had proposed, and solicit trade. But Harry forbade it. "I don't *want* you to try to obtain commissions! You must continue to be *seen!* You must be *talked about!* You are not just a pretty little dressmaker, you are *the* dressmaker! You are *la belle Liane,* and you don't go running after clients—clients come begging to *you!*"

"Strange, I hadn't noticed."

Putting aside my doubts, I continued to design or sew every hour of the day and appear in public every evening. But as week followed week with no sign of progress, I could not help but feel that there was something fundamentally wrong with our campaign.

Finally the truth dawned on me: Céleste and I simply were not taken seriously as *couturières.* For one thing, though my designs were *à la mode,* they carried the cachet of a distinctly new personality, which put their worth in question. Therefore, until some public favorite took us up—a popular actress, or someone comparable—all others would be reluctant to do so.

But even more limiting was our dubious position in the world. I had become aware of some raised eyebrows and whispered jokes about us—Harry might call us his "hostesses," but we were regarded by many as a pair of cocottes or, at best, *poules de luxe.* How could we expect society to regard us as anything but a passing novelty, *très amusante* but hardly to be taken seriously?

By May, we could scarcely have been more discouraged. But then we had a bit of luck—or so we thought.

Near the end of the month the great composer Gioacchino Rossini, accompanied by his mistress, Olympe Pellisier, arrived in Paris for a four-month stay. Though Rossini had come to consult medical specialists about his health and would spend most of the four months in seclusion, he had literally thousands of visitors during the first and last days of his visit. Thus it was that Harry and Eugène were invited to a dinner party at the Rossini lodgings in the place de la Madeleine, and Céleste and I accompanied them.

I liked Olympe Pellisier—today, of course, she is Mme. Rossini—from the moment we met. At forty-six, she was a round-faced beauty with a small, perfect mouth, fine wide shoulders, and knowing eyes. She had started life, Céleste had told me, as little better than a common prostitute, but her extraordinary beauty, wit, and intelligence had made her the leading courtesan of her time, with one of the most brilliant salons in Paris. Few women had had so many distinguished lovers, but for the last seven years she had attached herself exclusively to Signor Rossini and had devoted all her thoughts and efforts to his well-being.

Like George Sand, Olympe had the gift of drawing one out, and after dinner I found myself sitting with her and Céleste and chattering as if we had been friends for years. I told her how Céleste had taken me to meet Eugène, how much he had taught me in the last year, how Céleste and I aspired to be quite simply the finest *couturières* in the world.

"And the gowns you and Céleste are wearing, Liane—you say you designed them both?"

I nodded. "And Céleste made the patterns."

"You owe it to yourself to see more of Liane's designs while you're in Paris, Olympe," Céleste said.

Almost imperceptibly Olympe stiffened, and for a moment I thought Céleste had gone too far: a dinner party was not the occasion for selling dresses, and I was certain that Olympe's wise eyes saw through us. But then she smiled and said, "Why, of course!"

"I'd be flattered to show them to you. Any time that's convenient for you."

"Well, then—three o'clock tomorrow?"

Was it possible that, after all these weeks, we were about to get our first commission? We were up for hours that night, arranging a portfolio of designs and talking about our prospects. We were so excited, it was dawn before we fell asleep.

The Rossini house was crowded with visitors when we arrived the next afternoon, but Olympe took us to a room where we could be alone and she could look through the portfolio. There was one formal gown she particularly liked: a cloud of gold silk, off the shoulders and quite décolleté, to be worn under a wide mantle of red silk.

"It's beautiful," she said, "but it does look expensive. What would it cost?"

"Four thousand francs," Céleste said.

Olympe almost jumped. "My God, you can't be serious!"

Céleste's face pinkened. "Quite serious. Oh, we could make and sell the gown for much less than that, of course.

But what a shame to take a masterpiece and ruin it with shabby material and poor workmanship. Eugène says that if we use any but the best materials for that gown and have so much as one stitch out of place, he will never again speak to either of us.''

A knowing smile had come to Olympe's face. ''Eugène says that, does he? Well, I'm sure he's proud of his protégées, but . . .'' Olympe shifted some of my designs about on a table, looking at them again. ''Let's face it, I'm a woman of a certain age, and I'm afraid that some of these dresses would be a little young for me.''

''Oh, no,'' Céleste said, ''and certainly not the gold gown!''

''What do you think, Liane?''

''I think you could only make *any* of my dresses look lovelier.''

Olympe threw back her head and laughed—a rich, full laugh. ''I love you both! But four thousand francs for a gown? Oh, darlings, I'm afraid not.''

Céleste's eyes had a slight look of desperation. ''Olympe, may I be frank with you?''

''Why, my dear,'' Olympe teased, ''I had no idea you were being anything else.''

''You know how much it would mean to us to do a dress for you. But if our dresses are expensive, it is simply because we are the best dressmakers you'll ever find—''

''And the most modest!''

''—and we cannot afford to lower our prices. However . . .''

Olympe, still smiling, nodded. ''However . . .''

''As long as you agreed not to tell anyone, I think we might *return* part of the price to you, say a thousand francs—''

''So that I could truthfully say that I had paid all of four thousand francs for my magnificent dress and you could say that you had sold a dress to none other than Olympe Pellisier for that high a price.''

''Exactly.''

Olympe sat chuckling and shaking her head. ''Tell me the truth. How many dresses have you sold?''

''Quite a few. Really, Olympe, does it matter—''

''My dear, can you give me the name of even one satisfied client?''

''Of course.''

''Who?''

Céleste shrugged. ''Marie-Sophie Taglioni.''

Ah, if only I could have lied that smoothly! Olympe repeated the great dancer's last name two or three times as if considering it, then nodded.

"Very well. I shall commission you to do the gold gown for me. I shall pay the full price of four thousand francs—and you shall immediately return *two* thousand to me."

Olympe and Céleste both looked at me as if asking for my agreement. I said, "We shall make you the most beautiful dress in the world!"

We had done it! Received our first commission! Never mind that we had had to cut our price in half and would receive only a fraction of what our labors were worth—we were now truly *couturières,* and with a most distinguished client!

We arranged to take Olympe's measurements and show her swatches of the materials the next morning at eleven. "No, don't bother to come here," she said, "I'll come to see you. It will give me an excuse to get out of this madhouse for an hour or two."

When we were on the street again, I was ready to go home, but Céleste said, No! We must pay a visit to Marie-Sophie Taglioni! And we headed for her house on the place d'Orléans.

"Marie," she said, when we had arrived, "we are so sorry to burst in on you at this late hour in the afternoon, but we are showing a few select friends some of Liane's latest designs, and we simply *must* have your opinion. . . ."

Clearly, of the two of us, Céleste had the talent for trade. When Marie-Sophie pointed to the gold gown, Céleste said in an offhand way, "Oh, yes, that's the one we're doing for Olympe Pellisier," and Marie-Sophie's interest deepened instantly. True, she also winced when she heard our prices, but the promise of a thousand-franc rebate brought a commission for a three-thousand-franc gown.

Two commissions in one afternoon!

We had at last reached a turning point. Now all we had done in the past months—the long days of hard work, the endless evenings of putting ourselves on exhibit and parading our wares—would bring its rewards. One client would lead to another, and each of those to still others, until . . .

There was no telling where it would end. Our designs were the best (We *had* to believe that! Modesty was fatal!), our prices were the highest, and there would be no more rebates. Within a year, I was sure, we would be the most famous, the

most exclusive, the most demanded *couturières* in Paris.
And all we had to do now was to go home, sit down to meals
we were far too excited to eat, and wait through the long next
morning for Olympe's arrival. For that, really, was when it
would all start. With Olympe's arrival.

She never came.

As eleven o'clock became twelve, and twelve became one, I
felt a foreboding, but I tried to keep up hope. Céleste, her
knuckles white as she tore at a linen handkerchief, said,
"She'll be here soon, it's just that she's so busy, and perhaps
Signor Rossini has had an attack." But somehow I could not
believe that. Something had gone wrong, terribly wrong.

At three in the afternoon, a messenger brought a note from
Olympe:

> . . . On reconsideration, I have decided not to go ahead
> with the dress. I am sorry if this comes as a disappoint-
> ment, my dears, but I am certain you will have no
> difficulty in finding another buyer for it. Why don't you
> try the lovely Taglioni? She told me yesterday evening
> that she had expressed interest in the dress to you. Odd,
> but she did not seem to recall the first dress you made for
> her. . . .

So Olympe had found out. I could not tell from the note if
she was amused, angry, or merely annoyed. Whatever the
case, I certainly did not blame her, but I doubted that she had
any idea of how she was punishing us for our little deception.

"It's all *my* fault," Céleste said, tears in her eyes. "If only
I hadn't told her that stupid lie!"

"It wasn't stupid. I suppose it was wrong, but I would
have done the same thing if I had had the chance. And we
could hardly know that she and Marie-Sophie would meet last
night and talk about us."

"All the same . . ."

The second note arrived minutes later:

> . . . have decided to wait until next fall before buying
> any new clothes. By the way, if what Olympe tells me is
> true, it was very naughty of you to use my name as you
> did. . . .

I hardly felt the second blow, for I was still so numb from the first.

"You do know what this means, don't you?" Céleste said bitterly. "By this time, they'll be spreading their funny little story all over Paris. Now no one will *ever* take us seriously. We'll be lucky if we ever sell a dress!"

I tried to reassure Céleste, but I knew she was right. We had all but destroyed our chances for success.

Our fears were justified. When Harry returned to the rue Saint-Honoré that evening, he told us that all fashionable Paris was laughing at the tale of the two little would-be dressmakers who had tried to sell their shoddy goods at the most outrageous prices by telling lies.

"I will grant you that lies make the world go 'round," he said, hiding his anger behind a façade of supercilious boredom. "I will even grant you that if you had got away with it, I would have been amused. But it was nonetheless a foolish thing to do. What on earth made you attempt such a thing?"

"We thought we saw an opportunity to sell—"

Harry's anger began to show through the façade. "I have told you repeatedly that you are not *supposed* to sell your work. Why should you *want* to accept any commissions this spring? People are already leaving Paris for the summer, and the effect would be lost. I did not *want* you to accept any commissions until next autumn, when everybody will be coming back. *Then*, my darling children, *I* would have obtained for you all the commissions you could possibly have handled, and the world would have been yours."

"But we thought if only we could get started this spring—"

"You thought, you thought. Very well, I'll be leaving for England next week, and you can continue to do the thinking for the next few months."

Somehow, despite the bleakness of our spirits, Céleste and I managed to get through the next day. Coward that I was, I could not stand the thought of facing Eugène or George, so I stayed home and, for the first time in weeks, earned some of the money Harry was paying me. He was holding a dinner and card party that evening, so Céleste and I had an excuse not to go out.

There were, as I recall, about a dozen male guests of various nationalities at the party—an American named Jackson, a couple of Englishmen, a German, a Swede, and perhaps three or four Frenchmen. And, of course, M. Paoli.

Céleste and I had little to do until the gentlemen had had their coffee and moved to the card room. Then we were required merely to look pleasant, engage in occasional bantering conversation, and make sure that cigars were lit and glasses were always filled. M. Paoli hardly seemed to notice me, for which I was grateful.

But I should have known he was merely waiting for his moment, as he had done for more than a year. And late in the evening, during a break in the game when the players were relaxing, it came at last.

"Mamzelle Liane," said Mr. Jackson, the American, after I had lit his cigar, "I must say you surely are a fine figure of a woman. Yes, sir, ol' Lord Harry certainly knows how to pick 'em."

"Why, I thank you, monsieur."

"In fact," said Mr. Jackson, winking broadly at the others, "meaning no offense, mamzelle, but you are so special, I don't know but what I wouldn't give a hundred American dollars just to spend a single night with a sweet little lady like you."

I merely smiled. Mr. Jackson was an amiable man, elderly and grizzled. Sober, he probably never would have said such a thing. Besides, Céleste and I had become somewhat hardened to suggestive remarks, and Harry had never allowed anyone to become openly insulting to us. I looked across the room to see if he had heard, but he was deep in conversation with one of the Frenchmen.

"Yes, sir," Mr. Jackson said, grinning up at me, "a hundred dollars for a single night. What do you think of that?"

"She thinks it's insulting," said Mr. Rodale, a young, dapper Englishman. "The very least you could do is make it pounds."

"A hundred pounds," said Herr Peters, the German, pink-faced and porcine, "how much iss dot in German money?"

"More than you can afford, Fritz," Mr. Jackson said, still grinning, and Herr Peters reddened. A few heads turned our way.

"Pounds, francs, dollars—vot ever it iss, I don't care, I bid it!"

"Sorry," I said pleasantly, "not enough."

"Indeed not," said Mr. Pearsall, the older, more courtly Englishman. "Dear Madame Duhamel, I herewith formally tender you an offer of *two* hundred pounds for a single night's exclusive enjoyment of your company with all its unrivaled charms."

"Prettily put, sir, but I fear still not enough."

"Ah, the price of pleasure. Two hundred fifty?"

I smiled and shook my head. By this time, everyone in the room was aware of the mock auction. A little nervous at this turn of events, I looked around for Céleste, but she had left the room some time before.

"Two hundred fifty—my God, what's that in dollars?" asked Mr. Jackson. "Over a thousand?"

Herr Peters was working something out with pencil and paper. "Two hundred seventy-five pounds?" he asked, looking up at me. He sounded as if he meant it.

"Sorry," I said.

"Six thousand francs," said one of the Frenchmen.

It seemed to me that the jest was going a little too far. "Gentlemen, I am afraid that none of you has reached an acceptable price, and the bidding is now closed. If I may pour someone a glass of wine . . ."

"Three hundred fifty pounds," said the dapper Mr. Rodale, and for the first time I saw a glint in his eye as if he, too, might mean what he was saying.

"Gentlemen," I protested, "I am *not* for sale!" but it was as if my words went unheard.

"Four hundred," said Herr Peters.

"Four hundred fifty—"

"Six hundred," Paoli broke in, his voice strong and hard. "Six hundred pounds for one night, payable in any currency the lady wishes."

The room became completely quiet. Every eye but Harry's turned toward Paoli, and Paoli's gaze held mine. His face was stiff and challenging, a muscle twitching in his cheek, no trace of a smile. This was the moment he had waited so long for, come at last. There was not the slightest doubt that he meant what he said, that he meant to have what he bid for, and everyone in the room knew it.

"Hey, Harry," Mr. Jackson called nervously across the room. "Did you hear what Louis said? He's willing to pay your lady friend here six hundred pounds for a single night."

Harry, help me!

Harry looked around indifferently. He shrugged, then turned a contemptuous eye on me. "Whatever the market will bear, I suppose. You can hardly blame the poor working girl for turning an occasional honest penny."

For a moment I went numb with shock. He meant it! He was angry with me over the matter of the dresses, he was tired of the game he had been playing, and he was casting me off. He was letting Paoli have me.

Paoli rose to his feet and glared about the room as if defying anyone to outbid him. "Six hundred pounds," he said in a low hard voice. "Six hundred pounds for a single night."

No. I would not let him do this to me. Not Paoli, not Harry. I felt a rising tide of anger, but I dared not let it show.

"No, Monsieur Paoli," I said as gently as possible. "Not for six hundred pounds or for ten times that much, and you need bid no longer."

Paoli's face paled, and his eyes seemed to burn with hellfire. His shoulders bunched powerfully as he reached for the cane that was never far from his hand. "And why is my money not as good as any other man's?"

I tried to keep my voice as sweet and reasonable as possible, but my anger would not be denied. "Because I do not like you, Monsieur Paoli." I felt a wave of consternation go through the room at this insult, but I went on: "I have said that I am not for sale. But even if I were, no price in the world would put me into your arms. I would die first, Monsieur Paoli—or you would."

My words seemed to sweep through the room like a whirlwind, as everyone moved and spoke at once. Then Paoli stepped toward me, staggering as if he had been struck.

"You dare to insult me!"

"I repeat: I do not like you, Monsieur Paoli. No, more than that, I despise you beyond all other men."

"I have warned you, madame. And now I have bid six hundred pounds, and you shall honor—"

"A thousand pounds," Adam Trevayne said quietly, stepping into the room. "I bid a thousand pounds. For a single night."

Oh, no, I thought, why had he returned at this moment? I would willingly have gone to Paoli with a knife beneath my cloak, rather than have Adam endangered. But I could not will Adam away. He stood by the door as casually as if this were the most ordinary evening imaginable.

"A thousand pounds," he repeated.

Once again the room was silent. Harry's eyes were bright with amusement. For a few seconds, Paoli merely gaped. Then: "You are too late, monsieur," he said. "The bidding is closed."

"A thousand pounds—"

"A thousand pounds has it," I said.

"You continue to mock me, madame—"

"The lady says a thousand pounds has it," Adam said, his gaze never leaving Paoli.

"The *lady!*" Paoli exploded. "Then take your *lady,* monsieur, but I shall have her at my pleasure. I buy and sell better than she, and a whore is a whore at any price. Have her as my gift to you, monsieur, and when we are *both* done with her, perhaps she will still fetch a few pesos in South America!"

As Adam rushed forward, Paoli stepped back and raised his cane, gave the handle a twist and showed steel—a swordcane! At the same moment, Harry threw a table aside and rushed toward Paoli, and I realized this was the moment that he, too, had awaited: the moment when Paoli was vulnerable. His indifference to me had been a pose, a bluff, to lead Paoli on, and now—

But Adam reached Paoli first. As Paoli tried to draw the sword, Adam snatched the cane from his hands and slammed the blade back into place. I cried out as a tall Frenchman, Paoli's lieutenant, drew a pistol and pulled back the cock. Adam twisted toward him, bringing the cane down on his wrist, and the Frenchman screamed as his wrist broke and the falling gun exploded harmlessly. Without an instant's pause, Adam took the cane in two hands and brought it down against the edge of a table, snapping both the blade and the sheath. He tossed the pieces aside in a gesture as casual as his entrance into the room, and turned to Paoli.

"Your pleasure, monsieur?"

For a dangerous man, Paoli suddenly looked surprisingly helpless. But appearances were deceptive.

"Pistols, I think," he said. "But our seconds will discuss the matter."

"As you wish. And now if you will kindly pardon me . . ."

For the first time since entering the room, Adam turned to me. And smiled.

7 ~~~~~

Paoli left the house at once.

"I say, Adam, old boy," Harry said a few minutes later, "are you very good at killing people?"

"I don't know, Harry. I've never done it before."

"Pity. It's not very difficult, actually, once you get the hang of it. But the first time . . ." Harry shrugged. "Ah, well, tomorrow I shall coach you. I shall be your second, of course."

"How disappointing for poor Louis!"

The party was over. The guests had either gone to their rooms or departed for their own homes. Now Harry left for his apartment, whistling like a schoolboy, and Adam and I found ourselves alone together in the same small drawing room where we had talked the previous November. Without a word, we walked into each other's embrace, not to kiss but merely to cling together.

"You are mad," I said, "completely mad to challenge that terrible man. Oh, Adam, I'm so frightened!"

"Don't be, my darling. Time the world was rid of him."

"But if he should hurt you—"

"He won't."

He lifted my face then and kissed me, and I melted in his arms, melted like snow in a warm spring rain.

"Augusta, Céleste told me," he said a moment later. "She told me something of what you've been through. About Tom's death . . . and about Scarborough . . ."

"Don't speak of it. That's over, that's past."

"I never should have left you here. But you're free now, Augusta, and this time I shall not leave Paris without you."

Slowly, I withdrew from his arms and sat down on a sofa. I was remembering something Harry had said to me.

"What will you do with me, Adam? Tuck me away in a comfortable little villa in St. John's Wood?"

"My darling, I only know that after I've finished with Paoli, I'm going to take you away from here, and I'm going to keep you where you'll be safe forever."

"Safe, Adam? Is there any place in the world that is safe forever?"

"I'm going to hide you from the world, my darling—"

"No. There is no way to hide from the world. Oh, for a few hours, perhaps—a day of peace, a night of love—but then it always finds you."

"I shall protect you, I swear!"

I shook my head. "We mustn't let ourselves be blinded by sentiment, Adam. I've let that happen to me too often. If the day ever comes when we can love each other freely and fully, love each other as equals, with no shadow of another between us . . . well, we'll see then. But until that day comes, I must take care of myself, my darling. And I have sworn that I shall do so."

"But how can you, a woman alone in a man's world?"

I laughed. "I don't know. And I must admit that so far I've made a poor job of it."

He wanted to argue, but when he tried, I leaned forward to press my lips against his, and felt the star-filled whirl of the heavens.

"Augusta," he said, when our mouths had parted, "I'm staying at my friend's apartment again. Stay with me there tonight."

I hesitated, torn. I wanted to be with Adam, but in spite of the feelings his kisses brought to me . . .

How could I explain to him something I myself hardly understood, something I had tried desperately not even to think about since that terrible night in the Scarborough house? How could I explain to him the coldness that, until this very night, had invaded my body? How could I make him understand the fearful shrinking in on myself, the hardness within me that had replaced all tenderness, the sensation of cold stone and acid that was at my very core?

In the face of that, how could I ever be what he wanted me to be, what *I* wanted to be *for* him?

". . . Adam, I just don't think it's time yet."

He reached out to touch my cheek. "My darling, I know you've been through a terrible experience. Perhaps one beyond any man's full comprehension. But I've felt your lips on mine, I've felt you trembling in my arms, and I think you're wrong. There does come a time for healing, and I think the time is now.''

"Oh, if only I could believe that—"

"Believe it. I told you last November that I wanted to make love to you as you have never been made love to before in your life. I'm going to do that, Augusta. I'm going to make love to you before I leave Paris, and when I do leave, I pray you'll leave with me.''

"But not tonight, Adam, please?" I begged as he embraced me again. "Let me dream of it a little first."

"Yes, darling. Dream of it. And so shall I. . . ."

I lay awake late, and slept late, and when I arose, Céleste had long been up.

"Welcome to the day, sleepy head," she said as I entered the drawing room where she was having coffee. "Do you know it's almost noon?"

"What's happening? Where's Harry? Has Adam sent any message?"

Céleste handed me an envelope. I took out the note and read it.

My Dearest,

Harry and Mr. Jackson have met with Paoli's seconds. They have agreed that Paoli and I shall face each other tomorrow at dawn in the Bois de Boulogne. So I now have the virtually impossible task of putting my affairs in order, and I shall be tied up every minute with lawyers.

Harry tells me he is giving an informal supper party for me at his "hunting lodge" this evening. The guest of honor will necessarily be quite late, if indeed he can attend at all, but will you wait for me there? I promise you that, if at all possible, I shall come to you.

With all my deepest love, my darling, until we meet again and for all time beyond,

Your Adam

My knees went weak as I read, and I had to sit down.

"Oh, my God, it really is going to happen, isn't it!"

"Yes, my dear," Céleste said gravely, "it really is going to happen."

"Do you think Adam has any chance at all against Monsieur Paoli?"

Céleste patted my hand. "Of course he does. Harry says Adam is an excellent shot. He will be all right."

"Adam says there's to be a supper party."

"Yes, I've been attending to the invitation list."

I tried to smile. "Not an Adam-and-Eve night, I hope."

Céleste laughed. "No, nothing like that. Just food and drink and perhaps a little dancing, and a few people staying overnight. Just an ordinary country evening."

Ordinary: waiting for two men to fire on each other, to wound and perhaps to die.

I dreaded returning to Harry's château, but when I arrived, it was as if I were seeing the big, rambling ivy-covered mansion for the first time. Guests wandered over well-tended lawns and through spring-fresh gardens and groves. A small orchestra played under a peaked pavilion of green and yellow canvas, and the fountain of stone nymphs and fauns sent water sparkling high into the bright, clear air. The place held no memory of the night I had spent there more than a year earlier.

My thoughts were entirely on Adam, and I recall little of the hours that followed. People came and went. The sun began to paint the sky pink, mauve, and indigo. The sound of the orchestra, playing unceasingly, frayed my nerves. Suddenly I was painfully hungry, and yet the smell of food nauseated me: after a few bites, I fled from the dining room. *Adam, Adam,* I thought, *when are you coming to me?*

The evening wore on and the party grew smaller and quieter. The musicians were dismissed. Those guests who had come expecting some kind of Dionysian revels before death at sunrise were disappointed. Yet the thought of what was to come did have an odd effect on the party, as if this night presaged the last night for all of us, and life must be seized while we still had it. Eugène was there with his cousin and sometime mistress, the Baronne de Forget: they would share a bedchamber, and from the way she clung to his arm, I knew he would have an exciting partner that night.

The evening lengthened, and it became evident that Adam would not appear. Though disappointed, I thought it was probably just as well: he would need all his strength, his energy, his concentration at dawn. One by one, or in pairs, the guests went up the stairs, I among them.

I could not sleep; too many thoughts whirled through my

head. Where was Adam at this moment, what would happen tomorrow, what would my life be if he died? Finally I slid out of bed, pulled back the drapes, and flung wide the windows. Settling down in a chair, I looked out at the moonlight, brilliant on treetops and fields.

How long did I sit there? Once I thought I heard a carriage, perhaps a guest departing. Then, a little later, music floated through the air, the distant sound of a piano.

For a moment I thought I was dreaming. The moonlight was more brilliant than ever. Where was the music coming from? It drifted through the night as if somewhere outside an angel were playing. And the melody was so familiar. . . .

The "Moonlight Sonata"!

I leapt from my chair. This was no dream! I found my slippers and, tying my robe around me, hurried out into the hall. There the music was much fainter, but once again I followed it, as I had done at Huxton Hall on that night so long ago. Along the dark passage I went, and down the stairs, the music growing a little louder with each step. . . .

The music room was on the same side of the château as my bedchamber. The windows nearest the piano had been opened wide. And at the piano, playing, sat Adam.

Oh, how it all came back to me then! He had been wearing a robe that night at Huxton Hall, and nothing more. He had risen from the piano and come to me, he had held me in his arms and kissed me and moved his hand over my bare breast, he had laid me back on a couch and thrown open his robe and—

I knew what he was here for, I knew what he wanted, but I was not ready! My wounds were still too new, still unhealed!

With a cry, I ran from the room.

I did not run for my bedchamber, I simply ran, ran, ran through one doorway and out another, out of the château, down the steps and into the moonlit gardens—ran so hard that a slipper went flying off behind me.

I did not stop until I reached the fountain, still throwing its jet of water high into the air. There I leaned back against the fountain's basin wall to catch my breath. Under the brilliant moon, the clearing around the fountain was bright as day. Except for the cool sound of falling water, the night was silent.

Fool, fool, fool! I thought. *You* know *you want him! Fool! Hypocrite! Coward!*

My breath calmed—then caught, as I saw something dimly white and ghostlike moving in the shadows of some trees.

Adam emerged into the moonlight. He was wearing only dark pants and a white shirt, and a gentle breeze lifted his wide Byronic collar and billowed his full sleeves. In one hand he held my missing slipper. I did not breathe as he crossed the clearing toward me.

Holding up the slipper, he smiled at me. Then he knelt and took my bare foot into his hand. "Such a narrow foot," he said, as if to himself, "so fine-boned, so delicate." When his lips brushed over the arched surface, a deep, warm shiver ran through me.

He put the slipper back on my foot. He stood up, keeping his hands away from me, careful not to touch me further.

"Are you really so afraid, Augusta?"

"Oh, Adam, it's just that . . . I'm not sure . . ."

Slowly, as if afraid he might startle me, he put a finger under my chin and tilted my head back. He lowered his head toward mine, giving me time to turn away if I wished. Our lips met, and his kiss seemed to flow, hot and burning, into every hidden part of my body.

"Not sure, Augusta?"

I could hardly speak. "If you knew how I've fought loving you . . ."

His lips stilled mine again. His fingers moved around my throat to the nape of my neck, then down beneath my robe and gown. Slowly, very slowly, as he kissed me, his hand moved robe and gown aside, his palm covering my bare shoulder.

"Are you fighting me now, Augusta?"

"Oh, Adam, I don't know! I don't know what I want! I don't know—"

"Then let me teach you."

Our mouths met a third time. As his arm went around my back and drew me closer to him, the hand on my shoulder slipped down to cup my breast and flick the rising nipple. Moaning, I found my arms encircling his waist and pulling him closer to me. "I love you," he whispered, his lips against mine, "I love you, my darling, so much, and now at last . . ."

My hands slid under his shirt and up his back, and, oh, God, I thought, he was everything I had ever imagined he would be, everything I had ever dreamed of, and how could I resist him? My robe came open, and I found myself arching against him, swaying and pressing, seeking the hard power of his body. As I drew his shirt over his head, he sent silk and lace slithering over my body, drawing it over my aching breasts and between my longing thighs, kissing me, stroking me, tasting every part of me, first through the thin fabric and then under it, searching out every secret, every tender bud and fold and hiding place, leaving nothing unkissed, unawakened, undelighted.

I felt him unveil me further, felt his buckle loosen, and what mattered my dim protests? I was powerless to resist. . . .

Only when he swept me away from the fountain did I realize that he had cast off the rest of his clothing. Then, lying back on the soft grass, my gown in complete disarray, I saw him as I had not since that night so long ago at Huxton Hall—once again the Greek god leaning over me in the moonlight, but a god of warm, powerful, desiring flesh, a god of bone and muscle and blood.

His words came back to me: *"I'll make love to you as I've never before made love to any woman. You are the temple wherein I'll worship. . . ."*

Even as I protested, "No, no, no!" I reached for him and drew him to me between the gateway of my raised thighs. His body cast a moon-shadow across me, and in the darkness between us, I led the worshiper to the door of the temple. For a moment the worshiper lingered there, pressed to the door, a moment of the most ecstatic dread and anticipation.

And suddenly all remaining fear, all reluctance, all restraint was swept away. I *wanted* him to make love to me! How long, how long it had been! How long since I had given myself up thoughtlessly, mindlessly, heedlessly to love! How long since I had been in the arms of a man I truly cared for and desired! How long since I had been with a man who was neither devil nor demon but simply my caring, needing, passionate lover!

The door opened and the worshiper entered, entered to the farthest reach.

Why had I feared this, I wondered afterward, when we lay quietly in each other's arms, listening to the soft babble of the fountain. James Scarborough and Harry had ceased to matter. Even Tom had become part of a past so distant that the pain he had given me had vanished. I knew now I was still capable of love, and I had Adam, and nothing the future might bring mattered in the slightest as long as I did not lose him.

A little later he found his clothes and slung them over his shoulders, then picked me up, cradling me in his arms. Still naked, he carried me back to the château, through the front hall, and up the stairs to my room, as indifferent to being seen as if he were some pagan prince.

In my room he pulled the remains of my tattered gown off—stripped me naked and washed away the stains of our late-night frolic, while we whispered and laughed like naughty children. When we were clean, he lay back on pillows in the middle of the bed and drew me into his arms.

"Do you love me?" he asked, his touch moving over everything intimate that was now his.

"Oh, yes, yes, I do love you, Adam."

"Tomorrow, darling, I'm going to ask you to leave Paris with me—"

"Ask me now, Adam, ask me now!"

"No. I don't want you to answer because of the magic of the night or from fear of the dawn. I'll ask you tomorrow, darling, when the worst is over. And I want you to know that even if you refuse me, I shall not cease to love you. I'll return to you again and again, you'll never be free of me, and one day I shall take you away to our Greek isle, and there I shall . . ."

"Oh, dear Adam . . ."

I made love to him then, as fiercely as he had made love to me. Kissed him until his body glistened in the moonlight, made every part of him tremble with pleasure and desire, led him to the brink and back from it and to the brink again. Tried to repay him in the only way I knew how for his kindness and love and the great gift of himself. Tried to give joy and take it, as never before in my life.

Then, in his arms and exhausted at last, I sank into sleep. Sank down, down into peaceful darkness.

But there was no escaping M. Paoli, not even in sleep, and he came to me that night like a creature from hell.

But such a strange creature. He loomed over me, a huge wooden doll, brightly enameled and hinged at the hips, a sinister and monstrous doll contrived by the Devil himself. He was standing at the top of a grassy slope, staring down at me. I was unable to tear my gaze away from his dark unblinking eyes. Slowly, at first, he moved. He took one step forward toward me on the slope, stiff-legged. Then he lurched another step. And another and another, tottering from side to side, faster and faster, while I stood directly before him. Adam was trying to drag me out of Paoli's path, and I was trying to protect Adam, but I could not move, and the giant doll of M. Paoli was lurching ever-faster toward us, to fall on us and crush us, to destroy us. . . .

"Liane! Liane, you're dreaming! You're dreaming, dear, wake up!

I awakened, gasping and crying and tearing at the sheet. Céleste was holding me in her arms; I clung to her.

"It's all right, Liane, dear, it's all right. . . ."

Gradually I calmed, but the nightmare feeling stayed with me. Paoli would destroy me, he would destroy Adam. . . .

Adam! What had happened to him? I rolled out of Céleste's arms and looked around. Where Adam had been, there now lay only low-slanted moonlight.

"Where is he, where's Adam? Oh, Céleste, what's happened? What time is it?"

"I don't know. Almost four, I think. They've gone, dear . . ."

Almost four! It would soon be dawn!

"But why did no one awaken me?"

"They thought it best if you slept until . . . after."

I leapt from the bed. "How long ago did they leave?"

"A half-hour or so, not long—"

The thought that something might happen to Adam and that I would not be there was unbearable. "I can't stay here! I've got to find them!"

"I told them you'd say that. If I were you, I'd want to be there too."

"Then help me! We've got to hurry! We've got to find them before . . ."

We dressed hastily and hurried out to the stables, rousing up a sleepy-eyed boy to help us. Most of the carriages were gone, but we found a small, light cabriolet which the boy soon had hitched to a horse. Harry's château was to the north of Paris, and the Bois de Boulogne was to the west, a considerable distance away, but fortunately Céleste was familiar with the roads. She would drive.

The ride seemed endless. Long before we reached the Bois the sun was staining the eastern horizon. Céleste assured me that, large though the Bois was, there were not many places where duels were held, and she would have no difficulty finding Adam and the others. But by the time we entered the forest, it had filled with a deep fog that became strangely luminescent as the sun rose higher.

"I can hardly see the road," I said. "How will we ever find them?"

"Don't worry. Perhaps the fog will delay—"

Ahead of us, two pistol-shots sounded, one on the other so quickly as to seem almost one, and I cried out as if I were the victim. Adam, for all I knew, was at that very moment lying dead or dying.

"Look!" Céleste said. "Look ahead!"

We could barely make them out at first, but as we got closer, the fog thinned. There were some two dozen men, divided into several groups. Two of the men, one of them tall and slim, the other short and stocky, were in shirt sleeves, and I recognized Adam.

"Oh, thank God," I cried out in relief, "it's over! And he isn't hurt!"

"No, Liane," Céleste said worriedly, as she reined up. "I don't think it is over . . . yet."

Eugène was hurrying to me as I stepped down from the carriage. "Eugène, he's all right, isn't he? Let me go to him, I must speak to him, I must—"

"No!" Eugène said sharply. "You shouldn't be here. You'll only upset him."

"But it's all over, surely it's over—"

"No, it's not over! Paoli was barely scratched and Adam not hurt at all. Paoli insists on continuing. There will be at least one more . . ."

He broke off as a stillness settled over the party. Adam and Paoli stood fifty feet apart, each with his right side to the other, pistols aimed at the heavens. Paoli's seconds and friends backed away from him and moved toward the center ground. Harry and Mr. Jackson and some others moved away from Adam. Fog swirled between Adam and Paoli but not so thickly as to hide them from one another.

"Stop them!" I said, "Eugène, you must stop—"

His hand covered my mouth.

A judge called out a signal: *"Allez-y!"*

Everything happened so slowly and yet so quickly: The pistols swung down on extended arms. The pause of a fraction of a second seemed to go on and on—until broken by the crash of the pistols, each spitting a hot red flame.

Adam's body lifted, twisted, fell back.

I screamed.

Harry ran and caught Adam before he hit the ground. Blood was pouring from his side, staining his shirt. I was at his side without knowing how I had gotten there.

"Easy, old boy," Harry said.

"A flesh wound, I think," Adam said, his voice strained. "A flesh wound, nothing more."

"Best let the doctor look at it."

Adam gave no sign that he was aware of my presence. His eyes never left Paoli, who stood grinning across the fifty-foot clearing.

"A crippling shot, my friend," Paoli called, "but I leave you with your life." He nodded toward me. "And I claim the prize."

"We're not finished yet, Paoli," Adam said.

Paoli laughed. "As you wish, my friend."

Eugène dragged me to one side, and I watched with horror as Harry and Mr. Jackson steadied Adam on his feet and a doctor tore away his shirt to bind a pad to his ball-torn side. I was weeping, crying out, begging with no real idea of what I was saying. I knew only that this deadly game must end, and I would have done anything in my power to end it. I would have given Paoli his night. I would have faced him with a pistol myself. But nothing I could say or do would stop what was happening: a judge put another pistol into Adam's hand and pointed it skyward, as if Adam lacked the strength to lift it himself. Someone put a pistol into Paoli's hand, and once again everyone was backing away from the two duelists.

"Allez-y!"

Again the pistols swung down. Adam looked as if he were about to fall forward on the ground. Paoli's pistol held level, but Adam's did not, and they both went off, booming and spitting flame.

Adam fell back. And this time, Harry failed to catch him.

Crying his name, I ran to him, and no one had to tell me his fate—I knew the moment I reached him. His chest was already bathed in blood, and when he tried to raise his head, crimson poured from a corner of his mouth. The doctor did not try to stop me when I gathered him into my arms. When I looked up, the doctor nodded slowly, his face grim.

" 'Fraid he got me, Augusta." Adam's face was ashen, his voice a whisper.

"Don't try to talk, darling, it's all right, don't talk!"

"Want to talk. Must tell you once more . . . I love you. One last time."

"No! You're going to be all right, it's not bad, darling, I'll nurse you, I'll take you back to England as soon as you're well, I'll take you back and never leave you."

" 'Fraid not. 'Fraid it's me leaving you, but—but—"

"Hush, darling, no, you're not leaving me!"

"Did I get him for you, Augusta? Did I get Paoli?"

"Oh, yes, sweetheart," I lied, "yes, you did get him, and he'll never bother us again! Never, ever again!"

"Then you're safe. That's what matters, darling. You're safe. Don't mind dying so much, if I know you're safe."

"You're not going to die, my darling. I love you too much ever to let you die!"

". . . love you . . . darling . . . Augusta."

He died.

There in my arms in the Bois de Boulogne, while the dawn fog still swirled about us.

They tried to lift me away from him, but, failing, let me cling to him for a time. I was only dimly aware of what happened next, and I don't know now if I remember truly or if I only imagine certain things I have been told. I *do* remember that Harry, kneeling near me, stood up and walked away. He said something then, and it might be that I really do remember his words: "I say, old boy, wouldn't care to try your luck twice on the same morning, would you?"

Paoli's laughter, after a moment, was loud and sharp. "I have been expecting this, Harry. I have seen it coming ever since you welcomed the whore into your house."

"Of course. It's no surprise to either of us. Our dear friend Adam was only an intruder in our little contest. This morning was meant for us all along."

I suppose I did hear the pistols going off.

It was later, when my tears had ceased to flow but still lay wet on my cheeks, that Harry touched my shoulder.

"He's dead, Harry," I said.

"I know, dear girl. But he won't go to hell unaccompanied. The dog trots quickly after him."

I let Adam go then. I released him gently, laying his head back on the ground, and, with Harry's help, stood up. He held me swaying in his arms. I looked across the field of honor to where M. Paoli, too, lay on the ground, propped up in his seconds' arms. Even through the fog I could see those soulless black-button eyes.

Shrugging off Harry's hands, I walked toward Paoli. His eyes stayed on me every instant until I was standing directly over him.

"Whore!" he suddenly said, his voice harsh with loathing. "Whore! Pig! Filth! That I, Louis Paoli, should die for such as you! You—you—you—" He searched desperately for the filthiest, most dishonorable name he could possibly call me. "You . . . *woman!*"

I leaned down over him. I smiled. With all my strength, I struck the dying man's face.

BOOK FOUR

A Woman of Independence

~~~~~~

To strive, to seek, to find, and not to yield.
—Alfred, Lord Tennyson, "Ulysses"

A life without love . . . is nothing but a mere magic-lantern show.
—Goethe, *Elective Affinities*

1 ~~~~~~

I remember little of the rest of that day. Harry put me into his carriage and took me back to Paris in a state of near-collapse. As Céleste helped me up to my apartment, all I could think was that Adam was dead . . . Adam was dead. We had shared our love for such a little time, and now he was taken from me forever. Adam was dead. . . .

I awakened the next day to find that I was, if not famous, then certainly notorious. Two duels had been fought over me on a single morning, and two men had died. No longer was I Liane the supposed cocotte, one of the wicked Englishman's harem. Oh, no, now I was Liane the dangerous beauty. I was Mme. Duhamel the grand courtesan for whom men went to their graves. I was *la belle dame sans merci*. And all at the cost of Adam's life.

That afternoon I began to understand the full import of what had happened. First there was a note from Olympe:

> . . . poor, dear child . . . my deepest sympathies . . . and if I can be of help to you in any way . . .
> . . . and about that dress, dear, I find that I simply *cannot bear* to do without it. Now, you remember that it's mine, and don't you dare sell it to anyone else, because I want you to go ahead with it at once. And, dear child, if you should need me . . .

It was very kind of Olympe, I thought, but of course I could not let her spend so much money on one of my dresses merely out of sympathy.

But then, once again, there followed very quickly a note from Marie-Sophie Taglioni:

> . . . afraid you misunderstood me completely about the dress. . . . didn't intend to cancel the order but merely

to put it off until next fall! But darlings, I find I cannot wait. . . .

A little later Céleste came to my apartment. Her face was pale, her eyes large and unfocused. "People keep coming and asking for you," she said. "A lot of them, we hardly know at all. I tell them you're not ready to receive visitors, and—and, Liane . . ." There was no triumph in her voice, no jubilance, and she looked close to tears. "The women . . . half of them . . . all they really want to talk about is your dresses. They want to see your designs. Some would place orders right now, if they could. They have even offered me money to put them first."

Wickedness, death, and scandal had won the prize where all our efforts had failed. Success was ours, if only we cared to grasp it. But how could we care at that hour? How could we care at that price?

My mourning was necessarily private, if not solitary. I could hardly accompany Adam's body back to England, but neither could I bear to stay in Paris. And so, after a few days, I boarded a railway train for the first time in my life and, at George Sand's invitation, set off for Nohant.

We lived quietly that summer, George and Frédéric and I. George's son, twenty-year-old Maurice, was away visiting his father. Her daughter, fifteen-year-old Solange, had been left at her boarding school in Paris. There were few visitors, though Eugène came down for a few delightful days. Frédéric spent hours at his piano, and George lounged about the house in a dressing gown, when she was not hard at work on her new novel, *La Comtesse de Rudolstadt*. When the weather was good, I put my hair up in braids and, with George's encouragement, donned pants and spent hours roaming the countryside. I soon had an unfashionable spray of freckles over the bridge of my nose, but I could not have cared less. One day we went on an outing together, George on foot, Frédéric on a donkey, and I on a horse. I delighted George and terrified Frédéric by jumping timber while riding astride and bareback. After that, George took to introducing me as "Pocahontas, my wild Indian daughter."

Only one disturbing incident occurred during my visit. Toward the end of July, I happened to be out in front of the house one afternoon, when a carriage arrived in the courtyard. One of the two men in the carriage was wearing a pearl-gray broad-brimmed hat. It was one of those nightmare moments when one thinks: *This cannot be!* I had had hardly a glimpse of him—those dark, heavy-browed eyes, that strong jaw—when I whirled through the front doorway and slammed the door shut behind me. I rushed to find George.

"Please, you've got to help me!"

George's eyes widened. "Liane, what is it?"

"There's a man outside! I'm almost certain he's an American, a man named Gannon Murdock. I can't think why he would be here, except—to look for me! Please, George, don't tell him I'm here. Tell him I left a few days ago for—for Italy!"

There was a knock at the front door, and I hurried away to hide on the staircase.

I could hear little of the conversation down below, but I was right: the visitor was Gannon Murdock. He spoke a crude but serviceable French, and when that was not sufficient, his companion translated. Unable to follow the conversation, I went to a front window and waited almost two hours, until the carriage rolled out of the courtyard and disappeared down the road.

"What a charming man," George said mischievously when I went back downstairs. "And what a pity I couldn't persuade him to stay longer!"

"George, please, what did he say!"

"Apparently he was very fond of your Adam, and he's extremely curious about this mysterious Liane Duhamel his dear friend died for. He's been in Paris, looking for her and questioning everyone who knows her. He's talked to Eugène and Céleste and goodness knows who else."

For a moment I could only hold my breath. The good Lord only knew what tales, both true and false, Gannon might hear about Liane Duhamel. And if he were to uncover her true identity, if the good people of Charleston were ever to learn that their own Augusta Welles Raveneau was supposedly a notorious Parisian courtesan . . .

"What did he find out?"

"Very little, apparently. He says he has to return to America soon, but someone told him Liane had come to Nohant to visit me, and so . . . ." George shook her head in puzzlement. "Dear child, I don't understand. Why should you go to such lengths to avoid the man?"

In the next hour I told her in strictest confidence more about myself than I ever had before.

"An American? Oh, my God, Pocahontas, and I never guessed! What a serial I could write for the *Revue indépendante—*"

"George, no, you promised!"

"—but nobody would ever believe it!"

A few days later, in August, I felt ready to leave Nohant. The evening before my departure was star-strewn, with a quarter-moon low in the sky, and as we wandered about the front courtyard enjoying the fresh country air, I told George of my intention to visit Adam's grave.

"I know you still feel the pain," she said, taking my hand, "and you will continue to feel it for a long time to come. But believe me when I promise you, Liane, one day there will be another love in your life."

I shrugged. "Perhaps. But why should I want one? I've already known the best and the worst of love."

"It's true," George said, "that you have been through far more than most women your age, but to give up love . . ."

I laughed. "Oh, I won't 'give up love,' George, any more than you have. But I don't think love will find me again very soon, either. Meanwhile, I'll be like Céleste. I'll have my dear, good friends, and if I wish, I may even take a lover now and then, and I shall care for all of them very much. But no more than that."

"And you think that will be enough for you?"

"George, even before Adam died, I vowed that never again would I be at the mercy of men. I swore that, one way or another, I would make my own fortune, and that's what I'm going to do. When I left Paris, I was too sick with grief even to think of such things. But no longer. I'm going back there, and I'm going to bring that city to its knees. You're going to be proud of me, George."

She put an arm around my shoulders and hugged me. "Pocahontas, I am already proud of you."

I arrived back in Paris to find a new life awaiting me. Céleste had proceeded to set up our dressmaking business, and she was hard at work and aglow with the pleasure of it. She had rented an atelier not far from Eugène's studio, and as she led me through the reception room and past the offices to the big workroom with its cutting tables and bolts of fabric and mannequins and screens and half a dozen seamstresses hard at work, I had a feeling of awed disbelief. All this was *ours!*

"I hope you approve," Céleste said anxiously. "These women are the very best I could find. You may think I'm overpaying them, but I don't tolerate the slightest flaw in their work. And Liane, there is so much to do! Everyone is getting ready for the fall season, and your dresses are in such demand—"

"Oh, you make me feel so guilty for going to England right now!"

"No, don't. I know it's something you have to do. I'll keep things going, and when you get back—Liane, would you like to share an apartment with me? I've been looking at some places, and there's a nice one very near here. . . ."

Never in the wildest dreams of my childhood would it have occurred to me that one day I would be a young business-woman in Paris, sharing an apartment with her best friend, a French countess!

The next day I left for England, with one of Harry's maids as my traveling companion. We were crossing the Channel, on a day so clear we could all but see France behind and England ahead, when Lisette, the maid, took out a poke of breadcrumbs and, standing by the rail of the packet, started throwing them to the gulls that circled in graceful arcs against the cloudless sky. As I listened to the gulls' cries and watched them plucking the crumbs from midair, a marvelous thought came to me. With an almost painful surge of happiness, I realized for the first time that I was *free!* I was no longer dependent upon Harry's bounty. M. Paoli's threatening shadow no longer lay over me. I no longer had a husband or even an overly protective lover to keep me from doing exactly as I pleased. I was earning my own way by doing work I enjoyed, and I could come and go when and wherever I wished. I was free as the gulls themselves, and who on this earth had any right to ask for more? When Lisette noticed the smile on my face, it so pleased her that she laughed aloud. It seemed immoral to be happy so soon after Adam's death, but I could not help myself.

London was in the midst of its "season" when we arrived, and for a few days Harry, who had also returned from Paris, tempted me with party after party. But I had not come to England for that. Finally I tore myself away and late one afternoon arrived at Adam and Jewel's country house.

From the way Jewel embraced me, one would have thought I was her closest friend in all the world.

"Oh, Augusta, dear, where have you *been* all this time?"

"Traveling, Jewel, traveling."

"I heard that you and Tom had gone to Italy—so suddenly, as I recall." She broke off as she realized that I, too, was wearing black. "Augusta, is it true what I heard . . . that Tom . . ."

"Yes. Less than a year ago." There was no reason to tell her that my mourning was not for Tom. "He had gone back to America on business."

"Oh, then you're alone too."

Embracing me again, she burst into tears. I led her into a drawing room, where we settled together on a couch and she wept on my shoulder. Oh, irony, irony, I thought, that Jewel and I should try to comfort each other.

She asked me to stay the evening, stay the night, but I refused. There was nothing more to be said between us, nor did I wish to endure more of her emotions or to share my own. We parted at her door with a dozen promises to see each other again soon, knowing quite well that we might never again lay eyes on each other, and, with Lisette, I went to the inn in the nearby village.

In the morning I went to the church graveyard where Adam had been laid beside his forebears. I had little difficulty in finding the grave. The stone was freshly cut and the new grass was delicate and tender.

I knelt. I said a prayer of sorts and a few words I thought Adam might wish to hear. I was still on my knees when once again I heard that unforgettable voice, that soft Carolina purr: "Well, princess . . . so we meet again."

If there was anyone in the world I did not care to encounter at that time, it was Gannon Murdock. I had a new life to lead, and I wanted no intrusions from the past. I wanted only to be left alone to begin my life over again.

But there he stood behind my shoulder, frowning slightly, his dark eyes moving swiftly from me to the headstone to the grave and back to me, as if seeing too much—far more than I wanted him to see. Ignoring the hand he extended to assist me, I rose to my feet.

"What are you doing here, Gannon Murdock?"

He grinned. "My, my, what a warm greeting. Well, for

one thing, yesterday Harry told me you were on your way to see Jewel, and I thought I might corner you here more easily than in London.''

"You've nothing to do with me, and I've no wish to see you ever again."

His grin faded. "And I've no wish to intrude on you, Gussie. But when Tom came home without you and proceeded to get himself killed, and then you still didn't come home, and nobody seemed to know what had happened to you . . . well, I couldn't help worrying about you a little."

That deserved a laugh. "You? Worry about me?"

"Does that seem so strange?"

"After all you've done to us? After what you did to Tom?"

He shook his head. "I didn't force Tom to gamble with me, Gussie, and I didn't stack the deck."

"You were determined to take the Barony, *my home*, away from him—"

"You're damn right. And I did it. And as for you, you were his responsibility, not mine."

"And I don't need your concern now, Mr. Murdock. I am taking care of myself quite nicely, thank you."

"Good."

So he said, but his eyes searched mine, as if looking for the truth. Why, I wondered, did I not simply walk away? And yet something—so many old memories—held me there beside him. I remembered that evening in London, he in my carriage, his lips on mine . . . and that night at the Barony, years earlier, when he wept on my shoulder. Dear Lord, I thought, what was he to me now, that I should remember and feel this sense of loss?

He turned to look at Adam's headstone.

"I liked Adam, Gussie. I suppose I liked him as much as any man I ever met. We had some fine times together. And anybody who thought that Adam's pretty face didn't belong to a hell of a man was making a bad mistake. I'm going to miss him."

As I did, so painfully. At least Gannon and I had that in common, even if he did not know it. The breeze that whispered through the graveyard was like our shared prayer.

". . . And all because he had to get himself cut down for some fool little trollop."

It was as if he had slapped me. "I beg your pardon?"

"Harry must have told you."

"Adam was killed in a duel—"

"Over one of Harry's girls. A 'seamstress,' she calls herself, an 'artist's model.' " He made the words a mockery.

"And what's wrong with that?"

He smiled. "You're still pretty naive, Gussie. That's what French doxies often call themselves—seamstresses and models. Apparently this one is a little beauty with a lot of well-placed friends—mostly artists, bohemians, you know the type—but her dressmaking was a joke until Adam got himself killed over her. And now she's making a small fortune, it seems—peddling her goods over our dead friend's grave."

Of course. What else could a man from Charleston be expected to think? And in a sense, wasn't it true?

"Whoever she is," I said, fighting back my tears, "and whatever she is, she can't be *all* bad, or Adam would never have defended her." Grief brought a touch of anger. "And whatever she is, I won't have you saying Adam threw his life away like a fool."

Gannon looked at me curiously. "Well, well. I never knew you cared for Adam so much. And now I find you at his grave . . ."

"He was a friend," I said weakly. "A very good friend."

He shrugged and turned back to the grave. "Maybe you're right. I'd hate to think Adam died out of some damn-fool mistaken sense of gallantry. There must be something special about this—this Liane Duhamel, she calls herself—that two men would die for her on a single morning. Anyway, I'm going to find out."

"What do you mean?"

"I'll get back to Paris sooner or later, and the next time I'm there, I intend to meet this Liane Duhamel. I want to know who and what the lady is. I want to know why a good man—my friend—should have died for her."

No, I thought, he must not. I said, "Leave her alone, Gannon."

He looked at me curiously. "Why should I?"

"Adam must have meant something to her, and she to him. Surely she's suffered enough."

"I'll let you know, when I've met her."

". . . Yes. You let me know."

He turned away from the grave. "I'm going to call on Jewel now. Do you want to go with me?"

"No. I've already talked to Jewel." Without thinking, I held out my hand, and he took it. "Goodbye, Gannon."

He frowned, as if not quite convinced of something. "Gussie, I know we've got no reason to love each other, but . . . are you sure there's nothing I can do for you?"

"Nothing. And I can't imagine why you should ask."

He laughed. "Neither can I." He looked at our hands, still together. "Well, then, if we don't meet again . . . good luck."

I withdrew my hand. "Good luck to you, too, Gannon."

"Goodbye, Gussie."

"Goodbye."

He walked away and did not look back.

How can I recapture the quality of the next year and those that followed? On returning to Paris, I threw myself into my work. I was at my drawing board seven days a week, and often enough slept in our workshop. If ever will or energy flagged, my dreams of recovering the Barony were sufficient to renew them. I intended to make my fortune, and I hated the thought of wasting a single hour while I did it.

It was amusing to see how one commission led to another. Because I had designed for Olympe Pellisier, I was invited to attend one of the most exclusive salons in Paris, that of Delphine de Girardin, wife of the influential *Presse*'s publisher. Not only did Delphine and her friends buy our dresses, but at her salon I met Alexander Dujarier, her husband's partner, which led to commissions from his mistress, Lola Montez. And Lola led us to still other sales. It soon became apparent that to be fashionable one simply *had* to have a dress bearing the *belle Liane* label—and few people questioned our prices.

We were not at all surprised, then, when one afternoon the courtesan Marie Duplessis urgently summoned us to her apartment on the boulevard de la Madeleine. I recall that it was always filled with whatever flowers were in season—except for roses, which made her ill—but her favorites, of course, were camellias. Great banks of dozens upon dozens of camellias. On that particular day the apartment was crowded with visitors, but she soon separated us from them and led us into her bedroom.

"My dears," she said, when we were alone, "you simply *must* make me the most beautifully dressed woman in Paris!"

It was that commission, more than any other, that made our
names. Not that we played favorites with our clients, but
Marie was a joy to dress. Three years younger than I, she was
tall and very slender, with black hair in long ringlets, a
pink-and-white complexion, and catlike eyes—a Dresden fig-
urine come to life. Even the feverish glow of her cheeks,
portending an end that would come all too soon, added to her
beauty. And for the next year or two, until she went into her
decline, no other woman in Paris could match Marie Duplessis
for sheer elegance. There were few who could resist our
dresses after that, and our atelier was often bright with light
and abuzz with activity twenty-four hours a day.

Ah, but I must not make too much of the work. There was
also the fun—being recognized at the Opéra, being invited to
the most exclusive salons, having lunch at Very's or dinner at
Vefour's. I remember sitting in the Café de Paris one afternoon, Lola Montez with Dujarier at one table, Marie Duplessis
with the younger Dumas at another, and I with Alfred de
Musset at a third, each of us a cynosure. The Café de Paris
was favored by literary people, and on that single afternoon
Balzac sat with us for a time, Victor Hugo appeared and
snubbed Sainte-Beuve, Alfred de Vigny quarreled with Roger
de Beauvoir and Eugène Sue, the elder Dumas flirted with
every woman in the room, and I was introduced to the great
poet-statesman, Alphonse Lamartine. What young woman of
imagination would not have given a year of her life to be in
my place?

And then there were, occasionally, certain special men in
my life.

How often after tragedy we think we shall never feel a real
emotion again! We shall never laugh or cry. We shall never
love, never hate, never freeze, never burn. Though the spirit
still haunts our bones, the flesh is a dry husk. We are the
walking dead, like those creatures in the voodoo tales of
Charleston and New Orleans.

That was how I felt that year, after Adam's death. I had
had enough emotions to last me forever, or so I thought, and
despite what I had told George, I had not the slightest desire
to take a lover. I was willing—eager—to lose myself in the
pleasures of hard work and social life and to settle for a
gentler happiness and quiet affections—a smile exchanged
with Céleste at the end of the day, a touch of Eugène's hand

when I went to his studio. Nothing more was needed or wanted.

But every frost is followed by a thaw, every winter by a spring. One can work so hard and unceasingly as never to mark the passing of the seasons, but one day you are walking up the Champs-Elysées toward the great mass of the Arc de Triomphe, and suddenly as you raise your eyes heavenward you see the sprays of fresh new green in the dazzling sunlight, and you seem to hear the opening chords of a great symphony, and you think, *Oh, dear Lord, it's happened again!*

In exactly that way I discovered spring—and love, of a kind—in 1844.

Having a number of errands that day, I walked about the city, rather than riding, in order to enjoy the fine weather, and toward dusk I found myself near Alfred and Madeleine's building. I had seen neither of them for several weeks, though I had promised to stop by. This seemed like the perfect opportunity, so, hoping they would both be at home, I made the long climb up the steep, dark stairs to their garret room.

Did I sense that something was wrong even as I stood there on the landing? Did I hear a stifled sob from the other side of the door?

I knocked twice before Alfred called in a subdued voice, "Who is it?"

"It's Liane."

Alfred opened the door without a word and turned away before I could see his face. I followed him into the room. As always, it was scrupulously neat, the bed made, the cabinets closed, not a crumb on the table. A gentle breeze wafted the thin white curtains at the open window, and the waning light outside was gold. But there was a grayness about the room that had nothing to do with the hour of the day.

Alfred sat on the side of the bed, his head hanging down, his big stonecutter's hands on his knees.

"Alfred," I said, "what is it? What's wrong?"

"She's gone."

"Who? You don't mean—"

"Madeleine. She's gone." A sob burst from him, and he wiped his eyes. "I'm sorry. I can't help myself. It's been almost a month, and I should be used to the idea, but sometimes it dawns on me all over again: she's gone."

"But where?"

"With a Spanish painter. The went to Madrid."

"Oh, Alfred, I'm so sorry."

"I suppose I knew it would happen sooner or later. But I always pretended it wouldn't. I even pretended that nothing was wrong these last few weeks when—when she acted so strange and sad and always on the verge of tears and—and—" another sob burst from him—"when she wouldn't even let me touch her."

"Oh, Alfred . . ."

What could I do to comfort him? All too little, it seemed to me. I could only sit beside him on the bed and, leaning back against the bolster and headboard, draw his head down to my breast.

"Dear Alfred," I said, "I've loved you and Madeleine both for so long. I wish I could love you now the way you deserve."

I should have realized that my ice-bound heart was thawing even then. I held big, gentle Alfred in my arms, rocking him like a child, kissing his forehead and wet eyes, and I should have realized that spring had come. But I knew nothing of that until much later, when Alfred's convulsive sobs had stopped and he lay quietly against my breast. Then, carefully, as if afraid of crushing me, he encircled me with his arms. His shirt had come loose, and my hands wandered over his broad, hard-muscled back and his smooth chest. He raised his face to mine. And for the first time, we kissed fully, passionately, one open mouth to the other.

Oh, God, I had not meant this to happen. But now that it had . . .

Yet I grew frightened as he unfastened the top of my dress and drew it down off my shoulder. The male was still such a strange creature to me, and I knew I would never entirely solve his mystery, would never know for certain if he was about to give me the greatest pleasure or the deepest pain. I trembled through my entire body and nearly cried out as Alfred bared my breast.

How much more shall I say of that evening? No woman could ever have wanted a more tender lover. Under his burning lips and gentle fingers, my fears gradually vanished. Growing bolder, I returned his caresses. Clothing slipped away, first some of his, then some of mine. "Taurus," I said, laughing softly and fondling him, "Taurus, my bull."

"Yours, Liane," he said, "yours for as long as you want me."

And then it occurred to me: those men who had loved me most in all the world were dead. Two men who had lusted so loveless for me were also dead. Was that to be my fate—to be a kind of angel of death?

"Oh, Alfred," I cried out, "don't die! Don't ever die!"

"How can I die," he asked, "when you are here, bringing me back to life again?"

"Taurus, I cannot be Madeleine for you. And I don't know that I'll ever be able to give you all the love you deserve. But I do care for you so much."

"And I love you, darling Liane," he whispered. "I love you so much."

For a time we were still, kissing gently. Then we began the next task of love.

2

Oh, the year that followed!

The previous autumn I had written to Aunt Nickie, telling her not to worry about me, that I was doing quite nicely. I had told her that Tom had left me a few francs (true enough) and that I had found surprisingly lucrative work as a dressmaker (also true). Under the circumstances, it struck me as wise to remain in Paris at least for the time being so as to be no burden to my family. Some weeks later, through my Paris solicitors, I received a reply. Uncle Thad, said Aunt Nickie, did not approve. How could I ever expect to be accepted back into Charleston society and into a respectable household when I persisted in behaving in such a questionable manner?

A questionable manner? Oh, Uncle Thad, if you only knew!

After that, our correspondence faltered and, within a few years, virtually died. Uncle Thad disapproved of letters from Aunt Nickie that were not stern and admonitory, and I—I certainly dared not tell what was happening in my so different world.

Meanwhile, I had my work. No matter what my other interests, my work *always* came first.

Céleste and I were well aware of the fickle nature of the public and the precariousness of our position. Favorites came and went. Therefore, throughout the next year we lived on the very edge of our nerves. I had to keep coming up with fresh, new designs that would appeal to our clients, and Céleste had to keep adding illustrious names to our client list. And somehow we did it. I would go to my drawing board without an idea in my head except that surely never again would I conceive of a fresh design, and yet the design would appear, as if from my fingertips, surprising me more than anyone else. And Céleste would burst into my workroom to announce excitedly that she had added yet another famous beauty to our client list—Alice Ozy or Atala Beauchene.

My escape from all this was Alfred—or Taurus, as I had come to call him. Almost every Sunday afternoon, I would go to his room, and there the world of fashion would be forgotten. We would gossip about our friends and make jokes. We would eat a simple meal, perhaps no more than some sausage and bread and cheese, and drink a glass or two of wine. Sooner or later, when the urge came to us, we would reach for each other and kiss and feel the familiar rise of excitement. Then we would make love, for the next hour or two forgetting the rest of the world entirely.

Lovely, lazy Sunday afternoons! Afterwards, I would lie on his bed, content as a cat, and watch him walk naked about the room. With his great, powerful sculptor's shoulders and arms, his broad back, his sinewy thighs, he was less a figure of classical beauty than that of an ancient gladiator, still unscarred. "Taurus," I would whisper, "Taurus, the gladiator of love," and he would turn to me and smile.

Then perhaps he would get out a board and a bit of modeling clay. Just as I always had my sketchbook, he always kept a bit of clay in his room, and I would watch, fascinated, as he sat at a table beside the bed, his clever fingers producing one figure after another—a dog, a horse, a man and woman embracing, a caricature of a friend.

But now I remember the afternoon that my own features appeared in that clay.

I lay there on the bed, stunned, as I saw my own head

taking shape. There was no mistaking those long-lashed eyes, that full mouth with the down-turned corners. The likeness was so perfect, the execution so sure, that I knew Alfred had practiced it to surprise me. But I wanted no such surprise.

"Please, no!"

He looked at me and laughed. "What?"

"Don't do me. Destroy it. Please!"

He was dumbfounded. "But why?"

How could I tell him? How could I explain that Liane Duhamel had a secret life in which she was an American woman named Augusta Raveneau? And that she had a dream of one day returning to that life? I had little worry about any sketches of me from my modeling days—likely they would long ago have been destroyed—but people from Charleston did appear in Paris from time to time, and though I had managed to avoid them, if one of them were to see and recognize a portrait of the notorious Liane Duhamel. . . . No, there must be no portrait, no bust in clay, no daguerreotype. I pretended it was a superstition, an eccentricity, but I insisted upon it absolutely: only those who had met Liane Duhamel face to face knew her features.

"I've told you, Taurus," I said, getting up from the bed, "I don't like being done! Please destroy it!"

He, too, rose to his feet, protective as any artist of his work. "But this is the best one I've ever done of you. I want to keep it."

"No!"

In a kind of panic, I lunged toward the clay, but he fended me off with an arm. "Liane, for the love of God, I thought you'd be pleased!"

"Well, I'm not! And if you have any respect for my wishes . . ."

Somehow I got past his arm. I brought both hands down on the clay head, then threw myself onto the table, rolling on the head and crushing it. Taurus snatched me up and held me by my upper arms, bent back over the table. His face was a mask of rage, and his entire body trembled visibly. He held my arms so tightly that they would be bruised for days.

"That was my *work!*" he said between clenched teeth, his face almost touching mine.

"But it's my *life,* Taurus! I love you, but please, respect my life! I ask you to promise me!"

His hands relaxed on my arms. As he looked over my

shoulders at the crushed head, the rage left his face, and his eyes were those of a hurt child. "Don't worry," he said. "If that's really what you want . . ."

I soothed him, and before long, still spattered with clay, we made love again, but things were never quite the same between us after that. There was always afterward some resentment on his part for what I had done, and guilt on mine for having done it, because, however I tried to justify my act, I was enough of an artist myself to understand Alfred's reverence for his work. If he had done to me what I had done to him, I would have been outraged.

Hence our unspoken feelings began to separate us after that, and we saw less of each other. I would put off my visit to his room for a week or even two weeks. Finally, over a month had passed without my visiting him when the incident occurred that separated us for good.

I truly had not expected it. Like a fool, I had deluded myself that all was going well between us.

It happened on a Saturday evening in May, one of the few free Saturday evenings of my busy life. It occurred to me that it had been considerable time since I had last visited Taurus's room—we had seen each other from time to time for a quick luncheon or a hurried hello, of course—and now I had an excellent opportunity to spend the night with him. Since his studio was on the way to his room and he frequently worked late, I thought I would stop by and see if he was there. And sure enough, a dim light showed through one window.

The front door was open, and so was the inner door that led to the "practical room," where the assistants and apprentices worked. I entered and looked around. There were the usual blocks of stone, the armatures, the clay figures covered with damp cloths, and the smell of marble dust and plaster and wet clay that I loved so much.

Apparently most of the staff had gone home, for the room was deserted, and the only light came from the next room, where all the preparatory work—the sketches and designs— was done. I was about to call out when I heard the sound of a woman's voice.

That sound—a moan, a sob, like a soul in pain—stilled me. For a moment I merely stood there, holding my breath. When it was repeated, I forced myself toward the next room. Fearfully, I looked through the doorway.

I should have known the meaning of that sound. Their

clothes abandoned, they were on a couch at the side of the room. I recognized the girl, a pretty little thing named Otille, and I had seen the light in her eyes when she looked at Alfred. I felt less shock, unexpected though the sight was, than a sudden overwhelming sadness, as if I had lost something more precious than I knew.

They were beautiful together. Fools deride the postures of love, but every artist knows they can be beautiful. And Alfred was giving his mistress such deft care and tenderness as he had not shown me in months.

My Taurus. . . .

I could not move until he slowly turned his head toward me and opened love-glazed eyes. Then I turned and walked silently out of the studio. There was no outcry behind me, only the fading sounds of a girl's rapture.

That ended it between us, of course. The next morning, early, he tapped at my apartment door.

"May I come in?"

"Of course. But be quiet. Céleste is still asleep."

We went into the dining room, where I poured coffee.

"I'm sorry about last night, Liane."

"What have you to be sorry about? I was the intruder."

"For what it's worth, I intend to marry that girl. I'm doing pretty well now, and I can afford to marry. And she means so much to me."

"I see. And I meant so little?"

He gave me the smile I loved, and I hated him for it. When he put his hand on mine, I had all I could do not to snatch mine away.

"Liane, it had to end and you know it. You've known it for months. A modestly successful stonecutter has little place in the life of Liane Duhamel."

"You were the only man in my life—"

"And you would not even let me portray that face I love so much. It's yours, and you keep it to yourself. Always. Your love for me was only a Sunday love, Liane, and not always then."

"My work—"

"Comes first. I understand and respect that. And I'll always be grateful to you. When I hardly wanted to live, you gave me something even better than what I had lost. But not yourself, Liane, never really yourself. Just a small part of yourself."

"And of course *she* will give you so much more."

"Yes. And she will accept more from me. That's even more important. Now . . . can't we be friends?"

I nodded.

He smiled and patted my hand and got up to leave. I stayed where I was, as he headed out of the apartment.

"Taurus," I said when he reached the door.

"Yes?"

"What does she call you?"

"Not Taurus," he said. "Never Taurus. No one but you will ever call me Taurus."

And he left.

There were few men in my life after that. I responded to the loss of Taurus as I did to all disappointments—by throwing myself deeper than ever into my work. In a curious, perhaps perverse way his loss merely increased my determination to be completely independent. And I was too busy, much too busy, to commit myself wholly to a love, however promising. Like many a young man who is driving himself mercilessly to build a career, I was married to my work. I *refused* to fall too deeply in love. Whatever a man might want of me, I would give if I could; but, as Taurus correctly understood, my work always came first.

By the spring of 1845 we felt thoroughly established, with every likelihood of keeping our clientele as long as we maintained the quality of our designs and workmanship. During our second year in business, Céleste and I cleared almost fifty thousand francs each, with prospects of making more in the year to come. But dreams such as mine cost money, and I was far from satisfied. After all, Marie Duplessis was reputed to *spend* in a year twice what I was earning, and Dumas the elder was said to earn four times as much.

I was ambitious. There had to be a way to make more money. And I thought I knew how to do it.

In 1838 a number of businessmen had gotten together and opened up the Galeries du Commerce et de l'Industrie on the boulevard Bonne-Nouvelle. The idea was to bring a number of different types of shops together on a single premises so that customers could conveniently visit them all. Unfortunately, the Galleries were not very well organized, and the experiment failed, but it was replaced in 1841 by the Palais Bonne-Nouvelle, which soon proved successful. In fact, it was so successful that more of these so-called department stores were opening up every year.

And who patronized them? The ladies. The ladies of Paris, looking for well-made, fashionable clothes at a reasonable price. They were our future customers, the potential source of a fortune.

When I first told Céleste my idea, she was skeptical. "It's not the kind of thing you're known for, Liane."

"That doesn't mean we can't do it."

"But do you think that the wife of Victor Hugo, say, is going to buy a *belle Liane* gown when any butcher's wife can buy one at the Bonne-Nouvelle?"

"We won't call them *belle Liane* gowns. We'll find a different name. We'll go right on doing our originals for our regular clients just as before. But for the department stores, we'll do the same dress over and over again with variations and in different sizes, and they'll be sold right off the rack. Céleste, darling, believe me, it can be done! And there's *money* in it, my little cauliflower! Money, money, money, money!"

Céleste's blue eyes brightened. She smiled.

Of course, I was not the first dressmaker to notice the possibilities of the new emporiums, nor would I be the last. But I intended to be the best and the most successful, and that meant that Céleste and I had to study the situation thoroughly before committing ourselves.

During the next year, we did exactly that. We spent hundreds of hours learning everything we could about the merchandising of clothes through these new stores. We visited them regularly. We talked to the saleswomen and the customers. We noted the quality of the materials, the designs, the workmanship that was selling—and that which was not. Céleste even went to work in a store for several weeks. We took careful and precise notes of everything we learned, and later we discussed every point.

After several months of these investigations, I learned a crucial lesson which should have been obvious to me from the beginning. In an experimental vein, I turned out several possible designs for our new line. They were simple, tasteful, and, I thought, very attractive, and I was certain that we could manufacture them at a competitive cost. I picked the three I liked best to show to the manager of the Bonne-Nouvelle, who seemed to be particularly knowledgeable in these matters. He received me cordially in his office and served coffee. An assistant, a woman who dealt with women's clothing, was sent for. With a feeling of great pride, I produced my three designs.

I could see their faces falling as they looked at the watercolors one by one.

"Is something wrong?"

A sad shake of the manager's head. "I am sorry, madame, but—but—but—"

"But what?"

"These are very lovely, but they won't sell."

"But why not?"

"No flounces," said the assistant mournfully.

"No *what?*"

"No flounces," the manager said. "Too simple, too unadorned. More and more, our customers want flounces."

I was appalled. "Do you mean to tell me you cannot sell a dress of superior design, a really lovely dress, a charming dress, a *reasonably priced* dress, merely because it doesn't have *flounces?*"

"It's true. Madame has the artist's eyes. To her, fashions may come and go, but what is truly good is always good. But right now, the ladies *think* that flounces are the loveliest things in the world, and that's what they want from us. If we can't provide them, someone else will. Therefore—flounces!"

Oh, what I learned that afternoon! Obviously, if I wished to seize the fortune that I sensed lay at hand, I was going to have to make my peace with flounces. But how? How could anyone with the slightest taste make peace with a flounce?

Well, I did. And a lucky thing, too, because in the years that followed, flounces became increasingly popular with even my most tasteful clientele. And eventually I was forced to admit, on the evidence of my own designs, that, yes, flounces *could* be beautiful.

Our studies led us in some directions we never anticipated. For example, children's clothing. While working in a department store, Céleste had noticed something interesting. When madame was shopping for a new gown, what was more natural than that she should also pick up that new dress little Annette needed and a new jacket for little Pierre? Therefore, before the winter was over, we were investigating children's clothes, and I was turning out my first designs in that field. I do believe we were the first, at least in that period, to turn out matched mother-and-daughter dresses. The idea appealed to me about as much as a flounce, but Céleste said the dresses would sell, and they did.

By the spring of 1846 we were ready for the coming fall season. We had our designs, we had our contracts. But after a great deal of thought, we still had not come up with a name for the new line. What, what, what should we call it? My partner looked at me diffidently one day, bit a fingernail, and finally suggested: *"Belle Céleste?"* Perfect! Our ladies' dresses would be called *belle Céleste* and our children's clothes *par belle Céleste*. Once again we were ready to take on the world.

I am afraid I have portrayed my relationship with Céleste as more one of milk and honey than it actually was. The truth is that, though we generally got on quite well, at times there was considerable strain. Céleste had periods of intense depression which I did not yet understand and which came to annoy me terribly because they had no apparent cause. And my inability to talk about anything other than our work at any hour of the day or night sometimes brought her to the verge of hysterics.

The situation grew worse that spring. Finally we agreed that I should find my own apartment so that we could have a little time away from each other and more easily enjoy separate social lives. Céleste helped me find and decorate a place not too far away, and this immediately eased the situation between us. But it also intensified the feeling I had, late in the spring, of being at loose ends—of being lost somewhere between the planning and the acting—of with nothing to occupy a mind that begged for activity.

That, I suppose, is why I paid such acute attention to the remarks I overheard at Harry's dinner party.

Céleste and I had continued to serve as his hostesses from time to time, and that evening it was my turn. The party was enjoyable enough but hardly different from a hundred others, until dinner was over and the gentlemen had left the table to join the ladies in the drawing room. Then, as we circulated through the room, I happened to hear one of the English guests speaking to Harry: ". . . simply impossible to preserve more than six pounds of meat in a glass jar or an iron canister or anything else. It inevitably putrifies . . ."

Why did those words hold me? Why did I suddenly wonder what in the world the man meant? Impossible to preserve more than six pounds of meat? Of course, it was possible.

"Someday, Sir Jasper," Harry said, "someone will find the answer, and when he does, he'll make a fortune."

Sir Jasper Fitzwarden shook his head. He was a fat, elderly man with flaring side whiskers and quivering dewlaps. "No, no," he said, *basso profundo*, "I am convinced that it cannot be done. It is against the laws of nature. It has been tried and tried, and no one has yet . . ."

I moved on, but Sir Jasper's words stayed with me. He was something-or-other important at the British Admiralty and an intelligent man. Why should he say a thing that seemed so contrary to common sense and to the little I knew about preserving food? I might have dismissed the whole matter from my mind but for one thing. Harry had said, *"Someone will find the answer, and when he does, he'll make a fortune."* And if that were the case . . .

The question continued to haunt me long after the last guest had departed. For convenience, I usually stayed in my old apartment after these affairs, and I did that night. And as I got ready for bed, I kept thinking about what I had heard. Was it really possible that they did not know the answer? I kept telling myself that I must not understand the problem.

Finally curiosity got the best of me. Donning a robe, I went to Harry's apartment.

"I don't suppose I dare hope that you've come here to seduce me?" he asked, as he opened the door.

"Some other night, Harry—I only want to talk to you for a moment. But if you'd feel safer on neutral ground—"

"Don't be silly, puss. Do come in."

After he had settled me into a chair with a glass of brandy and thrown another stick on the small fire that took the night chill from the spring air, I asked my first question: Why had Sir Jasper said it was impossible to preserve more than six pounds of meat in a canister or a jar? Harry, sitting opposite me in his smoking jacket, shrugged. "Simply because no one has yet found out how to do it."

"I don't understand. What is the problem?"

Harry smiled in the usual superior masculine way. "Augusta, dear, what do you know about preserving food?"

"Not much. At home, when we put up preserves, we usually cooked the fruit with sugar-house syrup, then poured it into jars and put brandy-soaked paper on top. Or sometimes we just put the fruit into the jars and corked them lightly, then cooked them in an oven till the juice was boiled down. Then we pushed the corks in and sealed them with resin.''

"Very good. We give you a pass. Now, listen to me." He gave me a donnish look, and proceeded to lecture. "There are, in my view, basically five means, and combinations thereof, of preserving foodstuffs." He ticked them off on his fingers. "Cooking and sealing, which you have just more or less described. Chilling, as in a root cellar or on ice. Dessication, as when one makes dried fruit. Chemical treatment, as when one pickles a cucumber, salts meat, and so forth. And sealing and heating.

"Now, sealing and heating food in jars, as you may know, began only some thirty-five years ago, when a Frenchman named Nicolas Appert invented the process. Actually, an Englishman named Thomas Saddington invented a very similar process at about the same time or a little earlier, but Appert's investigations and treatise were much more thorough, so he gets the credit. Both processes were very like the one you described, except that the jars were heated, not in a dry oven, but in baths of hot water.

"However, there is one great drawback to the use of jars or bottles. Because no one has ever devised an adequate way of securing or protecting them, they rattle about on railway trains and on ships at sea, and a great deal of good food is lost to the musical tingle of breaking glass. But early on, an engineer named Bryan Donkin—I know the old boy, by the way—began experimenting with tin-lined canisters, and they worked out quite well. And then some years ago another Englishman, Peter Durand, also worked up and patented a tin-lined iron canister that is so satisfactory that its use has spread as far as America. Any questions thus far?''

I stared at him. "Harry, how in the world do you know all this?"

Harry looked hugely self-satisfied. "In the same way that I know a great many things that might surprise you, my dear Augusta. You see, I do not share the common prejudice against trade, not when I see a potential profit. And I see a veritable *fortune* for the man who solves the mysteries of food preservation.''

Of course. Tom had long ago told me that Harry was "in railways, mills, real estate, half a dozen other things," and I had come to realize that behind the wicked dandy there was a tradesman as shrewd as any Yankee merchant.

"How, Harry?" I asked. "How is there a large potential profit?"

Harry leaned toward me as if to emphasize his answer. "Augusta, if I could find a way to preserve large cuts of meat, say up to fourteen pounds, in canisters, and then obtain an exclusive contract to supply the Admiralty, you have no idea how much profit could be made by that alone."

"But Sir Jasper says it's impossible."

Harry settled back in his chair. "Donkin's canisters held up to six pounds of meat. His rivals tried larger quantities, using the same process, and the meat spoiled."

"But why?"

"My dear girl, nobody knows why food spoils. We only know that under certain conditions it does and under others it does not. It is a complete mystery."

Perhaps. But I still could not get over the feeling that I knew the solution to the problem Harry had posed. Oh, not in detail, perhaps, but in principle.

"Is the meat packed hot or cold?" I asked.

"The meat is simply put into the cans, air is excluded, and the canisters are tightly sealed. And they are then subjected to a period in hot water."

"How hot and for how long?"

"A boil, or very close to it, but for no longer than necessary. After all, the idea is merely to *preserve* the meat, not to cook it. And if the canisters are subjected to too much heat, they explode."

I shook my head: I had a feeling of unreality. I was certain I was right. I had the solution to the problem.

I do not suppose there is any harm in disclosing my solution, such as it was, to these pages. As I have said, when I heard Sir Jasper speaking of the impossibility of preserving more than six pounds of meat in a canister, his words seemed to contradict both common sense and my own experience. I knew very little about the process of tinning meat, but the thought of it brought a flood of memories back to me. I remembered Matty, our cook, putting up preserves. I remembered her saying she could "puhserve 'most any fruit, but you got to get it done right and done all the way through, or it don't keep."

You had to get it done all the way through.

Something told me that that was the answer. It was not enough simply to "expose" the meat to heat by putting the canister into boiling water. The heat had to penetrate *every part* of the meat, even the innermost, sufficiently to inhibit deterioration at every point. And just as it took much longer to roast a large piece of beef than a small piece, it took much longer for the heat to penetrate a large, fourteen-pound tin than it did a small one of six pounds or less.

But how could the answer possibly be so simple and obvious? How could a plantation cook possibly have more insight into these matters than the wise tradesmen and engineers of London and Paris? Ridiculous! How could I ever dare to believe that I was right?

You see, my solution to the problem was not arrived at through any streak of genius on my part, but rather through the natural confusion and childish ignorance of a mere woman's mind. All I had, really, was the kind of irrational intuition of which women are often accused and for which they are so often scorned by wise, ever-logical men.

Ha!

I had meant to spend only a minute or two with Harry; instead, we talked for almost an hour, and everything he told me seemed to confirm my theory. But that was not enough. I had to put it to the practical test and prove it was true.

And perhaps the best place to do that would be in London. Because if I could get that Admiralty contract . . .

"When do you plan to go back to London, Harry?" I asked, as I got up to leave.

"Oh, sometime next week."

"Would you like a traveling companion?"

"I'd be delighted." He narrowed his eyes and smiled at me. "My dear, you've asked a great many questions. Do you perhaps have some idea that you can solve the great conundrum of the fourteen-pound meat canister?"

"Why, Harry," I said innocently, "how could I, when minds so much wiser than mine have failed?"

"You're probably quite right. But I've learned not to underestimate you. And, young lady, I am going to keep an eye on you. I've been looking for a solution to this problem for a long time, and you may be of use to me."

And you to me, Harry. And you to me.

3 ⌁⌁⌁⌁

Céleste was dubious and I could hardly blame her.

"How can you be sure, Liane?"

"I can't, really, until I prove I'm right. And yet I *am* sure, and I am going to prove it. The question is, will you mind my leaving you alone here the next three or four months? Do you think you can spare me?"

"Well, I'll miss you, of course, but don't stay for that reason. We're all ready for fall, and I'll keep things going. It will do you good to get away and think of something else for a change."

We left for England a few days later. I did not care to use my French identity in London, but neither did I care to revert to Tom's name: I was not there for the social life, and I intended to avoid old acquaintances and distant cousins. Therefore I decided to use my maiden name. I would be Mrs. Welles. Mrs. *Gustava* Welles. The idea amused me, and I wished Mrs. Gustava Welles a long and active life.

Harry had lent me Lisette again and invited me to stay at his Belgravia house. Once settled in, I did not waste a day before going to work. I obtained a copy of Mr. Appert's treatise, *Art de conserver les substances animales et vegetales*, and pored over it. I bought one book after another on cookery, though I found them all to be quite vague on matters of heat, cooking time, and measurement. I talked to every cook I could contrive to meet, and still I learned all too little. But I was certain I was on the right track. Somehow I would find a sure way to preserve canisters of meat, no matter how large or small.

I needed a kitchen. To his cook's consternation, Harry said that I could use the huge one in the Belgravia house. Fine. I would borrow his kitchen and his cook too, but meanwhile I wanted Harry to find me something even larger. I would need a place where I could prepare meat in large quantities and have it sealed in canisters, a place where I could store the finished product for a long time to come—for a year or more.

"Augusta," Harry said, "I know what you're trying to do, but before you spend huge amounts of money—do you have any idea of the complexity of the problem?"

"Not yet, Harry. But I do know the simplicity of the solution."

Oh, such dazzlingly confident words!

As I had had little experience of tinned meat before, my next step was to learn everything about it I could. To that end, I purchased a variety of meats in different-sized canisters and examined them carefully. How well cooked were they, if they were cooked at all? I found, as I suspected, that, to some degree at least, the meats *were* cooked—more so on the outside than at the center, but even at the center they were not what I would have called blood-raw.

Next I took roasts of equal sizes and tried to cook them to the exact degree of "doneness" of the tinned meats. No doubt a lot of this effort was not strictly necessary, but I was learning about cooking meat, not just about preserving it. I took careful notes on everything we did, weighing the meat before and after cooking and carefully observing all cooking times. The cook and his staff thought I was quite mad.

"Well, at least the poor of London have reason to be grateful to you, Augusta," Harry said, when I had been at this for several days, giving most of the food away.

"I'm not doing this for the poor people of London, Harry. I'm doing it for little Gussie." We were sitting in the garden, where I had taken an hour off for tea. "Have you found me a factory yet?"

"I have indeed, through the good offices of Sir Jasper. A disused Admiralty warehouse on the Thames."

I was surprised. "Sir Jasper?"

"We want that Admiralty contract, don't we? Sir Jasper's support will be crucial in obtaining it. Therefore we subtly make him a party to our cause by enlisting his aid."

"What am I going to have to pay for this warehouse?"

"We've already bought it. I am sure we can work out an arrangement—"

"*We*, Harry? You keep saying *we*."

"Exactly. We'll put in sufficient equipment for our present needs, and later we'll turn the entire building into a combined factory and warehouse. We'll have inexpensive river transport, and—"

"*Why* do you keep saying *we?*"

"Because we are partners, of course."

He returned my long stare smilingly while I tried to control my temper.

"Harry," I said, when I dared speak, "I am grateful to you. You've welcomed me into your house and even given me the use of your kitchen. You've introduced me to many persons and taken me places I might have found difficult to reach. You have gone out of your way to be helpful. But this is *my* business. Forgive me, Harry, but I don't need you."

Harry's smile never faded. "Don't *need* me, pet? But how can you do without me? Do you think you have a prayer of getting that Admiralty contract without my help?"

"I don't see why not."

"Forgive me, Augusta, but you are out of your depth. The Royal Navy is perhaps the most conservative organization in the world, and people like Sir Jasper *know* you cannot tin more than six pounds of meat. To them, it has been proved for all time, and a twenty-five-year-old widow lady, no matter how attractive, is never going to persuade them otherwise."

"Then what makes you think that *you* can?"

"Because I have had a long and fruitful association with Sir Jasper and a number of other gentlemen at the Admiralty. I am trusted. I am respected. Again, forgive me, my dear, but though you may have the solution to the problem, *I* shall secure that contract. And, for that matter, any number of others you could never get on your own."

I believed him. But I was still angry. I did not like being manipulated and used like this.

"All right, Harry. What do you propose?"

"Even down the middle. We both put up an equal amount—"

"*Damn* you!" I cried, leaping up from my chair. "*I* have the idea—*you* put up the money!"

His eyes widened. "*All* of it, Gussie?"

"*All* of it, Harry!"

He smiled as if that were exactly what he had had in mind all along, and extended his hand. "Agreed."

My anger with Harry soon vanished, as I realized that he was going to be an extremely useful partner. And since he was financing our endeavor, I retained my money for other investments.

The warehouse Harry had purchased was in excellent condition, and he had already hired people to clean it and rid it of rats. For my immediate purposes, I needed only a little equipment—a meat locker, a cooker, a sealer, and the like—and it was quickly obtained. But since, if we were going into commercial production, we wanted to do so as soon as possible, we decided to start planning the conversion of the warehouse at once. And to this end, we needed professional help.

"Algernon Collins," Harry said.

Mr. Collins, who was destined to become a permanent member of our firm, was a young member of a recently dissolved engineering company. Harry had met him in connection with some textile mills and had implicit faith in him. I, when I met him, was skeptical. Far from my image of an engineer as a big-fisted giant capable of managing a bunch of drunken navvies, he looked more like an eager young gnome with dirty-blond hair, bright hazel eyes, and far too wide a smile for his boyish face. About thirty, he appeared less than half that, but he did seem to vibrate with intelligence and energy.

"What do you know about tinned food?" I asked, when we met at Harry's office in the City.

"Nothin', mum!" he replied with an enthusiasm that made his ignorance sound like a positive asset.

"What do you know about cookers—"

"Nothin'!"

"And canister sealing equipment—"

"Nothin', mum, nothin'!"

"Well—what can you do?"

"Anythin'! Build you a railway locomotive. Build you a suspension bridge. Build you a steamship. Build you a—"

"Our Mr. Collins," Harry said, "is a veritable Brunel."

"Mr. Collins, we are looking for someone who can build us a meat packing plant."

"Fine, fine! Build you anythin' you please, mum!"

Since Harry was paying the bill, I allowed him to override my doubts about Mr. Collins, and a few days later I found that the engineer had already learned more about meat packing than I had in three weeks. When I explained to him that we did not want simply to duplicate other plants, but that we had certain experimental equipment to build and certain improvements in meat packing in mind, his enthusiasm only increased.

"Fine! Fine! Let's 'op to it!"

To help with my experiments in the warehouse, I hired a couple of assistants who could be trusted to follow orders without trying to understand what I was really up to: to them, I was simply studying the art of meat packing. But no secret purpose could ever have been hidden for long from Mr. Algernon Collins. One day, after watching me silently for half an hour, he suddenly burst out:

"As I see it, you're studyin' the effects of two important temperature variables, the outside and the in. Now, in 'alf the plants I've visited, the temperature gauges are either busted or missin', and they just go by the boil of the water, which is a kind o' rough temperature equalizer, so to speak. *Our* cookers, though, are gonna have the most reliable gauges, and they ain't never gonna fail us. And as to the interior temperatures o' the meat, what you need instead of all this guesswork is some kind of gauge that will extend through the wall of the canister so that you get an exact measurement."

That shrewd little man knew exactly what I was up to. I think he had even guessed my theory.

"We've got to take him in, Harry," I said one evening back in Belgravia. "We really have no choice."

Harry was irritated. "I don't see why. If you want to keep him on permanently, fine. We'll give him a generous bonus from time to time, and I'm sure he'll be satisfied."

"No, he will not. He's far too ambitious, and we have to give him a chance to satisfy that ambition—an incentive to stay with us. Harry, everything I am learning, he is learning too. And since the basic idea is far too simple to be protected by a patent, he can walk off with it anytime he wishes. And where are we then?"

Besides which, Mr. Collins was just about the best engineering help we could possibly have found.

Not long after he had joined us permanently, my suspicion that Mr. Collins was quite capable of taking care of himself was confirmed.

"The canister sealin' equipment, mum," he said one day when he was showing Harry and me his drawings, "I wonder if you'd mind me deviatin' from the normal and usin' me own design. I've come up with something quite a bit better than what's usual, I'm 'appy to say."

"If you say it's better, Mr. Collins, that is quite satisfactory to me."

"Fine, mum," Mr. Collins said, and added in an offhand way, "I'm 'avin' me little idea patented."

"Ah, now, one minute," Harry said quickly. "You're in our employ. You do realize that the patent to any sealing device you invent while in our employ belongs to the company."

"Beg to differ with you, sir," Mr. Collins said cheerfully, "but this 'ere little device was developed by me on me own time."

"Oh, come now, Collins—"

" 'Tis a fact, sir. But I'll tell you what. Just so there's no 'ard feelin's and to show that me 'eart's in the right place, I wouldn't dream of chargin' our own company 'ere for its use. But the patent stays in me own name, or," he flashed a disingenuous smile, "it's me *honor*, sir. Me *honor* obliges me to walk."

Harry rolled his eyes heavenward and sighed. I laughed, we all laughed, and Mr. Collins stayed on.

My principal impression of the rest of that summer is one of sweat. I did not perspire, I did not glow, I sweated—there in that waterfront warehouse, where we kept the fires roaring under our boilers twelve hours a day. I do not know how many times I was burned or scalded or nearly lost a finger in the machinery, but we got the job done.

We were working with every common type of meat, mostly in large cuts. There was so much we had to find out. We did not know if every ten-pound cut of beef, say, had to be subjected to heat for the same length of time or not. We did not know if pork, as we suspected, had to be heated longer than other meats. But thanks to Mr. Collins's ingenious thermometers, we were soon getting much more accurate ideas on the subject than we could have in any other way.

Early in July we put up a number of sample canisters. Two weeks later we opened twelve of them. Harry laughed at my insistence that we first test the meat on dogs rather than on human beings. "There are beggars in London so hungry, my dear, they would thank your for any scrap of maggoty meat you might throw to them."

"Not if they're dead, Harry."

But of course sooner or later we had to test our tinned meat on human beings, and that being the case, there was only one thing I could do. I arrived at the warehouse early one morning and started a fire in the iron stove. I opened a can of beef, cut a thick slice, and fried it in its own fat. A little later Mr. Collins arrived, to find me sitting at a table, forcing down one bite after another.

"My God, Mrs. Welles, mum, what are you *do*ing!"

"Having breakfast, Mr. Collins. Would you care to join me?"

Later I forced myself to work, rather than contemplate my imminent illness or extinction, and by the end of the day I had quite forgotten my breakfast. After that, I never asked anyone to eat anything I was not willing to eat myself.

Every two weeks throughout the summer we opened more tins and tested the contents. The meat was always good, and when September came, there still was not a single swollen or otherwise suspect tin in the warehouse. "You've done it, Augusta," Harry said. "You've proved your theory and worked out a way to apply it. Now we can go ahead—"

"Go ahead, Harry? Why, we've hardly begun."

"Oh, you don't really think you still need more testing!"

"This is only where the real testing starts."

"Right she is, milord," Mr. Collins said. "We've got to be real scientific about this. I come up the 'ard way, and I mean to make my fortune with this firm, but I ain't gonna do it poisonin' the poor dumb brutes I rise up over."

"How much meat do you think we'll need for the next series of tests, Mr. Collins?" I asked.

"I figure we'll need a minimum of two and a half tons."

Harry looked shocked. "Two and a half tons!"

"Of highest quality, freshly butchered, boned and trimmed beef, pork, mutton, and veal. As you say, Mrs. Welles, just to start."

I looked at Harry.

He sighed. "Order it."

We began our final task of the summer, the packing of some five hundred canisters with various-size cuts of meat. Harry saw to it that the meat was purchased and transported to us under Admiralty supervision. When all the canisters were ready, they were taken to an Admiralty warehouse where they were placed in a locked and sealed room. They would remain there, under guard, for a year.

Then it was back to Paris for me. Mr. Collins and I had drawn up a detailed schedule of tests he was to make during the following year; but I, having been away from Paris longer than I had planned, had to give my full attention to our clothing business.

The first thing I learned on my arrival was that Gannon Murdock had recently been in Paris looking for Liane Duhamel. Unfortunately for him, Mme. Duhamel had been on an "extended holiday," touring about Europe, but once again he had talked to a great many people and asked a great number of questions.

"Oh, that man!" I said, exasperated. "He caused me enough trouble when I was Augusta Raveneau! And now Liane Duhamel! Will he never leave me alone?"

"But why do you care?" Céleste asked, amused. "Why is it so necessary for you to avoid this Mr. Murdock?"

Although I had tried several times to explain, she never really seemed to understand. "Céleste, to the people of Charleston, it was bad enough that my husband left me behind all by myself in a foreign city—"

"But you were *not* all by yourself. You were with friends, I was with you."

I shook my head. "If they should ever learn about my life here—"

"But what is so terrible about your life? You are now a respected—"

"Widow lady with a *very* active social life. A former courtesan, if one believes half what one hears. And to the good people of Charleston that would make me forever a 'bad woman,' no better than a common prostitute. I could never go back there."

"Oh, Liane, I cannot believe that the people of your Charleston could ever be so uncivilized!"

"Believe me, Céleste, please believe me. And one day I *do* hope to go back."

But I had no more time to think of that than I did of my tins of meat in London. I had clients waiting for new designs, new dresses. More stores were opening, and Céleste had already made contracts to supply them.

We had far outgrown our original workshop, but fortunately, additional space was available in the same building and in those next door, and we expanded until our shops became a veritable factory. I found myself wandering through it, looking about in amazement at the pattern and cutting tables, at the draped fabrics, at the mannequins, at the ladies with the pins in their mouths and the flashing needles in their fingers. Could this possibly be what Céleste and I had started less than four years before? Surely not—we had never anticipated, never dreamed, of such a thing, not even in our most optimistic moments. Surely it was too good to be true.

Yes, it was.

We had both seen the problem coming but, because we did not wish to face it, had said nothing. Silence would make it go away. But of course silence did nothing of the kind, and the problem grew more formidable each day.

In our youthful confidence, our exuberance, our pride, we had simply taken on more than we could handle.

By December we could no longer deny this. The holidays were coming—Christmas, the New Year, carnival, Mardi gras. Among both our individual clients and our store clients, demand was at its peak. And we could not supply it.

I walked into Céleste's office one morning to find her sitting at her desk, her face pale with strain, her eyes wide and unblinking, and I knew the cause was not simply the hard work of the preceding months. She was looking at orders, letting the papers fall from her fingers. Suddenly weak-kneed, I sank into a chair beside her.

"What is it?" I asked, even though I knew.

"We can't do it. There is simply no way we can do it."

"Fill the orders, you mean."

"Orders worth thousands. Orders worth a small fortune."

"But we have the materials—"

"But not the people!"

"There are always seamstresses in Paris. We'll find them, we'll train them—"

"There is no time! Liane, it's the busiest season of the year, and all the best people we know already have work!" She thumped her hand down on the papers that cluttered her desk. "There is *no way* that we can fill these orders!"

We sat there for several minutes. I knew that every word she said was true. But I could not accept it. We had worked too long and too hard. To fail during this season could be our ruin, as far as the store trade went.

No, I could not accept that.

I stood up.

"Where are you going?"

"Out."

"Liane, we must talk about this!"

"You've just convinced me that talking isn't going to do any good."

"Then what are we going to *do*?"

"Find a dozen trained seamstresses where there aren't any. Hire them away from another workshop. Or better yet, hire a whole shop. I don't know. But I do know that somewhere out there, there's an answer, and I'm going to find it."

Sometimes the gods smile on us. As I spoke, the ghost of an idea came to me, but I must admit I did not even recognize the answer when Céleste and I went out into the reception room and saw it in front of us.

There stood Mme. Colombier, her bosom more magnificent than ever, and her small, dark eyes bright with the hungry look that I remembered from our last encounter.

"My dears," she said before we could speak, "so good to see you again. I trust you remember our last meeting."

"Vividly," I said.

"Madame Duhamel, you have vindicated my faith in you. You will recall that when others doubted, Monsieur Delacroix and Madame Colombier said, '*This* little girl has talent.' "

"You tried to rob me!"

Mme. Colombier smiled as one might at a bright child. "If you choose to think so, my dear. I am sure that by now you have learned that in the rag trade theft is the first law of survival. I have long looked forward to laughing with you over that little incident."

"What are you here for, Madame Colombier?" Céleste asked.

Mme. Colombier looked pained by this abruptness. "May we sit down?"

I was quite ready to show Mme. Colombier the other side of the door, but to my surprise, Céleste was suddenly very polite and attentive. She insisted that we all go into her office and have coffee.

"And now to business," Mme. Colombier said after a few minutes of social chitchat during which I was mostly silent. "I believe it is possible that you have a small problem."

"A problem, Madame Colombier?" Céleste asked innocently.

"You must realize that, like a kindly aunt, I have been keeping a very close eye on you—and so have all those other vultures out there! Within the trade, it is no secret that you have so many contracts that no one knows how you can fulfill them and yet maintain quality.''

"Oh, yes," Céleste said in a bemused voice, "I know some people have that impression."

"Since some of your clients are friends of mine, I've had the opportunity to examine your work, and I must say it is excellent. By the way, speaking of theft—so naughty of you, my dears, to have stolen my client, Delphine de Girardin.''

"Oh," said Céleste, wide-eyed, "if only we had known . . .''

"I'm sure. But to the point. You do need help, don't you?''

"Oh, we could use a few good seamstresses, I suppose—"

"Of course. And I have them."

My wits were returning, and I began to realize that my vague idea—of somehow hiring not individual seamstresses but a whole workshop—might very well turn into a reality right there in Céleste's office.

"What exactly did you have in mind, Madame Colombier?" I asked.

"Ladies," she said in her best *grande dame* manner, "as you may know, I have been in the trade since I was fourteen— over thirty years. I know it inside out. I have built up an excellent organization. I have a staff of a dozen ladies who never lack for work, and I have on call more fine seamstresses than I care to tell you about—housewives, mostly, who are glad to pick up a few francs for part-time work.''

"And you propose . . .?''

"Even at the height of the season, I know more good people than I can keep working. You, on the other hand, admit that you need some first-rate seamstresses. I propose that we combine forces—permanently.''

I was seeing Mme. Colombier in a new light, but I was still wary of her. "Madame, with all respect, you did try to cheat me once. How do I know that won't happen again?''

Mme. Colombier drew herself up in her chair with dignity and glared at me with offended eyes. "My dear, when we first met, you were, as far as I could see, just a wealthy young chit, all silk and satin, who was ready to take food from the mouth of a *real* designer. Of course, I now know that you were not quite what you seemed, and if I owe you an apology, you have it. But if we were to meet again under the same circumstances, I would do precisely the same thing. We may be thieves in this business, but *some* of us, at least, take care of our own.''

The Welles gorge rose. ''Now, just one minute, madame, if you're implying that *others* of us don't—''

''Ah—Liane!'' Céleste said quickly, hopping up from her chair. ''I forgot to tell you, you have an appointment!''

''I do?''

''Madame Colombier, if you will excuse us for a minute . . .''

Céleste bustled me out of the office and closed the door. She turned excited eyes on me.

''We're going to be all right. I learned a lot about the trade while you were gone, and Félicie Colombier is one of the best.''

''Félicie?'' I could not believe that name, not on Mme. Colombier.

''I'll make a deal with her.''

I nodded slowly. ''If you think we can trust her.''

''It doesn't matter. She'll get us through the year. And if she tries to cheat us in some way . . .'' Céleste shrugged. ''By then we'll have our own permanent staff of part-time workers—hers!''

I looked wonderingly at Céleste. ''My dear, this business is turning us into a couple of pirates!''

''Rich pirates! Like her!''

''Make a deal.''

''Trust me. Now, you get back to your drawing board, girl!''

Mme. Colombier did not cheat us in any way, and we had no need to steal any of her staff. She was a wise and tough old bird who saved us from many a mistake in the years that followed, and once we were allied together, nobody could have had a more loyal friend.

What a year that was—1846 and 1847! Eugène decorated the library of the Luxembourg, and George wrote *Lucrezia Floriani*. In America, the United States went to war with Mexico, gold was discovered in California, and Dr. Morton used ether as an anesthetic. We attended Berlioz's *Damnation de Faust* at the Opéra-Comique, and Adolph Thiers held the first reform banquet in Paris, presaging the revolution to come. And that was the year they installed electric arc lights at the Opéra. Electric lights—who could have conceived such a marvel!

But what I remember most vividly is the death of Marie Duplessis.

Such a short time before, she had been the toast of Paris, the very figure of mirth and love, of pleasure and gaiety. She had laughed and danced and loved the nights away and slept through the days, while her cheeks had grown ever rosier with the flame that was consuming her life. For all that time, Death was looking over her shoulder, and in the last year those cheeks suddenly paled. She knew the end was coming. Weaker each day, she began to seclude herself in her apartment on the boulevard de la Madeleine. That lovely body for which so many adoring men had paid hundreds of thousands of golden francs grew so thin and weak that she no longer allowed anyone to see it. She supported herself by selling all her treasures, one by one. At the end, no old lover was allowed to see her—only we women who took turns holding her hand.

She died on February 3, 1847, at the height of carnival, while the oblivious crowds were singing and dancing in the street below.

As I held those lifeless fingers, I reminded myself that Marie had chosen the life she led, but was it possible that she never truly lived at all? Why did I feel so desolate—not only for her, but for myself as well, as if her death were a warning, a prefiguring of my own possible fate? She was as elusive as a flame, and as dangerous if held too long, and so soon snuffed out. And the heart of the flame was never truly known. . . .

I had only one weapon to use against my melancholy. Work. More work. Always more work.

We had to have new dresses ready for our clients before Easter. New orders from the stores had to be filled. Mr. Collins's long, detailed reports arrived weekly—I had to study them closely and reply, suggesting new experiments. As always, I contrived to fill every hour.

I received one piece of news that cheered me considerably that spring. My Charleston lawyers, whom I had asked to give me any news regarding the Barony, wrote that Gannon Murdock had considered an offer for the plantation, turning it down only when he learned that it had come from my Uncle Thad. That meant Gannon was *not* absolutely unwilling to let the Barony go! I could understand his not wanting to sell to my uncle, but Gannon and I had not been on such bad terms the last time we had met. Then, might he not be willing to sell to me one day? Oh, if only I had already made my fortune! I wrote to my lawyers, asking them to continue watching the Barony for me, and to keep me informed.

Summer arrived and Céleste took a long-deserved holiday. Later, in July, George's sullen, evil-tongued daughter, Solange, arrived in Paris with her new husband, a black-bearded ne'er-do-well sculptor named Clesinger, both of them to malign George to Frédéric Chopin. Frédéric, long susceptible to Solange, believed her slander and sided with her against her mother, with the result that after nine years of the closest friendship the two parted. Another cause for sadness. In August I hurried down to Nohant, hoping to console George.

Then it was time to return to England. I found that Mr. Collins and Harry, anticipating total success, had already completed the conversion of our old building into a factory-with-warehouse—rows of gleaming cookers and sealing equipment! To my eye, it was all beautiful.

I had one bad moment when I saw a swollen canister. Mr. Collins laughed and for the first time called me by my first name. "It's supposed to be like that, Gussie. Do you realize that we can now predict infallibly which tins will spoil and which will not?"

"Then we know more about packing meat than anybody else in England, Algie."

"More than anybody else in the world!"

Though I would like to make a drama of it, the rest was almost anticlimactic. We opened some tins that had been sealed a year before, at the same time as those we had stored with the Admiralty. We tested the meat on animals, then ate it ourselves—with far less apprehension than I had felt at that breakfast more than a year earlier! Soon after that, we went to the Admiralty warehouse and, in the presence of Sir Jasper and other officials, opened up the sealed room. The schedule called for a test on animals, but a stove had been set up, and I amused myself by frying and eating a piece of pork from the first tin opened, while the others looked on.

"Really, madam," Sir Jasper boomed, his wattles quivering, "really, I would not!"

"Sir Jasper, this food was meant for human consumption.

And I would not supply provender even for Her Majesty's pet dog unless I were willing to eat it myself.''

We won the day. We had succeeded where all others before us had failed. Let the Admiralty open the other canisters and make all the tests they wished, I thought, as Harry, Algie, and I left the warehouse and walked to our carriage that afternoon. I was already growing bored.

But something had been tickling at the back of my mind for months, and I finally spoke about it. ''Harry, what was that that you said to me—oh, it was long ago, over a year—about nobody having figured out a good way to pack jars and bottles so they won't break?''

4 ~~~~~

On reading the foregoing pages, some might think that success followed automatically. But of course anyone acquainted with recent history would know that was not the case.

We could hardly have started our *belle Céleste* line of dresses at a worse time. A famine had beset northern Europe in the middle forties, and the harvest failed again in 1847. France was in a severe agricultural and industrial depression, which could hardly fail to affect the sales of our goods. Fortunately, however, our clothes were designed for customers who had reached a level of affluence where many could still afford them, and so we did not fare too badly.

But then came the events of 1848. All Europe was thrown into turmoil in that stormy year—revolutions in Berlin, Milan, and Parma; three revolutions in Vienna alone; war between Sardinia and Austria, between Austria and the Czechs. Revolution in France.

No need to recall it all here. Thousands of workers were starving, and they blamed the government for being unable to give them relief. In late February, three days of revolt in Paris brought an end to the monarchy. Louis Philippe, our ''Citizen King,'' abdicated and fled with his family to England. Never again would we see that underestimated little man strolling about Paris with his green umbrella under his arm and talking to his subjects.

That evening, while Céleste and Félicie and I sat in Céleste's darkened apartment listening to the wild shouts and cries in the streets, the Chamber of Deputies, terrorized by a mob, proclaimed a republic.

The upheavals continued. The new government began setting up national workshops, devoted to public work projects, for the unemployed of Paris, but soon ran out of money to finance them. Business came to a standstill. A huge radical demonstration in March nearly overthrew the new government. In the April election, the moderates won control of the national assembly, but in May the workers invaded the assembly hall and again tried to overthrow the government. The moderates, by then thoroughly terrified, decided to abolish the national workshops, which they saw as hotbeds of revolt. And the result, as we all know, was a bloodbath.

Until then, George, always an ardent socialist, had enjoyed herself immensely. She had written manifestoes encouraging the rebels; she had written a dramatic dialogue, celebrating them, for the Comédie Française; she had founded a new radical weekly, *La Cause du Peuple*. But she had a romantic vision of a bloodless revolution in which no one was seriously hurt.

The June Insurrection disillusioned her: it gave Europe the bloodiest street fighting it had ever seen. Paving stones were torn up and trees were felled as the workers of Paris constructed barricades. Troops were called out, and in the next few days almost five thousand rebels and soldiers lay dead or dying in the streets, and God alone knows how many thousands were wounded, scarred, and maimed for life.

But somehow order did return. Paris, sickened of blood, for the most part accepted the repressive measures of the next few months. The assembly agreed on a constitution, and in December a long-time pretender to the throne, Prince Louis Napoleon, soundly trounced his opponents in the national elections and took office as the president of the French Republic.

"The best way to survive a revolution," Céleste had told me, "is curled up in bed with a good book, or a good friend." She was right, and we survived. Not only survived, but were soon thriving again. Even in the bad first five months, we had had some call for our *belle Liane* dresses, and by autumn the orders for our *belle Céleste* and *par belle Céleste* lines were coming in again.

France's troubles were by no means over, but we could begin looking to the future. I always liked to plan ahead, and as early as 1849 we were considering the feasibility of selling our goods in all the larger towns of France. I was thinking, too, of starting a new line of dresses, one less exclusive than the *belle Lianes* but considerably more expensive than the *belle Célestes*. I forsaw increasing prosperity in the near future, and with it a demand for such dresses. And I was right.

"You know," I said to Céleste one evening when we were working late, "if we can succeed this well with our dresses in Paris, I see no reason in the world why we shouldn't open a workshop in London."

"Liane!" she said as if I had knocked her dizzy. "Do you want to sell *all* the dresses to all the women in the world?"

"Why not?"

In England, too, we had difficulties, though not on the scale of those in France. The contract Harry had made with the Admiralty was not quite what we had anticipated. But that was far from heartbreaking—we soon had contracts with the Army and other parties, and in less than two years we were not only expanding our London factory but studying the possibility of opening another in Paris.

But perhaps the most important thing about our success with meat packing was that it put us on the road to preserving other foods. For Harry and Algie and I were not going to be satisfied with a single triumph, no, no, no! Sooner or later our rivals would figure out our process, but meanwhile we would have established Wycherley-Welles Foods and no longer be dependent upon our tinned meats.

And so, indeed, it worked out. When we heard that the Admiralty was considering building its own factory rather than contracting for tinned meat, it bothered us very little. Nothing was going to stop Wycherley-Welles from thriving and growing.

It did seem that I had practically everything a woman could ask for. I had the Midas touch, and despite all setbacks, my investments succeeded, my business ventures flourished. I had a thousand acquaintances, a few close friends, a hundred admirers. I was to be envied as much as any woman I knew. And I was rapidly approaching my goal—to be forever capable, God willing, of standing on my own, never again a dependent or a victim. And yet, and yet . . .

Was more missing from my life than I knew? And if so, what could it be? What was this feeling of hopelessness that sometimes swept over me in the middle of the night, this sense of corners of my soul left unexplored, this loneliness?

Never mind! If loneliness was the price I had to pay to attain my goal, then I would willingly pay it.

Be strong, Augusta, I told myself. Be strong!

I continued to avoid people from my British and American past, for the most part successfully. But one evening at a dinner party in London I found myself being introduced to Mrs. Humphrey Cobbett, a pretty woman whose brow was no longer pinched by a frown, whose full lips were no longer compressed, whose brown hair was no longer pulled back to give her round face a severity it otherwise lacked. Millicent Scarborough! She recognized me instantly, saw my panic, and was quick to reassure me. Later, when she called on me, I confessed some of my history to her, and we renewed and deepened our friendship.

Less amusing were those visitors to Paris from Charleston. Gannon Murdock, like a number of others, was in the habit of coming over every two or three years, and in the autumn of 1849 he nearly caught me in Harry's house. I had just entered the hall and was about to go upstairs to my usual apartment, when Harry entered from the drawing room. When he saw me, he whirled around and said loudly, ''Really, Murdock, since you continue to be so fascinated by our Madame Duhamel, I am sorry you missed her again.''

Fortunately I had my wits about me, and I dived through the doorway that led to the back of the house. Through the door I heard Gannon's voice.

''. . . been interested in her ever since Adam died . . . some of the stories I've heard . . . damned if I know why I have such bad luck meeting her.''

''She said she was going to visit the Rossinis in Bologna, then go on to Rome. Try the Caffè Greco on the Via Conditti— it's one of her favorites.'' Harry's voice perked up impishly. ''By the way, I've been wondering. Whatever happened to Tom Raveneau's pretty little wife? Agatha Raveneau, I believe the name was.''

"Augusta. I have no idea, Harry. I haven't seen her since
. . . my God, it's been over six years!"

"My, my," Harry laughed, "how time flies."

With relief, I heard the front door close.

I had an even narrower escape the next spring. Usually it
was easy enough to avoid Charleston people, even when they
came to our workshops to be fitted for dresses. But on that
particular sunny day, there was not the slightest chance of
escape. I was in the rue de Rivoli, walking toward my
carriage, when another carriage stopped behind it. The door
opened, and a big, laughing, red-faced man in his early thirties
got out. He turned to help a woman down. She, too, was
laughing unrestrainedly—they were both obviously too happy
with each other to give the slightest thought to decorum. For
an instant, as they walked away from their carriage, they both
looked directly into my eyes, and I froze. There was no doubt
about it. They were Beau Legree and Zelda Butler.

Their eyes moved on. They moved on. I moved on.

Oh, the sadness that swept over me then! They had not
recognized me, and I should have been so thankful, yet I
could not be. Beau and Zelda. Would they have known me if
I had been as happy as they? I had forgotten that people could
be so happy.

But never mind, I thought. I had my own well-earned
rewards. I was content.

Wasn't I?

A few months later, toward the end of summer, Céleste's
mother-in-law died.

Odd, but for years I had not thought of Céleste as having a
relative of any kind, and certainly not a *belle-mère*, as the
French say. Then one day a messenger came to our offices,
asked for her, and handed her an envelope. She tore it open
and paled as she read the message. She handed the letter to
me. It was from the old comtesse's lawyer, who said he
wished to discuss Céleste's inheritance.

Her inheritance! It had never occurred to Céleste that she
would receive an inheritance—surely Valentin's mother would
see to that! But no, the lawyer explained to her the next
afternoon, all that had been left in trust for Valentin now went
to his widow. There were no other claimants, and the entire
estate was hers, without let or hindrance.

A few days later we went to see the de Laurence château. It

was a lovely place, with its high mansard roof and dormers, its age-darkened stones, and its surrounding ancient oaks. There was a small staff, worried for their futures, whom Céleste quickly reassured. Then she took me for a tour through those rooms, which she had not seen in years. She was smiling, but her eyes had that old, haunted look which I knew so well.

Later we went for a walk through the fields. It was a glorious day, with puffy white clouds scudding across a sky of deepest blue, the air brisk with the coming autumn, and the leaves just beginning to turn. When we came to a stone wall, Céleste boosted herself up to sit on it and looked around.

"Well, Comtesse," I said, "how does it feel to be mistress of all you survey?"

"Oh, I don't know, Liane. I'm not displeased, of course. But everywhere I look I see reminders of what might have been and now can never be . . . of the happiness Valentin and I might have shared. And I think of that old woman, my *belle-mère*, living alone here and hating me."

I looked at this woman with her wind-tousled blond hair and her sky-blue eyes and wondered how anybody in the world could possibly hate her. This woman who for nine years, almost a third of my life, had been both the sister I had never had and the cousin I had lost. My comrade.

"Liane," she said suddenly, putting her hand on mine, "I'm sorry for the way I've acted toward you at times."

I knew what she meant—a certain bitchiness that we had in common. It was one of the reasons we had taken separate apartments. I smiled and said, "You're no worse than I am."

"Oh, yes, I am. And lately I've been worse than ever."

"Well, we've both been working so hard—"

"No, I don't think it's that. I'm older than you, don't forget, and maybe it's just something that happens to some women at my age. You realize that never again will a shop-girl call you mademoiselle. When you look into the mirror in the evening and see that weary little wrinkle under you eye, you know it won't be gone in the morning. And you think, 'Good-bye, girl-in-the-mirror. Goodbye, whoever you are. . . .' " She smiled, not very happily. "Maybe it's just vanity, but let's face it, Liane—women on their own like us can use good looks as well as intelligence, and beauty does fade.

"Or maybe it's not that at all. Because let's face this too. For some women, not even a hundred lovers, no matter how handsome, rich, and adorable, will ever make up for a well-loved husband and a family.''

I felt a familiar pang. ''Céleste, if that's what you really want, I'm sure that someday—''

''No. I told you long ago that I'd never truly love again, and now I know I was right. The years are going by so fast, and all that has passed me by. And now it's almost time to buy a pussy cat and a saucer for the milk.''

Her voice wavered, and she looked away from me. It had never occurred to me that she felt so strongly about such things.

When she looked at me again, her eyes glistened, but she wore a brave, bright smile. ''Never mind! I'd be a fool to feel sorry for myself. I've had so much that other women miss, things that other women only dream of. *I* am the original *belle Céleste*, and all Paris knows it!'' She reached over and mussed my hair. ''You and I, we're a match for them all, aren't we, Liane?''

''Any time. Just bring them on!''

She hopped down from the wall and gave me a hug, and we started back for the château. But, oh, she was right. The years were going by so fast, and was there a pussy cat and a saucer of milk waiting for me too?

The following autumn and winter were very good indeed. I went to London briefly on business for our packing-case company, which was developing rapidly. We knew that customers preferred to buy certain foods, such as marmalades and preserves, in crocks and jars, and after a good deal of experimentation with various materials—wood, paper, hemp, even gutta-percha—we had worked out a compartmentalized case that minimized breakage and which, most important, we could manufacture cheaply. Our competitors in the preserved-foods business were our best customers.

Back in Paris, life continued at its usual hectic pace. I was at my drawing board, in meetings, at fittings for hours every day, and out with friends almost every evening. I enjoyed the attentions of a young banker who could not have been a wittier or warmer companion. In fact, my life could hardly have been more successful, more crowded with entertaining events. And yet, and yet . . .

I have written of the periods of depression which overcame Céleste and which, for so long, I failed to understand. But increasingly, such periods darkened my life as well. For the most part, I fought them off with work, telling myself to be strong. But in February of 1851 there occurred an incident which, though trivial in itself, plunged me into a melancholy that was worse than anything I had experienced in years.

It involved three of the most beautiful and popular young women in Paris, all members of the Russian aristocracy: Countess Lydia Nesselrode, her cousin Marie Kalergis, and their good friend Princess Nadejda Naryschkine. All three were married, but their unloved husbands were far away, and in Paris they felt free to do exactly as they pleased. They were known for their gay lives, their expensive tastes, and their wild escapades. But I had had no idea of how wild those escapades were until that February afternoon when Lydia and Marie visited me in my apartment.

Perhaps the wine I smelled on their breath had loosened their tongues, or perhaps they had been drinking to bolster their courage. In any case, their chatter, which was frequently bold, was even more so than usual that afternoon. Had I ever attended one of Lord Harry's famous Adam-and-Eve nights? No, I had not, and as far as I knew, he had not even given one in years. Did I think he might give one for them? Why not ask him themselves the next time he was in Paris? Had I ever—oh, you know, Liane—"done it" in front of somebody else? Had I ever "traded partners?"

The questions, the first from Lydia, the second from Marie, were so unexpected that I faltered in answering: "Why . . . no. . . ."

"She *has!*" Marie said, delighted.

"No, I have *not,*" I said, angry with myself for feeling that I had to deny or affirm anything.

"Oh, Liane," Lydia said, "everybody knows that you and Céleste do *every*thing together."

"And *share* everything," Marie added, tittering.

"And everybody knows that everybody in Paris sleeps with everybody else. Why, George Sand has gone down on her back for so many men—"

"Oh, *that* old whore," Marie said, contemptuously.

"That 'old whore,' " I said, "is my friend!"

"Marie doesn't mean it that way," Lydia said placatingly. "She likes George as much as you or I do. The point is that as long as everybody is constantly exchanging lovers, why not just admit it and do it openly?"

"Do it *together*," Marie said.

I tried to retain my sense of humor. "Somehow I don't think you'll find many subscribers to that idea."

Marie tittered again. "You might be surprised."

"Tell us the truth, Liane," Lydia said, "haven't you ever wondered what it would be like to make love with Alex Dumas?"

I had a sense of history repeating itself. How many years ago had I heard almost those same words from Jewel Trevayne? And quite likely these girls thought they were the first to say them.

Finally, with much giggling and many requests for secrecy, their story came out. I confess I was curious—who is not about such matters?—but the tale was hardly original.

Lydia sometime before had taken the young Dumas as a lover, and Marie had taken Alfred de Musset. It was no secret—all Paris knew it. Each woman had been curious about the other's lover, but since the men—Alex especially—had been reluctant to make any kind of exchange, the women had finally settled on a course of action. Having invited the gentlemen to a late supper in Lydia's apartment, the ladies had greeted them *en déshabille*. After a quantity of pheasant and champagne and a good deal of teasing during which most clothes were shed, Marie had without much difficulty persuaded Alfred to make love to her on a couch while Lydia and Alex looked on. Alex had then been obliged to follow suit with Lydia.

Her cheeks aglow, Lydia looked at Marie. "Shall I tell the rest?"

I was beginning to think that both young ladies were *quite* drunk. "Really," I said, "I'm afraid you'll regret—"

"I don't mind," Marie said.

"After that," Lydia went on, "it was easy. . . ."

To put the matter briefly, Lydia had then set out to seduce Alfred in front of the others, and when it became apparent that she was succeeding, Alex, in excitement or jealousy or both, had thrown himself on Marie. "Practically raped her," Lydia said, and Marie tittered at the memory. "And from then on, it was back and forth, back and forth, for the rest of the night."

"All right," I said with a weak laugh, "I have heard enough."

"Now, don't say that you and Céleste haven't done the same—"

"We have not. People have vivid imaginations."

Lydia obviously did not believe me. "Anyway, we had a wonderful idea. Two couples aren't really enough. It's better to have three or four or even five couples, so you can go all night without repeating partners—"

"So we brought in Nadejda and some others," Marie said, "but we need you and Céleste too so that we can always be sure of having enough couples—"

"So if you and Céleste will join us . . ."

Saying I could not speak for Céleste, I declined the invitation, and eventually the ladies left.

The outcome of this little affair is well-known. The secret of the lovers' circle could never be kept, and whispers concerning it swept through the city. About a month after the ladies had visited me, Count Nesselrode, claiming his wife to be an innocent who had been compromised by a scamp, had Lydia removed from Paris by force and brought back home. Alex, who truly loved her, tried to follow but was turned back at the Polish-Russian frontier and never saw her again. Eventually he learned that she was going from lover to lover and no longer had the faintest interest in him. Disillusioned, he then fell in love with Lydia's friend, Princess Nadejda, who left her husband for him, and they have been living together ever since—while Alex composes grim tales of the evils of adultery. Other people's adultery, that is.

But of course, when Lydia and Marie left my apartment that afternoon, these events had still to take place. From my window I watched them enter their carriage and ride away. What did I feel as I stood there? Amusement? Distaste? Sadness? I had no idea.

As if I were observing a stranger, I noticed that my hands were trembling. My hands, my face, my body. . . .

And then it welled up in me—something between rage and grief. How dare they come to me with such an invitation! How dare they think that our friendships and affairs, Céleste's and mine, were in any way comparable to theirs!

I was Mme. Liane Duhamel, artist, designer, the finest *couturière* on the Continent. I was also, though they did not know it, Mrs. Gustava Welles, a leader in industry. I was a woman of achievment and dignity. How dared they think that my life was so shallow, so unfulfilled, so forlorn that I would

waste myself on their endless, trivial pursuit of pleasure!
How dared they!

And yet, if their invitation were so wildly inappropriate,
why was I not laughing instead of standing there trembling,
eyes wide, hands pressed tightly to my mouth to hold back a
cry?

Was it possible that Lydia and Marie were in some fashion
a mirror image of Céleste and me, however distorted?

Was I *really* so much better than they, so different?

Oh, God!

How I got through the months that followed, I shall never
know. Never before in my life had I experienced such a sense
of futility, of utter emptiness. Not even my dreams of recovering the Barony helped me, and my universal remedy, work,
became impossible. I found myself sitting at my drawing
board for hours on end and never moving my hand.

The spring passed, and the summer. I went to London to
attend the Great Exposition and to study the garment market,
but nothing raised my spirits. Céleste had some idea of what
was wrong and tried to help me, but to no avail. George
questioned me, but how could I explain to her what I hardly
understood myself?

Autumn came, and the leaves fell from the trees. What was
missing from my life? Dear God, what was missing, that I
should sicken and wither so?

At last one day I found out.

On that cold, bright November afternoon, after a dress-fitting
appointment, I happened to find myself near the rue Notre-
Dame-de-Lorette, where Eugène had had his studio for the
last half-dozen years, and it occurred to me that I had not
seen him for several months. The thought gave me an excuse
not to return to work, so I gave the driver Eugène's address.

As Jenny led me into the studio and called out my name, I
had a wonderful feeling of homecoming. Why had I stayed
away so long? Had I not known I would find comfort here?
As always, the studio was exceptionally neat, and a big iron
stove kept it tropically hot. It was a long room with a very
high ceiling, a long, wide skylight, and a huge window at one
end, so that it was marvelously bright and airy. A large well-
cushioned purple divan stood on a posing dais in the center of
the room, but the model, if there had been one, had left.

Eugène appeared from behind a canvas and easel, wiping

his hands on a turpentine-soaked rag. He was in shirt sleeves and slippers, which was unusual for him: even close friends rarely saw him so casually attired. He had reached his early fifties by then, and as he came toward me, I noticed for the first time that his thick dark hair was touched with silver. Though the lines about his eyes suggested weariness, the dark eyes themselves were still charged with feverish energy, and his handsome, taut-lipped mouth under the full mustache was almost cruel. With his narrow waist and hips and his white shirt open over his deep chest, he made me think of some exotic warrior chief.

"I thought you had deserted me forever," he said, tossing the rag into a basket with some others and coming to me. "Why didn't Jenny take your hat and coat?"

"I can't stay long, Eugène."

He laughed, took my hands, and kissed my cheek. "I'm not sure I'm ever going to let you go."

His words touched something in my heart that had not been touched in a very long time, and I felt more than ever that this was a homecoming.

Eugène took a moment to wash the turpentine from his hands and to hang up my outer garments. Then, with an arm around me, he led me to the purple divan, where we sat down together and I settled against his side.

"And now, my dear, you must tell me about yourself."

"If I say I've been melancholy, Eugène, you'll laugh. You'll tell me again that a woman isn't capable of melancholy."

He smiled at the memory. "Do you realize, Liane, that it must be . . . almost ten years since that winter afternoon when Céleste first brought you to my studio?"

"You sound melancholy yourself, Eugène."

"I suppose I am. I look about me, and I see . . . Balzac dead last year . . . Chopin the year before . . . and they were both younger than I. And I still have so much to do."

"That simply means that, for you, the best is still to come."

In the next hour as we talked, sharing old memories and anticipating the future, I felt like a creature that had too long been dreaming bad dreams in its dark, dank cave and was at last emerging into the warm, bright sunlight. Why had I been so sad and listless these past months? What were Lydia Nesselrode and Maria Kalergis to me that I should let their foolish invitation wound me? I was Liane Duhamel, a woman with dear, good friends, a woman of accomplishment, a woman with the strength and determination to succeed where most others would have failed. Then why my months of dejection?

Perhaps Eugène felt and reflected my rising happiness, for I saw joy spreading over his face, and I had to fight back the impulse to kiss him on that cruel, beautiful mouth.

"I have an idea," he said suddenly, rising from the divan. "You can stay a while longer, can't you?"

"Why I suppose . . ."

"Good." He hurried to the door and called out, "Jenny! I am at work! I am not to be disturbed under any circumstances!" Returning, he picked up a sketchbook and began looking at me in a special, intent way that I knew well.

"Eugène, you're not going to—"

"Yes. I've put off doing your protrait for too long."

I felt a surge of panic and held up my hands. "Please, no!"

He ignored me. His pencil was already at work. "Do you know that at one time I made a number of portrait sketches of you? Some from life when you weren't aware of it, others from memory—"

"Eugène, you mustn't!"

"—but I didn't care for any of them. I think now, though, that I can get what I want."

"Please, Eugène, no! You *know* I don't want my portrait done!"

He lowered his sketchbook and looked at me with amused exasperation. "My dear woman, do you still cling to that superstition of yours?"

"Yes, Eugène, it's—it's bad luck for me! If my face is portrayed, my dreams may not come true! I believe that!"

He shook his head wonderingly. "Most women would give their souls to be captured on my canvas, but *you* refuse to be portrayed by the great Delacroix! Is it because those old fools still haven't admitted me to the Institut des Beaux-Arts?" He was joking, but there was a note of genuine irritation in his voice.

"Please, Eugène, indulge me. Perhaps someday I'll let you portray me—when I'm very old and very ugly and you want to do the three witches of Macbeth. I'll be happy to be a witch for you."

He laughed and made a gesture of surrender with his

sketchbook and charcoal. "Very well, I won't do a portrait of
you, at least for now. But I'm going to make use of you
nevertheless. Take off your clothes."

"I *beg* your pardon?"

"Take off your clothes. I'm interested in your anatomy,
not your dress. Please take off your clothes."

"Are you serious?"

"Of course I'm serious. Liane, don't act as if you've never
posed in the nude before. Just *take off your clothes*!"

"Five francs?"

"Three. You're still very inexperienced. You may use the
screen over there, if you wish."

I went behind the screen and slowly undressed, feeling as
shy as a virgin schoolgirl who had never before done such a
thing. When I had my clothes off, I edged out from behind
the screen, feeling more naked and vulnerable than I had in
years.

At first Eugène, seated at a drawing table and always the
professional artist, did not even give me a glance. "Get up on
the dais," he said, "in front of the divan," and I, trying to
hide modestly behind two small hands, scurried past him,
to do as I was told. I stood slightly averted from him,
hardly daring to look at him until I heard him speak.

"Good God." It was little more than a whisper.

"Is something wrong?" I asked worriedly.

"No. But I had forgotten."

"Forgotten what, Eugène?" I looked around to see him
still sitting at his drawing table but now staring at me almost
reverently.

"I have always said that a great work of art should be a
feast for the eyes and that nature merely provided the raw
ingredients for the master chef to work with. But now and
then one sees something, a field in sunlight, a child's smile or
an old man's eyes, or perhaps the body of a beautiful woman,
which is almost like God's reproof to the artist. 'Man, be
humble. There is only one true Creator.' " He smiled. "However, I *do* think you've lost a bit too much weight."

We both laughed.

He stood up from the table and came toward me. He stood
facing me with his arms crossed over his chest. In those
moments something was happening between us that had nothing to do with his art and only a little to do with my nudity,
something that had not happened to me in a very long time,

and I found myself with a quaking body and my breath catching in my throat. Eugène saw; he knew. But he spoke only of his art, as if not to frighten me further.

"How shall we use you?" he asked. "A protrait is one thing, but that body. . . . One of my 'amorous nudes,' an odalisque, a new version of *Woman with a Parrot*, perhaps? Or another *Nude on a Divan?* What could possibly do justice to you? God would never forgive me if I did less."

"As long as you don't do my face, Eugène."

He shrugged. "It's a pity. In your case, the face and the body go so beautifully together. But I can always alter the face, if you wish, so that you won't even know yourself."

He walked back and forth and around me, looking at me from every angle, and wherever he looked I felt as if he were touching me. "Odd," he murmured, "how two people can know each other for ten years, and yet . . ."

He sat down behind me on the divan and leaned back on the pillows. "Sit down if you wish," he said.

He was giving me a chance to decline without embarrassment to either of us. Instead I slowly sat down, near him but with my back to him. I curled a leg up under me. When he put his hand on my shoulder, I stiffened for an instant, listening to my heart, then put my hand on his.

"I have loved many women, both lightly and deeply," he said. "At my age I would be very foolish to fall in love again."

"Surely, Eugène, that would depend on whom you fell in love with."

"My work has always come first. It always will."

"I know, I understand."

"I have always thought of women as delightful but disturbing creatures who, if permitted, would devour all one's time and strength."

"I know. You think we're all potential Delilahs."

"Exactly. However . . ." He moved closer, until I felt his warm breath on my bare shoulder. "If one might be permitted just once to kiss an old and very dear friend . . ."

Still holding his hand to one shoulder, I turned my head back over the other. Our mouths met.

There are times when, no matter how old or experienced a woman may be, she becomes an innocent child again. I kissed Eugène as if I had never kissed a man before—lips trembling, teeth chattering, an unbidden cry in my throat. I turned, twisting in his arms to be held and caressed, and then, and then . . .

I knew the meaning of the hopelessness I had so often felt, the longing for something more, the dark nights of my soul. I was strong, but strength was not enough. I was a conqueror, but victories were not enough. I was not meant for mere casual affections and petty amorous games. I was meant for love, for passion, for the enduring heart.

Eugène's hands were like flames on my naked body, and for the first time in so long, I gave myself up entirely to another. This was not merely my dear friend in my arms, we were not merely seeking comfort and consolation in each other's embrace, we were not merely hiding together from the shadows of eternal night—this was my beloved. And, his mouth to mine, he laid me back on the purple divan to make me his.

5 ~~~~~

What more should I say of that November afternoon? I rediscovered delight as Eugène's kisses blessed every part of my body; I rediscovered ecstasy as his lips explored every mound and hollow; I rediscovered the profound difference between mere pleasure and the passion of unstinted, unguarded, unmeasured love. Flinging off his clothes, Eugène took me, there in the waning daylight on the purple divan, took me and raised me to the heavens, raised me again and again, until I could stand the bliss of our lovemaking no longer and came floating down to earth again, exhausted, depleted, light as a feather.

"Oh, Eugène," I sobbed afterwards, "I do love you, I do love you so."

He still lay over me, nestled between my thighs, his body lightly touching mine while my hands coursed up and down his back. He laughed softly and pressed deep, his strength, amazingly, as yet unexpended. "And I love you, my dear

Liane," he said. "I love you as I have not loved in a very long time and may never love again."

"Never again, Eugène, for either of us."

His fingertip traced my cheek under my eye. "Never again is a long time for you, darling. And I'm much older than you."

"Don't speak of it. I'm going to keep you with me forever."

He laughed again, a tender skeptic, and kissed me, moving within and against me slowly, gently, pleasingly.

"Do you know," he said after a moment, lying still again, "I just realized something."

"And what is that?"

"I do think I owe you a few francs."

"Monsieur," I said, pretending offense, "no matter what you may have heard to the contrary, I do not do this for money!"

"A thousand pardons, madame. I was not referring to this particular exercise. When you first modeled for me, and again today, I told you you were worth only three francs a session. I confess, I was wrong."

"Five francs?"

"Well . . . four."

We laughed together, and he nuzzled my throat. After a moment, he lifted himself from me and pressed back again.

"More?"

"Oh, Eugène," I laughed, "I couldn't!"

"You're certain?"

"Certain."

"Then . . . may *I* madame?"

"Monsieur, please do!"

He closed his eyes. Purring like a cat, a tigerlike smile on his face, he began again. And I found that I was wrong. As I tried to help him, as I tried to give all that love could give, I received in return. The evening light that came through the great skylight turned orange and crimson and purple, and we seemed to rise up and become one with it. And when at last his moment came, I was with him—two lovers locked together and lost in their ecstasy, sharing for a little while a glimpse of heaven.

The world was bright again. And why had I ever thought it otherwise?

Great events were happening in those months, but Eugène

and I were almost too wrapped up in each other to notice them. We did, of course, know that Louis Napoleon was not going to be satisfied with being president of the French Republic, and certainly not with a single four-year term. A few months before, he had tried to get a revision of the article of the constitution which forbade two successive terms for the president, but had failed. Nevertheless, he had had a clear majority of the assembly behind him, if not the three-quarters necessary for constitutional revision, and a return to empire seemed imminent.

The coup d'état came on December 2, just a few weeks after Eugène and I had discovered our love. I arose that morning to find soldiers in the street, the newspapers shut down, and posters announcing the dissolution of the assembly. The Army, it seemed, had occupied the Palais Bourbon, where the assembly met, and hundreds of deputies were being arrested. I hurried to Eugène's studio.

"You shouldn't be out on the streets on a day like this," he said. "Anything can happen."

"But most people have been expecting this. And the streets seem quiet enough."

"So does gunpowder—before someone puts a match to it."

He was right. The next day there was a popular uprising, barricades were thrown up, and troops clashed with the working people of Paris. And on the third day, troops fired on an unarmed crowd—the Massacre of the Boulevards—and once again blood flowed over the cobblestones. But repression was stern, and quiet soon returned to the city. A plebiscite gave Louis Napoleon the right to draw up a new constitution, which he did, putting virtually all power into his own hands and giving himself a ten-year term. In effect, France was once again an empire, and another plebescite would confirm this the following November, when Louis Napoleon would assume the title Napoleon III.

But we had so much else on our minds, Eugène and I. How could I have known that love could make a thirty-year-old woman feel like a sixteen-year-old girl? All the magic had come back to my days, and I seemed to hear music wherever I went. Had the church bells really rung during those bleak past months? Only now did I hear them, and night and day I wanted to sing.

I did do my best not to take up too much of Eugène's time.

He still had his work, the work that always came first, just as
I had mine. But his studio had been open to me since I had
become his pupil, and now I spent more time in it than I had
in years, frequently joining his other pupils and receiving his
merciless criticism. He never spared me, any more than he
did the others, nor would I have wanted him to. Every word
he spoke to me was part of the music of my life.

But of course the best times were when we were alone.
Only then would I pose for him. Eugène would call to Jenny
that we were not to be disturbed, he would close the door,
and I would disrobe. But his discipline was rigid, and seldom
could I persuade him to make love right away.

"A few sketches first . . ."

It was like those early days when I had first posed for
him—I on a couch or a chair or the floor itself, changing
positions on his command; he working rapidly, eyes intent,
rarely speaking a word. But just as he had never used those
first sketches, he found nothing he could use now, and after
an hour or so he usually threw his pencil to the floor in
disgust.

"I am not getting what I want! I find myself doing the
same sketches over and over again!"

"You're trying too hard, Eugène. Relax, think of something else. Don't pursue it, let it come to you."

"Ha! Now the pupil is giving the master lessons."

"Only those I learned in your studio."

I would drape any handy sheet around me, and Jenny
would bring tea and biscuits, and we would relax for half an
hour. Then it was back to work again, until . . .

"No more. Come to me, Eugène. It's time now for something else."

And we would make love.

Glorious days, glorious nights. He was different from any
other man I had ever known. Whatever he might have lacked
of the youthful vigor of one lover or the passionate drama of
another, I never missed it. The vigor and the drama of his
soul went into his painting, while for me he reserved a
gentleness, a tenderness, a sensitive finesse such as I had
never before experienced. Oh, dear Lord, I sometimes prayed,
only let me express my love for him as beautifully as he does
his for me.

Not that we did not have our little differences and our share
of spats from time to time—of course we did. Several times,

when I had been posing for an hour or more, I got up and glanced over his shoulder to find that he was not doing a figure study at all but a portrait sketch.

"Eugène, I have *asked* you—"

"All right, all right. It's for my own amusement, and nobody is going to see it. You see, I'm tearing it up."

.The third or fourth time this happened, shortly after the New Year, he became angry. "What is this strange obsession with guarding your image! Have I harmed your face in some way? Am I causing you pain? Even if I showed this drawing to all Paris, would you be hurt? But I have no intention of showing it to anyone in the world!"

"Then why must you—"

"Because that face presents a challenge to me! Because I am an artist first of all, and both the artist and the man in me are in love with that face! You say, 'Don't portray my face,' and it's as if you were saying, 'Put out your eyes and cut off your hands!' "

The silence between us was charged with pain.

"I'm sorry, Eugène. But it's something I can't help. Perhaps I had better leave now."

When I started toward the screen where I had left my clothes, he stepped in front of me. "You are not going to leave."

I did not care for a peremptory tone, even from Eugène. "And why not?"

"Because I know you. And if you leave now, you may decide not to return until I ask you."

With alarm, I heard myself saying, "That's very possible."

"And I may be too big a fool to do so. Don't leave, Liane, unless you truly wish to be done with me. Is that what you wish?"

His eyes, ablaze with dark fire, frightened me. But the fact that I was close to losing something so precious to me frightened me even more. Then his arms were around me, his cruel lips were on my throat, and once again I found myself melting, melting. . . .

Until that quarrel, I had seemed to dwell in an eternal present, as if life either before or after our love were unimaginable. That I might lose Eugène? Unthinkable!

But the incident brought me at least a little bit back to

common sense. Would we really go on just as we were, I wondered, for the next ten or twenty or thirty years?

"Eugène," I said one Sunday afternoon, "Why don't you marry me?"

Eugène gave me a quick, startled look. I was once again lying naked on the purple divan while he worked at a nearby table.

"Why should I marry you?" he asked.

"I could live with you. I could take care of all your needs."

"Jenny takes care of all my needs very well, thank you."

"Not *quite* all of them, I hope."

He smiled and did not answer.

"Would you be pleased," I asked, "if we had a child?"

"No."

"Why not?"

"Because a child, like a talkative woman, is a distraction. And I have no time for distractions."

"Any child of yours would be very sweet."

"Nonsense. All children, without exception, are little demons. I remember distinctly that, as a child, I was the worst demon imaginable."

"But if I were accidentally to bear you a little demon—and it could happen—would you mind?"

He looked at me coolly. "Are you pregnant?"

"No."

"And you are not the kind of woman, surely, to plan a little 'accident,' are you?"

I could be as cool as he. "No, Eugène, I am not. And I resent your suggesting such a thing."

"I didn't introduce the subject, but since it has come up, let us have an understanding. I love you, my dear, as much as any other woman I have ever known. But I am not just starting out in life, and neither are you. I have worked very hard to contrive a comfortable mode of existence, and I know that you have done the same. We have achieved, or are achieving, what we have dreamed of. And on top of that we have been blessed with our love. That seems to me to be a most marvelous arrangement, and I see no reason in the world to change it."

"No. Of course you're right."

So I said, but why did I think at that moment of a sun-warmed stream in South Carolina and my own old dream of taking my children to it as my mother had taken me so long before? It did seem increasingly unlikely that I would ever have children, by Eugène or anyone else.

I looked up, as I heard Eugène's chair scrape away from the table, and saw him coming toward me.

"You look sad," he said, smiling at me.

"I'm sorry. I'm not."

"You are." Sitting down on the divan, he drew me into his arms. "But I know a way to take the sadness from your face. And silence a chatterbox at the same time."

I smiled back at him. I would not think about the next ten or twenty or thirty years, but simply accept my happiness. But one thought did nag at me, marring my contentment.

Why did I not allow Eugène to paint my portrait? If I were committing myself wholly to him, why should I not call a halt to the masquerade I had lived for so many years? Surely it no longer mattered if Liane Duhamel were recognized by someone from Charleston.

And yet when I contemplated revealing the truth, I found my hands growing damp and my breath coming short. To reveal myself as Augusta Welles was to bring her to an end. From the day I let the truth be known, I would be Liane Duhamel forever, and Augusta Welles would never again go home.

Hence, I delayed saying anything to Eugène, though I told myself I intended eventually to do so. Delayed, as it happened, too long.

I think I intended to tell him that February day during carnival when I went to his studio. *"Eugène, if you still wish to paint me . . ."* Or perhaps I only *wanted* to tell him. In any case, I knew I could not delay much longer: to do so was mere weakness and unworthy of my love for him.

When I arrived at the studio, Eugène was gone but expected back soon, and Jenny, as usual, let me in and left me to my own devices. I hung up my outer garments, adjusted the draft on the stove, and wandered about the big room, looking for something to occupy my time.

Was I meant to find the big portfolio? Was it Eugène's way of letting me know? Of letting me make the decision?

I had never snooped through Eugène's possessions, had never opened cabinets or drawers. But—unusual for him—the portfolio had been left out in the open on one of the tables. I, without a thought in my head, opened it up.

And found myself staring at my own face.

It was a pencil drawing, a three-quarter view, life-size. A line led from the brow to a comment: "No!" Other lines pointed to the mouth and the chin—features not rendered to Eugène's satisfaction.

Feeling slightly stunned, I turned the drawing over to see what lay beneath it.

There was another drawing of my face, from another angle.

And beneath it, another . . . and still another . . .

Pencil drawings, charcoal drawings, watercolors . . .

Besides the portrait studies, there were sketched out a number of scenes which meant little or nothing to me—composition studies, all very tentative. Amidst these studies, I found a list headed: *"The L. D. canvas."* It read:

> Paola & Francesca?
> Abélard & Héloïse?
> Tristan & Iseult?
> Anthony & Cleopatra?
>   Caesar & C.? No, no, no! Then
>   *what? who?*

Eugène's words, repeated time and again, came back to me:

"I'm not getting what I want!

"I don't know what to do with you!

"My work has always come first. It always will."

Oh, what a fool I had been!

The evidence was there, indisputable. From the very beginning Eugène had intended to use my face for a major canvas. And knowing I would not permit it, he had made his studies secretly.

"But sacristi! I don't know how to use *you!"*

How to use me. Oh, yes, he had used me, certainly, or tried to, just as he had used others—the models he had bedded and kept satisfied until he was finished with them.

Hardly knowing whether to rage or to weep, I found I could do neither. For a time I sat there, sick at heart, wondering what I would say to Eugène when he arrived. When he did not appear, I acted, as I thought, within my rights: I reclaimed what was mine. My features, my face. I took only those studies which clearly showed my face, and I fed them into the big cast-iron stove. When I had finished, I put my outer garments back on and, not daring even a word to Jenny, I left.

I felt old and tired, and every hour that passed seemed to add another year to my life. Back in my apartment, I had the fire in the fireplace built up, and I sat close by it, feeling as if I would never be warm again. My heart was slowly turning to stone, and my bones were cold, cold, cold.

What a fool I had made of myself, thinking that I was someone special to Eugène, thinking that there still might be a great love in my life. Why had I not been wise enough to accept what I was and what I already had? But, no, that had not been enough for me. I had had to have "true love." I had had to love the great Eugène Delacroix—and delude myself that he could love me in return.

It was late when he came to my apartment, but carnival singing could still be heard outside in the streets. When the maid brought him into the room, his eyes were dark with fatigue, but he seemed quite in control of himself. He was heavily dressed against the cold weather, and was carrying what appeared to be a tube of rolled drawing paper about two feet long. I stood braced against his onslaught, but he merely smiled.

"Don't be afraid. I am no longer angry. I came to apologize."

"Take off your coat."

"My carriage is waiting. I can stay only a moment."

Nevertheless he did take off his coat, and I poured two brandies. We settled facing each other before the fire, which provided the only nearby light, and Eugène dropped the tube of paper by the side of his chair. He smiled at me again.

"As I said, I came to apologize."

"I thought you loved me, Eugène."

"I do. But I have told you often, my dear, my work always comes first. Before anything else in the world."

"And that was a sufficient reason for betraying my trust?"

"I'm not sure. If I were, I would not be here now, saying I am truly sorry."

"Eugène, admit it. All you were interested in from the very beginning was using me for a painting."

"No, Liane. That was not all."

"But you admit that that *was* the most important thing to you."

He shrugged. "Everything has its place. Work, love, pleasure. . . . But yes, from that first day I wanted to use you, felt I *had* to use you. But I didn't know how. I kept looking for the perfect vision and never quite finding it."

"Then nothing is lost, is it?"

"Oh, yes. A great deal is lost. A masterpiece, perhaps."

"I'm sorry, Eugène."

"And I keep asking myself, why, why, why wouldn't you let me paint you?"

"I have told you—"

"No, I mean the true reason."

"I think I would have let you, in time, Eugène. In fact, I was going to tell you that when I went to your studio this afternoon."

His smile was sympathetic but unbelieving. "Liane, we have been lovers for over three months. And friends for how many years? And it took you this long?"

"I'm sorry you don't believe me."

"Tell me, do you still love me?"

"Yes."

"Are you willing to let me paint you now?"

"I don't know."

I said the words before I thought, and they were honest. And that threw everything into question, even the depth of my love for Eugène. But I had *wanted* so much to love him. . . .

He leaned forward to touch my hand. "My dear, I have no idea why it is that you choose to keep the image of your face to yourself. I only know that there is some part of your heart, some part of your soul, that you keep inviolate—even from the man who loves you. And perhaps that is good. People like us, Liane—we need that. It is one of the sources of our strength. The place where we keep our secret dream. The place that can never be revealed until the dream is completely fulfilled—even though that may never come to pass."

He leaned back in his chair, sipped his brandy, and laughed quietly. "I've heard you and Céleste refer to me as a 'glorious monster'—no, no, I wasn't offended. Because it's true. People like us—you and me, my dear—we *must* appear to be monsters to the rest of the world in order to accomplish what we do. Our dreams, our hungers, our ideals, are so much larger than those of most people. And we must fulfill them or die. We *are* monsters!''

"Even when we love, Eugène?"

"When we love, my dear, it is dragons who mate." He drank the last of his brandy. "Well, it is late, and I must be going."

We stood up and put our glasses aside on the mantel. I helped Eugène into his coat, and he turned toward the door.

"Oh, Eugène . . ."

I had noticed the roll of paper still lying by his chair, forgotten, and I handed it to him.

"Oh, yes. This wasn't in the portfolio, so you overlooked it. It doesn't matter now, but I thought it was the best idea I had thus far."

He unrolled the paper and held it up so that we could see it by the firelight. For a moment my heart stopped.

It was a drawing of a male and a female, nude, done with ink and brush, and unfinished. It had been done quickly, almost slapdash, but its very crudeness gave it vitality. The female was sitting and leaning back on something that had hardly even been sketched in, perhaps the purple divan with cushions. Her eyes were half-closed; her full mouth, with its downturned corners, was swollen with desire. Her arms were flung out, her thighs spread apart. The male was well above her, his back arched, his face turned away so as not to distract the viewer's gaze from hers, his near arm held out wide. One knee was on her far side, on the divan by her hip; the other leg was extended between her thighs; but he touched her nowhere except with a hand supporting the back of her head. He was not yet conventionally draped, as he surely would have been in a finished painting, and Eugène's sketchy brush strokes suggested that he, too, was the captive of desire.

In a hushed voice, I said, "It's beautiful."

And it was. The male, clean-lined, graceful, and powerfully sinewed, was the classical ideal. But he was not the true subject of the drawing. The true subject was the female; and whoever the woman she was supposed to represent—Francesca da Rimini or Héloïse or Woman herself—she was a symbol of every woman who had ever offered her soul through her body. In the flickering firelight, both figures seemed to come to life, seemed on the verge of moving together to consummate their passion. It was one of the most perfect drawings I had ever seen, one of the most sensuous, one of the loveliest—in its own small way, a masterpiece.

"Ah, well," Eugène said, and he tossed it into the fire.

I cried out and, without a thought, reached for it, but Eugène pulled me back. In that instant, I saw the sad, weary, contemptuous, amused look in his eyes. His act had been at once a gesture of propitiation—and of revenge.

"Now you needn't worry," he said, drawing me into his arms. "That's the last of them. Am I forgiven?"

"Of course, my darling."

"And you do still love me a little?"

"I always will."

We kissed and I went with him to the door. We kissed again and parted.

I returned to the fireplace to watch the last corners of the drawing darken and curl in the flames and crumble into ashes.

6 ~~~~~

There was no more love after that, not really.

Oh, yes, Eugène and I would always have a kind of love for each other, and the deepest mutual respect. But I never again posed for him, and we drifted apart. We never ceased to be friends, we met socially, and I visited his studio from time to time. But I never again entered it alone.

"What's become of Eugène?" Céleste asked.

"Oh, I gave him up for Lent."

For Lent, and for good.

Not only Eugène, but all other men as well. I was determined to put all that behind me. Perhaps, I thought, I was not even capable of the kind of grand love of which a young girl dreams. Was that not what Eugène had told me, the same thing that Alfred had told me years before, that mine was only a "Sunday love" and sometimes not even that? (Damn them both!) If so, too bad, because I was no longer willing to settle for that. And if on certain lonely nights my longing seemed more poignant than ever, well, perhaps that was punishment for my sins, and by sheer will power I would bank my fires. And I would allow myself no more melancholy, no more despondency. I would work. I would be strong.

Certainly there was plenty to do. I was studying the advantages of sewing machines, for instance. Their use in the garment industry was not new—M. Barthelemy Thimmonier had had about eighty in operation back in 1841, but a mob of workers, fearing for their jobs, had destroyed them. I was acquainted with the Elias Howe and the Wheeler and Wilson machines, I had seen M. Thimmonier's latest machine at the Great Exposition, and I had heard about Isaac Singer's recent patent. I was certain that such machines were soon going to change the industry, and I was determined that nobody was going to get ahead of *belle Liane*.

And there was the matter of our first London workshop. For over a year, even during my period of melancholy, we had been studying the London garment market. We had come to realize that we could not simply move our lines of dresses, unmodified, from Paris to London, no matter how admired they might be. The average London housewife with a few shillings to spare might *think* she liked the latest fashions from Paris, just as Parisians thought they were interested in the latest from London; but actually the two cities were distinctly different markets, and we had to design for them accordingly. In London, some of our "latest from Paris" dresses would be very English indeed.

I spent most of the summer and part of the autumn in London, and both Céleste and Félicie Colombier made trips across the Channel to help me. But I myself had to do most of the dealing with shops owners, mill owners, and others, because they did not altogether trust a French accent. Fortunately my English accent helped them forget I was *Mme*. and not *Mrs*. Duhamel, and I also received much help from my friend, Mrs. Humphrey Cobbett—known to me earlier as Millie Scarborough. Millie did not need the money, but she enjoyed the challenge.

Naturally, while feigning indifference, Harry watched our activities with great curiosity, and one evening after dinner at the Cobbetts' home, he got to his point of interest.

"This business of opening a new atelier," he said, when

he had cornered me in the conservatory apart from the others, "it must be costing you ladies a great deal."

"Nothing ventured, nothing gained, Harry."

"But do you think it's wise to risk so much?"

"We really have no choice."

"You could take in a partner, you know."

At last! I had been waiting for him to make the first move.

"Oh, I think not. This is *our* venture, and I believe we ladies would prefer to keep it among ourselves."

"If you take in a partner, you'll decrease the risk."

"But if we don't, we'll increase the gain. Besides, Harry, a social occasion is hardly the proper time to talk business."

"Now, see here, Augusta—"

Conveniently, Mr. Cobbett chose that moment to join us.

But Harry was not easy to evade, nor did I wish him to be. The next day he appeared in my office at our meat-packing plant.

"Perhaps we can strike a bargain," he said, dropping into a chair. "Allow me into your new venture, and I'll allow you into mine."

I had not expected that. I had expected him to be so persuasive that I could only yield gracefully and take his money—as I had intended to do all along. "I don't think so, Harry."

"Hear me out. Thus far you have tried to reach only the more affluent markets, even in the goods you turn out for the emporiums."

"Simply because that is where the money is."

"That is true. But the relatively poor must be clothed too; and in the coming years there is going to be a growing market for the kind of factory-made clothes that can be turned out just as cheaply as possible."

"The sweat system, you mean? Dealing with contractors and subcontractors, exploiting women and children—"

"Now, you know those women and children need work."

"I don't care. I won't do it."

"Very well, then, don't. But somebody is going to, and whoever takes your share of the market is going to sweat those workers far worse than you ever would."

I shook my head. "In that kind of trade, Harry, you've no choice but to sweat your people or go under. And that's not going to change for a long time to come."

"Oh, I don't know. Up in Leeds, for example, you don't

have all this cheap female labor whenever you want it. That means less homework and higher labor and factory costs, perhaps, but other costs are lower. London is not the only city in England where one can manufacture, you know.''

Leeds. I had not thought of that.

"Even so, Harry, I honestly don't think—''

"You're right, don't think yet, just listen. Augusta, there are a number of people I could go to with this, but I want to work with you. And what I have to offer, once again, is money—and contracts. And I refer, of course, to the Admiralty.''

"The Admiralty?''

"Uniforms. Thousands of uniforms. Enough uniforms to pay for my initial investment, make a tidy profit for both of us, and establish us in the cheap-clothing business. And up in Leeds you can keep the sweating to a minimum. Do I have your attention, my dear?''

"Keep talking, Harry.''

It was fortunate that I could leave our newly established London workshop in Millie's capable hands, and during the past five months I had found them very capable indeed—because I had been back in Paris for only a few weeks when trouble began.

At first we thought it was just one of those maddening incidents. In transporting our goods from our workshops through the filthy streets of Paris to the stores, there were bound to be accidents: a dress of two might easily be dropped into a gutter or splashed by a passing carriage. In this particular case, an entire rack of dresses was shoved over by three of four boisterous drunks and trod into the dirt.

The same thing happened two days later.

And again the next day.

That afternoon one of our seamstresses came to my office, frightened and weeping. Like many of our people, she worked in her own home—it was convenient for her and reduced costs for us—and on her way to us with a dress, she had been assaulted by a couple of youths and robbed. As they had run away with the dress, one of the thieves had yelled, "If you don't like it, don't work for that bitch, Duhamel.'' At that point we realized that several of our homeworkers had not brought work in recently.

Félicie said, "I'm going to find out about this.''

It did not take her long. The next morning she came to my office and told Céleste and me what she had learned.

It seemed that one of the principle dressmakers in Paris, Mlle. Dubufe, had been doing very poorly that season.

"And so," Félicie went on, "Apparently two or three weeks ago she decided to correct that situation."

"Eliminate some competition," Céleste said.

"Exactly. She came out of the gutter, la Dubufe, and part of her still dwells there. It seems she enlisted the aid of her brother, Etienne Dubufe, and his gang of ruffians. Their game is to scare off seamstresses and damage goods so that the rest of us will find it difficult or even impossible to deliver orders. They started on Madame Roget and Madame Cadol and only just got around to us. Other dressmakers have had their work damaged or stolen too."

As Félicie spoke, I felt the strength draining out of me. We had all been wearing ourselves to the bone in preparation for Christmas and the New Year, but if Félicie was right, if these attacks were going to continue and even get worse, our efforts would be for nothing. For weeks I had been sleeping only four or five hours a night and sometimes less, and I did not see how I could possibly face this new problem. Why did I not simply close up shop, I thought, burying my face in my hands, and say, Devil take it. Both Céleste and I were now wealthy enough that, if we wished, we needed never again lift a hand.

But did I really want to let all our efforts here in Paris go to waste? And what about Félicie? What about the women who worked for us? What would they do, with Christmas coming? Most of them needed every franc they earned.

Somehow—for the ten thousandth time, it seemed to me—I gathered up my strength.

"What are the other dressmakers doing about all this?" I asked.

"Nothing very effective, as yet. Roget thought Cadol was responsible and got some bullies to attack Cadol's people, and Cadol swears she is going to get even with Roget and Dubufe both. I suspect this whole thing is going to turn into a cat-and-dog fight, and in the end we're all going to lose."

"No, we won't," I said. "If anyone wants a fight, we're going to give it to him. And we're going to win. Félicie, do you have any idea of how we can get some bullies of our own?"

Félicie nodded. "The same man who gave me my information. Dirty Sylvestre."

"Dirty *Sylvestre?*"

"You smile, my dear, but Dirty Sylvestre is a true savage. And, I might add, a very close friend for a number of years. He has an army of loyal followers—thieves, cutthroats, and brutes—and he would like nothing better than to tangle once again with his old enemy, Etienne Dubufe."

"Then bring him to me."

Thus began the garment-trade war of 'fifty-two and 'fifty-three.

I did try to talk sense to some of the other dressmakers that evening, but Mmes. Roget and Cadol were too angry to listen, and Mlle. Dubufe refused to see me. By the time Félicie brought Sylvestre to my office the next morning, I was quite ready to do battle.

Sylvestre looked like an overgrown rat from the sewers of Paris. Of indeterminate age and hairier than any man I had ever seen, he was tall and wiry, with a huge, long torso and very short bandy legs. His eyes glared out from under eyebrows as thick and shaggy as his beard, his teeth resembled those of a horse, and a badly mutilated left ear flapped idly at the side of his head. He saw me staring at the ear and laughed.

"Long time ago my old friend Etienne, he bite it off." Sylvestre's voice was a low, hoarse growl, and his accent that of the lowest criminal haunts. "My luck is, my little turtledove Félicie is near and she sews it back on. Everyone says it gonna turn sickly and kill me, and for weeks I *do* get sick as hell. But I never give up my ear! And today . . ." He flipped the hinged ear with a fingertip. "Today, good as new!"

"And," said Félicie worshipfully, "my Sylvestre soon took his revenge."

"What was that?" Céleste asked.

"You gotta ask, madame?" Sylvestre grinned wickedly. "Today my old friend, he don't hear so good. Not for nothin' they call him Earless Etienne!"

We had found our man.

In the next few weeks, the situation became one of all-out war. We had one or more spies near every important dressmaker's workshop, watching the comings and goings, and no doubt they had their spies watching us. We guarded our people and our goods as well as we could, though there could be little protection from roving gangs, fast-driven carriages, and filth thrown from rooftops. But we gave as good as we got—and better. A rack of our dresses was destroyed in the street by a gang of bullies? Very well, Sylvestre soon knew who was responsible, and if it was, say, Etienne Dubufe, then Mlle. Dubufe could count on losing two or three racks of dresses. A couple of our seamstresses were prevented from reaching our workshops by Mme. Cadol's bullies? Very well, that was worth a dozen or so of Mme. Cadol's dresses. Short of murder or arson, we were ready to make almost any kind of reprisal.

Though Sylvestre liked to play the clown when among friends, he proved to be not only a ferocious fighter but an intelligent general. "Now, I want all of you to remember," he told his men, "nobody is paying you to bust skulls or get your own busted. You're being paid to get our goods to market and keep their goods away. If you got to bust skulls to do that, fine. But if you can't do that, nobody is gonna give a damn whether you get your skull busted or not."

Sometimes Céleste and I were even more ferocious than Sylvestre. "I want you to go after those sons of bitches," Céleste roared at him after one of our ladies had been hurt by a couple of Mme. Roget's bullies, "and when you find them, I want to hear the sound of splintering bones!" And when Sylvestre suffered one of his rare defeats, I found myself telling him, "The next time you meet Etienne Dubufe, I want you to come back here with either his head on a platter—or your own!"

An ill-chosen image. As soon as Sylvestre had left the office, Céleste and I broke into wild laughter at the thought of his returning from battle, sheepish as a schoolboy, with his own head on a platter.

So it went, through November, December, January. Though we had not wished for a war, once it was thrust upon us we were in no hurry to end it before Mlle. Dubufe and the others had learned their lesson.

By February, I thought that time had come. The services of Sylvestre and his men had been well worth their cost, and we were far better off than our enemies. Our *belle Liane* trade had not suffered at all, and our other lines were making at least a small profit. On the whole we were coming out of the war in a stronger competitive position than we had gone into it.

One afternoon, therefore, Céleste, Félicie, and I called on Mme. Cadol. She cursed us in three or four languages and then listened to reason. Neither she nor we had wanted this state of affairs, and there was no reason why we should not be allies and protect each other. That agreed, we then persuaded her that we should approach Mme. Roget and some other dressmakers. Very quickly we built up a strong alliance. And finally we called a meeting of all the leading dressmakers of Paris and announced that they could either stop fighting and join our "protective society" or take their chances and face ruin. Naturally, they joined. As for Mlle. Dubufe, who had started the whole costly conflict, I did not wish to deprive her of her livelihood, but I used my growing influence to guarantee that never again would she get an important contract—unless she worked for me.

At that point I wanted nothing in the world so much as a full week's sleep, but there was no time for that. We had to complete our preparations for Easter, then hurry to London to do the same there. And on the Monday following Easter, Céleste, Harry, and I departed for Leeds, where we were expanding our garment factory. I thought of it as a factory rather than a workshop because I intended to use the latest and best machinery—such as the new Singer sewing machines.

"And what about all these cottons and woolens we're buying?" I said to Harry one afternoon. "Somebody's making a profit on them. Don't you think we should consider having our own mills? We could make a profit on the material as well as on the finished uniforms."

Harry gave his head a quick shake, as if to clear it. "Gussie, don't you ever stop? I mean, I do know that this factory was my idea, but there is such a thing as spreading oneself too thin."

"But I'm not suggesting that we risk anything, Harry, at least not right away. I'm only suggesting that we *think* about it."

Think and, eventually, do. But meanwhile we had to get back to London for conferences with Millie and Algie. Our *belle Céleste* line was a resounding success in London, and both our preserved foods and our packing-case firms were expanding rapidly. In June, Céleste and I returned to Paris to work on the fall designs, but in August I was back in London. There would be no vacation at Nohant that year—in fact, it had been several years since I had had any real vacation at all.

September. Back to Paris. It was by far our biggest year, and we had to expand our workshops. Special Christmas commissions for *belle Liane* gowns were already coming in, and I was working on designs for the next spring. October and November passed so rapidly I never knew what happened to them, and then Christmas and the New Year were on us. A day or two of recuperation, and we began making costumes.

And then once again it was carnival.

Carnival and Mardi gras gave us a few days' respite, for we closed up shop through Shrovetide and Ash Wednesday. The evening of our closing was a time of celebration, and the last hour or so was devoted largely to the consumption of champagne. One of the nicest things in the world, I thought, was simply wandering through our workshops on the evening before a holiday, listening to our ladies' laughter and the popping of champagne corks.

On that particular evening, Harry had stopped by to wile away an hour before going to the theater, and Céleste and Félicie were there with me. When the lamps started going out and the ladies moved toward the door calling "Goodnight, goodnight!" I had an idea. "Why don't the three of us," I said, turning to Céleste and Félicie, "go somewhere and have a nice supper together."

"Oh, I'd love to, dear," Félicie said, "but you see, Sylvestre and I had already planned . . ." And sure enough, who appeared at that very moment but Sylvestre, trimmed, tailored, and top-hatted like the most stylish boulevardier, and Félicie was whisked away on his arm.

"Céleste?"

"I am sorry, Liane, but . . ." She smiled naughtily. "I met someone quite wonderful last week, and it's been so long since I've, ah, well you know . . ." The brightness in her blue eyes faded as she looked at me. "Liane, are you all right?"

"Of course. Why wouldn't I be?"

"You look tired."

"I am. I shouldn't have suggested supper. I'm going straight home, have a bite to eat, and go to bed."

Céleste frowned. "My friend has a box at the Comédie, and we're going to supper afterward. Why don't you join us?"

"Oh, no, that would hardly make a romantic evening."

"Perhaps he can find a friend for you, if you like."

"No, no, no, you go on and have a good time."

"Well, if you're sure . . ."

While Céleste said goodnight to the last of the ladies and waited for her escort, I went to look out a dormer window. The workshop was in the loft of a building so situated that I could see out over many of the rooftops of Paris—could see lights twinkling in distant windows and the glow of the gas and oil lamps in the streets below. Another carnival, I thought. So much in my life had happened around carnival time. Last year we had ended the garment-trade war. The year before that I had ended my affair with Eugène. And the year before that . . .

Had it really been seven years since I had sat at Marie Duplessis's bedside, holding her hand and waiting for her death, at carnival? *Seven years?*

I was almost thirty-three years old, and where had the time gone? Where, dear Lord, where? Marie was a legend now. She had hardly been cold in her grave before Alex Dumas had begun his novel about her, *La Dame aux camélias*, and followed it with his play. And now Verdi had turned her story into an opera, *La Traviata*.

Well, nobody is ever going to turn your story into an opera, my girl, I thought—you didn't have the good luck to die young.

It was a maudlin thought, born of champagne, and unworthy of a grown woman. But it brought tears to my eyes all the same.

"Yes, you've done it, haven't you, Madame Duhamel?"

The soft voice at my ear startled me. Looking around, I found Harry at my shoulder.

"You've done it," he repeated. "Look at those lights. That's Paris. And you've made it yours."

"Have I, Harry?"

"I remember a dozen years ago, when you were little more than a waif in this city, deserted by your husband and all but penniless. And look what you've done since. Is there a woman in Paris who doesn't feel a spark of envy when she thinks of you? Or a man who wouldn't take pride in having you at his side?"

"Oh, come now . . ."

"It's true. And of course they don't know half of what I know. May I make a little confession to you?"

"I'd rather you didn't. I don't like confessions."

"This one won't hurt you, at least not as long as you don't take it too seriously. You see, for almost as long as I've known you, I've been just a little bit in love with you . . ."

I felt stunned. What he said explained so many things. Why had I never suspected?

". . . But of course I knew I didn't have a chance, and I'm not a man to make a fool of myself. As I say, please don't take this too seriously, because God knows *I* don't. Love is such a *gross* inconvenience."

"No, Harry, I won't take what you say too seriously. And I do agree with you about love . . . so inconvenient . . ."

"It really has little place in the lives of the truly strong, people like you and me and Eugène—and even George, if only the old cow knew it. Oh, it's fine and dandy for the idle hour or the weekend diversion, but we, the strong, were meant *do* things—to make and build and create. And you, Augusta, are without doubt the strongest woman I have ever known."

"Am I, Harry?"

"You've taken on the worlds of art, science, and business enterprise and mastered them all. You virtually *invented* modern meat-packing—took the first important steps forward since Nicolas Appert, and our competition is still trying to find out how we do it. You are the leading designer and *couturière* of Paris—which is to say, of the world. In Leeds you are revolutionizing mass-produced garment manufacture, and when we get our own mills . . . tell me, Augusta, where will it all end?"

"I don't know, Harry, I don't know."

"I've never known anyone like you. You're not afraid of any idea, any possibility, and the thought of failure never daunts you. And when either friend or enemy opposes you . . . Oh, I know you think of yourself as a gentle and reasonable woman, but the truth of the matter is that you can be ruthless. Completely and utterly ruthless—as when you ruined Mademoiselle Dubufe. I think that you are not only the strongest, but also potentially the most dangerous woman I have ever known. Yes, Augusta, you can be frightening."

I tried to smile. "You certainly do know how to flatter a girl, Harry."

He laughed. "Well, I must say you've added zest to my life. I hardly even have time to play my 'Wicked Man' games any more. Of course, most games pall after a time, but not the ones I play with you, Augusta. Not the ones I play with you. . . .

"Well, good evening, my dear. Do have a nice holiday."

"Thank you. The same to you, Harry."

I felt his lips brush my cheek, something that rarely happened. Somewhere behind me in the near-darkness of the loft he said good evening to Céleste, and a door closed.

For a time I merely continued to stand at the dormer window, looking out at the lights of Paris. Never in the world would I have expected Harry to say such things as he had just said to me—not about anybody. He had actually sounded respectful, almost in awe of me. But what, really, had I accomplished in the last dozen years? Oh, a great deal, on the face of it, but why did it all seem in some way unimportant and even unreal? Why did it all seem like a mere playing of games, as Harry had put it? There were few things I had done that I would have changed. Then why did I once again sense a void in my life? Why this vast, dark emptiness in my soul? Why? Why?

Words, my own and others', echoed out of the past:

George: *"One day there will be another love in your life."*

"Perhaps. But why should I want one? Even before Adam died, I vowed I was going to be a free and independent woman. . . ."

Alfred: *"Your love for me was only a Sunday love, and not always then."*

"My work—"

"Comes first. I understand and respect that. . . ."

Eugène: *"People like us—you and me, my dear—we must appear to be monsters to the rest of the world to accomplish what we do. . . . We are monsters!"*

And now Harry: *"You, Augusta, are without doubt the strongest woman I have ever known. . . ."*

And he had asked: *"Where will it end?"*

Yes, where *would* it end? Once upon a time, I had had dreams. Whatever had become of them? Were they dead? Did the past dozen years forecast the true pattern of my future? Was my life to be forever nothing more than acquiring one more workshop, one more factory, one more mill? Was I to end my days, an old lady confessing to a priest, "Forgive me, Father, for I have sinned. All these years I was wrong. God gave me a life, and—I don't know what happened— somehow I threw it away!''

At that moment, standing by the dormer window and gazing out at the lights of Paris, I broke.

I felt like a bird that had been flying for years on end without ever touching earth; a bird that had struggled to stay endlessly aloft while flying toward some destination that had long before been forgotten; a bird that had survived storm after storm, each time renewing its will and forcing itself to fly still higher and farther on aching wings—until a single puff of wind robbed it of its last remaining strength and sent it hurtling earthward, to crash on the rocks below. And oh, the pain, the pain!

I felt it like a sudden bursting within me. It wrenched and racked and tore at me. It bent me and twisted me. It wrung tears and cries from me until, like a child, I could not catch my breath, and I felt Céleste shaking me. "What is it?" she asked, as I looked into her alarmed eyes. "What is the matter? What is it?"

"I want to go home," I said in English.

Yes. That was my forgotten destination. Home.

"What? What are you saying?"

"I want to go home."

"Go home? You want to go home?"

"Oh, I'm so tired."

"Of course you are! Of course you are, darling!"

"I'm so tired of being strong. I'm *not* strong."

"Oh, Liane—"

"And I *don't want* to be ruthless and dangerous, I *don't want* to be a monster. I just want to be Gussie Welles of the Barony, and go home!"

"Home—you mean—"

"I want my Aunt Nickie and—and Pearl and Rufus. I want my mamma and daddy. I know I can't have them, but I want them. Oh, Céleste, I so much want to go home!"

For a moment Céleste held me at arms' length and stared at me as if she could not quite believe what she was hearing. Then she gave me a hard shake. "Well, if that's all you want, you silly woman," she said, "for goodness' sake, *go* home!"

Her words had the same effect on me as if she had suddenly thrown a bucket of ice-cold water in my face. For a moment I could only gasp for breath and stare back at her.

"Go home?" I asked.

"Yes, *go* home! Can you think of a single reason why you shouldn't?"

I shook my head. "I don't know. I . . ."

"I'll *take* you home! We'll start packing in the morning!"

"You mean . . . just . . . go home?"

"Why not? I've always wanted to see America. We'll go together."

"Just . . . go home." The thought was hard to comprehend.

"Yes! Yes! Time we both had a holiday, isn't it?"

"Yes!"

"Very well, my dear, it's settled! *You* are going *home!*"

Yes. Yes, I was. I was going home at last . . . going home.

The next morning, when Céleste came to my apartment to see how I was, I was embarrassed by the memory of my performance. "Oh, you know me," I said, trying to excuse myself, "things pile up, and every couple of years I have to have a good cry so I can forget about them afterwards. Besides, I'd drunk a lot of wine," I added scornfully. "Champagne tears!"

Céleste looked doubtful. "Then you should feel better now. Do you?"

"Yes!"

But I did not, and she knew it. The only thing that made me feel better was the thought of going back to South Carolina, to Charleston, and, yes, to the Barony. To see the Barony, at least one more time.

"Then we're going," Céleste said, when I had confessed this to her, "and I'll have to practice calling you Gussie."

My heart rose at the thought, rose and began to sing again. But there was so much to be done first! "Oh, I *can't* go back now!" I told Céleste half a dozen times in the next few weeks. "I'm needed here! Maybe *next* spring—"

"*No,* Li—Gussie! If you put off going now, you'll do the same thing next year, and you'll keep on putting it off forever. And you don't think I'm going to miss a chance to see America, do you? The Battle of Bunker Hill! Don't fire till you see the whites of their eyes! To arms, to arms, the British are coming, one if by land, two if by sea, and don't tread on me!"

"Why, Céleste," I said, laughing, "I had no idea you were interested in American history!"

She looked astonished at my ignorance. "My dear woman, don't you know that the French Revolution began at the Lexington Common?" She burst out with a few glorious measures of *La Marseillaise*.

We spent a few weeks in France preparing for our trip, then went to England to do the same thing. We went up to Leeds. We returned to London. We spent hours in conference with Millie and Algie, who, like Félicie in Paris, were to keep us informed with regular dispatches. The period was hectic, and I kept saying, "I *can't* go now!" and delighting in the fact that I *was* going now. We planned to spend at least four months in America and return in September or October.

A few days before our departure, I confessed to Harry what was in my heart, almost hidden even from myself.

"I think you should understand, Harry, that there is a possibility that I shan't come back."

It took a moment for the meaning of my words to sink in. We were having after-dinner coffee in his Belgravia house, and his hand shook, almost spilling coffee from his cup.

"You can't be serious."

"I am, Harry, quite."

"You've spent half your life over here. All your accomplishments are over here. Your business interests, your livelihood is over here. I can understand your wanting to visit America, but why in the world would you want to return to some little tidewater village for good and all?"

"I don't think you understand, Harry, that in my heart of hearts I have always been, and shall forever remain, one of those barbaric Americans."

Harry's voice rose. "But you're needed over here!"

"Nonsense. You people will all do quite nicely without me."

"Augusta, that simply is not true. *Belle Liane* gowns, for instance, cannot exist without Liane Duhamel. Nor can *belle Céleste*."

"Harry, I'm quite willing to let *belle Liane* die a natural death. And as for *belle Céleste*, we've developed a couple of marvelous young designers. As a matter of fact, Harry, I'm considering selling out all my interests over here"

"No!" Harry leapt up from his chair. "No, I shall not allow it! You belong here with us, and you cannot throw yourself away like this!"

"Dear Harry," I said gently, "I only remarked that there was a possibility, not a certainty."

"I know. But I also know that when you get an idea into your head, it sometimes becomes an obsession and you cannot let go of it until you make it a reality."

That was true. And the more I thought of my return to America, the more it seemed to me that I would surely find my true destiny there.

Harry accompanied us to Liverpool, and at last the great day came. He boarded the S.S. *Atlantic* with us—how fitting that we should voyage on an American ship!—and inspected our flower-filled stateroom. At the last warning he went back down the gangplank and stood among the crowd, while Céleste and I managed to find a place on deck at the rail. The great steam whistle blew—*boooommh! boooommh!*—and the gangplank was lowered.

"Goodbye, Harry!" we shouted.

"You'll be back!" His words pierced the tumult. "You'll be back by October, mark my words!"

"Goodbye, Harry! Goodbye!"

"Never goodbye! You're coming back!"

"Goodbye, Harry! . . ."

Goodbye, goodbye, goodbye . . . and at last I was on my way home to America!

BOOK FIVE

To Xanadu

~~~~~~

Oh, I'm burning! I wish I were out of doors! I
wish I were a girl again, half savage and hardy, and
free . . .

—Emily Brontë, *Wuthering Heights*

Who would have thought my shriveled heart
Could have recovered greenness?

—George Herbert, *The Flower*

1 ᪫᪫᪫᪫᪫

Our crossing could hardly have been more comfortable. Our stateroom was rather small and stuffy, but the *Atlantic* had a dining room and a drawing room, each almost seventy feet long and marvelously well furnished; we dined on turtle soup, filet of pigeon au Cronstaugh, and almond cup custard; and the trip took only ten days. I could not understand why so many people still preferred sails to steam. For me, the sway of the grand saloon!

We arrived in New York City in early April, and how wonderful it was to hear American voices all around one again! The very air seemed charged with peculiarly American energy, and somehow that energy became connected in my mind with a new word which had come into widespread use during my years abroad. That word was "okay." One heard it everywhere. "Okay!" "Okay, okay, okay!" "Okey-dokey!" America, I thought happily, you're okay!

We spent several days in New York City, during which time we had a *very* interesting conference with Mr. Isaac M. Singer, but Céleste insisted that in the main we forget business and simply enjoy ourselves. I was amused to realize for the first time in years that she spoke English with a slight French accent. We had been so close for so long that I had actually stopped *hearing* her accent. But in America there was no denying that, when she called me Gussie, the name somehow emerged as Goosie, and I must admit that I did not find myself altogether charmed.

Our New York sojourn at an end, we again boarded a packet, this time traveling south on the final leg of our trip, and on Wednesday, April 19, we reached Charleston. When we entered the harbor and passed Castle Pinckney on its shoal, we saw the long line of Charleston wharfs, facing east into the Cooper River, and I found myself bouncing up and down at the rail like a child and bubbling over with joy. After seventeen years I was home at last!

As we disembarked, I looked about the crowded wharf, half-expecting to see familiar faces. But of course I saw no one I recognized, and I breathed a sigh of relief. I was not yet ready to meet old acquaintances.

I had given a great deal of thought to our arrival. Because we had no wish to advertise our wealth, we were traveling modestly and without servants. No one knew we were coming, for I did not wish to give Uncle Thad time to make arrangements for us that we might find unsuitable. I was dressed fashionably but conservatively, as Charleston might expect of a very proper widow, and Céleste was too. I had recently acquired a long-handled lorgnette, which dangled from a ribbon around my neck, and with its aid I could be truly formidable. Indeed, I knew I could, because I had practiced in front of a mirror!

With the help of my lorgnette, a very English accent, and a few My-good-man's, I soon had a carriage and help with our steamer trunks and bags, and we were on our way to the Planters' Hotel.

We had supper in our rooms and spent the evening and the next morning putting our clothes in order. The truth is that, now that we had arrived in Charleston, I was almost terrified at the thought of venturing out into the streets and seeking old friends and family. What would have changed? Aunt Nickie and I had not exchanged so much as a letter in years. She might be dead, for all I knew, and so might Uncle Thad and little Lucy. What insanity had inspired me to return to Charleston without first sending word ahead? At the very least, it was a rude and inconsiderate way to treat Aunt Nickie.

Céleste understood my apprehensions, and she prodded me out of the hotel. At her suggestion, we hired a carriage and set out to explore this city I had left so long ago.

Ah, Charleston—changed, yes, and yet so much the same. There was a new French Huguenot church right across the street from our hotel, but Saint Philip's, up the street in the next block, was exactly as I remembered it. I showed Céleste the City Hall, and Saint Michael's and the Fireproof Building, and the Old Powder Magazine, and I cannot recall what all—and all the time she teased me about my beloved city.

"Gussie! It is a be-yew-tiful city, but why does it *smell* so bad? *Mon Dieu*, it smells worse than *Paris, Londres, et Rome tous à la fois!* Does nobody ever sweep up the horse sheet?''

"Say *merde*, Céleste. *Shit* is a vulgar word in English.''

She grinned and pretended to wave the odor away from her nose. "Sheet, *merde, Scheist*—call it what you wish, my dear friend, it still smells the same.''

Finally I told the driver to go up Meeting Street toward Wraggboro. I was not yet ready to meet my relatives, but I wanted to see the house in which I had once lived. It was just as I remembered it, a magnificent three stories of Adam architecture. It was surely one of the half-dozen finest houses in Charleston—Wraggboro, I had learned from our driver, had been incorporated into the city—but I saw not a sign of life, not so much as a servant, anywhere.

But at least it still existed. It was not merely a child's dream. It was still there.

I had our driver take us south again by way of King Street and then East Bay. As we neared the same wharf where we had landed the previous day, I saw what I was looking for: a warehouse building whose every corner I had known in childhood. In those days the big, long sign in front had read WELLES & SONS. Now it read THADDEUS WELLES.

I told the driver to stop. We remained in the carriage, while I looked across the street at the building. My uncle might be inside at this very moment, and quite likely was. The thought gave me a curious feeling.

A gray-haired man, thin and slightly stooped, stood in shirt sleeves just inside the doorway, squinting at us through his glasses. There was something familiar about his appearance. Charlestonians are nothing if not polite and helpful, and after a moment he pulled on his coat and, smiling, crossed the street toward us.

"Are you ladies looking for some place? Perhaps I can help you.''

His name was . . . of course: Mr. Walters. He had been with the firm for years. And now he was looking at me with increasing curiosity, as if he, too, were on the verge of recognition.

"We're visitors to the city,'' I said, "and we were given the name of Welles. Mr. and Mrs. Thaddeus Welles. But we don't wish to disturb Mr. Welles during business hours.''

Mr. Dawson laughed. "Well, you can't very well do that,

seeing as Mr. Thad isn't here right now. He went down to
Savannah on business and took his missus and his little gal
with him. Be back in about ten days, I'd say. Care to leave a
message?''

I masked my relief. "Oh, no, we won't trouble you. I'm
sure we'll still be here ten days from now.''

"Anyone else I can help you find?''

"Well . . .'' Odd, that I should think then of one person
only. And after I had avoided him for so many years. But was
not the desire to see the Barony one of my principal reasons
for returning? Perhaps I might even buy it!

"I don't suppose you know a Mr. Gannon Murdock, do
you?''

Mr. Walters looked pleased that he could be of help.
"Why, I certainly do. 'Most everybody knows Mr. Murdock,
or at least knows of him. He's likely at one of his plantations
this time of the year, but you just might find him at his house,
over on Meeting Street.''

When Mr. Dawson had given us directions, we thanked him
and set off. We left him standing in the street, looking after
us and scratching his head, as if wondering, wondering. . . .

When I saw Gannon's house, I remembered it from my
childhood, though it had belonged to someone else then. It
was three stories and of brick; and in the Charleston fashion,
it had not its front but its side to the street, and faced south. A
high brick wall, broken only by a wrought-iron gate to the
courtyard, hid both the garden in front of the house and the
outbuildings and courtyard behind.

Hoping we would find Gannon at home and alone, I lifted
the brass knocker and thumped it down. The door was opened
almost at once by a well-dressed black man who said "Yes,
ma'am?'' and looked at us with polite curiosity.

"I am Mrs. Raveneau and this is Mrs. de Laurence. I
wonder if we may see Mr. Gannon Murdock, please.''

"Of course, ma'am. Please come in.''

The door led not into the house but onto the long, broad
piazza which looked out onto the front garden. The azaleas were
still in bloom, and the camellias were glorious. The butler
opened another door for us, and we entered a broad hallway
that ran through the center of the house to the courtyard
behind.

"If you will kindly make yourselves comfortable in the

parlor,'' the butler said, indicating a doorway, "I am sure that Mr. Murdock will be able to join you in a few minutes.''

Céleste and I entered a room, furnished largely with Queen Anne furniture, that managed to seem formal and restful at the same time. As I went to an open window and looked out at the long stretch of gardens beyond the house, an odd feeling of displacement came over me. *There must be something wrong*, I thought with a touch of panic. *I'm not supposed to be here. Somehow I have arrived here entirely by mistake.*

Céleste touched my arm. I turned away from the window.

For the first time in eleven years I found myself looking at Gannon Murdock.

In a way, it was as if I were seeing him for the first time. This was no seventeen-year-old boy, no twenty-five-year-old youth. This was a man, matured and seasoned and in his prime. His forehead and jaw were ever nobler than I remembered, his hands bigger, his shoulders broader. His black mane was as thick as ever, but touched with gray at the temples. His brows were drawn to a frown over those dark eyes I knew so well—no, the eyes had not changed—and his mouth was hard, as if ready to issue a challenge.

For a moment we could only stare at each other.

"Gussie,'' he said. Only a murmur, a low rumble, like distant thunder.

"Gannon?''

Then he was coming toward me, smiling at me, and my knees were so weak I could not move. "Gussie,'' he said again, and I, like a fool, tried to look at him through my lorgnette, but it slipped from my fingers as he took my hand.

Incredibly, I found myself laughing, and on the verge of tears. "Gannon,'' I said again, "Gannon Murdock!''

"You've come home.''

"Yes. For a little while, anyway.''

He looked at Céleste, and I saw the shock of recognition in his eyes.

"Gannon,'' I said, "this is my dearest friend, Mrs. Céleste de Laurence. Céleste, I'd like you to meet . . .''

Céleste smiled and held out her hand. "I told you I thought I had met Mr. Murdock before, Augusta, and—am I not right, Mr. Murdock?''

"I believe you are, Mrs. de Laurence.''

Céleste was superb: "The first time was, oh, a dozen years ago, when our mutual friend, Lord Harry, sent Mr. Murdock to me. Mr. Murdock was seeking an introduction to Marie Duplessis, but unfortunately she was away from Paris at the time. Do I remember correctly, Mr. Murdock?"

"Not quite, Mrs. de Laurence. The lady I was looking for was Madame Liane Duhamel—whom I never found, by the way. Madame Duhamel seems to be a remarkably reclusive woman, at least where I'm concerned."

"Oh, she really is quite shy. But if you have a message for her, perhaps when I return to France . . ."

"Just give her my compliments and say I wish her well."

I was glad to hear that.

"And now, ladies, if I may offer you some coffee . . ."

The hours that followed were more pleasant than I ever would have expected. While the coffee was being prepared, Gannon showed us the lower rooms of the house and took us out into the garden, and there I caught up on some history. His sisters had both married quite well, it seemed, and his younger brother, Ross, after graduating from Princeton, had gone to work for a Charleston law firm. Gannon's parents now made their home in Savannah, and Mr. Murdock helped manage "our plantations." The Murdock family had done very well indeed.

"And what about you, Gussie?" Gannon asked, when we were back in the parlor drinking coffee. "What would it take to keep you here with us?"

"Why, I don't know. I no longer have a home here, after all. Unless, of course," I added with a smile, "you were to sell me the Barony."

For a moment his face went blank, and Céleste, too, looked startled, for I had not yet confided my thoughts to her. But Gannon recovered quickly, and his eyes seemed to reappraise me.

"Now, don't tell me you came here this afternoon to make an offer for the Barony."

"No, though the possibility of doing so has occurred to me from time to time."

"Well, I'm sorry, but the Barony is not for sale."

"But wouldn't you be wise to at least listen to any offer made? I've heard that good businessmen always do that."

Gannon smiled patiently. "Perhaps you're right. But you

would be most unwise to bid on a plantation, even the Barony, sight unseen, wouldn't you?''

"Why, I suppose—"

"Then I have a suggestion. I'm planning to give a little party at the Barony in a couple of weeks. Why don't you and Mrs. de Laurence come out and spend the night?''

How could I refuse such an invitation? It meant an opportunity to see Pearl, Rufus, Aunt Polly, all the others of the Barony whom I had never ceased to love! When I looked at Céleste, she nodded.

"Gannon, we'd love to come."

"Good!" Gannon rose to his feet. "And now I'm going to tell the cook you're staying for supper."

"Oh, we couldn't impose! Besides, we should be out looking for an apartment or a house, someplace we can rent for the summer.''

Gannon frowned. "At this time of the year, that may be a little difficult. But maybe your cousin Horace can help you. He knows so many people, if anyone can help—"

"Oh, poor Horace," I said, feeling guilty at not having given him more thought. "How is he?"

"Why . . ." Gannon hesitated. "Why, he's all right, Gussie.''

"Aunt Nickie wrote me that he had left home and was earning a living sweeping out stables, offices, and shops.''

"Well, look at it this way, Gussie. Somebody has to do the sweeping out, and we all like Horace."

"I'm so glad."

"And now shall we go see him?"

Our carriage, hired for the afternoon, was still waiting out front, and the three of us rode though the bustling city streets the few blocks to Broad Street. There Gannon helped us down from the carriage and escorted us into the offices of a law firm where Horace had worked for many years. "They've been as good to him as you could ever wish, Gussie, and in return Horace is nothing if not loyal. Nodding at a couple of clerks who seemed to know him well, Gannon led us into an inner office where several more clerks sat at desks. We looked about, but there was no sign of Horace.

"Horace Blakely," Gannon called out. "Anybody here seen poor old Horace, the fellow that sweeps up evenings?"

A tall, slender blond man, leaning over a clerk's shoulder, straightened up and smiled at us. I heard Céleste's breath catch, and I could hardly blame her. With his frank, open features and his lively hazel-green eyes, he was a most attractive man. "What can I do for you, Gannon?" he asked, coming toward us.

Then, seeing us, he halted as if he had been hit in the stomach. His eyes opened wide. His mouth gaped.

"G-G-G-Gussie!" he said. "Is that r-r-really you?"

I had forgotten how Gannon could laugh. Great whoops that would knock him out of the saddle when he was a boy, and which threw him back against the wall now.

Later he told us how Horace had worked to overcome his stuttering—until he realized what an asset he could make of it. "When old Horace hooks his thumbs in his waistcoat armholes and tells a jury, 'Now, y-y-you all know me, I'm justa-justa local boy, b-born and r-raised here,' Gussie, it isn't one full minute before he's got 'em eating out of his hand. Old Horace turns stuttering into sheer eloquence." The rebellious youth who had left home to sweep out offices and stables had, it seemed, turned into one of Charleston's finest lawyers.

Horace joined us for supper at Gannon's house. "It'll just be something simple," Gannon had said, and it turned out to be beans cooked with chunks of ham and goose and sausage— "Cassoulet!" Céleste said, delighted—and served with cornbread hot from the oven and a rich nutty-flavored butter. Gannon and I took turns telling stories of our childhood, and few meals were ever enjoyed with such laughter.

Afterwards we sat out on the piazza, and while Horace and Céleste chattered and flirted, I caught up on some more history—who had married whom while I had been away and how many children they had. As evening came on and windows lit up in the surrounding houses, Gannon led me down from the piazza and into the darkness of the garden.

"Gannon," I said, as we strolled among the flowers, "Why are you being so kind? The last time we met, I do not think you were overly fond of me."

He was silent for so long that I thought I might have offended him.

"In a country graveyard," he said. "By Adam Trevayne's grave."

"Yes."

"I reckon I've got to ask your forgiveness for that day, Gussie."

"My forgiveness! Whatever for?"

"Gussie, I pretty nigh broke Tom. Took the Barony from him and left him with the hounds at his heels. I'm not saying I did wrong in that. But then I kept telling myself that you were his responsibility, and I just sort of walked away from the whole thing."

"Well, I certainly wasn't *your* responsibility."

"Maybe not. All I know is, I kept worrying about you. That day in the graveyard, I should have made sure you were all right."

"I can't imagine why."

He shrugged. "Habit, maybe. When we were kids, I was taught to always look after the little ones, no matter what."

"I know. And you always did."

"Anyway, I got into my carriage that day and rode off. Saw Jewel and headed back for the city. And all of a sudden, on the road to London, I asked myself what the hell I was doing! I turned the carriage around and laid on the whip and damned near ruined a good horse, riding back hell for leather. But you weren't at the village inn when I got there. I even went back to the graveyard, but of course you weren't there either. I remember standing in that graveyard and feeling so . . . disappointed. After a while I got back into my carriage and rode away. I've always sort of wondered, what if I'd turned back in time—and today, when I walked into the parlor . . ."

"What did you think, Gannon?"

"Frankly, Gussie, I never knew I could be so glad to see you."

Nor I you, Gannon. Nor I you.

A movement in the shadows attracted my attention, and I looked around to see a figure approaching us from the courtyard. "Ross," Gannon said, "my brother. He works for the same firm as Horace."

The young man who came to a halt before us was a more slightly built version of Gannon. His face was thinner, his features finer, his eyes more darkly intense.

"Ross," Gannon said, "I don't suppose you remember who this is."

Ross smiled. "Of course I do. It's Miss Augusta. Welcome back home, Miss Augusta."

"Why, how could you possibly remember?" I asked, delighted.

"Had to be you. Only one person in the world Gannon would ask me about remembering who'd have eyes something like . . . like Lucy's."

Gannon laughed, pleased at his brother's sharpness, but I was considering how Ross had pronounced my cousin's name. That told the whole story.

"Have you stopped by the Barony lately?" Gannon asked.

"Had dinner there." Suddenly his voice was curiously flat.

"Everything all right?"

Ross shrugged. "Why wouldn't it be?"

"Miss Gussie is thinking of making an offer for it."

Gannon's voice had an undertone of challenge, but Ross's answer was indifferent, almost contemptuous, as if he knew he had no say in the matter: "Then sell it."

I could feel Gannon's anger flare, but Ross appeared not to notice. He smiled at me again. "Nice to have you back, Miss Augusta. Hope we'll be seeing a lot of you. Now, if you'll excuse me, I think I'll go look for some supper."

When Ross had disappeared into the shadows of the piazza, I said to Gannon, "I take it that Ross doesn't want you to sell the Barony?"

"You're wrong. He meant exactly what he said. He doesn't give a damn whether I sell it or not. And," Gannon added bleakly, "it's getting so sometimes I feel the same way."

Then sooner or later you are going to sell, Gannon, I thought. *To me!*

By the following Monday, Horace had found three houses for us, and we chose one on Bull Street, near Coming. It was a two-story wooden "single house," facing west. As with Gannon's much larger "double house," the street door opened onto the piazza, and the piazza door opened into a hall. To the front of the house was the parlor, and to the rear a small dining room, and stairs, with a landing midway, led from the hall to two bedrooms upstairs. The furnishings in the house were worn but pleasant and comfortable, and the whole did not give the impression—which I wished to avoid—of great wealth. Horace found us some well-recommended servants living nearby, and we quickly settled in.

Our social life began at once. Perhaps because of my family's prominence, gentlemen from the *Mercury* and the

Courier had interviewed us while we were still at the hotel, and their newspapers had advertised our presence. Julie Anne Legree Raveneau, all hugs and kisses, was the first to arrive at our door, and, yes, she had married Dexter Raveneau, and, yes, we were practially sisters-in-law even if I was widowed, and, yes, Mrs. de Laurence and I must come to dinner that very evening.

Other invitations followed, to intimate suppers and large dinner parties, one for almost every evening of the week. Somehow Horace contrived to be Céleste's dinner partner three or four times, and Gannon was twice mine. Good, I thought. The better terms we were on, the more chance I had of persuading him to sell me the Barony. But how strange it was to see Zelda Butler Legree, who almost twenty years earlier had dismissed Gannon with a disdainful, "Don't touch me, boy," now flirting with him as if he were a dear old friend.

When we had been in our house a week, we ended one of our evenings in Céleste's room. While she sat cross-legged on the bed brushing her hair, I sat in a chair with my bare feet up beside her.

"I do think you've quite captured Cousin Horace's heart," I said. "Why, he hardly took his eyes off you all evening."

"Nonsense, Gussie. He was only being gallant."

"Now, you know the poor boy is helplessly in love with you. Why do you lead him on so?"

She ignored my teasing. "He's really a very wonderful man, you know. Did he tell you he's been abroad twice, studying law?"

"He did say something about it."

She stopped brushing her hair and stared into space. "Just think, Gussie. If what you've told me about him is true, we could have passed him in the streets of London or Paris and you would never have recognized him. It's not unlikely, you know . . . Horace Blakely and I . . . passing each other on the Champs-Elysées . . . or sitting in the same restaurant, perhaps . . . and never knowing . . ."

Something between alarm and joy flooded through me. "My God! You are in love with him!"

She looked at me with misty eyes. "Don't be silly. I wouldn't dare let myself fall in love with Horace. I must be three or four years older than he, at least. How could I expect him to love an older woman?"

"Céleste, don't talk like that!"

"Well, it's true." She blinked the mistiness away and smiled at me. "And speaking of hearts, dear Gussie, do I detect a warm spot in yours for Mr. Murdock?"

"Gannon Murdock?" I said derisively. "Oh, great balls o' fire!"

Looking puzzled, Céleste inquired as to "what is this *great bawls afar?*" When I explained, she laughed and said, "Oh, Gussie, you are becoming more American every day!"

The next morning the inevitable happened—the moment I had looked forward to with anticipation and dread ever since our arrival in Charleston. I was upstairs in my bedroom, when I heard a knocking at the door, followed by the sound of a youthful female voice: "Hoo-hoo! Anybody home? Hoo-hoo!"

I hurried down to the landing, and when I looked at the open doorway, my heart nearly stopped. The girl who waved to me could not have looked more like Melinda—the same eyes, the smile I had adored. When she saw me, she gave a squeal of pleasure and came into the house with open arms, and a moment later she was followed by a svelte-figured woman with a heart-shaped face who looked at least ten years younger than her fifty-odd years. I nearly fell down the rest of the stairs in my eagerness to get to them. I was back with my people at last.

They had arrived back from Savannah the previous afternoon and only this morning learned of our presence in Charleston. Was I back for good? No, only for the summer. But what were we doing in this house? We must move into the Wraggboro house, and do so at once! No, I thought not. Céleste and I were used to living independently, and we thought it best to continue doing so. Aunt Nickie understood. She and Céleste took to each other immediately—two Frenchwomen in this American land which would always seem a little strange to Monique de Garinet, even though her French accent had all but vanished.

Lucy was a delight, and every moment she reminded me more of Melinda. "I met a young man," I said, "who paid me a wonderful compliment. He said I looked a little like you."

"Ross," she said, and her answer, her eyes, her tone of voice all told me what I wanted to know.

"You're going to find you're something of a heroine to Lucy," Aunt Nickie said a little later.

"But why?"

"Because you defied your uncle, her father, and lived your own life, and," her eyes appraised me, "obviously have prospered. And I must warn you, I do not think Thad will approve of such a state of affairs."

"Oh, dear!"

We both laughed, women who shared a certain understanding of men.

It was agreed that Céleste and I would come to dinner at the Wraggboro house that evening, and with a certain breathlessness I looked forward to my first encounter with Uncle Thad in almost thirteen years.

When we faced each other in the entrance hall some hours later, I found myself looking at an older, heavier man than I remembered, one whose hair had turned entirely white. He embraced me and kissed my cheek and murmured a welcome. He welcomed Céleste politely. He smiled at me, but his smile was thin, and he did not laugh; he was gracious but not cordial. Had I expected anything else?

First of all, I had some gifts to present, I said, just a few little things I had picked up. Actually, they had been selected with great care, nothing obviously expensive, but all quite nice: a stickpin for Uncle Thad, a brooch in the form of a carved ivory flower for Aunt Nickie, and a silver necklace with some semiprecious stones for Lucy.

"It is beautiful!" she said, putting it on and looking at herself in the mirror. "Oh, Mamma, isn't it beautiful?"

Aunt Nickie agreed that it was indeed beautiful.

"I'll keep it always and think of you, Cousin Gussie, whenever I wear it." She seemed as pleased as if I had given her the Kohinoor.

Later, as we ate, Lucy bubbled over toward me, and Aunt Nickie and Céleste shared constant laughter, but Uncle Thad said little, and though the faint smile never left his lips, his eyes told nothing. He was a man, I decided, with the habit of keeping his own counsel.

Finally, as I knew he would, he turned to the question of my "place" in Charleston and in the family.

"Your aunt tells me that you are in Charleston only for the summer."

"Yes, just for the summer holiday. Céleste has long wanted to see America, and . . ."

"Have you considered returning for good?"

"The possibility has occurred to me, but I really don't know yet."

"In either case, your proper place is in this house. There is no excuse for your wasting money on a rented house when you have a home here."

"But I could hardly leave Céleste to pay for a whole house—"

"Mrs. de Laurence is invited to stay here, too, of course. I suggest that you move in tomorrow."

I exchanged looks with Céleste and sighed. "Uncle Thad," I said, "we do thank you, but Céleste and I have for many years been in the habit of living on our own and taking care of ourselves. I think it would be best if we continued our present arrangement."

For the first time, the room was completely silent—a tense silence—while we waited for my uncle to answer.

"I'm afraid I must insist," he said. "It is not proper for you to be living alone."

"But we are not alone, we have each other—"

"Oh, now, Thad," Aunt Nickie said placatingly, "you know that *many* widowed ladies live alone."

"Not in this family."

Céleste's eyes twinkled. I knew she was enjoying our little altercation.

"Uncle Thad," I said, patting his hand, "I'm more pleased than I can say that you're so concerned about Céleste and me. But you see, I have made a decision. And the matter is not open to debate."

Again the room was silent, as we attended Uncle Thad. Finally, with a sigh, he said, "As you like. But you know my wishes."

I had won my first clash with my uncle. I was certain, however, that the years had not taught Uncle Thad to be a graceful loser, and I was not unprepared when, after we had left the table, he took me aside. "Augusta, if you would step into my office with me for a few minutes, please.

"I am not altogether surprised," he said, when we were alone, "to find that you are as willful as ever."

"A strong will can be useful to a woman on her own in this world, Uncle Thad."

Uncle Thad pulled a chair out from the desk and sat down. I remained standing before him like a schoolgirl.

"I understand that you have been seeing Gannon Murdock."

Apparently tales were spread every bit as quickly in Charleston as in Paris. "Aren't you going to ask me to sit down, Uncle Thad?" I asked.

"Please do."

I settled into a chair.

"I need not tell you, Augusta, how . . . inappropriate it is for you to be seeing Murdock. He's the man who corrupted your cousin, the man who caused her death. He's the man who vowed revenge on us all and who cheated your husband out of the Barony. I don't care how many friends he's acquired in Charleston, he's a thief and a villain, and I've put my curse on him and his whole filthy clan."

So much for Lucy and Ross's romance.

"Is that what you called me in here to tell me, Uncle Thad?"

"No. I want an explanation about you and Murdock. As head of this family, I'm entitled to it."

I smiled. "Perhaps you are. Very well: To say I have been seeing Mr. Murdock is misleading. We have encountered each other twice at dinner parties, and I called on him once to inquire about the Barony."

"What about the Barony?"

I considered how to answer the question, and decided I had best come to an understanding with my uncle at once. "Uncle Thad, there is something I think you should know. Mr. Murdock has invited Céleste and me to visit the Barony, and since I wish to see it and our people again, we have accepted. Now, I have no wish to embarrass or scandalize you, Uncle Thad, but I have been my own mistress for a very long time, and I have not returned to Charleston to be held accountable for my every act."

Uncle Thad's brooding gaze rested on me for a moment. Then to my surprise his eyes warmed with amusement, and he actually laughed. "As willful as ever and as stubborn! Augusta, if you had been born a man, you might have carved a real place for yourself in this world!"

"I'm pleased that you think so, Uncle Thad."

"Now, what's this gossip I hear about your making an offer for the Barony?"

Yes, he would have heard about that too. What should I

tell him? I preferred to have him know as little as possible about my affairs, but on the other hand I had always believed it best to stay as close as one could to the truth.

"I suggested to Mr. Murdock that I was interested in purchasing the Barony. He told me he was not interested in selling it."

"A dressmaker—even one who can afford to live on her own and give handsome gifts to her family—is hardly in a position to buy one of the finest plantations in the state."

"Surely that depends on the dressmaker. I happen to have a friend in England who is acquiring some textile mills. He will want a great deal of cotton at the best possible price. He has suggested that he might give me financial backing if I sell cotton exclusively to him."

"May I ask who this friend is?"

"Certainly. His name is Henry Wycherley. He's the Earl of Huxton, and quite wealthy. But I really don't think anything is going to come of this, at least as far as the Barony is concerned. Mr. Murdock was quite adamant about not selling."

"I'm sure he was. He won't even listen to an offer from me." His eyes morose again, Uncle Thad drummed his fingers on his desktop for a moment. "The Barony should have been mine, Augusta. I suppose you know that. But due to a little misunderstanding with your grandfather—"

"Well, what's past is past, Uncle Thad."

"No, it's not. I'm not the kind of man to let the past die. And it occurs to me that maybe, just maybe, Murdock would sell to you, when he never would to me. That would at least put the Barony back into the family, and you wouldn't need the backing of your English friend."

"Then who—"

"Me."

And how long then before the Barony would fall into Uncle Thad's hands? Was that what he was thinking?

"I doubt that Mr. Murdock would agree to that."

"He wouldn't have to know." Smiling, my uncle leaned forward and patted my knee. "You're quite right, Augusta, it is unlikely that you can get Murdock to sell. But I sense that you've become quite a woman of the world, and I'm sure your powers of persuasion are great. So make your visit to the Barony, and who knows? Perhaps it will be ours again even sooner than we expected."

Not ours, Uncle Thad. And not yours. Mine.

2 ◡◠◡◠◡◠

My old hunger for the Barony had been reawakened that evening in Paris when my strength failed; and now it was growing. But I realized that Uncle Thad might prove to be a threat to my ambition and that I had best seek legal advice. I decided that as soon as possible I would call on Cousin Horace.

However, before I could leave the house the next afternoon, there was a knocking and a "Hoo-hoo!" at our door, and Céleste ushered Lucy in. She had hardly greeted me, when she was looking about the parlor as if expecting to see someone hiding behind the furniture.

"Oh, he's not here," she said, disappointed.

"Who is not here?"

"Ross. Ross Murdock."

"Why would you expect to find him here?"

"You won't tell?"

"*I* am asking the questions, young lady."

"I sent word to him that I was going to be here in an hour and to meet me if he could."

"Lucy!" I said with more indignation than I felt, "you don't think you're going to use our house for a lovers' assignation, do you?"

"Oh, don't be angry! You're not angry with me, are you, Miss Céleste?"

"With you, dear, never."

"It's just that we hardly ever get to talk, even at church, and Daddy doesn't even like me to go to parties when he thinks Ross may be there. And when we *do* meet, nobody will let us be alone together for more than ten minutes at a time."

"And quite right they are," I said.

"Oh, Cousin Gussie, when *you* were young—" children

do know how to wound!—"didn't you look for ways to spend just hours and hours with the man you loved?"

"My dear, I'll have you know that *I* was a most proper young lady at all times."

Lucy smiled impishly. "Oh, yes, I've heard. Riding your horse astride instead of sidesaddle. Dipping in the stream in your birthday suit. Screaming your head off at cockfights—"

"Lucy Welles, whoever told you such stories!"

"My mamma. And my daddy too. My mamma with a smile on her face, and my daddy with a frown." She frowned in imitation of her father. " 'No doubt she came to a bad end, and no wonder. No discipline. Ran loose like a gypsy brat.' "

"Your father said that?" Céleste asked, delighted.

"Over and over. I was *not* to end up like poor, awful Cousin Gussie. Maybe I shouldn't be telling you that, Cousin Gussie, but I guess it's all right, because," she shook her head wonderingly, "you certainly have changed his mind!"

"I have?"

"You must have. Before, you'd have thought he'd never even allow you in the house. But just this morning he told Mamma that we should give a big dinner party for you as soon as possible. What did you say to him in the office last night to change him so?"

"Why, I really don't know," I said innocently.

"Anyway, Mamma says she's sorry not to give you more notice, but can you and Miss Céleste come to dinner again Friday evening?"

I looked at Céleste, who said, "Of course," and I said, "You tell your mother we'll be delighted to come."

But dinner on Friday evening was the last thing on Lucy's mind. "Oh, why couldn't Ross have met me here!"

"Don't you worry, Lucy," Céleste said. "The maid just opened the street door, and I think I hear male footsteps on the piazza right now."

She was right. Seconds later the maid escorted Ross into the parlor, and though he was polite to Céleste and me, his dark gaze at once went to Lucy and stayed on her.

"I hope you all don't mind my coming here like this," he said. "I got a message from Lucy to meet her here."

"Oh, dear," Céleste sighed, "and I had hoped it was my ancient crumbling beauty which had drawn the boy to our little house."

Lucy laughed at Ross's blushes, and I thought she was going to embrace him.

"Now, see here, you two! I hope you don't plan to make a habit of meeting here. I have no intention of courting trouble with Lucy's father or with Gannon Murdock."

"Oh, Gannon doesn't mind my seeing Lucy," Ross said. "He figures nothing can come of it, on account of her old daddy, but he's going to learn different."

His voice had taken on an edge that reminded me of something. "Ross, forgive me for asking, but is there any trouble between you and Gannon? Last week at your house, I sensed—"

"Oh, mostly we get along fine. It's just that he's got stuck on this idea about me being a planter like him."

"And Ross wants to be a lawyer," Lucy said, with a touch of defiance that clearly put her on Ross's side.

"But is there any reason why he can't be both? Many professional men are planters as well."

"But I don't want to be a planter," Ross said. "I'd be a terrible planter. I don't even want to own slaves. Miss Augusta, I hope I don't offend you, but I don't believe in slavery."

"You don't offend me at all. But an abolitionist lawyer is going to have a hard time making a living in Charleston."

"That's right. Horace Blakely says he's bitten his tongue till it's dang near ready to fall off. He says he's about ready to give up and go north."

"I didn't think Horace would be afraid to speak his mind."

Ross laughed at my naiveté. "Miss Augusta, you've been away too long. Around here, speaking up against slavery is the surest way in the world of getting yourself horsewhipped. That's because in their hearts everybody with any sense knows that slavery is doomed, and they're afraid to face up to it. The modern world, the world of the future, isn't going to be happy darkies picking cotton in the fields—machinery is going to do even that one of these days. The world of the future is the world of steam power, and right now that world is mostly in the North."

"And you want to go north too."

Ross nodded. "Northwest, me and Lucy. To Ohio or maybe even Indiana or Illinois. There's a need for lawyers up there, and Horace says I'm a good one even if I'm still learning."

Once again I had that old familiar feeling of history

repeating itself. I remembered lamplight in a barn late at night, and I heard a young man's voice: *"There's a future in the West. . . . And don't you worry none about Melinda, Gussie. I'll take care of her . . ."* Oh, God, I thought, surely that terrible night need not be repeated.

"Well," I said, "I don't mean to encourage you—I'm not at all certain I should—but tell me, what's to stop you from just up and going?"

"Money," Lucy said flatly.

"That's right," Ross said. "We've got to have enough to at least get there and keep us going until I find work. I save every penny I earn, but right now that hardly amounts to anything."

"And your brother won't help you."

Ross shook his head. "He's determined to keep me here and make a planter of me."

I felt sorry for them, but there really was nothing I could do but urge them not to give up hope. "Sooner or later things usually take a turn for the better," I said, "and I, meanwhile, have to go down to Broad Street."

Lucy's eyes beseeched me. "Cousin Gussie, since Ross and I are already here, would you mind, just this once . . ."

"You want to stay here together for a little while?"

"Please?"

"Very well, for a little while. In the parlor, with the curtains open." Lucy's face lit up with pleasure, and Ross's cheeks pinkened. "But mind you, Céleste is going to be nearby."

"Why, Cousin Gussie!" Lucy's eyes were a little *too* wide with innocence. "I wouldn't *dream* of doing anything improper with Ross!"

"Just be sure you confine your improprieties to dreams, my girl. And as for you, young man, we allow a few chaste kisses in this house, but mind your hands."

"Why, Miss Augusta," Ross said, trying to hide his embarrassment with a jest, "I wouldn't *dream* of doing anything improper!"

"And don't you get uppity with me, my lad," I said, tapping his chest with my lorgnette. "I've changed your nappies in my day, and I am familiar with the contours of your backside. And if it should need paddling . . ."

On which auntlike note I took my leave.

*   *   *

As soon as I had been conducted into Horace's little book-lined private office and the door had closed, I came directly to the point.

"Horace, I need a lawyer, and I hope you'll accept me as a paying client."

"N-now, you know I'm always at your disposal, Gussie. You'll never have to pay me a cent."

"But I want to. There are two things I hope you will do for me, and I want to keep them both confidential. And one of them, at least, will take some time and effort."

"All right, what can I do?"

"Prepare an offer for the Barony."

He looked at me as if not quite certain he had understood correctly. "You mean an offer to *b-buy* the Barony?"

"Exactly."

"Have you spoken to Gannon about this?"

"I have. He said the Barony was not for sale."

"Well, then—"

"He may not *know* it's for sale. Now, Horace, Uncle Thad has heard a rumor that I've already made an offer for the Barony. I've admitted to him only that I expressed an interest in the plantation and that I might be able to obtain financial backing. I don't want him to know—"

"Whoa, now, wait a minute." Horace leaned back in his chair and looked at me pensively, as if all this were going too fast for him. "You're serious about this."

"Quite serious."

"You say you may be able to get financial backing."

"Actually, I don't think I'll need it."

"Not need—! Gussie, do you have any idea of the m-market value of a plantation like the Barony?"

"Only vaguely. That's why I need you, my lad, to prepare an offer. You'll have a better idea of the market, and you'll do a better job than I ever could."

He shook his head. "Gussie, I d-don't even know how much acreage Gannon has now. Or how many people he has out there. But I'll bet the people alone are worth a hundred thousand dollars."

I was becoming a little impatient. "Horace, real-estate sales are a matter of public record. Find out what the Barony was valued at when Gannon took it over—there must be *some* kind of record. As for the people, find out the going price for hands, prime, three-quarter, half, and so forth. Then make an educated guess at the Barony's population so that we have a rough idea of what it's going to cost us. Horace, you know how to do these things!"

He looked at me for a long moment, then said, "I think I shall assume that I am dealing with a m-madwoman."

I laughed. "Do that. But humor her."

He stood up and paced, as nearly as one could pace in that little room. "All right, I shall d-do that. Can you give me some idea of what you're willing to pay?"

"As much as necessary, but as little as possible."

"That's no answer. I'm merely trying to determine if you have the slightest idea of what you're getting into."

"Horace, will you please sit down? I'd like to give you a slight idea of what *you* are getting into."

He sat down. From my reticule I took a folded piece of paper. I said, "This is absolutely confidential, of course," and handed it to him.

He unfolded the paper. He read it, or at least stared at it, for quite a long time. When he spoke, he sounded almost angry—or in shock.

"Gussie, what the hell is this?"

"Precisely what it looks like. A summary of my financial position, more or less, as of last month. A listing of some of my holdings, my investments, together with current valuations."

"*Some* of them?"

"Enough, I hope." I had listed only those which could in no way lead to Liane Duhamel.

The paper dangling from his fingers, Horace leaned back in his chair and stared at me, a funny little smile on his face. "Well, well," he said.

"As you'll have gathered, my principle interest is in preserved foods—the name of Wycherley-Welles is no coincidence. But I have also been fortunate in my other enterprises and investments. I'm sure I'll be equally fortunate in investing in the Barony."

He was not listening. "Deserted in Paris by her husband. Living as a seamstress, Aunt Nickie said. A long silence, as if she had disappeared from the face of the earth. And then, after a dozen years," he waved my financial summary in the air, "she comes home with this. If only Uncle Thad knew. If only Charleston knew."

"Well, Uncle Thad and Charleston had better not find out!"

He shook his head as if to clear it. "Jesus—excuse my language, but I'm having difficulty believing we're having this conversation. Is th-this really the same old Gussie?"

"Same old Gussie, willful and stubborn, or so I'm told. And now: do you think I can afford the Barony?"

He waved the paper again. "With this kind of collateral? No question. Except that I doubt that Gannon will sell."

"Horace, dear, you just put together an offer. When the time comes, *I* will do the negotiating."

"How soon do you want this?"

"As soon as possible."

We talked for another hour, and before long, Horace began to show some enthusiasm for my plans.

"You said there was a second thing you wanted me to do for you," he reminded me.

"Oh, yes. I need advice. I told you Uncle Thad has heard of my interest in buying the Barony. Last night he offered to supply the financial backing—"

"Don't let him. If you do, he'll sure as hell find some way to foreclose and take the place away from you."

"Exactly. In fact, he'll try in any case, and," I said, pointing to the paper I had shown Horace, "that's true of everything I have. My question is—can he do it?"

Horace thought for a moment. "It's not as if he were your husband—a husband pretty much controls his wife's property even in those states with a Married Women's Property Act. But he is your closest living male relative, which gives him a certain power over you. Since you're a widow, Uncle Thad could claim responsibility for you and argue that you're incompetent to manage your own affairs. But considering that you've done very well without his help for a number of years, he'd find that difficult." A flush came to Horace's cheeks. "Especially with me fighting the old b-b-b-bastard. Not to brag, but with me behind you, I really don't think you have anything to worry about."

"Then I won't."

"But a word of caution, Gussie. Don't sign anything he gives you without showing it to me first. Don't sign, no matter how harmless it seems or how persuasively he argues it's in your own interest. If you give him power of attorney over you, you might as well have signed away your life.

We'd still give him a hell of a fight and maybe win, but you'd know you'd been in deep trouble.''

I knew Horace was right. And I would not forget.

For a dinner party given at the last moment, the one Aunt Nickie and Uncle Thad gave for Céleste and me was quite large and most successful. There were eighteen or twenty guests, some of whom I had known well in my childhood—the Blanchards, the Legrees—and others who had been more distant—the Draytons, Traggs, Pinckneys. They were all of the older generation, people who had known my parents.

The dinner itself was excellent, and afterwards Céleste and I amused ourselves by talking with the ladies.

''Your uncle tells us,'' said the ancient Mrs. Tragg, ''that you have done ex*cep*tionally well. If you will excuse me, my dear, how does—uh—a dressmaker—ah—''

''Do exceptionally well, Mrs. Tragg? By making exceptionally expensive dresses for people who can afford them, and then by investing prudently.''

''If you'll excuse my saying so, my dear,'' said hawk-faced Mrs. Joinder, a less than pleasant woman, ''I am sure you are quite talented, but French designers do have a certain *je ne sais quoi* that all others in the world lack.''

''Mrs. Joinder, I could not agree more.''

''I *never* go to Paris without buying at least one *belle Liane* gown.''

Céleste gave a little squeal of pleasure. I laughed and explained, ''Céleste is an associate of Madame Duhamel, you know.''

The ladies gaped. ''Why, Countess,'' Mrs. Tragg said, ''you are *that* Céleste? I never dreamed . . .''

When we had first arrived in Charleston, I had been afraid that some well-traveled lady, recognizing Céleste's name or face, would add up two and two and make a shrewd guess about my own identity. By that evening, however, I had realized that never in the world would Charleston ever be able to conceive of me as being anyone other than its own Gussie Welles.

''I heard so much about Madame Duhamel when I was in Paris some years ago,'' Mrs. Tragg said, ''and I went to her ateli*yay,* but I never met her. Did you, Eliza?''

''Only in passing,'' Mrs. Joinder said, more truthfully than she knew, ''only in passing.''

"Tell us, Countess, what is she like?"

"Why don't you ask Augusta? She's a much better judge of character than I."

"Do you know her, too, Augusta?"

"I've been employed by her from time to time, and I've benefited from her comments on my work."

"Liane Duhamel is very shy with strangers," Céleste said, "but she has the most generous heart in the world."

"*I* have heard," said Mrs. Joinder "that she has led a rather—ah—disorderly life."

"Oh!" Pained, Céleste brought the back of her hand to her forehead. "The things that people will say!"

"A truly generous heart, Mrs. Joinder," I said. "Generous and noble and brave."

"A saint, to those who know her," Céleste said. "Truly a saint."

"Truly," I agreed. "Being a dressmaker myself, I have for years looked to Liane Duhamel for inspiration in every way."

"*Quelle femme!*"

"*La patronne des couturières!*"

The ladies were beginning to look at us a little oddly. Time to change the subject!

The evening passed quickly and more enjoyably than I had anticipated, but as Céleste and I had a long day ahead of us, we left as early as possible.

The next morning Horace arrived at our door with horse, carriage, and driver to take us to the Barony. The day was as beautiful as it had been on my first trip, so long ago, and, as we traveled the dearly familiar road, I found myself taking a journey into memory. There were the same gnarled old oaks, festooned with gray veils, and beyond, the vast cotton and rice fields, and I could almost hear my father's voice, so happy as he pointed out everything to my mother and me for the first time.

Then came the moment I had awaited for so long, had dreamed of for so many years: my first sight of the Barony big house—the long white four-columned façade, the two sets of stairs leading up to the grand piazza, the four chimneys that had seemed to me as a child to touch the sky. And, oh, Lordy, I thought, almost in tears, they still did!

As we rode up the road of crushed white shells that led

through the long, broad park and gardens to the house, Gannon Murdock came out to meet us. Our carriage came to a halt on the circle in front of the house, and he helped us step down.

"I guess I should say, 'Welcome home, Miss Gussie!' "

"You do, Gannon Murdock, and I shall weep!"

Three boys scurried about us, taking our bags and carrying them into the house. Gannon led us up the long stairs to the piazza and through the open double doors into the entrance hall, where a handsome Negro woman awaited us. Her arms were folded over her bosom, and her expression was aloof.

"Well, Gussie," Gannon said, "do you know who this is?"

I knew, but I could only stand and stare, until the woman's mouth began to tremble from suppressed mirth and she broke into a smile. We threw ourselves into each other's arms. I did weep then.

When I could be coherent, I introduced Pearl and Céleste to each other. Then I asked, almost fearfully, "And your mamma? Is Aunt Polly all right?"

"Oh, Mamma is fine. She's the housekeeper now."

"And Rufus," I said. "What about Rufus?"

"Why, Miss Gussie, honey, those was our boys, brought your things in. Rufus and me got three fine boys and a girl!" She held me at arm's length as if inspecting me. "But what about you? Way back, we all heard you had some real bad times. But it do look to me like you come through all right."

"Oh, yes. I came through all right."

She showed Céleste and me up to the room Melinda and I had shared, and as far as I could see, not one thing had been changed. There was the bed, in exactly the same place, and I even recognized the counterpane. The chairs, the table, even the pictures on the walls were the same.

As soon as we had freshened up, Pearl showed us the rest of the house. Everything was so familiar, so much as I remembered it, and yet somehow I felt like a ghost wandering through those rooms—the parlors, the ballroom, the library. Could I ever really *belong* here again?

I had to meet all the others, of course. I had to hug Rufus and his parents, Sarah and Nathan. I had to be ordered out of the kitchen by old Matty, who still tyrannized over her domain. I had to hug David and Ben and Aunt Polly. Then it was time for dinner, thank heavens, for I could not have stood any more emotion.

After dinner, I put on a bonnet and Gannon took me for a walk about the plantation. The first place we visited was the stables, where a brown horse with a familiar white blaze on his forehead was browsing in a far corner of the paddock. He took one look at Gannon and came running.

"Recognize him, Gussie?"

I rubbed the horse's nose. "He can't be!"

"He sure is. Your own Wanderer."

"He must be over twenty years old!"

"Don't tell him that. He thinks he's a colt."

We strolled on, not quite aimlessly, under the hot Carolina sun, through fields, through woods, until we came to the stream. My favorite of all streams.

It had changed, of course. Some of the surrounding trees had grown much larger, others had died, and the cleared area on the bank where we had played and where Aunt Polly had sat with her needlework seemed smaller now. Yet it was recognizably the same place, a place of clear-running water shimmering in the sunlight.

Gannon, now in shirt sleeves, put an arm around my waist. "Remember, Gussie?"

"The time you pulled me out because of the cotton-mouth. . . . Oh, yes, I remember."

"You couldn't have been more than fourteen."

"You were so handsome that day."

Gannon laughed. "I was a damn fool every day."

"Do you have any idea of how I've dreamed of bringing my own children to this stream, Gannon? But I don't suppose I'll have anything like that now."

"I don't see why not."

"I never remarried and now I doubt that I ever will. And pretty soon I'll be too old to be starting a family."

He leaned his head against mine. "Aw, no, Gussie."

"Yes, Gannon."

"No, Gussie."

Putting a finger under my chin, he tilted back my head and kissed me.

A quickening sensation, an awakening.

His lips moved on mine again, gently, tentatively, tenderly. As if careful not to frighten me.

"I think not, Gannon," I said weakly.

"I think so, princess," Gannon said, and his mouth moved harder against mine, as he drew me into his arms.

Oh, if he had had any idea of what he was doing to me! After two years and more of self-denial, after telling myself a hundred times I was past all this, after vowing a hundred times, *never again!*, I found myself taking his head in my hands and kissing him back, kissing him longingly and hungrily, while he pressed the whole hard length of his body against mine.

Finally I wrenched myself away from him. He tried to draw me to him again, but I held him off. "No, Gannon, no more. This isn't for us, and you know it."

"Gussie, I only know I'm glad you've come here."

"So am I. But now we've got to get back to the house. Your guests will be arriving soon."

"To hell with them."

"No, Gannon. Please. Please, let's go now."

He kissed my forehead and stroked my cheek. "Just one thing."

"What's that?"

"Do you still hate me for . . . what happened in England?"

"Oh, Gannon, I was angry with you, I resented you, I feared you. At times I wanted to kill you. But how could I ever really hate you?"

Hand in hand, we walked slowly back to the house.

Gannon's "little party" that evening was grand beyond anything Céleste and I had been led to expect. We were the guests of honor, it seemed, and Gannon had invited everybody he could find whom I had known in my childhood. The house was soon filled with happy voices, music, food and drink, and I must have been hugged and had my cheek kissed a hundred times in the course of the evening. "Ain't been a party like it here," Pearl told me, "since yo' folks went away."

I spent most of the evening in the ballroom, never missing a dance, and my greatest pleasure was watching Céleste and Horace in each other's arms, watching almost enviously, as I had watched Tom and Melinda years before. But the moment I shall never forget is the one when Gannon entered the ballroom. He had been looking out for his guests, and I had seen little of him. But then, just as the orchestra, led by old Ben, was starting a waltz, there he was, taking command of the room simply by the force of his presence. And, oh, how I recognized the look on his face! His eyes swept the room as if he were searching for someone, just as they had done at my fifteenth birthday party. But this time when they stopped, he was not looking at Julie Anne Legree. He was looking at me.

It was that meaningful look that I remembered so well—a long sideways look, and an amused, half-suppressed smile, that said he knew what I wanted and needed better than I knew myself. Then he was coming toward me—"My waltz, I think?"—and before I could say a thing, his arm was around me and I was whirled away. And caught between laughter and indignation, I could only think, *Damn you, Gannon Murdock! Damn you, don't you* do *this to me!*

A wonderful ball, a wonderful night. It must have been nearly dawn when Céleste and I went wearily up the stairs to our room and slipped into bed. She fell asleep mumbling something about wishing I were Horace, and my last thought was that I had been kissed and waltzed and after seventeen years was sleeping in my own bed at last. I had never slept better.

We awakened late, and when we went downstairs, Gannon was seeing off the last of his other guests. Pearl set the table for us, and Gannon and Horace had coffee while Céleste and I ate breakfast. Gannon wanted us to stay over another night, and Céleste and Horace might have been willing, but I declined. I could not deny that I found Gannon very attractive—I suppose I always had—and I had an idea that, if I did stay, we might once again find ourselves on the stream bank. But lovely as that might have been, I had no intention of having an affair with him or with anyone else. Besides, I had business with Gannon. I did not wish to complicate that. Our visit had been very pleasant, but it was time for me to depart.

We left that afternoon with invitations to return and also to visit Gannon's two plantations down the coast. We all agreed to have dinner together in Charleston very soon. Our carriage started down the long white road and back toward the city.

But my heart stayed at the Barony.

3 ~~~~~~

There was no happier woman than I in all Charleston the next afternoon, when I went down to Broad Street to call on Horace and take the next steps in my plan. I had formed a general strategy, and I predicted that the Barony would be mine within a month.

"*If* Gannon accepts your offer," Horace had said.

"Oh, he'll accept. Not our first offer, of course not. Our third offer, I should say."

On my way to Broad Street, I stopped at the post office and was given two letters, posted separately but arrived together. The earlier one was from Harry. ". . . have successfully concluded negotiations for the mills, and in effect they are now ours." *Good!* "However, we are having some problems at Leeds. The workers are unhappy with the way Collins has been reorganizing them for efficiency. Really, my dear Augusta, this is a matter that calls for your fine touch. Certainly I cannot deal with that damned horde of women. . . ." *Oh, Harry!* I thought angrily.

The second letter was from Millie. She had been having a dispute with a cooperative store over the pricing of our *belle Céleste* dresses, it seemed, and really thought I should be there to take charge, and please, please, I should not be angry with her if she did the wrong thing.

Damn! I thought. *Damn, damn, damn!* They were like children! Well, they were just going to have to get along without me for the rest of the summer. Sooner or later, I would have to answer both letters and give my best advice, but meanwhile I tried to put them out of mind. Nothing was going to lower my high spirits that day.

Horace was amused by my buoyancy. "I l-love to see you feeling happy, Gussie, but I don't see how you can be so c-confident."

"If you're going to make a deal," I said, "you have to believe in it. Now, shall we get to work?"

There was so much to be done, and I was determined to act quickly, if only to give Uncle Thad the least opportunity to interfere. Horace arranged for meetings with bankers, emphasizing to them the need for confidentiality. A title search had to be made for the land Gannon had added to the plantation. Fortunately, Horace had located an old inventory of the Barony, which aided us in framing our offer.

The task was more formidable than I had anticipated, but by the following Monday, in the middle of May, we had completed it. Horace sent a message to Gannon saying that we would like to see him as soon as possible about a business matter, and the answer came back that Gannon would be pleased to see us at five o'clock that evening and of course he would expect us to stay for supper. We sent our acceptance, and I also sent word to Céleste that I would not be home until late.

When the butler showed us into Gannon's parlor that evening, however, Céleste was the first person we saw.

"I hope you don't mind, Augusta. Mr. Murdock asked me to join you all for supper, and I thought—"

"Of course she doesn't mind," Gannon said, entering the room, "and neither does Horace. We're all friends here." He turned to the butler. "Luke, I think the ladies favor the dry madeira, and Mr. Horace and I will have some of that fine sour mash. Gussie, Céleste, please sit down."

I should have realized then that our coming to an agreement was not going to be easy. I had little of Céleste's patience and tact in business negotiations, and Gannon had not become one of the South's wealthiest planters by having no mind or will of his own.

"Now," he said, when we had sat down, "a few weeks ago you said something about making an offer for the Barony. Is that what you have in mind?"

"Yes, it is. In confidence, of course. I would prefer that my uncle not know."

"I understand."

"I think you're going to like what I have to say, Gannon, and before I go into the details—"

"Excuse me for interrupting, Gussie. Have you put your offer in writing?"

"Yes, we have." I signaled Horace, who took a thin sheaf of papers from his leather case and extended it to Gannon.

"Very good." Gannon took the papers and, without a glance at them, set them aside.

"Now, as I started to point out—"

"You needn't bother, Gussie. I'll read your offer as soon as I get time. Meanwhile, here's Luke with our refreshments, and I think I can promise you a pleasant supper."

"Gannon," I said, annoyed, "you promised to *listen* to my offer—"

"Gussie," Horace said, breaking in hurriedly, "I'm sure Gannon would much rather read your offer at his leisure."

"I promise you, princess," Gannon said, "I will read your offer carefully, and I won't keep you waiting for an answer any longer than necessary."

This was not at all the way I had envisioned our negotiations taking place. Gannon was obviously determined to turn our business meeting into a social occasion, but what could I do?

We had, as always, a very pleasant evening together, and I even managed to forget that I was waiting for an important decision. But the next several days were a strain. I did not expect Gannon to accept our first offer, but I wanted to know his reaction and to make a second offer as quickly as possible.

We got our answer the next Monday morning. Horace drove up to Bull Street to give it to me. I was not surprised to learn that Gannon had refused the offer.

"All right, Horace, now I want you to send our second offer to him just as quickly as possible."

"He'll have it this afternoon."

We had already worked out the details of the second offer, which was about ten percent better than the first. This time I expected a fast answer from Gannon—either a fast *yes*, after a little dickering, because the offer was too good to refuse, or a fast *no*, because he was tempted and wanted to be done with the matter quickly.

The next afternoon I went to Horace's office to learn if he had heard from Gannon.

"Gussie, I'm sorry. I delivered the offer myself. Gannon took a quick look at it and said he'd let us know in three or four weeks—"

"Three or four weeks!"

"—when he got back to Charleston. He left this morning to look after his two places down the coast."

I felt an unexpected pang that Gannon should leave the city for so long and without telling me he was going. I would miss him. But more important, everything seemed to be going wrong with my plan to acquire the Barony, and as Horace spoke, I think that in my heart I knew that Gannon would refuse any offer I might make.

But I could not accept that. I was as determined as ever to make the Barony mine.

I bided my time. We entertained frequently at our little house in Bull Street and were entertained in turn. We dined once a week at the Wraggboro house, where I carefully evaded my uncle's questions about Gannon and me. Céleste saw Horace constantly. Twice Lucy and Ross met at our house, though I had asked them not to. Lucy visited us frequently, and one day she brought bad news.

"All this time my daddy has said I couldn't marry until I was eighteen, and now that I'm nearly there, all of a sudden he's talking about my settling down. He talks like I ought to get married this fall or next spring at the latest."

"And you're afraid he won't change his mind about Ross?" I asked.

"I *know* he won't! I swear, he's got a list in his head of who I can marry and a list of who I can't."

"Well," Céleste said, "I don't think he's different from a lot of papas in that. But he can't make you marry someone you don't love, can he?"

"Oh, Miss Céleste, you don't know my daddy!"

We gave her what encouragement we could, but I must admit that my own thoughts were elsewhere. By that time, the month I had given myself to acquire the Barony had passed. And soon after, toward the middle of June, I learned that Gannon had returned to Charleston.

The next day, Horace told me that our second offer had been turned down.

Again, I was not surprised. I had told Horace that Gannon would most likely accept my third offer, and now, sitting in his office, I told him what that was to be.

"What do you think?" I asked. "Will he accept it?"

"With Gannon, I r-really don't know. I do know that most

planters in his position would consider such a deal mighty tempting.''

''Then let's tempt Mr. Murdock. I want you to arrange another meeting with him, but this time I'd like to have it right here.''

A meeting was arranged for the next afternoon, and Gannon was already in Horace's office when I got there. We exchanged amenities and got down to business.

''Gussie,'' Gannon said, sitting at ease in a far corner from me, ''I don't want to waste your time or mine. So let me say at once that your first offer was more than adequate and your second was more than generous. But the fact remains that I am simply not interested in selling the Barony.''

''But you are willing to hear me out.''

''As a matter of courtesy, yes. But first I'd like to know a thing or two. Horace says your uncle isn't behind you, but he won't tell me who is.''

''I hardly think it's necessary for you to know. I can raise the money. Isn't that enough?''

''No. You may not *think* Thad is behind you, but, unless you can prove it, that doesn't make it true. He can be pretty devious.''

''Very well,'' I said, ''but you do understand that this is in the strictest confidence. I don't want my uncle or anyone else to know.''

''I understand.''

''You have visited England in recent years, I believe. One of the largest food companies is called Wycherley-Welles. Have you ever heard of it?''

He looked at me without moving, his face blank. Then: ''My God. You and Harry.''

''I had the idea and he had the money.''

Gannon shook his head as if to clear it. ''No wonder you don't want Thad to know!''

Horace laughed. ''If Gussie has cleared up your doubts as to her backing, m-may she present her offer?''

''I'm here. It won't hurt to listen.''

''Good!'' I said. Though Gannon's manner was offhand, I felt that at last I truly had his attention. ''First of all, my last offer stands, just as I presented it. However . . .''

''However?''

''Gannon, I understand that in South Carolina alone you have three large plantations, all producing cotton.''

"Cotton and rice, mostly cotton."

"And of course you sell it through a cotton factor."

"Of course."

"Suppose you could cut your factor's percentage in half. Wouldn't that mean a great deal of money for you?"

"Certainly. Just how would you cut the percentage in half?"

"A friend of mine in England has recently acquired some textile mills and will probably acquire more. He is going to need a great deal of cotton, and insofar as you can supply his needs, he will purchase cotton exclusively from you to the capacity of his mills. He will buy at the current market price, minus half of your factor's percentage. In other words, you'll split the commission, which will be a significant saving for him and a significant gain for you."

The room was silent and Gannon sat motionless. I assumed he was thinking it over.

"She's right, you know, Gannon," Horace said after a moment. "No matter how you look at it, it's a nice arrangement."

Gannon nodded. "It is nice. Who is your friend, Gussie? Harry again?"

There was no harm in admitting it: Gannon had to know sooner or later. "Harry and I are partners. You see, Gannon, we all benefit."

"Yes, we do. I like the arrangement, Gussie. I like it very much."

For a moment I could only hold my breath. "Then you agree—"

"But since it benefits us all, I don't see why it has to be tied to the sale of the Barony."

"Because I want the Barony."

He nodded, and I waited.

"But I don't want to sell it," he said at last, flatly, as he rose to his feet, and I knew I had failed.

"Wait!" I said quickly. "Think about it! Gannon, I am offering you—"

"Gussie, I don't want to think about it. I told you right at the beginning that I was not interested in selling, and if I ever gave you any other idea, I apologize. Now, if you'll excuse me—"

"Gannon, damn it!" I jumped to my feet. "The very least

you can do is make a counterproposal! We're both reasonable people! We'll work something out!''

"Gussie, I don't like being shouted at."

"Just name a price!"

Gannon's face darkened. "All right, ten percent more than you're willing to pay! That's my price!"

"In other words, you're holding onto the Barony for sheer spite!"

"There are other plantations, princess—go buy one!"

"I want the Barony! Gannon, you know it's not really yours! You practically stole it—"

"I'm no thief, Gussie!"

"The Barony is *my home!*"

"*Your* home!" Gannon's laugh was acid. "The Barony was *my* home for years before you even saw it. I was born there, remember? And I've told you: the Barony is not for sale!"

As he headed for the door, I nearly broke. "Gannon, don't you understand? The Barony is *my last dream!*"

He hesitated, and for an instant his eyes seemed to soften. But then they hardened again.

"If that's true, princess, I'm sorry for you."

He left.

I did not know whether to scream with anger or just sit down and weep. Horace remained silent until he thought I had regained control of myself.

"I'm sorry, Gussie," he said then. "I'm sorry to see you disappointed, and I'm sorry to see two of my friends angry with each other."

"What would you advise me to do, Horace?"

"Ordinarily I'd tell you to go home and dream up a still better offer. B-but after the way you b-blew up at Gannon, I really don't think there's much point."

"Then you think I should just forget about it?"

"Well, for now, anyway."

But I could not. No matter what Gannon had said, the Barony should have been mine—in my heart it had always been—and I meant to have it. There was more than one way to skin a cat, I thought grimly, and if Gannon Murdock thought he could get the best of little Gussie Welles—the woman who had helped found Wycherley-Welles, the woman who had won the Paris garment-trade war—he had a lot to learn.

"Horace," I said, "I want to know about Gannon Murdock."

"Well, wh-what do you want to know? I suppose I know as much as—"

"I want to know his business dealings. I want to know who his friends are, who they have been. I want to know where his money came from, how much of it was honestly earned, how much stolen. I want to know everything—"

"Now, w-w-wait a minute, Gussie. I can get you any information that's on public record, but I can't dig up—"

"Find me somebody who can. There are such people, aren't there? I recall reading about the Pinkerton National Detective Agency. Get me a detective. I suspect that Gannon Murdock has a lot in his past he'd like to keep hidden, and I want to know what it is."

Horace looked at me as if seeing me anew—and as if he did not care for what he saw. "Gussie, I'm sorry, but I can't help you. Gannon Murdock is about as good a friend as I've got in this world, and I intend to k-keep it that way. If you insist on this, you're going to have to get yourself another lawyer, one not connected with this firm."

I was sorry too. I hoped I was not losing Cousin Horace as a friend.

"Can you recommend a lawyer who will help me?"

He wrote a name and address on a piece of paper and handed it to me. The lawyer was a Mr. Daniels, and the address was just down the street.

"Thank you, Horace."

I stood up to leave. When I reached the door, Horace said, "Gussie, I wish you wouldn't."

"I'm sorry, Horace."

I left to see my new lawyer.

Mr. Daniels was very helpful. A graying, hollow-cheeked, middle-aged man, weary-eyed from seeing so much of the world, he understood my problem at once.

"Yes, I can get you an investigator," he said. "But this kind of work can become very expensive, Mrs. Raveneau. I suggest that, for now, we put my man to work finding out whatever he can about Mr. Murdock right here in Charleston. Then, later, if necessary, he can look farther afield."

"That will be most satisfactory, Mr. Daniels."

By the time I was back out on Broad Street, my anger and

frustration had turned into a kind of elation. So Gannon Murdock thought he could keep the Barony from me, did he? Well, one way or another, I was going to show him just how wrong he was. Somewhere Mr. Gannon Murdock had a weakness, and I was going to find it. And when I did, I was going to *squeeze* Mr. Murdock, I was going to *twist* Mr. Murdock, I was going to *tear* at Mr. Murdock, until he screamed bloody murder and begged for mercy. And then I was going to *take* the Barony!

I was utterly certain I would succeed. But then I made one of the worst mistakes of my life. Though I have sought any kind of excuse for myself, I still cringe with shame at the thought of it.

As I started along Broad Street toward Meeting, the very first person I encountered was hawk-faced Mrs. Joinder. I had no particular wish to speak to her—I was much too busy enjoying my own seething emotions—but to do so was unavoidable. So we both stopped and smiled and said a few conventional things, the busy crowd swirling around us, and while I was looking for an excuse to be on my way, Gannon came riding along the street in a carriage. As he passed us, he touched the brim of his hat and nodded.

"Such a nice gentleman," Mrs. Joinder murmured.

"Gentleman!" I said. "Gannon Murdock, a gentleman?"

Mrs. Joinder looked surprised. "Well, I only meant—"

"If Gannon Murdock is regarded as a gentleman, I must say that Charleston has certainly lowered its standards since I was a girl."

"Well—well—" Mrs. Joinder tried to regain her footing. "Of course, you're right, we must maintain standards, but—"

"Mrs. Joinder, that man was the son of my father's overseer."

"Oh, I know. But the Murdocks were very highly regarded at one time, and—"

"Nevertheless, as my father used to say, it takes a hundred years to make a peasant into a gentleman but only one generation to make a gentleman into a peasant. As far as *I* am concerned, Mr. Murdock is evidence that my father was right."

It is an unfortunate truth that few vices in this world are as competitive as snobbery. Even as I spoke, I could see Mrs. Joinder revising her estimate of Gannon Murdock. If *my* "standards" were so high that I looked down on this oaf of an overseer's son, *her* "standards" were at least as high or even higher.

Oh, Mr. Murdock, I thought, amused, *if only you knew how vulnerable you are!*

Even so, I honestly had no intention of conducting a rumor campaign against Gannon. As far as I was concerned, I was simply setting the record straight, and I had another chance to do so the next evening, when we had a few friends in for dinner.

Somehow the conversation among the men had gotten around to the skills and merits of various planters—not surprising, since they all had plantations—and the elderly Mr. Blanchard expressed the opinion that Gannon Murdock was one of the best. "Look what he's done. Lifted himself by his bootstraps. Three plantations in South Carolina alone, not to mention all that land out in Mississippi."

I could not let that pass. "Why, Mr. Blanchard, what's that got to do with being a good planter? You know how Gannon Murdock got his start, don't you? With a deck of cards! I was always taught that a gentleman gambled only for sport, but Gannon Murdock is an outright professional. Gannon didn't buy or earn the Barony, you know." I did not attempt to hide my scorn. "He *won* it with those cards of his."

"There is some truth in that," Mr. Tragg said to Mr. Blanchard. "When we traveled to England on the same packet with Gannon some years back, he certainly concentrated on parting the rest of us from all the money he could. But," he said to me, "I think you'll find that, however he started out, he's pretty well thought of by most people who know him."

"Well, not by me!"

I do not know how many such incidents occurred in the next week, and I have no wish to remember, but there were several. Céleste was present at one or two of them, and she tried to warn me that I was speaking too freely, but I refused to listen. After all, I was only speaking the truth, wasn't I? And when little Gussie's blood rose to a boil and she went on the warpath, nobody, but nobody, was going to shut her up!

Or so it seemed, until the very last incident. It occurred at a dinner party given by Zelda and Beau Legree near the end of June, and, oh, how I blush to remember!

Gannon, absent because of a previous engagement, was mentioned favorably several times during the evening, and

Hamilton Butler spoke admiringly of his skill at cards. Really, I thought, it was too much!

"Now, don't tell me you actually play cards with him!" Dinner was over by then and we were out on the piazza, taking the cool evening air.

"Why not?" Ham asked. "Gannon's a challenge. He's the best cardplayer in these parts."

"A common sharp!"

Ham laughed. "Well, maybe. I know he got his first stake gambling. But I don't think he'd actually cheat anybody."

"Wouldn't cheat?" I said indignantly. "Why wouldn't he cheat? A man who would steal would certainly cheat, wouldn't he? And *that* is how he got his first stake, not by gambling, but by stealing a diamond necklace, the Tear of Venus, from my father. Don't tell me everybody has forgotten?"

I did not realize how quiet the piazza had suddenly become.

"Now, Augusta," Ham said, "you know that was never proved."

"Never proved! Ham, there were witnesses who saw him and his father come back to the Barony after they had supposedly left. Why else had they come back? They set the overseer's house on fire to get us out of the big house, then they stole the Tear."

"But those witnesses were slaves, hardly trustworthy—"

"They were *witnesses!* Honestly, I do not understand this forgive-and-forget attitude everyone seems to have toward Gannon Murdock. Even if he hadn't taken the Tear of Venus, it would have been something else—he once told me he wouldn't take anything from a Welles that he didn't earn or didn't steal. He took the Barony away from me—my home—and he won't even sell it back, and as far as I'm concerned, he's nothing but a mean-minded, arrogant, thieving, no-good . . ."

Dear God, what was I saying?

Everyone else was utterly silent. Every eye was turned toward me. And for the first time I realized what I had been doing for the past ten days.

"I . . . I'm sorry," I said fumblingly. "I'm afraid . . . I get carried away on the subject of Gannon Murdock. I . . . I do apologize."

I left the party soon after that. I could not stay there while feeling such an utter fool.

Of course, I spent the next hours lying awake and trying to convince myself that what had happened was not really my fault and that Gannon deserved every word I had said against him and that I was completely justified in every respect. But in my heart I knew perfectly well that I had behaved shamefully.

I was still unhappy the next morning when Horace arrived to take Céleste to church. He had never ceased to be polite to me, if only for Céleste's sake, but I felt his disapproval, and when the two asked me to go to church with them, I declined. Besides, I did not wish to see anyone who had heard me at the dinner party the night before. It was much better to sit quietly in the parlor while watching the Sunday activity outside the window.

That was how I happened to see Gannon's arrival.

The instant he brought his carriage to a halt in front of the house, I knew he must have heard about the things I had been saying—had I ever imagined he would not?—and my first impulse was to run and hide like a guilty child. But of course I would do no such thing: I would face Mr. Gannon Murdock. After all, I told myself, I might have been a fool to speak my thoughts publicly, but it was not as if anything I had said were untrue.

Gannon came up on the piazza and passed a window. I awaited his knock at the door.

But he did not knock. The door was flung open, and suddenly he was standing, hat in hand, in the parlor doorway. Never had his eyes looked darker or fiercer under the thick black brows.

"Mrs. Raveneau," he said between clenched teeth. His voice was a soft, low rumble.

"Mr. Murdock," I said breathlessly, "this is my house! Don't you even have the decency—"

"Don't you speak to me about decency, woman. I came here to give you some information. You can call off your detective—yes, I know about him—because you're wasting your money. I don't give a damn what he digs up—"

"You have nothing to say to me!"

"I have plenty to say. There was a time, Gussie, when, if I'd decided to sell the Barony, you would have been the first person I turned to. But now I wouldn't sell it to you for anything in the world. I'd even sell to Thad Welles before I'd sell to you."

"How dare you! How dare you come into my house—"

"Let me tell you something else, Gussie. When you first came back to Charleston, I was glad to see you. Hell, that first evening I was delighted. But you've spoiled it all, Gussie. Spoiled a hell of a lot of good memories as well. And for that reason I wish to God you'd never come back.''

"Gannon," I said desperately, "I'm sorry if I've hurt you, but you've hurt me, too. For so long I've dreamed—"

"Other people have dreams, too, my dear, but maybe you're too damned wrapped up in yourself to understand that. You're a spoiler, Gussie, just a miserable spoiler!''

"Gannon, listen to me. I am sorry, but—"

"And who the hell are you to sit in judgment on me? Who the hell are you after all these years to go around telling people that I'm some kind of sharper and thief?''

I could hardly see him through my gathering tears. "I never said a thing that wasn't true!''

"Well, let me tell you one thing more. Maybe you can hurt me with a few people, but not the way you're hurting yourself. Some people are getting a little tired of the way you've been behaving lately. In fact, I've been given to understand that you are getting to be a real pain in the ass. So why don't you just give it up, Gussie? Why don't you just pack it in and leave? Why don't you just pick up all that money of yours and go home to London like a good girl? You're not needed here, you know. We've been doing just fine without you. You're unwanted, Gussie. Go home!''

At that moment I could have killed him. "You—you—you— you are everything I said about you! You are nothing but a—a thieving—cardsharping—good-for-nothing—*overseer's son!* You—you are—''

"I think, my dear," he said softly, skimming his hat across the room, "the time has finally come.''

He came toward me slowly, his arms hanging loose at his sides. His shoulders seemed to bunch up and grow larger as he approached. His clenched jaw worked, and his dark eyes were utterly merciless. I knew he was capable of anything at that moment, and I should scream for help, but I could not. My voice caught in my throat, and I could only cringe away from him as he came closer, ever closer, until he seemed to tower over me.

I managed a short hoarse scream as his hand shot out and seized me by the back of the neck. Whirling me around, he sat down on the edge of the nearest chair, and the next thing I knew, I was on my stomach across his knees.

Suddenly I knew what he was going to do, and I managed

a single "Damn you, don't you dare!" before his broad hand came down on my backside with all the force and fire of a bolt of lightning.

I kicked. I screamed. I struggled. But I could not escape, and that big hand came down on me again. And again. And again.

I cursed. I wept. I clawed at him and tried to bite him. But that hand kept coming down, mercilessly, cracking like a whip and filling my backside with such pain, such fire, as I had never felt before in my life.

"Stop it, damn you," I wailed, and at last lay limp over his knees and silent except for my weeping, and *still* that hand kept coming down.

He did finally stop. Standing up, he dumped me sprawling on the floor. I lay there weeping while he picked up his hat and walked out to the hallway and the front door. There he turned to give me one last long unrelenting look. Then he opened the door and left.

4 ~~~~~~

For almost an hour I lay where I was on the floor and wept. The maid, frightened by the commotion, came into the parlor and asked if there were anything she could do for me; when I shook my head, she scurried away. Each time I thought my tears were ending, a new flood came welling up.

Gannon had made me face the truth, and I knew he was right. He had *not* stolen the Barony, and he was not under the slightest obligation to sell it to me. And as for the Tear of Venus, for all I knew the theft of the necklace was more Laird Murdock's responsibility than his son's. In any case, whatever his sins in the past, Gannon had earned a respected place in the community and I had impugned it. He had every right to be angry with me and to refuse even to consider selling me the Barony. I had hurt no one more than myself, and I deserved what I had gotten.

Fortunately Céleste and Horace were not due back at the house until evening, so I had most of the day to compose myself. Even so, they had hardly walked in the door when Céleste realized that something was wrong.

"Now, tell *Maman*," she said later, when we were alone in the parlor. "What has happened?"

By then I could even laugh a little as I told her, though my tears were still close.

"You mean to tell me," she said, her eyes sparkling, "he actually gave you a—how do you say it?—a spanking?"

"A spanking," I confirmed, rubbing my backside. "I won't be able to sit comfortably for a week."

"But how marvelous!" she said, clapping her hands. "Forgive me, my darling, but I did try to warn you!"

"My dearest friend," I said despairingly. "A brute invades our house and turns me over his knee, and she stands here laughing!"

"But it's priceless! Oh, how I wish I could have been here and watched!"

"And cheered that devil on, no doubt."

"No doubt." But she was not so unsympathetic as she sounded. When my mouth quivered, she murmured, "Oh, my baby" and enfolded me in her arms, and once again my tears flowed, this time on her comforting shoulder.

"I've spoiled everything, haven't I?" I said, when I could speak again.

"Oh, no."

"Yes, I have. And we were having such a good time—you and I and Horace and—and Gannon."

"Ah," she said, "I was right. You do like him, don't you?"

"Like him?" I said, withdrawing from her arms. How could I explain to her? "*Of course* I like him! B-b-but I also *hate* him! Because he's—he's—he's *Gannon!*"

"I think I begin to understand," Céleste said softly.

I sat down, hunched in a chair. "I only mean that he's been a part of my life for so long, ever since we were children. I can't say that we were ever really close, but he was always *there* at the Barony, and at twelve I secretly adored him and at fourteen, when he got whipped, I tried to comfort him. I've spent years avoiding him, and yet a world without Gannon in it somewhere just wouldn't be the same."

Céleste knelt before me and took my hands. "Gussie—Liane, may *Maman* make a little suggestion?"

"Of course."

"Forget about buying the Barony."

I laughed miserably. "Have I a choice?"

"And make up with your Gannon. Go to him and tell him you are very sorry you have been a bad girl and it won't happen again."

"He'd never listen to me. He'd just think I was still trying to get him to sell the Barony."

Céleste shook her head. "No. Tell him what you've told me. Tell him there is a grown woman who cannot help being disappointed that he won't sell, but that there is also, within that woman, a very young girl who still loves him very much, and you don't want him to be angry with her."

"Do you think he'd listen? Do you think he'd care?"

"My dear, I've come to know Gannon quite well this summer, and, yes, I think he would care very much."

Oh, if only that were true! I did not want to return to England to be remembered only with bitterness—the witch from London with the evil tongue. It would not be easy, but if only I could put aside pride for once and dissolve stubbornness in sweet reason and say, *Gannon, I'm sorry! And I'll never bother you about the Barony again.*

"Will you?" Céleste asked. "Will you, please, for your own sake?"

"Yes."

Oh, please, I thought, at the sound of the knocker on the street door; if only the day could end right now. But the knocker sounded again, so I went out onto the piazza, where a youthful voice told me it was "Mr. Thad's boy Isaac," and I opened the door. A horse and carriage stood waiting in the street.

"Mr. Thad say give you this, ma'am," Isaac said, handing me a note. "He say I s'pose bring you back right away."

I unfolded the note and read it by the light of the parlor window:

My dear Augusta,
    Come to the house at once. Isaac will bring you. This is extremely important, so do not keep us waiting.
                                                            T. W.

What in the world could be wrong, I thought, alarmed, and I showed the note to Céleste, who had followed me out.

"Do you want me to go with you?"

"No. I think I had best go alone."

It was probably just that Uncle Thad had learned that I had made an offer for the Barony, I thought, as the carriage bore me toward the Wraggboro house. But even for Uncle Thad, the note had seemed needlessly abrupt.

Nothing about the house seemed unusual as we pulled into the courtyard, except perhaps that an extra light or two was burning. Henry, the butler, opened the entrance hall door before I reached it, and as I stepped inside, my uncle appeared in the parlor doorway.

"You took your time," he said. "Come in here."

I followed him into the parlor. Aunt Nickie was walking the room, her face drawn with strain. Before I could say anything, my uncle thrust a piece of paper toward me and said, "You can start by reading this."

It was a letter. It was addressed to me, but that had not stopped Uncle Thad from opening it.

Dear Cousin Gussie,

By the time you read this, I reckon you'll know what Ross and I have done. Maybe you'll think it's awful, but there just doesn't seem to be any other way. My daddy will never give his consent, and you know how much I love Ross.

I'm terribly sorry about the necklace you gave me, and Ross is sorry too. We know you never meant it for this, and Ross says to tell you he'll pay you back for it just as soon as possible. I had no idea how valuable it was until my friend's mother looked at it and said she was shocked at my wearing such expensive jewelry. Then I found out, and with what Ross has saved, we can go just about anywhere we want and live for months and months.

Please forgive me if I'm doing something wrong, Cousin Gussie. I thank you more than I can say for encouraging Ross and me and letting us meet at your house. Please wish us happiness the way I wish you happiness. I want us to be like you—strong and independent and good, and I want you to know that I shall always look up to you as an inspiration. God bless you.

Your loving cousin,
Lucy

Lucy could hardly have written a letter more certain to damn me in my uncle's eyes. But surely she had not known he would see it.

"I don't understand," I said, looking up from the letter. "What—how—"

His hands behind his back, Uncle Thad paced the room as if threatening to burst through the walls with his anger at any instant. His face was expressionless except for the narrowness of his eyes.

"She deceived us," he said. "On Friday she told us she wanted to stay at a friend's house for a few days. She was supposed to be home by this evening. When she didn't return, I went to her friend's house. That little lady, pretending great innocence, gave me a letter addressed to your aunt and me. There was another addressed to you, which I took, as you see, and apparently there was a third which had already been dispatched to Gannon Murdock." He stopped pacing and faced me, his eyes still slitted. "And now, Augusta, do you have anything to say for yourself?"

"Please, Thad, please," Aunt Nickie said quietly, but Uncle Thad ignored her.

"Uncle Thad, I had no idea that Lucy would put that necklace to such use, and I told them clearly that they were not to consider our house their meeting place."

"Yet they did use it. And you even encouraged them—"

"Stop it, Thad," Aunt Nickie said, "please stop it. Augusta isn't responsible. And at least those two children love each other. They'll be all right!"

"They'll be all right when I have them back here. Because I'm going after them, and when I find them . . ."

"Uncle Thad," I said, "let them go."

"She's my daughter. He's a Murdock—"

"Let them go! They love each other. And they're not children any longer. Ross is a fine young lawyer with a promising future, and he'll take good care of Lucy. He'll be a son-in-law you can be proud of."

"Listen to her, Thad," Aunt Nickie said. "Please listen."

"She has nothing to say to me. She has forgotten what the Murdocks have already done to us."

"Not Ross," I protested. "Ross has done nothing!"

"He has stolen my daughter. He's ruined her by now, most likely, the way Gannon Murdock ruined her sister. He's a Murdock, and that's enough!"

He was interrupted by a commotion in the entrance hall. The butler said something, and the muffled voice of Gannon Murdock answered angrily. Gannon appeared in the parlor doorway. "I'm sorry, Mr. Thad," the butler said. "I open the door to see who it is, and I can't stop him."

"Murdock," Uncle Thad said, "what are you doing in my house?"

"You know why I'm here, Mr. Welles, sir," Gannon said in that angry, scornful way I knew so well. "You and I have got business, whether we like it or not."

"That's right, we do. That pup of a brother of yours has run off with my daughter, and—"

"I don't give a damn about your daughter. If you can't keep her home, that's your problem. But I do care about my brother throwing himself away when I have plans for him."

"Well, I have plans for him too. When I catch up with him, Murdock, I'm going to do to him what I should have done to you seventeen years ago. Would to God I'd done it to you both and made you the last of your breed."

As Gannon stepped toward my uncle, he was shaking as if he had a fever. "Welles, we're going after those two. They'll leave a trail of some kind, and we'll bring them back. But I am telling you here and now, as God is my witness, if you so much as touch my brother—"

"Don't you threaten me, Murdock."

"You'll answer to me, Mr. Welles. I promise you, even if I hang for it, you'll answer to me!"

Dear God in Heaven, I thought, had they learned nothing from that summer night so long ago? Would they never learn?

"All right," Uncle Thad said, "let's get moving. After we've got them back here, we'll settle once and for all."

"No!" I cried out so sharply that Gannon looked around at me as if noticing my presence for the first time. "No, you mustn't! If you can't help them, at least leave them alone!"

"You keep out of this, Gussie," Gannon said. "You've done enough already."

I shook my head. "Leave them alone! Uncle Thad, when

are you going to stop? You don't own your children! Why can't you just love them and take care of them and let them lead their own lives?''

"You shut your mouth in this house, woman—"

"No! If it hadn't been for you, Melinda and her child would be alive today. They'd both be alive and happy and . . ."

I heard a cry from Aunt Nickie, and my hands flew to my mouth. For a moment there was utter silence in the room. But I had already said it, spoken the truth after all these years, the truth that I had vowed to keep buried forever, the truth that could only bring more grief and pain. And as I looked at Aunt Nickie, something strange and terrible was happening to her face. It was falling apart, aging, turning into an ancient tragic mask before my very eyes.

Uncle Thad turned on me a face scarcely less terrible than Aunt Nickie's. "How do you know? How could you possibly know, unless she told you . . ."

"I don't know," I said desperately. "It—it was just a way of speaking! I only meant . . ." But it was too late. My words could not be unsaid.

". . . and you lied to us that morning in the library."

Such a heartbreaking wail as I had never heard before came from Aunt Nickie then. Uncle Thad went to her and held her before she could collapse. When I turned toward Gannon, he was giving me the same look of shocked disbelief, of sick dismay, as he had in the barn that night when he thought I had betrayed him and Melinda.

"Gannon . . ."

He turned away from me very slowly. He left the parlor without saying another word. I heard the click of the door as he left the house.

Aunt Nickie was sobbing in my uncle's arms. When I went to her, hoping to comfort her, my uncle's arm shot out, thrusting me aside.

"Don't you touch her."

"Uncle Thad, please!"

"I curse the day you came back to Charleston. I curse the day you returned to this house. Get out. Leave. You're no niece of mine."

I could only stand there and look at him for a time. My uncle. My father's brother. Turning me out of his house with a curse.

When I left, Aunt Nickie was still sobbing in his arms.

*   *   *

On returning to the house, I went straight to my room and put on my nightgown, for I wanted only to escape into sleep. But Céleste came in and sat with me on my bed, and I told her what had happened.

"Tomorrow," she said, "it won't look nearly so bad."

I shook my head. "I meant never to tell. Now Gannon knows he lost not only the girl he loved but their child as well. Aunt Nickie knows she lost not only a daughter but also a grandchild. Uncle Thad knows for certain now that his worst suspicions were true. Céleste, I came back home with such hopes, and I've brought nothing with me but pain. Even for the people I love."

"Chèrie, I think you blame yourself too much."

"I should never have come back. What did I think I'd find? My girlhood again, my innocence? Oh, God, how lost they are!"

"Tomorrow," Céleste said soothingly, her arm over my shoulders, "tomorrow will be better."

I shook my head again. "Tomorrow I think I shall pack my bags. You won't mind, will you? We can still spend some time in the north, if you like, visiting the places you wanted to see. And maybe I can start forgetting."

I broke off as I saw the stricken look on Céleste's face and realized what it meant. How could I have been so thoughtless?

"Oh, I'm sorry," I said. "Of course we're not going to leave. We'll stay just as long as you wish."

She looked at her hands in her lap. "I love him," she said.

"I know, dear."

"I keep telling myself to be sensible, that I can't possibly be in love again after all this time, and yet . . . he means everything to me, Gussie. These past two months . . . it's as if I had been reborn."

"I know."

"And I'm so afraid of losing him. Afraid that he doesn't love me and never will."

"How can he keep from loving you?"

She laughed, not very happily. "Men have been known to resist, you know. And these Charleston men . . . You were right, Gussie, the people here, they are even more proper than our European bourgeoisie! The idea of a woman living as freely and independently as a man—appalling! And when I tell Horace more about myself . . ." She shook her head.

"Maybe you shouldn't tell him too much."

"Oh, I have no intention of 'confessing all,' believe me. That would be ridiculous. But he must understand that I am not one of his innocent Charleston belles. I am a woman who has been about the world—"

"And," I said, "who takes pride in the fact."

"Exactly. I want him to love me for what I really am, not for what he may think I am."

"Then, he will." *Would he?*

Céleste closed her eyes. "Oh, I hope so!"

Though I was concerned for Céleste, for the next few days I thought of little other than Lucy and Ross. Where were they? Were they all right? I expected Uncle Thad to come question me about their possible destination, but I heard neither from him nor from Aunt Nickie. I decided he was probably on his way north in pursuit of the runaway pair—he and Gannon Murdock together.

Then on Wednesday afternoon I received a message from Gannon.

A young black man named Virgil, dusty from the road, delivered it to me on the piazza. "Mr. Gannon, he say I s'pose bring'n answer from you in the morning. Bring you back to the Barony, too, mist'ess, if'n you want."

So Gannon had not gone after the runaways after all. I opened his letter. It was written in a nicely formed hand that, like the wording itself, seemed slightly out of control:

Dear Gussie,

For what it's worth, I regret our argument in Horace's office—standing there shouting at each other like a couple of spoiled brats. I also apologize for anything out of line I may have said at the Welles house the other night. God alone knows what I might have said. I don't.

I must talk to you about a very important matter. Will you please come out to the Barony? I'll be very grateful. Come as soon as you can. Bring Mrs. de Laurence if you wish. Perhaps Horace will drive you out again. Or Virgil, the bearer of this letter, will bring you. But please come, Gussie. Again, I shall be very grateful.

                                        Gannon Murdock

I read the letter twice, then showed it to Céleste. She read it and said, "We're going, of course."

"What in the world could he want?"

"We'll find out when we get there."

And so, on a steaming hot Saturday at the beginning of July, I found myself arriving with Céleste and Horace at the Barony again. As we got out of the carriage, Pearl and Céleste greeted each other like old friends, and Pearl's boys came running to take our bags. Gannon, pulling on his coat, came out of the house and down the steps. He greeted Céleste and Horace cordially, then turned to me. I had feared this moment. I knew Gannon would be nothing less than polite, but beyond that? I had no idea.

He took a step or two toward me, and my heart beat faster. The breeze moved an unruly lock of black hair over his forehead, and it seemed to me that he had never looked more handsome than at that moment—a sun-bronzed, London-tailored, American savage. I looked for some sign of the anger, shock, and dismay that had been in his eyes when we had last met, but I could see nothing.

For a moment he merely looked at me. Then he smiled, and his eyes were warm, and he said quietly, with his heart in it, "I'm glad you've come."

I said, "I'm glad too, Gannon."

He ushered us into the house. As soon as we had freshened up in our rooms, dinner was served, and though the talk and the laughter flowed easily over the table, I cannot say it was as if the events of the previous two months had not occurred. Despite his welcome, there was a tension between Gannon and me we all felt.

Half an hour after dinner, Horace announced that he was going to take Céleste down to the landing and let her dangle her feet in the water. Gannon then suggested that, if I could stand the heat of the day, he and I take a walk in another direction and "discuss some things." With my permission, he left his coat and cravat behind, and we wandered out through the flower gardens to the same vine-covered gazebo where Tom and I had met so many years before. Gannon smiled and tossed his hat down on the bench seat. I took my bonnet off, and for a moment we just stood there looking at each other as if wondering how to begin.

"Gannon," I finally said, forcing myself to look into his eyes, "I just want to tell you that I am very, very sorry."

"For what, Gussie?"

It was harder than I had expected. I looked down again. "You know for what. I shouldn't have . . . talked about you the way I did. I'm ashamed of myself, Gannon. I don't know what devil got into me, but I have no excuse. I can only hope you'll forgive me." Pressing my palms together, I touched my fingertips to Gannon's chest just below the open neck of his shirt. His hands enclosed mine.

"Do you expect me to apologize for turning you over my knee?"

I shook my head. "No."

What happened to us in that moment? I think we realized anew something of what we meant to each other—not as friends, exactly, and certainly not as lovers. Perhaps as souls. I found myself slipping into his arms and laying my head on his shoulder, and we held each other close. He was still my Gannon. And I suppose I was still his Gussie.

After a minute we separated. "Now," I said, "what was it you wanted to talk about?"

"Oh, that," he said. "Gussie, does your offer for the Barony still hold?"

"Of course."

"Good." He held out his hand. "It's yours."

Just like that, on a handshake, the Barony was mine again. My dream had come true. I felt as if I were reeling; I could not catch my breath. In a near-faint, I slumped down onto the bench seat.

"Gannon," I said, as he sat down beside me, "I'll thank you forever for this, but I don't understand. Why?"

"Oh, lots of reasons. The world is changing more than the South knows or wants to admit, and before the sky comes falling down on us, I'm getting rid of a lot of my holdings. I'm going up to Virginia soon to sell some property, and in the fall I'm going out to Mississippi. I hope to sell all I've got out there by spring. If you want the Barony so damn bad, I figure I might as well sell that too. To you."

"Fine," I said. "Now tell me the real reason."

For a moment, he seemed to withdraw into his own thoughts, and his face saddened. When he spoke, he seemed to do so as much to himself as to me.

"First, I want to tell you that you were right about Ross and Lucy, Gussie. In the note he left for me, Ross said he'd let me know when they were settled up north. When he does,

I'm going to send him some money. Try to help them out. And I'll get Lucy's necklace back if I can.''

"I'm so glad, Gannon. But what changed your mind?"

"You did. Gussie, you're sure it was true about Melinda having a baby?"

"Yes. She didn't want to worry you."

He closed his eyes and touched his forehead, and I could feel his reborn pain.

"I might have had a sixteen-year-old son today," he said wonderingly, when he had opened his eyes again. "Or a sixteen-year-old daughter. I would have liked that, Gussie. I really would have *liked* that."

"I know."

"Anyway, I wouldn't want to do to Ross and Lucy what Thad Welles did to Melinda and me. And the other night at Thad's house you made me realize that that was exactly what I was doing. I was trying to give Ross the kind of life *I* wanted for him, not the kind *he* wanted. And who was I to say that my dream for him was better than his own?

"You see, Gussie, I was brought up to be a man of the land. You could be a doctor, a lawyer, anything you wanted, but a good name and good land came first. And I hoped to see Ross settled down here at the Barony.''

"Ross!" I said, surprised. "Not yourself?"

"Myself at first," he said morosely, "but the last few years it's seemed less and less likely that I'd marry and have children to leave the place to. And I always wanted to see Murdocks on this land. Figured that either Ross or I, one of us, would put the Murdock name back on the land again and keep it there. Well, it looks like I was wrong."

"I'm sorry, Gannon. It's a dream I can understand."

"I know you can, Gussie. In some ways, we were brought up two of a kind. But," he smiled, "don't be too sorry. With our old house burned down, I find the place doesn't mean quite as much to me as I thought. And I've got a damn fine place down the coast that I built myself. Bought up the land, cleared it where I had to, improved it. Built a big house on a high bluff at the mouth of the river where you can see the ocean. In the summer it's even nicer than Sullivan's Island. And as I said—I built it myself."

I liked his quiet pride. "What do you call it?" I asked.

"I call it No Name."

"No Name! But why?"

He grinned. " 'Cause it ain't got no name."

I laughed, and he put an arm around me. "Just the same," I said, "we had some mighty good times right here at the Barony."

"We certainly did."

Then his mouth was on mine, and it was a very nice kiss, gentle and tender and caring, and lovely warm waves went through me, and at sixteen I, in my innocence, would have thought of earthquakes and volcanoes. Now it was simply a very, very nice kiss.

Ah, what a lovely afternoon that was! We traded a few more kisses, even nicer than the first, until my inner tremors suggested that maybe there *was* something to the idea of earthquakes and volcanoes and we had best leave the gazebo. We walked out to the field quarters and spent an hour with people I had known in childhood, then went again to my favorite stream, and finally back to the big house.

Supper was as pleasant as it always was when we four were together, and the others made a lot of jokes about the "new mistress of the Barony" and proposed toasts to her. Later, as the evening drew toward an end, we went our separate ways, Céleste with Horace and Gannon with me—we were all behaving quite *wildly* by Charleston standards!—and Gannon and I eventually found ourselves outside on the upstairs piazza. He had brought out a settee, and I sat comfortably in the circle of his arm while we looked out toward the landing and the moonlit river.

"No," I said, when he tilted my head back. "No more kissing games."

"Why not?"

"Because they can lead to nothing."

"Are you so sure?"

"Yes."

He kissed me anyway, and I damned him silently and kissed him back.

"Gussie," he said a little later, "have you given any thought to coming back here permanently?"

"Yes, but . . . oh, Gannon, since I've come home, I've realized that, except at the Barony, I'm *not* really at home. My dear, I am simply not a Charleston lady anymore."

"Well, to be perfectly honest, Gussie, I've never quite succeeded in turning myself into a Charleston gentleman."

"I think you're a perfectly lovely gentleman," I said. "If

anyone says anything against my Gannon, I'll scratch his eyes out.''

He laughed and rubbed his cheek against my head. "Tell me something. Why didn't you ever marry again? A woman as beautiful as you must have had a thousand chances.''

"Why do people always assume a woman *wants* to marry? You know I've been a very busy woman. I've become an—an—I've become an *industrialist*.''

"Do you mean to tell me that, after Tom, you never fell in love again?''

"Oh, once or twice, perhaps. But what about you, Gannon? Why have you never married?''

"I don't know. Like you, I've been mighty busy, and when I'm not working, I like to travel. Still, hell, if I met the right woman. . . . What about you?''

I had no illusion that Gannon had any serious interest in me, but in case he did, it was time to nip it in the bud.

"Gannon, I have lived alone for so long and fought so hard to get what I wanted that I have become a very independent and willful woman. Call me selfish, call me sot in my ways. I am forced to admit that I have become an old termagant who yields not one inch to any man on anything that remotely interests her. And I like it that way. Do you understand me, Gannon? I would be an absolute fool to marry any man, and any man would be a fool to marry me.''

Gannon sat in silence for a moment or two while we gazed at the moonlight on the river, and I smiled to myself. There, I had said it, and he had got it straight, once and for all.

Finally, he sighed. "Yes, you're right, of course. I'm afraid I'll have to admit I'm pretty much the same. Just so damn used to living in my own way that I doubt that I could make any woman happy. Or that any woman could make *me* happy, for that matter.'' He shook his head. "It's sad in a way, but I really don't think there's a woman in the world who could make it worth my while. Yes, when I think about it seriously, I don't suppose there is a single woman in the whole world who could even *tempt* me! You're absolutely right, Gussie. I've got to agree with you a hundred percent.''

We sat quietly.

"Thank you," I said, after a moment.

"Why, you're welcome," Gannon said.

"Thank you very much.''

He turned his head to stare at me. "Is something wrong?''

"Oh, no, not at all. Should something be wrong?"

"Gussie, if I said something I shouldn't have—"

"Why, what could that have been?"

"You sound angry—"

"I am not angry!" Not in the slightest. Just very slowly becoming completely *furious!*

"Then why—"

I stood up. "It is so reassuring to know that chivalry is not dead!"

"Chivalry not—Gussie, I was only *agreeing* with you! Why are you angry?"

"Good night, Mr. Murdock," I said, trying to sound blithely indifferent. "Good night! *Thank* you for a pleasant evening!"

Gannon began laughing. "Gussie! Please! Don't be angry! Please!"

I went into the house, pursued by his idiotic laughter. It followed me until I reached the door of my bedroom and slammed it. Hastily I pulled off my clothes, flinging them about the room, and pulled on a nightgown. I blew out the lamp and slipped into bed.

Damn him, damn him, damn him, damn him! I thought furiously. *Damn him!*

I fell asleep dreaming of Gannon's mouth on mine.

5 ~~~~~~

The next afternoon the four of us rode back to Charleston together. By then I had regained my equanimity and could pretend an indifference to Gannon I did not feel. Often when he looked at me, he seemed to be on the verge of laughter, as if—maddeningly—he saw through all my pretenses. And I, with all my heart, wanted nothing more than to kiss his beautiful mouth and slap his handsome face.

"Must you look so superior all the time?" I asked, late in the day when we had stopped to rest and water the horses.

We were in a pleasant grove at the side of the road, and Gannon and I had wandered off by ourselves.

"Superior?" he asked, surprised.

"You know what I mean. As if I were some kind of endearing idiot child and you had all you could do not to burst our laughing at me."

"But I do want to burst out laughing. But not *at* you, Gussie. It's just that I'm so fond of you. You make me feel good, and I want to laugh, I want to sing. My God, woman, is it possible that I'm falling in love with you?"

"I certainly hope not!"

"So do I. Jesus, an old termagant like you, selfish as hell and sot in her ways—"

"You . . . bastard!"

Gannon cackled gleefully as I tried to swat him, and before I could stop him, seized me and kissed me.

The two men stayed for supper that evening, but we sent them home soon afterwards. While Céleste said good night to Horace in the parlor, I went out onto the piazza with Gannon.

"Don't," I said, as he tried to pull me into his arms. "The neighbors."

"The neighbors will mind their 'north-side manners,' " he said. "Nobody in Charleston looks out his back window into his neighbor's front yard, remember?"

Well, maybe some did not, but . . . oh, well, I thought, let them look. I slid into Gannon's arms.

"You are fond of me, too, aren't you, Gussie?" he asked a minute later.

"Of course I am. How could I not be, you sweet old bear?"

He gave me a kiss then that could have led to a lot more, but I pushed him away. "Now go home."

Horace came out of the house, and the two men left together. I went back into the house and found Céleste sitting in the parlor, looking as if she wanted to cry.

"Why, what in the world . . .?"

She shook her head and looked away.

"Céleste, what is it?" I asked, but I had the feeling I already knew. I sat down with her and took her hand. "Have you and Horace quarreled?"

"No."

"Then tell me."

Her next words took visible effort: "Gussie, he doesn't love me."

"Oh, Céleste, I'm sure that's not true . . ."

"We've been seeing each other constantly ever since you and I came here. Other men have hardly existed for me. And right from the beginning he's acted as if I were the only woman in the world for him. But he's never said a single word about marriage, and now I don't think he ever will."

I tried to think of something encouraging. "But you've got to give him time. Two months isn't so long."

She shook her head. "He doesn't even want to go to bed with me any more. Not that we ever have, but we both wanted to, almost from the instant we first laid eyes on each other. Did you know that Gannon gave us adjoining bedrooms at the Barony last night?"

I did know, of course.

Céleste laughed mirthlessly. "A wasted gesture, believe me. Dear Horace didn't even come in to kiss me goodnight, let alone try to seduce me."

"But, dear, some men are very shy—"

"No. I can assure you that Horace is not shy. That's not the trouble at all. Gussie, you did warn me about these very proper Charleston people. . . ."

Oh, no. That was what I had been afraid of.

"I told you I wanted Horace to love me for what I really am and not for what he may think I am. So this past week I've tried to tell him a little bit more about myself. And it wasn't long before I realized that I was making a mistake. I could *feel* him pulling away from me, as if . . . as if . . ."

As if she were not good enough for a Charleston gentleman. Céleste turned away from me to weep for a moment. What a sad way to end such a wonderful weekend, I thought. But of course it had not been wonderful for Céleste.

"Dear," I said, "I don't want to give you false hope. I have too much respect for you to do that. But if you truly love Horace, don't give up. Maybe he needs a little time to think about what you've told him, and to get to know you again as you really are. At least give him that chance. Give *yourself* that chance."

She nodded. Good.

But Céleste's experience was a forceful reminder of an important truth. I had spent years keeping the identity of Liane Duhamel separate from that of Augusta Welles Raveneau, because I was certain that a woman of Liane's background and reputation—"disorderly," as Mrs. Joinder had put it—would be less than acceptable to Charleston society, no matter how admired her dresses might be. And I had been right.

Furthermore, I was right in not allowing myself to become emotionally involved with Gannon Murdock: to do so would have been the height of folly. He would have had to accept and love and, yes, take pride in me for what I was—a *parisienne* of imagination and spirit and an independent way of life. But Gannon—like Horace—though intelligent and traveled and hardly provincial, was nonetheless a gentleman of Charleston background and standards.

And Charleston gentlemen did not marry women like us.

As far as Horace and Céleste were concerned, I hoped I was wrong, and certainly he did not seem any less fondly attentive to her in the days that followed. The four of us spent Independence Day together, and both he and Céleste showed every sign of having a wonderful time. We listened to patriotic speeches and watched the militia parade through the streets, all of us cheering when the flag went by. Like schoolboys, Gannon and Horace flung firecrackers about, bursting eardrums and scaring horses. In the evening we all went out to the Washington Race Course and watched the fireworks, yelling our approval at each spectacular burst of a rocket. And when in a flash of light I saw Horace gazing at Céleste, I could not believe that he was any less in love than she.

Ah, but that Gannon Murdock, what a persistent lad he was! When the gentlemen took us to our door that evening, he refused to go home. We sat together in the dark parlor and talked about the fun we had had that day, and we remembered other Independence Days, from childhood. We listened to Céleste's and Horace's murmurs and quiet laughter out on the piazza. (*Oh, dear Lord*, I thought, *please make him love her!*) And we kissed, at first gently and nicely, and later not at all gently but *ever* so nicely, until my head was abuzz and my body felt adrift in a warm sea of pleasure, and I whispered, "Oh, Gannon, go home, go home, go home!"

"When you promise to visit No Name with me."

"Oh, no . . ."

"We can go down next week, after we get our business done and before I have to leave for Virginia. Bring Céleste. Horace too, if he can get away from the office."

"Gannon, what are you trying to do to me? I have to go back to England in a few weeks—"

"Come down to No Name. We'll walk barefoot on the beach and go out to dive through the waves, and you'll never want to leave."

"Oh, Gannon . . ."

"Come with me, Gussie. Come down to No Name."

In the days that followed, he invited me repeatedly, but I was wise. I was sensible. I firmly resisted. Meanwhile, the transfer of the Barony was concluded, and the moment the papers were signed in Horace's office, I hurried off to tell Aunt Nickie the good news. I knew that Uncle Thad was still away, searching for Lucy and Ross, so I thought I could safely go to the Wraggboro house without incurring his wrath.

When I arrived, I was pleased to see that Aunt Nickie had largely recovered from the terrible evening two weeks earlier, though the pain seemed to have aged and weakened her. She took me into the parlor and listened, smiling, while I told her everything—well, not *quite* everything!—that had happened between Gannon and me. Then, embracing me, she said, "Oh, I am so happy for you, Liane. Does this mean you'll be staying on in Charleston permanently?"

"No, but I do hope to get back at least once every two years—"

I gaped at her.

What had she called me?

Liane?!

"How did you know?" I croaked out, when I could speak.

"Oh, I have my ways," she said, laughing. "After all, I've talked to Céleste—"

"Did she tell you?"

"Of course not. But—you, Paris, Céleste, that Lord Harry person, the way you and Céleste teased those poor women at our dinner party, so many things. I simply made a guess."

"But if *you* can guess, then others—"

"Never. You forget, Augusta, they don't see you as I do. Your secret is as safe with me, dear, as it is with Céleste." She whispered: "We shall be three civilized Frenchwomen among these primitive Americans!"

I was glad Aunt Nickie knew; she was perhaps the only woman in Charleston who could have understood my story. I said, "I want to tell you all about it."

"And I want to hear. There were so many rumors when your husband came back—"

She was interrupted by the sound of a door. She gave me a startled look and stepped out into the entrance hall.

"Thad, dear! Oh, I'm so glad you're back. Did you . . .?"

Uncle Thad's voice was soft and weary. "No. I followed them up to Washington . . . followed some false leads . . . no use . . ."

"I'm sure Lucy will be all right. We'll hear from her soon."

There was no point in delaying the inevitable. I stepped out into the entrance hall.

"Good afternoon, Uncle Thad."

He said nothing, did not move, did not smile. We might have been two statues facing each other.

"Augusta has brought the most marvelous news," Aunt Nickie said. "She has just bought the Barony from Mr. Murdock."

And still my uncle merely looked at me, his face a perfect blank.

"Isn't that marvelous news, Thad?"

"Isn't it?" Uncle Thad walked toward the stairs.

"Just think, Thad, the Barony is back in the family at last. Isn't that wonderful?"

"Wonderful," Uncle Thad said, going up the stairs and never looking back. "Wonderful."

He disappeared from sight.

Aunt Nickie came to me. "I'm afraid he's still angry, dear. But he'll get over it."

No. I did not think that Uncle Thad would ever get over it. The question was, what would he do now?

Gannon left for No Name a few days later. When he asked me why I kept refusing his invitations, I simply told him that I had my own life to lead and had no wish to become more deeply involved with him than I already was. He then gave me the sweetest smile in the world and a kiss that made my objections seem quite silly, and repeated: "Come down to No Name. We'll have the place ready for you. I'll be waiting."

Still, I might not have gone if it had not been for Céleste. "Please," she said, "let's go. I want to get away from this city and far, far away from Horace. Please, Gussie, do I ask so much of you?"

"We can go to the Barony," I said, alarmed by a request I knew I could not refuse.

"No. I want to see No Name. And besides, in your heart don't you really want to go?"

"Nonsense!"

But be honest: wasn't Céleste right?

She and Gannon had everything arranged, it seemed. Virgil, his young driver, arrived at our house with a carriage early Saturday morning. I was still half-asleep when we were ferried across the Ashley River and started on the long, bumpy road down the coast. Few days in my life had seemed longer, and it was close to sunset when we arrived at our destination.

"Dere duh house," Virgil said, "jes' ahead."

It had been built on one of the very highest points of this low-lying country. As we drew around in front of it, I saw that, in the traditional fashion, it faced down a long slope to the river and the landing and—seen distantly through the evening haze—the ocean. It was a great brick block of a house, painted white, with piazzas completely encircling it, making it look broad and airy and comfortable.

As Céleste and I struggled creakily out of the carriage, Gannon came running down the staircase to greet us, whooping his pleasure and embracing Céleste as affectionately as he did me. He noted Horace's absence but tactfully did not refer to it again.

"Well, what do you think of the place, Gussie?"

"Oh, Gannon, it's lovely. I'm so glad you invited us!"

"Come inside. I have a surprise for you."

He led us up the stairs and into a central passage as broad and high-ceilinged as any I had ever seen, and then into a parlor. There I found myself facing a handsome, sun-darkened country woman of about my age. She looked at me a bit mischievously, I thought, and with feigned shyness said, "Ah know yew. You're Augusta. Will yew play with me? Mah name is—"

"*Janthina!*"

"Oh, the look on your face!" Janthina said, laughing, as we embraced. "Well, take your shoes off, lady, and stay a while!"

The evening that followed was one of our happiest since coming to America. We had to meet Janthina's husband, Mr. Ridley Ames, of course, and her children. Céleste looked at the children with such naked desire that I knew she would have been heartbroken if the two-year-old had not taken to her at once. This, I thought, was the life she should have led.

We had a fine supper—chicken and gumbo and two or three other things, as I recall, for Gannon set a sumptuous table. Janthina's three oldest, two girls and boy, ate with us. They were a lively bunch, well-mannered but filled with high spirits. Mr. Ames, a lean, wiry man, no taller than Janthina and I, told us stories of sailing on the schooner-yacht *America* under Commodore John C. Smith in 1851 and beating fourteen British vessels in a race around the Isle of Wight. I had been in England that summer and had *seen the America!* I had seen the crew standing on her deck! I had seen Janthina's husband and never known it!

After supper, while the others sat down to a game of cards, Gannon took me for a stroll along the piazza. "Mr. Murdock," I said, "did you invite Céleste and me here to show us how much in life we've been missing?"

He didn't answer. He said, "A lot of people say I was crazy for building a house this big. It's nice when my sisters and their families visit, but mostly it just stands here, empty and wasted."

My words of two months earlier came back to me: *"Pretty soon I'll be too old to be starting a family." "Aw, no, Gussie." "Yes, Gannon . . ."*

I said, "Don't make me fall in love with you, Gannon."

"Why not?"

Because it won't work, my darling, it won't work, it won't work, it won't work . . .

Knowing that, why did I let him kiss me? There in the darkness of the piazza, he drew me into his arms and held me with inescapable strength and yet such incredible gentleness that I wanted him never to let me go. He drew me to him and kissed me, and I kissed him in return. He laid his head against mine, and when I opened my eyes, his were still closed, and the expression on his face was one of pain and longing. I felt him tremble as his arms tightened around me.

Oh, my darling, I thought, *don't fall in love with me! Don't!*

If he should somehow learn the truth about me, about the life I had led . . . that I was the woman who had cost Adam Trevayne his life . . .

But he must not. Ever.

*   *   *

The sun was already high and the day was bright when I awakened the next morning. For a few moments I lay still in my bed, feeling marvelously good. Then I remembered. The piazza. Gannon's kisses. I had been right to resist coming here. But it was too late now. And how could anybody feel as desperate and miserable and gloriously happy as I did, all at the same time?

Céleste and Janthina were having coffee when I went downstairs. Janthina took one look at me and shook her head disapprovingly. "Thought Gannon said to put old clothes on this morning. He's taking us sailing."

"These are the oldest I brought."

"I keep a few things here. After you have breakfast, I'll get you something better."

The "something better" turned out to be an old dress, worn paper-thin and held together in front by a couple of safety pins. My costume was completed by an old wide-brimmed straw hat, held on by a ribbon around my chin, and a pair of soft-soled shoes, making me, Janthina said, "The very picture of the latest from Paris! Now, why don't you go down to the landing and see what Gannon is up to?"

Feeling very much the country girl, I strolled down the green slope toward the landing, where the sloop was moored. A couple of servants were putting food hampers aboard, and Gannon was stowing them away in the cabin. I reached the landing and was saying "Request permission to come aboard, sir," when I realized there was something familiar about the boat. She was some thirty feet long, rather beamy but fine at bow and stern, and freshly painted, with brasswork gleaming.

The *Maid of Athens!*

"Oh, Gannon, she's beautiful!"

"I thought you'd be pleased," he said, helping me aboard. "She's in as good shape as when you left."

The hours I had spent on my little ship as a girl, and how I had loved her! She had a lot of cockpit and not much cabin, because she was mainly a working vessel, built for transporting supplies along the coast and upriver. But she was surprisingly fast, and I would not have traded her for another, not even to win the *America*'s Cup.

Having looked her over, I settled down in the cockpit to look at the far shore. The mouth of the river was wide and peaceful, and the boat rocked gently as I leaned over the side. We seemed to be drifting, drifting . . .

I looked around to find that we were at least fifty feet from the landing and moving away fast. And Gannon was hoisting the mainsail.

"Gannon, what are you doing!"

"Taking you sailing."

"But Janthina and Céleste—"

"I'll take them another time. This time it's just you and me."

Oh, no, it was not!

Jumping to my feet, I tore off my hat and kicked off my shoes. I pulled my dress up to my waist and knotted it.

"Gussie, what are you—"

"Swimming ashore!"

Stepping up on the rail and gripping with my toes, I bent my knees for a dive. But in that very instant, a hand grabbed me from behind, and to my consternation, *r-r-r-rip!* went my drawers, and a breeze cooled my backside. Then an arm encircled my waist, and I fell tumbling back into the cockpit with Gannon.

"You bully!" I screamed. "You knave! You rascal!" He was laughing his head off. "You—you villain! You rogue—"

"Having fun, Gussie?"

Scrambing to my knees, I struggled to get my dress unknotted and back down where it belonged. "Kindly turn your back, you—you laughing hyena, while I fix my drawers!"

I managed to fasten them with a safety pin from the front of my dress. Men may talk all they wish about the miracles of steam power and modern engineering, but every woman knows that civilization reached its *real* summit just a few years ago with the invention of the safety pin.

While Gannon finished hoisting the sails, I assessed the situation. It was perfectly disgraceful, of course. Ladies simply did not go out sailing along with men who were not their husbands. (And they certainly did not get their drawers torn half off!) But on the other hand, who was to know? Céleste and Janthina would never tell. Should I continue to protest, or—"

"Take the helm, Gussie," Gannon said, "she's all yours!" *What* had he said?

"I said, take the helm! Make this lady behave!"

With a cry of delight, I leapt to the tiller. *No*, I was not going to protest!

There is absolutely nothing else in this world like it: You have one hand on the tiller and the other grips the mainsail sheet, and as you draw the sail tight, bringing it into perfect harmony with wind and rudder, you feel your vessel come alive and lift in the water and *go!* You have harnessed the wind, and you ride it. It is yours. You are its mistress. Your concentration is so complete and absolute that any cares you may have in this world vanish and you might as well be sailing the seas of the moon. My crew, at the jib, crowed his joy, and at the top of my voice I cheered back.

The *Maid of Athens* was mine that day, and the wind was mine, and it is a measure of Gannon Murdock as a real man that he let it be so. We ladies were generally supposed to be timid, helpless, and appreciative passengers. An occasional wife or tomboy daughter who had been raised to sails might be allowed to handle the jib sheets in fair weather, but nothing more. My father was one of the few men I had known who would allow me to take the helm by myself. But Gannon that day put me on my own. We practiced tacking and jibing dozens of time, until my hands were raw and forgotten muscles were aching, and I do not think he offered so much as a suggestion. "You're the captain, Gussie," he said, "just shout your orders loud and clear," and by early afternoon we had our skills perfectly coordinated. Together, we made our little ship *dance* on the sea!

Gannon took over when he saw weather coming—which I had not. Suddenly the sky was dark and we hardly had the sails stowed when the deluge came. It came straight down, driving, pouring, more like a vast waterfall than a rain, and bone-chillingly cold. The shoreline disappeared. From the cockpit we could not even see the bow of the boat. "Better go below, Gussie," Gannon yelled over the roar, but I turned my face up to the heavens and yelled back, "No! I wouldn't miss this for anything in the world!"

It rained for perhaps half an hour and stopped as suddenly as it had begun. The distant shoreline reappeared, the sun broke through, and once again the day was scorching hot. Gannon and I looked at each other, sodden messes, laughing. He pulled off his sopping shirt, and I might as well have pulled off my dress, for all the good it did me, but within minutes we were both dry.

"Oh, Gannon," I said, "that was marvelous."

"Are you hungry?"

"Starving!"

As soon as the cockpit was dry, he rigged a canopy over it, for we had had enough of the sun as well as the rain. Then he brought out a vast number of cushions and blankets for our comfort, for it is a fact that nothing in the world gets quite as hard as the deck of a boat. And finally he brought out the food hampers: fowl and shrimp and wine and all manner of lovely things.

Hardly saying a word, we ate and drank. Ate and drank until we were stuffed, and my head was muzzy with sun and wine and good food and fatigue. At exactly the same moment, we both released a great sigh and lay back on our heaped-up cushions, laughing softly at each other. I rolled into his arms, and when we kissed, he tasted nicely of white wine and curried shrimp. We laughed some more and kissed some more, and I thought, *Oh, this is wrong, I must have drunk too much!* but I did not care, I only wanted to go on and on lying in his arms, half-asleep and kissing him. When he slipped his hand into the torn front of my dress, I did not even try to stop him.

"Oh, Gannon, Gannon," I murmured, as he touched my nipples, "did you bring me out here to seduce me?"

"The thought had crossed my mind."

"I remember you vowed that one day you would have me."

"I didn't know then that I would fall in love with you."

I must be completely mad, I thought, as his mouth moved against my throat while he pulled open the front of my dress. *Completely mad or besotted or asleep and dreaming.*

"Gannon, don't," I said, as he laid me on my back and kissed my breast. "Please, no more."

He raised his head to look into my eyes, unsmiling. "Gussie, I'm not going to lose you."

I shook my head. "It's just a nice day at No Name. A nice day out sailing, and I've drunk a little too much wine. Don't try to make more of it than that."

"It is more than that."

Before I could say another word, his mouth covered mine, our tongues met, and I was powerless to protest. We lay together for a time, thighs entangled, playing gently, trading kisses and caresses, while desire and need mounted. But when he reached under my skirt to pluck at my underclothes, I pushed him away and sat up, shaking my head to clear it. It was quite time to call a halt to our pleasures before they went too far.

"I do think we had better start back now, Gannon."

He sat up and moved close to my side. "We have the rest of the afternoon. Gussie, do you remember the day I pulled you out of the stream because of the cottonmouth?"

"How could I forget?"

"I think I wanted to make love to you even then." His arms slid around me. His lips moved over my eyes. A hand lifted my bare breast and drew at the swollen nipple. "I still want to make love to you, Gussie."

God knows, I, too, wanted him to make love to me. I ached for him, yearned for him, more every minute. Yet I forced myself to be wise.

"We mustn't. Gannon, I'll be leaving for England soon—"

"No. I'm keeping you here."

"I must. I have responsibilities, people dependent on me. Even if I wanted to stay, I could not."

"I'm giving you no choice," he said, drawing me closer.

"Oh, Gannon, please!"

He was merciless. A half-dozen times, escaping his embrace, I tried to kill passion with jests and derision and laughter, and once when he tried to kiss me, I put a grape between my lips. But then, as he pressed his mouth to mine the sweet juice ran down our chins, I was back in his arms, and I found myself snuggling my breasts into the hair of his chest and returning his kisses. I tried to resist him, tried to calm my heart, but he seemed to know everywhere I was most vulnerable, everything that would weaken my will. "No more, Gannon, no more," I begged time and again, but I might as well have protested a storm at sea. His mouth moved over my throat, my shoulder, my breast, his hand moved over my belly, along my thigh, over every tender place, until I was a mindless, whimpering, wanting thing, no longer resisting, but helping him slip off my underclothing so that I could give myself up to his invading touch. Then I was tugging his clothes away too, until he lay naked beside me, as sunbronzed and beautiful as I remembered him from his boyhood. But this was no boy beside me now, with his long, clean-lined limbs, his powerful, rippling muscles, and his aroused and seeking manhood.

"Oh, God," I moaned, reaching for him, stroking him, "Gannon, why are you doing this to me?"

"I love you."

"No, no."

"Forever, Gussie. As long as I live. Till the last sunset. Till the last damn tick of the clock."

"You mustn't."

"But I do. And you love me."

"No." *I don't, I don't!*

"You do. Say it."

"No!" *But, oh, if he doesn't stop! . . .*

"Say it!"

"Oh, Gannon . . ."

It was as if everything that had ever happened to me were but a prelude to this moment, to this hour. And there was no turning back. Nothing but complete surrender was possible, as he lifted my dress up over my head and laid me back on the cushions, complete surrender to him and to myself. Complete surrender, as he slid his hands under me and lifted me, kissed my body, held me as easily as if I were a child, covered me with his mouth on breast, on belly, on thigh, raking me with his teeth, exploring, tasting, fondling, as if to learn every part of my body, until, as he kissed me between raised thighs, his tongue pressing hard against me, I could wait no longer, and I cried out, begging, quickly! quickly! and he raised up over me, spreading my thighs wider and bringing his manhood to bear on my yielding flesh, but my mind was aflame and I hardly knew what was happening as he thrust himself in, in, in, in.

Oh, that moment! That long, sweet, body-wrenching, mind-shattering moment! In all my life I had not known it could be so beautiful, I had not known that I was capable of such passion, and I was lost, lost, lost. . . .

Then, slowly, slowly, my mind cleared, and I found Gannon lying over me, careful not to crush me. He was kissing me gently, so gently, and I could feel him within me, filling me, and now and then moving a little. When I opened my eyes, the light blinded me in spite of the canopy. Water made lapping sounds, sweep lapping sounds of love, as the boat gently rocked and I returned Gannon's kisses.

He looked into my eyes. And smiled. Then, carefully, staying with me, he lifted himself from me so that we could look at each other. Was it possible that I had ever performed this same act before, gone through these very same movements? No! Never! The past was a dream, and this was the only reality. As if he were seeing me for the first time, Gannon's gaze moved down over my body to where we were joined. And my gaze moved over him—my gaze and my fingertips—over the broad shoulders glistening with sweat, over the deep, sun-darkened chest with its diamond of crisp black hair between the nipples, over the flat armor-hard belly and the lighter tan of the loins, through the hair that was entangled with my own, to the dark, heavy-veined flesh that speared into me.

Holding him, I looked back at his face.

And suddenly I did not know him. It was as if I had never seen him before.

Who was this man who was performing the most intimate of all shared acts with me? Who was this dark stranger who was making such use of my body, who was giving me such bliss? Who could he be?

I thought of the fifteen year-old-boy whom Janthina and I had teased so mercilessly, of the seventeen-year-old who had lain beside me at the stream on the Barony, of the young man who had kissed me in a hansom cab in London, and of another who had bid me farewell in an English graveyard. I thought of the man I had returned to America to find and who had asked me to come to this place.

And in that moment I knew that I had them all, all the Gannons I had ever known and ever would know, I was making love to Gannon through all the years. And I was also making love to the Dark Stranger whom I would never know, the Dark Stranger who is in each of us and who can never be known. But I would try to love the Dark Stranger no less than the others—and perhaps, if I were wise and good, I would one day come to love him most of all.

"Say it, Gussie. You love me."

"Oh, Gannon . . ."

I gave up. Like a madwoman throwing herself off a cliff, like a fool leaping in the dark. I gave myself up, gave up to Gannon, gave up to love.

"Yes, I love you. I love you, Gannon. I love you!"

It was done. No turning back. We belonged to each other now—as Gannon had said, till our last sunset together, our last tick of the clock.

My breath caught as he lowered himself on me again, and together we sought the final moment when we would be lost in our fire.

"I did it," Gannon said afterwards in a voice filled with wonderment. "After all this time. I made love to Gussie, and I love her more than life."

"Yes, darling, you did. We did, you and I together." And, as our boat gently rocked us, he drew me to him again.

He was wise. He did not speak of marriage or of the future that afternoon. We dwelt in the present in our own private world. We floated in our little boat as in a dream, lying naked together on our cushions, eating fruit and laughing softly and making love. "You taste of salt, Gussie," he said, as his mouth moved over my quivering breast. "Salt is the taste of love, my darling," I said, "didn't you know that?" Then I gave myself up to sighs, as his mouth moved on.

But the sun was lowering in the west, and soon the wind would fall, and we saw the sadness in each other's eyes at the knowledge that, for a time, our private world must be left behind. I kissed my lover and whispered, "Time to raise the sails, darling."

He pulled on his pants, I pulled on my dress. We hardly spoke as we sailed in, he now at the helmsman's station and I resting against him in the circle of his arm. The sky in the west was a half-dozen shades of blue and green, and a few puffs of cloud turned flamingo pink. As we neared the mouth of the river, Gannon pointed to his house, high and white on the green bluff. "No Name," he said.

For some reason, the lines of a Coleridge poem came to my mind, and I found myself speaking them aloud: " 'In Xanadu did Kubla Khan/A stately pleasure dome decree . . .' "

Gannon, who never ceased to surprise me, carried them on: " 'Where Alph, the sacred river, ran/Through caverns measureless to man/Down to a sunless sea.' Well, I don't think our river runs through any caverns, and our sea is anything but sunless. But I think you've given me a name for the house, Gussie. Xanadu. We'll call it Xanadu."

I pressed my cheek against his chest.

That evening Céleste and Janthina's eyes sparkled with curiosity, silently asking a hundred questions, but the ladies had had the tact not to meet us at the landing or to look at me too closely until I had been to my room. We had another delicious supper, and soon after that, Janthina announced that she and her family had best start for home.

"Why don't you come visit us, Céleste?" she asked. "Come see our place."

"Why, I'd love to."

"Come on, then, come tonight and stay as long as you like."

"Well . . ." Céleste's eyes, still curious, turned to mine, and I nodded. "Well, for a day or two . . ."

And she was supposed to be chaperon to Gannon and me. Scandalous! Scandalous! She caught me alone in the upstairs hall and whispered "Well?" but I merely suppressed a smile and looked very secretive and wise.

They left in two carriages. While Gannon saw them off, I went back into the house. I went up to my room, undressed, and put on my most beautiful nightgown. (And what had been in my mind when I had packed that?) I plumped up several pillows to sit back against and, the lamp still lit, slipped between the sheets.

I did not have long to wait. Gannon, wearing a robe, tapped at my door and entered. For a moment we only looked at each other. Then he crossed the room and sat down on the side of the bed. We embraced and kissed.

"Come to bed, Gannon," I whispered.

"Not yet."

"I want you beside me."

"Soon. But first I have something for you. A gift."

He took it from his pocket. Strands of gold hung glittering from between his fingers. It was a necklace. As he stretched it out, I saw that there hung from it a diamond like a single great teardrop from the eye of a goddess, a diamond in a nimbus of gold and silver, a diamond that flashed every color of the rainbow and the purest white fire.

The Tear of Venus.

Carefully, Gannon fastened the necklace around my neck.

"Yours," he said. "With my heart. Forever."

Later, when the necklace was the only thing I wore, we made love.

We had planned to stay at Gannon's plantation a week. We stayed two.

When Céleste returned after a few days at the Ridley

plantation, she still wanted to know about Gannon and me, of course, and after I was ready for bed that evening, I went to her room and happily confessed all. Yes, I was in love with Gannon, I loved him with all my heart.

"Oh, Gussie, I am so happy for you!"

"But I'm frightened, Céleste. I try not to think about it, but I'm frightened of what he'll think of me when he learns who and what I am. And I must tell him—even if I could keep it a secret, I'm not one to sail under false colors, any more than you are. Sooner or later he must know."

"But he won't love you any less. How could he?"

I nearly blurted out, "And what about Horace?" but I bit my tongue in time.

She read my thoughts. "Gussie, Gannon is not another Horace."

"But Horace does love you," I protested. She smiled wryly.

We stayed together in her room for a while, giving each other comfort and encouragement: our men loved us; they would always love us. Then I returned to my room, happy in the thought of what was yet to come that night.

I was afraid Céleste might become bored, but somehow Gannon managed to round up some gentleman callers—most of them, unfortunately, little more than pink-cheeked school-boys—to take her on outings. Janthina came calling now and then and took her to visit those neighbors who had not yet departed for the summer, and Céleste returned to the Ridley plantation for a few more days' visit. All in all, she was well enough entertained to allow Gannon and me to spend a great deal of time alone together, and I had no doubt that word of that scandalous fact soon reached Charleston.

Not that I cared terribly, and nether did Gannon. We were on our honeymoon, and we spent our time doing the things honeymooners have always done. We walked lonely beaches, as Gannon had promised, and went out to dive through the waves. We went horseback riding. We bathed in a clear-running stream and ate from a hamper beneath the trees, and afterwards, when the urge came . . .

We did have a quarrel or two. Gannon wanted us to be married as soon as possible and go to Mississippi together.

"But, darling, I have *told* you, I *must* go back to England this fall. I am *needed* there, I have *obligations!*"

"Goddamnit, *I* need you! Hell, we can go to England just as soon as I've finished up in Virginia and Mississippi."

"But my business won't wait! I am needed in England *now!* Darling, please try to understand!"

"I am trying to understand. It's just that I'm going to hate being apart from you, even for a day. Gussie, whatever else, I want us married right away. Just as soon as I get back from Virginia."

"Oh, yes!" I said happily. "Oh, yes, darling, I do want to marry you just as soon as possible!"

I lived in a sweet agony. I was going to be married! First, however, I had to tell him certain things, and I had no idea of how to go about it. But there had to be a way, there *had* to, I thought desperately, and somehow I would find it!

Meanwhile, we had our days and nights of love, days and nights that passed all too quickly. The last Sunday in July arrived, and it was time to return to Charleston. Gannon put Céleste and me aboard the *Maid of Athens* for a nice smooth journey back.

It was long after dark when we entered the Charleston harbor. Gannon had sent Virgil ahead with the carriage, and he met us on the wharf, then drove the three of us to Bull Street. With some surprise, I noticed there was a light burning in our parlor.

Virgil took our bags into the hall and returned to the carriage, and Céleste went into the house while I lingered a moment on the piazza with Gannon. We had offered him supper, but he had refused.

"I wish you were going to Virginia with me."

"Oh, so do I. But I'd best stay here with Céleste. We've been quite naughty enough."

"I plan to be back in a week or ten days, two weeks at the most. And then . . ."

We embraced one last time. Two weeks, even a single week, seemed like an eternity, and I wanted to cling to him, wanted never to let him go. But we kissed and he slipped away from me, and I stood watching as his carriage vanished into the darkness down the street.

I went into the house.

The first thing I saw as I stepped into the parlor was Céleste, her face white and drained, her eyes large. Then, over to one side, I saw the man sitting in the chair.

He was hollow-eyed and bearded and at first glance appeared older than he was. His hair was light brown and sun-bleached, a kind of gold. When he stood up, trembling as if the room were cold, and smiled at me, I knew his face, but I thought, *It cannot be! It's someone else, a Raveneau cousin, perhaps! It cannot be!*

He said in a soft, shaky voice. "Good evening, my dear Augusta."

It was he. My husband. Tom Raveneau.

BOOK SIX

Portrait of a Woman

~.~

Let us live, my Lesbia, and love, and value at a
penny all the talk of crabbed old men.
—Catullus, *Odes,* V, 1

All these woes shall serve
For sweet discourses in our time to come.
—Shakespeare, *Romeo and Juliet,* III, v

1 ~~~~~~

The room seemed to darken and I felt myself swaying. Céleste rushed to support me as I struggled not to faint.

I still thought I had to be mistaken, this *had* to be some other Raveneau. After all, the beard, the hollow eyes, the tremor . . . no, no, no, this must not be Tom, it must not! I could not entirely comprehend in that one instant what his return would mean—the destruction of all my dreams once again, of marriage plans, of the very fabric of my life—but I knew his reappearance would be far more catastrophic than even his desertion. No, it must not be he!

Tom's voice seemed to come from a great distance: ". . . sorry . . . should have realized this would come as a shock."

I managed to say, "We thought you were dead."

"I know that now. But I had no idea until I arrived in Charleston a few days ago. My brother and I separated when I came back to America, and neither of us has heard from the other in years."

"What . . . what are you doing here?"

"Augusta, may I sit down? I've been very sick—"

"What are you doing here?"

"I'm sorry," Tom mumbled. "Of course. You want to know—"

"What are you doing in our house?"

"Please!" His eyes bright with alarm, Tom held up a hand as if to ward off a blow. "Please—"

"Tell me!"

"I will! Please, I'm sick, I'm weak, but I want to tell you!" A spasm of shivering so overcame him that he could not go on. He stood with his arms wrapped around himself like a man in a freezing wind.

"Gussie," Céleste said, "I think he really is ill."

"All right," I said, "sit down."

Tom fell back into his chair. "Just a fever. I had malaria a while back, and—"

"Now, tell me what you are doing here."

He nodded. "I was in Columbia on business. Thought I might as well see Charleston again, see my brother, maybe see you too, if you were here. Dexter wants nothing to do with me, but he told me you were back in Charleston and had gone off visiting somewhere. So I went to your Uncle Thad—"

"*You what?*"

"I went to Thad. Told him I wanted to see you. At first I thought he was going to gun me down on the spot, but then he seemed to think it was all very amusing."

Oh, I was sure he had.

"Did my uncle tell you you could stay here?"

"Yes. I was coming down with fever and needed a place to stay and someone to look after me. Your uncle persuaded your servants . . ."

He would have had no difficulty in doing that. No black servant would have dared to defy my Uncle Thad.

"Augusta, I swear to you I have no intention of giving you any trouble. I'm only glad to know that you're all right. I haven't done badly since we parted—if there is any way I can make amends to you, I want to do it."

"There isn't. You've never lifted a finger for me in all these years, and there's nothing you can do for me now."

Tom shook his head. "Really, that is not quite true. I wrote to you several times, but you never answered. I can't blame you if you never even opened the letters, but I did—"

"I never got them."

"That's quite possible."

"I don't believe you ever sent such letters. And I don't believe you didn't know that we all thought you were dead."

He shrugged helplessly. "Augusta, I can only guess at what happened. I had just arrived in New Orleans from Natchez, when I was robbed. Evidently the thief was killed and identified as me through my possessions."

"I don't believe you. I don't believe a word you're saying."

Tom closed his eyes, a penitent accepting his punishment. "I can hardly blame you. Though why I should lie?"

I had to get away from him. I rushed out onto the piazza and huddled in a chair as if hiding in the darkness. After a moment, Céleste came out and sat down beside me.

"What should I do?" I asked.

"Shoot him."

My laugh was uncontrolled. "I'm tempted. Céleste, do I owe him anything?"

"Nothing."

"He is my husband."

"Is he?"

"Oh, God, what has happened to my life!"

Céleste put her hand on mine. "We don't know yet."

My mind was still benumbed by shock, and I had to struggle to understand the situation, to grasp the reality.

"I don't suppose we can put a sick man out into the streets in the middle of the night."

"We shall at least try, if that is what you wish."

"No . . ."

Oh, God, what to do?

And what did he know?

What did he know about Liane Duhamel's life? About Gustava Welles's life? What had he learned while he was alone in the house?

"Gussie, what is it?"

"Come . . ."

We hurried back into the parlor. Tom appeared to be sleeping, but he stirred when I spoke.

"Which bedroom have you been using?"

"The front one."

Mine. Not that it mattered. If he had searched one room, he had searched them all.

Taking a lamp, I went up the stairs, with Céleste right behind me. Fortunately my most important papers—the list of my assets, the deed to the Barony—were locked up in Horace's office, but I kept the letters and reports from Harry and the others in a chest of drawers in my bedroom. When I looked at them, they appeared to be untouched, but I could not afford to trust Tom. I glanced through a few pages and was relieved to find that, while they did suggest that I was a woman of considerable substance, they did not reveal how considerable. I assumed that, since his arrival in Charleston, Tom had learned of my purchase of the Barony; but I could tell him, as I had Uncle Thad, that Harry was backing me. Perhaps all was not lost.

In any case, I would fight. If Tom meant to make trouble for me, he had no idea of how I had learned to fight.

But how would that allow me to marry Gannon? There was no divorce in South Carolina, and even if I could get an English divorce decree, which was questionable, I was certain that South Carolina would never recognize it. What would Gannon and I do?

I thought my head would burst. "Céleste, may I sleep with you tonight?"

"Of course. Share my room for as long as you wish. But are you sure . . .?"

"I'm not sure of anything."

"I think you should speak to Horace as soon as possible."

"I intend to, tomorrow. But right now I just want a few hours of peace."

In retrospect it seems to me that from that point on I did all the wrong things. But perhaps there was no right thing I could have done. Perhaps the whole terrible drama simply had to play itself out.

In the morning Tom was, if anything, worse; he was almost delirious with fever. Telling him to stay in bed, I sent for a doctor.

"Is it malaria?" I asked, when he had seen Tom.

A bald, roly-poly man with a sardonic air, he shrugged his shoulders. "I think not. But in any case, he's a mighty sick man."

"Can he be moved?"

"Out of the house? Absolutely not. A fever like this one could lead to complications and kill him."

"But when will he be well enough to leave?"

"Mrs. Raveneau, a fever can last two days or two weeks. In these matters, the science of medicine consists of classifying our various species of ignorance, and the art of healing consists of giving the patient bed rest and liquids and otherwise leaving him alone."

In short, he claimed to know little, and he did nothing.

That afternoon I went to see Horace at his office. He greeted me cheerfully.

"Augusta, I wonder if you realize h-how you've set the gossips of this old town b-buzzing. You know, it's one thing to go on an overnight trip with your cousin and a female friend to visit your old home, the Barony. It's another to go off two whole weeks to a bachelor's plantation and to have your duenna abandon you with him for d-days at a time. Oh, yes, word got back—''

"Oh, Horace!"

Horace laughed and settled me into a chair by his desk. "Don't take it seriously, Gussie. But t-tell me, are you in love with our friend Gannon?"

"Oh, yes!"

"Good! Then I trust that we'll soon hear the p-peal of wedding bells, Romance will have been served, and the g-good people of Charleston—''

"Horace. Tom Raveneau—my husband—has come back."

Horace's face went blank. He sank into a chair behind his desk.

"Oh, my God!"

When he had recovered his composure, I told him every detail of what had been done and said since our arrival home. He listened intently, asking questions and making me repeat myself.

"And Tom gave you no idea of his plans?"

"No. He says he's only here for a visit, and he seems to want me to think he's a changed man."

"Do you trust him?"

"No."

"Neither do I." He pounded his desk in frustration. "If only you had sent for me last night! I would have gotten him out of your house. By force, if I had to."

"But he's sick!"

"I don't g-give a damn if he's dying. We want to reduce any legal claim he has on you after all these years. I can't get you a divorce, but I might have gotten you some kind of legal separation—hell, I still will, I'll fight it clear through the legislature if I have to!"

"But what am I supposed to do now? Go back to the house and throw a sick man out of his bed and into the street?"

"I'm afraid it's one day too late for that. You're in a position of 'damned if you do, damned if you don't.' On the one hand, the doctor has told you that Tom must not be moved, and if you force him out of the house, you're in a position of willfully endangering his life. On the other hand, if you don't, you will be sleeping under the same roof with a man who legally happens to be your husband. In fact, you have already done so. Evidently you have taken your husband back under your care. You are living together as man and wife—''

''But we are not!'' I felt as if I were being pummeled from all directions. ''If only he hadn't come down with a fever . . .''

Horace shook his head. ''If he's up to no good, he'd have found some other way to get at you. As your husband, he'd have plenty of opportunity.''

''But there must be some way I can protect myself.''

''For the moment, all we can do is k-keep an eye on him and wait.''

Horace warned me that as long as Tom was with us I had best be very circumspect in my behavior—give him nothing he might be able to use against me. I was to report any new developments immediately, and if Horace had anything to tell me, he would send some harmless message giving me an excuse to come to his office. Somehow, he assured me, I would come through this crisis all right. But I knew he was not really certain, and neither was I.

When I got back to the house, Tom's fever was still raging, and he showed little improvement for the next several days. Toward the end of the week, when he was feeling a little better, Dexter and Julie Anne Raveneau paid a call. While Dexter went upstairs to see his brother, Julie Anne talked to me.

''You do know, don't you,'' she said, her eyes bright with excitement, ''that you've got this whole city talking?''

''So I've been told.''

''Well, you can hardly blame people. First you and Gannon are seen together quite a lot, then suddenly you are ripping him up and down with your claws like you just purely hate him, and the next thing you run off to his plantation to spend two weeks practically alone!''

''People . . . exaggerate.''

''And meanwhile, your husband comes back after all these years. Honey, it is all so *scan*dalously ro*man*tic! Gussie, is it true what they're saying, that you refused to come back to America with Tom because you preferred that French woman—I mean Céleste—and her friends?''

I looked at her aghast. ''Julie Anne! I never refused to return to America with Tom!''

''Oh, they say he blames it all on himself—his gambling and all—''

"But I never—! I *begged* Tom to bring me home! But he deserted me in Paris! And that is all I am going to say!"

Dexter, coming down the stairs, had overheard us.

"That son-of-a-bitching brother of mine been telling lies, like always?"

In his late thirties, Dexter was as mean-eyed as ever, and he had developed a manner to fit his looks: we find a way to make our peace with whatever features the good Lord gives us. But I had learned that there was no kinder, more decent man in Charleston, and in the days that followed he stopped by the house regularly to be sure that Céleste and I were all right.

Now he said, "Listen to me, little lady. If that polecat gives you any trouble, you come running to me, and I'll bust his ass." He shook his head. "I swear to God, he can charm you like a snake charms a bird, when he wants to, but I knowed him for poison since we was kids. So I just kept my mouth shut and bided my time till I got him out of my life, and I ain't letting him back in. And you better not let him back in your life neither."

But he was already back in my life, wasn't he?

In the next day or two Tom's fever dropped, but his weakness kept him in bed.

"Augusta," he said in a faltering voice, when I went to see how he was, "I can't tell you how sorry I am to cause you this trouble."

"You're sick," I said. "That's not your fault."

"I know, but I'm still in the way. And I don't really deserve . . ." He looked close to tears. "Augusta, I want you to know you won't be out anything. I am a—a moderately wealthy man. My plantation . . . in Louisiana . . . oh, Augusta, you were right about so many things."

"Please don't talk. Rest."

On Sunday morning Horace came by to take Céleste and me to church. We were about to leave the house when, to our surprise, Tom appeared on the landing, making his way slowly down the stairs. He was fully dressed and had shaved off his beard, leaving only his side whiskers and a thin mustache.

"Last night," he said, "I heard you say something about going to church. I do hope you don't mind if I go with you."

"Mr. Raveneau," I said angrily, "I certainly am *not* going to church with you!"

He smiled sadly at me and shook his head. "Augusta, I fear that you have still not discovered the great consolations of religion. Well, if I must go by myself . . ." Slowly, weakly, he made his way out the door and onto the piazza.

Céleste's eyes blazed with anger. "That—that—*Tartuffe!*"

"Probably," I said, feeling sick, "though we can't really be certain he's a hypocrite."

"*I* can be certain!"

"Gussie," Horace said, "I think it would be best if Céleste and I took Tom to church and kept an eye on him. Then we can report back to you."

"I would appreciate that."

What they reported back was that after church Tom had charmed the parishioners—particularly the Mrs. Traggs and the Mrs. Joinders—right out of their skins. Oh, yes, they heard him say, it was so good to be back home again among the finest people on earth, and really there was no other city in the world that was a match for Charleston. No, unfortunately he could not stay long—he had to return to Louisiana, where he had wrested a plantation from the soil with his own hands. But he was so glad to know that Augusta was safely home again, for there were some ties that time and youthful mischief could not dissolve, not till death do us part. And *he* was not one to carry grudges, not when his own mistakes were so manifold, and he did hope that time would bind up old wounds. . . . Oh, the prodigal had returned with a vengeance—and got religion!

Oh, Gannon, I thought, *come home! It's been a week—please, please, come home!*

When Tom returned to the house that afternoon, he immediately went to bed. But each afternoon after that, he got up and dressed and, though he still appeared weak, left the house. I had no idea of where he went, and he volunteered only a few vague words about "some business" he had to take care of. He was never anything other than polite, self-effacing, and appreciative of the care that was being given to him. But in the middle of the week an incident occurred that gave some indication of the true man.

He was about to leave the house when a boy came bearing a message and asked for a reply. Telling the boy to wait, he came into the parlor as he read the note. "Actually," he said, "this is for both of us. The Traggs are inviting us to a dinner party this Saturday evening. How nice of them. Really, Augusta, I do think we ought to accept."

How dared he, I thought. How dared he!

"Tom," I said, "I assumed we had an understanding. This is my house and Céleste's. You are a guest here until you are well enough to leave, and I think that time has come. I bear you no ill-will, Tom, but you have been out of my life for a long time, and I prefer to keep it that way."

His smile was polite, even sweet. But his blue eyes had a metallic glitter that I remembered all too well.

"I quite understand, Augusta, and I can hardly blame you. But perhaps this is the time to increase our understanding. Why don't you sit down?"

"I prefer to remain standing."

"Well, then, if you'll forgive me . . ." He settled himself into a chair and, still smiling, looked at me. "My dear, you have been very patient with me, and I appreciate that. And since I am not one to remain where I am not wanted, I look forward to leaving this house—and Charleston—as soon as possible. But meanwhile, as I have been recuperating, I have developed some rather profitable business dealings here in Charleston. They should be concluded very soon—"

"How soon?"

"In less than a week, I should say. I shall then leave, and I very much doubt that I shall ever return. Meanwhile, I think we should try to accommodate ourselves to each other. And since I would like to attend this dinner party—"

"I have no intention of appearing anywhere with you as if I were your forgiving and everloving wife!"

"Very well, I shall accept for both of us, but when I go, I shall present your apologies and say that you are ill and had to remain at home."

"I may be elsewhere—in public!"

He was still smiling, but his eyes had narrowed and a flush had come to his cheeks. I had all I could do not to flinch from him when he stood up.

"Augusta, I am going to write an acceptance to this invitation. And you will do nothing to embarrass me in any way." He started toward the escritoire, then turned back. "Oh, by the way, that reminds me. I gather that you have resumed your affair with Gannon Murdock."

"I never had an affair with Gannon Murdock!"

He shrugged. "I won't argue the point. I am told he's out of the city right now. When he returns, please avoid him or I shall have to take steps. I am still your husband, after all, and as I say—I do not like to be embarrassed. Do we understand each other?"

Why had I not thrown him out that first night? Why had I not screamed and raged and driven him from our house?

"You will leave next week?"

"I promise you."

"Until then, I shall try not to embarrass you."

"Thank you, my dear."

With the arrival of that invitation, I realized to what a degree Tom had managed, in only a few days, to regain a place in Charleston society—as my husband. But why had he done it? If he were really planning to leave, why should he bother? Why?

Oh, please come home, Gannon, I prayed, please come home! And on the following Monday, two weeks after he had left, my prayers were answered.

A boy delivered Horace's message Tuesday afternoon, soon after Tom had left the house. The messenger had been told to avoid tom, but all the note said—in case it should be intercepted—was, "I have time to discuss your will this afternoon, if you should care to do so." He had a carriage waiting, and a few minutes later we set off for Broad Street.

The first thing Horace said when I entered his office was, "He's back," and I nearly leapt into the air as I hugged myself and sang joyfully, "Oh, I knew, I knew, I knew!"

Horace laughed and kissed my cheek. "I've been watching for him, and he got in late last night. He's waiting for you at his house. The boy and the carriage are his."

A fearful thought: "You told him about Tom?"

"I sure did." Horace shook his head in awe. "Gussie, I thought he was going to burst into flames and burn the city down. I have never seen such an enraged man in all my life!"

"Oh, that's my Gannon!"

His smiled vanished. "Gussie, what are you going to do?"

I sank down into a chair. "Oh, Horace, I don't know, I just don't know. I've had the feeling that Tom was up to something, but he's said that he'll be leaving in a few days. Maybe after that . . ."

"Don't underestimate him in any way, Gussie. Whatever else he is, Tom is a d-dangerous man. And I don't want you getting hurt."

"Dear Horace."

Ah, but I was wasting time. Of course I had no intention of obeying Tom's order that I avoid Gannon—Gannon would be waiting for me, and the hours were precious.

But as I got up to leave, I realized that for the past month I had been so involved with my own circumstances, first with Gannon and then with Tom, that I had hardly given a thought to Céleste and Horace.

"Horace, before I go, may I ask you a rather personal question?"

"Why, I think you have that right, Cousin Gussie."

"I hope you won't be offended, but . . . Horace, the first weeks we were here, I had such hopes for you and Céleste. And you both did seem to like each other so much. But then . . . what happened?"

Suddenly his face was that of the bewildered little boy I had known years earlier. He slumped behind his desk and looked away from me without speaking.

"I really thought you were falling in love with her."

"I was," he said softly. "I did."

"Then . . .?"

He shook his head. "It's no use."

"But why not? Céleste cares for you, too, you know."

"I know she does—up to a point. But Gussie, what am I?"

"Why . . . you're Horace!"

"I'm a Charleston lawyer. I'm a d-damn good lawyer and something of an authority on international law—I'm not ashamed of my accomplishments. But when you get down to it, I'm still just a little Charleston lawyer."

"But what does that mean?"

"Not much, in her eyes."

"Why, that's not so!"

"Now, l-listen a minute. Think about it, what kind of woman is Céleste? She's a woman from another world. A French countess. A figure in high artistic and social circles. Victor Hugo! Alfred de Musset! Hector Berlioz! The Dumases, both of 'em! From what she's told me, I get the distinct impression that she's even *slept* with some of those b-b-b-bastards!"

Blood rushed to my face. "And does that offend your Charleston morals? Did you expect her to be some kind of widowed virgin, just waiting all these years for dear, kind, noble Horace to come along?"

"Of course not! But B-b-b-balzac, for Christ's sake!"

"Balzac is dead," I snapped, "and Céleste never slept with him! And you, little man, are lucky if that woman gives you the time of day!"

"Gussie," Horace shouted back, "you are missing the p-p-point! That is exactly what I am saying! I am just a little Charleston lawyer, and what does a woman like that want with a man like me? When I got too close to Céleste, she let me *know* that!"

"She did *what?*"

"She let me know there was no permanent place in her life for me. Oh, she didn't say anything directly, she did her d-damnedest to spare my feelings, because there's not a mean bone in that beautiful body. She likes me, we have wonderful times together, but she just d-doesn't w-w-want-want-want—"

"Why, you damn bloody fool!" I could not believe what I was hearing! "You idiot! You dunce! You simpleton!"

"Gussie, what—!" Horace looked as if I had shot him between the eyes. "Gussie, what—"

"Is *that* what you think she was trying to tell you? Are you really that witless, Horace? Or is this just your cowardly way of avoiding any more involvements with Céleste? If it is, I can only say, For shame, Horace Blakely, for shame! Treating poor Céleste like that!"

"Gussie, I don't know what the hell you are talking about!"

"Well, if you can't figure it out, Cousin Horace," I said, yanking on my bonnet, "you're certainly not a good enough man for my best friend!"

I dashed out of his office and headed for the carriage. If *that* didn't turn the trick, I thought, grinning to myself, nothing would!

There had been little risk in visiting Horace's office, but going from there to Gannon's house was a different matter, and all the way along Meeting Street I kept careful watch for Tom or anyone else I knew. However, I saw no familiar faces, either white or black, and I felt safe as the boy drove through the gateway and the gate clanged shut behind us. Pulling off my bonnet, I rushed into the passage of the house.

And into Gannon's arms.

"You villain," I said, as I kissed him, "to stay away so long!"

"If I had known about Tom. . . . Horace sent a letter to Richmond, but somehow it missed me."

"There's nothing you could have done. But Tom says he'll be leaving in a few days, and then—"

His face grim, Gannon held me at arm's length, as if examining me. "He hasn't hurt you in any way, has he? That bastard hasn't tried to . . . touch you?"

"No, darling," I laughed, "he hasn't harmed me in the slightest, and no man but you has touched me in a very long time. But," I grew more serious, "that does bring up a problem."

"What problem?"

For the first time I put into spoken words a thought that had grown more urgent each day since Gannon had left.

I said, "I don't want to alarm you, darling, because I can't yet be certain. But I think I may be pregnant."

He just looked at me. Then his hands slipped under my arms, and very slowly he lifted me until I was looking down into his face. He lowered me enough to kiss me, then lifted me up again. His face split into a grin.

"You see, Gussie," he said. "I told you it wasn't too late!"

"But you damn fool," I wailed, loving him so much it hurt, "I am married to another man!"

His smiled faded. Slowly he lowered me so that I slid down against his body, and wrapped his arms around me.

"Now, you listen to me, princess. As far as I'm concerned, you're not married to anyone but me. Tom's being alive doesn't make one damn bit of difference. There's nothing and nobody in the whole world that can take you from me. You're my woman, and I'll battle my way through heaven and hell before I'll let anyone change that."

"Heaven and hell are one thing," I said, weeping from happiness. "You may find the good people of Charleston a little more difficult."

"To hell with them. We don't have to stay here. We can go any place in the world you want."

"Right now, I only want to be here with you."

"How long can you stay?"

"Long enough to make love."

"Good. You'll come here and we'll make love every day."

"No, just this once, my darling. Tom has warned me to stay away from you—for fear he'll be embarrassed, he says. And maybe he doesn't frighten you, but he does me. So just this once, dearest, until he leaves."

He kissed my tears away.

"Gussie, have you ever wanted to be carried up a long flight of stairs and across a bedroom threshold?"

"My love, I have *dreamed* of being carried up a long flight of stairs and across a bedroom threshold!"

He swept me up in his arms.

But our lovemaking that afternoon was haunted by a sense of impending tragedy. For, no matter how we tried to reassure each other, we knew that Tom's presence threatened us, and the thought kept coming to me, *What if this is the last time? What if he is taken from me, or I from him?*

The day wore on, the sun lowered and the sky took on its evening cast, and I knew I had stayed too long.

"Oh, God, I should go!"

"You don't ever have to go if you don't want to."

"Oh, I must! I must!" Unwillingly I forced myself from the bed.

"You're sure you don't want me to go with you?" he asked, while we hurriedly dressed.

"No. If he saw us together, I think he'd kill you."

"If he tried, I'd fling the silly bastard into Charleston Harbor!"

"My darling, Tom is an experienced duelist. And if you refused to duel with him, he would simply shoot you down under the 'unwritten law' and almost certainly go unpunished."

In the courtyard we clung together for one last kiss. Then he checked the street and signaled the boy to drive me out the gateway and home. The boy took the less trafficked streets when he could, but all the way back to Bull Street I looked fearfully about, expecting to see Tom and have him guess where I had been.

When we reached Bull Street, I saw with relief that there was no light in our house: that meant Tom probably was not home yet. With a shiver up my back at the thought that he might be watching, I rushed from the carriage through the piazza door, and the boy drove away.

Safe at last—I hoped.

When I went into the hall, Céleste came out of the unlit parlor. "Gussie!"

"Is Tom here?"

"No."

Oh, thank the Lord!

"Gussie, I've been waiting for you! The most wonderful thing has happened!" Even in the dusky evening light of the hallway, Céleste's eyes were lit up and her face was aglow. "Oh, Gussie, you will never guess!"

"Then tell me, what is it?"

"This afternoon, just a little while after you left, Horace came here—"

"He did?"

"He came charging in here like an absolute madman! And he asked me to marry him! He *demanded* that I marry him!"

"Oh, Céleste!"

We embraced, and once again that day I felt the tears of happiness.

"He was so wonderful. He stayed all afternoon and left only an hour ago!"

"Oh, I'm so happy for you!" We were almost dancing together in the hall. "And I just know he was tender and sweet and gentle—"

"Oh, if only I could tell you!"

"But at the same time—"

"*D'autre part, ah, Dieu!*" Céleste rolled her eyes. "*Quel étalon! Vraiment, le cheval entier!*"

"Oh, I'm so happy, so happy!" I said, laughing.

"We'll be married as soon as possible, and he's going back to England with us in September. And after our honeymoon, he'll teach and study in London and Paris, and oh, we have such plans! . . ."

I hardly heard her as she babbled on, laughing with me, almost singing, for I was thinking that some dreams *did* come true, and this was one that Tom could do nothing to spoil.

I was wrong.

We both jumped, startled, as we heard his voice at the door: "How nice to see the ladies in such high spirits. I wonder what could account for it?"

We stood perfectly still as he came through the doorway.

Then we saw that he was not alone. Three other men followed him into the hall. One of them, a lawyer I had met a time or two, gave me an embarrassed nod.

"Please make yourselves at home in the parlor, gentlemen," Tom said, "and light some lamps. I'll be with you in a minute."

Without a word, the three men filed into the parlor.

Tom smiled at me. "Did you really think you could deceive me, Augusta?" he said in a voice too low for the other men to hear. "Did you think I wouldn't keep an eye open for Gannon Murdock? How many pennies do you think it costs to have a man stop by his house once or twice a day and bribe a servant for information? Well, haven't you anything to say, Augusta?"

Someone lit a lamp in the parlor, and I saw that Tom's face was either smudged or bruised: there was a mark on his left jaw and another high on his right cheek.

"What's happened?" I asked, my heart racing. "What have you done to Gannon?"

"Nothing—yet." As he brushed some dust from his clothes, Tom looked at Céleste. "I happened to meet the French bitch's lover a little while ago. He resented some remarks I made about her and behaved like a ruffian. Our seconds will meet tonight, and I think I can confidently say that within the next twelve hours our old friend H-h-h-horace will be shaking hands with Jesus."

Céleste's hand flew to her mouth. Her face grew twisted. Her eyes, so happy a moment before, now saw only horror. With a cry of grief, she threw herself out the doorway and ran for the street.

Tom laughed.

"You're inhuman," I said. "To expect decency from you is beyond reason. Do you know what you've done?"

"Far better than you do, my dear. Now, go upstairs to your room and wait for me. We have some things to talk about."

"Dear God," I said, "no wonder that even your own brother has nothing but contempt for you."

"Augusta . . ." Before I could move, his right hand shot up to seize my face, his left took my arm in an iron grip, and he thrust me into the darkness in the back of the hall. His face above mine was taut with anger, his eyes burned, his voice shook. "Augusta, you will do as you are told. You will go upstairs and wait. I shall not be long. And then you and I have some business to attend to. Do you understand me?"

His fingers dug into my flesh until I whimpered with pain. Perhaps that satisfied him, for he flung me away.

"Now, go!"

I went up the stairs, feeling his eyes on me, just as I had felt Paoli's so many years before.

Stumbling into the darkness of the back bedroom, I had the feeling of reentering that nightmare world, the world in which Adam had died trying to release me from its dangers. And now Horace was about to die, for I had little doubt that Tom would kill him. Céleste's gentle Horace, a man who would never dream of fighting a duel except under the greatest provocation.

But first, what did Tom have planned for me? And for Gannon?

I thought of getting away through a window, but I was not sure I could do it, and I knew I could not escape for long. And surely, for the moment, Tom did not plan anything too terrible, not with three witnesses downstairs. So I stayed near the door of our room, trying to hear what was happening, but all I could make out was some muffled talk and a little laughter. Then I saw lamplight from just beyond the landing. Tom was coming.

He appeared on the landing. In one hand he carried a lamp, in the other, pen and ink from the escritoire. The lamp, lighting his face from below, made him look like a demon from hell. Once again he smiled at me. And slowly, as if savoring the thought of what was to come, he mounted the stairs.

2 ⁓⁓⁓⁓⁓

"No, Augusta," Tom said, as he entered the bedroom, "you should not have disobeyed me. I told you to avoid Gannon Murdock. It was bad enough to arrive here and learn of your escapade on his plantation. If anyone were to find out about your afternoon in his house—well, that hardly fits the picture of a husband and wife long separated but happily reconciled, now, does it?"

"We are not reconciled."

"Oh, but we are. Or we soon will be."

He set the lamp and the pen and ink down on a table at the side of the bed. Though his skin was still fever-ravaged and thin against his skull, he now looked more like the man I had once known: golden Tom Raveneau, one of the handsomest young men in Charleston. But grown older and harder. Older and harder and merciless.

From his coat pocket he took some papers and spread them out on the table. "Now, Augusta, I have a few things here that I want you to sign."

Horace's words with respect to my uncle came back to me: *"Don't sign anything . . . might as well have signed away your life."*

I said: "See my lawyer."

"Don't be foolish. Aren't you even curious as to what these papers are?"

"Not in the slightest."

"My dear, that simply shows how desperately you are in need of a husband's guidance. Let me explain. One of these papers appoints me your attorney in fact. That is to say, it empowers me to transact any and all business matters for you."

"I won't sign it."

He ignored me. "Actually, it is probably quite uneccessary. I am your husband, and though we've been separated for a number of years, we are now together again and living under one roof. Incidentally, if you haven't gotten around to paying this month's rent yet, you can forget it. As your husband, I took over the lease and paid it before you came home, so *you* are now living in *my* house.''

"You . . . filth!''

"For one who pretends to be a lady, you have developed a charming vocabulary. But to continue. Aren't you going to ask me why I want your power of attorney, Augusta?''

"You can go straight to hell!''

"It's a matter concerning the Barony. These papers include a properly drawn-up deed, which I want you to sign.''

"You're not going to take the Barony from me!''

"Of course not. I am merely going to sell it for you, and you'll be happy to know that it will remain in the family. Your Uncle Thad has made a truly generous offer for it. The minute he learned that you had purchased it, he sent for me, of course—''

"Sent for you?" Now he had truly surprised me.

"Naturally. As your husband, I think I can safely let you in on a little secret. Your Uncle Thad and I have been business partners for a number of years. You may recall that he had an interest in the slave importation trade—as I have myself. After your grandfather disinherited him, he continued that interest. We happened to meet in New Orleans, and just as I told you, at first he was ready to shoot me on the spot. But then I told him *my* side of the story—how his slut of a niece had refused to come home with me, how she had actually deserted me to remain in Paris with her degenerate French and English friends. . . . What's the matter, Augusta? Nothing to say?''

And you believed him, Uncle Thad, I thought, sickened. *But how could you?*

"Very well, to continue. Your uncle and I came to an understanding. Neither of us wanted his interest in the slave trade disclosed. As traders, we each had a secret identity to protect—I more than he, perhaps, because for all I knew, that damn Paoli was still after me. Our common interests quite naturally led to our partnership.''

I found my voice again. "You knew that Paoli was after you?''

"I knew somebody was after me. I've long had the habit of looking back over my shoulder, my dear, and when I was in

New Orleans, soon after coming back to America, I noticed a certain pair of gentlemen in my vicinity with suspicious regularity. After a day or two I managed to lead one of them into a deserted alley. The damn fool actually said, 'Louis Paoli sends you his greetings.' At least I think that was what he was trying to say—he never finished. I put some identification on his body and left him to be found. After that, it was easy enough to persuade his partner to notify Paoli of my death and collect the full payment for himself. Naturally, as a simple precaution, I dispatched him too, soon after that, and the money became mine. It amused me to be rewarded for my own execution.''

''As easily as that, you killed them.''

''It was self-defense.''

''I'm sure. Just as it will be self-defense when you kill Horace tomorrow.''

''I'm glad you share my confidence. My dear, I long ago lost my schoolboy pride in never having killed a man in a duel. Now my pride is in never leaving an enemy alive.''

Not Horace, not Gannon. And not me, quite likely, when I had outlived my usefulness.

''Shall we get on with it, Augusta?'' Tom said, motioning toward the pen and ink and the papers. ''We don't want to keep the gentlemen downstairs waiting too long, do we? If you'll just sign—''

''I am not signing anything.''

Tom looked very patient. ''You will sign, and afterwards they will witness your signature.''

''I won't—''

He caught me completely unaware. His hand swung up in a smashing blow across my cheek. Then, grabbing me, he pushed me against the side of the bed, and his hand smashed across my face again. As I opened my mouth to cry out, his palm covered it.

''I am sure, Augusta, you do not wish to embarrass yourself, or me, by any silly screaming. But if you do, I can assure you that the gentlemen downstairs have a pretty good idea of the kind of woman you are and know that you may need a husband's firm hand. Now, to be sure we understand one another . . .''

His bared teeth flashed in the lamplight. He removed his hand from my mouth, and before I could utter a sound, twice more his hand whipped across my face. My lips began to swell and blood flowed over my tongue.

"You are going to sign those papers, my dear."

"They won't do you any good!"

"If you are so positive of that, then sign them and spare yourself pain."

"Horace will stop you!"

"Horace will be dead. Face it, Augusta, you are putting off the inevitable. You are my wife, and you are going to do as I say!" Abruptly, his hold on me relaxed, his face softened, and his voice became gentle and reasonable. "And, after all, what's so terrible about selling the Barony? I told you, I have a plantation in Louisiana—I find it useful for bringing slaves into the States—and eventually we'll be going there. I don't yet know the terms of your purchase from Gannon, but—"

"I'll stop the purchase!"

"No, you won't, my dear, because I am managing our family affairs from now on. As I was saying, your uncle has guaranteed that we'll make a very nice profit on the sale. So you see, you have no reason in the world to be difficult."

"I'll sign nothing!"

Stepping away from me but carefully remaining between me and the door, Tom sighed and shook his head. "Thad told me you hadn't changed much. Stubborn, stubborn, stubborn." He paused, as if considering what to do. "Well, tyke, I certainly don't want to mark you up too much, not my own dear wife. So I think you had better take off your clothes."

I wanted to shout my defiance, but I could only whimper: "No."

"Where I come from, when we want to docile or discipline a slave, we work him naked. Man or woman, they never feel more vulnerable than when they're stripped naked, like animals. And I think that's what you need. Take off your clothes, my dear."

"No!"

Again, a hand flashed painfully across my face, but this time, before I recovered, both of his hands were on my dress and tearing at it. *"I said, take off your clothes!"*

For a man who had recently been so ill, he was stronger than I would have believed, but anger and fear added to my own strength. Knocking his hands aside, I raked my nails across his cheek, and saw blood spring from the furrows. As he clutched at his face, I slammed my knee toward his groin with all my strength, but the blow glanced off his thigh as he leapt aside. With a snarl, he threw himself at me. His hands encircled my throat as he shoved me back onto the bed. His face was insane in the lamplight, the sounds that came from him completely animal. His hands tightened, I could not breathe, and for a moment I thought he was going to crush my throat, break my neck. My lungs ached and the room began to darken, as if the lamp were burning out. Then his hands left my throat and began tearing at my clothes again. Pulling me from the bed, he stripped me to the waist and threw me to my knees on the floor.

"You bitch!" he said in a low, tight voice, a furious whisper. "You bitch! I'll teach you to turn your claws on me! I'll make you regret you ever touched me! By God, you'll never again—"

Lifting me by my hair with one hand, he slapped the other back and forth across my face until it felt bathed in fire. I could see nothing, could hardly hear his voice.

"Bitch, I'll make you beg, I'll make you beg!"

Still lifting me by the hair, he pulled me halfway onto the bed again. His hand went to my breast.

I screamed, as pain filled the tender flesh. Screamed until his hand released my breast and clamped down on my mouth.

He threw me back onto my hands and knees on the floor, and his hands continued ripping at my clothing, pulling it down to my thighs.

"I'll make you pay, I'll make you beg . . ."

Half-blinded by tears and pain, I nevertheless saw that he was taking off his thick, wide leather belt.

"Now, you bitch, beg!"

Oh, the fire then. Nothing I had ever experienced could compare to it. Breath sucked back horribly in my throat, then I could not breathe, and the fire came again across buttocks and thighs, came again and again, until a monstrous howl burst from my throat and Tom's hand clamped across my mouth.

He laughed with satisfaction.

"Is that enough, tyke? Learned your lesson?"

"God curse you—"

Straightening up, he kicked me in the belly. All my insides

felt suddenly displaced, the most horrible nausea I had ever felt spread through me, and hot liquid spilled from my throat.

He kicked me again.

Oh, no, not that! The baby, I thought, *the baby!*

"Please," I whispered.

He kicked me still again.

"Please!"

Brought the belt down on my buttocks.

"Please!"

Say it again. I can't hear you."

"Please!"

The belt, the fire.

"Please! please! please! please!"

Again he laughed with satisfaction. No, with happiness.

"You'll sign?"

"Yes," I wept. "Yes. But get me a gown first. Please."

"Of course, my dear."

Drawers clattered open. Clothes rustled as they were thrown about. A nightgown landed on the floor in front of me. Tom yanked my clothes the rest of the way off, then helped me up onto my knees and pulled the gown over my head.

"I hope, Augusta, that you've learned your lesson," he said, trying to sound very calm and sensible. "There was no need for you to go through all that, if only you had done as you were told in the first place. Now, isn't that true?"

"Yes."

He helped me to my feet. "Now, you just take your time. I told those gentlemen downstairs they might have to wait for a while, so there's no hurry. Think you can sit on the edge of the bed by the table, honey?"

Somehow, in spite of the pain, I managed. Tom was gentle and soothing, the loving husband who wanted nothing more than to comfort his wife. "Now, don't you even make a move toward that pen until you feel ready. I want a nice, firm, steady signature."

I wanted only to sign the papers and be rid of them. I read nothing, had no idea of how many times I signed. I simply signed. Slowly. Carefully. Trying to do it right.

"That's good, Augusta, honey," he said when I had signed the last paper. He folded them and put them into his coat pocket. "You've learned to be a good girl. And now you're going to get your reward."

Putting an arm under my legs, he lifted me and laid me on the bed, and I accepted his help almost with gratitude.

"Yes, tyke, your reward," he said, as he began unbuttoning his pants.

When I realized what he meant to do, I cried out and tried to throw myself off the far side of the bed. Grabbing me, he pulled me back. He climbed onto the bed with me, and pulled my gown up as far as it would go. I tried to fight him, but most of the strength had gone out of me. Without much difficulty, he settled on his knees between my thighs, finished opening his pants, and held my wrists.

"Don't know why you're fighting me, when you can just lie back and enjoy it. Maybe it's because you didn't stay away from Murdock, the way I told you, is that it? Maybe you think I'm punishing you. In any case, tyke, I am going to teach you that you belong to *me!* You are still my wife, honey, and whatever you got, whether it's love or money, it's *mine!* And I am now going to take it!"

Dear God, I thought, what kind of madman was this who was forcing himself on me? as if I were nothing more than a body that belonged to him and to him only and certainly not to myself?

The law was on his side. The law said that a married man and woman were one flesh.

And the flesh belonged to the man.

No! No, I would not accept that! I belonged to myself! To myself and to whomever I chose to give myself in love! And I would fight, I would fight . . .

But I could not. He was too strong for me, he had weakened me too much. When I tried to twist away from him, when I tried to claw him, he struck me until blood ran over my face and my skull seemed to burst. And as my mind cleared again, I felt him opening me up and sliding into me.

He stretched himself out over me. Holding my wrists, he looked down at my face as if to see what he could read in it, and slowly, slowly, he pleasured himself with my body. "You know," he said, "looking back, I can't understand why I didn't do this to you more often. Why did I spend so much time gambling and so little with you?" He sounded honestly puzzled. "Well, tonight it's not going to be like that last time, back in Paris, tyke. Oh, no. No, we're going to take our time. I can't say you're contributing much as yet, but pretty soon . . ."

He laughed, and his voice grew husky, as he continued his pleasure. "You remember how, that last time, I told you how bad you were in bed? Well, now I'm going to tell you something else, Augusta. I lied. The truth of the matter is that you were the very best that ever was. I've had plenty of others, more than I can count, I've had them everywhere from Europe to South America. But when you get going in bed, when you really get going . . ." He groaned with pleasure. ". . . There's no one else anywhere that can match you, honeychild. Not even Jewel, and God knows she was good. But you . . . I'm not exaggerating . . . when you get going, you are the best in the world!"

Eyes narrowed with lust, he laughed again. "And do you know why? Do you know why you're the best?

"Because at heart you're a whore, Augusta. Nothing but a whore with a lot of whorish bed-tricks. The sweetest little whore I have ever met in my life, but still just another goddamn whore."

I had to make him stop. I had to be rid of him. Surely I would die right where I was if I did not get rid of him. So I did it the only way I knew how.

"Oh, yes!" he moaned, thrusting faster. "Finally caught fire, didn't you, oh, yes! I knew you couldn't help but love it, a whore like you. Only a whore could love it the way you do, and you're the . . . oh, God!"

At last, at last, he was finishing. But even that seemed to take forever.

He slowed and stopped, then lay heavily on me, panting. Finally he rolled off me and onto his back. "You're mine again, honey," he said contentedly. "We've now had what they call conjugal relations, as a husband and wife should, and you're mine again for as long as I want you."

I lay quietly. I felt nothing. No pain, no degradation, no sorrow. Nothing. I was beyond feeling of any kind.

"Oh, we're going to have some fine times together, Augusta, I can promise you that. Wait till I get you down to Louisiana. But first we've got to go to Europe, don't we? Don't we, Augusta?"

I did not answer. I pushed my gown down between my legs, then lay perfectly still, gazing up at the ceiling. I felt the bed move as Tom adjusted his pants and rose up on an elbow to look at me.

"Yes, first we've got to go to Europe," he said, stroking my cheek. "Those are mighty interesting letters that Harry and those other people have been writing to you. Can't say I can altogether make them out, but it sounds like you and Harry have been doing some mightly interesting things in the last dozen years. You must have made a pile of money, to be able to buy a place like the Barony. Isn't that right, Augusta?" When I did not answer, he gave my cheek a little slap. "I said, isn't that right?"

Still I lay silent, staring at the ceiling.

"Augusta, I think I'd better make something clear." Tom's fingers moved to the base of my throat, kneading the flesh and slowly closing. "You're lucky I came back, lucky you've got a husband to look out for you. And if you do as you're told, you may go on being lucky for a long, long time. But if you try to defy me . . ." As his hand tightened, I began to choke. "If you ever again raise your hand against me, Augusta. . . . Do you understand me, my dear?"

I could not breathe. I grabbed his wrist and tried to pull his hand away.

"I said, do you understand me?"

His fingers loosened, and I managed to say yes.

"Good." His hand moved up over my face, stroking it gently. "Do you know your trouble, Augusta? You never really learned a woman's place in this world. Even as a girl you were headstrong and rebellious. Isn't that so?" His hand tightened on my face. "I said, isn't that so?"

"Yes."

"Trouble was, in the old days I was too easy with you. But I've learned a lot, Augusta, and now I'm going to teach you. And God, how I'm going to love doing it!"

I could not hold back the words: "May your soul rot in hell."

He stiffened. "What did you say?"

"May your soul rot—"

His hand closed over my mouth and nostrils.

"What did you say, Augusta?"

Again I grabbed his wrist and tried to free myself, but his fingers tightened on my face.

"What did you say?"

He was too strong for me, and I lay still, determined not to give him the satisfaction of a struggle. But the seconds went by, each one longer than the last, and he merely grinned down at me.

"You have something to say to me, honeychild?"

My lungs began to ache again, and suddenly, after a moment that seemed to last forever, my body rebelled. I found myself kicking, flailing about, fighting desperately for air.

Tom laughed. "What did you say, Augusta? Just tell me what you said."

My lungs were in torment, my chest seemed about to explode. I tried to slide out from under his hand and off the bed, but he hooked one leg over mine and slipped an arm over my head and around my neck, locking me in his grip, while the pain grew.

Tom's eyes were bright with amusement. "Let's just call this your first lesson in good manners, Augusta—the first of many."

But dear God, was he mad? Didn't he know what he was doing to me? I was in screaming agony—didn't he know?

"Now what do you say, Augusta?"

I reached blindly toward the bedside table for something—a hand mirror, a jewelry box, anything—to save myself. Tom's face above me was a grinning death's head in the lamplight. "What do you say . . .?"

The whole world was turning into a great blur of pain, and I knew I had only seconds left. Then my hand found the base of the lamp, and I did the only thing I could. With all the strength I had left, I lifted it and swung it at Tom.

As he saw what I was doing, he threw himself back from me. He struck out at the lamp, trying to thrust it away, but he succeeded only in knocking off its chimney and tipping it over. For an instant, as the fuel oil poured out over him, the flame looked as if it might die. Then it flared up. Tom's chest caught on fire, and screaming, he shoved the lamp away, causing fuel and flame to spread down his body.

He knocked the lamp from my scorched hand. It flew across the room, broke on the floor near a window, and the spreading flames instantly set the draperies on fire.

"Help me!" Tom cried, as he beat the flames on the front of his body. "Help me!"

He struggled off one side of the bed, and I, fighting for air, threw myself off the other. He grabbed at the corner of the counterpane to beat at the flames, but the bed, too, was on fire, and the flames were spreading fast.

"Help me!"

I stared at him. What could I do? I was still in pain and almost too weak to move. He was trying to beat the flames down from his face and at the same time struggle out of his coat, but his arms were caught in the sleeves.

"Help me!"

Like a maddened animal, he threw himself from wall to wall, and another set of draperies caught fire. The faraway brutish thought struck me: *Who would have thought he would burn so well?*

"Help me, help me, help me! Help me-e-e!"

Coat, pants, shirt, almost all of him was in flames, and the more he fought the fire, the faster it spread. He screamed one long *"HE-E-ELP ME-E-E!"* and then, seeing me merely standing there, he threw himself at me, a fiery demon with all the hatred of hell on his face. He missed his grasp, but the impact of his body knocked me through the bedroom door. I screamed when I saw that my gown was on fire, and as I beat at the flames, I fell down the stairs to the landing. One of the three men who had been with Tom came rushing up the stairs past me. When he reached the second floor, he screamed "Oh, my God!" and came running down again, leaping over me and down the rest of the stairs. "Fire!" he shouted. "For God's sake, he's on fire, the whole damn house is on fire! Get the fire company! Sound the alarm for the fire company!"

As I looked up, Tom ran out of the back bedroom. He was encased in flame, even his hair ablaze. For a moment he stood there, writhing and screaming.

Then he fell. Fell, or threw himself at me. A great mass of fire, a human torch, he seemed to drift down through the air as slowly as a burning leaf, yet I barely managed to roll aside before he crashed onto the landing. I threw myself down the lower flight of stairs to the ground floor, and when I looked up, the human torch was still writhing, and the curtains on the landing window were aflame.

My gown was burning again. I beat at the flames and rolled across the floor, catching the edge of the rug and pulling it over me. My body felt as if it were burning in a dozen places. Struggling out of the rug and to my feet, I staggered out through the doorway onto the piazza and toppled over the rail, hardly feeling the jolt as I struck the ground.

I crawled away through the darkness. When I looked back, the entire second story of the house appeared to be on fire, brilliant against the black night sky, and it seemed to me that distantly, through the dull roar of the flames, I could still hear Tom's screams. Then I could bear no more: I sank into my own blessed darkness.

The clang of fire bells, the rumble of engines, the clamor of voices brought me back to consciousness. "Is she alive?" Who is she, anybody know?" The Raveneau woman—she lives here." "Look, she's moving!" Dark shapes hovered over me, and between them I saw the roof going up in flames as the entire house became a funeral pyre.

"Tom," I moaned, "my husband . . ."

"We know, lady. But what happened?"

"Please . . ."

"Somebody help her. Bring a blanket. Get her away from the house."

Hands lifted me to my feet, and a blanket was wrapped around me to cover my burnt gown. We were so close to the house that I could feel the heat of the flames. Half-led, half-carried away through the crowd, I closed my eyes and let happen what would.

I found myself in the parlor of a house down the street, being cared for by a woman with whom I had become slightly acquainted during the summer. Several men, apparently officials of some kind, tried to question me: How had the fire started? "Getting ready for bed," I told them. "My husband brought up a lamp . . . wanted to talk . . . lamp dropped . . ." If I was evasive, actually there was little I could say at that time, for my body felt as if, like Tom, I were being burned alive, and my mind was still benumbed by the horrors of the night. My neighbor told the men she would look after me until someone from the Welles family came for me, and they departed. I retreated behind closed eyes.

When I opened them, Céleste was leaning over me, and Gannon and Horace were standing nearby. They were the dearest faces in all the world.

"Oh, thank God we've found you!" Céleste said. "I knew something terrible. . . . I went for Horace, of course, and Gannon, and when we saw the flames. . . . are you badly hurt?"

"I don't think so. Burnt a little."

"Has a doctor looked at her?" Gannon asked the lady of the house.

"No, not yet."

"Horace, would you look for a doctor? I'm going to take Gussie to my place."

Even I, in my half-conscious state, saw the look of shocked disapproval on my neighbor's face. "No, take me to Aunt Nickie. Please, Gannon. To Aunt Nickie."

"Whatever you want, Gussie."

Gannon picked me up, still wrapped in the blanket, and carried me out to his carriage. When we arrived at the Wraggboro house and he carried me in in his arms, Aunt Nickie looked as if she might faint.

"There's been a fire," he explained. "I don't think she's too badly hurt, but Horace has gone for a doctor. Can you take Gussie and Céleste in?"

"Of course!"

"Thad won't—"

"This is her place," Aunt Nickie said firmly, "hers and Céleste's too, if she'll stay. Now, take her into the parlor while I get a room ready for her."

Céleste said, "Thank you, Nickie. I'll help you."

In the parlor, Gannon very carefully and gently laid me down in my blanket on a couch and put a pillow beneath my head. He knelt beside me, kissed me, and took my hand. "What happened," he asked. It was our first chance to talk alone. "Céleste said Tom had come with some other men, and she was afraid . . ."

I said, "I killed him."

For a moment he was utterly still. Then he said, "I think you had better tell me exactly—"

"He said Uncle Thad sent for him and told him about me . . . and the Barony—"

"*Thad?*"

"They're partners. In slave trading. Tom said he had made a deal to sell the Barony to Uncle Thad. But I wouldn't sign the papers, so he . . . he did such awful things . . ."

"What did he do, Gussie?"

"Tore off my clothes . . . and hurt me . . . beat me with his belt and then . . . called me a whore and . . . forced me."

Gannon's eyes closed. In a rush he gathered me into his arms, and for a time we were silent.

"You should have let me kill him," he said. "How did it happen?"

I shook my head. "It was like a terrible dream. He was angry with me, and began smothering me with his hand. I reached out for anything I could find to hit him, and somehow I picked up the lamp, and . . . then he was on fire, and . . . oh, God, how could I do such a thing!"

"You were only defending yourself, Gussie."

"But I killed him!"

"No." Gannon rocked me soothingly in his arms. "The truth of the matter is that, after all these years, Tom Raveneau just plain ran into the wrath of God."

Gradually he calmed me. When Aunt Nickie and Céleste returned, they saw that he and I needed only each other at that hour, and they left us alone again. As I looked into Gannon's dark eyes, my tears ceased, my breathing eased, and something like peace stole over me. I kissed him and ran my fingers through his unruly hair, touched his cheek, his mouth, the gray at his temple. Smiled at him. Knew that somehow we would survive and be happy. Was certain that this night of horrors was ending at last.

And then Uncle Thad appeared.

I had heard the click of a piazza door but had given it no thought. Now I looked over Gannon's shoulder to see my uncle standing in the parlor doorway. His eyes widened slightly and he stood perfectly still; nothing else betrayed his surprise.

Gannon saw my face stiffen. Slowly he looked around at my uncle. He stood up.

"Good evening, Mr. Welles," he said in a soft, flat voice so meaningless that it almost became a challenge.

Only my uncle's eyes moved, as he took in the situation: I lying on the couch in a tattered, scorched nightgown and an old blanket, my face bruised and swollen; Gannon standing by me.

"What are you doing in my house, Murdock?" Uncle Thad's voice was as flat as Gannon's.

"I brought your niece to her Aunt Nickie. At her request."

"How good of you. You may go now."

"Not yet." Gannon's voice hardened. "Not quite yet, Mr. Welles."

No, I thought, please, God, no more. I said, "Gannon, you had better leave."

"You heard my niece, Murdock."

Gannon ignored us both. "You brought Tom Raveneau here. Do you know what he's done?"

"Whatever it is, Murdock, I doubt that it is any of your business." Uncle Thad stepped aside from the doorway and motioned toward it. "Now, if you will kindly—"

"He *beat* your niece, Mr. Welles."

A smile flickered over Uncle Thad's face. "As her husband, he may have exercised a little—"

"He stripped her naked, beat her with a belt, called her a whore, and raped her."

In that moment, my uncle lost something vital; his face sagged. His mouth moved before he found words. "He—he's her husband—it's hardly rape—"

"Her *husband?* A man who deserted her years ago? Who came back only to steal everything she has? He has the right to beat her, to abuse her, to force himself on her? Is that how you keep your women in line, Mr. Welles, sir? With a leather belt, a dirty word, and a little loving rape?"

"You'd better get out of here, Murdock." Uncle Thad's voice was hoarse and strained. "You'd better—"

"I don't think you do, Mr. Welles. You may be one fine son of a bitch, but I really don't think you do, and you wouldn't do it to your niece either. No, you'd just get a man like Tom Raveneau to do your dirty work for you."

"Tom Raveneau will answer to me! Now, you get—"

"Tom Raveneau is dead."

Uncle Thad stopped as if shot, the blood draining from his face.

"That's right, Mr. Welles, Tom Raveneau isn't going to answer to anyone but his Maker. He got careless with a lamp tonight, it seems. I'm sure you heard the fire bells."

Uncle Thad looked at me without appearing to see me. He looked about the room as if not quite sure what he was looking for. He wandered to the fireplace and kicked aimlessly at the andirons and fire tools.

He looked at me again. "Did he . . . did he . . ."

"Did he what, Mr. Welles?" Gannon asked. "Did he leave anything that would put the Barony into your hands? No, he did not."

Uncle Thad did not answer, and I thought I knew why. *"The Barony is mine!"* he had said years earlier, in my childhood, and he had vowed, *"I am going to have it! One way or another!"* He could no longer believe that. He had thought his chance had come at last, and it had failed. There would be no further chances. He was seeing the death of his fondest dream.

"The Barony is still Gussie's," Gannon went on. "It will always be Gussie's, even after I marry her. And as for you, well . . . you can join your friend Tom Raveneau in hell where you both belong."

Uncle Thad lowered his head like a man defeated—or like a bull, too long tormented, about to charge. "I've had enough of you." He spoke so softly that I barely heard him.

Gannon turned to me. "Princess, I'd better get out of here before I say anything more. I'm sorry that damn doctor isn't here yet, but maybe I can find him. I'll be back in the morning."

"Murdock."

Gannon turned to my uncle.

With a wide-sweeping blow, all his strength behind it, Uncle Thad slapped Gannon's face.

Gannon worked his mouth as if it hurt. He touched his lip, then looked at the blood on his finger.

"Mr. Welles," he said, "I don't duel."

Again Uncle Thad's hand swept up and across Gannon's face, so hard that I myself could feel the flash of pain, the spreading numbness.

"I told you once, I don't duel. And if you do that again—"

A third time Uncle Thad's hand came up, full-strength, and slammed into Gannon's face.

Gannon roared. His big left hand closed on the front of Uncle Thad's coat and lifted him; his right fist plunged like a cannon ball into Uncle Thad's belly. Uncle Thad's eyes bulged, his face crumpled, and he retched violently. Gannon lifted him higher and then, his right hand cocked, carried him across the room and pressed him to the wall. And there Gannon returned the slaps—*One! Two! Three!*—while I screamed, "Don't, Gannon, don't, don't, oh, please, don't!" Gannon whirled my uncle away from the wall and raised a fist to hit him one more time, a blow that might have killed, and again I screamed, "Don't!"

Gannon held my uncle perfectly still. His eyes moved briefly toward me.

He flicked my uncle away, tossed him to the floor like something small and filthy, something disgusting, to be discarded. He strode from the room.

And I saw the glint of lamplight on the pistol Uncle Thad was drawing from his pocket.

I cried a warning to Gannon. I never would have believed my uncle could move so quickly. With a catlike movement he was on his feet and through the doorway. I leapt off the couch and grabbed the only weapon I saw, a poker from the fireplace, and followed after him. "Murdock," I heard him call out, "you'll meet me on the field or you'll die right now. Which will it be?"

I stopped in the parlor doorway, afraid to go farther. Gannon was at the piazza door, his back to us. Uncle Thad stood in the center of the hall, his feet apart and his knees bent, the pistol thrust out in front of him, straight at Gannon and perfectly steady.

"Uncle Thad, no!" I begged.

"Which will it be, Murdock?"

"Why, Mr. Welles, sir. I never dreamed that you would deign to challenge a mere overseer's son."

"Don't, Uncle Thad, please!"

"Which, Murdock?"

"Mr. Welles, I am going to walk out this door—"

"Then I'll shoot you in the back. Do you want it in the back like a dog, Murdock, or are you going to turn around and take it like a man?"

Aunt Nickie's soft, reasonable voice broke in: "Neither. Thad, put that gun away."

I looked toward the back of the hall. Aunt Nickie stood there with a large wicked-looking pistol in her hand. It was one of several weapons that had been around the house for as long as I could remember. Behind Aunt Nickie stood Céleste, her face distorted by horror.

"Get out of here, Nickie," my uncle commanded, his eyes never moving from Gannon.

"Thad," Aunt Nickie said gently, "we have all had enough. It is late. Augusta has been through a terrible experience. Gannon was kind enough to bring her here—"

"This man caused your daughter's death, woman!"

"No, he did not." Aunt Nickie sounded very weary. "He loved my daughter. As he now loves Augusta. You are going to let him go, Thad."

"He's going to pay—"

"No! You have done enough to him! You kept Melinda from him, and you've put Augusta, the woman he loves,

through hell. You've tried to keep Lucy from his brother—
driven her from this house, as you did Horace. You even put
the blame on him for stealing the Tear of Venus—''

''*Woman!*''

''—when you took it yourself! I know you did, Thad. I
saw you when you came back to the house to take it.''

''Woman, you don't know what you're saying. The diamond was taken from me like everything else was, even my
daughter. Both my daughters!''

''You stole it, Thad,'' Aunt Nickie said, gently insistent.
''Stole from your own brother to restore your fortunes. I think
you set the overseer's house on fire, too—''

''Murdock, turn and take it face on.''

''Thad, don't!'' Aunt Nickie commanded sharply, her voice
rich with pain. ''Don't, or I'll have to shoot you!''

For a moment the hall was utterly still. Then a tremor like
an earthquake swept through my uncle's heavy body.

''Nickie, what the hell are you saying!''

''I must stop you. Somehow I must stop you once and for
all, even if I have to kill you to do it.''

''Woman, this is your husband you're talking to. This is
Thaddeus Welles, and you know no man ever loved you
more. Can you really say such a thing to me?''

Aunt Nickie's only answer was the clicking of the pistol as,
with her thumbs, she drew back the cock.

''Nickie . . .''

''Please, Thad,'' Aunt Nickie wept. ''Don't make me do
it. If you make me do it, I'll die too.''

Again, silence. Uncle Thad's face glistened with sweat.
His pistol shook. His entire body trembled, as if he were
being pulled two ways. As if every muscle in his body were
pulling against another.

He raised the pistol higher and steadied it. For a moment I
was certain he was going to fire.

Slowly he lowered it.

For the first time, he looked away from Gannon. He turned
toward Aunt Nickie. Stared at her and at the weapon in her
hand.

''Get out of here, Murdock.'' His voice was a harsh croak.

Gannon looked at me. He nodded. He started to open the
door. Unlce Thad turned toward him again to watch him go.

And could not let it happen. Could not. Snarled and raised

his pistol toward the ceiling, then thrust it out to draw a bead on Gannon.

Céleste screamed. I hurled the poker. Both pistols roared.

Perhaps the poker saved Uncle Thad's life as well as Gannon's. His shot went wild. He twisted and staggered as Aunt Nickie's shot hit his side. Clutching at himself, he fell against a wall.

Aunt Nickie made no sound. Her head was back, eyes closed, tears streaming down her face. It was the face of a woman who thought she had lost all she loved most. Her arms hung loosely at her sides. The pistol dropped from her fingers.

Slowly, still clutching at his side, Uncle Thad went to her. He put his arm around her shoulders.

"Now, it's going to be all right, Miss Nickie," he said softly. "Don't you fret. You hear me, Miss Nickie? There's no harm done. It's going to be all right, everything all right."

He looked around at Gannon, still at the door, unmoving.

"Murdock, I'd be obliged if you'd go find that doctor you were talking about."

He turned back to Aunt Nickie. "It's going to be all right, Miss Nickie, you'll see. Everything all right . . ."

3 ～.～.～.～.～.～.

I lost the baby—if indeed there had ever been one. Impossible to know, of course. When I told Gannon the next day, he was even more disappointed than I, but as it turned out, the loss was for the best.

Meanwhile, Horace had finally arrived with a doctor, who supplied me with unguents for my burns and said that, except for a small patch or two, I was unlikely to have scars. I gave thanks. Uncle Thad was hurt worse than I—his wound was passed off as an accident—but as I learned in the days that followed, the injury was far more to his soul than to his body.

Finally I was put to bed in my old room with ever-faithful

Céleste at my side, for she refused to leave me, fearing I might want something during the night. I slept deeply and dreamlessly—no burning houses, no flaming bodies—and did not awaken until the next afternoon. Céleste, refusing to allow me out of bed, brought me a breakfast tray. When I was finished, she brushed my hair and tied it with a ribbon, and soon after that, she announced that Gannon had come to see me, his second visit that day.

He came in and sat on the edge of the bed, and for a long time we simply embraced. Then I told him about the baby. He said it was all right, that there would be other chances, but he clung to me a little tighter, his face hidden on my shoulder, and I wondered if he were thinking about that sixteen-year-old son or daughter he had never had. *Never mind, my darling, I'll give you one yet.*

"And now, Gannon Murdock," I said, pushing him back from me, "I want an explanation. How did you get the Tear of Venus?"

"Looked for it! It had belonged to my family, and I wanted it back, so I looked for years. I had a very good description of it which my family had hung on to—a kind of memento, I suppose—and I gave copies of it to jewelers and diamond dealers wherever I went. Everywhere from New Orleans to Rome. I had almost given up hope, but then I heard from an Amsterdam dealer, so the last time I went to Europe, a couple of years ago, I visited him. And he had it. The Tear of Venus."

"But there were witnesses—"

"Coaxed, threatened, and bribed. It wasn't hard for your uncle to arrange that."

I shook my head in wonder. "And you simply let me go on thinking you had stolen it. Why didn't you tell me the truth?"

"Gussie, if I had told you the truth, would you have believed me?"

"Why, I . . . ." Would I have?

"And if you had had any suspicion at all that I might be lying to you, wouldn't that have soured things between us, at least a little?"

He was right.

"Princess, I probably would have told you the truth sooner or later, when I was certain you'd believe me. But meanwhile I'd a lot rather have you think I was a reformed thief—than an unregenerate liar."

No wonder I loved him, I thought, and how could I bear to be parted from him? He must have been thinking something similar, because he said, "Gussie, is it *really* necessary for you to go back to England?"

"I'm afraid it is, darling."

"And *I* have to go west!" His voice was disconsolate. "This is going to be the damnedest marriage. How are we ever going to work it out?"

"We will, darling. Trust me. There is an answer to every problem. We will always find a way."

"All right, we'll find a way. But meanwhile we're going to be married."

"Oh, yes!" *Just as soon as I tell you . . .*

"As soon as possible."

"Oh, no, you're not," Horace said grimly from the doorway. "You t-two are not going to get married now—or for a long time to come!"

Horace came into the bedroom, followed by a pale Céleste, who sank into a chair. "Horace," I said, alarmed, "what is it? Why shouldn't Gannon and I be married?"

"Gussie, you have got to realize that a lot of people are going to consider Tom's death suspicious."

Of course they would. It *was* suspicious!

"Are you saying that Gussie is in danger of being indicted for murder?" Gannon asked.

"I r-regret to say, very much so."

"What can we do about it?"

"What *I* am going to do about it is to use every bit of influence I have to get this whole thing quashed. But if you and Gussie get married, you will simply confirm the suspicion that Gussie, maybe with your help, took steps to rid herself of an unwanted husband. And I must remind you that the State of South Carolina has no great p-prejudice against hanging a woman."

Céleste cried out.

"And aside from not getting married right away, what can we do?" Gannon asked.

"Do exactly what you were going to do anyway. You, Gannon, let it be known that you are going west as soon as possible and going alone. Then go."

"And I'm to return to England," I said.

"That's right. I want to put an ocean between you two and keep it there for at least a year."

"A year!" Gannon sprang to his feet. "You're asking for a year out of our lives?"

Horace nodded. "For Gussie's sake."

"We don't have to throw away a year!" Gannon said angrily. "We can run away together! We don't need South Carolina—we have all the rest of the world to live in!"

Horace matched Gannon's anger. "Gannon, you're talking like a schoolb-b-boy! You've got family, friends, investments in South Carolina! And so has Gussie. And the world you want to live in really isn't all that big. The law would follow you and sooner or later catch up with you!"

"Gannon," I said softly, "until spring. You said you might not finish your business in Mississippi until spring anyway. And I don't want you to make a winter passage."

"Spring," Horace agreed, compromising. "You can go to Gussie in the spring. If you're discreet!"

It was agreed. We would meet in the spring.

Tom's remains were buried a couple of days later, and this time there could be no doubt—he would never trouble me again.

Now all I had to do was to make one or two interesting little revelations to my love, and gain his understanding, and all would be well.

I confess to being a coward. I delayed. Stalled. Procrastinated.

My evasions were made easier by the fact that our visit to America was rapidly coming to an end, and there was so much to do! Not only did we have to prepare for the trip back, but also for Céleste's wedding, and I was determined to make her the most beautiful bride Charleston had ever seen. Since we had only a few weeks, that meant a lot of hard work.

And there was the matter of Uncle Thad. Céleste and I continued to live under his roof—at Horace's and Aunt Nickie's insistence—and I could not leave Charleston without coming to some kind of terms with him. It is to his honor that he took the first step.

Though his wound was superficial and he recovered from it quickly, he moved about the house like a distracted ghost, tending to avoid me. Then one afternoon he once again asked me into his office.

"Augusta, there is something I must say. I hope you'll believe me when I tell you that I had no idea that Raveneau would treat you as he did."

"Why, of course I believe you, Uncle Thad."

"If I had had even a glimmering of such an idea, I never would have sent for him. I mean that."

"I know you do."

"I have in my time done certain things . . . taken certain steps . . . to correct what I saw as injustices. I am no longer totally certain I was right in every instance. But whatever I did, I never wanted anything bad or harmful for any of you children."

"Uncle Thad, I'm sure you only wanted what you thought was right for us all."

"But the other night, some of the things your aunt said . . ."

As he repeatedly clenched and unclenched his fists and a sheen of perspiration appeared on his forehead, I began to understand what this conversation was costing him.

"About Horace, for instance. It's true that I . . . well, I drove him away. I never understood the boy. To be honest," the words came out painfully, "I never really tried. So I missed the chance of having the son I always wanted. And today Horace doesn't even know I'm proud of him."

"Why don't you tell him, Uncle Thad?"

He went on as if I had not spoken. "But that is not the point of this discussion. The point is that when Tom Raveneau told me certain things about you some years ago, I believed him. And now I keep asking myself *why* I believed him, *why* I allowed him to go unchallenged. I really don't know why, except that I found it convenient to do so."

"Please, Uncle Thad, you needn't—"

"Allow me to finish. If anyone had spoken in such a way about your Aunt Nickie or her daughters, I would have killed him. And I should have done the same for my brother's daughter. If I had called Raveneau out and disposed of him as he deserved, you would never again have suffered at his hands." His voice shook. "I can only say that I'm sorry, Augusta. Truly sorry."

What does one do? He was my uncle. And he was trying so hard. I could only say, "Thank you," kiss his forehead, and leave the room quietly.

*   *   *

Oh, the days were passing so rapidly! August was gone, it was September, and then it was Céleste and Horace's wedding day. We were to sail for the North and for home the next morning—and *still* I had not told Gannon everything about myself!

The wedding, at Saint Philip's, was beautiful. Afterwards there was a reception on the lawn of the Wraggboro house—a pavilion, an orchestra, long tables of refreshments—and half of Charleston came. But how odd to see Uncle Thad and Gannon, guarded but on their best behavior, standing together with hands locked behind their backs and nodding gravely as they muttered wisdom about crops and market prices in lowered, consciously male-baritone voices! These two who three weeks earlier had been ready to kill each other. Fools! Clowns! Children, playing their little games! Thank heaven there is so little justice in this world—or where would most of us be?

The afternoon wore on, and the hour came for the bride and groom to depart. In a shower of rice and shouted well wishes, they rode out of the courtyard and down Meeting Street, with Gannon and me following in another carriage.

Ah, the relief of reaching Gannon's house, where the bride and groom were to spend their wedding night! Buttons and laces were unfastened at last, clothes were loosened and shoes kicked off, and "Who wants a drink?" Gannon asked. "Madeira, Céleste?" "Booze, Gannon, booze," Céleste said, now very American, "great bawls afar!"

It was to be one last happy evening together for the four of us—and for Gannon and me—before Céleste and Horace and I departed. On Horace's instructions, Gannon and I had, as a matter of caution, been alone together precious little during the past three weeks; but surely, I thought, there could be no harm in our spending this last evening together, even if I dared not stay the whole night.

As always, the chatter and the laughter were warm and easy over the supper table, but we all knew we were waiting for a certain moment, and, when the sun was well down, it came. A silence fell over the table, where we were still sitting, having our coffee, and after a moment Gannon turned to me.

"Gussie, I just realized I've never shown you my paintings. Would you like to see my gallery?"

"Why, I'd love to, Gannon." It was, of course, a stratagem to leave the bride and groom alone. They already knew where the bridal suite was.

"How about you, Céleste? Would you like to see my gallery?"

"On my next trip to America, Gannon," Céleste said grandly, and a mite tipsily, "on my next trip!"

"Well, then, Gussie . . ."

We left the table and went upstairs to the gallery.

Now I absolutely *must* have my little talk with Gannon, I thought. I simply could not make him wait eight or nine months and travel all the way to England before he learned the truth!

"I'm afraid the light won't be the best," Gannon said, "but at least you'll get an idea . . ."

Lamps had already been lit for us, and as I looked around at the walls, I was wonderfully surprised. I do not know what I had expected, but Gannon had a truly fine collection. Among the contemporary artists represented, I suppose Corot, Courbet, and Millet would have been most admired, but I was delighted to see several Daumier paintings. Everybody knows Daumier's lithographs, but only a very few of us have learned to appreciate his wonderfully expressive canvases. I could hardly wait to show Gannon mine.

That is to say, Liane's. Oh, Lord . . .

"Gannon," I said weakly, "your collection is wonderful. But there is something . . . something . . ."

"Yes, Gussie?"

Looking desperately about the room for a reason to delay, I realized, with a feeling of gratitude, that I had been so interested in the Daumiers that I had failed to look at one of the paintings. Or at least I assumed it was a painting—it was about two by three feet and covered by a white velvet curtain.

"Why, what's that?" I asked, pointing.

"Oh, that? I meant to take that down. These aren't all the paintings I own, and I change them from time to time. Gussie, darling, it's getting late. Why don't we—"

"But what is it?"

"Oh, nothing that would interest you, really."

Anything to delay the inevitable. "But I'd like to see it. Why do you keep it covered like that?"

He seemed embarrassed. "Because it's a picture for nobody but me. Most people wouldn't understand it. They'd either be offended by it or consider it a joke. Maybe both."

"I'd like to see it."

"Gussie, it's really not even finished. The artist didn't even want to sign it. He had some ideal in mind, and it was just too much for him, so he gave up. And I persuaded him to sell it to me. I think he wanted it off his hands so that he wouldn't keep returning to it, forever trying to accomplish the impossible."

"You make it sound more interesting all the time. Please, Gannon, I won't laugh or be offended, I promise you. Please let me see it."

"Well . . ."

Reluctantly Gannon stepped to the wall and drew back the drapes that covered the painting.

"There she is, Gussie, your rival, if you had ever had one."

I stared.

I knew that picture!

This time it was in oils: a nude woman lying back on cushions on a purple divan, her eyes half-closed, her full mouth, with its downturned corners, swollen with desire. And as before, the male, not yet draped, was arched over her, one leg extended between her spread thighs and a knee on her far side, but he touched her only with a hand supporting the back of her head.

But how in the world could Eugène have been dissatisfied with the painting? To me it was magnificent, a complete fulfillment of the promise of the sketch. Eugène had always been superb with light on flesh, but in this painting the light actually seemed to come *from* the luminescent female figure. It lit up the front of the male—his back was shadowed—and seemed to hold back the darkness, full of evil shapes and forces dimly seen, which completely surrounded the two figures. I saw the painting as a kind of allegory of love: though the woman might be the victim of her own passions and those of the man, it was nonetheless her love that created all that pure, serene, and lovely light, her love that lit up the darkness for them both.

But my God, the women portrayed, the woman herself . . .!

"Well, what do you think of it?" Gannon asked.

I tore my gaze away from the painting to look at Gannon. I tried to read his expression. His eyes had a distant, brooding look. But surely he was teasing me! He must have known about me all the time!

"It was inspired by Liane Duhamel, of course. Céleste's partner."

"Oh, yes."

He *had* to be teasing me! Granted, the painting was not a precise rendering of the subject, but that mouth, those eyes! How could he miss them, how could he *not* know?

"I thought for a moment you didn't recognize her. I don't suppose it's a very good likeness—the artist worked from memory."

"It's . . . not too bad."

"There was a time, Gussie, before you came back, when . . ."

"When what, Gannon?"

"Oh, nothing. I understand that you've met her. Do you know her well?"

"Sometimes she seems like a complete stranger to me."

"I looked for her for years, every time I went to France. I think she avoided me because she figured I blamed her for Adam's death. And maybe I did at first. But I talked to everyone I could find who knew her—friends, lovers, everyone—and even without meeting her, I . . ."

Fell in love with her! His brooding eyes, his lowered voice, the twist of his mouth—everything about him told me. Gannon Murdock had fallen in love with Liane Duhamel!

Oh, this had to be Gannon's idea of a joke! It *had* to be!

". . . I came to admire her very much. She's quite a woman, Gussie. You've probably forgotten, but you once implied that there must be something special about her, and you were certainly right."

But what if it *wasn't* a joke?

Gannon sighed. "Looks a little like Melinda, doesn't she?" As reluctantly as he had opened the drapes, he drew them closed again.

No! He *didn't* recognize her! He honestly did not recognize her!

And furthermore, in some corner of his heart, Gannon Murdock—the man I loved—*was still in love with that woman! He was in love with Liane Duhamel!*

Then what was *I* supposed to be? Some kind of . . . *consolation prize?*

Stunned, I just stood there, feeling like an idiot while he put out the lamps. "And now, my dear," he said, when the last one was out, "don't you think we've wasted enough time?"

I was of half a mind simply to walk out. To say to hell with Gannon Murdock and put on my hat and *go!*

But of course I did nothing of the kind. So I was a consolation prize, was I! Very well, I would *show* him what kind of consolation prize I was, I thought, as I slid into his arms. If he didn't know already, I would just *show* him!

"Kiss me, you fool," I said, "and take me to bed!"

After a revelation like that, was I going to tell Gannon about Liane Duhamel? I certainly was not! When we sailed the next day, waving to Gannon who stood on the wharf, he still had no idea of my secret.

A few days in New York and then ten days on a steamer packet, and we were in England again. And how good it was to be back! How good to be in London and dealing with Millie's troublesome store managers! We talked about prices and designs and display methods, and before I was through with them, they had doubled their orders. And how good it was then to go up to Leeds and solve Algie's labor problems! And while I was at Leeds, I was struck, not for the first time, by the slowness of the cutters as compared to the sewing-machine operators: it took a number of cutters to supply a single machine. Now, if only we could devise a machine for cutting that was as efficient as those for sewing . . . I would have to give that matter a great deal of thought.

And then back to Paris at last, and how good to see Félicie and Sylvestre again! And to get back to my old familiar drawing board, my watercolors, my crayons. All summer my brain had itched with ideas, and now they came spilling out.

Then back to London on business for Wycherley-Welles, and out to Huxton Hall, since the weather was crisp, for a ride to the hounds. Talleyho! While there I discovered that, though Harry had mellowed over the years, he had not entirely given up his wicked ways. Among the guests at Huxton Hall that weekend was a particularly attractive young couple who seemed just a little to eager to explore the ways of the world and a little too dazzled by the company they were in. And when I saw Harry secretly smiling at them and stroking his chin and looking every moment more like a ginger-haired Satan, I suspected it was time to take steps. "No, Harry," I said.

He contrived to look very innocent. "Why, no *what*, Augusta?"

I frowned at him through my lorgnette. "No, Harry. No, no, no-o-o!"

He shrugged and laughed. "Oh, well, I'm rather too busy for that sort of thing these days, anyway . . ."

Oh, I wondered, how could I ever have thought that I would be content to live out my days as a quiet Charleston widow and plantation owner! Surely a summer back home every two or three years would be quite enough for me. I needed change, I needed challenges, and all winter long as I have been writing these pages, scribble, scribble, scribble, till my middle finger has an aching callous and my hand cramps painfully, I have been asking myself, *What next? what next?*

And now I think I know.

Why should Wycherley-Welles not extend its operations to America?

Look at a map and consider the city of Chicago, Illinois. It bids fair to become the greatest railway center in the United States. It is already the largest corn market and wheat trade center, and the Illinois and Michigan canal makes it possible to bring in unlimited produce from the southwestern farmlands. My guess is that within a few years Chicago will be the greatest distributing center in the United States. Perhaps in the world.

Now, doesn't that sound like a perfectly lovely place to build a meat-packing plant?

And if we're going to do that, why not our own stockyards?

And why stop there, why not raise our own cattle?

Why stop *anywhere?*

Oh, God, the world is my oyster! When I think of how it is changing and of all its possibilities! When I was a child, we got rid of our old wooden plows in favor of cast iron, and now we have given up cast iron for steel. Railways, so new to us then, are now spreading their webs over continents. We now have daguerrotypes and rotary presses and magnetic telegraphs and McCormick reapers and adhesive postage stamps.

Not to mention the safety pin!

And this is only the beginning! And, I do want my part in the fun! I still have half my life to live, and I want to scratch my name on the face of the earth: *Gussie Welles—she was here!* Oh, the tales I shall be able to tell my grandchildren!

And, of course, the tales I shall *never* tell!

* * *

Ah, but spring is here at last, and I have looked up to see the burst of green and to be dazzled by the sunlight and to listen to the opening chords in the latest movement of an everlasting symphony. I wish Céleste could be with me at this time, but she and Horace are at her chateau awaiting their first-born— how I envy them!—and I am once again in London. Waiting for Gannon.

Because he is coming, he is on his way, he will be here any day now, and every promise in his lovely letters—who would have dreamed he could be so eloquent, so passionate, so thrilling!—we shall make come true. And as he holds me in his arms, he will ask me to marry him.

I, of course, shall refuse.

"*No*, I won't marry you, Gannon Murdock! How dare you think that, just like that, at a flick of your finger, I would marry you!"

He staggers back from me. He gapes. "Gussie—"

"How dare you think that I would share your heart with another woman!"

"Gussie, what the hell are you talking about!"

"You know perfectly well what I'm talking about! I saw your eyes, I heard your voice! Do you think I don't know that you're in love with that—that—that *French hussy* in that— that—that *lewd picture* of yours?"

He groans and sinks into a chair. "Oh, I *knew* I shouldn't have shown you that picture!"

"Well, thank heaven you did!"

"But, Gussie, I don't even *know* that woman!"

"That, my dear Gannon, is precisely the point. How can I, mere flesh and blood, ever hope to compete with an unknown ideal? All our lives you will think of her, and somewhere in your mind will lurk the question, *What if . . . what if . . . what if . . .?*"

"Gussie, I love *you!*"

"But you also love *her,* Gannon Murdock, and don't you deny it! And you are going to have to choose between us!"

"But how can I choose when I don't even *know* her!"

"You are going to have to *find* her!"

"But I have *tried!*"

"Then for my sake, try again, at least one more time. Find her, know her, make love to her. Seduce her, if you must. Do *that*, Mr. Murdock, and *then* make your choice!"

"But if I can't even find her—"

"If you fail, I don't see how I can marry you. No, I really don't see how. Now, *go*, Gannon Murdock! To Paris! *Go!*"

And off to Paris he will go.

Ah, I can see him now, charging about Paris in search of Liane Duhamel. First, of course, he will go to her offices, where he will confront the redoubtable Mme. Colombier.

"Ah, *Dieu*, it is the Mistair Murdock again! I had hoped we had seen the last of you. No, monsieur, Mme. Duhamel is not in. Yes, that is still her office, the door with her name on it, but I can assure you she is not in there. Yes, she is in Paris, but she has a meeting today with the directors of the Bonne-Nouvelle. . . ."

He will look for Liane at the Bonne-Nouvelle, but somehow he will just miss her. Having obtained the address of her apartment, he will go there.

"No, monsieur, she is not here," Liane's maid will inform him. "No, I have no idea when she will be back. She is out almost every evening, and she frequently stays overnight with a friend—Mme. Sand or another. I am so sorry. . . ."

If George is in the city, he will, without a doubt, go to her.

"Oh, it is the charming American again, the one with the somewhat fractured French. No, monsieur, she is not here. I believe she is in Paris, but I have not seen my Pocahontas for several days. Perhaps Monsieur Delacroix . . ."

"Murdock, *sacristi!* you gave me your word you would take that painting out of France and show it to no one who might recognize Liane!"

"Calm down, M. Delacroix, Mme. Duhamel will never know about that picture. But I must find her. If you can please tell me . . ."

"But I have no idea. . . ."

Up and down and back and forth across Paris, searching, always searching, for Liane Duhamel, until he can think of no other place to look, no other person to question, and once again he goes to her offices.

"I have told you repeatedly, monsieur, Mme. Duhamel is not here!"

"Who is in that office?"

"No one, monsieur!"

"Why is there *never* anyone in that office?"

"Mme. Duhamel is a very busy woman. She must frequently visit her clients—"

Gannon steps past Mme. Colombier, steps toward the door marked *Mme. Duhamel,* while madame tries to restrain him.

"Monsieur!" she says. "Monsieur, you cannot go in there! That is Mme. Duhamel's private office! Nobody is allowed to enter that office without permission! Sylvestre, come here, quickly! Monsieur, you cannot—"

But this time Mr. Murdock will not be denied. Nobody can stop him, not even Dirty Sylvestre, whom he effortlessly tosses aside as he charges toward the office. He throws the door open with a crash, and whatever poor woman may be in there at the time rises from a drawing table, startled, even frightened, as Gannon Murdock rushes in, looking for Liane Duhamel. And what do *you* think, Gentle Reader . . .

"Monsieur?" says the woman, her brown eyes large and luminous, the corners of her mouth pulled down in apprehension, her lip atremble. "Monsieur?"

. . . This time, will he find her?

Bestselling Books
for Today's Reader —
From Jove!

Chasing Rainbows

A novel of love, enduring courage and soaring triumph!

BY
ESTHER SAGER

They grew up on a lush estate in Virginia—Winna, the selfish blonde beauty, and Libby, the lovable auburn-haired lass. Then, at ten, an accident left Libby to face life against towering odds. Yet Libby is a survivor, and it is she who captures the heart of sophisticated Adam Bainbridge.

Suddenly Winna invades their perfect world—with malice and betrayal in her heart. Libby and Adam must learn that love is, like a rainbow, so very hard to catch and keep.

_____ 05849-1 CHASING RAINBOWS $2.95